THE HOUSE OF TUSK
Book One of Lanterns

A FANTASY NOVEL BY
R. J. LUCK

Published by R. J. Luck
ISBN: 978-1-5371-1516-0

Copyright © R. J. Luck, 2016-2019

Visit R. J. Luck's official website at www.slowjinn.com for the latest news, book details, and other information, or find him on Facebook.

Cover art, 'Rune Master', by Susan Seddon-Boulet, courtesy of Turning Point Gallery and the Boulet family.
www.susanseddonboulet.com
© 1988 Susan Seddon-Boulet. All Rights Reserved.

Illustrations by R. J. Luck
Cover design by Lieu Pham, covertopia.com
Book design by Guido Henkel

This is a work of fiction. Names, characters, places and incidents either are products of the author's imagination or are used fictitiously. Any resemblance to actual events or locales or persons, living or dead, is entirely coincidental.
All rights reserved. No part of this publication may be reproduced, distributed or transmitted in any form or by any means, including photocopying, recording, or other electronic or mechanical methods, without the prior written permission of the publisher, except in the case of brief quotations embodied in critical reviews and certain other noncommercial uses permitted by copyright law.

Table of Contents

Acknowledgements 9
Special Thanks 10
About the Author 11
Characters 12
Map 1 – The Lantern Universe 13
Map 2 – The Fantastical Atom 14
A Note from the Writer 15

Snow Fell Farm
    Chapter 1 – Frost 19
    Chapter 2 – The Yakreth Warrior 30
    Chapter 3 – Memory in the Sword 36
    Chapter 4 – Dream Room 41
    Chapter 5 – The Inkwell 45
    Chapter 6 – Pandora's Box 56
    Chapter 7 – Mad Bill and the Archer 72
    Chapter 8 – Renlock 83
    Chapter 9 – Black Hole 105

The House of Tusk
    Chapter 10 – Potential's Graveyard 123
    Chapter 11 – Himassisi 132
    Chapter 12 – The Governor-General's Residence 140
    Chapter 13 – Gods 150
    Chapter 14 – Atomic Glove 162
    Chapter 15 – Destroyers and Heroes 168
    Chapter 16 – Prophecy of the Norns 174
    Chapter 17 – Fateful Revelation 190
    Chapter 18 – Roots 195
    Chapter 19 – To Dream or not to Dream 199
    Chapter 20 – Rufus 201
    Chapter 21 – Ominous Gust 217
    Chapter 22 – Zarzanzamin 221
    Chapter 23 – Fateful Kiss 229
    Chapter 24 – Ravenous 242
    Chapter 25 – The Invite 263
    Chapter 26 – Forbidden Fruit 268
    Chapter 27 – Marvellous Bath 282
    Chapter 28 – Fury Rose 297
    Chapter 29 – War Room 300

Chapter 30 – Loyalty's Limits..311
Chapter 31 – The Pirate and the Dagger....................321
Chapter 32 – Sea-ing Sphere 338
Chapter 33 – Sifting for Secrets 342
Chapter 34 – Doors of Hell..346
Chapter 35 – Net of Light..349
Chapter 36 – Battle of Beauty......................................359
Chapter 37 – Tricky Friendship 364
Chapter 38 – Spying on the Spies 372
Chapter 39 – The Tell-Us Scope..................................384
Chapter 40 – Emotional Whirl.....................................394
Chapter 41 – Wilderspin's Wizardry 401
Chapter 42 – Light Interrogation 423
Chapter 43 – Asclepius's Hunt 440
Chapter 44 – Devil in the Detail 447
Chapter 45 – Frost Manor...453
Chapter 46 – The Three-Part Key...............................468
Chapter 47 – Hide and Seek...470
Chapter 48 – Vault of the Naga 472
Chapter 49 – Tainted Saint and the Puritan 480
Chapter 50 – The Art of Duelling................................489
Chapter 51 – Ocean of Eden 503
Chapter 52 – Vicar's Tea 507
Chapter 53 – Pain and Potential 514
Chapter 54 – The Prophet...517
Chapter 55 – Rage 520
Chapter 56 – A Miracle 523
Chapter 57 – Council of Shadows...............................530
Chapter 58 – Paradise..536
Chapter 59 – Glabrous 545
Chapter 60 – Go Ladies to..550
Chapter 61 – The Only Way Out.................................561
Chapter 62 – Power of Acceptance 570
Chapter 63 – The Fall...573

The Holygate of Hunter

Chapter 64 – Stone Circle 585
Chapter 65 – The Wolf...593
Chapter 66 – Thin Air 602
Chapter 67 – Song of an Ancient Blade 610
Chapter 68 – Jaded Endurance 622
Chapter 69 – Acceptance and Deceit 628
Chapter 70 – The Second Eagle...................................635

Chapter 71 – Braysheath's Request...........................638
Chapter 72 – Best Seat in the House 643
Chapter 73 – The Mission 645
Chapter 74 – Deadly Patience 650
Chapter 75 – Old Hag...652
Chapter 76 – Morrigan and the Staff 659
Chapter 77 – Rufus's Secret......................................665
Chapter 78 – Mother of Shocks 674
Chapter 79 – Lawrence's Demon..............................682
Chapter 80 – Oblivion..690
Chapter 81 – Sinful Eyrie 700
Chapter 82 – Sylphilanthropy 710
Chapter 83 – Feast and Rebirth 717
Epilogue   – Too big to Believe................................736

Glossary of Terms 744

For the dwindling forests and all the life that depends upon them

May they once again flourish

ACKNOWLEDGEMENTS

Sources of inspiration that shine out among so many are Carl Jung, Bhagwan Sri Rajneesh, Joseph Campbell, Hermann Hesse, Friedrich Nietzsche, Eva Pierrakos, Daniel Quinn and Sri Prem Baba. I must also thank Ted Andrews for his fine books on the wisdom and symbolism of nature.

SPECIAL THANKS

For their invaluable guidance: Roisin Heycock, Clare Havens, Sanne Burger, Laura MacDonald, Andy Burroughs, Alan Durant, James and Alice Rose, and Griffin Parry.

To dear family and friends for endless generosity and warmth, especially Dad and Hilary, George and Jane Luck, Jim Luck, Peter and Gina Knox, Peter and Eiluned Slot, Keith and Lucy Richmond, Fraser and Katy Rees-Durham, James and Alice Rose, Vinny Taylor and Shirin MacDonald, Lawrence and Mele Clarke, Toby and Katie Gordon.

To the bright star that brought me into this world—beloved Mum. Jenny. And an extra thank you to dear Dad who showed me *The North*.

And for all the humbling grace I have received along the way, particularly from the people of Kurdistan, Iran, Pakistan, India and Colombia.

ABOUT THE AUTHOR

As a child, Robert Luck planned to spend his life in the crown of a tree. As an adult, he found himself employed in an investment bank. God knows how that happened. Yet, on a visit to Tibet, something magical stirred to life—an irrepressible urge to explore the great mysteries. He left the bank in Manhattan, returned to Britain, bought an old motorbike and rode eastwards on what has become a long voyage into the unknown. Exploits in places such as Iran, Uzbekistan, Pakistan, India and along the Andes, were only the surface of more thrilling adventures in the inner-worlds. Ultimately his journey has brought him back to the boy in the tree and the reality of magic on Earth.

Main Characters

Jake — A schoolboy aged 16 from Northern England
Luna — An ancient destructive power stirring from the depths
Lord Boreas — Lord of the Sirens and God of Greed
Rani — Warrior of the Yakreth, born in Kashmir
Frost — Jake's remarkable new friend
Braysheath — One of two surviving *shepherds*
Rufus — A Scottish flying carpet
Geoffrey — An ancient lizard and master of dreamtime
Lawrence — Jake's father, reported dead in Egypt

Other Characters

Nestor — Jake's gregarious but missing grandfather
Ti — Tao god and staff member at the House of Tusk
Asclepius — Greek god and staff member at House of Tusk
Bin — A giant osprey and Rani's confidante
Bill — Manager of Snow Fell Farm and mad man
Wilderspin — The Pigeon Lord of Renlock
Count Frost — Frost's father and something big in finance
Merrywisp — Pixy and chief cook at House of Tusk
Glabrous — A thorsror and Commander of the North Gate
Tancred — Sprite and butler to the House of Tusk
The Sylph — A mythical being, capable of destroying energy
Morrigan — A sword of untold power

Map 1—The Lantern Universe

Outside worlds reflect worlds within

Map 2—The Fantastical Atom

Worlds

1-4 The Outer-Peregrinus, including the Earth's surface, along with death planets Roar, Leaf and Hunter.

5-7 The Inner-Peregrinus, including the planets Fear, Greed and Pride.

8   The Core, symbolised by the Sun. Also known as heaven, nirvana, infinity, God, the Higher Self...

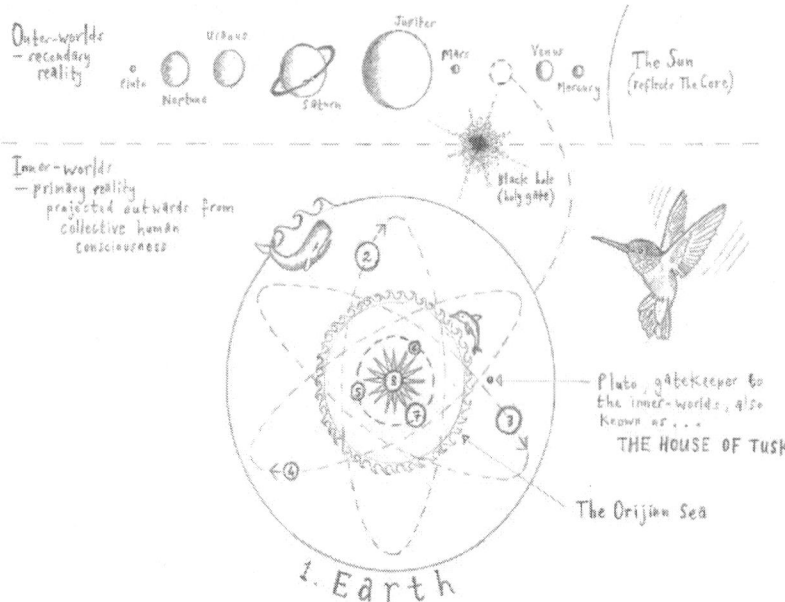

Notes

1. Earth's surface is the testing ground of the Lantern universe. Its shadow planet is Saturn, the task master who forbids shortcuts. The rest of the universe is contained within Earth, synonymous with the human body.

2. The Orijinn Sea is the Mother of All Seas. Located at the mid-point of the universe, it is created by the clash of inner and outer forces and is carried to the surface of Earth through the dreams of whales.

See Glossary at end of book for more details

A NOTE FROM THE WRITER

You are reading this story at the perfect time. It's our story at its most exciting, most terrifying, most magnificent moment. It's a story of what human beings really are and what we are a part of, which is very different from what most of us have been taught.

The following adventure is raging and romping inside of you. Each and every character is there. Some are uniting to seek a treasure buried so deeply that it's almost beyond reach, while others strive to keep it hidden, misunderstanding the vastness and inclusiveness of its value.

The world you see through the window of wherever you find yourself is just the surface of unfathomable depths that our greater reality is bursting to reveal. On offer is a golden age, perhaps more dazzling and magical than any other that has gone before. But it can't surface unbidden, not easily, certainly not smoothly. It requires our invitation, which can only be given by uniting through our hearts and acting out our most beautiful vision, restoring Earth to the pristine world we were entrusted with.

This tale, full of doors, is a strange map into our darkest and brightest depths. It requires stillness and an ear for the silence between the voices—a silence that becomes a deeper conversation.

Robert
Britain, 2019

SNOW FELL FARM

CHAPTER 1
FROST

Jake knew nothing about objects of power, except for one thing—that they existed. He hadn't known it until that very moment as he stood just an arms-length away from one. The knowing was visceral. He could feel its power thrumming through his bones, both threatening and inviting. It demanded his full attention and for a fleeting moment he forgot the pain in his heart that had drawn him to that hallowed place.

The object was an old-fashioned inkwell on his dad's desk. Its bulbous, brass surface mirrored his amber-coloured eyes and shaggy blonde hair, colouring him with a golden hue that made him look even more lion-like than he already did—sixteen years old and moments away from chaos.

He reached out for its lid. His fingers tingled. An inch from contact, energy surged up his arm. A sharp pain prickled between his eyebrows. He winced and pulled away as the edges of his vision fractured like shattered glass.

Part of Jake was desperate to flee from the object, but his curiosity was too powerful. He clasped the lid and pushed. With a blinding light the inkwell snapped open. Its innards gaped wide into a terrifying portal and a monstrous force hauled him through it.

Compression. Expansion. An almighty flex of energy. One followed the other in the blink of an eye.

Then silence so intense that a shiver ran up his spine.

He was standing on a grassy plain between mountains he didn't recognise. It was dusk and cold. A great tension hung in the air. Then Jake felt it. Something was racing towards him, though he couldn't tell what—loping through the grass, powerful, relentless, inescapable.

He saw it too late. It came out of nowhere. A great white wolf, blue eyes blazing, leapt for Jake's chest.

With a surge of adrenalin, he swung away, except he was no longer outside, but back on the train where he had been just moments before, dreaming of the inkwell in his dad's study.

Jake had knocked over the tea of a passenger, but he didn't notice. He was light-headed. His eyes felt different—sharper, deeper-seeing and he had the strange sense that the wolf in the dream had in some way leapt inside of him and gifted its vision.

Jake gazed out of the window into the dusk. The train was racing between the wintry mountains of the northern England. But something wasn't right. Despite being inside, he felt bitterly cold.

Again he recoiled. As though the window didn't exist, a light passed through it—the light of a lantern held up in scrutiny of Jake's face, the glimmer of an eye within its flame. Holding it was a ghost. Sombre-faced and grey robed, he appeared like an old knight without his armour. The only colour was his ageing red beard.

It can't be! panicked Jake in thought, gripped by a fear he had long forgotten.

'Jake,' said the ghost in a tomb-like voice. His presence grew powerful. 'You must die...'

The ghost spoke with chilling calm, just as it had in Jake's nightmares when he was a boy. It had spoken the same words. Next, the ghost would pass inside of Jake and he would sink through his own grave then freefall into a writhing darkness until he awoke yelling.

'You must die,' repeated the ghost as it passed through the window. 'Die before—'

'No!' barked Jake and struck the pane of glass. The jarring partially brought him back. He was about to strike a second time when the lantern flashed so brightly that he was forced to shield his eyes.

Something grabbed his shoulder. He spun around. The ghost was inside the train. Jake jumped to his feet and swung at the lantern, but struck something else.

The ghost had disappeared. In its place was the conductor of the train. He, along with all the other passengers, was regarding Jake as though he were mad.

'Steady on, mate! You all right?' he asked.

His heart racing, Jake peered out the window into the fields of snow, though found no sign of the ghost, the wolf or anything else unusual.

He took several deep breaths and turned back to the carriage.

'Yes. Yes I'm fine. Everything's fine. Sorry I hit you. I, erm... I was just dreaming,' stammered Jake, passing his ticket for inspection, desperate to restore some dignity. 'Let me buy you another tea,' he said to the man beside him who declined the offer awkwardly.

Confused, shaken and embarrassed, Jake sank back into his seat. An elderly woman sitting opposite studied him with a dubious expression before returning to her book.

The weight of the rest of the passengers heavy upon him, Jake sought respite in the gathering darkness beyond the window.

Could I have really seen it? he wondered.

Part of him wanted to dismiss it as imagination, but it had felt too real.

What's the wolf got to do with that bloody ghost? And why has it come back into my life now? 'Die before...' Before what? A certain date? A certain person or place?

Jake regretted having struck the window, wishing he had been brave enough to hear what the ghost had had to say.

He was so preoccupied that when the train next jolted to a halt, to his surprise it was Harkenmere, the station of his home town. He jumped up, grabbed his bag and made for the door.

No one but Jake stepped from the train. It had started to snow again, the large flakes covering the station in a stillness so enchanting that Jake joined it, barely conscious of the train departing. He gazed up at the mountains that he had spent most of his young life climbing and drew a deep calming breath.

By the time he had exhaled, it all came flooding back—the pain, sharpened by the joyous memories of all the homecomings that had gone before. This time, however, someone would be missing.

Your father has died, in Egypt...

Jake hadn't heard the rest of what the headmaster had had to say just the day before. He had bolted from the school in the Scottish Highlands, raced up the nearest mountain and roared to the sky until he collapsed exhausted, shivering, sobbing and feeling decades older.

It was the second time death had knocked at his door, the first when he was only a baby. That time it had stolen his mother. Now that it had his dad too, all that remained of a home was a wandering granddad and a farm manager who was so eccentric that most thought him mad.

As grief threatened to consume him, Jake recalled what his dad had often said—that life is a great gift no matter what it brings us, that our responsibility is to understand the heaven-sent lessons and to evolve, not to suffer. Jake also recalled something he had once read in a book on Native American Indians—*Death is a sacred passage, life on Earth just one part, tiny yet vital, of a far greater reality.*

Jake's sadness fought back. Such a grand idea was wishful thinking. *We arrive at random and we leave at random*, he decided and though a small voice deep inside of him cried out in protest, the blunt thought suited his heavy heart.

A breeze blew from the stillness and swept about him so softly that it felt like an embrace.

It was swiftly followed by a stiffer breeze. Bitterly cold, it blasted from the opposite direction and whisked up the snow. With a shiver, Jake pulled his coat tight about him. He felt a menacing presence as though someone were standing just behind him, staring at him intently. He spun around. There was nothing but snow, yet his skin tingled and his heartbeat sped. Jake stood his ground, waiting to see if something emerged. When nothing did, he set off for the stairs and the station exit.

THE SIGHT OF THE HIGH STREET OF THE OLD MARKET TOWN WAS a welcome one. A big Christmas tree covered in lights had been erected next to the war memorial while carols and roasting chestnuts suffused the dusk with a cheer so rich that Jake was almost swept up by it. But not quite. He couldn't shake the feeling that he was being followed. As he proceeded along the pavement he glanced back several times, though each time saw nothing unusual.

Why would anyone spy on me?

He couldn't think of a good reason, until the image of the ghost filled his mind. Jake stopped. He scoured the crowded street, refusing to be spooked.

Finally Jake gave up worrying about it, helped by the sight of a chocolate éclair. He was staring through the baker's shop window, wondering whether to buy one or not when a voice from behind him made him jump.

'What are you doing here?' it demanded.

Jake spun around to find a boy standing uncomfortably close to him and immediately took a step back. The boy looked about Jake's age and had a similarly lean build, but where Jake's charm was rustic and rugged, the other boy was striking. He had a wild and exotic air—dark rakish hair, tanned skin and hazel eyes that sparkled with such mischief that he reminded Jake of a fox.

'What am I doing here? What are you on about? I've never met you before.'

'What? You mean I have to know you in order to ask you a simple question? Ha!' cried the boy and caused Jake to take a further step backwards.

There was something about the boy's presence that both captivated and repelled Jake in the same instant. Not only did he seem older than he looked, but there was a sprightliness about him, as though he might leap into a tree at any moment. He was so vivid, so alive that he seemed unreal.

'Well?' pressed the boy. 'What are you doing here?'

Jake didn't answer. He was thinking back to the ominous sensation he had felt since disembarking from the train.

'What's the matter? Are you one of those pompous types?' accused the boy. 'Emotionally repressed? Is that it? After all, it's a common enough disease. Or do you think you're too clever for me? Ha! Well, you might be clever by school standards, which isn't saying much, but you're hardly wise—'

'Have you been following me?' broke in Jake, who would have excelled at school if he applied himself, but he found it all too dull and irrelevant and so he did the minimum and saved himself for sports.

'Me? Follow?' barked the boy. 'Certainly not! I'm not one to follow. However...' he trailed off in a mysterious tone and looked in the direction of a rooftop across the street. 'I have a feeling *someone* was.'

Jake followed the boy's line of sight, but saw nothing but snow dancing about the slate-tiled roofs.

'Why would anyone be on the roof in this weather?' said Jake, struggling to take the boy seriously. 'And why are you bothering me? I'm really not in the mood—'

'Bothering you?' exclaimed the boy. 'More like why am I, Frost, for that is my name, bothering *myself* in talking to you? And as for your *not being in the mood*, one doesn't rise to the glittering challenges of life by not being in the mood. One remains relaxed but ever alert to the signs and synchronicities, ever ready to respond. In an instant! Have you never heard of forbidden fruit? Know what it is? I bet you don't.'

'I've never thought about it,' replied Jake amid Frost's barrage.

'Of course you haven't. It's presence! That's what's forbidden. Presence and spontaneity, the two keys to life. And anyway, who are you to ask me a question when you've yet to answer mine?' he drove on mercilessly. 'But it doesn't matter because I already know what you're doing here. I just thought I'd give you chance to be interesting which, not surprisingly, you've failed miserably. I'll forgive you, however, if you buy me a cake. How about a custard tart?'

Somewhat embarrassed by the encounter, Jake looked about to see if others were watching, but no one paid them the slightest attention as they scurried past with hoods and umbrellas up.

'You're mad,' he said flatly, any idle curiosity as to Frost's identity giving way to the call of home. He made to leave, but Frost blocked his way, a flash of a danger in his grinning eyes.

Jake was more than capable of looking after himself, but he considered fighting a last resort and especially with someone like Frost. Unlike oversized thugs who were usually slow and ran off crying after two hard punches to the nose, Frost was lithe. Behind his every movement was the quiet confidence of someone who knew his strength.

'Mad or not, what I really am is a synchronicity,' said Frost, breaking the awkward silence. 'Won't you wake from your dreary existence and explore it?'

Just then a text message rang out from Jake's phone. Hoping to use it as an excuse to break away from Frost, he withdrew it from his coat pocket.

No sooner had he done so than Frost swiped it from him. In the same movement he tossed it over his shoulder.

Jake watched in disbelief as it spun poetically through the air and disappeared down a road drain. It couldn't have been a more perfect throw. Jake would have congratulated Frost had it not been his own phone that had cost a small fortune. Instead, it took all of Jake's strength to keep his cool.

'Why did you do that?' he growled.

'You'll thank me for that one day,' said Frost airily. 'Probably as soon as tomorrow.'

'Not before you've replaced it,' warned Jake.

'That's precisely what I've already done!' declared Frost.

Not sure how to deal with Frost, Jake said nothing.

'I've replaced it with reality.'

'What are you on about? *This* is reality,' said Jake, gesturing to their surroundings.

'You clearly have no idea about reality,' declared Frost. 'If you did, if you knew how to truly see and hear, then you'd realise that what you call reality is just the surface of it. The greater part is hidden beneath it, within it, along with great power. Not power as most people know it, which is child's play and makes one look ridiculous, but real power. Some call it magic,' explained Frost.

Jake looked down at his empty hand and back at Frost, about to offer a succinct opinion of Frost's version of reality, but Frost cut him short.

'The first thing you must do, however, is to stop dumbing your wits with things like phones and TV—rubbish things which clutter you up with nonsense and fear when you need to be empty and trusting to let power flow through. Not to mention how their poisonous signals are killing off the bees and when the bees are gone, when the trees are gone, humans also will disappear.'

'Magic, power flowing through us?' laughed Jake.

'Of course! Magic is not the privilege of just a few, but available to all. But these walking dead…' said Frost with a sweeping gesture to the passing public. 'Look at them. Zombies! Robots! Certainly not human. Too afraid to even look each other in the eyes. There! Look at that idiot!'

Frost was pointing at a boy about their age. He was gazing into his phone, writing something, barely looking where he was going, while a girl stopped what she was doing and watched him pass. Her expression was one of wonder as though she had felt something deeply mysterious.

A sparrow swept under the boy's nose. A dog barked. A passer-by clipped his shoulder. All were signs to alert him, but he missed them all. Not even a dump of snow freeing itself from a roof and covering his phone could grab his attention. He simply wiped it away and continued to type while walking.

Frost barked with laughter. 'He's so busy looking online for a girlfriend, one that'll drive him mad, that he's missing one right beside him that'll give him joy.'

Jake studied the girl. The deeper he looked, the more he saw her beauty—not fashion beauty, which was boring, but real beauty. It was in her manner and movement as much as anything else.

'See what I mean?' said Frost with a grin.

Jake looked back at his empty hand and had to concede that Frost had a point. 'Look, I'm not interested in power, I just—'

'Oh, aren't you?' challenged Frost, his eyes glinting. 'I know you are. Everyone is.'

A chill ran up Jake's spine. He thought of the wolf and the ghost and their powerful eyes and also wondered at the mysterious appearance of Frost.

Could they be connected?

Frost's presence was so strong, however, that Jake couldn't think straight. He craved to be on his own in order to make sense of it all.

'Look, I've had a long day. I'm heading home,' he said. 'So if you wouldn't mind—'

'Home?' barked Frost. 'That's exactly what I'm talking about! Your *real* home! It's right here in this moment. But to find it you must be silent. Stop thinking!'

'Silent?' scoffed Jake. 'You hardly strike me as silent.'

'Oh, but I am. I may be talking to you, out of pity I might add, but on the inside I'm thoroughly silent. How else could I sense a gust of wind just a moment away to your right,' said Frost and a gust blasted from an alley and ruffled Jake's hair. 'Or know that a raven is about to land on that sign over my right shoulder?'

To Jake's astonishment, a raven did just that.

'Tell me, raven,' said Frost without turning to see it, 'one caw for yes, two for no, is what I say true?'

The raven released a single resounding caw, its beady eyes fixed on Jake.

'And tell me something else, raven, except this time, because our friend here is such a doubter, caw five times for yes—should he be honoured that I, Frost, am taking my time to offer him some guidance? That I am, as far as he's concerned, a gift from the gods?'

Without a moment's hesitation the raven released five quick caws and flew off through the snow.

As Frost stood smugly, Jake stood stunned.

Finally he found his voice and decided to put Frost to the test. 'You said you knew why I was back in Harkenmere.'

'You're back for a funeral,' stated Frost matter-of-factly. 'Your dad's. He was the Egyptologist mentioned in the papers. Died under a collapsed wall while doing some restoration or something, not that I believe anything I read in the papers.'

His words struck Jake like a stab to the heart.

'You're doubtless wondering how I could possibly know so much about you. Well, I can see it, plain and simple,' continued Frost, leaping ahead of the anger behind Jake's sadness so that in order to keep up, Jake had to do the same. 'For those of us who aren't so superficial it's quite normal to see deeper things and there's a big cloud of death about you. The bigger question, however, is why are you *really* back? What's really calling you from the void created by your dad's death?'

'What do you mean?' asked Jake in a sceptical tone, though his interest had been piqued.

'Your soul's mission, of course. Your quest!' announced Frost. 'Very few wake up to their destiny, so wake up!'

Though part of Jake wanted to walk away and be alone with his sadness, there was a growing part that couldn't—a part that cared not for gentle manners or sympathy, but truth, no matter how brutally delivered and waved away anger as childish. As for his feelings about Frost, he was so arrogant that it was almost enjoyable. And there was something else about him, something Jake couldn't quite put his finger on, for which words like charm and charisma weren't quite enough. Whatever it was, the longer Jake spent in Frost's company, the more powerful it became.

He looked back at the rooftop across the street.

'Did you really see someone watching me?' he asked, his trust and suspicion of Frost in equal measure.

'I felt something,' said Frost.

'Like what?'

'Oh, an assassin probably,' said Frost nonchalantly, as though it were the most ordinary thing in the world.

Though he thought Frost's reply absurd, Jake suffered the same ominous feeling he had felt on the platform.

'Who are you?' he asked. 'Why have I never seen you around town before?'

'As I've already explained, my absent-minded friend, you've been wandering around fast asleep, just like everyone else.'

'Where do you live then? Which school do you go to?'

'Go to school?' exclaimed Frost. 'After all I've said, do you think I would go to school for my education? Ha! Certainly not. Nature is my teacher, because unlike you I don't wish to be programmed like a machine, filled with lies by fools. As for home, I live in a house larger than the Queen's. My father is extremely rich. The rest you know. I'm devilishly handsome and *far* brighter than you.'

'After what you said about power, I wouldn't have thought you'd be interested in money. Makes one look ridiculous, isn't that what you said?'

'Oh, I'm not interested in it,' declared Frost. 'Nor is Father. To him it's just a tool for making others look ridiculous.'

'If your house was as large as you say it is then I would know about it.'

'Another statement which only goes to show just how blind you are,' announced Frost. 'But at least you can see cake. Come on, let's have some!'

Again Jake felt himself split in two. His adventurous side was fascinated by what else Frost might say. He was exhausted, however. Above all, he was keen to get back to the peace of the farmhouse and see his granddad.

'Another time,' he said. 'I expect our paths will cross again.'

'Only if they're meant to,' replied Frost, his eyes sparkling with knowing.

With a nod, Jake passed Frost.

'Watch out for bats!'

'Why?' said Jake, turning back for a moment. 'What have bats got to do with anything?'

'If you see one, either while awake or in a dream, you know, under auspicious circumstances, then it means you're in for a shock. A big one! An initiation, in fact.'

'I've already had a shock,' said Jake ironically.

'Oh no you haven't,' challenged Frost. 'Death's not a shock. Or it shouldn't be. It's the most natural thing in the world, the pinnacle of one's life! Physical death, that is. Death's a time for celebration. There are, however, other types of death. Ones that are far more interesting. Anon, Lord Burton!'

Another chill ran through Jake. He was about to question Frost when a second gust of wind appeared and Frost was momentarily concealed in a mini-blizzard. By the time it cleared, he had disappeared.

'Lord Burton? What's he on about?' muttered Jake for there were no peers in his family. *He must mean landlord. Now that dad has... * Jake struggled with the admission... *passed on ... Frost probably assumes the farm is mine.*

Jake stared into the space where Frost had stood. It had been such a bizarre encounter that he wondered whether it had actually happened and yet, like the sighting of the wolf, he secretly hoped it had—a strange light had been shone into the darkness of Jake's grief and while it had, things had seemed less final.

Shaking his head in wonder, Jake finally set off for the bus stop.

Halfway over the bridge that crossed the river he suddenly stopped. A bird swept past him, so close that they almost collided. It was odd because it was night time and still snowing and birds usually took shelter at such times.

It happened again, except this time there were several birds. They appeared from under the bridge and flew about him in a tight circle with great agility.

'I don't believe it!' he gasped. 'Bats!'

CHAPTER 2
THE YAKRETH WARRIOR

THE WOODLANDS OF WRATHLABAD COVERED THE ENTIRETY OF that immaculate world. It was a world in which, like any other, nature ruled supreme. The difference in Wrathlabad was that every specie knew it. They dared not challenge her balance for they understood the consequences, both for the cosmos as a whole and their own journey through it.

All elements, all life were revered, but especially the trees. Ancient and life-giving, they were worshipped for their shelter, their shade, their medicine and wisdom. Above all, they were worshipped for holding the world together in every way, especially through their roots, which prevented soil from being blown away.

Many tribes dwelt there in peace. One, however, stood out. They were called the Yakreth, a tribe whose skills in hunting were legendary, not only in their own world but in many others as well. Like all exceptional hunters, they made exceptional warriors. Some called them assassins, though not in the conventional sense, for they fought for nature, for balance and for wholeness. In a cosmos where so many forces created destruction, few were pure enough to hire the Yakreth, and so they largely worked for themselves.

Two of their tribe were currently descending through a rain storm. One was a giant osprey, its fierce yellow eyes and outstretched magnificence undimmed by the weather. Riding on its back with brown eyes just as fierce was a girl on the verge of womanhood. At first glance, one might have thought her primitive. Across her back was a bow and her clothing was made of leather. On closer inspection, the clothing was exquisitely made, leaf-patterned and fitted her like hornbeam bark to the trunk of a tree, perfectly complementing her rich earth-coloured skin.

Finally they broke through the rain. Greeting them amid a canopy of green was a vast amphitheatre of waterfalls.

'Ah, Bin!' exclaimed the girl. 'How good it feels to be back! That snow up there on the Surface,' she said referring to Earth, for that's how those of the inner-worlds spoke of it, 'it's so beautiful, but, brrr, cold! I'm much more suited to here.'

'You were born somewhere far colder,' said Binshia the osprey, who to Rani was like an older sister.

'Kashmir,' said Rani, a word she liked the sound of.

'A troubled place in a troubled world,' said Bin, 'where humans, like all humans in such times, fight for ownership of what cannot be owned, but only known, only worshipped.'

'Land,' sighed Rani, for she loved it as much as she loved the air and the sea. 'But why was it just me who was brought here after the earthquake? My parents weren't the only ones who died. I still don't understand. Why did the Ancient One go there and select me, bringing me to a world far away from the Surface?'

Only twice had Rani seen the being she called *the Ancient One*, but she had never forgotten the green of his eyes blazing with secrets beneath the hood of his cloak—secrets too great to tell.

'Braysheath, you mean. You're old enough now to call him by his real name.'

'Braysheath, then. But why did he do it?' pressed Rani. It was her favourite subject.

Bin released a sigh. 'Who can guess at the behaviour of one so powerful,' she said. 'But I'm glad he did.'

'The nature up there, like here, it's breathtaking, but why do the people there make such a mess of it? Why do they insult the Great Mother so? Don't they realise?'

'For now they've forgotten.'

'It's as though they can't stand the sight of her, the way they chop her down. I don't understand it. They cause so much destruction. And yet, to observe the way they move in those things called towns, they look powerless. The men don't move like men. The women don't move like women. There's no polarity. No tautness. They all look the same—isolated and scared, rushing from building to building.'

Rani thought back to the secret mission, her first proper one. She and Bin, who was able to shrink down to the regular size of an osprey, had been charged with keeping watch on a boy called Jake as he returned home from Scotland. She hadn't been told why she had to. Her instructions were simply to ensure that no harm came to him. Everything had been going fine when, from the rooftops through the snow, she had spotted someone following him. The sight of the follower had caused her hairs to stand on end. She had immediately recognised what he was. In an instant her bow had been loaded. It had taken great restraint not to fire, but to have done so might have caused chaos, hence her reluctant return to consult her chief.

'Hurry, Bin,' she said. 'We've taken a big risk leaving the boy unprotected. We must get our instructions and return to the Surface as quickly as we can.'

Bin tucked in her wings and shot towards an especially large tree that commanded a view of the entire waterfalls and the jungle that fell away beyond them.

As they flew towards it, Rani reflected on her conversation with Bin.

I'm from the Surface and my first mission is also up there—to protect this new lord to the House of Tusk.

Yet it wasn't a mission she could embrace wholeheartedly. There was something about this Jake that left her cold. It wasn't his appearance, which seemed innocent. It was something she perceived in his energy, a type of old darkness she didn't understand that reminded her of mandrake forests, places of deep initiation. But it had been difficult to judge in the town. She would have to wait until she saw him in nature and observe its response to him.

Bin swooped down towards the upper boughs of the tree. She landed on one of its giant branches in front of a gaping archway that lead into the trunk. Stationed on either side of it were two black panthers. Close to each of them were bows and arrows, for Yakreth panthers were able to shift into human form if battle required it. But they weren't humans, unlike Rani who was the only real human among them. So too was Bin the only osprey in the tribe, selected especially for Rani since she couldn't shift shape into a panther. Regardless, she embodied their ferocity and valour and aspired to the panther's ancient symbolism of reclaiming one's true power.

On seeing Rani and Bin, the panthers gave short bows of their stern-faced heads.

Rani slid off Bin and laid down her bow in a customary mark of respect. Also customary, for her at least, she kept possession of two curved kukri-like knives that she wore criss-cross through the back of her belt.

She and Bin passed through the archway into a large circular hall, magnificent in its simplicity. Torches burned from the burnished insides of the tree, casting menacing shadows about the towering statues of heroic panthers past. A fountain flowed at its centre. Beyond it at the far end was another archway. Sitting majestically within it, looking out across the waterfalls through the rain, was a particularly powerful-looking panther.

Rani, followed by Bin, crossed the hall and stopped a small distance short of it.

'Chief Ezram,' she said, bowing her head to his broad back.

'Warriors Rani and Binshia,' replied Ezram in a deep and dignified voice without turning round. 'Why are you here and not on the Surface?'

'I wouldn't have left my watch, my chief, were it not for a complication. Something which I believe warrants your council.'

Ezram said nothing.

Rani visualised his face in human form, whose features were known on the Surface as Tibetan. Framed in long greying hair, it would at that moment be expressionless, his wise eyes half-closed in contemplation. She knew it well, for it was Ezram that Braysheath had entrusted with her upbringing.

'My chief, the lord-in-waiting has returned from that place where they imprison children and make them blind and stupid. *School* they call it. But he's been approached by someone… someone who's trying to become his friend, though only so he can lead him astray. It is this that I have come to consult you about.'

Still Ezram remained silent, continuing to look out over the falls.

'It's the way he moves and the look in his eyes,' explained Rani. 'I think he's a—'

'He is,' interrupted Ezram.

'So you know! But how can that be?' she asked. 'The Ancient One, Braysheath, surely he would have intervened. Surely he knows?'

'Naturally.'

'Then why… ?'

'Destiny is a rich tapestry made up of many threads. One can never be sure how things might play out or who will play which role.'

Rani's head swam with the scale of his words and the implications of what she had witnessed.

'My chief, we are nature's warriors, protectors of balance. The House of Tusk has a similar role. Is it not so? But if this Tusk boy, Jake, were to be allowed into such a powerful place under the influence of this other one, then I can't imagine how anything but destruction will follow.'

'From destruction comes creation. And as for imagination, the reason yours is currently failing you is because you're too far from your quarry to empower it. The Yakreth are strong when they are close. Only then do we observe the subtleties and know whether and when to act,' said Ezram, his reprimand all the more cutting for its calm delivery.

Rani wished to take issue, but Bin nudged her with a wingtip and gently shook her head. Besides, Ezram was right. A warrior had to be as close and as fluid and natural as the wind in order to be effective as nature's right hand, a role that had once been humans until that hand was severed by a mysterious series of events ten thousand years earlier.

'Then, with your permission, Chief Ezram,' she said, her tone betraying her injured pride, 'we will take leave and make haste for the Surface.'

'Since you *are* here…' began Ezram and finally turned to face them. His eyes were so powerful that all but the most fearless would shrink before them, but Rani knew him too well. 'I have further instructions for you. When the lord-in-waiting descends to Himassisi to take up residence at the House of Tusk, you're to follow him. Stay close but out of sight. Your mission remains to protect him.'

'What?' exclaimed Rani, dropping all protocol. She couldn't believe her ears. Her eyes shone with excitement. 'You mean we should actually *enter* the fort? Enter the House of Tusk?'

Chief Ezram nodded.

'But how will we get in? I've heard it's impossible unless invited.'

'When the time is right, you'll have access. Follow your instincts.'

She shot a glance at Bin whose proudly puffed up feathers were a perfect expression of Rani's own feelings. Euphoria coursed through her. Not only was the House of Tusk said to be a place of untold power, but the natural beauty surrounding it was unsurpassed by anywhere else in the cosmos, even Wrathlabad.

'Of course I will go, my chief,' she said, recovering her composure, 'but what I don't understand is why I'm required at all. Surely the House of Tusk and Braysheath himself have enough resources and power to protect the new lord.'

Ezram was silent, though he held her in his unsmiling gaze.

'Braysheath does know about this mission, doesn't he?' she asked, once again forgetting herself.

Rani, who knew every subtlety of Ezram's face, panther or human, noticed the twinkle in his eyes.

'Has he been here recently?' she asked excitedly. 'Was it he who asked you to send me?'

'I knew it!' she cried, reading Ezram's silence. 'I wish I could have seen him! Why didn't you tell me, Father?'

'No one is to know,' he said, maintaining his serious tone, while his eyes betrayed a glimmer of pride.

'But I still don't understand why me? I'm not yet a full warrior,' she admitted, and modestly, for it was widely known that she was one of the tribe's finest archers.

'Consider this your initiation,' he replied.

Rani positively trembled with excitement on hearing this and would have leapt up and hugged Ezram were it not for her lingering concern surrounding the new lord and Braysheath's choice of her as protector. It was deeply mysterious, like his taking her from the Surface all those years ago and his knowing about Frost, but doing nothing about it.

'If it's a secret, even from those in the fort,' pondered Rani, 'then Braysheath must consider the fort at risk from the inside?'

'Perhaps,' said Ezram.

'And maybe he has chosen me because this Lord Jake and I will be the only two humans in the inner-worlds, though why that would make me better at protecting him, I don't know.'

'I am not privy to Braysheath's thoughts. Time will reveal why he chose you,' said Ezram, marking the end to the discussion. 'In the meantime, take care not to lose your balance.'

Rani frowned. 'What do you mean?'

'You are a woman now. But never forget your first love,' said Ezram, before turning away again.

Rani knew only too well that a Yakreth warrior's first love was always nature, though why Ezram had sought to remind her she had no idea.

'Of course not, my chief,' she said somewhat pompously. 'Nothing will *ever* challenge that.'

CHAPTER 3
MEMORY IN THE SWORD

THE FARMHOUSE STOOD TEN MILES FROM HARKENMERE, FIVE miles out along the main road that headed west and over a pass before turning off onto a narrow lane that wound northwards, all the way up a little-inhabited valley. The Burton's farmhouse was right at the very end. It lay beyond the oak-fringed lake, amid the last fields before they finally surrendered to the mountain wilderness.

Jake had caught a bus that went as far as the final hamlet. From there he had to walk another mile to reach home.

By the time he stepped from the bus the snow had stopped and left in its wake a silence so striking that it stilled the mind—and Jake's had been very busy. His chief preoccupation had been Frost. The meeting had been so strange that it had pushed aside graver matters, not to mention the casual way in which Frost had spoken of death.

What did he mean by types of death which were far more interesting than physical ones? pondered Jake as his footsteps crunched through the snow. *He mentioned an initiation. For what?*

Though he tried to dismiss it all, he couldn't. Aside from the raven and the appearance of the bats, there was something about Frost that was too intriguing. He had challenged Jake's view of the world. His granddad Nestor, who lived in one of the farm outhouses, constantly did the same, but Nestor, fascinating and great fun though he was, never forced his views. Frost, however, had spoken with such magnificent authority that he had appeared like a giant. As Jake reflected on their meeting, he realised it had nourished a part of him that had been neglected, albeit with a strange aftertaste.

Jake glanced up at the moon. It was full, gracing the valley and mountaintops in a silver so serene that it stole his attention even from Frost and held it until he arrived at the farmhouse.

He stood at the end of the drive and beheld the familiar sight so dear to his heart. The raw nature, the old drystone buildings, the stillness, the fierce weather whenever it came, he loved it all. It was a place of memories. And though he had no memory of his mother, he had grown up knowing her as the wind in the trees, the swaying grass, bird song and the play of sun in crystalline pools and everything else that was beautiful in nature, for that's how his dad had described her.

A gentle breeze blew about Jake. He inhaled deeply, imagining her love filling his lungs.

But who, he wondered, would replace his dad?

He let it go. He was too tired for such heavy thought. Instead he simply dwelt on his dad's image.

The newspaper had been incorrect in labelling him just an Egyptologist. He had worked on ruins all over the world. It was the reason Jake had seen so little of him while growing up. But when his dad had been back, his presence had filled the house like lamplight in a cave.

His attention returned to the house. The only light shone from the kitchen.

Bill's probably at his second home, propping up the bar, assumed Jake, referring to the farm manager and The Tiger's Tail pub in town. Mad or not, the thought of him brought a glimmer of warmth to Jake's heart, for Bill was like an uncle and if ever Jake needed him, he had always been there.

An owl hooted from the copse of ancient trees beside the house. In the half-light cast by the moon the trees looked twice their usual size. So too did the colossal boulders in the fields. Other than the occasional bleat from the hillsides and stirrings from the cowshed, the farm appeared deserted. Even Nestor's outhouse was locked up, which was strange given the circumstances.

Perhaps Granddad went to Egypt to collect Dad's... Dad's body. But why hasn't he called?

Though keen to see him, Jake was relieved to have the house to himself. It had been a long and strange day and there was something fitting about entering the house alone.

A raven cawed from the great cedar tree, interrupting Jake's musings, reminding him of Frost. It was swiftly followed by a gust that shunted him forward. Obeying its command, Jake made for the kitchen door just as three bats shot out from the trees and flew in circles about the house. Frost's warning of an initiation returned to his thoughts. So also did the image of the wolf and a shiver ran up his spine.

Once inside, Jake felt a strong pull towards his dad's study. He resisted it, not yet ready to enter such an emotionally-charged place.

Tomorrow, he thought.

A wave of tiredness swept through him. Without wondering why it had hit him so suddenly, he headed straight for bed and fell into a deep sleep.

After his first encounter with the inkwell, when it appeared again Jake felt fear, even though he knew he was dreaming. Yet he had to know what the ghost had meant about dying, so he flipped open its lid before he hesitated. Once again he was hauled through the ominous portal.

This time there was no sign of the ghost. Jake stood before giant pyramids silvered by the moon. His attention was drawn towards a great sphinx close by and a temple beside it. He only had to think of being inside of it and he was there.

On top of the altar lay a sword—exquisitely made and obviously ancient, it had about it an air of power, like a sword carried by a king.

Am I supposed to hold it? he wondered, both excited yet wary.

Yes, said an ethereal-sounding female voice from inside his head that he accepted without alarm. *Yes, hold the sword. It's important.*

What was it Dad once said about swords in stories? thought Jake. *That what they really represent is opening one up to truth, cutting away false ideas. Swords aren't about killing, but the truth can feel like death if we don't want to face it.*

He remembered something else his dad had said, quoting a Sufi mystic named Rumi. *Die before you die. Die as many times as you can in one lifetime—to old beliefs and customs which no longer serve you so that you may become who you truly are.*

'Is that what the ghost was going to say?' he wondered excitedly.

Bracing himself for blinding flashes of light and a rush of power, Jake clutched the sword's hilt.

But nothing happened. Not immediately.

Rather than power, he felt something else flow from the sword—emotion, something between sadness and shame and the temple's insides became an earth-walled chamber that Jake instinctively knew lay beneath the sphinx. It was an image from the recent past. The sword was revealing a memory.

Jake jumped when he saw the white wolf, though it appeared unthreatening. It sat on its haunches, watching on as part of the wall transformed into a great swirling mass of darkness. It reminded Jake of the inkwell, except this gateway felt sinister and somehow wrong.

'Look at you. How pathetic!' spat a voice as deep as thunder.

A tall man dressed in black stepped in front of Jake and radiated such power that he appeared like a god. He was holding a Samurai sword, except that he wasn't Samurai. With long dark hair tied back in a single tress, he looked more like a Viking mixed with a Greek, for he was swarthy and ruggedly handsome with piercing blue eyes.

Emotion surged through the sword in Jake's hand. Sadness and shame were swept aside by anger, exhaustion and excruciating pain. He gasped. On his knees, Jake was living the memory. Deep gashes covered his body. He was aware of speaking, though couldn't hear the words, as though something were blocking them.

'You're time is over, Tusk,' continued the man. 'The time for *all* humans is over.'

He glanced over his shoulder at the vortex of the gate. 'Destiny awaits. I would wish you farewell, but that would be pointless.'

With lightning speed he swung his blade.

Adrenalin surged through Jake, but before the blade struck him, a colossal force tore through the memory and cut it short. He was no longer in the chamber, but at the entrance to a cave. Disorientated, his heart racing, Jake peered inside.

If the man with the sword had seemed god-like then the character Jake was studying was in a different league all together. Dressed in a dark cloak with the hood up, he sat in a cave in front of a fire, smoking a pipe. All Jake could see of his face was a bushy grey moustache and the rich brown of his skin. It clearly wasn't the ghost. Combined with his hawk-like features he reminded Jake of Arabian nomads he had once seen in a documentary.

He looked peaceful, yet his presence electrified the air. When he inhaled, the atmosphere grew light. When he exhaled, it grew so heavy that it felt to Jake that the world might implode, as though the man's very breath determined the fate of the universe.

This cave, thought Jake as he studied it. *It's in the mountains above the farmhouse!*

A gust blew into the cave and shunted Jake forward. Taking it as a sign, he stepped from the shadows into the cave.

As quick as a hawk, the stranger glanced up from the flames and fixed on Jake. His eyes were a dazzling green. They widened as though in recognition or shock, perhaps both, and shone with terrifying wisdom. Jake grew dizzy. He feared that were he to gaze into the eyes for more than a moment, they would swallow him whole.

Only then did Jake notice that coiled about the neck of the stranger was a cobra. It reared up and hissed venomously. It was swiftly followed by a shriek and a great flapping of wings. Out of nowhere a mighty eagle flew at Jake and planted its talons against his chest. Its surprising bulk knocked him off balance.

Jake glanced backwards. Where moments before had been solid ground was now a hole. It was deep—so deep that it passed through worlds. He had but an instant to flail his arms about in panic and to try and wake. But neither worked.

The stranger smiled.

And Jake plunged.

CHAPTER 4
DREAM ROOM

SOMEWHERE DEEP WITHIN THE INNER-WORLDS, THAT IS, somewhere deep within Earth's psyche, for Earth contained many worlds beneath its surface, a new room had appeared. It was one of a kind and could only be seen from the outside by those who were truly awake or those who had created it.

The room was round, its only furniture an old wooden table and two chairs. On the table burned a single candle, barely enough to reach the room's wall which contained twelve doors. Though their positions remained fixed like the hours on a clock face, the doors and their frames constantly changed, rarely the same for more than a moment. There were old doors, new doors, lavish doors, plain doors, doors of every kind, some framed in creeping plants, others in ancient symbols while some were adorned with a torch or a lantern casting the occasional flash of extra light. They were as infinite as the thoughts of the being who had created the room, for that's what they reflected: thoughts available for exploration, though most of the time there were so many that they were more like a maze to become lost in.

That same being sat on one of the chairs, gazing into the candle flame. He sat not as a human. That body had been destroyed battling a god. Instead, he sat in his spirit form—a wolf.

A white wolf.

'I'm too old for this,' grumbled a lizard resting on the table, the wolf's only company. With a drooping crest and heavy-lidded eyes, it looked ancient. 'I was enjoying the four hundred and fifth year of what was intended to be a five hundred year snooze when you rudely awoke me. Why didn't you summon one of the younger lizards?'

'Because I need experience not youth, Geoffrey old friend,' said the wolf, who had also seen better days. 'And when it comes to dreamtime you're the best there is.'

'With or without me, you're buggered,' said Geoffrey, his attention on the bats that flitted through the shadows. 'You'd have been better off if you'd just done the decent thing and died, rather than crying out for me from the void.'

The wolf's eyes twinkled with humour.

'What were you thinking?' continued Geoffrey. 'First chasing a god then fighting the bloody thing, and if that wasn't enough, half-dead you dive after it through the god gate when you know full well it's only designed for one being at a time.'

'There was no time for thought. Not even time to send a message,' said the wolf. 'That I happened to be in the chamber beneath the Sphinx, hidden in the shadows at the very moment Boreas arrived and summoned the gate was remarkable.'

'Isn't Boreas meant to be a noble god, responsible for the world Greed?' asked Geoffrey, referring to one of six worlds through which all souls must ultimately pass on the long journey from Earth's surface to the Core, a destination some called Heaven. 'Not to mention God of the North Wind and Lord of the Sirens.'

'*Supposed* to be. Yet there he was summoning the god gate, a gate designed to corrupt humans, tricking them with the promise of great power—a false power which ultimately brings about their downfall, though not before they've created great destruction.'

Geoffrey sat in ruminative silence, eyeing a moth fluttering about the candle flame.

'It didn't make sense,' continued the wolf, 'why a god with true power would bother passing through the gate... unless... unless he had been corrupted and had plans on the Surface, for the gate would recalibrate his power so that it could be used there too. When I tried to stop him, his bragging confirmed as much. He claimed that a powerful spirit disguised as a fertility goddess by the name of Luna, with him as her henchman, intends to rob the Surface of energy, stealing as many souls as she can.'

'And going where with them exactly?'

'That's the question.'

'One you intend to investigate?' asked Geoffrey dryly.

'With your help, I hope. Come on, Geoffrey, think about it. What were the odds that I would survive?'

The wolf closed his eyes for a moment and shivered at the recollection of being impaled through the chest with Lord Boreas's sword. His life had flashed before his eyes. Confronted with the choice of living or dying, it had been the image of his son, Jake, that had drawn his will power towards life. With a Herculean effort he had staggered forward and fallen through the gate after the god.

'I knew only one body could emerge from the gate,' he went on. 'But I took a gamble—that two souls entering the gate at the same time would confuse it, at least long enough to allow a battle of wills, between one that was corrupted against one that was less corrupted. As a human against a god, my one advantage was the ability to dream and so access the potential of the cosmos and the power to co-create. As you know, when a being chooses to become a god, a false god through the god gate, they lose this and become reliant instead on the fickle belief of their followers. They choose short term individual power over the infinite power of the communal heart.'

'And where is Boreas's soul now?' asked Geoffrey.

'It exists, but in the void—lost. As I summoned you and requested the creation of this place, I heard his cry of anguish. We have the initiative. The cosmos supports us. With your guidance, and if I can remain focused,' explained the wolf as he glanced uncertainly about the ever-shifting doors, 'my soul can occupy Boreas's body that lies uninhabited somewhere. I have the chance to move close to this Luna, impersonating Boreas in order to find out what she's up to. Can't you see what a lucky throw of the dice it is?'

'Perhaps,' muttered Geoffrey. 'But the stakes are extreme. For a start, your soul is fractured from the stress of the gate. I see it. You will not last long—'

'All the more reason to get moving,' pressed the wolf.

'Second, assuming you can fool this powerful spirit, Luna, which is unlikely, each mistake you make, each time you attempt to access Boreas's power, which you might need to, you leave a scent. Right now he can't find this room. We're travelling at light speed through a void, perhaps a separate one from him. But the moment he senses you, desperate for his body back, he'll be onto you like a rash.'

'Risks I'm willing to take. What else am I to do?'

Geoffrey released an exasperated sigh.

'As for you, old friend,' assured the wolf, 'you can leave whenever you wish. But please, at least help me get started.'

'And how will you start?'

'Before impaling me, Boreas also bragged of something Luna had instructed him to steal—from the House of Tusk no less.'

Geoffrey groaned with dismay. 'And what dreadful thing would that be?'

'Pandora's Box,' said the wolf.

Geoffrey stiffened.

'Boreas claimed there was much more to the box than the Greek myth about disease and pestilence. He said it holds a key of some sort, to something ancient that Luna needs for her plans.'

'Of all the objects of power hidden within the fort's vault,' said Geoffrey in a distant voice, 'that and one other, a sword, are the most dangerous. All that is known of them is hearsay. Some talk of the box containing a key to something—a perversion of nature say those strong enough to hold the thought, modern in making, ancient in essence, an essence now so bitter that it has the power to destroy energy, something supposed to be impossible.'

The wolf stared into the candle flame as though it held the answer.

'And so you're going break into the fort and then deliver it to her, is that it?' said Geoffrey sardonically.

'If I don't do it, and if she's as powerful as Boreas claimed, then she'll get it anyway. It's far better that I do it. First, because of who I am... who I *was*,' corrected the wolf with a wistful light in his eyes. 'As the most recent Lord Tusk I have a better chance than any of stealing it while doing minimal damage to the fort. I can then use Pandora's Box as a way of moving close to her and, with a bit of luck, scupper her plans.'

Geoffrey closed his eyes and looked more tired than ever.

'You do realise what this means, what's at stake?' pressed the wolf. 'Earth's surface is the testing ground of humanity—the laboratory about which the entire cosmos revolves. It's already stretched to breaking point. If it falters, which it certainly will if Luna is allowed to steal energy unchecked, then the entire cosmos will falter with it.'

Geoffrey's eyes remained closed, his body motionless when finally he spoke. 'Then perhaps you should let it.'

CHAPTER 5
THE INKWELL

EVERYTHING WAS HOW JAKE REMEMBERED IT—THE WALLS crammed with shelves of books, the red Persian rug patterned with green dragons and the antique desk that had once belonged to an Indian king. His dad's study, a place where classical music never quite faded and the smell of pipe tobacco forever hung in the air.

Jake took a deep breath. It was a his favourite room. Whenever his dad had been back from his long spells overseas he had always had time to tell Jake a story. Incredible stories. A mug of hot chocolate in hand, he had sat by the fire while his dad told tales of high adventure on magic carpets in far off lands where gods and goddesses were common.

He wiped away his silent tears and crossed the threshold with his breakfast, followed by Trifle the cat who leapt upon the green sofa and made himself at home.

Placing the tray on the desk, Jake sat down behind it. He closed his eyes and took a slow sip of his tea. When he opened them, his gaze fell upon the old brass inkwell sitting at the far corner of the desk. Excitement and fear shivered through sadness in equal measure.

'I had a dream last night, Trifle,' he said.

If Trifle was listening, he made no show of it. He was curled up licking a paw.

'It felt very real,' continued Jake and took a pensive bite of toast. 'But how could it be real when it was so fantastical? And if it was real then what is a portal doing in Dad's study? Maybe my mind is just creating a fantasy out of all of his stories, inventing a secret way to access them and somehow Dad.'

It then occurred to Jake that the characters he had seen through the inkwell of his dreams had never been part of any of his dad's tales. A chill ran through him when he thought of the stranger in the cave, along with being knocked into a deep shaft by an eagle, a fall he had no recollection of.

'There's only one way to find out,' he said and jumped up and reached towards the inkwell.

Just like the time he encountered the inkwell while dreaming on the train, Jake stopped an inch short of touching it. This time there was no tingling in his fingertips. Emboldened, he took a deep breath and flipped open the lid.

Nothing. No flex of energy. No gaping portal. Just the glass receptacle for ink.

With an exhale of relief, Jake slumped back in the chair. The relief was short lived. It was swiftly followed by disappointment.

'Dreams are just dreams, Trifle. It's a shame. Imagine if the inkwell really was a portal to another world!'

As he took another bite of toast, a moth appeared, fluttering in and out of a light beam. To Jake's delight, it flew about his head—not just once but three times, before settling on an envelope. It was propped up against an antique pot on a small table beside the sofa. Jake was too surprised by his name written on it to wonder at the behaviour of the moth.

'Granddad's writing!' he exclaimed, leaping up from the desk. 'But...'

Without further thought he tore open the envelope and withdrew a single sheet of writing paper. He was about to read it when a voice from over his shoulder caused him to cry out in shock.

'What you got there?' it said.

Jake spun around, his heart racing. It was Frost, looking as mischievous as he had in town.

'Bollocks!' barked Jake. 'What are you doing here?'

'I've come to save you.'

'Save me?' exclaimed Jake and cursed a second time. 'What are you talking about?'

'From yourself, of course!' beamed Frost. 'From a lifetime of tedium and drudgery and pretending to be something you're not.'

'Pretending?' exclaimed Jake.

'Of course! Pretending to be a know-it-all. Pretending to be oh-so-terribly handsome.'

'I was right the first time,' scoffed Jake. 'You *are* mad.'

'Well, you're neither bright nor handsome,' continued Frost, ignoring the insult. 'In fact, you're rather ugly.'

'How did you get in here?' demanded Jake, unnerved at how Frost had managed to sneak up on him without making the slightest noise.

'Who's that letter from?' asked Frost, his eyes glinting with intrigue. 'Read it out.'

'It's none of your bloody business!' retorted Jake.

'Come on, don't be boring. Look, I brought éclairs!' announced Frost, holding up a box as though it explained everything.

'I thought you said éclairs were for girls.'

'Only when *you* eat them.'

Jake tossed back his head in dry laughter. 'Anyway, you can't have éclairs for breakfast.'

'You can. I'll prove it,' said Frost. He grabbed one from the box and ate it in two bites. 'There, see? Delicious!'

Jake did his best to look unimpressed, but he was secretly delighted to see Frost despite his audacity—perhaps because of it.

'Seriously,' said Jake. 'How did you do that?'

'Simple. I took an éclair out of the box like so,' said Frost, taking another. 'And ate it!' Frost stuffed it in his mouth.

'No, you idiot. How did you creep in here so quietly?'

'An idiot, hey?' said Frost with a cream-filled grin. 'Well, at least I can hear.'

'The floorboards creak. How did you do it?' pressed Jake.

'You were too wrapped up in that letter of yours to pay attention to anything else,' said Frost as he swanned past Jake. He leapt into the chair and put his feet upon the desk. 'So come on, read it out.'

Jake glanced down at the letter before folding it up and putting it in his pocket.

Frost snorted with amusement and took another éclair.

Jake studied him. In the confines of the study he was even more aware of Frost's presence than he had been in town. It was magnetic, so much so that part of Jake wanted to share the contents of the letter even though Frost was a total stranger. Instead, he wondered why Frost was in his home trying to befriend him. Jake had nothing to hide and though the farm was obviously worth something, the Burton's had nothing of interest to a typical thief. Neither did he think Frost a thief. Jake had only to look at his clothing to tell that. The quality of the cloth was high and fitted him as though it had been tailored specially, though he wore it with an air of disdain, adding to his sense of style.

Frost was grinning at Jake. 'Seen any bats lately? Had any dreams?' he ventured and finished off the last éclair.

Jake thought for a moment before answering. The letter was real and private. The dream less so, or so Jake thought. He was intrigued to hear what Frost might make of it.

'Actually I did,' he admitted, reclaiming his tea before Frost drank it. 'It was incredible! It felt so real!'

'Ha!' cried Frost. 'Of course! Let's hear it!'

Standing in the centre of the study as though on stage, Jake proceeded to recount his dream.

As he did so, Frost leaned back and gazed out the window, his eyes brightening with each new detail.

Finally Jake finished. 'What do you think? Meaningless rubbish, right?'

'Far from it!' shot back Frost and thwacked the desktop to press the point. 'It's a brilliant dream and very, *very* important.'

'But it's just a dream,' insisted Jake, part excited, part disturbed by Frost's enthusiasm. The image of the stranger in the cave loomed ominously in his mind. 'They're not real. The contents don't actually mean anything.'

'Not real?' exclaimed Frost who leapt atop the desk with surprising agility. 'Not meaningful? Dreams are more real than anything!'

'Balls,' said Jake.

'Dreams are the language of nature! An insight into your primordial psyche!'

'Primordial psyche?' said Jake doubtfully.

'A psyche of symbols. Dreams are honest for a start. No masks, no contradiction, no inhibition nor hypocrisy. None of the deceit of daytime! Not to mention how they access the great repository of the unconscious which, by the way, forgets nothing, *nothing* at all and contains all wisdom, all secrets of all time! Dreams are where the soul and the distorted ego fight an illusory battle and dance their merry dance. Dreams are everything!'

'Distorted ego?' asked Jake.

'The conditioned mind, my overly-conditioned friend.'

'What are you talking about?'

'Brainwashed.'

'I'm not brainwashed!' said Jake.

'Actually, it's more like contaminated than washed,' corrected Frost. 'What was once a wonderfully simple, wonderfully practical mind has been rewired, reprogrammed and re-everything else that's mad and ridiculous and utterly imbalanced.'

Jake scoffed. 'Reprogrammed? I'm not a computer.'

'Not originally. Before, you were something truly miraculous, infinitely superior to a lifeless and rubbish computer, confined to the limits of its witless inventor. But you've allowed yourself to become one, doing exactly as you're told—what to think, what not to think, what to see, what not to see, what to feel, what not to feel, what to touch, what not to touch, not knowing what's real and what isn't. Your mind has been reprogrammed to believe that only mind and matter exist and that spirit is hocus-pocus. In other words, you have been programmed to be thoroughly stupid and thoroughly, *thoroughly* dull. Not to mention powerless.'

Jake was about to take issue but smiled instead, amused at Frost's impressive performance.

'So, who is it who's done this reprogramming?' he asked, deciding to humour Frost.

'Oh the usual suspects. The cultured lot. Anyone *respectable* but not worthy of respect. Anyone who claims to have your best interests at heart and especially those who claim to love you. Ah, modern love! How wonderful it is.'

'And why would these people do such a thing?'

'Because they're even more asleep than you,' said Frost and jumped back down into the chair. Arms behind his head, he stretched back with a satisfied grin.

'Anyway,' he said a moment later, 'blaming gets you nowhere. As for your dream, it was far more than just a dream. It was an initiation! Pyramids, caves, serpents and eagles, your plunging through a hole into the lower realms—these are all *massively* symbolic. And you saw bats, didn't you? Ha! I knew you would. Didn't I tell you?'

'An initiation for what?' asked Jake, unconvinced.

'You'll soon find out. Except you're not allowed to know just yet. It's why you remember nothing of the fall into the hole. That character in the cave was checking you out, taking a peek into your darkest secrets.'

'You're not telling me you think he actually exists?' mocked Jake.

'Of course he does.'

Jake shuddered at the thought.

If he is real, what on Earth could he want? he wondered.

'Most characters in dreams usually reflect yourself. They're different aspects of your many personalities and fears,' explained Frost. 'But sometimes an actual being appears, independent in its own right—a guide, a gatekeeper or, if it's a very auspicious dream, someone higher ranking.'

Jake studied Frost whose eyes glinted with mystery, wondering if he might be right. 'Why did you say *up here on the surface*?'

'You live on the surface of life—not only literally but more importantly, symbolically. When you finally start to wake, what's hidden beneath the surface comes up to greet you, one world after the other, until the whole cosmos is here before you, all dimensions merged into one,' claimed Frost and his grin broadened. 'If you could see what I can see right now, what surrounds you in this room and outside, you'd die of shock!'

Jake looked about the study uncertainly. 'Where do you get all these ideas?'

'I spend my time knowing *useful* things,' said Frost, 'not memorising dates about who murdered who and who stole what, playing with abstract equations or worrying about how to spell properly. Such things are for fools! For followers! And when you get the answer *right*, whatever it may be, in truth you're wrong! Life is a mystery waiting to be danced with, not analysed.'

On this point Jake agreed with Frost. Exams were a menace. *Who set the questions anyway?* he had often wondered and who were the markers to judge the quality of an answer?

While Frost was studying him, a cawing raven drew Jake's attention to the copse beside the house.

'What about the wolf in the dream?' he asked.

'The wolf is simply brilliant and quite the opposite of all that nonsense you've been told. They're playful, intelligent, loyal and are the epitome of wild spirit. Not wild in a savage sense, but in the sense of being in balance and true to their nature.'

'So what was one doing under the sphinx temple?'

Frost's eyes flashed with intrigue. 'Well, that's the question, isn't it?' he said. 'A visit from an animal in a dream could mean several things. Often they're encouraging the dreamer to embody their nature in order to help that person in daily life. Sometimes the animal might represent a specific person—you or someone else. How did you feel about it at the time?'

'I don't know. It didn't seem to be a threat. And the sphinx?'

'Some archaeologists believe there's a hidden chamber beneath one of the sphinx's paws. Even more interesting, there's an old legend known only to a few that states it contains a portal, assuming you know how to summon it. And you saw it! It's said to lead to another world. Many have sought it, but none have found it. Only a select few have been led to it by special gatekeepers.'

'What other world?' asked Jake excitedly.

'A world of power, of course,' explained Frost, still leaning back in the chair. 'The idea is to pass through the portal then return to the Surface to rule the world.'

'If it's known only to a few,' said Jake, 'how come you know about it?'

'Because I'm brilliant,' replied Frost unashamedly.

Jake studied Frost. He appeared to know a huge amount about incredible things and yet left Jake with a sense that he was holding back, a feeling confirmed by the humour that never left Frost's eyes.

With a deep breath, Jake glanced about the shelves of books. His gaze fell on two books in particular. The first was titled *Janus—The God with Two Faces*. The second was *The Tibetan Book of the Dead*.

'What do you think about reincarnation?' he asked.

'Oh look!' cried Frost pointing above Jake's head. 'A moth! Very auspicious!'

'A moth?' said Jake excitedly and looked up at it. *Perhaps it's the same one that showed me Granddad's letter!*

'She's coming over here!'

The moth left its circling above Jake's head to do the same over the inkwell. Frost's eyes were wide with anticipation as it changed its flight to a hovering. It was only an inch or so above the lid when something extraordinary happened—with a loud snap and a powerful pulse of energy the moth was gone.

Jake's eyes shot wide. 'But it was just a dream...'

'If it was just a dream then open the inkwell,' challenged Frost.

'I already did.'

'Then do it again.'

'Why don't you?'

'Because it's your inkwell,' said Frost. 'It wouldn't do for me to interfere in such matters.'

'If it is a portal then it probably goes to Egypt, right? That would be amazing! I've never been. I often begged Dad to take me, but he would never let me come on his work trips.'

'Egypt would be far too boring,' said Frost, deflating Jake's hopes. 'If it's a portal then it will take you to another world entirely, one with great tests of courage.'

Jake studied the inkwell, wracking his brain for an alternative explanation as to where the moth had gone.

'Come on! What are you waiting for?' cried Frost. 'Stop being a coward!'

'Alright, shut up will you,' said Jake and reached for the inkwell lid.

'By the way,' said Frost, interrupting Jake, 'if you follow the moth you do realise you might never come back and if you do then this world will never seem the same again. It can't do. Such is the nature of the hero's quest. You do have a quest I assume?'

'A quest? Of course I don't have quest other than to shut you up.'

'Oh dear, it's worse than I thought,' sighed Frost. 'You must have a quest before entering a portal and the stronger your faith in it, the better you chances of survival.'

'You mean like saving a girl or something?'

'Are you talking symbolically?'

'God, not symbols again. I've had enough of this,' said Jake and once more reached for the lid.

'Wait!' cried Frost. 'You *must* have a quest! So if you like the idea of saving a girl, so be it. You don't have a girlfriend up here do you? That would make the quest less powerful because the girl you seek is in the inner-worlds.'

'No,' replied Jake. 'I had a girlfriend in town, but—'

'Then your quest is to save a magical woman from dreadful peril.'

Jake laughed, taking Frost's drama as a joke. 'Yes,' he agreed. 'That's the quest.'

Frost glanced out of the window and up at the mountainside, a mysterious light in his eyes. 'I'd be careful what you wish for if I were you,' he muttered.

'Why do you say that?' asked Jake and followed Frost's line of sight, but saw nothing unusual on the mountainside. 'What are you looking at?'

'Nothing. It's just the standard disclaimer before entering a portal,' said Frost smiling and nodded at the inkwell.

Jake focused back on the mysterious object. He repeated his quest in his mind. Then, before losing his nerve, he grabbed its lid

It didn't budge.

'That's odd,' he said. 'It opened before.'

'Try harder,' said Frost. 'Put your back into it.'

Jake did so, but it refused to give.

'Think about something appropriate,' suggested Frost. 'If it's a portal to another world, you can't just expect it to open to anyone. You must focus your intent on something—something which acts like a key to your quest.'

'Like what?'

'Try the moth. Like the butterfly it's a symbol of rebirth because they transform from a grub into something that flies.'

Jake thought of the moth as he pushed with all his might against the stubborn lid.

He was about to give up when the image of the ghost filled his mind. Shrouded in mist, it turned in Jake's direction and held up the lamp. A vibration spread from the inkwell up through Jake and grew in intensity as once again the eye appeared in the flame. It was closed. The vibration grew so intense that Jake was shaking. He tried to let go, but couldn't. Suddenly the flame brightened.

An instant later the eye shot open and with it the inkwell.

A pulse of energy shook the study.

Seeing the portal in everyday life was terrifying. Its power was immense. The more he resisted it, the more powerful it grew. He felt like he was been shaken to pieces.

'Frost!' he snapped. 'Do something!'

Frost had collapsed in hysterics. The sight of Jake bent over the desk, his legs and backside convulsing wildly was too much for him.

'Do something!' repeated Jake, staring with horror into the swirling darkness of the void. His body was consumed by a terrific heat. The pull was so great that it felt like his eyeballs were being wrenched from their sockets.

'Jake!' howled Frost. 'If you could just... oh, ha-ha! If only you could see yourself!'

Adding to Frost's entertainment was the storm of books hauled from the shelves and sucked into the inkwell, thwacking Jake as they went. The hefty shelves were threatening to follow, as was the furniture, while Frost was unaffected.

'Stop resisting,' managed Frost between guffaws. 'Let go! Dive in! Surrender!'

Within the darkness were nebula-like flecks of pink and green. Their beauty was so bewitching that Jake felt himself split in two. While part of him continued to cling to the desk, another part of him imagined sticking his head into the portal to see what he could see.

The things he had seen before through the inkwell flashed through his mind's eye—the wolf, the sword, the powerful man in front of the swirling gate, and the even more powerful stranger in the cave. This time, as though he were still in the dream, instead of the eagle knocking him off balance, Jake willingly leapt into the bottomless-seeming shaft. He shot past doorways he intuitively knew were entrances to different worlds.

His curiosity was taking him deep at great speed. With a flash of light, he crossed a critical threshold into more mysterious and darker places. Faces, many of them, grave and powerful feeling, strange yet somehow familiar, emerged from the darkness and studied him as he raced past them one by one.

For a split second, the travelling part of him wondered if he was going too deep too quickly. The instant it did, fear rushed in. Prickling, hot, crushing, it almost consumed him. He felt the exhaustion in the part of him that clung to the desk.

'Frost! I can't... I can't hold out much longer! Help!'

His eyes streaming with laughter, one hand holding his stomach, finally Frost got to his feet.

'Oh, for a camera,' he wheezed. 'Such a shame to stop it.'

Despite the urgency, Frost didn't rush forward to Jake's aid. One moment laughing, the next he was poised like a wild animal alert to danger.

'One can't be too careful with private portals like these,' he muttered, though Jake was too embroiled to hear him. 'Especially one to the august House of Tusk. I doubt my welcome would be as warm as the one for our new lord here.'

As a test, he took a step closer but contrary to the forces working on Jake and the study, Frost was repelled backwards.

'Thought that might happen,' he said.

As Jake plummeted deeper through fear, everything turned black. Then flashed bright green—a giant eye of ferocious wisdom loomed before him. It reminded him of the stranger in the cave, except it was different. Its pupil was like a ravenous black hole that consumed worlds. There was no escaping it.

'F-Frost,' stammered Jake on the verge of passing out. 'I... I'm...'

Frost scoured what remained of the study, fixed on a lamp straining against its plug. With lightning speed, he ripped free the cord and swung the socket end lasso-style towards the inkwell lid. Remarkably, it took hold.

'Such a shame,' he repeated. 'Still, off he'll pop soon enough and if my instincts serve me, which they always do, an invite will follow. It's my only way in.'

Grinning smugly, Frost gave the cord a sharp tug.

As Jake drew what he imagined was his last breath, an instant from being sucked into the abysmal pupil of the giant eye, the lid of the inkwell snapped shut and he collapsed in a heap.

CHAPTER 6
PANDORA'S BOX

GEOFFREY WAS PERCHED ON THE WOLF'S HEAD. LIKE A SKIPPER at the helm scouring the clouds of an approaching storm, he glanced about the dream room, noting how the doors about the circular wall changed at great speed. Finally he had agreed to help the wolf, starting with the theft of Pandora's Box. Where words had failed, cake had succeeded—chocolate cake, Geoffrey's weak spot. As long as the wolf could dream them up and Geoffrey was content with the quality, he would do what he could to prolong the great human experiment known to some as evolution.

'Calm your mind,' commanded Geoffrey. 'Stop worrying about what you ought to have done and what might happen. You must be completely present. Focus on one thought and one alone—entering the vault.'

Seated on the chair in front of the burning candle, the wolf closed his eyes and did his best to be present. He dared not think of the two people dearest to his heart. Strong emotions in the dream room, which demanded objectivity, were a great risk—they could tear the room apart and much more besides. Instead he thought of nature, of crystalline rivers and green mountains, of balmy breezes on spring mornings and one by one the pace of the changing doors slowed down.

He also dwelt on the brilliance of Geoffrey's plan—to dream a way directly into the vault rather than attempting entrance from the outside. The House of Tusk's vault was the most secure in the cosmos. Not only was it guarded by Naga serpents, fatal to both mortal and immortal alike, but it was composed of special rocks that allowed passage only to those with permission. It was also full of weapons and other objects of power. Confiscated over thousands of years, most were highly unpredictable, some containing souls which could possess an intruder and use their body to fulfil their own wicked desires.

There was a loophole, however. Given the fort was based in a world known as Himassisi, it was designed to repel gods, mythical creatures and other such powerful beings, but not a soul from the Surface still encoded as human with the human gift to dream —extremely potent if mastered. So it was for the wolf. Despite appearances, his soul was still human. It was the soul of Lawrence Burton, Jake's dad.

'That's better,' said Geoffrey as all the doors stabilised.

Lawrence's gaze was fixed on the one directly ahead. His hackles rose. Strong and strange-looking, it sparkled ruby-red, except they weren't rubies but garnets, a powerful mineral able to deflect the subtlest of negative intent. Framing the door were writhing knots of red serpents—the Naga.

'That's it,' said Lawrence, his voice betraying a tremor of fear. 'The door to the vault.'

'Now materialise Lord Boreas's body,' instructed Geoffrey from the table, having left his perch on the wolf's head.

Lawrence closed his wolf eyes, this time focusing on the image of the god. Strain flickered across his brow as he battled to steady his emotions. His only memory of the god was from their fatal duel beneath the Sphinx, but he managed to recall it as a detached observer. He watched Lord Boreas leap into the swirling portal of the god gate followed by his mortally-wounded self, visualised their souls cast into chaos by the confused gate as they battled for possession of the god's body left in limbo. He imagined Lord Boreas's body slumped in the shadows on a stone floor which might have been anywhere and, visualising his dream-body in the same place, stepped into it.

Lawrence shivered with the reality of what he had done. When he opened his eyes, to his astonishment he was no longer the wolf but Lord Boreas standing almost seven feet tall in the dream room.

'You'll need to brush up on your attitude,' said Geoffrey. 'Drop Lawrence the romantic saviour. Boreas is not only God of planet Greed, but God of the North Wind, the bringer of winter, tempestuous and devouring. As Lord of the Sirens he is fire and lust behind a mask of charm. In both forms he is a destroyer. You need to sizzle and chill to carry it off.'

'I'll work on it,' said Lawrence as he got accustomed to his new body.

'And I'd work on those feet, too,' suggested Geoffrey dryly.

Lawrence looked down and barked with laughter. He still had the feet of a wolf. 'I thought they'd be better for stealth!'

A moment later he had visualised them into the feet of Lord Boreas.

'And the tail,' added Geoffrey.

Lawrence glanced over his shoulder and released another bark of laughter. He had forgotten how wonderful it felt to laugh and his spirit soared.

Having dealt with the tail, it was then he noticed that part of his spirit still existed as the wolf sitting on the chair, its form ethereal like a phantom.

'It's the part of you that must remain in the dream room,' explained Geoffrey. 'It's your lifeline back from wherever you venture in your dream-body.'

'How many worlds is it possible to inhabit in a given moment?'

'In theory the number is infinite, depending on the power of one's imagination and ability to sustain it. In your case I'd say two, if you're lucky.'

Lawrence practised shifting his focus between himself in Lord Boreas's body and the wolf until his presence in the two was roughly in balance.

'Remember,' said Geoffrey, 'this is dreaming and it's very real. Anything less than total presence will betray you. There are no masks in dreamtime. It's not like daytime up there on the Surface. Deceit doesn't exist. If you feel anger you'll become it. If you feel lust you'll become it and so on. Neither is this like ordinary Surface dreaming where what seems like death is simply symbolic and becomes a door to a deeper dimension within your psyche. This far down into the unconscious it's visceral. The wounds are real and so is death. It doesn't matter that you appear to be Lord Boreas. It's your dream body that counts.'

Lawrence nodded gravely.

'And I needn't remind you,' continued Geoffrey, 'what will happen if the real Lord Boreas finds this room or even worse, uses it to enter the fort's vault. All hell will break loose. Literally.'

'I wonder what totem he'll use.'

'Something befitting his vanity. Something bigger and fiercer than a wolf. But don't get lost in appearance. The wolf totem is what was sent to you in your moment of crisis and what is sent is always what's needed. Its sense of loyalty, its stamina, will serve you well. The medicine of the wolf, which resorts to ferocity only as a last resort, reminds you of your true nature and nothing, *nothing* is more important than that. I dread to think what demons Lord Boreas might unleash. Remember where he rules. Planet Greed has many faces, all an obsession with quantity. Fall prey to these and you fall prey to Lord Boreas. Show him a flaw and he'll rip it wide open and create an abyss. The wolf, however, roots you in quality.'

To better ground himself in the dream room Lawrence inhaled deeply of its rich scent, a scent as complex as the imagination which had given birth to the multitude of places behind the doors.

'You ready?' asked Geoffrey from Lawrence's shoulder.

'As ready as I'll ever be,' replied Lawrence, focusing on his breath to steady his heartbeat.

'If you survive this then you might have a chance of fooling this so-called Luna who, make no mistake, is an extremely powerful being. But the chance is slight. I certainly wouldn't bet on it.'

'What else do you know about her?'

'No specifics, which is why we know she's powerful. There is little that can be hidden from lizards who see clearly through most illusion, so her power must be ancient. That she conceals herself, that she's rising up from the depths of the cosmos, can only mean one thing—she's after light. After energy.'

Lawrence felt grateful to have the grumpy old lizard as a guide. His wisdom and frankness gave Lawrence courage.

'Are you sure you still want to deliver Pandora's Box into her hands?' challenged Geoffrey. 'Whatever lies inside of it, you'll be handing her an instrument to channel and amplify her own chaos.'

'Only if it co-operates with her. You mentioned before that some say it contains something highly destructive. It might decide to destroy her.'

'And then destroy the rest of us.'

'We've already been over this.' Before he lost his nerve, Lawrence held his palm just short of the gem-encrusted door. Power tingled through his fingers. Following a final glance back at the wolf, he pressed his hand to the door.

Gems blazed an angry red.

Serpents reared and hissed.

His body jolted with the surge of energy.

An abyss of fear yawned before Lawrence and threatened to consume him. Believing the fear was just an illusion, he took a resolute step and passed through it.

They emerged through a gilded tomb of a pharaoh. It stood upright and opened like a door into what, at first glance, appeared like a museum. They were inside the main vault of the House of Tusk.

On the outside, it was a rectangular-shaped lump of sparkling red rock that took up most of the space of one of the many halls within the fort. Despite its enormous bulk, it floated in the air while red snakes slithered on guard across its surface. The insides, however, were far greater than the dimensions suggested by its outer appearance. It contained many halls on many levels, all brimming with objects of power from all over the cosmos. The more powerful ones were contained separate vaults.

Lawrence, disguised as Lord Boreas, Geoffrey still upon his shoulder, glanced around the vault. Sensing his presence, weapons bristled. His body tingled with the awesome power of the place. Lawrence and Geoffrey had entered into one of the more powerful halls where the weapons and other objects were wiser and plainer than those elsewhere which glimmered with gold and jewels and wasted energy on pointless jeers and insults.

The atmosphere calmed. As Lord Tusk, lord of the fort and thus keeper of certain gates that were critical to the smooth functioning of the cosmos, Lawrence belonged there, as did Geoffrey, and the objects sensed it. Lawrence took a moment to steady himself, balancing his focus on both the vault and the part of his spirit still with the wolf in the dream room.

'That was easier than expected,' said Lawrence.

'It's getting out that you need to worry about,' said Geoffrey and strained his hearing for any movement. 'Let's not linger. You know where it is?'

'Yes,' said Lawrence, having got his bearings. 'This way.'

He sped off from the hall and passed through two others. He was about to activate a hidden door within a grand fireplace when he froze—a slithering sound came from the adjoining hall.

The Naga!

Heart racing, Lawrence pressed himself into the shadows of the fireplace. He shifted the balance of his awareness to the wolf in the dream room so that he was less present in the vault.

A large red Naga serpent slithered to the centre of the hall and stopped. Sensing something, it reared up. Green eyes blazing, it licked the air.

Though it was several paces away from Lawrence, it felt like it was right beside him. He battled to stay calm. Taking a great risk, he shifted yet more of his awareness to the wolf. Only a phantom of him remained in the fireplace and the doors in the dream room began to quake in their frames, threatening to betray its existence to the real Lord Boreas lost in the void.

Following another lick of the air, finally the serpent slithered from the hall.

Once Lawrence was certain the Naga was out of hearing, he rebalanced his presence and the dream room became calm again. He pulled the hidden lever in the fireplace to reveal a long staircase of stone steps dimly lit by a flaming torch. Not wasting an instant, he fled down them.

They arrived in a dank corridor like one of a dungeon, except instead of cells there were vault doors, behind which lay the most powerful weapons. Lawrence stole towards the one at the very end.

Though it was similar to other doors in having no handle or keyhole, its metal surface was iridescent and shimmered with a light of its own making.

'Are you sure this is it?' asked Geoffrey.

'I'm sure,' said Lawrence and once more glanced back through the strangely dancing shadows, half expecting one of them to rush forward and attack him. Before one did, he withdrew a knife from his belt and drew the blade across his right palm.

'Last chance to reconsider,' said Geoffrey calmly. 'What you're about to do will change the cosmos forever. But in which direction there's no telling.'

'I understand,' said Lawrence.

'I doubt it,' replied Geoffrey. 'But what the hell, it'll liven things up.'

His mind still racked with doubt, Lawrence focused within and listened to his heart. Its voice was clear—*Do it*. Before he had second thoughts, Lawrence pressed his bloodied palm to the door.

His heart raced. He prayed the blood from Lord Boreas's hand would be encoded not with the light of the god but with his own and that the vault would recognise him as Lord Tusk despite his disappearance. If not, the alarm would sound, the corridor would seal and they would be trapped. Lawrence couldn't afford to be caught. Too much was at stake. He was more useful to the fort if thought dead, but the deception would only work if it remained a secret to all but Geoffrey. Besides, the Naga might strike before Lawrence could explain.

For moments that felt like eternity nothing happened. Then something shifted in the surface of the door. His heart raced faster. He thought he glimpsed a face in it, several in fact, but the movement was too fleeting.

Finally, with a great gasp, the door unlocked and noiselessly swung open. As Lawrence released a sigh of relief, he and Geoffrey were lit up green by the room, its walls made up of the same iridescent metal as the door. Its only contents were a simple stone altar on top of which stood a rectangular shape about the size of a jewellery box.

'I've never been in this vault,' said Lawrence, both awed and terrified by the sight of Pandora's Box. 'I wonder if there are any traps.'

'An object like Pandora's Box doesn't need any. Only a fool would pick it up, let alone open it,' remarked Geoffrey.

'Enter the fool,' said Lawrence and, bracing himself, took a tentative step into the vault.

Before his foot had even touched the ground, a dreadful chill shot through him.

Back in the dream room, his wolf spirit whined with fear. Doors changed at great speed, reflecting Lawrence's racing mind.

Stay present, warned Geoffrey telepathically, digging his claws into Lawrence's shoulder.

The air prickled with a power beyond Lawrence's darkest imaginings. An immense presence inhabited the room. He felt his life-force in the balance and knew Geoffrey's hearsay to be true: that whatever was inside the box, it had the power to destroy energy.

Keep going, commanded Geoffrey. *If you submit to your fears we're done for.*

The prickling power grew heavier and denser. It slithered through Lawrence like a plague of vipers, challenging his existence, each leaden step like a passage through death: deeper, darker. He focused on his tremulous breath and on the wolf—a fraying lifeline back to the reality he knew.

Sweat broke out on his brow. His vision blurred. By the time it had cleared, the vault had transformed into a vast cemetery at dusk—soundless, lifeless, with tombs the size of small houses. It wasn't a place of rest and peace. It was a place of doom.

You're getting a glimpse of what's inside the box, said Geoffrey. *Stay present.*

Like the fort's vault, the dimensions inside Pandora's Box were far greater than those of its outside.

His legs about to buckle, Lawrence managed a final step. A dark and mighty grey pyramid loomed up amid the tombs. His mind reeled at the sight of it. His soul gasped. He was on the verge of passing out when he bumped into something solid. The jolt brought him back to the reality of the vault. He had reached the altar.

It took Lawrence several deep breaths to restore himself, enough to stand straight with the help of the altar.

'That was the easy part. Now try picking it up,' said Geoffrey, referring to Pandora's Box.

The moment Lawrence focused on the time-ravaged surface of Pandora's Box, a biting wind blew up and tore about him in a storm of whispers—several voices, both male and female, conspiratorial, as though making a momentous decision.

'You act with ignorance!' hissed a female voice that gripped Lawrence like an icy hand about the innards.

'I act with uncertainty,' gasped Lawrence boldly, 'but I act from my heart.'

The wind grew so violent, so bitterly cold that it felt like an arctic whirlwind, the whisperings like curses in an ancient tongue.

Geoffrey was silent. The decision to pick up the box had to come from Lawrence alone.

The cursing tempest grew worse. The longer it raged, the weaker he became. It was now or never. Intention was key. He needed a pure thought. Unable to think of anything but the artic gale, he used it to his advantage. He visualised a pristine landscape of snow, except there was no wind. It was blissfully still. The only movement was a stag and doe foraging beneath a solitary Scots pine. It was a powerful image of grace and harmony and the wolf in the dream room released a wistful howl.

Buffeted by the gale, Lawrence could hold it only a moment. Before it faded he took a deep breath and made the fateful move. He placed his hands on the box.

The cursing gale ceased instantly. Lawrence braced himself. The vault was as still as the snowy landscape lingering in his imagination.

When the stillness remained, Lawrence released a sigh of relief.

Geoffrey moved to the altar. He closed his eyes in concentration.

'What do you think?' asked Lawrence. His hands were still holding the box he hadn't dared move.

The lizard didn't answer. He was trying to see through the mystery of the box.

Seconds passed. Lawrence relaxed a little more. He shifted the box a fraction.

Geoffrey's eyes shot open in shock.

The box vibrated, glowed then blazed an ominous green. So did Lawrence.

'Don't let go!' ordered Geoffrey.

Fear coursed through Lawrence on such a scale that he scarcely recognised it as his own. It felt like the fear of an entire world, the collective fear of an endless cemetery clinging to his own fears.

With a yelp, the wolf in the dream room leapt to its feet but collapsed right back again, clawing frantically at the floor with its front paws.

Lawrence battled to hold on to Pandora's Box. He could no longer tell where he was or what he was holding when an almighty pulse burst from the box, shook the vault, shook the fort, shook Himassisi and every world throughout the cosmos.

For the moment it lasted, Lawrence ceased to exist. At least, that's how it had felt when he returned, as though his every atom had been blasted to a different direction of infinity then sucked right back again.

In some worlds volcanoes had erupted. In subtler ones, beings stopped mid-conversation and wondered why, feeling that something huge had taken place deep within them though couldn't say what exactly.

Lawrence's life flashed before him. Not the acts of heroics he had expected, not the battling of beasts or demons but the smallest things—acts of tenderness he had long forgotten.

His past was probed, the future divined. Not only his own but the entire web of life with which he was connected. In less than an instant the value of his life was weighed and measured then cast aside as the presence in the box focused on one event alone —his duel with Lord Boreas. The intensity of its interest coursed through Lawrence like wildfire.

Back in the dream room, doors shook in their frames. The wolf floundered about blindly, barely conscious of its movement. The presence in the box saw both Lawrence and the wolf, saw everything, saw through Lawrence's disguise and plan, saw what had become of the real Lord Boreas. Its interest leaped to feverish levels when it sensed another being of great power connected to the god.

Luna! thought Lawrence, though his consciousness was too weak, too slow, to see the details the box saw. He felt only the immensity of its awareness, himself a mere pawn in the mind of a master chess player, while the board it played upon was the entire cosmos.

Fury, excitement, its emotions swept through him like tsunamis. And finally a laugh—vengeful, healing, wicked and joyful, its dryness rich with irony.

As the laughter subsided, an image formed.

Lawrence gasped and staggered back, releasing the box.

He was no longer aware of the vault, the altar, or even Geoffrey, only a peculiar being framed in twilight. It had the ashen face of an old man, so wizened it was as if the history of the world were etched within its folds—a face that had seen history's best, but especially its worst. It lent him an air of sadness. And yet it was so perfectly matched by a subtle expression of wry humour that his face was impossible to read. It was almost comforting, grandfatherly. Yet in that deception lay the greatest of dangers. It was the face of someone who knew power to its deepest roots, had nothing to lose and would risk everything for nothing more than a moment's amusement.

As the image grew brighter, Lawrence noticed it had wings but they were charred as though they had been set alight.

An angel? he wondered.

No ordinary one, he heard Geoffrey reply telepathically.

A fallen one?

Geoffrey shook his head. *More complicated.*

The angel released another humourless laugh, apparently privy to their thoughts.

'Who are you?' asked Lawrence in a reverent tone.

The angel smiled subtly. 'A name? I do not have one.'

'Then what are you?' pressed Lawrence.

'A tester of your faith,' replied the angel.

'How will you test it?'

The angel merely smiled.

'May I ask what's inside this box?' asked Lawrence.

The angel held out its hands, indicating itself. 'A surprise. Nothing. Everything. The choice, ultimately, will be yours.'

Lawrence was desperate to know as much as possible about the being and the box, but knew its only answers would be more riddles or silence. He was also painfully aware that the shock he had just suffered would have been felt far and wide, not least in the fort. Only minutes remained before the source was identified and the Naga were upon them. He couldn't, however, simply leave. He needed the box, needed its permission to take it, suspecting the angel would play out the time for maximum suspense.

'You've seen Luna,' started Lawrence, recalling the complex sensation that had washed through him from the angel, especially bitterness.

The angel smiled.

'I don't know who she is, but she means to create chaos,' continued Lawrence. 'By delivering you, this box, to her, I have a chance to move closer and perhaps foil her plans.'

The angel released another dry laugh.

Lawrence glanced over his shoulder to the vault door which he could only vaguely make out, expecting to see a Naga about to strike.

'May I take you to her?' he asked.

The angel shrugged. 'If you can carry me.'

Lawrence nodded his wish to try.

The image of the angel faded and the reality of the vault fully returned.

'We've got to get out of here,' said Lawrence, both emboldened by the angel's mood, but also daunted.

'After you,' said Geoffrey, eyeing the box.

Expecting it to be impossibly heavy, Lawrence lifted it with remarkable ease and placed it carefully in a shoulder bag he was carrying.

With Geoffrey back on his shoulder, he darted from the vault, along the corridor and back up the steps to the fireplace.

Having checked the way was clear, he stepped from the fireplace and stole back to the hall they had arrived in.

Fortunately that hall was also empty.

Lawrence opened the pharaoh's tomb and cursed. The portal had closed.

'I was afraid that might happen,' said Geoffrey. 'It was one-way only. We'll have to find an object which can act as a portal.'

Both scoured their memories, though even Geoffrey knew only a fraction of what the vault contained.

'The Arch of Canisp!' cried Lawrence. 'It's in a vault one floor up from here. A druid's gate, it can be relied upon. It should take us anywhere we wish, even the dream room.'

No sooner had Lawrence said so than a chilling hissing echoed through the halls.

'The Naga! They're close!' he cried.

As he raced from the hall and up a flight of stairs, the hissing grew louder. It was a terrible sound and a cold sweat broke across his brow.

Without warning, he stumbled and crashed into the bannister.

'The box!' he panted. 'It's suddenly heavy!'

'Your fear creates a gateway for collective fear and its weight is great,' explained Geoffrey. 'Stay focused.'

The image of the cemetery loomed in Lawrence's mind as he staggered up the remaining stairs and along the corridor. He was halfway along it when, yet again, the box grew heavier and he veered into the wall and collapsed. With a snarl from the wolf in the dream room, he realised why. Among the many doors, a new one had fixed into place. It looked innocent—plain and wooden like one to a garden. What bothered Lawrence was the ice spreading out from its frame.

'Winter,' he muttered as an icy chill ran up his spine. 'It's Boreas. He's onto us.'

'The surge of energy when you touched the box has alerted him,' said Geoffrey. 'The stench of fear you're drawing from it is leading him right to you. Get to the arch, you don't have long!'

Lawrence suspected the angel had foreseen the appearance of the new door. It was intervening to raise the drama.

Back in the vault, Lawrence scrambled to his feet but the bag was too heavy.

With a sickening hiss, three of the Naga appeared at the top of the stairs. The shape of cobras, the size of pythons, they reared up and bared their fangs.

Only thirty or so paces stood between them and Lawrence and another twenty to the vault containing the Arch of Canisp.

'Release your fear and the bag will lighten,' advised Geoffrey.

'Oh, just like that?' cursed Lawrence as he strained to lift the bag.

'Find a happy memory.'

Under the pressure, Lawrence's mind went blank.

As the Naga darted forward, he remembered how his life had flashed before his eyes when he first touched the box. One image stood out. Following the torture and trauma of losing the woman he loved during the birth of Jake, finally Lawrence had held his only son. His emotions had been in turmoil. But when Jake, eyes closed, had reached out and touched Lawrence's face, joy had tingled through him, so sweet that all the bitterness had dissolved.

So too in the vault. A great lightness came over both Lawrence and the bag. The Naga only metres from him, Lawrence picked it up and bolted for the end of the corridor and the vault door containing the Arch of Canisp.

As he sprinted, he redrew his knife across his palm. He had but a moment to press it against the stone door, leap inside as it swung open and slam it shut in the Naga's faces.

Chest heaving, he changed the code of the door using his will-force.

'Well done,' said Geoffrey, 'but it won't hold them for long.'

'We don't need long,' panted Lawrence.

'Are you sure about that?'

Lawrence spun around. Towards the far end of the vault was an archway made up of two megaliths and a capstone, similar to the ones at Stonehenge—the Arch of Canisp.

Lawrence, hand to the hilt of his sword, scanned the vault for anything unusual when a leaf, orange with Autumn, danced in the air between him and the arch. It was swiftly followed by several others until a great swirl of leaves blocked the view of the arch.

He knew what the leaves meant and cursed.

'Ti,' he muttered, referring to Yu Huang Shang Ti, the Taoist god, staff member of the fort and a master with the sword.

'He mustn't learn the truth,' said Geoffrey. 'Prepare to fight.'

'Against him I haven't a chance.'

'You do if you access Lord Boreas's power. You need only open that door in the dream room.'

'What?' exclaimed Lawrence. 'Boreas will be on us in seconds!'

'You run that risk or blow your cover. Besides, Boreas already has the scent. With luck, you may have minute, but no more,' said Geoffrey, who darted for cover on the wall.

The air grew charged, the leaves glowed then swept outwards to engulf Lawrence in the whirl.

Standing before him, the epitome of poise, understated in human form, was the Chinese god. He was dressed in the traditional style of ancient China: his dark hair tied up in a bun, and dark robed.

As the leaves continued to dance about them, Ti calmly studied Lawrence.

'Lord Boreas,' he said in a genial tone. 'You appear different from when we last met.'

Lawrence had no idea how long ago that might have been. He remained silent, fearing his words would betray him. He was under great pressure. The Naga were behind him, busy cracking the new code into the vault. Racing through the void, beyond the arch, threatening to enter not only the dream room but also the fort, was Lord Boreas. In between, amplifying both threats, stood Ti.

Shifting his presence to wolf, Lawrence focused his attention on the ice-framed door. The dream room was his creation and responded to his will power. He had only to will the door open and, ice or no ice, it would open. Whether his wolf-spirit could survive the blast of Boreas's power and channel it to Lawrence in the vault remained to be seen.

As Ti took a step closer, his hands crossed peacefully at his waist, Lawrence took deep and gentle breaths to remain calm. At least Pandora's Box in the shoulder bag remained light despite his anxiety, confirming Lawrence's suspicion that the angel didn't take sides and cared little for ethics. It provided support where needed only in order to heighten suspense.

'Give me the bag, Lord Boreas,' said Ti and slowly reached out a hand.

Get ready, said Geoffrey in thought. *Remember—no flourishes. End the fight as quickly as possible, then leap through the arch.*

Ti cocked his head as though he had sensed Geoffrey without knowing what it was. He returned his attention to Lawrence, moved closer so that only a step remained between them.

The god's sense of calm, aided by the dance of the leaves, was contagious and Lawrence battled to remain alert.

Ti gently reached for his shoulder which bore the bag.

Now! said Geoffrey.

As Ti's hand touched Lawrence's shoulder there was a questioning look in his eyes.

Forgive me, thought Lawrence for Ti was dear to him. Then, casting aside all doubt, he exerted his will-power.

The door exploded open.

A blizzard of Lord Boreas's power tore through the wolf.

Ti was hurled back by a great pulse that burst from Lawrence who, far from being torn to pieces, felt supreme.

The shock lasted only a moment. Before Ti had a chance to draw his sword, Lawrence was upon him.

They collided as masters of martial arts. Totally centred, each anticipated and blocked the other in a rapid series of otherworldly thuds. Their gazes locked, the clash of their energies was poetically reflected by the swirl of leaves.

Stop dancing, said Geoffrey. *Boreas is closing in and fast!*

The Naga's hissing grew excited at they got close to opening the vault door. A terrible growl reverberated through both the dream room and Lawrence—like that of a lion close to the kill.

You need more power to break the stalemate, said Geoffrey. *Half-step through the door.*

Doing so, however, would strengthen the link with Lord Boreas, reducing the time it took him to find the dream room. But if Lawrence could end the fight more quickly, he had a better chance of making it back to the room before the god.

Trusting Geoffrey's wisdom, the wolf leapt forward through the blizzard, crossed the threshold of the door and planted its front paws into the snow.

A great quake shook both dimensions. The wolf convulsed with the surge of power and Lawrence's lifeline back to the dream room began to fray. Yet while it held, a surge of power it remained. His blows shot up to lightning speed. His skill was flawless. The dance of leaves became a storm.

Barraged by so much power, the Taoist god's serenity wavered—a flicker in the eyes, a bead of sweat, a desperate grab for a knife. It was all Lawrence needed. An instant later the wrist was snapped. Following three more blows Ti went down in a heap.

As the leaves joined him on the ground, the Arch of Canisp came back into view. Through it Lawrence could see the dream room. His wolf-spirit dragged itself back into the room. When he willed the door closed, however, it refused. A stronger willforce was keeping it open.

'The Naga are almost in,' said Geoffrey who had reappeared on Lawrence's shoulder. 'Time to leave.'

Ignoring the feverish hissing through the door to the vault, Lawrence took a tentative step towards the arch. The image between the megaliths zoomed in to reflect his interest. Filling its frame was the door leading to Lord Boreas's world. The blizzard had calmed to reveal a snow covered forest.

'Boreas is too close,' said Lawrence. 'I can't close it.'

'Then get your arse back there and close it in person,' said Geoffrey.

Just then something emerged between the trees. Fifty or so paces from the door into the dream room was a creature—one of legendary strength and fierceness and Lawrence had his answer as to what spirit animal Lord Boreas had chosen. It wasn't a lion, but a Siberian tiger. It's powerful ice-blue eyes penetrated the wolf's, saw through the channel it represented and fixed on Lawrence in the reality of the vault. Realising the scale of the prize within reach, the tiger released a roar so mighty that it shook the dream room and covered it in frost. A moment later it leapt forward and charged for it.

In the same instant Lawrence sprinted for the arch, the Naga cracked the code and appeared in the vault. It took them only an instant to assess the scene, before darting after Lawrence.

Lord Boreas had fifty human paces to cover to Lawrence's fifteen or so, but a tiger's paces were larger and faster. The Naga wouldn't be able to follow Lawrence through the arch—it obeyed the will of the first through it—but if they caught him before he reached it, he was done for.

Summoning every ounce of his strength and courage, Lawrence ran for his life, blocking out fear in case Pandora's Box suddenly grew heavy and slowed him down. It wasn't easy. He was running head on towards a tiger as it raced through the snow, growling victoriously

There was nothing the wolf could do but watch on anxiously, standing clear of the door so that when Lawrence dived into the room he could slam it shut. Assuming he made it.

Only a few paces remained for both the tiger and Lawrence.

As he sprinted, Lawrence once more felt the memory of baby-Jake's hand against his cheek, felt the joy, the lightness. It came at the perfect time. The Naga were almost upon him. But as they lunged for his legs with their poisonous fangs, he leapt through the arch and disappeared.

CHAPTER 7
MAD BILL AND THE ARCHER

JAKE HUNG FROM THE OVERHANG OF ROCK BY A SINGLE HAND. Beneath him gaped a sheer drop of a hundred metres, yet he used no ropes. It was how he climbed. His lean body had been honed by the sport. Nestor, Jake's granddad, likened him to a lizard for he had started climbing as soon as he could walk. But it was mid-winter. The rock was cold. His legs and arms burned with fatigue and his hands were almost numb.

Regardless, Jake was calm. It was the strange calm born of abandon, poured from a world turned upside down, a brand of abandon whose essence was wild.

Few mountaineers attempted the extreme overhang even in summer. It required four moves while upside down and thus great strength, skill and confidence. Usually Jake did it in one fluid movement. Anything less sapped strength at alarming speed. This time, however, at the farthest point of the overhang, he simply hung there by one arm and stared down at the distant crags.

Peppered in snow, they looked like freeze-framed waves dashed against a cliff, like Jake, no longer fluid. There was something enchanting in their appearance. They seemed to beckon Jake, daring him to let go.

Normally when Jake felt out of balance, his mind cluttered with the concerns of school, the moment he stepped onto a mountain, clarity embraced him like an old friend.

Not this time.

Despite the excitement of the inkwell, something had shifted deep within him. It was as though in opening the inkwell not only had a great mystery been unleashed but something else, for though Jake mourned his dad, an older sadness had escaped and followed him up the mountain, gusting from the crags and swirling about him. It felt ancient. He couldn't explain it, but it was like a sadness deep within the earth had risen up and filled him.

He had the sense that were he to let go then far more than his own destiny would be affected, as though he were central to some great mystery he couldn't know.

Another gust burst from the crags and he almost lost his grip. His arm burned with exertion. Yet he didn't relieve it with the other. Being so close to death he felt incredibly alive. To court death, as sadness courted him, to not fear it, seemed the most natural thing in the world. Yet to succumb to it, to throw away a life before its time, struck Jake as the worst of crimes, that if there was life after death then such a blasphemy would warrant the severest of punishment.

Something wafted past him. Its flight was so silent that it was like a phantom. It was a barn owl. Despite his precarious position, Jake was spellbound. His heart soared at the sight of it. The bird was so out of place that high up, so mystical, so weightless-seeming amid a land laden with snow that Jake finally opened up to Frost's idea of synchronicity. To be open to such a reality was to be open to guidance, to the idea that one was never alone.

Life's amazing! he thought.

Nature was glorious yet he knew so little about it, about anything it suddenly seemed, and a great thirst for discovery welled up within him and forced everything else aside.

Rather than descend, the owl flew higher, beyond the overhang and out of sight. Jake glanced down once more at the crags. Down was the past, he decided: regret, self-pity, a bewitching plunge which, despite the crags, he knew to be endless. Up was adventure. Up was life, Frost, the sizzling mystery of the inkwell, his granddad whose letter he carried in his pocket and still hadn't read.

Rather than plunge into sadness, he invited his sadness to lighten up and join him on a great adventure. Digging deep into his reserves of energy, Jake swung up his fresh arm, swung up a leg, heaved himself over the overhang and picked his way to the end of the ascent.

Having rediscovered his zest for life, the world unfurled before him. No longer an obstacle to battle with, life was a breathtakingly beautiful afternoon of snow-capped summits, soft sunlight, blue sky and mournful bird cries.

Beautiful or not, it was cold. He found a sheltered spot on the summit, tugged on an extra shirt and jumper and finally settled down to a packed lunch and a flask of coffee.

His thoughts returned to the inkwell. What had taken place only that morning couldn't be brushed aside as easily as a dream. In fact, because of the inkwell, the dream felt more real.

'The stranger in the cave,' he muttered.

His body tingled with the idea that the mysterious character actually existed, that perhaps his dad had known him in a secret life.

He was about to take another sandwich when he remembered his granddad's letter. Jake snatched it from his pocket. He noticed that the envelope was without a stamp, suggesting it had been hand-delivered, but by whom he had no idea.

The message was surprisingly short.

> *Dear Jake,*
>
> *Thought you'd enjoy a couple of ditties I've written. Not up to much, I'm afraid. Neither is the local plonk, which is probably why! Keep up your poetry. There's no better tonic for the soul.*
>
> *Love,*
> *Granddad Nestor*
>
> *Two lords a leaping, one known, one knot*
> *Untied or Titan'd, in Hades a plot*
> *Inside the risen, the Muses' second kiss(?)*
> *In words, pain for some, for others perhaps bliss*
>
> *Go ladies to lotus to Greek god seek*
> *Imagining things of which none can speak*
> *They follow their hearts and know their minds*
> *Accepting in action is both the cruel and the kind*

The letter was so different from what Jake had expected that he didn't know what to make of it.

A second chill ran through him.

'Hades,' he muttered, as he recalled his lessons on Greek myth and connected it with what Frost had said of the inkwell. Hades was the underworld where all spirits went when the body died.

'Titan'd... that's a play on the word *tightened*!'

He remembered something about the Titans being old gods who preceded the Olympian gods of Greece and how their dad, paranoid of being toppled from power, banished his Titan children to a hell called Tartarus, one that lay deep beneath the underworld of Hades. One of them, however, had escaped, returned home and in revenge had chopped off his dad's balls. He then had his own children. Later, suffering from the same disease as his dad, he also tried to get rid of his children, except rather than send them to a hell, he ate them instead.

Jake recalled the reaction of the class. Some had thought it brilliant. Others were appalled. The teacher had informed them that history was full of such father-son betrayal.

He stared at the letter. *But why has Granddad written me these poems without even mentioning Dad's death?*

Jake looked back out at the mountains. *They're more like riddles than simple poems,* he reflected. *Perhaps he's mentioning Dad, but not directly because to do so would be too...*

He shuddered as he connected the letter with all the other inexplicable events of the past day or so.

... too dangerous?

Looking back at the riddles, he noted another play on words —the part about two lords, one known and one 'knot'.

A knot, like a tangle, perhaps a puzzle he means for me to solve.

A raven flew over and cawed so loudly that Jake jumped. It was as though the raven agreed.

'Untied,' he repeated. *Its place in the riddle suggests it has a double meaning, as though one of these lords, whoever they are, has either gone to a place like Tartarus, or been... untied.*

If the idea of hell wasn't bad enough, Jake dreaded to think what being untied might mean.

He was then struck by a crazy idea. *Could dad be one of the lords in the riddle? Is that why Frost called me Lord Burton when we first met? If so, how the hell could he know about such a thing?*

Another chill ran up his spine. If his dad had been some sort of lord in another world, had the title passed to Jake? The idea was thrilling and terrifying at the same time.

He made a mental note to grill Frost when they next met. Confirming Jake's earlier feeling, Frost clearly knew a lot more than he was letting on. As for the inkwell and where it led—*I have to pass through it,* he decided.

A stiff gust tore from the crags and almost blew the letter from Jake's hand. It had blown with such force from such stillness that he was reminded of the gust of wind on the train platform and the strange feeling that someone had been watching him, someone other than Frost.

Like then, he was gripped by an ominous feeling. Jake glanced about to make sure he was alone. All he found was the orange sun as it set majestically over the mountains and some ravens soaring about the crags.

Better get going, he thought. Before he did, he skimmed the riddles one more time.

Inside the risen. 'No idea what that means,' he said. *Muses' second kiss...* 'The Muses?'

Jake had a vague recollection of his dad having once spoken of them in one of his many stories.

'The Sphinx!' he cried out. 'The Muses had something to do with the Sphinx!'

His skin tingled as the link between the letter, his dream and the inkwell grew tighter, along with the idea of a hereditary title—if his dad had been a lord, then his granddad might also have been, despite still being alive.

Where is he? wondered Jake. He had to speak to him.

Jake fought back a terrible dread that something had also happened to his granddad Nestor. He glanced through the second verse. Though it made little sense to him, the last two lines felt more like a warning than a clue.

Why did Granddad leave me the letter rather than simply wait to tell me in person? And without all the riddling.

It was so unlike him. The gregarious Nestor, rarely seen without his deerstalker hat, never wrote or phoned if something could be said in person. He loved company. Given Jake's dad had spent so much time away, Nestor and Jake were especially close.

In light of the letter, he questioned his granddad's frequent wanderings around Europe and whether they were really what Nestor had claimed them to be—Vienna for the opera, booze-ups with chums in Paris or sailing about the Mediterranean with beautiful women. Nestor was such a good storyteller that one could never quite tell what was real or not.

The thought of losing his granddad as well as his dad in the same week was too much for Jake. He jumped up, wishing to be free of such heavy thought, stowed the letter in his pocket and raced off to the steep path down the mountain.

With the sun sinking behind the summits, shadow raced up the mountain side like a horde of doom. The symbolism was not lost on Jake as he tore off defiantly towards it.

Despite the fading light he descended even faster than he usually did, hopping from rock to rock with the ease of a mountain goat. It was his way to disengage from a busy mind. Like rock climbing, it required a different sort of awareness to thinking, otherwise one tripped or twisted an ankle.

About halfway down the mountainside, Jake stopped a moment for a breather. He glanced up through the dusk for a final glimpse of the upper crags.

His heart leapt.

Someone was up there. Their body was silhouetted against the sky a hundred or so metres higher and looking directly at him.

It's a girl! But what's she doing up there alone at dusk? thought Jake. It was reckless to be up so high so late in the day, especially in snowy conditions.

She hasn't got much gear with her. And what's she got across her back? It doesn't look like an ice-axe.

He was torn between calling out to make sure everything was fine and turning away, but there was something about her which prevented him from doing either. It was a sort of intensity, a stillness. She stood as though she belonged there.

Still Jake stared. *Why is she watching me?* he wondered

Then it struck him—the strange sensation he had felt with the gusts of wind, both up on the summit and on the station platform, along with Frost's mysterious behaviour in town when he had looked up to the rooftops, claiming that someone was watching Jake.

And there was the time in the study, remembered Jake when Frost had announced Jake's quest as a search for a magical woman. *Be careful what you wish for,* Frost had warned while gazing out the study window up at the mountainside as though he had seen someone.

I wish I could see her face and know who's spying on me, thought Jake, fascinated by the idea that she might be the very woman of his quest.

Something bright flashed through the sky—too large and bright to be a shooting star.

'A comet!' he gasped, marvelling at how its tail lit up the sky.

It lasted just a moment or two. Before it disappeared, Jake tore his gaze away from it to make use of its light and catch a glimpse of a dark-skinned girl.

He was dumbstruck. Dressed in leather and furs, armed with bow and arrows, she looked like a warrior from the ancient world. As she stared at the comet with a perplexed expression, she seemed to shine just as bright.

The comet's light lasted just long enough for her to glance back at Jake. Despite the distance, it was as though she were right in front of him, her eyes so bright and fierce that Jake struggled to hold her gaze.

As the light faded, he scoured the mountains to check she was alone. By the time he looked back, she was gone. He caught only a glimpse of something large and dark diving down and away into the shadows, flying like an eagle, yet it looked much larger, even larger than the one in his dream. Stranger still, the girl was riding on its back.

Jake stood there, his heart racing. He scoured the dusk for any sign of her but found only stillness.

'Another mystery,' he muttered under his breath.

This time, however, instead of tension there was lightness. He had only glimpsed the girl, but he could still feel her, as though she had leapt through his eyes and was beating a trail to his heart.

FOR THE REMAINDER OF THE JOURNEY BACK TO THE FARMHOUSE, Jake was in a daze. Before he knew it, he was approaching the farmyard, stirred from his reverie by singing. It was the all too familiar voice of someone Jake considered best locked up and who often was. More than once he had been caught by the police after the pubs had closed, galloping down the high street like Don Quixote crying *Charge!* It was Bill, the farm manager. He was roaring in accompaniment to Christmas carols blaring from the kitchen radio.

By the time Jake was outside the front door, *Oh Come All Ye Faithful* was playing. Jake braced himself as he barged in through the door to the welcome warmth.

'Oh come let us a-d-o-r-e h-i-m, Christ look who's arrived!' sang Bill, twisting the end of the verse to suit Jake's arrival. 'Well, well, look who's here! Look, Trifle! Look what's just *wafted* in through the door!' he bawled through a chaos of spluttering pans, a glass of wine in hand.

Jake collapsed into a chair beside the fire and tugged off his snow-covered boots, regarding Bill with a wry smile. He hadn't changed. He too was wild eyed, though unlike the girl on the rocks whose eyes had seemed more like a cat's, Bill's reminded

Jake of a March hare—alert, but with a glint of madness. A hare with a shock of thick dark hair flecked with grey.

'I'm cooking bangers and mash!' announced Bill. 'Stand back!'

Bill was highly dangerous when at the stove. Yet he cooked with a passion to behold, flourishing and thrusting wooden spoons with the fervour of a conductor at the Proms. The wall about the oven was a collage of porridge, stew, various other things which couldn't be identified, along with an occasional meteor of cake.

'Bugger! These bloody beans are sticking to the pan!' he cried as though the world had ended. 'What's wrong with the damn things? They don't make them like they used to. It's a conspiracy, I tell you. Those damned trixy-pixies have infiltrated the bean factories!'

Jake had heard Bill blame the trixies countless times before. Whenever something dreadful happened, it was those *blasted bloody trixy-pixies*. The worst of their apparent crimes was their constant meddling in Bill's golf game, chiefly by removing his ball from a plum position on the fairway and hiding it in the rough.

Bill threw the contents of his wine glass into the pan as a remedy before refilling it and taking a large gulp. He made some hurried adjustment to the hob, covered the pans with lids and spun around to face Jake.

'I may make it look easy, but don't be fooled. It's the Devil's work, cooking! Stay away from it! Leave it to the professionals!'

Bill took another gulp of wine and sat down at the table.

'Anyway, dear boy, how are you?' he enquired calmly, his mood suddenly transformed.

'Bill, why are you wearing a cat-shaped tea cosy on your head?'

'Keeps the nerves steady. Cat magic,' said Bill glancing up at the shelf. 'Isn't that right, Trifle? What's that, Trifle? Jake's a lazy oaf for not helping out on the farm today? I suppose you're right. What? Now steady on, Trifle old fellow! Ha! That was rather fruity! I know he's not particularly pleasant to look at or witty or charming or anything else of use, but there's no need to lower the tone. Even if it is true. Ha! There you go again! My God, that one would make a pirate blush!'

'Talking to animals, especially cats, is a sign of lunacy,' said Jake, choosing to exclude his own conversations with Trifle, which didn't count because he didn't believe Trifle understood a word, whereas Bill clearly did.

Bill poured out another glass of wine and slid it across the oak table. 'Cup of tea?'

Jake took a sip.

'Where's Granddad?' he asked. 'I haven't seen him since I got home.'

'That old goat? God knows. Probably run off with some floozy.'

'I'm serious, Bill—'

'So am I! You know what he's like.'

'Actually,' said Jake. 'I'm not so sure I do.'

'Oh?' said Bill and shot Jake a piercing look. 'And what's that supposed to mean?'

Jake immediately regretted his cryptic comment, not yet ready to confide his encounter with the inkwell or his granddad's riddles.

'Nothing,' said Jake peering into his glass. 'Nothing, I simply, you know, it's a confusing time.'

Bill maintained his gaze on Jake while taking another gulp of wine, looking unconvinced.

'What's that all about?' said Jake, glancing over at the TV which was on mute, grateful for the distraction. It was the news. Jake switched off the radio and turned up the volume of the TV.

A reporter was standing in Trafalgar Square outside a giant contraption of scaffolding covered in plastic wrapping. It stood beneath a crane and loomed high above the London skyline.

'Though it's not unusual to see restoration work going on in an old city such as London,' said the reporter, *'what's caught the public's attention is not only the fact that the scaffolding is twice the height of the building beneath it, but similar reports of exactly the same thing going on in other high profile capitals around the world. Not to mention the heightened level of security.'*

The camera zoomed in on a particularly fearsome set of guards, each armed with a truncheon.

'The Mayor's office has refused to comment while at a similar site in Delhi, one local has actually managed to get a look inside and claims that, far from restoration work, the historic building has been completely demolished, the rubble apparently carried away through a large hole in the ground. Which begs the question—what are the cranes for?'

The report finished with the crane framed in the camera.

'Weird,' said Jake as he turned down the volume. 'What do you make of that?'

Bill was still staring at the blank screen, having shown an uncommon level of interest.

'How could they be taking away the rubble through a hole in the ground?' continued Jake. 'They'd have to dig a hole in the first place and then where would they put the earth?'

A strange light flashed in Bill's eyes.

The mysterious broadcast unsettled Jake. He thought of the inkwell and all the other strange happenings.

'Maybe they're going to carry all the rubble through the earth's crust and rebuild whatever it is in some secret other world,' he said, making light of it.

'The crust,' muttered Bill, the strange light in his eyes intensifying.

'Yes, you know, that thick layer of rock that surrounds—'

'I know what the bloody crust is you little punk!' shot back Bill and caused Jake to smile. 'It's *you* who doesn't know what it is.'

'What do you mean?' retorted Jake, intrigued by Bill's mysterious manner.

Bill coughed and shifted in his chair, as though having second thoughts.

'Nothing. Nothing, just… that things aren't always what they seem, that's all.'

'Rubbish! That's not what you were going to say!' cried Jake, not to be denied one of Bill's nutty theories. 'Come on—out with it!'

Again Bill studied Jake with uncomfortable gravity.

'How can the crust be anything other than the crust?' pressed Jake.

'Gypsy blood. Gypsy intuition,' was Bill's sparse reply.

'You're not a gypsy!' snorted Jake.

'We're all gypsies,' said Bill, his tone far off. 'At heart, we are.'

'Speak for yourself.'

'I do! And I certainly wouldn't speak for a snotty-nosed jumped-up whippersnapper like you!' retorted Bill.

Jake was enjoying himself. It wasn't the first time they had locked horns. 'You'll be telling me there's a God next.'

Bill's gaze turned steely. 'You would do well to use caution when referring to such things,' he warned icily.

'Why?' challenged Jake.

'Because!' exploded Bill and made Jake jump. 'To use such words is to invite the very flames of hell!'

He had barely finished his sentence when a powerful hissing issued from the grill pan behind him, shortly followed by a flame. The sausages erupted and set light to the back of Bill's hair which went up like a torch, tea cosy included.

Just like Frost that very afternoon, rather than helping, Jake roared with laughter.

'Fff-boll-follicles!' cried Bill as he leapt up from his chair and bolted outside for the snow.

'Bloody sausages!' he yelled as he went, causing Jake to laugh even harder. 'Bloody trixies!'

CHAPTER 8
RENLOCK

LAWRENCE WAS BACK IN THE DREAM ROOM SITTING AT THE TABLE. Still in the form of Lord Boreas, his wolf spirit resting at his feet, he finished dressing a gash to his left arm. He was greatly relieved to be back. Having leapt through the Arch of Canisp, he had arrived in the dream room just in time to slam closed the door on the real Lord Boreas, though not before he slashed Lawrence with his lethal claws.

'Just because the charred angel allowed you to take Pandora's Box, it's no assurance of further help,' warned Geoffrey between mouthfuls of chocolate cake.

'At least we survived.'

'So far. But by showing yourself to the angel and taking the box you have committed to confronting your deepest fears. You've simply taken the first step along a path which I predict will be extremely short and extremely painful.'

'You mentioned before that Pandora's Box contained a perversion of nature, ancient in essence with the power to destroy energy,' said Lawrence, eyeing the box before him. 'Do you think that's what the angel is?'

'Part of it,' said Geoffrey polishing off the last crumb of cake. 'The voices you heard in that strange wind in the vault, of which I counted five, are in some way related to what presented itself as a burnt angel. But whatever the angel is, your destinies are now entwined. Inextricably.'

Lawrence ran a hand gently across the box. 'If there's a small chance it will help me... if I can somehow inspire it to choose our side then the risk to my soul will be worth it.'

'The risk is to all souls.'

Lawrence was about to say something but was cut short by a pulse of energy through the room.

The wolf and Lawrence leapt to their feet.

One of the many doors of the dream room had fixed in position.

The other doors followed suit.

'Did you do that?' asked Geoffrey.

A hand ready at his sword, Lawrence shook his head.

For the first time all the doors looked the same—plain oak. All except the one. Both the frame and door were made of a cold rough-hewn granite that exuded a raw sense of power. It was as though the other doors had stopped in obedience to it.

As Lawrence took a cautious step towards the door it ground open. A salty gust blasted into the room and almost blew out the candle. Mist followed.

His grip tightened about the sword. The wolf growled. Its hackles rose. Geoffrey's eyes were almost closed as he sniffed the air with a sixth sense.

Lawrence braced himself for ambush. The mist, however, retreated, creating a vast clearing over a stormy sea. Towering high into a grey sky like a fortress stood a granite cliff. Lawrence shivered at the sight of it.

It was no ordinary cliff. Delineated within it by a multitude of lights was the image of a giant Buddha in meditation. The lights were portals like those in a dovecot and through which streamed a continuous flight of birds.

'Renlock,' said Geoffrey grimly.

Lawrence had heard of the place, though had never seen it. In the life of the cosmos it was a modern thing, created by the Pigeon Lord, a spy master, and rented out to the highest bidder—lesser gods for the most part, looking to topple those above them.

'The remnant of a plundered world,' said Geoffrey. 'Stripped of its outer-sparkle, reclaimed by an angry sea, that cliff is all that remains of a once abundant land. This far down there's no illusion. Here we see a reflection of the work of man.'

Lawrence knew the distinction—*man* was modern man, a distorted energy that affected both men and women alike, distinct from the motherly, nurturing energy it had forced aside. Man sought to own the land, own everything, strip it of all value without understanding the true worth of things, without realising that in plundering the land he plundered himself. Beneath his expensive robes, man was a miserable beggar, a spoilt child, though he lacked the awareness, the honesty and the courage to admit it.

A shiver ran through Lawrence. He recalled the vault in the House of Tusk.

'The cemetery I saw as I approached Pandora's Box—it's a reflection of the lost souls that inhabit the Surface,' he deduced. 'This place shows the same reality but through a different lens.'

'Anything else?' prompted Geoffrey.

'Renlock and the god gate—they're both modern in the making, only as old as the retreat of the last Ice Age, a mere ten thousand or so years. They're part of the same cursed act that caused the pre-historic tribes to fall from balance and wisdom.'

'And?'

Lawrence lowered his gaze to the box.

The penny dropped.

'Of course! Pandora's Box! Whatever's inside of it, its bitterness is also modern and so probably born of the same event!'

Lawrence's mind was cast back to the angel's flash of anger on sensing Luna through the body memory of Lord Boreas.

'My God!' he gasped as an even greater realisation dawned on him. 'This Luna—whatever it is she's planning, it's not new. She, he, or whoever the powerful being is behind the mask of Luna, it must be the same one who started this bloody mess in the first place.'

'Bravo,' said Geoffrey.

Lawrence fought back a sense of dread as he stared at the waves crashing up against the distant cliffs of Renlock.

'The opening of this door is not my doing. Luna is summoning Boreas. She intends to use Renlock and its unscrupulous resources to finish off what she started—the toppling of the Overlord. She means to rule the surface of Earth, along with the rest of the Outer-Peregrinus,' said Lawrence, referring to the outer part of the cosmos and what geographers termed Earth's *outer-mantle*. 'She has come from so deep down within the Peregrinus that she needs tools like Renlock and Pandora's Box to physically manifest her plans. Initially, at least, until she's acclimatised to denser realities.'

'With you at her side. Another tool,' smiled Geoffrey sardonically. 'A dispensable one. Feeling up to it?'

Lawrence drew a deep breath. 'But if she's so powerful, why is she bothering with the surface of the Peregrinus?'

'If you want to know the answer...' said Geoffrey, looking out of the granite-framed door to Renlock.

Lawrence followed the lizard's line of sight before turning to the wolf who sat proudly. It looked him straight in the eye with a powerful unflinching gaze. He smiled gently in return. Lawrence then collected his shoulder bag, placed Pandora's Box inside of it and approached the granite doorway. Beneath it was a long drop to the sea.

'You must approach Renlock as Lord Boreas would,' said Geoffrey. 'He travels by a winged horse, completely white.'

'As white as winter,' muttered Lawrence as coldness once more threatened to seize his heart. The wooden doors trembled in their frames, echoing his fear. 'Do you think Luna is a goddess?'

Geoffrey closed his ancient eyes.

'What is a goddess or a god? he asked rhetorically. 'The meaning of things has become so distorted. There are false gods, greedy humans who seek the short cut through the god gate without realising they take the longest path to authentic power, and there are those more noble, like Brock, the current Overlord, an advanced human who was asked, begged, to take on the role. But all types are part of the same journey towards what cannot be named, only felt.'

'Do you think she has already been a goddess?'

'No. She's beyond gods and goddesses.'

A deeper dread stirred in the pit of Lawrence's stomach.

The door to the left of the granite one instantly shifted.

A terrible roar shook the room, accompanied by a blast of snow. Lawrence leapt back. Framing a patch of darkness where the door had been was the giant head of the Siberian tiger, its piercing eyes promising ruin.

'A reminder,' remarked Geoffrey, observing the new door, 'that following your episode in the vault, Boreas has your scent. Succumb to fear and he'll be through that door in a flash. Fear attracts the very thing you fear. And the charred angel, if that's what it is, will not protect you. It's sick of human fear dressed up as courage.'

Lawrence took a steadying breath. Though the snow stopped falling within the portal of its jaws, the tiger head, the threat of Lord Boreas's presence, remained.

Lawrence closed his eyes as he prepared himself.

I must find something to celebrate in this moment, he thought, desperate to restore some presence. *I'm alive.* He took a deep breath. *I must be thankful for that. I'm here because I'm meant to be here. Despite the terrible odds there has to be a chance. And with love in my heart, anything is possible.*

For a moment the gusts calmed. A gentle breeze enveloped Lawrence. His skin tingled at its touch and the wolf whined with pleasure.

The arrival of a new sound drew him back—the flapping of large wings. He gasped at the sight of a beautiful winged horse hovering beyond the door—white, not as winter, but glowing like a beacon in a dark night. It was a pure sight and Lawrence felt the same light shine within himself.

The horse whinnied and tossed its mane, encouraging Lawrence to mount up.

As Lawrence wondered how to reach the horse, a granite walkway extended from the doorway towards it.

'You coming?' he asked Geoffrey.

'And how do you think you'll survive without me?' replied the lizard and darted up Lawrence's outstretched arm.

Once Geoffrey was upon his shoulder, Lawrence gave a final glance back to the stoic wolf then strode out and leapt atop the horse. With another whinny they were off, racing over the sea.

AS THEY APPROACHED, LAWRENCE WAS ASTONISHED AT THE NEVERending stream of pigeons flying in and out of the many portals, each a separate department within Renlock—responsible for intelligence from different parts of the cosmos, especially the Surface. The pigeons were spies. Given their proclivity for gossip and the fact that pigeon was an almost impossible language to learn unless you were a pigeon, they made excellent spies. Almost every pigeon on the Surface was one, loitering on window sills of places of power or listening in on secret conversations in city parks. Though in theory they were mercenary, in practice all worked for Renlock, who paid the most—in light, the only currency of worth.

With Geoffrey hidden within his robes, Lawrence landed on one of the many landings amid the multitude of portals, some way towards the top of the Buddha image.

'Ah, welcome!' cried an approaching man through the cacophony of cooing. Portly, pinstriped and bald—save a fastidiously groomed strip of dark hair that ran about the back of his head and connected his ears—he looked like a banker. His dark eyes shone with a lively light.

'Welcome to Renlock! General Communications Headquarters to the Outer-Peregrinus!' he beamed.

As he stooped in a deep bow, Lawrence studied the Pigeon Lord. He was famous for his passion for Surface fashion, hence the suit, along with being an appalling creep who, like all creeps, was not to be trusted. How he came to be Lord of Renlock when it was created thousands of years before was a mystery to all save Wilderspin, along with the power that had supported him. Regardless, he had two roles. As landlord of Renlock he rented it out to those who sought power and could afford the rent. Whether it was occupied or not, his bread and butter was his spy business. As a spy master, he knew more than most about what went on day to day throughout the cosmos, though the subtleties perceived by the truly powerful were beyond him.

'The august Lord Boreas, I assume. Lord of Much, if I may be so bold and abbreviate all your titles into one of my own, not to mention prospective tenant of Renlock. An honour! Yes indeed, it is an immense honour to receive you! Wilderspin at your service—a god long since fallen, 'tis now my *great* privilege to lord over this most fundamental of institutions.'

Lawrence simply nodded in acknowledgement.

'If you don't mind me saying so,' continued Wilderspin, 'I had expected a more dramatic entrance. You know, a blast of snow, a flock of sirens swirling about you. In fact, I was rather looking forward to it! Haw-haw! Not that I'm disappointed of course. And what a splendid steed!'

'Not even a god can afford to waste energy,' said Lawrence down his nose in a wintry tone, doing his best to play the part of Lord Boreas. 'As a *fallen* god, I would've thought you understood that.'

'Quite, quite,' replied Wilderspin, unabashed by the jibe. 'Alas, we all fall sooner or later, do we not, my dear Lord Boreas? Still, I count myself lucky to have ended up here, rather than having to start back at square one on the Surface. What a bore that would be!'

Though part of Lawrence took an immediate dislike to Wilderspin, the other part almost burst out laughing at what an arse he was—a jumped-up civil servant to aspiring gods. As Wilderspin gazed out to sea as though he expected someone else, Lawrence's eyes glistened with amusement.

Wilderspin was on the verge of saying something when his eyes shot wide. He had sensed something and stood electrified with boyish excitement.

Wilderspin wasn't the only one who had sensed something. At any given moment, in and about Renlock was up to a quarter of the cosmos's entire population of pigeons. The din was astonishing. It never stopped. This time, however, pigeons were silenced as though commanded by a powerful switch. Even the boisterous gusts which forever eddied through the many entrances to the cliff had ceased. It was as though the whole of Renlock held its breath or had it taken away.

Lawrence closed his eyes, unable to hide the tension in his brow, a subtlety noted by the ever-watchful Wilderspin.

In the stillness of that immeasurable moment it was Wilderspin who first perceived a change. He spun around and gazed at the granite wall. Something had appeared in its otherwise perfectly-polished surface. It was a lichen. Despite its tiny size its birth resounded through Renlock as though a forest were sprouting up. The single lichen spread to become a collage of sorts, shaped like a human face, except green and fibrous, summoning the rock to life.

Spellbound, Wilderspin stepped closer. And leapt right back again when a pair of abysmal eyes shot open, shortly followed by a mouth. It gasped with such depth that as pigeons took flight in panic, it inhaled a whole stream of them and didn't stop until its eyes lit up like emeralds.

For a moment that seemed like aeons they blazed green when, just as suddenly as they had opened, they clamped shut again with the death-like clunk of a sealed tomb, one that consumed every light in Renlock.

The stillness was complete. Not even a wingbeat disturbed it, not even a breath, until the entire cliff was shaken by a boom so base that it might have come from the Core itself. It was a boom of such power that had Wilderspin's face been visible it would have revealed an uncharacteristic flicker of fear, for though he loved to flirt with power, even the Pigeon Lord had his limits. He buckled on the verge of prostration.

Finally light returned, though it came not from the lanterns. Where the face had emerged just moments before was now an archway. Approaching from a distance was something that glowed. It moved as though floating.

Luna, thought Lawrence and his heartbeat raced.

Sensing his tension from inside his cloak, Geoffrey dug his claws into Lawrence's ribs as a reminder to stay present.

Back in the dream room, the wolf leapt up onto the chair and gazed into the flickering flame of the candle.

As Luna moved closer, Lawrence noticed that it was her cloak that glowed. Inside was a ghostly shadow, the features of her face nothing more than different tones of grey. She approached through an arbour of roses. They were so red that they too seemed to glow then withered and died as Luna passed. A moon rose up in the peculiar space of the archway, but like the roses, it shone for an exquisite moment before the light it reflected was stolen away.

Luna exuded vast power. Lawrence's hands trembled with the pressure. He discreetly clamped them together to try to control them.

She's absorbing the light, the life, of all she passes, he observed. *She needs it in order to arrive here from the darkest depths.*

Nightingales also appeared about the arbour. They had just a moment to sing a few sweet notes before they too were leached of life and fell from their perches.

Such was Luna's presence that by the time she reached the archway both Lord Boreas and Wilderspin were visibly suffering despite doing their best to hide it. They stood at the edge of her aura—a turbulent twilight within which all was challenged, probed, stripped of energy or mercifully left to exist, though in a state of fear.

Luna stood at the threshold of the archway acclimatising herself to her new surroundings.

Lawrence struggled to look into the shadow beneath her hood. She appeared giant even though she was shorter than him and physically frail.

Her mouth yawned wide in a deathly gasp and inhaled another stream of pigeons.

'I say!' cried Wilderspin. The shock of seeing so many of his valuable agents disappear had jolted him back to his senses. 'My stars! What an appetite!'

There was nothing he could do but watch, however, as the stream of pigeons thickened. As it did so, Luna's appearance underwent another transformation. Following a momentary brightening in her cloak as the pigeon light was absorbed, it dulled to grey, though grew more lifelike. It became tattered and smattered in rotting leaves, while moths flew out through the holes. As for her face, only a chin was visible beneath the hood. Though it was no longer shadow, it was as grey as a tombstone, with moss and lichen creating the impression of a beard. It was as though a graveyard had come to life and condensed itself into a single being.

As her form shifted into place, the stream of pigeons lessened and the lanterns billowed back to life, though were not as bright as before. The wall returned to its former shape with no trace of the archway.

'What power!' gasped Wilderspin, his eyes shining with awe. To move through rock took great power, especially the rock of Renlock. 'And how... how striking!' he added as he marvelled at the now stooped figure, the moths taking the place of her aura. 'My Lady! Goddess Luna! Goddess of the Moon! Welcome!'

Luna responded by taking a step forward into the hallway. It was the uncertain step of one unaccustomed to walking. Despite her apparent frailty, it caused the granite to crack.

She turned in Lord Boreas's direction.

'My lady,' he managed, the weight of her attention commanding a bow.

The moths of her aura flew out and about him. His body tensed. Back in the dream room, the candle flame, which symbolised Lawrence's life-force, flickered wildly and shrank. The wolf whined and willed its restoration.

A pair of cat-like eyes glowed green from beneath Luna's hood.

With great effort Lawrence tilted up his chin and took her gaze straight on.

Luna's eyes flashed brighter at his boldness.

His head swam. The candle flame almost went out.

Snow puffed from the giant mouth of the tiger-framed door, announcing that Lord Boreas smelt his fear and was closing in fast.

Regardless, Lawrence's wolf spirit didn't waver. Its gaze was fixed on the flame with total presence.

I belong here, Lawrence reassured himself in thought. *The cosmos supports me otherwise I wouldn't be here. I belong!*

The candle flame flickered defiantly and lengthened a little.

In a testament to the power of the dream room, finally she appeared satisfied that Lawrence was Lord Boreas, her chosen henchman. She shifted her gaze down the hall to the wan light at its end. The gravity of her attention caused another flock of pigeons to veer off course into her aura. The instant they entered it they transformed to light that fed Luna through the moths.

Her composure bolstered, her next step was surer and, though it caused no cracks, it left an imprint as if the granite were mud.

Wilderspin stared at it aghast.

'Remarkable. Quite remarkable,' he muttered and looked up at Luna. Her gaze was fixed down the hallway. Getting the message, Wilderspin gave his hands an enthusiastic clap.

'Right then! As you're both doubtless pressed for time, how about a quick tour?'

Recovering his composure, Lawrence nodded his head in assent, greatly relieved that back in the dream room the snowing within the tiger-framed doorway had once again stopped.

'Excellent! Follow me!' exclaimed Wilderspin and set off along the landing through a broad tunnel.

'I must say, it's been an *age* since a decent usurper turned up, one sufficiently credible to take up tenancy. So it's a delight to have you here my lady and lord. A delight!' he cried with an exuberant wave of an arm. 'Needless to say, throughout its history Renlock has played host to many a successful coup, which is hardly surprising given the extraordinary resources at its disposal.'

They arrived at the landing's other end, a landing within a great wall which towered almost as high as the cliff outside, stairs zigzagging through its middle to connect the various departments of Renlock. Wilderspin led them up the final flight so that they stood on top of the great wall which commanded a view of a vast cavern. Together with the cliff outside, it gave the impression of guarding against some terrible threat that might arrive from either the sea or from within the land.

At first there was nothing to see, just shadows and clouds of pigeons going about their business. Wilderspin's eyes, however, were shining with excitement.

'Ready?' he beamed.

Not waiting for an answer, he waved a hand and the light of the cavern was fully restored.

Lawrence suppressed a gasp and stepped back.

Luna stepped forward, her step now light. Her aura of moths dispersed in playful flits. The lichens vanished from her face which, though ghostly pale, was suddenly more human. Her mouth opened but instead of words a snake slithered out, coiled about her neck and disappeared into her robes.

'The Hollow-gram of Brock!' announced Wilderspin proudly.

Lawrence couldn't believe his eyes. The cavern had transformed into a giant-sized grim city alley which led away from the great wall. Its source of light came from within a giant bottle of whisky balanced on top of a ramshackle house in the place of a water tank, the same source of the sickly light Lawrence had seen from the outside seeping through the portals in the cliff.

What shocked Lawrence was the sight of the man partially lit by its weak glow. Slumped, eyes closed, apparently drunk, was a tramp. Like the bottle of whisky, he was giant, Lawrence no greater in size than the tramp's nose.

'This is Brock? The ruling god of Earth and Overlord of the Outer-Peregrinus?' he asked. 'I thought he didn't manifest as one being but had split himself up into many of the creatures of the Surface.'

'Indeed, my dear Lord Boreas, that is how he maintains omnipresence on the Surface and an admirably humble way of doing so, I might add, for most gods are too vain. They prefer to appear as one all-powerful classic-appearing god and frighten the life out of people,' explained Wilderspin. 'But what we have here is a holographic monitor of Brock's health. And what better symbol than a downtrodden aboriginal?'

A deep sadness threatened to take hold of Lawrence as he studied the wretched state of Brock. The bottle of whisky required no explanation. He thought not only of the plight of the native Australians but of the Native Americans and other last gasps of tribes that had once inhabited the entire Surface, living in balance, nourishing the land that nourished them—keepers of wisdom. Then something had happened. With the retreat of the last Ice Age a new deluge flooded the world—one of ignorance. In a wave too great to resist, it had swept across the Surface, corrupting everything in its wake.

Whisky, he mused. *The enchanting poison if drunk to excess. The perfect expression for the dismal state of the Surface—the numbing of feeling, the abuse and rage, the pollution. A false gold exchanged for sacred earth. A deadly source of warmth on a cold winter's night that'll leave you frozen come dawn.*

While Luna stood motionless, apparently entranced by what she saw, Wilderspin watched Lawrence with a curious glint in his eyes.

'God made humankind in the image of God—divine and graceful,' he said dryly, 'and modern man reduced God to the image of modern man. Is it not so, Lord Boreas?'

Lawrence didn't answer. He was studying the bottle of whisky. Like a hospital drip, a tube ran from the bottle directly into the bloodstream of Brock's right arm. At the bottle's open top was a constant flutter of pigeons as they came and went.

'What are the pigeons doing?' he asked.

With another wave of Wilderspin's arm the hollow-gram shifted so that a magnified image of the bottle top filled the cavern.

'See that?' he said as a pigeon perched on the bottle's top, tilted its head and cried a single golden tear into the bottle. 'That drop of whisky represents yet another pitiful prayer from the Surface.'

'Pitiful?' said Lawrence, disturbed yet fascinated by what he saw.

'An ignorant, selfish prayer, one which enslaves rather than liberates, especially the person praying. Praying for quantity, praying for romance, praying for more offspring, rather than praying for spirit. In such greedy times as these, my dear God of Greed, praying is a tragic business. Why, were just one person to pray for the health of dear old Brock here rather than themselves, a hundred tears of whisky would disappear just like that!' said Wilderspin with a click of his fingers. 'Were that one person to put that prayer into action by treating all they met as manifestations of God, which of course they are, then Brock would be spared a thousand drops!'

And if all those who claim to worship him did the same? Lawrence dared to wonder and imagined Brock before he became Overlord, walking through an ever-changing landscape of pristine nature—serene desert, exuberant jungle, creaking arctic, ponderous mountains. He walked not in the rags of a tramp. He walked as a human being, a co-creator and caretaker of the world, radiating grace, radiating a sense of belonging, an aboriginal in a loincloth, his skin rich and vibrant, his every step, his every movement, a surrender to, and a fusion with, all that surrounded him. Snow, leaves and sand danced up at his approach. Bees and butterflies, birds and mammals of every type, along with passing humans—all streamed through one another and Brock in a joyous moment of recognition.

'Why did Brock become a god?' he asked.

'Because that infernal meddler Braysheath begged him to, in a vain attempt to fend off the election of another god of war and the fall of human consciousness. Alas, it happened anyway, as sooner or later it must. Golden ages are such a bore! All that human magic and too much peace!'

On hearing Braysheath's name, Luna's aura of moths tightened about her in angry flight. 'The Fall,' she croaked in a voice that grated through every living thing in the chasm.'

'Indeed, my lady!' beamed Wilderspin, casting her a shrewd look. 'The fall from Eden, from an age of truth into another round of hiss-tree. The start of all distortion, including the myth of the snake itself. Sensuality became a sin, for hiss-tree is a time of imprisonment in the mind.'

Despite the fact that Luna had finally spoken, Lawrence couldn't tear his gaze from Brock. The fall was too easy to picture—ten thousand years of war, of plundering nature to build war ships and sprawling lifeless cities, culminating in the madness of the past century when the world's population had shot up from one billion to seven billion, despite two world wars and so much disease. All the while, tribes and species who lived in balance went extinct every day, along with their valuable wisdom. Ancient forests were felled and rivers dried up with the coming of dams, mines, agriculture and the appalling wastage involved with feeding so many humans whose contribution to life was next to nothing. *Progress* it was called by those in science, religion, industry and politics, who to Lawrence's mind were all the same despite their different clothing. They were greed.

Geoffrey gently clawed his chest. Lawrence got the message. *Collect yourself!*

'The start of separation,' remarked Wilderspin, noting Lawrence's captivation. 'Men began to think of themselves as only men. Women only as women, when the secret of human magic is to be everything, plants, creatures and the elements included. Evolution had once again spiralled out of *we* and back into *I*, this cycle darker than ever before.'

Lawrence battled to ignore a new door that loomed large in the dream room. A dangerous thought knocked from behind it and demanded attention—why and how had Luna caused this fall?

The lower half of her face, which was all that showed from beneath her hood, now had colour. When she spoke, her voice had become more human though was so ethereal that it was heard with equal strength throughout Renlock. 'The bottle of whisky is almost full.'

'So it is!' exclaimed Wilderspin. 'When it's completely full, it means that the number of Brock's true followers has fallen to half the level of his heyday. It's an inverse measure, you see. As true faith falls, so whisky rises and poor old Brock, who is powerless to remove the needle from his arm, powerless to break the connection with the reality of Earth, grows even weaker.'

Lawrence looked back at Brock whose body was completely still, as though all breath had left him.

'Missionaries and schisms, my lady. Forced conversions by zealots, who claimed Brock for themselves and created an unsustainably high threshold. They then proceed to squabble over his name and here at Renlock we can account for only one name. Naturally we take the largest group, but still, it's a terrible business for an Overlord.'

'What happens when it's full?' asked Lawrence.

'He falls through the threshold of belief and so falls from his status as Overlord,' explained Wilderspin. 'Stripped of omni-status and earthly power. The energy that flows up through Renlock and up through the Surface temples is shut off then atomically re-encrypted for the new Overlord.'

'Brock required energy from Renlock?' queried Lawrence, realising that the energy Wilderspin claimed to control had been hijacked energy from its natural source, just as surface temples had been repeatedly built on top of ancient springs of power. 'Other Overlords, gods of war, I can understand using it. But Brock's power comes from nature, from the divinity within all things.'

The great weight of an awkward silence pressed in on Lawrence as both Luna and Wilderspin turned in his direction.

'Did you not just mention, Wilderspin, that missionaries of dogmatic religion have caused his downfall?' said Lawrence.

'Indeed I did, my dear Lord Boreas,' replied Wilderspin, quick to recover from the touching of a raw nerve. 'Brock might have lasted longer had he made better use of Renlock—the focused flow of power, our apparatus for controlling the weather and many other unique devices enabling a far more efficient means of controlling humans than a crude reliance on the power of will.'

'And a device to scour human dreams?' broke in Luna and caused Lawrence to wonder what else she was after, in addition to Pandora's Box.

'Yes, my lady!' exclaimed Wilderspin. 'Especially that! A wonderful device that allows an Overlord to search the collective unconscious of all humans on the Surface for the most secret of things. Anonymously, of course, for to sift through the dreams of others is to attract the attention of powerful souls.'

Wilderspin paused for thought before continuing.

'In fact, my most esteemed Goddess Luna, given the success of your liberation movement is as good as assured, I'd be delighted to permit you a sneak preview at your convenience. After all, it doesn't hurt to oil the wheels, does it, Lord Boreas?'

As Luna nodded her approval, Lawrence said nothing, relieved at least that his disguise as Lord Boreas had so far held.

'Well, I think that covers the most important matters,' enthused Wilderspin, turning back to Goddess Luna. 'If you do decide to rent the place, it'll be yours for the agreed term. I merely require my regular office, one down from the top, in order to manage my intelligence side-line—the pigeons you would've noticed on your flight in, Lord Boreas. The intelligence is for sale, should you have interest.'

Lawrence looked up at the highest part of the cavern where stairs continued to zigzag up to more offices and a final one at the very top.

Wilderspin finished with a satisfied clap of his hands. 'All that remains is the unsavoury business of payment. Naturally, the only currency we deal in is light, for light requires no belief. It simply is! As for the fee…' he continued, though was cut short by Luna who revealed a transparent flask from inside her cloak. It emitted the most glorious light and caused a billowing of pigeons throughout the whole of Renlock. Maintaining her gaze on Brock, she held it out in Wilderspin's direction.

His face lit up as he received the flask in reverent hands. Awestruck, he held it aloft to study it. 'Flawless,' he gasped. 'I can't remember the last time I saw such a magnificent sample. Awoken light. Completely awoken! May I enquire of its origin?'

Luna said nothing.

'No I suppose not,' he said merrily and carefully uncorked the flask.

The air filled with an exquisite ringing. He poured the tiniest sample onto a quivering finger and touched it to his tongue. For a moment or two Wilderspin was quite lost to the world as his eyes rolled upwards and closed in ecstasy. When he reopened them, they shone with a blissful light.

'Consider Renlock your own,' he purred and stooped into a deep bow.

'That is all,' said Luna, concluding their business.

'Of course, my lady. My lord. You know where to find me if there's anything you require. Anything at all,' said Wilderspin.

With a final bow, he departed.

Goddess Luna and Lawrence remained alone on the landing. They waited in silence until Wilderspin was out of sight.

Lawrence was the first to speak. 'If I may ask, my lady, with access to dreams, for what will you search?'

'A hunch,' she replied sparingly, still gazing at Brock. 'What news of Lord Tusk?'

'Disposed of, my lady,' replied Lawrence, mustering a smug tone. 'For one lifetime at least.'

'And the new Lord Tusk?'

'Just a boy, my lady.'

'Do not underestimate the young. They are more dangerous than their idiot parents.'

'When innocent, of course, my lady. But such is the Surface these days that by seven years old they have already lost their power, having learnt the idiocy you allude to.'

'All the same, watch him closely,' said Luna and eyed Lawrence's shoulder bag. 'I believe you have something for me.'

Lawrence knelt, bowed his head and held out the shoulder bag containing Pandora's Box.

Luna reached inside the bag.

Lawrence braced himself for a similar reaction to what he had experienced on stealing the box, remembering well the angel's anger at Luna.

Nothing happened. She slowly withdrew the box. As she held it up it shone. So too did Luna's face.

'Pandora's Box,' she said and lovingly stroked its surface. 'Well done, Lord Boreas.'

She gazed up from it to study Lawrence who was once again standing, the moths of her aura flitting about him.

'Your wish is my command, my lady.'

Luna relented her gaze and returned it to Renlock. 'I approve of this place. It will serve as your base, Lord Boreas. I will visit occasionally though I have other matters to tend to.'

'Nothing I can assist with?' asked Lawrence, keen to learn as much as he could of her plans.

'You'll be busy enough. I require you to re-enter the House of Tusk.'

'My lady!' gasped Lawrence, taken aback. 'The fort will be on heightened alert following my first visit—'

'Then use your imagination,' broke in Luna. Though her tone was composed, the flight of the moths grew agitated and pigeons took flight. 'Try something more dramatic, if you must. I care not for how you do it.'

'Of course, my lady,' conceded Lawrence, doing his best to hide his inner turmoil. 'What would you have me do once inside?'

'I want you to steal one of the eight holygates and bring it here.'

'Steal a holygate!' exclaimed Lawrence, forgetting his manners.

Holygates were a fundamental part of the cosmos's fabric—the gates that allowed souls to advance through the worlds of the Peregrinus from the Surface to the Core.

'Which one?' he asked having recovered himself.

'The gate from Hunter,' said Luna, referring to the gate which returned souls to the Surface from Hunter, the last of the three worlds of death. Together with the Surface they formed the Outer-Peregrinus.

'I shall do my best, my lady.'

'You shall succeed, Lord Boreas, otherwise I shall have your light.'

Lawrence said nothing. The threat was clear—to lose one's light was to lose everything. It was a fate infinitely worse than death, because without light one couldn't die, couldn't be reborn, couldn't exist, not as an individual.

'I also require all three of the secret backdoors the House of Tusk uses for private access to the three worlds of death,' added Luna.

Lawrence was lost for words.

'The gates are essential to my plan for toppling Brock. He will soon fall,' she said, surveying the tramp in the alley, 'but I have lost my patience. He must fall within the next few days.'

What Luna was asking was so incredible that Lawrence decided to go along with it.

'If I may enquire, my lady, what will you do with them?'

Luna studied who she believed to be Lord Boreas for a long moment before elaborating.

'They will serve two purposes. First I will jam the holygate, choking off the supply of souls to the Surface. All births will be stillborn,' she said with cold detachment. 'And since all those pitiful humans care about these days is their number of children—insurance for their old age that they call love, unable to find any deeper meaning to life—outrage will follow. When the scientists find no answer, when the consolation of priests wears thin, Brock, God Almighty, will be blamed and what remains of his followers will desert him.'

'And the back doors?' asked Lawrence, suppressing his shock.

'The holygates permit souls to flow in one direction alone and only when the soul is ready to move on. The secret backdoor gates, however, allow movement in both directions.'

'But only for one or two beings at a time, my lady, surely. Braysheath and—'

'Braysheath,' tittered Luna in a steely tone that chilled Lawrence to the bone. 'That relic of the old ways. It's time for a shift. I shall enlarge the gates, recode them, bring them together in one room here at Renlock and allow free movement for all souls.'

Lawrence struggled to keep up with the scale of Luna's plan. 'Such a thing will—'

'Be catastrophic, Lord Boreas. The meeting of souls not meant to meet before their time will cause chaos. War will ensue where war was never meant to be. And death in a place of death is a death most final. The souls, Lord Boreas…'

'Will become lost,' he muttered in disbelief.

'Whereupon I shall find a better use for their light.'

Lawrence gazed at Brock as his mind reeled.

She talks of the deeper meaning of life and is angered at human abuse of nature and in the same breath talks of a war of souls and stealing human light with complete dispassion. Her plan is bold beyond belief. It shows a profound understanding of universal law. And she scoffs at a being as powerful as Braysheath! Could she be older? Is that possible? A chill ran through him. *Whatever she is, she means to create chaos.*

'You amuse me, Lord Boreas,' said Luna. 'I thought you would approve.'

Unsure of how much protection the dream room afforded him, Lawrence chose his words carefully. Though she hadn't yet seen through his disguise, she would surely sense a lie.

'I am here to serve, not judge, my lady,' he said. 'I simply wonder why bother? Why not let evolution unfold as it will? If the time of humans is over then their energy will simply manifest as something else.'

Once more the heat of Luna's attention prickled through Lawrence.

'You are the God of Greed, are you not?' she asked.

Geoffrey gave Lawrence another dig of his claws, daring him to be bold. Luna had asked a direct question. It required a risky lie, that or a very loose interpretation of the words god and greed.

'I am,' replied Lawrence, choosing the latter.

The prickling heat intensified then finally relented.

'Then you should realise that human energy is central to the great experiment known as creation. I for one, however, have grown sick of humans and their pretence at humanity, these brats of all ages—their hypocrisy, their cowardice disguised as goodness and strength, their feigned ignorance, their filth, their pride at being so ugly.'

'What of potential, my lady?' ventured Lawrence.

'It has moved beyond reach,' she replied. 'Revolution follows so-called revolution but nothing changes, only the scale of their idiocy. Where have the elders gone, I ask you? Where are the real men and real women? Where are the lion-hearts amidst the sheep? They have become too few. How many I wonder? One real human per city, perhaps two.'

Lawrence wanted to say that it must be more but he wasn't sure and so said nothing.

'I'm bored, Lord Boreas. I intend to drain the Outer-Peregrinus of as much light as possible before it's too late—strip it of all identity and cleanse it completely. The only shame is that the suffering of humans will be so brief,' said Luna with a calm that was far more chilling than words of anger. 'Wilderspin is right. The Surface has become an ironic place. Humans have made their lives hell yet they're so ignorant, so arrogant, so unbelievably stupid that they don't realise it.'

Lawrence couldn't argue. Her sentiments reflected his own but like Brock he felt the solution lay in compassion and inclusion, not in blame and punishment.

'Is the situation so desperate, my lady?' he asked. 'Even if humans are the centre of some grand experiment in separation, nature will surely take its course. Tides will rise, land mass will shrink and with it food supply. With less food, the population will shrink and calm will eventually return.'

'Again your ignorance surprises me, Lord Boreas,' said Luna.

Lawrence's heartbeat raced as another wave of prickling heat coursed through him. His existence was in the balance. Another blunder and Luna might discover his real identity.

'Nature has become a reflection of human nature,' continued Luna. 'The pollution of the pristine world with which they were blessed reflects an inner-pollution—an unconscious self-hatred behind which is fear and shame, but humans are too cowardly to confront it, projecting it onto others instead. Its weight has become too great. I am here, Lord Boreas, to clean up, to salvage what I can.'

'And where, my lady, will you go with all this light? Where is there to go?'

In answer the air grew light and tingly. With a pulse of light the image of Renlock disappeared, replaced by a dazzling white. It lasted for only a moment before Luna controlled her outburst of euphoria, unaccustomed as she was to her new surroundings. But in that moment, Lawrence perceived an arctic landscape. And something else—a glimmer of darkness on the horizon, dancing like black flames that for some reason made him think of portals.

'You forget your place, Lord Boreas,' chided Luna as Renlock reappeared, but there was no anger in her voice.

Lawrence's mind raced.

Was it a portal? Can it really be possible to leave the cosmos?

An instant later he gave up. He had to be present and such a question was too great to ponder.

'I would never forget my place, my lady,' he apologised. 'Neither do I presume to know but a tiny fraction of the cosmos and its intricate workings. I merely wish to know what I may in order to better execute your orders.'

'Remember, Lord Boreas, I chose you for your charm and guile, not for compassion or the second-guessing of my plans.'

'Of course, my lady,' said Lawrence with a bow of his head.

Luna held out a hand. A pigeon landed on it and dissolved into a ball of light which then flowed in through her fingers and caused a momentary glow in her eyes.

'My lady, if I am to re-enter the House of Tusk and take these gates, will you permit me one last question?'

Luna nodded.

'The holygate from Hunter to the Surface—how will you block such a thing? If my understanding is correct, they are designed to permit passage for souls alone, nothing physical. I thought that tampering with such things was impossible.'

'Everything is possible, Lord Boreas. Such is Universal Law and the mechanics of time, much misunderstood though they are.'

Lawrence waited patiently for more.

Luna held up Pandora's Box. 'I shall do it with this.'

'Pandora's Box is nothing but an empty myth,' said Lawrence, curious to learn what she knew of it while assuming to know nothing himself. 'It has already been opened more than two and a half thousand years ago.'

'That is one version, but like all myths in this mythless time it has become twisted. The legend of Pandora's Box goes back beyond the epoch of the Greeks, though it was during their time that something was stumbled upon, something ancient and powerful in the extreme—a sylph. Something without a body or a soul. Its location and the key to its release are sealed within this box.'

'If it is without body and soul then it doesn't exist,' replied Lawrence.

'Not *one* soul,' continued Luna. 'For a sylph to exist, it must have more than one soul.'

With a shiver, Lawrence recalled the voices in the wind when he had approached Pandora's Box in the vault. Geoffrey had counted five. 'Then surely it is not a single entity,' he said, continuing to play ignorant.

'That is the genius of a sylph. If it exists, that is, which I will shortly find out. And if it does then I shall bend its will to my own. I will send it into the holygate. The nature of the sylph will confuse the gate and so jam it. Its wisdom under my command will keep it that way, long enough for Brock to fall.'

She doesn't fully understand what's inside the box, thought Lawrence with a flicker of hope. *She knows what it is by name alone but nothing else—not its fickle and bitter nature or where it came from.*

Neither did Lawrence know where it came from, but he knew that it knew her, was related in some way to her own actions and the feelings were far from friendly.

'That'll be all, Lord Boreas. Report back to me when you've done as I've asked,' she concluded.

'My lady,' said Lord Boreas. Following a courteous bow and with great relief he departed for his winged horse.

ONCE LAWRENCE WAS GONE, A PECULIAR-LOOKING DARK CLOAKED being emerged from the shadows—a man for the most part except that his skin was silvery. There was something lion-like in his features, in particular the long broad nose and a sweptback mane of silver hair. Most striking of all were his eyes. They glinted like sapphires and shone with icy indifference. He was a commander of the inner-force, one of the five forces which sustained the cosmos, one that originated from the Inner-Peregrinus and which challenged the positive flow of the outer-force.

'Bring Nestor Tusk here, Commander,' instructed Luna. 'Lock him up and appoint guards—just a few and only your best. And let no one else know.'

'Is not even Lord Boreas to know?' he asked in a steely monotone, notably lacking the unction of Wilderspin.

'No, Commander. Only you and your carefully selected guard. It is not wise for others to know all of one's plans.'

As the Commander disappeared back into the shadows, Luna returned her attention to the slumped form of Brock. A subtle smile returned to her face.

Only you sense who I truly am, she said inside Brock's head, *what I was and what I've become, for only you understand the value of suffering. And yet you are too weak to reach those who matter.*

She watched him closely but nothing stirred from the image of the Overlord.

You've been a worthy adversary, she continued. *A worthy guardian of humanity. But now a greater nature must take its course.*

CHAPTER 9
BLACK HOLE

IT HAD BEEN A LONG AND BIZARRE DAY. THE INSTANT JAKE ENTERED his bedroom a great tiredness swept through him. It hit him like a mighty wave crashing against the land, flattening him to the shore then dragging him out into an ocean of dreams too strange and distant to recall. There was only a vague awareness of a far off sound ushering him along. Sometimes it was like a female chant, subtle yet powerful. At other times it was like the wind and the mournful howl of a wolf.

Despite such a deep sleep, he awoke feeling fresher and more vibrant than ever before. When the cockerel crowed at first light, Jake sprang from bed, leapt into his clothes and up to the window. A robin was singing. Fresh snow had fallen overnight. It promised to be a glorious day and Jake's heart soared in greeting.

The bewitching eyes of the girl from the evening before flashed in his mind and the splendour of life's great mystery rocketed beyond all limits.

Famished, Jake bounded from his bedroom and down the stairs.

He swept through the kitchen in a polished routine—kettle on, bread popped into the toaster—and headed straight for the larder with a *Hey-ho Trifle!* en route.

His spirits couldn't have been higher as he grabbed the latch to the larder door.

Or plunged deeper on opening it. He leapt back in horror and cursed.

'Ah, hello there!' cried the stranger from the cave.

He was rummaging among the shelves and looked exactly as he had in Jake's dream.

'This… this can't be…' stammered Jake, his heart pounding. 'It's simply… simply not possible.'

'Everything's possible, Jake m'boy, I assure you,' said the man, maintaining his focus on the contents of the shelves. 'Given a sprinkle of time and an occasional stir.'

Shaking his head in disbelief, Jake edged back towards the sideboard.

'Here, hold this for me, would you?' said the man. With a wave of an arm something large and writhing shot from his sleeve.

Jake realised too late that it was the cobra. Horrified, he struck out his hands in defence but caught its neck instead. In an instant, its tail was coiled about his arm. It flared its hood and hissed furiously.

Heart thumping, Jake was too terror-struck to shout out. His stomach churned when it slithered through his grip and made a horrifying circuit about his neck, its chilling smoothness like a sliding kiss of death.

Finally it wound its way down his other arm and slithered off.

When Jake finally regained control of his body, he glanced about for the cobra, though found no sign of it. He rubbed his neck and shuddered at the recollection.

As for the man, if that's what he was, he looked like a giant hunched up in the larder. It wasn't only his height but his presence which, just like in Jake's dream, enlivened the senses. A chorus of exotic bird song erupted from the copse outside. Smells of food and spices filled the air with such richness that Jake's stomach rumbled in reply. Everything burst to life. Even Trifle had sprung from his perch and was coiling himself about the man's legs while his purring reverberated through the kitchen as though on loud speaker.

'Who are you?' asked Jake.

'I've had many names over the years, most unrepeatable in such august company as yours. But some call me Braysheath.'

'Brays-heath,' repeated Jake. 'Am I going mad?'

'I do hope so. It'll help enormously.'

'With what?' asked Jake nervously.

'Help me find something,' replied Braysheath, his attention still on a shelf of jars and tins.

'Find what?'

'Marmalade!' cheered the man, brandishing the jar victoriously.

'But it was just a dream…' muttered Jake for what felt like the hundredth time in less than two days, wishing he could find an explanation for what was going on, that the stranger really was just one of Bill's mad friends from the Tiger's Tail pub playing a foul trick on him.

Perhaps Bill used some strange technique of whispering the dream into my ear while I was asleep, thought Jake. Bill had done far crazier things.

'I too think I'm dreaming when I find a full jar of marmalade. I say to myself, Braysheath old fellow, sometimes life is just too good to be true! Now, how about some tea and toast?' he said and passed to the table, took a seat and proceeded to study the jar.

'Am I dreaming now?' asked Jake.

'Most certainly, yes,' said Braysheath as he opened the jar. He stuck his beak-like nose inside and inhaled deeply. 'Mmm! Scrumptious! Oh, how I love marmalade!'

'Then why does this feel so real?' asked Jake as the smell of oranges filled the air.

'Because it is,' replied Braysheath unhelpfully. 'Come on, let's see some toast!'

In something of a daze, Jake turned to check the toaster, making sure he kept Braysheath in his peripheral vision while also keeping an eye out for the cobra.

As he poured the tea Jake did his best to restore some reason.

'It can't be both,' he said at last. 'Not a dream as well as real.'

'Why not?' said Braysheath.

'Because this time I'm awake. I know I am,' he said as he placed the mugs of tea on the table. He glanced out the window, reassured by the sight of Bill in one of the fields putting out feed for the sheep. 'Now feels different from my dream in the cave.'

'Because it is,' said Braysheath and took a slurp of tea. 'That time you were awake while dreaming. That is to say, you became conscious within your dream. This time, however, you're asleep while being what you call awake. It's a simple matter of definitions, dear boy, and it's good to loosen them up—not to be so rigid about things.'

'That doesn't make any sense at all,' remarked Jake.

'Thank you for proving my point,' beamed Braysheath. He eyed the toaster and the toast popped up.

As Jake buttered it, he struggled to gather his wits. Having failed, he returned to the table with a plate of toast, where he finally took a seat himself, first checking under the table for any sign of the snake though found only Trifle. He was purring away on Braysheath's lap, not in the least bit perturbed by a snake being in the kitchen.

'Splendid! Thank you!' exclaimed Braysheath and set about the toast with the relish of a child, smacking his lips together excitedly as he smothered a slice with marmalade.

'Oh, delicious!' he cried on taking his first bite, his eyes rolling heavenward. 'Simply *delicious*!'

'I'm pretty sure I *am* awake,' said Jake at last. 'And I think you'll find the rest of the world would agree with me.'

'Of course they would. They're asleep too! Most of them, anyway,' said Braysheath between chomps of toast. 'But, dear fellow, don't take me so literally. We're talking on different levels. On yours which, dare I say it, is a rather crude level, naturally you're awake. But on a deeper level, you're not. You're fast, *fast* asleep.'

'How so?' enquired Jake, intrigued despite his disbelief.

Braysheath paused his chomping for a moment and regarded Jake, his eyes twinkling with humour. 'You're an *educated* fellow. Am I right?'

'I go to school if that's what you're asking,' said Jake.

'Yes. Very, very *educated*.'

There was something about the way Braysheath had enunciated the word that made it sound like an insult.

'And you're not educated?' asked Jake.

'Educated? Ha! Good heavens no. Ha-ha! Of course I can pretend. It's not difficult. You just talk very quickly and throw in lots of names of other *educated* people, along with a few numbers and dates, just for good measure. People love numbers, especially with those decimal point things. The more precise the better! And there mustn't be any doubt. Certainly not! One must have complete faith in the nonsense one talks.'

Jake took a long sip of tea. Despite his appearance, there was something extremely comforting in Braysheath's presence and utterly infuriating at the same time.

'Where are you from? And *what* are you?'

'That'll cost you.'

'What?'

'More toast!' cried Braysheath as two more slices popped up from the toaster.

Jake spun around. 'Who put those on?'

'Perhaps it was the cat,' suggested Braysheath.

'The cat?' scoffed Jake. 'He's on your lap.'

'Our friend the cobra then,' said Braysheath. 'But whoever it was, it was very thoughtful of them. Now, come on, chop-chop,' he said, rubbing his hands together in anticipation.

Again checking for any sign of the cobra, Jake got up to butter the toast.

'Now, I did promise myself not to explain anything to you, at least not up here,' said Braysheath.

Up here? Frost said exactly the same!

'It's always the same, you see. I'm never believed! Even if armed with acorn coffee.' On which note Braysheath took another slurp of tea. 'But I now see, given you're such a... well, sensible, *educated* fellow, that I must concede something.'

The gist of Braysheath's words sent a shiver up Jake's spine, for it appeared his visitor had a motive, over and above creating confusion and eating all the toast.

'So let's see,' continued Braysheath as Jake placed the toast on the table. 'I suppose there are quite a few names for what I am, but I think the most accurate is *shepherd*. Yes, that'll do.'

The word shepherd caused Jake to think of the Bible and Braysheath certainly looked as though he had stepped from its pages. Jake could imagine him walking serenely through the silver light of desert nights, at one with the land's mystique though he would look equally at home in the lively world of mountains, woodlands and the open sea. That is, were it hundreds ago. But it wasn't. And therein lay the problem.

'And what about your sheep? Where's your flock?'

'Ah, my sheep,' sighed Braysheath wistfully. 'They're lost.'

'Lost? When?'

'Oh, quite a while ago. In fact, I was rather hoping you might help me find them.'

'Me? Why me? You mean you lost them around here?'

'Lots of places,' replied Braysheath, determined to remain vague.

'Well, if you need help, Bill's your man.'

'You mean that mad-looking fellow outside? I don't think he'll be much use.'

Bloody hell! thought Jake. *He's calling Bill mad!*

'Ha!' barked Braysheath and caused Jake to jump.

Surely he can't hear my thoughts! panicked Jake. *No. No of course not. It's just proof that he's mad.*

Braysheath was rumbling with laughter.

'What is it?' enquired Jake as innocently as possible.

'Just laughing with joy for life,' said Braysheath, gesturing for Jake to take a seat. 'Have some toast.'

Why is he here? wondered Jake, daring to take his dream seriously. *The inkwell took me to a sword, to a fight in a chamber beneath a sphinx temple. At the point when a man was about to be killed, Braysheath seemed to cut short the memory in the sword.* A chill ran through him. Along with deep sadness. An earlier thought returned to haunt him—the identity of the man about to be killed.

'Did you know my dad?'

Warmth overflowed from Braysheath's eyes and embraced Jake's grief.

'I know him. And wherever he is, he's a splendid fellow.'

'You mean he didn't die?' stammered Jake, unable to believe his ears.

'Had he died then I would know where he is. He would be on the world of Roar, a place of honesty, reborn as one of the animal kingdom, enjoying some well-earned rest before eventually being reborn here.'

'What?' exclaimed Jake, struggling with so much strange information, not least how Braysheath could know such things.

'Alas, there are fates worse than death,' continued Braysheath, echoing what Frost had said to Jake at their first meeting.

'What do you mean?' he shot back.

'I wouldn't like to speculate.'

A line from his granddad's riddles shuddered through Jake— *untied or titan'd*. 'Has he gone to some sort of hell?'

Braysheath studied Jake with a look of surprise. 'That's a possibility, but not the only one.'

Untied, thought Jake, inwardly grimacing at what that might mean, though not yet willing to share his granddad's riddle with Braysheath. The word *plot* from the second sentence of the first part of the riddle made him wary.

'You said he hasn't died and yet, in the memory of the sword, a powerful man was about to stab him when the dream changed and I saw you in a cave. Did you interrupt the memory because you know what happened to him?'

'I did not. I believe the dream was showing you that if you wish to know what happened to you dear dad, your most fruitful course will be to follow my guidance.'

'So you don't know what happened to him?'

'I wish I did.'

'Was he a lord?'

'Humph! Well done! I'm impressed!'

'Well?' urged Jake.

'Of himself, yes—on his to way to becoming lord of his mind. What you might call a *true* lord.'

Jake approved, but the answer was evasive. 'Not any other type of lord? Of a place, for instance?'

The twinkle in Braysheath's eyes grew brighter. 'Yes. In fact, I'd like to show you where. After all, actions speak louder than words, do they not?'

Another image flashed through Jake's mind, this time of the inkwell. A nervous excitement coursed through him at the prospect of a second encounter.

'And what did he do in this other place?' he asked.

Braysheath rubbed the stubble of his chin in thought. 'I suppose he was a sort of gatekeeper.'

'That doesn't make sense. If you're a lord then you employ a gatekeeper,' challenged Jake.

'Really? Well I must say that would be a very frivolous lord.'

'And Granddad? Is he also one of these gatekeepers?'

'Have you seen him?' asked Braysheath, avoiding the question.

'Not since I got back. I hope he's okay.'

'Dear old Nestor is indestructible. Wherever he is, I'm sure he's coping admirably.'

The way Braysheath spoke left little doubt in Jake's mind that he was about to become embroiled in something highly disturbing yet thrilling at the same time.

'A moment ago you mentioned rebirth. If such a thing really exists then how do you explain the population?' asked Jake. 'It's been growing at an accelerating rate for ages.'

For a moment the room grew dark and a murder of crows flew out from the copse cawing wildly. Braysheath's eyes took on a distant look that left Jake cold.

A moment later the room grew light again.

'These are weighty matters,' said Braysheath, his eyes warming up. 'But for now, let's just say that not all beings, not the first lot, were born equal. Most, yes, in terms of that wonderful stuff potential, but not seven.'

'Seven what?'

'Beings.'

'If not born equal, what were they born?'

Braysheath thought for a moment. 'Concentrated,' he said. 'Yes, that's the word. Like wonderfully fruity berries. And *realised*. That is to say that their potential was fully realised.'

'In what way concentrated?' asked Jake, captivated.

'When the cosmos was created, so were they and each contained what you might call a fairly juicy amount of its energy.'

'How juicy?'

'Oh, the seven combined, about a half,' explained Braysheath.

'Half?' exclaimed Jake. 'Half the universe's total energy? Rubbish! And they'd be billions of years old!'

'Rubbish?' mused Braysheath. 'I rather like that word. It's rub-ish. I've obviously rubbed you up the wrong way. It reminds me of that other word *problem*. I suspect it's a contraction of *probably-lemon*, something which at first tastes bitter though is actually extremely good for you. Anyway, I don't know about all those numbers but yes, pretty old. But that's how it was.'

'How do you know?' challenged Jake.

'Excellent question!'

'Well what's the answer?'

'Not telling you,' replied Braysheath with childlike stubbornness. 'Anyway, if you'll permit me to answer your original question, the important point is that once there were seven, but now there are only two.'

'What happened to the other five?' asked Jake, deciding to humour Braysheath.

'Chopped up.'

'Chopped up? How could anyone chop up such powerful beings?' asked Jake, fascinated by the idea.

'The very question I've been asking myself,' replied Braysheath. 'They've simply disappeared you see, but whatever the method—chopped up, sliced or diced—that's what's happened.'

'Chopped up by who?'

'Another excellent question, Jake m'boy and I'm not sure I have the answer. Not yet. But the point is that by chopping up just one such being created a huge supply of new souls.'

'But that still wouldn't work,' countered Jake. 'How many humans were there originally? Let's say a hundred million. That means that adding the seven others would only double it to two hundred million. There are now almost eight billion humans.'

'Alas, humans were not an entire half of the universe's original energy. You're forgetting our fine friends the trees and rocks and the sea and everything that inhabits them, not to mention air and fire.'

'So the first five added billions?'

'Indeed, but on a sliding scale. Though there were but milliseconds between the births of each of the seven, the difference in concentrations was vast. Such are Big Bangs as you call them. The first of the seven to get the chop created a few hundred million extra souls. The fifth, which I regret to say is ongoing, is adding billions. And so you can imagine what would happen if the final two suffer the same fate.'

Jake's mind boggled, not only at what Braysheath was describing but that he was describing it at all. Regardless, he found the explanation too fantastic to believe.

'And that's only the numbers side of things,' continued Braysheath. 'The nature of the seven was different. Fully realised also means fully awake, fully conscious, while humans are born asleep, that is to say, born in a state of forgetfulness.'

'If that was the case then wouldn't the addition of souls from these seven special beings to the general population help humans wake up?'

'On the contrary, Jake m'boy. Too much power when one's not ready for it only makes matters worse. It's rocket fuel to the weak points, like high pressure through a cracked pipe. To see too much too soon would drive you mad. Waking up is a gradual process.'

'But waking up to what?' asked Jake. 'This is it! This is reality—planet Earth and the rest of universe.'

'Ah, yes, the universe,' said Braysheath, who reached into his bag, pulled out a long pipe and proceeded to prepare it. 'Appearances can be deceptive.'

'What's that supposed to mean?'

'Oh, you know...' said Braysheath who lit his pipe. As he took a deep draw of the rich-smelling tobacco he gazed out of the window at the mountainside.

While waiting for an answer, Jake took refuge in a sip of tea.

Before the mug reached his lips he cried out in shock. It had transformed into a giant black scorpion, the lethal sting of its tail just millimetres from his eye. He hurled it away.

As soon as it left his hand it became a mug again and tea spilt over the table.

'Are you all right, dear boy?' enquired Braysheath with a concerned expression. His lips, however, quivered with mirth.

'Wh-wh-what? How? Did you see?' stammered Jake.

'I haven't the slightest idea what you're talking about.'

'The mug, it... it turned into a bloody scorpion!' said Jake. 'What did you do? It was a magic trick, wasn't it? Are you some sort of circus magician?'

'Magician? Good lord, no!' cried Braysheath and barked with laughter. 'Don't tell me you believe in magic? I would have thought a fixation with mathematics was quite enough.'

'Of course not,' said Jake indignantly.

'I should hope not. Either everything's magic or nothing's magic but you can't have it both ways. That fellow Einstein said as much. I liked him.'

'That tobacco you're smoking...' ventured Jake as he mopped up the tea.

'Penumbran tobacco. Perfectly normal, though one never quite knows where it'll come out, or when for that matter. If it comes out of your ears within a day, you're lucky.'

'Then how do you explain the scorpion?' pressed Jake, craving an explanation.

'I don't. I didn't see one, though it's interesting you did. There's a myth about how the scorpion was sent to Earth to curtail humans' excessive pride.'

Jake studied Braysheath. He was looking out the window again, an air of amusement about him.

'Anyway, what were you saying?' continued Braysheath. 'Something about Earth and the universe. You do realise, of course, that the planets above are merely a reflection.'

Jake was growing tired of refuting everything Braysheath said, but he couldn't resist it. 'We've landed on the moon. Of course they exist.'

'Indeed they do—on that crude material level you so love to speak on, what you might call a *secondary* reality. Ultimately, however, they're nothing more than a map, symbolic of an inner journey you're already on. And one of those twinkling stars up there is you. Isn't that lovely?'

'You're not trying to say that the entire universe is inside of me,' said Jake, remembering a documentary on astrology he had once seen in which some spiritual nut had tried to claim just that.

'Exactly!' beamed Braysheath, turning to face Jake. 'Well done, Jake m'boy. Well done!'

'Now you've definitely gone too far,' said Jake who got up to make himself another cup of tea. 'Besides, the universe is expanding at an accelerating rate.'

'A bit like the population, hey? Not to mention the mozzies and rats. See any connection?'

'And there are millions of other galaxies...'

'Also symbolic,' said Braysheath. 'Of how human potential is slipping out of reach.'

'I think Newton would disagree with you. If he were alive, that is.'

'Oh, he is alive. And is that the same Newton who said, oh what was it? *I'm like the boy playing on the seashore, distracting myself with which shell is prettiest, while an ocean of truth lies before me undiscovered.* Something like that, yes. Splendid fellow Newton. Couldn't fail to be with a newt in his name. As for that Aristotle character...'

'You made that up,' accused Jake.

'He's still working on gravity, you know, dear old Newton, though goes by a different name and body these days. Subtle stuff, gravity. Of course, he's very sensibly given up trying to weigh and measure everything. One can't get very far with such limiting things, not in the primary world. Or rather, the inner world.'

'But science has come so far!' exclaimed Jake in exasperation.

'I've nothing against it, dear fellow, but are you quite sure about that? Sounds like blind faith to me and that's always tricky stuff. Why, I can't tell scientists apart from the priests. To make matters worse, they all dress up in white.'

'Blind faith? Science is based on *fact*.'

'Until a less shaky one is found. I assure you, it's nothing more than trial and error and a fact is nothing more than a matter of opinion. And wasting all that money flying up into space like scaredy-cats trying to escape responsibility for Earth when the real journey is inside. Extraordinary! You know they've been claiming the world is round?'

'Of course it's round!'

'My word, you are in a pickle. No, the Earth *used* to be round, but now it's flat again. It's to do with depth. Quality, you might say. There's a distinct lack of it these days. It's a cycle, you see. We're in a dark age and have been since the retreat of the last Ice Age. What those wonderful Hindus call the Age of Kali though I call it the *Great Game*. Now, were we in a cycle of the *Great Dance* you'd be quite correct in claiming the world was indeed round again, whole, the switch between the two being what our scientist friends would call a reverse in polarity.'

'You'll be telling me there are aliens next!'

'Naturally. But again, they're simply symbols of what humans have *alienated* from themselves—luminous beings, self-mastery rising up from the inner worlds. Truth in other words! It can no longer be suppressed. It's rising up again, reflected through human imagination as great spaceships zapping away at the illusory material world.'

While Jake shook his head in confusion, he secretly revelled in Braysheath's company. Whoever he really was, his presence was so immense that he somehow felt central to the flood of mystery that had burst into Jake's life. If anyone could answer all the questions cluttering his mind it was Braysheath. Assuming Jake could get a straight answer out of him.

As Jake returned to the table with his tea, he almost dropped it. The mug shone like a miniature sun. Orbiting around it was a ring of three smaller planets and a ring of larger planets outside of them. All were inside a bigger planet that encapsulated Jake, as though he were standing inside an atom.

'The primary universe inside of Earth,' explained Braysheath.

The sun shone brighter, projecting a shadow image of the planets throughout the kitchen that looked just like the way the universe was presented in science books.

'The secondary universe!' exclaimed an amazed Jake

'Precisely.'

Once again the mug returned to normal and the model of the universe disappeared.

Just then, singing could be heard from the yard. Having tended to all the animals, Bill was returning for his morning snifter, greeting the trees as he went.

'Oh hello there, Guinevere!' he cried as he greeted the old oak tree. 'Why thank you, my lady! Yes, I do feel rather handsome today now that you mention it. And might I say that you too are looking rather lovely.'

'Oh God,' groaned Jake. The thought of two mad men in the house at once was too daunting to think of.

'It is really? How jolly,' said Braysheath.

'The Devil would be closer to the truth.'

'Ah, even better! I haven't seen him in ages!'

Jake quickly weighed his options. None appealed. Thankfully, however, Bill had stopped for a moment to hug the cedar tree.

'That place you wanted to show me,' started Jake.

'So you'll help?' exclaimed Braysheath in delight.

'I didn't say that, I just wanted to know where—'

'Oh, I'm overjoyed!' beamed Braysheath leaping up and clapping his hands together. 'How wonderful! I was afraid I might have put you off. What with all that talk of chopping up.'

'I just—'

'You know, if we get cracking we'll make Himassisi in time for tea and there's nothing quite like a Himassisian tea!'

'Tea? You've just had breakfast!'

'Just a nibble. Besides, you scoffed most of the toast,' said Braysheath with a wink.

Jake didn't respond, too stricken by the sound of Bill resuming his journey towards the house, skipping with merriment.

'Follow me,' said Jake and made sharply for the hall.

'Tour of the house, oh super!' said Braysheath.

Jake had little doubt that Braysheath already knew of the inkwell. Though he hadn't yet decided what to do, he had to get Braysheath out of the kitchen.

'Ah, your father's den!' said Braysheath as Jake ushered him through the door.

Jake just managed to get him inside and lock the door as Bill bounded into the kitchen. 'Ahoy there, Trifle!' he cried.

'You know what this is, don't you?' said Jake, indicating the inkwell.

Braysheath gazed at it and sniffed the air. 'Ah, yes. A hoomsakhlawhoosh! What you would rather boringly call a black hole. Made it myself.'

'Where does it go?' asked Jake, in too much of a rush to fully digest what Braysheath had said.

'To Himassisi of course. Though if you know how to use it properly, it can take you anywhere this side of the Orijinn Sea.'

'Not to Hades?' asked Jake. Himassisi sounded better.

'Hades? Why yes, you might very well call it that! I wonder where you got that idea,' said Braysheath with a knowing glint in his eyes.

Jake was half-listening to Bill's conversation with Trifle. He was talking about some unusual bird he had seen and how he must look it up in a bird book which meant coming to the study. 'In fact, I think I'll look it up right now!' declared Bill.

'Will I find Granddad by going through the inkwell?' asked Jake quickly.

'Oh, you'll find everything in there,' said Braysheath. 'If you have the time to look, that is. Infinity is rather large.'

Suddenly the door shook in its frame as Bill turned the handle and tried to get in.

'What's going on in there! Is that you in there, Jock?' bawled Bill, deliberately mispronouncing Jake's name. 'Open the door this instant, you haggis-eating guttersnipe!'

Jake's devilish side was half-tempted to let Bill in and see what happened. *But what if Braysheath disappeared into thin air?* he wondered. He couldn't afford to miss the opportunity to find his granddad.

'If I go through the inkwell, I'll be able to return, won't I?' he whispered, for the thought of never returning to the farm was unimaginable, despite the thrill of visiting other worlds.

'Whenever you want. Though I should warn you, things up here will seem a little different,' said Braysheath, yet again echoing Frost.

'In what way?'

'A little more… more lively, yes. Which is a fine thing is it not? Unless you like being asleep, being a sheep, in which case you're quite welcome to stay.'

'Open the blasted door, you filthy little swine!' cried Bill as he virtually shook the door off its hinges.

'You still haven't explained why this is happening to me,' asked Jake, his heartbeat racing as the inevitable drew closer.

Braysheath looked surprised. 'Because you chose it! Why else?'

'I certainly did not,' protested Jake.

'You'll soon discover, Jake m'boy, that there's much more to childbirth than you realise. So, shall we dance?' said Braysheath, stepping toward the inkwell and taking its lid in hand.

'Right, that's it!' roared Bill as he padded off down the hallway. 'I'm going to charge this bloody door down and God help you when I do!'

'So let me guess,' said Jake, recalling what Frost had said about the *hero's journey*, 'by passing through the inkwell I'm setting forth on some epic journey, presumably to save the world which of course I do, and erm, let's see, what else? Oh yes, win the heart of a beautiful girl.'

The image of the girl on the crags flashed through his mind and the pull of the inkwell grew stronger.

'Something like that,' said Braysheath. 'But that would be only half the story and very much the boring half.'

'Charge!' roared Bill from the far end of the hallway.

Winking at Jake, Braysheath flipped open the inkwell and the flex of energy shook the study. He then glanced up at the ceiling, his eyes wide with horror. 'My God! Niffy-sprite!'

Jake wheeled round and looked up in shock. Before he had a chance to realise the ruse, he was swept up by his trouser belt and hurled from the surface of the Earth.

Seconds later, the door mysteriously unlocked and Bill calmly stepped into the study and looked about.

'Well there's a mystery,' he said with a glint in his eyes, left the bird book on the shelf and returned to the kitchen for a morning brew.

THE HOUSE OF TUSK

CHAPTER 10
POTENTIAL'S GRAVEYARD

PRIDE. IT WAS MORE THAN JUST AN EMOTION. IT WAS A WORLD —one very far down the road. Though proud were the footsteps taken to reach it, only those without pride could pass beyond, and beyond was the Core, a place of such lightness that no baggage could be carried, least of all pride.

It was also the most difficult to let go of, especially on the world of Pride, where to judge by appearances was fatal. In fact, the more splendid something seemed, the more fatal it was. And in that place so brimming with outward splendour, one place shone out—a woodland. Forever autumn, forever sunset, it shimmered red and gold, one tree in particular. It reached high into the sky and in the node of its uppermost branch was an archway. In the softly-lit hall beyond it stood a figure. Goddess Luna.

She looked different than she had at Renlock. Part human, part tree, her skin was as smooth and pale as silver birch bark and instead of hair was a blaze of orange leaves. She had emerged from somewhere so deep within the cosmos that acclimatisation was a gradual process. Like a deep-sea diver rising to the surface, it had to be done in stages—through mineral, through vegetable until finally she was able to inhabit the shorter wave frequency of water, of emotions, the frequency of humans.

In the twiggy hands of her branch-like arms was Pandora's Box.

Standing with her eyes closed, she appeared to have been there for quite some time pondering the mysterious object when green flames suddenly erupted from her hands and engulfed the iridescent box. The flames writhed about its surface, searching for a way in, attempting to decipher its ancient code.

Sensing something, Luna's green eyes flashed open and shone with power. They fixed on a small flask of light on a table. It popped open and left the same heavenly ringing in the air as it had in Renlock. She inhaled deeply. The light left the flask and snaked through the air until it reached her mouth. She inhaled it and her peculiar body bristled with strength.

A pulse of energy shook the hall as Pandora's Box sprang open, transformed and yawned into a giant mouth of a crocodile, sucking forth a storm of orange leaves from the woodland outside.

Scarcely visible amid the chaos, it would have sucked in Luna too had she not taken the precaution of drinking the light, which added to her gravity. With the aid of her root-like feet, she took a tentative step towards the passageway of the crocodile's throat. Step by step she passed inside.

At the end of the short passageway the leaves thinned out to reveal a gateway to a colossal cemetery—the deeper reality of what lay inside of Pandora's Box that Lawrence had glimpsed before taking it from the House of Tusk. The vast and varied tombs, some the size of small houses, appeared without end. It was no ordinary place of death, for though the vacuum relented to a gale, it absorbed all sound, sucked all life from the air. Even the ancient yew and holly trees, symbols of rebirth, were dead, their grey forms wrestled in unnatural silence by the violent gusts which eddied about the tombs.

Doing her best not to be harried by the strange wind, Luna made her way through the twilight of the grey maze.

She was some way in when something caught her eye. A little ahead the ghostly form of a man emerged from a tomb. In a trance, he headed deeper into the cemetery. Her eyes sparkling with interest, Luna followed a little distance behind.

It wasn't long before the ramshackle horizon of tombs was broken by the crisp lines of a new shape—a great pyramid, as grey as gravestone. The ghost was heading directly for it.

The approach to it grew even more cluttered, not just with tombs, but with ancient yew trees, as lifeless as the rest.

Finally, Luna broke through the tangle into a large clearing around the great temple, the area bathed in the light of a blue moon which emerged from behind clouds. Luna waited at the threshold of the yews as the ghost made for the temple entrance.

Once it had passed inside, she too crossed the clearing and crept in, careful to keep to the shadows.

The only light came from the moon, beamed in through a shaft in the top of the cavernous pyramid, along with a peculiar blue-flamed fire. It burned faintly in a large bowl on the floor. Sitting in front of it within the shaft of light was what appeared to be an angel, except that its wings were charred. He was leaning forward warming his hands against the flame.

Without a word, the ghost approached the angel and stopped in front of the bowl. The angel looked up. The weariness in his movement, the resignation in his dark and dignified eyes, belied a sense of great power. He smiled a wry smile at the vacant looking ghost who immediately underwent a transformation. Its phantom body suddenly glowed like a billion suns as its atoms dispersed and streamed into the blue flame. Their impact on the blue flame was barely noticeable. In just a few moments the ghost was absorbed.

'You hear that, sister?' said the angel in a tone rich with irony.

Luna's arrival hadn't gone unnoticed. As he spoke, a peculiar wind of whisperings closed in about her and rustled her foliage. Her eyes shone with fascination. There were five voices, the same five who had torn about Lawrence in the vault.

'Listen,' he added. 'Listen very carefully.'

In the stillness of the temple arrived a new sound—a disturbance, faint but momentous, like an explosion, but from a great distance off.

'A new galaxy is born,' announced the angel.

Enthralled, Luna emerged from the darkness and approached the flame.

Once there, she and the angel remained in a suspenseful silence in what appeared to be a stand-off of power.

The angel broke it with a dry laugh.

Luna smiled enigmatically though a perplexed light in her eyes suggested the angel held the initiative.

'The flame?' she said at last.

'To warm a heart of stone. If only for a moment,' he replied as he rubbed his hands near the flame.

Luna studied what had seemed like a bowl, though on closer inspection was shaped like a heart—a huge one and almost cleaved in two.

'A little large for you, isn't it?' she remarked.

The haunting whisperings reappeared and buffeted her yet again, which only added to her delight.

'Alas, it doesn't burn very hot,' said the angel, ignoring Luna's comment. 'Such is the case when potential sours.'

Luna watched the flames die down to their former flickering. 'Intriguing. But potential cannot sour. It can seem beyond reach, but—'

'It amounts to the same,' interrupted the angel in his calm tone. 'A human *avoids* its potential and so *a-void* is created, dressed up as a galaxy, though is nothing more than an illusion, dazzling the gullible, a dream to chase but never catch.'

'Emptiness created,' muttered Luna, clearly captivated by the novel idea. 'What is this place?'

'You mean to tell me you don't recognise it? Now that's what I call ironic. It's a reflection—of the Surface, of the walking dead, of the illegitimate and truly hopeless. This, sister, is Potential's Graveyard.'

Luna glanced out through the temple entrance with renewed interest. 'And where do *you* fit into this charming place?' she asked, returning her attention to the angel.

The angel studied Luna. The amused glint in its eyes grew brighter. 'I am they,' he said, gesturing to the tombs. 'Except that I am awake.'

'You mean to say that you're the collective consciousness of those who are unconscious—the walking dead?'

The angel simply smiled.

'Fascinating,' purred Luna. 'Of course you might be nothing more than a parasite, growing fat on the light of others.'

The angel's amused expression remained unchanged as it beheld Luna.

'And is that what a sylph is,' added Luna, 'this collective consciousness? Or are you merely a gatekeeper?'

'I am both,' replied the angel.

Luna said nothing, but there was a questioning light in her eyes.

'A sylph is my shadow,' clarified the angel.

Luna peered behind the angel, but no shadow was cast by the blue flame. 'I thought I was alone in having no shadow,' she remarked.

'Mine is outside,' explained the sylph, gesturing to the graves. 'It's made up of many.'

'Well,' said Luna, 'I would like to enlist its help.'

The whispering wind swept about Luna with such ferocity that it left her frosted. Luna smiled and the frost was gone.

'Your audacity doesn't surprise me,' said the angel who, unlike the wind, remained calm. 'But you have nothing of worth to offer me. Everything I need is here.'

'How about freedom?'

'From what?' asked the angel.

'Have you forgotten the sweet aroma of pure potential?'

'Unlike you, sister, I forget nothing. Besides, I've acquired a taste for the sour.'

'Maybe so, but appreciation wanes without the contrast,' said Luna. 'I should know. I too was once imprisoned.'

'You still are—by your vanity. It will be your downfall.'

Luna tossed back her head in laughter. 'Vanity?'

'Were you not such a slave to your self-image, were you able to trust rather than seeking to control evolution then the tension between light and dark on the Surface of Earth would still be within natural thresholds. Rather than being at snapping point.'

'The Surface of Earth had become dull!' declared Luna with a dismissive wave of a hand. 'It was created too beautiful. The tribes of pre-history worshipped it as heaven, made it even more beautiful, and kept reincarnating there rather than journey through the Inner-Pereginus towards the intended heaven at the Core. I was waiting there for aeons. It was driving me mad!'

'And so you projected that madness onto them. To harry humans from the Surface you created hell there through a population explosion. It was clever. In theory. By sacrificing most of the shepherds you not only created a vast source of souls, but reduced the extent of their guidance. Alas, you underestimated the effect of doing so.'

'And what would that be?' asked Luna, apparently enjoying the angel's perspective.

'Humans learnt to take pleasure in negativity in order to survive it. The natural cycle into introspection, known as the Great Game, became depression and a need to make sense of it. Never before have humans so delighted in destruction and squalor and a lack of consideration for living things. Nor have they been so ignorant of the consequences for their souls.'

Anger flickered through Luna's eyes.

'And this enrages you even more,' added the angel. 'Not only that your plan has backfired, but at how unconscious they have become, mirroring back to you the extent of your own ignorance.'

'Ignorance!' snapped Luna.

The angel laughed dryly. 'A raw nerve?'

Unsure of her power in the strange reality inside Pandora's Box and in need of the angel's help, Luna exhaled her anger.

'You and I are in the same sinking boat,' said Luna.

'Have you never wondered from whence the boat came? That perhaps you are but a pawn in a greater game, one in which everything is just how it needs to be.'

Luna scoffed at the idea. 'The boat, you and everything else came from my dreaming.'

The angel smiled. 'You'll remember in time. For now you've lost your faith, that's plain to see. And to lose faith, authentic faith, is a loss of great power.'

'Neither of us have faith and we are both bitter.'

'But I'm aware of the fact that I enjoy my bitterness. That makes all the difference. As for faith, mine has run its course. I no longer have need of it. So you see, sister, you and I are very different. You seek control. I'm content to simply observe. You covet light, while I'm happy to let it go. You seek an exit where none exists.'

At the mention of the word *exit*, Luna's eyes brightened. 'None exists for now, but...'

Luna looked up along the shaft of blue light and out into the expanding cosmos. 'One could and soon. I sense it. Don't you?'

The angel warmed its hands again in the blue flame. 'At the point where body breaks from spirit, where the conscious breaks away from the unconscious, when humans have completely isolated themselves from the very nature which supports them, their true nature—in the instant before the point of snapping, yes, it's possible an exit might present itself. A momentary tear in the fabric.'

'That would be quite a moment,' purred Luna. 'Think of the possibilities. If my intuition is right, whoever stepped into that tear, call it a temple, could create whatever they wished with the light they carried—a new cosmos, one radically different. Or perhaps even nothingness. Anything but this!'

Luna's leaves rustled with excitement.

'Fancy playing a part?' she asked. 'All the while watching here from your front row seat? Simply release your shadow. I'll provide you a host to allow its movement outside of Pandora's Box to where I've stored the holygate that leads to the Surface. All I require is the gate to be blocked. A week of stillborn children should be sufficient to topple the Overlord Brock. Then a little longer to trap souls in the worlds of death while I cause a war between them—long enough for their souls to become lost and for me to take them. What you do with your shadow afterwards is up to you.'

The whispering wind tore through the pyramid and enveloped the angel in a light breeze as it conversed with him.

'Can your shadow block it?' asked Luna. 'After all, a shadow is one's link to death and rebirth. And yours is the densest there is.'

'A human's shadow, yes,' agreed the angel, its attention fixed on the flame. 'But my shadow is the end. Eternal death. It's a modern idea, but belief is a powerful thing.'

'Then have some fun with it,' suggested Luna. 'I'm not fooled by your display of indifference. You're bored. You need to get out. After all, what do you have to lose? I sense no pride in you, no fear of humiliation. And I'm sure you'll approve of my chosen host—a noble heart and full of life, his name is Nestor Burton from the august House of Tusk.'

For the first time the angel expressed surprise. It was subtle—less in his expression than in the whispering wind which instantly ceased. The deadest of stillness gripped the cemetery.

'You've heard of him, I trust?' enquired Luna.

Finally the angel looked up at Luna. 'And where is this man?' he asked.

'I hold him captive elsewhere.'

'Then how do you plan to transfer my shadow to him?'

'*I* shall carry it,' announced Luna.

The whispering wind erupted from the stillness and burst out into the cemetery like a gale. Whether excited or agitated, it was difficult to tell.

'Have you forgotten the fable of the frog and the scorpion?' asked the angel. 'The frog agreed to carry the scorpion across the river, which stung it midway, dooming them both. A vicious nature, warns the fable, cannot be reformed.'

'So it would seem with humans,' said Luna. 'But unlike the frog I'm not afraid of your sting. Neither do I fear the river.'

The angel was silent, the wry smile ever-present upon its face.

'Can I take your warning as an agreement to co-operate?' pressed Luna.

The angel gazed out through the entrance to the yews beyond the clearing, wrestled by the silent gale.

'Not an agreement,' he said at last. 'I offer no such thing. I weigh each moment as it arrives. I can only say that if it amuses me then I may block the holygate. The moment I'm drawn elsewhere I shall leave. Assuming you can bear my shadow.'

'I shall take my chances,' beamed Luna.

The angel sat in thoughtful silence. It was impossible to know, let alone understand, the motives of a being so vast. It could only be known that the scope of its vision was very far, very wide and very deep, that were the angel to use potential rather than destroy it then, given the huge portion of consciousness it represented, it could create whatever reality it wanted. That consciousness, however, was bitter. It was more bitter than even Luna's, for the origin of each and every soul that made up the cemetery inside of Pandora's Box had been born of five bitter acts—the greatest sins ever committed.

It was those acts and Luna's part in them, a connection she hadn't yet made, which piqued the angel's interest. The irony, the paradox, was irresistible.

'Take my hands, sister,' said the angel.

Luna's eyes flashed with excitement. She stepped closer and reached forward.

The air grew weighty.

The moonbeam brightened.

The flames in the bowl billowed higher.

In the instant their hands touched both lights faltered. A tremendous pulse of energy shot out from the pyramid. The ground quaked. Gravestones cracked. A deathly gasp shook the air as every ghost of the mighty cemetery sat bolt upright in their tombs and were hauled through the air towards the pyramid. They streamed in through the shaft like a volcanic eruption in reverse, streamed through the moonbeam in a dazzling torrent of blue, into the crown of the angel's head, out through his arms and into Luna's.

Despite the torrent, the angel's face remained composed, his eyes closed.

Luna's, however, were wide with shock and growing misted. Her bark-like skin was turning to stone, first her arms and spreading outwards.

There was no way of telling how much of the angel's shadow Luna had absorbed. From her chin down she was stone. The formation of the sylph appeared to be sucking the life from her.

Her lips were turning grey when a moth fluttered past them. With a sharp gasp she inhaled it.

Despite its size, the moth's energy was no less than any other creature's. A trace of light flickered through Luna's misted eyes and out and about the branches of her crown.

Sensing the shift, the angel opened its eyes. He peered out through the temple entrance with a look of mild amusement.

Something was entering the cemetery from Pride—a dark cloud smothering the twilight.

With unnatural speed it raced into the clearing. The air jarred with an explosion of cawing and a vast cloud of crows burst into the temple, sacrificing themselves into the electrical storm about Luna's crown. Just as the pigeon light on Renlock had helped ground her, so it was with the crows. The mist cleared from her eyes. Her body returned to normal as the greyness sank to her feet and became a shadow.

The striking sight of the ghosts streaming into the angel and crows into Luna continued for a while longer until the angel calmly released her hands. As the remainder of the ghosts drifted back to their tombs, the crows returned to Pride.

'That is enough for what you require,' said the angel, apparently unaffected by the transfer.

Luna, however, shone with power as she admired the unusually dense shadow that stretched away from her.

'Feel any different?' enquired the angel dryly. 'Any compassion for our brethren above?'

A shameless smile spread across her face. 'Not the slightest.'

Following a bow of her head to the angel, she strode from pyramid and back to Pride.

CHAPTER 11
HIMASSISI

CONTRARY TO JAKE'S FIRST ENCOUNTER WITH THE INKWELL, the sensation of entering it was pure bliss—like diving into the sea at midnight and swimming through the reflected stars. It was so delightful that when he suddenly found himself hurtling downwards through a stone passageway of some sort, flying even, whizzing past countless archways, he revelled in the adventure, even when the rancid roar of a dinosaur burst out through one of them.

Jake's speed became impossibly fast. He only caught glimpses of what appeared to be different worlds, an icy blast from one almost hurling him into another, only to be followed by a belch of heat from a jungle.

He glanced back and caught sight of Braysheath racing along behind him, his face half-crazed with excitement.

His expression, however, suddenly changed to one of alarm. It immediately infected Jake. He wondered what could be wrong and braced himself for incineration or something worse.

Braysheath sped forwards and wrapped himself about Jake.

A terrific pulse tore through the black hole. Jake felt as though he were being torn apart.

An instant later it was over and he was flat on his back, the air thumped from his lungs.

When he finally opened his eyes, he found himself under a bright blue sky. He was on a sand dune in a great desert. In the far distance was a glorious mountain range which reached so high there was snow on its summits. Following the chaos of the journey through the gate, the stillness was stark. The sudden contrast with an English winter was like a dream.

Suddenly Jake recoiled in shock. At his feet was a large dark dog. Not only was it particularly hairy and panting but its coat was steaming.

'What the hell?' he exclaimed.

'Thanador is his name,' came the strained voice of Braysheath who was lying beside Jake and looking dazed. The cobra about his neck appeared to be unconscious. 'The keeper of nothingness, though not nothingness as you understand it. He's what you might call *well connected*. He's perfectly friendly and very useful indeed.'

'Are you all right? What happened back there?' asked Jake.

Braysheath heaved himself up to a seated position and took out his pipe. Not to be hurried, he slowly packed its bowl with tobacco, lit it and inhaled deeply before answering.

'Something I've never felt before,' he said at last.

'What?'

Braysheath simply closed his eyes and took another slow puff. Though it was still a mystery to him, it had been Luna holding the angel's hands which had caused the shock throughout the cosmos.

'Anyway, here we are,' he said, perking up. 'And in the right place, too!'

'And what exactly *is* a niffy-sprite?' asked Jake, recalling the ruse Braysheath had used to hurl Jake through the inkwell.

'Cowardly little things. You find them in the herbs. Enjoy the trip?'

'Apart from being thrown in and the last part, actually yes, I did.'

'Well, if you will dawdle, what do you expect?'

'It felt like…' said Jake, struggling to find the right words.

'You felt complete?' ventured Braysheath.

'Yes! That's exactly how it felt!' exclaimed Jake.

'That's why they're called holygates. They make one whole. And though it's only for a moment or two the memory inspires.'

'But why do they make you feel whole?'

'Because they're usually passed through when you leave one world for another.'

'After dying, you mean?'

'Precisely. Free of the body, in the form of spirit, you're no longer ignorant of your connection with the rest of the cosmos. You literally meet your maker.'

'A creator,' said Jake, unconvinced of the idea. 'If there is a creator then where did he come from?'

'Oh, how humankind gets caught up in the idea of beginnings and ends and the scale of things,' said Braysheath in mock despair. 'Creation is ongoing and a team effort.'

'Why is it so difficult to get a straight answer from you?'

'Because the answers aren't straight. They're curvy,' replied Braysheath and gave Jake a wink.

'Anyway, what do you think of Himassisi?' he added.

'The desert?'

'The oasis. Quite a sight, isn't it?'

'What oasis?' said Jake.

'Ah, of course! You're still stuck with those blunt old senses of yours,' said Braysheath and gave Jack a thwack on the back.

A great jolt shot through Jake as though he had received an electric shock. When his vision cleared he gasped. He was sitting on the last dune before a vast lush oasis. All the colours, the desert included, burst with richness.

'What did you do?' he exclaimed.

'Saved some time,' said Braysheath. 'Perhaps a lifetime or two.'

Jake was lost for words as he gazed about.

'Listen,' said Braysheath.

'To what?'

'To this,' said Braysheath, gesturing to everything.

Jake concentrated on the oasis, letting go for a moment of all his preoccupations about how such things were possible. Sounds exploded to life—the cries of birds, the screeches of monkeys, strange barks and roars and all sorts of other mysterious sounds, even what seemed like the creaking of trees.

'You're doing something again, aren't you?' he said.

'I'm not doing anything, other than drawing your attention to it. Too much thinking makes you deaf, not to mention blind,' said Braysheath, reminding Jake of Frost. Unlike Frost, however, whose presence was mischievous, being close to Braysheath brought Jake a sense of peace.

'With too much thinking,' continued Braysheath, 'you not only forget where you are but who you are! That's what that Descartes fellow should have said, had he been a *feel*-osopher instead of *fill*-osopher, filling people up with rubbish. *I think therefore I am.* Ha! What nonsense! *I feel therefore we are.* There, that's much better.'

Jake turned his attention to his own thoughts. He ran a hand through the sand. It felt so real. An ecstasy of imminent adventure coursed through him. Before he could fully surrender to it, he needed some answers.

'What am I doing here?' he asked. 'Back in the study you said I chose this. But how?'

Braysheath took another unhurried puff on his pipe before answering.

'I'm sure you're in no mood to go into the great intricacies of death and astrology though I assure you that both are highly scientific. Just take my word for it, Jake m'boy, that there's a very good reason why you chose to be born when you did.'

'Actually, I am in the mood to go into it,' lied Jake, just to see if Braysheath would finally answer a question.

'Well I'm not. It would take almost forever and my stomach is starting to rumble.'

'Then tell me why I chose now to be born.'

'Because *now* is an excellent and very exciting time to be alive! More momentous even than when dear old Buddha or Jesus were up on the Surface. This time round, not just one, but *all* must become saviours!'

'What type of leap?'

'A leap of faith. An absolute whopper. Which reminds me. There's always an exception and among all those confused fillosophers was a splendid fellow called Nietzsche. He hit the nail clean on the head when he said that humankind had strayed so desperately out of balance with nature that it would take a superhuman leap to get it back on track. In fact, he considered the whole thing rather fortunate.'

'How could it be fortunate?' asked Jake as he watched a bird of prey wheeling high in the sky.

'Because it gives humankind a chance to become super.'

'Super? In what way?'

'All-round super. Like Buddha. Like Christ.'

'Everyone become like Christ? Are you serious?'

'Christ consciousness, Jake m'boy. That is to say, to always be present and truly feel that all is one. To love thine enemy—ignorance, in other words. To understand it, to feel compassion and forgive it, to transform it. Takes practice though. Alas, like all fine messages, Nietzsche's idea of *super* was turned on its head by someone with less wholesome ideas.'

'You mean Hitler?' asked Jake, for he had learned about Nietzsche in one of his lessons at school.

'That's the one. Anyway, marvellous fellow, Nietzsche. Not like all those other miseries. Always inventing problems. Always claiming something's missing. Why, I'll never forgive Socrates for claiming that trees couldn't teach him anything. My God, if only he knew! If only he could remember having been a tree! Ha!'

'Having been a tree?'

'Yes, indeed, which is why unconscious chopping down of them gets you into serious trouble in the world that follows,' said Braysheath and sighed. 'Dear old Socrates. And he was one of the brighter ones. Still, it's all part of what the Great Game has become.'

'That still doesn't explain why I might have chosen such a time as now to be alive,' said Jake, gazing at the trees of the oasis in a new light.

'Of course it does. It means you're an excellent leaper. You've simply forgotten how to do it. And that's why you're down here. In no time at all you'll be leaping about like a leprechaun.'

Jake laughed at the idea.

'You'll love it!' cried Braysheath. 'And when one's dancing with all creation there's no need for all that meaning of life twaddle and all that talk of God because it's everywhere. You feel it! Everything's sacred. Everything's a wonderful mystery. And that's the trick, to dance your merry dance, to dance your heart's message in the midst of the Great Game and all its deceit, encouraging others to dance theirs until so many are dancing that it becomes the Great Dance—a Golden Age of Truth. Rivers run wide once more, water sparkles, trees grow tall and thick in celebration.'

Jake liked the idea and took a hearty breath of air.

'Right, come on. Stop being boring,' said Braysheath, getting to his feet. 'Time for tea!'

'But you still haven't explained why it's me that's here and not someone else. I realise Dad was here and Granddad too but why?'

Braysheath's eyes shone with amusement. 'My word, you're a demanding fellow. You're here because of Reggie Burton. An ancestor of yours.'

'I've never heard of a Reggie in our family.'

'Well, we're going back some years of course. But he was an inquisitive sort. Something called an alchemist which are rare types who like to get to grips with the nature of things. The real nature. To get beneath the surface, so to speak. How scientists *used* to be. Anyway, he achieved what no other human had done before him.'

'What was that?'

'Get here. Unassisted that is. And alive! In a physical sense. We hadn't thought it possible that a human could exist anywhere other than the Surface. Of course a soul can go anywhere but not with a body. Not an atomic one. Not one from the Surface. It's just not how things were set up. Though on reflection one wonders.'

'We?' enquired Jake.

'Me and what was it I said I was?'

'A shepherd,' said Jake with a sneaking suspicion that the term was a dramatic understatement of what Braysheath really was.

'That's it! And so, yes, the fascinating thing was that Reggie arrived when we were having a rather tricky time. Two of those seven powerful beings I mentioned had already been sliced and diced then a third went missing. Another sacrifice which took over a thousand years.'

'But how could a human be of help here?' asked Jake.

'A fine question, dear fellow. But for a human to be conscious in a place like this, far beneath the Surface, is a hugely powerful thing. After all, humans and consciousness are central to what the cosmos is all about. Not forgetting, of course, how human bodies are designed to conceal the soul, which can be quite useful down here. And dear old Reggie made such a difference that we decided to keep him on, build him a handy base from which to operate, including that natty inkwell to reach the farm. In fact, when it was time for Reggie to pass on, we kept our faith in the bloodline which, with the exception of only one or two not-so-good apples, has proved to be excellent.'

'So I'm here because of my bloodline.'

'Exactly.'

'But you said *I* chose it. Who was that *I*?' asked Jake, not sure he wanted to hear the answer.

'That's what we're here to find out! But not before a good hot cuppa.'

Jake certainly needed a cup of tea but he could tell that Braysheath, like Frost, knew much more than he was letting on. He then remembered something Braysheath had said before hurling Jake into the inkwell.

'When I asked you about saving the world and getting the girl, you said that was only half the story. The boring half. What did you mean by that?'

'Simply that the world is not quite as polar as you've been told it is.'

'Polar?'

'The manure contributes to the perfume of the rose, just as day follows night and night follows day, each evolving through the other with the help of that wonderful grey stuff called dawn and dusk.'

'Are you trying to say that things like good and evil are the same?'

'One can't exist without the other, just as no white knight can truly call himself a saviour unless he's journeyed through the dark night of his soul, the journey where true faith is forged.'

'Dark night of the soul?' said Jake uncertainly.

'Don't worry about all that now. Suffice it to say that for a good leap forward it's rather useful to take a step back beforehand. Or should I say a step down, a step deeper?'

At the mention of dark nights and steps downwards, Jake wondered what he was getting into, reminding himself that if his dad and granddad were involved then surely it was fine. *If*, he muttered in thought.

'Anyway,' added Braysheath, 'people get far too excited about darkness. All they talk about is mental depression, a modern business, quite forgetting that existence is born from the primordial womb of the Great Mother, that it's the night which blots out the distractions of daytime and brings us rest and peace. Something I wished you'd give me a bit of.'

At that moment something crawled onto Jake's right hand—another scorpion. He leapt up and shook it off.

'See what I mean about leaping?' said Braysheath, laughing. 'You're a natural!'

'It *was* you who played that trick with the mug, wasn't it?'

'Dear fellow, I told you, I'm not doing anything,' said Braysheath who strode off down the dune in the direction of the oasis. 'Are you coming or not?'

Jake looked down at the still-steaming dog. He was watching Jake and appeared to be grinning.

'What if I want to go back to the farmhouse?' wondered Jake.

'I'm not sure poor old Thanador's up to it,' said Braysheath without turning. 'Something strange happened on the way down.'

'What's Thanador got to do with it?'

'Where do you think you came out of?'

'What?' exclaimed Jake. 'Are you saying I came out of *that*?'

'Exactly. Thanador is very special. He's connected to the inkwell and one or two other gates on the Surface. Within a reasonable distance of the oasis he's mobile. You'll find him indispensable.'

A horrific image filled Jake's mind. 'Which end did we come out of?' he asked.

'There's little difference in Thanador's case. He eats anything and there's no end of treats about the oasis. Anyway, if you want to return, you'll have to follow me. There's another way inside the oasis.'

'Wait!' cried out Jake. 'I still want to know—'

'I refuse to say anything more until I've had a cup of tea!' announced Braysheath, lengthening his stride.

Jake focused on the oasis more closely. It thrummed with life in a way that was so vibrant that there was something magical about the place. A complex feeling stirred in his stomach. To pass inside the oasis was to pass yet deeper into a world far from the one he knew when there was still so much Braysheath had yet to explain. The image of the ghost with the lantern swept through his mind. A chill ran up his spine at the strange timing.

Could the ghost and the oasis be connected?

He wondered why the ghost filled him with such fear, over and above the fact that it was a ghost. He instinctively knew it couldn't be escaped. But why? Where did it come from? Why was it pursuing him again?

Remarkably, Braysheath had almost covered the hundred or so paces to the oasis and was about to enter its jungle.

The colours and sounds bursting from the oasis seemed to grow even richer as though beckoning Jake inside, colours so brilliant that they outshone any lingering fears. The air grew light. His heart leapt and cried out for adventure. He thought of his granddad and the need to find him and his mind was set. Braysheath was his best hope.

'Wait! Wait for me!' Jake cried out and charged off down the dune.

CHAPTER 12
THE GOVERNOR-GENERAL'S RESIDENCE

LAWRENCE IN THE FORM OF LORD BOREAS HAD JUST BEEN shown to his office in the uppermost part of Renlock. It was the office reserved for the Governor-General, the chief representative of whoever was renting the place. In other words, Luna. Her intention, like all of those before, was the toppling of the Overlord of the Outer-Peregrinus, the outer-part of the soul's journey to the Core.

The office was plain—large, circular and stone. A sumptuous fire burned at its centre, taking the bite off the chilly air. There were no plants. They couldn't be trusted, not in Renlock. Unlike rocks, their affairs and concept of time overlapped too much with humans and their roots reached far. There was, however, a hammock slung from the beams, adding a homely touch, while various instruments scattered about the room lent it the air of an observatory, albeit one with sinister intentions.

Most sinister of all was the view from the stairwell which entered the office through the floor. It looked directly down on the hollow-gram of Brock in the alley, whose slumped form looked even more wretched than before.

Wilderspin and his entourage had just left. Lawrence was tired. He took off his cloak and sword and sat down at the table next to a window which looked out over a sea of moonlit mist. For some time he simply sat there in silence, gazing out at the calming view, greatly relieved his cover was still holding. At least, he hoped it was. Wilderspin was known to be so devious that if he suspected something, he didn't immediately let on. Instead, he would let things unfold in order to catch the biggest fish possible.

Following a quick appraisal of the office, he looked down at the tray of tea and cake on the desk in front of him. With a weary smile he poured out a cup of tea. In a saucer he poured some more tea and placed a chunk of cake beside it. He reached into a cloak hanging over the back of the chair, withdrew Geoffrey and placed him next to the saucer of tea.

'About time!' he grumbled. 'It's intolerable being closeted up in that filthy rag. And under your armpit of all places!'

'Sorry, Geoffrey,' soothed Lawrence. 'Have some tea and cake.'

Geoffrey glanced about the room, looking unimpressed, before draining his saucer of tea and scoffing his cake. 'That was a very stingy portion,' he remarked haughtily.

Smiling, Lawrence served him some more. 'Can we relax here?' he asked, looking about the walls as though they had ears.

'Humph,' said Geoffrey between slurps. 'You can't afford to relax *anywhere.*'

'Can we talk at least?' clarified Lawrence. In between visits to Renlock they had been back to the dream room but hadn't yet discussed what they had learned of Luna for fear that she might somehow hear them.

'It's all right,' said Geoffrey. 'If someone's about I'll know it. Lizard medicine is more powerful than that of pigeons.'

'And Luna?'

Geoffrey shook his head. 'Not in Renlock. Not yet. Perhaps when she's more powerful.'

Lawrence took another sip of tea.

'You look dreadful, by the way,' added Geoffrey.

'You might take a look in the mirror yourself,' suggested Lawrence. 'Besides, are you surprised? We've got to get back into the House of Tusk. The idea has been quite a shock.'

'We?' mumbled Geoffrey through a mouthful of cake.

'I can't do it without you.'

'You need to ground yourself better,' said Geoffrey. 'Your emotions almost betrayed you when you saw Brock. Luna felt them.'

Geoffrey was right. Lawrence knew it was only a matter of time until Luna discovered his true identity, but he had to delay that moment for as long as possible.

'When I asked her where she intended to go with the stolen light, Renlock briefly shifted to an Arctic scene. Where was that?' he asked.

'Could be anywhere, but you can bet it's somewhere almost impossible to find. And I doubt it's her ultimate destination—just a shipment point.'

'Did you notice she had no shadow? How can someone be immune to the effect of light?'

'By being *from* light, directly that is. In other words from the sun,' said Geoffrey and caused Lawrence's eyes to widen. 'Whoever Luna is, she's from the Core. The sun is the symbol of the Core, its outer refection.'

'Are you sure she's from the Core?'

'Her gravity is too great to be otherwise,' said Geoffrey. 'What else could summon a guardian commander of the inner-force to do her bidding?'

'What?' hissed Lawrence, taking care not to raise his voice. 'A guardian commander? How do you know?'

'Whilst inside your robes I sensed a powerful whiff of the inner-force.'

'How you can be sure it was inner-force?' pressed Lawrence.

'Because it's the only thing powerful enough to out-pong your armpit.'

'But guardians, like dryads, are neutral. They can't be corrupted.'

'The same was once said of a certain tribe of trixies,' replied Geoffrey, referring to the guardians' counterparts on the Surface. Together they conspired to ensure the lives of humans were as tricky as possible, putting up obstacles along the most promising paths. The opposing force came from the Outer-Peregrinus, aided by the dryads and pixies. Combined, the two forces created the tautness called life and ensured that its lessons were learned thoroughly.

Lawrence knew the tribe Geoffrey was referring to. Its leader had a grand home hidden away in the countryside in northern England, disguising himself behind the title of count.

'I bet the corruption of that tribe occurred at the same time as the creation of Renlock along with the god gate,' deduced Lawrence. 'They probably made the god gate! Trixies are excellent gate-smiths.'

He released a heavy sigh. 'And now the corruption goes deeper. Guardians! God help us.'

'Which god? The one down there isn't much use to you,' said Geoffrey, meaning Brock.

Lawrence smiled, grateful for the relief of Geoffrey's wit.

His stomach suddenly turned. 'Do you think the commander saw me as I truly am? The inner-force is destructive. Surely a commander would see through the illusion.'

'Difficult to say,' said Geoffrey. 'Even if he did, he might not say anything. They don't think and rationalise in the same way as other beings.'

Only slightly relieved, Lawrence took another sip of tea, turning his thoughts back to Luna. 'You say she's from the Core, but only a flawless soul can make it there and only having passed all the tests on Pride. The few who have made that long journey who then decide to return to the Surface do so only in order to help the shepherds and humanity.'

'And yet here we are with an exception,' said Geoffrey. 'One who's seriously pissed off.'

Lawrence gazed out to sea, barely able to believe the scale of what they were up against.

'All the more reason for you to be grounded,' added Geoffrey.

Lawrence shifted his focus to the dream room and studied it through the eyes of the wolf. The door framed by the gaping jaw of the Siberian tiger was still there. Like a calling card, it was a reminder of the ever-present threat of the real Lord Boreas, that if Lawrence were to slip up, he would be on to them in no time, reclaiming his body and causing chaos. At least the door within its throat was closed—for now.

'You're about to be tested beyond anything you've ever known and you're far from ready for it,' continued Geoffrey. 'Your soul is still evolving through the Outer-Peregrinus. It has yet to break free from the cycle of rebirth and pass through the Orijinn Sea to the more severe tests of the Inner-Peregrinus. You know those worlds only by name—Fear, Greed and Pride. You've yet to experience them however. Not directly.'

Lawrence knew only too well what Geoffrey meant. It might take thousands of years until his soul had the strength and gravity to be ready for the extreme trials of the Inner-Peregrinus. Regardless, he felt Geoffrey was being overly dramatic. 'I think I can safely say I'm above greed,' he said.

'Ah, but greed is not only about money and food. Amongst other things, there's gluttony for thought, gluttony for attention, gluttony for pity, gluttony for spirituality, you name it. It's also about lust.'

Lawrence nodded gravely, though there was a sparkle of amusement in his eye. 'It's the same with lust, Geoffrey, you old doubter. There's only been one woman I've loved in this life.'

'And you don't lust after her?' quizzed Geoffrey.

'I meant I don't feel lust for other women and I'd hardly call my feeling for the woman I love *lust*. Passion, yes, but—'

'Semantics,' interjected Geoffrey. 'If you can be seduced by an image, Boreas will use it. As for your claims of having integrity, we'll soon see about that. It's easy to say such things in the outer-realms, but to hold it together at the deeper levels is much more challenging.'

Lawrence drew a deep calming breath.

'You're accustomed to astral dreams where different characters represent different aspects of yourself until you integrate them. But in dreams at the causal level, it's not just about you, and the lines between realities are wafer thin. Total lucidity is vital. If the will force is strong enough, not only can you be injured, but also killed—across all realities.'

'Are we talking about when I'm sleeping?'

'Your dream body can be hauled away at any moment, or something can appear in your reality. You must be prepared for it. In one dimension you might be fighting for your life. In another, you may be required to talk calmly on a matter of great intricacy with someone like Luna, a being with super-conscious perception.'

'What can I do to better protect myself?'

'You must reinforce you place of power,' said Geoffrey and took another bite of cake. 'I assume you have one—a memory, a place that brings you stillness.'

As Geoffrey spoke, something in the office shifted. It was subtle. Shadows altered slightly. The flames of the fire billowed a little higher. Lawrence was too absorbed in thought to notice it. Neither did he notice four lizards dart out from crevices and position themselves on the walls like the points on a compass.

Lawrence found a memory. He closed his eyes and smiled.

His stillness was short lived.

Thunder rumbled. There was a disturbance out at sea.

Lawrence looked out the window. 'My God!' he gasped.

A tsunami was racing towards the cliff of Renlock.

He glanced at Geoffrey. By the time he looked back at the wave it was upon them and a great white shark burst through the window, jaws gaping.

Lawrence dived to the ground.

The scene faded as quickly as it had arrived. The floor was dry, but Lawrence was drenched.

He pulled himself up, his heart pounding. 'What just happened?'

'Don't panic. No one else in Renlock saw it. I created the conditions for a deeper reality to merge with this one.'

'So it was real?' asked Lawrence, deeply disturbed.

'Your clothes are wet with sea water, are they not? Had I left the reality open a moment longer, they'd be drenched with blood. Might I enquire as to your place of power?'

'It's a place I associate with the woman I love. It's always brought me peace in the past. I realise the dream room is deep in the unconscious but still, why did it have such a strong reaction?'

'Curious. Very curious indeed,' said Geoffrey without elaborating. 'I suggest you find another. Find a time of stillness when you were alone. These are always stronger. When you're alone and cam you're all-one, connected to everything.'

Again Lawrence closed his eyes in concentration.

Moments passed when his face became serene. His stillness was so powerful it seemed to spill over into the room and Geoffrey nodded with approval.

An instant later, a great transformation took place. No longer were the two of them in Renlock, but far out to sea on top of an impressive pinnacle which rose up like a plinth. The ocean was in a different world, though like Renlock it was stormy. A battered old oak tree stood at its centre, its mighty trunk hollow with age.

'Good,' said Geoffrey who was perched on the lowest branch, his voice clear through the wind. 'The ocean is a symbol of union, a source of power for you. But to a false god, deluded as they are, the idea of its immensity will drain them.'

Lawrence studied the oak. 'Incredible! It's exactly as I remember it.'

'Of course it is. Now, maintain focus here, in the office *and* in the dream room. Walk around the tree while sitting down at the table in the office and pouring out a cup of tea. In the dream room, simply sit still. The dream room is your centre, your source. If grounded there, the greater your chances of remaining grounded in other worlds.'

Lawrence did as he was instructed. He was doing an admirable job until a woman's head popped out from the hollow in the oak and caused him to spill some tea. It wasn't just any woman's head, but one of bewitching beauty. A playful light in her wanton eyes, she grabbed Lawrence by the collar, hauled him into the hollow and planted a passionate kiss on his lips.

Back in the office, Lawrence was busy pouring tea over the floor.

'Unless you focus you won't last a second,' warned Geoffrey. 'Neither here nor in the office.'

Lawrence was having a tough time escaping the hollow trunk for there wasn't just one woman inside but three, all tearing at his clothes as they wrapped themselves about him, moaning and giggling.

The part of him in the office walked into the wall, staggered backwards and was about to trip into the fireplace when Lawrence finally tore himself free of the women.

Geoffrey was shaking his head with disapproval as Lawrence did his best to refasten his clothes.

'Bloody hell, Geoffrey,' he cursed. 'What sort of test is this?'

'Nothing compared to what Boreas will throw at you. Now clean up the spilt tea in the office and do it with presence and self-control.'

As the Lawrence in the office fetched a towel, the other Lawrence distanced himself from the tree, keeping a close eye on it.

'Looking for us, handsome?' came a mischievous voice that caused him to wheel around.

Floating in the air beyond the pinnacle's cliff were the same three women. Free from the confines of the oak they looked even more intoxicating, their windswept silks leaving little to the imagination.

One shot forward and wrapped herself about him. Arms around his neck, she clung to his back. 'There's nothing like a man who's hard to get,' she purred in his ear. 'Makes the conquest all the sweeter.'

While Lawrence in the office struggled to mop up the spilt tea, the other wrestled to free himself from the nymph. He hadn't got very far when a knife appeared in one of her hands.

At the sight of it, any rules of decency were hurled aside. Lawrence grabbed her by the hair and flung her through the air.

'Oh, you like it rough, do you?' said the other two, suddenly armed with swords.

'My sword?' muttered Lawrence. It was in the office.

'The only limit is your imagination,' said Geoffrey.

The nymph was back on her feet and also armed. Grinning menacingly, the three of them closed in.

Lawrence backed away, doing his best to imagine a sword into reality, but only managed the hilt.

'Oh dear,' said one of the nymphs. 'That's a little disappointing.'

'There must be more to it than simply imagination. What am I missing, Geoffrey?'

'Apart from a blade, you mean? Try presence, but it must be total. No preoccupations. No fear. It's as simple as that.'

Enjoying his fix, one of the nymphs flew past him and deftly nicked his arm with her blade. 'Just trying to improve your presence!' she cried back to him with a laugh.

Ignoring the cut, Lawrence placed his hand against the oak to steady himself and closed his eyes.

Another nymph flew past him and nicked his other arm. Again he ignored it. 'Ooh!' she teased. 'What a man!'

'Perhaps we should target something more valuable!' suggested the third and while the other two swirled about the tree laughing, she darted forward.

Despite the pressure, both Lawrences were thoroughly focused, one methodically wiping the floor, the other caressing the bark. Both faces were peaceful, so much so that they seemed to glow. The sky, meanwhile, grew darker.

The nymph cackled as she expertly swung her blade.

In the split-second before it struck there was a blinding flash of lightning. The ocean shone like an emerald. The oak bristled.

All three nymphs started in shock.

A sword appeared in Lawrence's hand. As the attacking nymph darted forward, he deflected her with a flash of steel.

'Better late than never,' said Geoffrey as the nymphs howled in fury and gathered in the air for a combined attack.

Lawrence gazed at his sword, delighted. Though the sky was grey with storm clouds, the oak beamed like a beacon. Its leaves shone green while its branches stretched outwards despite the wind.

In a blaze of blades, the nymphs attacked, one after the other in close formation, their strokes brilliantly coordinated as though they were one.

Lawrence, however, was equal to it, parrying like a master swordsman, belting the last across the backside with the flat of his sword. As he barked with laughter, the oak grew even brighter and the wounds on his arms healed.

The nymphs swept around like maddened hornets and attacked again, this time all at once.

Not only did Lawrence rise to the challenge, he thrived on it. His blade moved with such speed and precision that he found time to casually reach down and pick a rose that appeared at will. Lawrence in the office was dancing about the room with the tray of tea skilfully balanced in a hand above his head while humming a song.

'What a beautiful flower,' he remarked. 'If only there was a beautiful woman to present it to.'

The comment maddened the nymphs all the more.

'Too easy is it?' asked Geoffrey.

'Far too easy!' cried Lawrence.

No sooner had he replied than three more armed nymphs appeared on his other side. Lawrence simply willed into existence another sword and parried the new arrivals with equal ease, looking ahead and admiring the clouds.

'What wonderful cloud formations!' he exclaimed.

Sensing a shift, he glanced over his shoulder. Dozens more nymphs were sweeping in from the sea, all armed with swords.

'Excuse me ladies.' Following several flashes of his blade he disarmed the nymphs he was duelling. With six more strokes he left them without robes. 'New guests to greet!'

Puce with indignation, they re-armed and joined the rest as the island was beset by enraged nymphs.

Lawrence danced through the onslaught, flourishing his blades, laughing as though he couldn't be happier.

Reflecting his joy, the oak shone yet brighter.

'Still too easy?' enquired the lizard.

Lawrence answered by shaving off one of Geoffrey's whiskers.

As a mark of his indignation, someone entered the office. It was Wilderspin—the real one—accompanied by a cloud of pigeons.

Despite the risks of Geoffrey's test, neither Lawrence faltered. While one continued his merry dance in his place of power, on seeing Wilderspin the other roared with mirth.

'Are you alright, my lord?' enquired Wilderspin.

'Couldn't be better!' declared Lawrence between guffaws. He drained a cup of tea and bellowed with yet more laughter.

'Mad as a hatter,' muttered Wilderspin to his pigeons and promptly left.

'This is child's play, by the way,' said Geoffrey from his branch. 'Opponents from the Inner-Peregrinus constantly transform.'

Suddenly, every one of the nymphs became a cobra and reared up, poised to strike.

Before they did Lawrence vanished into thin air.

An instant later, a sea monster burst through the surface. Its mouth was so vast that, as it swept over the pinnacle in the manner of a phantom, it swallowed whole Geoffrey's illusion, before disappearing back into the sea. All that remained was Lawrence's reality—the pinnacle, the oak and a surprised looking Geoffrey.

Lawrence reappeared from the hollow of the oak. 'That'll do for today,' he said smiling.

'An above-average performance,' grumbled Geoffrey. 'But that duel was only in two dimensions. The more powerful your opponent, the more dimensions the battle takes place in—a number which proliferates at exponential speed. You must be totally focused in all. The first to falter is the first to fall.'

'One step at a time,' said Lawrence.

With a click of his fingers he and Geoffrey were fully restored to the reality of the office.

'Time is something you lack.'

'True enough,' conceded Lawrence, 'especially with this mission to steal gates from the House of Tusk. But that shark bursting into the office has given me an idea.'

CHAPTER 13
GODS

As Jake charged down the dune he was swept up in a wave of euphoria, stumbling over twice in the deep sand, each time bursting out in laughter.

'Wow!' he cried having arrived at Braysheath's side. He gazed up at the trees—they were vast with trunks as thick as castle turrets reaching high into the sky.

'Magnificent aren't they?' said Braysheath.

'Magnificent!' agreed Jake.

'During the times of the Great Dance all the trees on the Surface are like this.'

Jake shook his head in wonder.

'Hello there!' bellowed Braysheath and startled Jake.

Two of the mighty trees suddenly shifted. With a terrific rustling and creaking they lifted their branches to create a majestic archway. A blissful breeze blew through it and enveloped them in greeting.

Jake was halfway through gasping with awe when a terrific trumpeting shook the air. As though the sound had hands, it picked him up and hurled him on to his backside.

Braysheath roared with laughter.

By the time Jake had got to his feet two bull elephants had appeared and stood sentry-like in the entrance.

Jake had barely recovered from the shock when something large and orange pounced between them. Despite its size and speed it landed with alarming stealth and was, without doubt, the most fearsome creature Jake had ever seen.

At first he thought it was a tiger. Like the trees and elephants, however, it was at least twice the size of those on the Surface and instead of fur it had scales. Its head was longer too, as much reptilian as cat. To top it off, it spoke.

'Braysheath,' it said in a deep sibilant voice and bowed its head. 'Welcome.'

'This, Jake, is Glabrous. He's what we call a thorsror and Commander of the North Gate,' said Braysheath. 'And this, my dear Glabrous, is Jake, son of Lawrence.'

Jake was too overwhelmed by the beast's sleek power to respond.

Glabrous peered down at Jake with his great green hypnotic eyes. Jake's entire body tingled. It felt as though the thorsror were gazing right through him and could see his darkest secrets.

Glabrous raised his head, licked the air with a forked tongue and sent a dreadful chill slithering along Jake's spine.

Finally Glabrous made a cursory bow though his eyes maintained a steely glint.

Thankfully a distraction arrived in the form of a third elephant. Strapped across its back was a magnificent howdah—a canopied saddle almost the size of Jake's bedroom.

'Aha, here we go!' cried Braysheath.

Glabrous stepped aside, whereupon the elephant lowered its great bulk to the ground.

'Right, hop aboard!' cried Braysheath.

Jake gave Glabrous a bow of the head and clambered up the rope ladder to the howdah.

Once Braysheath was in, the beast rocked to its feet and lumbered into the jungle.

'Unbelievable,' muttered Jake as they moved through the oasis. The trees got even larger while the richness in colour and smell of the tropical plants was intoxicating, to say nothing of the song of so many birds which flashed between the trees. Jake felt like a maharajah riding through a fairy tale. The farm seemed a million miles away and for all he knew, possibly was.

'Aha!' cried Braysheath.

Jake turned to find Braysheath rifling through a hamper. 'Marmalade! Fancy a crumpet?'

'Good idea,' said Jake, revelling in the novelty of it all.

He reached forward to accept the prepared crumpet.

A loud screech and flapping caused him to jump and the crumpet was snatched from his hand.

'Ha!' laughed Braysheath as his eagle flew off. 'He is naughty.'

'What is it with marmalade?' said Jake.

'I've given up trying to work it out,' said Braysheath and wolfed back a spoonful. 'It's a delicious mystery!'

With another screech the eagle landed beside him.

Unlike the time it had visited Jake in his dream, he could now appreciate its beauty. Its plumage was brown, but when a ray of sun penetrated the canopy its feathers were iridescent, glinting all the colours of the rainbow.

'Enjoying yourself?' enquired Braysheath, having polished off his second marmalade-smothered crumpet.

'I am.'

'No more questions? You surprise me. You were bursting with them not so long ago.'

Jake thought for a moment.

'Actually, I do have one. The seven beings you spoke of. What did they do exactly?'

'Like any shepherd, they took care of things.'

'Of what?'

'Of Humpty Dumpty's great experiment.'

'Humpty Dumpty?' scoffed Jake, having not heard a reference to the nursery rhyme in years.

'The Creator in other words. It's a useful way to think about it. You see, Humpty knew that if he jumped off the wall he would smash into many pieces and that each piece would forget what it had once been part of.'

'I thought he fell. Why would he jump?'

'Because he was curious. He wanted to see if his separate parts could remember.'

'You mean all the humans?'

Braysheath nodded.

'How could they?' pressed Jake.

'By becoming kings. Kings of themselves, by taking responsibility for their own destiny rather than sending out all of their horses and all of their men to do a job which can only be done by oneself. You see, Jake m'boy, there's no real freedom without responsibility. Humans on the Surface today might think they're free, but they're nothing more than slaves—slaves to their shadow and all of its fears.'

'And the shepherds?' pressed Jake.

'Were there to watch over the process, to make sure the pieces didn't become too scattered. They're rather like Humpty's insurance policy.'

'But they *have* become too scattered,' remarked Jake, remembering what Braysheath had said earlier about five shepherds being chopped up and the need for great leaps.

'Almost. Someone rather powerful and in rather a foul mood has given the pieces a good boot.'

A chaos of squawking erupted from the canopy above as a flock of parakeets took flight as if Braysheath's words had spooked them.

'So are you a descendant of these original seven shepherds?' he asked.

'Descendant? Ha! Heavens no! Ha-ha!' cried Braysheath and slapped his thigh.

'Then a friend of the family?'

Braysheath released another bark of laughter.

'Then how do you know all this?'

'How does anyone know?' countered Braysheath. 'True knowing can only come from experience.'

Jake studied Braysheath to see if he was joking, but Braysheath simply gazed back at Jake, clear eyed.

Jake's body shivered with awe. 'Don't tell me you're one of the remaining two shepherds,' he said.

'Alright, I won't.'

Jake looked at the cobra resting about Braysheath's neck. Its eyes suddenly flicked open and fixed on Jake with such intensity that he grew light-headed. As the intensity relented, he noted that within the ferocity of its eyes was something else—a twinkle of humour, similar to the one in Braysheath's eyes as though its fierceness and everything else were just a game.

'But if you're a shepherd,' reasoned Jake, 'and contained all that energy then wouldn't I be fried alive or something just from being near you.'

'One learns to control oneself,' said Braysheath.

The amused glint in Braysheath's eyes grew brighter. 'You don't believe me? Oh well.'

'So which are you?' asked Jake, deciding to go along with the idea. 'The oldest or second oldest?'

'The second, thankfully. The oldest must always bear such weighty burdens. Takes away all the fun.'

'And if you don't mind me asking, if you were chopped up, how many souls would you make?'

'Well, one doesn't like to brag of course, but I should think I was good for, let's see—twenty billion or so.'

'Twenty billion?' exclaimed Jake.

'Thirty if they got me straight after breakfast,' added Braysheath. 'Anyway, I have a feeling that the chopping up strategy has backfired.'

Before Jake had a chance to pursue the point, something yet more fantastic presented itself. They emerged from the jungle onto a glorious savannah. It was peppered with trees and beasts, though what caught his attention above all else lay at its centre. Built on top of a large solitary outcrop of orange rock was a building more magnificent than anything Jake had ever seen. Only in a history book on Mughal India had he seen something that came close.

Carved from the outcrop itself, its colour was made all the richer by the setting sun. Above the towering ramparts were elegant arches and cupolas, crowning the fort with something palatial. Yet the fort had an air of something far older than a few hundred years. It was largely to do with the trees. They were everywhere, crowding about the base of the outcrop, lining the ramp that zigzagged up it and whose long shallow steps appeared to have been carved for giants. Trees had even become part of the ramparts themselves, be it sprouting from the walls or loitering on top. There were trees of all variety, from copper beeches to Scots pines, while oaks mingled with acacias, fig trees and palms.

The fort, however, was no ruin. Rather, the effect of the trees was one of reinforcement as though an alliance had been struck, its standard-bearer a mighty banyan that had become part of the archway of the main entrance and whose aerial roots hung down like a portcullis.

'The House of Tusk!' announced Braysheath as the elephant waded through the river.

'It's...' muttered Jake, struggling to find the words.

'Really rather pokey, but it does the job,' said Braysheath, completing the sentence.

'And what job would that be?' asked Jake, trying to get to the bottom of what was expected of him.

'Gatekeeping,' repeated Braysheath, without elaborating.

'It's a bit large for a gatekeeper's lodge, isn't it?' remarked Jake.

'Is it? We were aiming for something modest,' said Braysheath. 'You see, after the first sacrifice I mentioned, each of the remaining six of the shepherds contributed a portion of their energy to create this place. We moved the holygates of the Peregrinus here where they'd be safer.'

'Peregrinus?'

'That inner-journey I spoke of,' said Braysheath, reminding Jake of his earlier claim that the cosmos was nothing more than a reflection of something inside of all living things.

'The holygates allow the movement of souls from place to place, though only when each soul is ready,' explained Braysheath. 'And there are other gates, rather like backdoors, which only the shepherds use. You might call them secret. And over the years we have added many other things to the fort.'

'Is the Peregrinus what flashed past us in the inkwell?' asked Jake.

'Not exactly. They're part of it, but more like padding—various worlds that have cropped up for various reasons, catering for misfits, overflows, that sort of thing, some with less than wholesome intent behind their creation, though all in the name of maintaining balance.'

'But how can a world just crop up?'

'Evolution, Jake m'boy. The cosmos is alive—one giant dynamic intelligence, a mansion with an infinite number of rooms. The key to all of them is imagination.'

'A mansion with a gatekeeper's lodge,' said Jake more to himself than Braysheath, his granddad's riddles in mind. 'One called Hades.'

'Hades was a Greek god and gatekeeper to the inner-worlds,' said Braysheath. 'So, yes, you could call it that.'

'But why does evolution need shepherds and gatekeepers?' asked Jake. 'What happens, happens. If the universe exploded into even smaller pieces surely that would all be part of evolution.'

Braysheath studied Jake, a curious gleam in his eye. For a moment Jake felt the same strange sensation he had when he touched the inkwell—a blissful ache which seemed to make sense of everything, though not quite.

'True,' said Braysheath. 'But each of us have our roles in whatever unfolds. Mine is a shepherd.'

'And my role is gatekeeper?'

'Indeed, dear fellow, but ultimately your role is also a shepherd, just like everyone else, all helping to get Humpty together again, though not necessarily in the same form as he was before. In fact, that would be rather boring.'

'But what does it mean to be a gatekeeper in this place?'

'This place is full of gates that are critical to the cosmos. Its potential power is vast, not only to keep the gates safe, but to see that they are used to elevate evolution to its highest frequency—

the frequency of union. But the realising of that potential requires a pure human heart to be resident.'

'Why?'

'Because of everything I've told you. This cosmos and especially Earth is all about consciousness and its evolution. Though humans are ultimately part of every other species, they are the vehicle for this great experiment.'

Jake studied Braysheath and smiled. 'I think you've got the wrong person.'

'We'll see about that, Jake m'boy.'

'Either way, I'd like to see more of the place before deciding to become a gatekeeper. Is this the place Dad was lord of?'

'Indeed!'

His heartbeat racing, again Jake thought of his granddad's riddle mentioning *two lords a leaping* and how one of the lords might be referring to his dad. He also thought of Frost addressing him as *Lord Burton*.

'Everything all right?' enquired Braysheath.

'Yes. Yes, fine,' said Jake, still not yet ready to confide the riddles. 'So, now that Dad's passed on does that make me Lord Tusk? Assuming I accept the role.'

'Acceptance is only the first stage. You must earn the title.'

Jake gazed about the savannah. Many of the creatures were staring at him. Grazing antelopes looked up. Lions stirred from siestas under trees. Just like Glabrous, their intelligent expressions were far from welcoming.

'Why are they looking at me like that?' he asked.

'Oh, I expect they were hoping for something plumper,' said Braysheath.

Jake focused instead on the mountain goats and monkeys leaping about the boulders of the outcrop, relieved when their elephant finally entered the cover of the copse about its bottom. Even there, however, he couldn't escape judgement. In an expression yet more haunting, the trees creaked and rustled as they journeyed between them.

Having passed two elephant sentries at the bridge, crossed a moat and after many twists and turns up the cypress-lined steps, they arrived at the top. There, across a drawbridge over another moat, lay the banyan-clad entrance.

'Hello there!' bellowed Braysheath as they passed through the arch into the cool of the tunnel whose staggering girth made for the perfect megaphone, startling Jake back to life.

'Why do you say it like that?' he asked.

'What, *hello*? Because, my dear fellow, it's a most excellent greeting. It's a contraction of holy-be-thou, just as goodbye was once God-be-with-you.'

'Hello?' asked Jake, mystified.

'Why thank you! Hello to you too!' cried Braysheath and caused Jake to shake his head.

They passed into a glorious, huge courtyard, containing a great lawn with a giant cedar in a far corner, a spinney of ancient trees at the centre, while elegant colonnades festooned in bougainvillea and other creepers lined each of the fort's levels.

Jake was jolted from his marvelling by the elephant lurching forward as it knelt down. By the time he jumped off on to the lawn, they had been joined by two men.

The first thing Jake noticed was an enigmatic-looking Chinese man with a wispy moustache and beard. He was dressed in dark robes, his long dark hair tied back in the traditional bun. His presence was peaceful, which was more than could be said for the other person. A warhorse of a man, he reminded Jake of a Greek statue, albeit one that was roughly hewn and whose toga was black. He had an especially impressive head. With steel-grey hair and a fulsome beard, he would have been magnificent to behold were it not for the disdainful glint in his dark eyes.

'Allow me to introduce two of the House of Tusk's greatest assets! This fine fellow,' beamed Braysheath, gesturing to the Chinese man, 'is Yü Huang Shang Ti, a name I personally have a devil of a job remembering. So instead we simply call him Ti, pronounced like a cup of tea, for what could be finer?'

'Hello, Ti,' said Jake.

Ti bowed his head to Jake, his expression impassive.

'And this cheerful scamp is Asclepius,' said Braysheath, referring to the other, a name Jake was sure he had come across before though couldn't recall where. 'Famed for his unrivalled powers in medicine.'

Asclepius for some reason ignored Jake completely, looking instead at a tree as though bored.

'Jake is doubtless raring to explore the place and since he's clearly taken a shine to you, Asclepius, perhaps you'd take him on a tour,' suggested Braysheath. 'I, meanwhile, must talk with Ti on a matter of urgency.'

'I'm sorry,' said Asclepius, in a gravelly disinterested voice. 'Who am I to take on a tour?'

Braysheath, however, was already striding across the lawn with Ti.

'I see only this overgrown sprite,' continued Asclepius, clearly referring to Jake. 'You, sprite—has Lawrence's son arrived yet?'

More bemused than offended, Jake didn't know what to say and so said nothing.

Asclepius muttered a curse in a foreign tongue and strode off in the other direction.

The greeting from Asclepius was so frosty that it called into question the warmth of Braysheath. As Jake watched Asclepius disappear into the shadows of the cloister he wondered whether he had been led into a trap. An uneasy feeling stirred in the pit of his stomach. Then he remembered the fort had been a second home for his dad and granddad. Keen to explore the fort, he waved away his doubts and Asclepius's mood and dashed after him.

By the time he reached the hallway inside, the only evidence of Asclepius was the sound of his footsteps descending a broad spiral stairwell. Jake had but a moment to marvel at how the trees were also inside of the fort. Their arching boughs formed fantastic corridors. Leaves blazed autumnal red while daffodils and bluebells graced the space between them in the same happy contradiction that reigned outside.

Jake raced down the stairs, reached the next level and again gasped in awe. Aside from all the hallways and the mystery as to where they led, directly below the courtyard above was another, this one a giant parlour-bazaar with a high vaulted ceiling. Cleverly arranged shafts beamed in what remained of the day's light, while lanterns held sway elsewhere. There was also a fountain at its centre though it was barely visible amid the hive of activity as baskets were bustled from chutes to stores, carried by people who were human in shape but half-sized like those in fairy-tales. Tearing himself away, Jake made haste for the lower levels.

On the third floor down, the stairwell showing no sign of coming to an end, Jake found Asclepius. Though he had arrived at another great hall with a fountain, this one was white marble and full of strange contraptions. Some were vast and contained animals. It was as though he had wandered into a natural history museum that had come to life. He soon realised that it was a hospital for animals. Not only was there an elephant with a leg in plaster-cast, but a winged antelope with both wings spread out in traction.

Asclepius was standing in a far corner.

Jake approached.

There, beneath the tranquil shade of a lemon tree, was a slab of stone covered in a nest of tropical leaves. When Jake saw what lay within them, he drew back in shock. Only the head was showing. It was neither wholly human nor wholly beast, but something in between. The left side was that of a beautiful Indian lady. The skin of the other side was red and scaled like a snake. Both her eyes were oddly clouded.

'What is it?' he asked.

At first Asclepius ignored Jake as he bathed the patient's head with a damp cloth.

'It's one of the Naga,' he said at last, his tone still terse. 'They guard the fort's vault. They're serpents but can shape-shift into human form and are extremely powerful.'

'What happened to this one?' asked Jake.

'A few nights ago, not only was the fort broken into, but also its vault. Yet more remarkable, the intruder escaped with an object of immense power. Have you any idea what that means—how powerful that being would have to be? Of course you don't.'

Again Asclepius's words caused Jake to doubt Braysheath who hadn't mentioned the break-in.

'What was stolen?' he asked calmly, encouraged by the gentleness with which Asclepius bathed the Naga.

'Pandora's Box.'

Pandora's Box! thought Jake. He had heard of the intriguing object in a Classics lesson at school. It jogged an even more disturbing memory—where he had heard the name Asclepius.

Asclepius! The Greek god of healing! Son of Apollo! he exclaimed in thought. *Perhaps he's just named after the god,* he thought optimistically. *After all, he looks human but then so does Braysheath. And Asclepius is doing exactly what he's meant to be doing—healing!*

He thought of Ti and wondered whether he too was a god.

The sense of foreboding doubled with another deduction. He recalled a line from his granddad's riddles: Go ladies to lotus to Greek god seek, Imagining things of which none can speak.

Granddad wrote of a plot in Hades. Does he mean Asclepius is part of it?

Jake drew a deep inward breath to stay calm. Holding on to the thought that he was possibly his granddad's only hope, Jake summoned his courage and decided to test the water.

'If the fort is so secure, do you think it's possible the intruder had help?' he asked and watched Asclepius for any reaction.

None came. His focus remained on the patient.

'When I say *help*, I mean help from...' Jake hesitated, sensing a tension in the air but pushed on regardless. 'Help from the *inside*.'

While Asclepius appeared unmoved, a head burst through the foliage of the tree and roared.

Jake leapt back and cursed in shock. It was a leopard. Heart thumping, Jake dared not move as its eyes blazed into him. Finally it retreated back into the foliage of the tree.

On Asclepius's face was the wryest of smiles. 'Do you believe in God?' he asked.

'What?' asked Jake, still recovering. 'What do you mean?'

'It's a simple question,' said Asclepius. 'The god of the Surface. Do you believe in him?'

Until boarding the train for Harkenmere, Jake had avoided expressing an opinion either way on the matter of God. Now it could no longer be avoided.

'I don't know about a god of the Surface, but I liked the way Braysheath spoke of an ever-evolving dynamic intelligence that we're all part of.'

'Well then, you're in for a surprise,' said Asclepius, 'because God Almighty, otherwise known as Brock, is about to fall.'

Before Jake could respond, Asclepius strode off. 'The tour's over!' he said as he went.

'God Almighty about to fall?' muttered Jake, for though he didn't fully understand what that meant, it sounded momentous. 'What the hell have I got myself into?'

'Deep shit,' came a small voice from above.

Jake looked up to discover a robin on a branch.

'Thanks for the encouragement,' said Jake, still not quite used to animals speaking.

'I could tell you everything will be fine if you like.'

'Yes, that would be better,' said Jake.

'Everything will be fine,' said the robin. 'Once you're dead. Everything's fine in death.'

'Very helpful,' said Jake.

'You're most welcome,' said the robin who evacuated his bowels and flew off.

Jake felt like doing the same. Instead, he decided to escape the oppressive air of the healing chambers and return to the lawn.

By the time he got there dusk had arrived, the courtyard was deserted and no lights shone from any of the rooms. His only company were the cicadas and the eerie screeches and barks issuing from the savannah below, all of which added to a mounting sense of gloom.

Jake twice called out for Braysheath but no answer came.

In no mood to explore more of the fort, he wandered into the spinney at the centre of the lawn. It was a perfect circle of trees. Inside it was a pool of clear water and a circular hearth where a fire had regularly burned, though not on this occasion and it was getting chilly.

This is ridiculous, he thought. *I'll go and search for a blanket, or even better, find a room to sleep in.*

Yet when Jake stepped from the spinney, in a bizarre warp of reality, he stepped right back into it as though nothing existed except the spinney. Deeply disturbed, he marched over to the other side of the spinney where exactly the same thing happened. By the third attempt to leave, he gave up.

Jake did his best to stay calm. Instead of pacing about, he sat down against a tree and tried to convince himself that everything would be fine. But as dusk thickened to night, Jake's mood darkened with it. He tried to shake it off, focusing on all the marvels he had seen on the journey in but it was no good. Everything was viewed through the ominous lens created by Asclepius's words. Jake felt trapped. His dad was dead, his granddad was missing—the one person he could trust and who, in turn, had entrusted Jake with an important riddle. Yet he couldn't escape the feeling that not only had he walked straight into a trap, but into the hands of the prime suspect—the Greek god, Asclepius.

CHAPTER 14
ATOMIC GLOVE

LYING LOW AND WAITING PATIENTLY SEVERAL DUNES BACK FROM the oasis were Rani and Bin. Night had fallen several hours before.

When the time is right, you'll have access, Ezram had told Rani in answer to her question as to how she and Bin would be able to enter the impregnable oasis fort.

Rani was disciplined and brave. Some said she was fearless, yet she couldn't deny feeling anxious. This wasn't only her first big mission—it was her initiation into becoming a fully-fledged warrior.

When the time is right, she repeated in her head, lying still, alert to the slightest movement or signal.

Though hours had passed without any clear sign, she had barely moved or said a word. Neither had Bin.

Suddenly Rani sat up a little. The moon was rising up over the desert, so close and so bright that it appeared to be rising out of the oasis itself.

'That's the sign!' whispered Rani excitedly.

'But if we fly now, in the light of the moon, we'll definitely be spotted,' cautioned Bin.

'It's a test of courage, a test of faith,' said Rani. 'Look at its position! The oasis is directly between us and the moon.'

Bin weighed the situation.

'The moon reflects the sun, Bin,' said Rani, 'and the sun is the symbol of truth, the Core, whose gravity draws us towards it, inside ourselves, inside the fort! Don't you see?'

Rani hopped up onto Bin's back. 'We must surrender to its gravity.'

'It's not strong enough to carry us over the oasis,' said Bin, 'yet we must fly close to the jungle canopy to avoid standing out and I can't risk flapping my wings. Too many others will hear them.'

'Faith, Bin!' repeated Rani. 'We're in Himassisi. Who knows what its moon can do, especially with Braysheath involved. Now get going. I have a feeling we must reach the fort before the moon fully crests the oasis.'

Reluctantly, Bin took flight, staying low to the desert, weaving between the dunes.

'Get up as much speed as you can then swoop up just before we reach the trees,' instructed Rani.

As they approached the edge of the oasis, butterflies in her stomach, Rani lay as flat as she could, pressing her cheek to Bin's neck.

Bin put in a final burst of speed before stealthily gliding up towards the jungle canopy.

Rani took a deep breath and held it.

The moment they flew over the oasis threshold she felt a surge of energy. It flowed through her with such power that she released a blissful sigh.

Ancient trees! she thought and inhaled their earthy fragrance.

'Bin,' she whispered, 'this woodland—it has more smells than even Wrathlabad. Can you feel its power?'

Bin gently nodded her head.

They had crossed the most dangerous part. Rani raised her head slightly. Just as she had hoped, despite Bin not flapping her wings, they weren't losing height, but gliding a few feet above the trees in a perfect line for the moon.

'You see, Bin! And look at the moon!' she whispered in the osprey's ear, marvelling at the full moon, half of it already showing over the trees. 'I've never seen one so large!'

The way it lit up the vast trees doubled their effect on Rani. Her heart soared and her eyes welled with joy.

A short while later her reverie was interrupted by what sounded like a strange wind. As she listened closely it was more like breath which then became an eerie-sounding chant.

'Bin, do you hear that?' she whispered.

'It's him. It's his song that's carrying us. We must be close.'

Suddenly the savannah and fort loomed into sight and Rani gasped at the sight of the enticing shadows—the mighty outcrop, the powerful elegance of the fort, the dozing elephants and so many other wonders.

The chanting, which Rani assumed only they could hear, grew more pervasive. A mist appeared as though from nowhere and swallowed up the savannah. All that remained above the mist were the turrets of the fort, the top of a cedar between them and Rani flying on Bin.

Straining her eyes, she suddenly saw him—the silhouette of the Ancient One, Braysheath, standing motionless on the turret of the nearest tower. Her heart leapt. She felt him too. His presence was in the very mist, which seemed to seep through her skin, tingle in her chest and flow through her very thoughts. It made her feel both tiny and vast in the same instant, insignificant yet vital.

Rani had glimpsed him just a few times in the past. Never before, however, had she sensed his presence so strongly. He felt terrifyingly powerful and wonderfully wild, though what she perceived was only a tiny fraction of his whole being.

It was so overwhelming that for a moment she closed her eyes. When she opened them again he was gone.

Seconds later, Bin landed quietly on the great turret where he had been standing.

'Where did he go?' whispered Rani, sliding down from Bin, her heart racing with excitement.

'We'll have to make our own way from here,' said Bin.

'We must find a hideout where we can base ourselves,' added Rani, then spotted a piece of cloth on the ground.

She picked up what appeared to be a glove made of a soft red material. Its surface was made of the exquisite plumage of some sort of bird. Her hand tingled at its touch.

'What do you think this is?' she asked.

Bin prodded it gently with her beak.

'He must have left it for us. Put it on and touch something,' she suggested.

Rani slipped her right hand into the glove. She gasped as it shrunk to fit her hand and the feathers became red fish scales, shimmering as though alive in the sea.

Thrilled, she pressed her hand against the wall of the turret. The glove tingled. Her heartbeat raced. The tingling intensified until it became a steady vibration then, to her astonishment, a portion of the wall's surface suddenly transformed into particles.

Eyes wide with disbelief, she tentatively pushed her hand through what felt like a mini-sandstorm.

'Look!' she gasped.

Gripped by excitement, she took a deep breath and cautiously passed through the peculiar wall, hoping it didn't suddenly reset and trap her halfway through.

She arrived onto the narrow steps of what looked like a secret passage between the walls.

'Come on!' she whispered, poking her head back outside.

Shrinking to the size of a normal osprey, Bin followed.

Once they were both inside, Rani passed her hand back over the vibrating particles and the wall miraculously resealed. She gaped at the glove in awe.

'This glove will take us anywhere!'

'Perhaps. Though if what I've heard is true, there are parts to the fort that we'll not even be able to see, let alone enter,' said Bin and hopped onto Rani's shoulder.

'Right, come on, let's find a base.'

They descended the steps, having picked up traces of fresh but surprisingly faint footsteps in the dust of what appeared to be a little used passageway.

Occasionally, Rani peeked through a wall using the glove in order to get her bearings. The passageway crossed with other secret ones, though she managed to keep track of the footsteps which stayed close to the outer wall of the fort.

Somewhere around ground level the footsteps suddenly stopped and turned left into the wall. Using the glove, she took peek through to the other side.

She found a cosy-looking lantern-lit room, one which gave her the distinct impression that it was meant just for her and Bin. There were no doors. The only way in was with the glove—that or equivalent wisdom.

Rani indicated for Bin to follow and passed inside.

The walls were the same red sandstone as the rest of the fort though the outward facing one had been specially treated so that it was transparent, offering a view of the savannah.

'Do you think others can see in?' she asked as she laid down her bow and sheath of arrows.

'I doubt it,' replied Bin, eyeing up a solitary orange tree that lent the room some extra colour.

Rani turned to take in the rest of the room. There was a hammock strung up under the tree along with a divan of sumptuous-looking cushions. At the centre was a gently flowing fountain. Beside it, on a red-patterned rug, was a jug of water and a glass.

'I wonder where he went,' said Rani, though the floor was too clean to show any sign of footprints.

She ran her ungloved hand slowly over the walls until she discerned a trace of the same tingling she had felt through the mist. With her gloved hand she opened a head-sized hole in the wall and once more peered through.

The first thing that hit her was the aroma. There were many smells, all delicious.

'Bin, it's a pantry!' she whispered. 'We must be next to the kitchens. It's perfect. And I'm famished after the journey.'

She scoured the many shelves of fruits and nuts, vegetables and other delights, selecting their dinner. Before making her move, she strained her excellent hearing. The kitchen on the other side of the pantry appeared to be empty. She stole inside and swept through it, skilfully pilfering, careful not to take too much of any one thing to avoid causing suspicion.

Job done, she hopped back into their secret lair and resealed the hole.

'There's fish, Bin, but it's smoked,' she said settling down on the rug with her haul of food. 'Will you go for a fish later?'

Bin nodded from her perch in the tree. 'I'm fine for now.'

'You're probably full of energy from Braysheath,' said Rani and turned her attention to the food. She closed her eyes and thanked Mother Nature for her glorious bounty, thanked the intelligence inherent in everything before her—the lettuce, the tomatoes, the carrots, the wheat of the bread and the fish—and thanked the nature spirits which had nurtured their growth.

That done, she tucked into the food with great relish.

'Well,' said Bin, 'at least we're in without being seen. And now—'

'And now,' interrupted Rani, having wolfed down a mouthful of bread and fish, 'we observe this Tusk boy and see what we're up against. I want to see how nature responds to his presence, especially here. I didn't like what I saw of him on the Surface.'

'Are you sure about that?' questioned Bin. 'I sensed a disturbance about him, an inner-turmoil, which is hardly surprising given his circumstances, but I wouldn't call it darkness. Besides, he's here in the fort. That wouldn't be possible unless nature accepted him.'

'Well you obviously weren't paying close enough attention,' said Rani imperiously. 'Perhaps you ate one too many fish from that lake up there. You know they put all sorts of poisons in the water? Probably made you a bit wonky. Anyway, I definitely sensed something shadowy about him and so we must do a *full* investigation of the fort—find its weak points, just in case we need to destroy it or something. As for the nature here accepting him, it's too early to say that. I expect it's already planning how it's going to test him.'

Bin studied Rani with a quizzical expression. 'Don't you think you're getting ahead of yourself?'

Rani thought back to the second time she had seen him, in the mountains. She had almost been impressed by the way he had climbed the cliff face—his movement had been smooth and flowing, the rock appearing to welcome his touch, but then rocks were difficult to read. Rani was more familiar with trees. Rock thought was longwave which meant their decisions were based on patterns covering vast expanses of time. Thus, what they might think positive could prove destructive for those on shorter cycles. Regardless, she had watched him with interest. Then he had hung by one arm from the overhang, wasting valuable energy, as though part of him was tempted to drop to his death, confirming her first impression that he was unstable.

'Better to be ahead than behind,' she said finally and tore off another hunk of bread.

'At least that other one isn't down here,' she added, referring to Frost. 'And if he does turn up we shall have to kill him.'

'Kill him? Isn't that a little dramatic?'

'It's the sensible thing to do,' declared Rani. 'One less of *them* the better.'

What *them* meant exactly, she dared not say. To name something was dangerous and could draw their attention. That's how it was on Wrathlabad, the world she was from—on Himassisi more so.

'But Rani, brilliant archer though you are—'

'Not *only* an archer,' cut in Rani, glancing at the two curved knives she wore through her belt.

'Brilliant young *warrior* though you are,' continued Bin, 'you've yet to kill someone. It's not something to be taken lightly.'

'Well, that one will be an excellent place to start. Besides, apart from his size, it's no different from killing a rabbit. It's all life, is it not? In fact, it's easier, because a rabbit is beautiful and in balance. *They* are not.'

'Either way, I think that one might prove a little trickier than you realise.'

'Humph,' said Rani and took a defiant chomp on a carrot. 'We'll see about that.'

CHAPTER 15
DESTROYERS AND HEROES

WHILE JAKE FINALLY SUCCUMBED TO DEEP SLEEP IN THE SPINNEY, Braysheath joined Asclepius and Ti in one of the House of Tusk's many halls. They were sitting on rugs around a fire which burned at its centre—the sole source of light in an otherwise dark room.

'Ahoy there!' he cried, as he strode over. 'Forgive my tardiness. Where are we?'

'Where are we, indeed,' replied Asclepius dryly. 'Brock is just days away from being replaced as Overlord by a destructive spirit posing as a fertility goddess, Pandora's Box has been stolen from the vault, Lawrence has gone, Nestor is missing and, to supposedly make everything right, we have a mere boy as the new Lord.'

Braysheath took out his pipe and tobacco. 'Appearances can be deceptive,' he said.

'You're referring to this boy or to Luna?' asked Asclepius.

Braysheath packed his pipe, lit it and took a long puff. 'Perhaps everything.'

Ti sat slowly rotating his healing wrist, broken by Lawrence in front of the Arch of Canisp during the theft.

'Nestor's about somewhere,' said Braysheath. 'I've felt his presence, though only fleetingly and very faintly. We must stay alert for any signs or any messages he might send. But Lawrence —are you certain he has gone?'

'Gone from the Peregrinus and so possibly gone forever,' said Ti. 'None of us here or any of our sources have felt his presence. His body hasn't been found. We fear his soul has been stripped of light, perhaps by this Luna. Either that or he's lost to a hell beyond our knowing.'

Braysheath took another puff on his pipe. 'You know, I'm still intrigued how Pandora's Box was stolen from the fort. The burglar dreamed his way in, am I right?'

'Yes,' said Ti, his serene expression ruffled with surprise. 'How did you know?'

'I've sometimes wondered if it were possible. Each time I concluded that only someone with a particularly strong destiny might manage it and from a particularly powerful place.'

'Along with a little help,' said Ti.

Asclepius turned sharply to Ti. 'What are you suggesting?'

'One of the lizards has been taken from the fort's library,' said Ti, referring to the Lizard Library which housed some of the cosmos's most ancient wisdom.

'Which one?' asked Braysheath.

'One called Geoffrey. He's not the oldest, though according to the other lizards he's the most gifted dreamer. He went missing a few days before the break-in, though it's hard to imagine a lizard aiding anyone outside the fort.'

'Taken?' said Braysheath. 'How?'

'No one knows,' said Ti. 'One moment he was there, the next he was gone.'

'If he was taken through skilled dreaming,' said Asclepius, 'one wonders how Lord Boreas managed it. As a rule, gods can't dream. Some have tried, but I know of none who have succeeded.'

'It had been quite some time since I last crossed paths with Lord Boreas,' said Ti, 'but when I encountered him in the vault he was different from how I remembered him.'

'How so?' enquired Braysheath.

'His presence—it was more extreme. He appeared hesitant as though battling with his conscience, something else gods are not known for. Once decided, however, the outburst of power and skill took me by surprise, which got stronger the longer we fought. Ages have passed since I was defeated in battle, but he beat me easily.'

'The manner of his departure?' asked Braysheath.

'The Arch of Canisp.'

'There's little doubt Lord Boreas is Luna's henchman,' said Asclepius. 'We've yet to gauge her power. Perhaps this is our first taster.'

'Second,' corrected Ti. 'The monks of Pride have reported that the goddess of that world, Rowena, has been acting out of character and that a dark energy has fallen over her woodland.

It's their belief that the spirit behind Luna has possessed her body.'

'First Lord Boreas is corrupted and now this—rulers of the two most powerful worlds of the Inner-Peregrinus,' said Asclepius. 'It's a display of great power.'

A weighty silence fell over the room as Ti and Asclepius stared into the fire. Braysheath continued to gaze into the shadows, puffing ruminatively on his pipe.

'Pandora,' he said in a distant tone. 'A modern telling of an old myth, commonly misunderstood. Like Eve, like Sita, to name but two of her many names, Pandora is a symbol of the first woman, a manifestation of the Divine Mother. Pandora's box, like the apple in Eden, is a symbol of the Divine Mother's potential within each and every human. In other words, the divine mind with all its knowledge and the power to create.'

He took another slow puff on his pipe, shifting his gaze to the fire.

'This box, hidden within each human, must be allowed to open in its own time, bit by bit, each piece of knowledge only released when one is worthy of it, just as an apple falls from the tree when it's ripe,' he continued. 'But if the box is forced open, if a human is taken too deep too soon, as happened during the retreat of the last Ice Age in all humans, then the power is used to destroy. The creative fire is abused. The human body, its waters, misused, much wasted, much laid to waste.'

'This forcing open of the Pandora's Box in each human,' said Asclepius, 'I take it that you are referring to the corruption of a certain tribe of trixies and what resulted—the god gate and shifting the balance of Surface forces in favour of inner-force.'

Braysheath nodded.

'The box you talk of is a metaphor,' said Ti, 'and yet an actual box, the one stolen, exists.'

'Indeed,' said Braysheath. 'It's my understanding that the creation of the stolen box was inspired by the myth.'

'But who was inspired to create it?' asked Asclepius.

Braysheath took an especially long puff on his pipe.

'Someone affected by the first opening of the box. Someone powerful,' he replied. 'Though I can't be certain.'

'You speak of revenge—on the corrupt trixies and the power which corrupted them?' asked Asclepius.

'Perhaps on everyone,' said Braysheath, 'for allowing themselves to also become corrupted. It blames everyone and so punishes all.'

'Do you have an idea who it could be?' asked Ti.

'Alas, no. I can only say that when I first brought Pandora's Box to the vault, the pain, the rage of whatever was inside was so powerful that I couldn't hold it directly with my hands.'

'A demon?' said Asclepius.

'The word doesn't do it justice, not by a long way,' said Braysheath. 'It was something unique. Something I'd never encountered before. But whatever it is, it's a being of immense intelligence, of great wisdom, though which suffered a shock, some desperately grave disappointment, which turned its wisdom into bitterness.'

'But from what world?' asked Asclepius.

'Not a world I remember,' said Braysheath. 'One beyond my memory.'

'I thought you knew all the worlds, even the most ancient,' said Ti.

'I do,' said Braysheath.

'Then…' started Asclepius.

Braysheath took another puff on his pipe. 'Then, my dear Asclepius, we're in rather a pickle.'

'Are you suggesting that whoever created the box is the very thing now inside of it?' asked Ti, not realising that he was referring to the charred angel that Lawrence had seen on holding the box and whose shadow, the sylph, Luna had now absorbed. 'Could it be that it took refuge there, biding its time.'

'*Was* inside the box,' corrected Braysheath. 'It was forced open somewhat auspiciously during Jake's and my journey through the inkwell. And if my intuition is right, by the same being that upset it in the first place.'

The two gods turned to Braysheath in surprise.

'If Luna is behind the turmoil on the Surface since the retreat of the last Ice Age,' said Asclepius, 'behind the premature forcing open of godly powers in humans by taking them too deep, turning them from creators into destroyers, then she herself is a destroyer, though one who withholds the seeds of rebirth. The same can be said for whatever she has released from Pandora's Box. But if what you say is true, Braysheath, that it seeks revenge, especially on her, then surely she doesn't realise the true nature of what's inside, otherwise why risk opening it?'

'We're guessing,' said Ti. 'We know not the nature of the being from the box, so we cannot know its intentions.'

'Quite right, dear Ti. These are just feelings. To have a better idea of what we're dealing with, we shall have to wait for the next move, from either it or Luna. Perhaps there are even greater forces at work of which this is just a part.'

'Meaning?' asked Asclepius.

'Pandora herself. Nature, in other words—the feminine energy in all humans. She has been waiting these past few thousand years to give birth to her daughter. Now the labour pains begin.'

Ti cocked his head questioningly.

'Luna plunged humanity into a dark age,' explained Braysheath, 'and from the womb of that darkness come the stirrings of an age of truth—perhaps the greatest ever. For when something as beautiful as humanity is hurled so violently into the shadows of ancient cravings by beings as powerful as Luna, then it's either lost forever or finally emerges in a blaze of beauty beyond even the most divine of imaginations, shattering all former moulds.'

Braysheath's eyes glistened as he continued to gaze into the fire.

'But to give birth to something so great,' he continued, 'is a difficult birth and giving birth is already a chaotic process. The mother can die. The child can die. Both can die.'

He took another puff on his pipe.

'Luna's strategy is not yet clear to me,' said Ti. 'First she engineers a population explosion by sacrificing five shepherds. Now it seems, by opening the box, she wants to cull the population. But whatever her intentions, it surely boils down to light. It always does. She covets human light and as much as she can lay her hands on. Though where can she hide so much light and to what use will she put it?'

Asclepius released a heavy sigh. 'In the Greek telling of the myth of Pandora's Box it is said that once the box was opened and disease and pestilence was unleashed upon the world, one thing remained inside the box—hope. And yet I struggle to see it.'

'What?' said Braysheath, his turn to look surprised. 'I thought you had already met our young Lord Tusk, bursting as he is to be put to the test, raring to get cracking with the great labours of his time.'

'Too young,' said Asclepius.

'Young?' questioned Braysheath. 'He's ancient!'

'You know what I mean. He may have been born many times before and achieved much, but the question remains whether he's physically and psychologically strong enough *in this life* to be awoken. And so suddenly given the pressure we're under. In fact he's a liability. Awoken or not, proven or not, as Lord of the House of Tusk he has certain powers. All previous lords were thoroughly tested before let loose. If he's captured, especially by Luna, there's no end to the trouble she can cause us.'

Braysheath gave his chin a pensive rub. 'The House of Tusk like the rest of creation is ever-evolving. Each time I visit this place some new marvel makes itself known to me. The fort is modern in the making, a counter-measure to Luna's meddling, but as the woodlands and the jungles of the Surface are mindlessly massacred, so the roots of this oasis reach deeper through the cosmos and hold it together. It is a place of staggering potential. But the key to unlocking it is the presence of a human being—one that's alive, spirited and waking up. It's how we designed the place, for as long as there is such a human in the cosmos there is hope. Remember what an awoken human is. It's something far greater than a god. It's a creator. A co-creator with nature.'

Asclepius looked like he wished to take issue but remained silent.

'I have great faith in Nemesis and the Scribes and the souls they select—souls for all humans,' added Braysheath, 'but especially the souls they chose for prospective lords and ladies of the House of Tusk. And the challenges of this great time of transformation call for an especially powerful lord. Someone of great potential.'

'That's what worries me,' said Asclepius. 'The realisation of such potential in such a short period of time is a great risk for someone in such a place as here. In our training of Jake, will we not be forcing open another Pandora's Box—forcing open his ancient knowledge too violently?'

'One must think positive, dear fellow,' said Braysheath cheerily. 'Besides, he comes with a couple of, how shall I put it? *Unusual* helpers.'

Ti and Asclepius looked questioningly at Braysheath but he didn't elaborate.

'There clearly isn't time for the usual character test of Jake,' said Ti. 'The forty days and forty nights in the desert. Will he be tested at all before his training starts?'

'I believe so,' said Braysheath. 'By the chief tester herself—Nemesis. And this very night.'

CHAPTER 16
PROPHECY OF THE NORNS

JAKE AWOKE WITH A START. HIS HEARTBEAT SPED—HE WAS STILL in the spinney of the House of Tusk. It was night time and deathly still. He scanned his surroundings, half-expecting to find a lion poised to pounce or a python eyeing him from a branch.

Satisfied he was alone, he stretched and took stock. Strangely, it wasn't cold. The spinney was how he remembered it except for lantern lights hanging from some of the branches. They lent a magical air to the vaulted space beneath the boughs, transforming the gloom he had gone to sleep with back into wonder.

Jake's attention was drawn to the pool. He kneeled down and stared into its dark surface, reassured to find his reflection staring back at him—something he knew. As he continued to study it, there was something about it that seemed different. Intrigued, he moved closer to the water.

His face was just inches from its surface when he froze in fear. Another face appeared in the reflection. Someone was standing right behind him.

Shock gave way to elation.

'Granddad!' he cried out.

Jake sprang up to find his granddad looking just as he always had—his kind brown eyes and distinguished-looking nose arching out beneath the brim of a deerstalker hat. The only thing strange was his tense expression.

'Jake!' he said urgently, grabbing Jake by the shoulders. 'You must come with me right this instant! There's not a moment to lose!'

'Wait! Where have you been?' asked Jake.

'There's no time to explain. You must trust me. Come!' said Nestor and wheeled around to the pool.

He placed his palms to its surface and muttered something.
'Granddad, the riddles—'
'Forget the riddles!' snapped Nestor, still focused on the pool.
'But...'
Before Jake completed his sentence, a gentle light pulsed through the pool that left it subtly changed.

'It's a gate,' said Nestor. 'A unique one. If you dive into it you'll re-appear in the farmhouse lake and none of this will matter—not the riddles, not the House of Tusk, not anything! Braysheath is the only other person who knows about it.'

Jake was confused. Despite his disturbing encounter with Asclepius, Jake was getting used to the idea of being in the fort. In fact, now that he was confronted with a choice of staying or leaving, he knew he wanted to stay—to explore the mysterious fort and understand how it was connected to the Surface.

'What does the gate do exactly?' he asked, trying to slow down the conversation.

'Whatever you want. There's no time to explain why or how,' said Nestor, glancing about as though expecting an ambush. 'Fame, fortune and all its trimmings if that's your wish. But more importantly, it can turn back time—as much as a thousand years or more or just a week,' explained Nestor with a glint in his eyes.

'To before Dad dying, you mean?' asked Jake, scarcely able to believe his ears.

'Exactly!' confirmed Nestor. 'Now go! Hurry! Focus your mind on what you want and dive in!'

If what his granddad said was true it changed everything. He would happily sacrifice all the adventure in all the worlds if it would bring back his dad.

Jake took a reluctant step towards the pool. As he gazed into it an image appeared which tugged at his heartstrings with such force that he almost dived in. It was the farmhouse a few summers before. Playing cricket on the farm track outside was his dad in bat, his granddad behind the stumps and Bill steaming in to bowl. Jake's eyes shone with longing and laughter as the ball missed its mark by several metres and shattered a car window instead. His dad roared with laughter while Bill cursed the trixies.

Jake was desperate to leap in yet something held him back. It seemed too good to be true, along with something else. From what little Jake had seen of Braysheath and the way he made everything seem possible, turning back time didn't fit. *One must accept what's happened with grace*, he could imagine Braysheath saying. *Then crack on and do one's best!*

'I don't understand, Granddad. What's such a thing doing in the House of Tusk?'

'Braysheath confiscated it ages ago and brought it here for safe-keeping. Now go! I'll see you on the other side. And then we'll have all the time in the world to catch up and explain.'

Jake studied his granddad. His hurried manner was a far cry from the unflappable man he so admired who, being a brilliant chess player, had always thought things through so thoroughly that there was never any need to rush.

Jake glanced about the spinney. Only then did he realise that it too had changed. Between the trunks of the trees was no longer the great lawn bathed in darkness, but a number of distinct paths, each leading into woodland, some overgrown, others less so. They exerted a strange pull on him.

'Jake! There isn't time!' hissed Nestor.

'Where did these paths come from and where do they lead?'

'Those? Oh, they're your destiny. You have an infinite number, but those are your twelve most probable. Though it could all change with just one act.'

'Such as diving into the pool?'

'Yes!'

'And if I do, will I forget everything that's happened, including Braysheath?'

'Everything since your dad passed on because he wouldn't have! Don't you see? Forget the paths!'

Feeling an odd sense of calm, Jake reflected on all that had happened since his dad's death. Braysheath, Frost and the mysterious girl spying on him from the mountains stood out in his thoughts. Suddenly Jake wasn't so sure what to do.

'Jake!' implored his granddad.

Jake looked back at Nestor. *Something doesn't quite fit*, he thought. *Could I be dreaming?*

'One moment, Granddad. I just want to take a peep at one of these paths,' he said and wandered towards the best tended path. Before diving into the pool he had to be sure he was doing the right thing.

'Jake, for heaven's sake, what are you doing?' cried Nestor, growing more agitated.

'Just a peep.'

Careful not to cross the threshold, he peered into the woodland. As soon as he did the scene shifted to one of daytime. The woodland was vibrant with birdsong while a short way along the path was a giant sea shell. Inside of it was a very different scene.

Cut off from the beauty outside was a gloomy man sitting behind a desk. It was cluttered with flashing screens, things that bleeped and newspapers covered in fearful reports. The in-tray overflowed and piled yet higher with each second that passed. The man looked terrible. His lifeless face was haggard and grey. Jake guessed he was around thirty years old, though he had the air of an old man.

'My God, it's me!' gasped Jake and stepped back to be rid of the sight.

'Of course it is. But it's just one destiny,' said Nestor. 'Your most promising one is right here through the pool.'

Jake was already peering up the next path. The woodland became the copse about the farmhouse, again revealing another of his destinies. Though this Jake had more life than the one in the shell, his eyes were still lined with worry. He gazed down the valley in the manner of a general awaiting an invasion, suggesting that there was no escape from whatever was coming. Again Jake stepped back into the spinney.

'All the more reason to dive into the gate, hey?' coaxed Nestor.

'But I don't understand, Granddad. If these paths are here now, aren't they reflecting what I can expect if I do dive through the pool?'

'Jake, stop thinking and trust me! Do you honestly believe I'd mislead you? Your own granddad!'

'But are you? Are you really my granddad? Or am I dreaming?' asked Jake.

'What a question!' exclaimed Nestor, before softening his tone. 'Jake, fella, I may not seem quite myself, but if you had seen the things I've seen, what's happening right now as we speak. There's still time to stop it. But only just. You must act now!'

Jake studied the paths on the adjacent side of the spinney and noticed one of them led back to the great lawn of the House of Tusk. But it was the one beside it which exercised the strongest pull. Of all the paths it was the most overgrown, so tangled that Jake could hardly see a way through the entrance.

'Jake,' said Nestor, gravely. 'Whatever you do, do not take that path.'

Jake turned to face him. Whether he was dreaming or not, the idea of turning back time suddenly struck Jake as inherently wrong, like cheating—something neither his granddad nor his dad would have supported. Jake recalled something his dad had once said: *the only way the past can be changed is in how we view it. A strong person finds the silver lining behind the clouds and understands what it is the past has taught them.*

Am I dreaming? he wondered more deeply as he surveyed his surroundings with a more discerning eye. What he was seeing was truly fantastic, but so was meeting Braysheath in the farmhouse kitchen in daytime reality.

Or am I being tested, perhaps within a dream?

Suddenly everything grew sharper as though to confirm his sharper awareness.

This person before me isn't Granddad, he decided and his surroundings grew sharper still.

Jake felt a flicker of sadness. Yet, seeing the image of his granddad renewed Jake's determination to find the real one and the best way to do so, he decided, was by doing what Nestor would do in the same situation—to ignore the fear of others and to take the path least trodden.

'Jake?' repeated Nestor as Jake returned his gaze to the tangled path.

The longer he gazed into the twilit mist of the ancient wood, the stronger became its pull. He thought he could hear enchanted whisperings beckoning him in.

'If you're my granddad,' he said calmly as he looked back, 'then you'll understand what I'm about to do.'

Following a deep breath, Jake stepped from the spinney onto the path.

'Jake, wait!' wailed Nestor. 'No!'

Jake swung round just in time to see the distraught image of his granddad transform into a thicket of vines and the path back to the spinney sealed up.

Panic gripped Jake. Heart racing, he forced his way back through the thicket, but found only more of it. The fort was gone. There was only the forest and the ringing of Nestor's cry which merged with the shrill bark of a fox.

Jake turned back to the path. Suddenly it was dusk. The air grew chill. An eerie mist seeped through the woodland. Fear threatened to overwhelm him.

Stay calm, he said to himself, closed his eyes a moment and took several deep breaths.

What are my options? he wondered, looking down at the vague trail. As an experiment he took a step off it. Immediately dusk thickened to night. The mist closed in. An owl released a shriek.

Vines reached up through the mulchy floor to ensnare him. A fearful chill ran through Jake and he leapt back onto the trail.

Not that way!

He took a moment for his heartbeat to calm down, reassured by night shifting back to dusk.

And what if I simply stay here? he asked and the already faint trail grew even fainter as weeds sprouted up and foliage fell over it.

He took a step forward along the trail and the process slowed, but not completely. In order to follow it he had to keep moving.

The trail it is, he decided and an owl released a soft hoot of encouragement. Focusing his mind on his mission to find his real granddad, Jake set off along the trail deeper into the wood.

Having gone some distance without event he began to relax when he heard movement. Jake slowed his pace and strained his hearing.

Someone was running through the woods in his direction, but the mist was too dense to see any more than a few metres in any direction. There were two people, in fact. Branches snapped and twigs cracked like gunshots. There was something desperate in the movement as though someone was being chased. He heard the panting of the one in front.

Jake's heart raced. It was less from fear than exertion. He had the strange sensation of being in two places at once as though he were one of the runners.

The chase was getting closer. Staying alert, Jake continued to move along the faint path. The encroaching pursuit seemed to come from all directions when he suddenly he saw it. Or rather, he became part of it.

To his horror, it was Jake himself who was in pursuit, though as a grown man, just metres behind another man, who glanced back in fear. Emotion coursed through Jake—the frenzy of panic, the morbid excitement, the electricity of life and death at close quarters. He tried to wrench himself free from the chase but couldn't. Whatever was happening was too strong.

The pursued man spun round for a final confrontation. He was hurled into a tree by the older Jake's hand. He felt the attacker's moves as though they were his own but he was powerless to change them—the grab, the throw, the quick exchange of deathly blows. He heard the crack of bones, though not his own, and a sensation in his left hand so gruesome that he almost retched. A knife blade had sliced through a throat. Jake saw the horror and disbelief in the slain man's eyes as his life force slipped away. The man slumped to the ground, twitched for a few moments then finally lay still.

The silence which followed was awful. Jake's temples throbbed. He looked down at his left hand. It was covered in blood. A moment later, the hand transformed to the one he knew. He was back with his true self having fallen to his hands and knees.

Battling to make sense of it, Jake ran over what he had seen. The man who had been chased was strong and clearly knew how to fight. Yet compared to the one who Jake had become, there was no match. The moves had been so skilful, so fluid and efficient that it was how Jake imagined an assassin would fight.

'But it was me,' he muttered in disbelief and wrung his hands together in a vain attempt to rid himself of the sensation of cutting a throat and the intoxicating sense of clarity, power and detachment that had accompanied it. *How can this path be one of my destinies?*

Jake recalled how the clothes of the murdered man had been from another era, perhaps the nineteenth century, along with something Braysheath had said about remembering. *Maybe this path requires me to remember—that to fulfil the destiny this path represents, I must first remember what I've been.* Jake shuddered. *Perhaps that's why the image of granddad told me not to choose it—because it's too intense.*

Shakily, he got to his feet.

'The path!' he gasped. It had gone. Without realising it, Jake had either strayed off the path or it had overgrown. Panic gripped him. Vines slithered towards him like snakes and started to coil about his ankles.

I've got to keep moving! he reminded himself as he tore his ankles free. *But in which direction?* In the mist everything looked the same. Keen to be rid of the vines, Jake made his best guess at where the path had been and set off.

With a curse he began to jog. The vines were growing fast. It suddenly darkened just like the first time he had strayed from the path.

Soon he was forced to run blindly through the mist, stumbling over roots, struggling to understand what was happening. Again he heard sounds which didn't belong to the wood. This time there were many. All were violent. At first they were distant but grew rapidly louder, closing in on him from every direction.

Jake accelerated in the hope of escaping them. The very act only accelerated the onslaught when out of nowhere something exploded and hurled Jake through the air. He scrambled to his feet to find himself on a waterlogged ship deck amid the chaos of war. Cannon erupted all about him. He could just make out the woodland. The two scenes were superimposed.

It's just a memory! he reassured himself.

He charged onwards before the vines took hold but ran clean into a bar-room brawl, ducking just in time to avoid a punch. Someone caught hold of his shirt. Jake spun round to find it was just the snagging of a branch then clipped a tree with his opposite shoulder, spun again to find a brutish-looking man drawing a gun and taking aim at him. Jake dived into an alley to escape and straight into an ambush where, with the same skill of the first vision, he disarmed and maimed all who got in his way.

Traumatised, Jake ducked and dived and charged on blindly as he relived yet more attacks, duel after duel in every conceivable context. The woodland was shot through with a chaos of scenes —exploding turrets, mountain blizzards, secret passages, murderous faces in all of them. Arrows, punches and blade strokes rained about him. More cannon erupted. Horses reared and whinnied. Every scrape and stab was perfectly synchronised with branches and thorns which tore at Jake as he crashed ever deeper into the wood.

Any momentary gaps in the violence were filled with faces staring at Jake—from tree trunks, branches and the forest floor, their expressions stern and curious.

Panting for breath, Jake ran on. Entangled in the forest, entangled in the past, he crashed through the barrage of emotions—euphoria, sorrow, love, fury and everything in between, all the while battling to revive his reason.

The clamour grew so intense that Jake was almost lost to it when a new level of awareness kept him alert a little longer. He sensed the presence of a woman. Regardless of the span of time, her presence was everywhere—a dangerous woman moving behind the scenes, sometimes at the forefront, sometimes seductive, at others times as violent as himself. Her presence was strangely familiar, as though Jake had met this woman many times and was destined to meet her again.

Her effect on him was worse than everything else. Like the sun, her gravity beckoned, while at the same time it threatened incineration. Yet on he ran, trying to escape but couldn't. The faster he ran, the greater he felt her presence, ever more youthful, ever more ancient, ever more powerful.

I must stop this! cried Jake in thought, aware that he was somehow running back through time in quantum leaps, afraid that he had already reached a point of no return. But the vines wouldn't let him stop.

He was on the verge of blacking out when a trumpeting shook the woodland. The shock was so great that it kept Jake on his feet long enough to see its source. It was a bull elephant. Furious-eyed and mountainous, with the largest tusks Jake had ever seen, it burst through all other images. Even the presence of the woman was cast aside. There was only Jake, the woodland and the elephant as it thundered towards him, intent on running him down.

Jake veered off in another direction, running as fast as he could, but it made no difference. Whichever direction he ran in, the elephant charged towards him.

The trees were too big to climb. In the moment left to him, Jake had two choices—to be flattened by the elephant or to be dragged beneath the earth by the vines.

That's it! he realised. *To go underground is to go within!*

The choice was far from appealing but Jake was exhausted. Finally he stopped. The vines coiled about his legs. A furious trumpeting erupted from the elephant. Its tusks were just metres from skewering him when, with a great tug, Jake was hauled through the woodland floor.

IT TOOK JAKE A WHILE TO REALISE HE WAS NO LONGER BEING dragged downwards but lying on his front, once again in woodland, but one he instinctively knew was different from the one before. Just as he had expected, it felt deeper.

Surprisingly, he wasn't out of breath despite having run to the point of collapse. Jake got to his feet and surveyed his surroundings. He was in a small clearing—a perfect circle. A shift in the clouds revealed a full moon which graced in its radiance the most glorious sight Jake had ever seen. Standing at the clearing's centre was a tree like no other, one of such extraordinary richness that it didn't belong to any one species but appeared to combine them all. Sprouting from its branches were all types of fruit, from pine cones to acorns, to lemons and figs and countless varieties of blossoms. Bees buzzed while all manner of birds sang as they flitted through the soft glow of light that appeared to come not only from the moon, but from the tree itself.

Between two of its mighty roots was an arched entrance the size of a cathedral's. Cautiously, Jake approached it, reminding himself that he was dreaming until he recalled something Frost had said—that dreaming was more real than what most people called being awake.

Jake reached the entrance and peered inside. His eyes widened. Sitting queen-like on a throne of contorted roots, her eyes closed, exuding a serene sense of power, was a sight even more splendid than the tree itself, except they didn't appear to be separate. Instead of hair, the woman had a tangle of vines which connected her to the trunk above. The rest of its cavernous insides were empty, except for creatures—bright blue butterflies flitted peacefully about her while birds, squirrels and even an owl perched in her vines.

Jake marvelled at her earthy beauty. *If Mother Nature exists*, he thought, *then surely she'd look like this.*

His reverie was interrupted by a great boom. It shook the ground. Panic gripped the tree and with it Jake. Creatures froze or fled for cover. The woman's eyes flicked open. Brown and gentle but grave with concern, they fixed on Jake then beyond him. Jake spun around to find a dense fog had enclosed the clearing though it hadn't crossed its threshold.

Another boom echoed through the wood, this time closer. Like a drum of war, it filled Jake with dread, both distant but also strangely familiar.

A dim light shone through the fog and sent an icy chill along Jake's spine. *A lantern!* The depth of his fear, the same fear he had felt on the train and as a child, suddenly made sense.

As the lantern moved closer to the clearing, to Jake's horror it became four.

'Jake,' said an ethereal female voice.

The woman was right beside him, or rather, a projection of her physical self which remained a part of the tree in a state of meditation. Creatures that hadn't already fled surrounded her like an aura—birds and butterflies, badgers, rabbits, foxes, mice and hedgehogs to name but a few. All shared her look of concern.

'Who are you?' gasped Jake, the awe of her presence helping to calm him.

'My most recent name is Nemesis,' she replied.

'Nemesis?' said Jake and took a step backwards. 'Aren't you a goddess? Something to do with punishment?'

'My role is to restore balance,' she said. 'So is yours. So is everyone's. In order to do so, you must return the way you came. Go back to the spinney and take the path to the House of Tusk.'

'I don't think I can,' said Jake, in no mood to leave the clearing. 'I'm not sure how I got here. I fell through the ground and the entrance to the fort is sealed up.'

Another dreadful boom quaked the clearing. Jake glanced back at the ghosts who continued to advance towards it.

'Who are they?' he asked.

'Now is not the time to take that path. One day, yes. One day soon perhaps. But not now. Do as I say. Return to the House of Tusk. Leave the clearing in the opposite direction to the ghosts. Remain calm and the way will open for you. Go quickly,' she said and returned to her physical body.

Jake was about to follow her instructions when another boom shot through him, the most dreadful yet. It should have sent him running but didn't. Something deep within Jake resisted. Part fascination, part defiance, he took a step in the direction of the ghosts.

Immediately the creatures that had formed Nemesis's aura danced and flitted about him, desperate to discourage him. The fox and badger tugged at his trouser legs with their jaws.

The ghosts reached the clearing and stopped, staying within the fog. There was something strange about the light in the lanterns—it shone on the ghost that bore it, but nothing else, as though it yearned to be with them.

One of them took a step forward to the very limit of the fog and held up his lantern. Another chill ran through Jake. The ghost had a fading red beard—it was the same ghost Jake had seen on the train. Like then, there was an eye of light within the lantern flame. It appeared for just a moment, though studied Jake with great intensity.

The longer Jake beheld the ghost and his lantern, the more the chill spread through him. But he didn't retreat. He refused to live in fear.

Despite the animals doing their best to hold him back, Jake advanced towards the ghosts who simply stood there with an old and expectant air, apparently waiting for him to enter the fog. As Jake advanced, confronting his fear, that same fear grew more complex. On one level, his fear of the ghosts partially dissolved, only to reappear on a deeper level with greater force—what was it they wanted from him? They were part of his past, part of his destiny, Nemesis had said as much.

She also said I'm not ready to take this path, he thought, *but I don't have time. I must save Granddad!*

Jake remembered something his granddad had once said—that fear is simply ignorance of the nature of what one feared.

Encouraged, he took another step when, just a few paces short of the fog, a stag appeared in front of Jake and halted him with its antlers. Before either had a chance to do anything another boom shook the woods, louder, more urgent than all the others. Screeches erupted from the tree as the remaining birds took flight, all except those about Jake which flitted ever more frantically, brushing him with their wingtips while the other animals clawed and tore at his clothes.

Finally, the source of the booming drew into sight. Unlike the ghosts, its source of light came not from a lantern but a pale sun which rose up behind him. It shot through the fog, silhouetting a huge man.

In comparison to Jake's chaotic journey through the first woodland, which had felt like recent history, the ghosts struck Jake as ancient. But what approached through the fog, the earth quaking with each portentous step, the ghosts stepping aside to make way for it, felt like it was emerging from another time altogether, perhaps another world, one where the extremes were far farther apart—of light and dark, the man appearing to belong to both, but in a way that was somehow terrible.

Horrified yet spellbound, as Jake watched he knew the difference between the theory of what his granddad had said and the practise of it, that knowing the nature of what one feared was easier said than done.

'You must leave!' warned the badger, between tugs on Jake's trousers. 'Every moment in their presence creates a stronger connection. Go back to the fort. Go now!'

Jake's newfound resolve was severely tested. His fear plummeted to a yet deeper level. As the man moved closer, Jake was beset with a vision.

He was in a dark tower, racing down steps with a torch, past archway after archway, each filled with darkness and marked with a chilling red symbol, one a spider, another an eye, and so on until he finally reached the archway at the bottom. Dank like a dungeon and marked with a red serpent, it reeked of the same pungent power as the man. Just the sight of it almost made him to faint.

To pass through it would be the end of Jake. He knew it. Yet it exerted a powerful force. Jake stepped towards it. Immediately the vision merged with the woodland. The stag and the rest of the animals bolted in fright. The archway now lead into the fog, the ghosts standing either side of it.

The silhouetted figure of the powerful man filled the space of the archway as he approached, blocking out the pale sun. His presence was immense. Not only was he tall and strong but he radiated a fierce intelligence.

'Who is he?' demanded Jake of the ghosts, battling to break the dark spell of the man, but the ghosts said nothing. They simply gazed at Jake with sombre faces.

'My granddad, Nestor Burton—where is he?' tried Jake instead, trusting there was a reason for what was happening.

The only response was the death-rattle of a laugh from the approaching man.

Despite his fear, Jake's heartbeat refused to race. Instead it slowed, matching the quakes of the man's footstep, as though they were becoming one. With each step the man took, Jake felt himself fill with darkness, though not darkness as he had imagined it. Rather, it felt as though he were inhaling raw power, a forbidden sort of wisdom, each step making terrible sense of all that had taken place—of the death of his dad, of disease, of famine, of all the suffering that blighted the world, a type of logic Jake instinctively felt would destroy him unless he broke free from it.

As the man's presence filled Jake, he felt himself slipping away, including his fear which he now wished back. He had gone too far. It was too late to flee. The man's presence was too strong.

Realising his folly, in a desperate attempt to restore himself as something separate, Jake closed his eyes and battled to breathe at a faster rate than the deathly slow rhythm of the man's footsteps.

He raced through his options. He couldn't pass through the arch, neither could he simply stand there helpless as the man possessed him with each step. All options spelt doom.

The man was only several paces from reaching the archway.

What can I do? panicked Jake.

Surrender, said the refined and powerful-sounding voice of the man inside Jake's head.

Who are you? demanded Jake, fighting the effect of the man's voice, which only weakened him further.

You already know, came the reply.

You are not my destiny! said Jake defiantly. *Not if you won't help me find Granddad.*

You waste your time with trifles, said the dispassionate voice prickling through Jake. *Your grandfather's spirit will soon be consumed.*

Consumed? thought a horrified Jake as his strength slipped away.

Your destiny is to end all of this, said the man.

Jake remembered what the ghost had said on the train—*die before...* Before something—and how Jake had wished he had waited to hear the full sentence before thumping the window. This time he desperately wished to ask the man what *he* meant. But with the man just a step or so from the arch and another into the clearing, Jake had only enough energy for one act—either to ask a question yet succumb to that destiny all the same, or to do something reckless in order to escape it.

Jake decided on the latter. The nearest ghost to his left was the one with the red beard. Jake lunged for his lamp, intent on casting it into the archway in the hope that it might explode and cast back the man.

His hand never reached it.

The moment it touched the fog, Jake was gripped by a deathly chill.

Suddenly heavy, everything went black and Jake plunged.

SOMEWHAT UNEXPECTEDLY, THE PLUNGE WAS SHORT AND INVOLVED a splash. Jake's momentum carried him to the bottom of what appeared to be a well.

Confused, relieved, the touch of the water refreshed him. He no longer felt the dreadful presence of the man. His strength returned.

If I wasn't ready to take that path, he reasoned as he focused on his surroundings, *then by touching the fog I've been dragged off to another place.*

Jake felt pleased with himself about his bold decision to grab the lantern. He made to spring up from the bottom of the well, but went nowhere. His body had lost its buoyancy. Unable to go up, Jake scrambled about the bottom for a way out. On his hands and knees, desperate for air, at last he discovered a rock which stuck out and which looked like it had been removed before. With a great wrench he dislodged it. Like a plug, it drained the well and spat Jake out on the other side.

Wherever he was, coughing and spluttering, to his great relief there was air. It was soon filled with a harsh shriek.

'Ooh! What've we got us 'ere, sisters?'

'Ooh! Nice little human from earth thinks me. Nice young flesh and enough for three!' said an equally ugly voice.

Having recovered his breath, Jake looked up. He was in a cave. Tree roots had forced their way through the rock from every direction, though rather than carry water upwards, water dripped from their ends and formed a pool at the centre of the cave. Hunched over it, sifting through its waters with their long filthy finger nails, were three old hags.

'What a treat, we'll have us some beers!' said the one with a large wart on her nose, rubbing her hands together gleefully. 'Bagsy the feet and both his ears!'

'Entrails and marrow, they be mine! Boiled for an hour with a twist o'lime!' said the hag who was missing an eyeball.

'Waste time with his innards? You must be crackers! They're all yours just save me his—'

'That's enough you gluttonous trout!' broke in the third hag, her voice the harshest. 'If we don't likes his credentials, you'll be supping on nowt!'

This final hag was the ugliest by far, her eyes beady and hard.

'Who are you?' asked Jake, having regained his composure. The scene he had arrived in didn't seem to fit the one he had left—like a leap from a horror movie into a fairy tale.

The first two answered in chorus: 'The Norns of Destiny if truth be told! Urd, Verdandi and the miserable Skuld! Watch the wise waters from the Tree of Life we do! Sniff and pick at its broth we do! Looking for those who'll write history, that's what! Those what've got it, not those what've not! La-la-la, la-la, la-lee, ha-ha-ha, ha-ha, ha-hee!'

Urd and Verdandi danced around in a hideous fashion, cackling.

'Shut up yer prattling, yer bags o'wind! Let's inspect him ere becoming unhinged,' interrupted Skuld.

She dipped her hand into the pool, took a step forward and cast the water across Jake's face.

The other two rushed forward to join Skuld in scrutinizing him.

As they studied the pattern made by the rivulets that ran down his face, their expressions grew more ugly. Skuld's was one of confusion, while those of the other two were of mounting horror.

Suddenly Urd and Verdandi leapt back and howled.

'Dragons' gizzards and Hade's fist! Devil's buttocks and evil mist!' screamed Urd.

'Snake-tongued and many-faced!' cried Verdandi. 'Ghost ridden, in darkness based! Satan's accomplice and gate of fire! Blood of mother and Creator's pyre!'

Ashen faced, they slowly shook their heads.

Jake felt dizzy with all the rhyming, though got the gist of what they were saying. *Satan's accomplice?* he thought. *They're mad!*

'What *are* you talking about?' he said at last.

'Why wasn't this in the pools, asks I?' said Urd.

'Destiny's ironic, but not want to lie!' added Verdandi.

While Urd and Verdandi continued their ranting, finally Skuld spoke, her voice calm yet icy:

'What we've got here is a complex brew. Many are the paths of destiny for you. Which you shall take, none can say. Grey are the clouds, much the dismay. Satan is there, of that I'm sure. So is a greater force, and so is a lure. But three things there be of which I can speak. Words of warning 'ere the havoc you'll wreak.'

Skuld's sober tone sent a terrible shiver through Jake. She closed her eyes and drew a deep breath. When she next spoke she was in a trance:

> *'On sinful eyrie your power buoyed, mind your intent and what's destroyed*
> *In Ark in ice, best think twice, if madness for a maiden is too dear a price*
> *At fiery gate when hope seems spent, love thine enemy and they'll repent.'*

Jake had been concentrating hard as Skuld had spoken, but he could make little sense of what she had said. He inwardly groaned at yet more riddles.

'Could you be a little more specific?' he asked.

As Skuld emerged from her trance her gaze hardened.

'Specific?' she spat. 'Destiny's our trade not career-planning, you ill-omened urchin. Now naff off or we'll see to it that you perish a virgin!'

Jake was more than keen to do just that and as Urd and Verdandi exploded into another bout of cackling, he looked about for an exit. It was then he noticed the hole he had arrived through had become a door. With Skuld still scowling at him, Jake skirted the pool, prayed for somewhere peaceful, opened the door and stepped through.

CHAPTER 17
FATAL REVELATION

Following his lesson with Geoffrey on the pinnacle in the sea, Lawrence was feeling more relaxed in his office at the top of Renlock. He was sitting at a desk engrossed in planning a second break into the House of Tusk. Luna's demand for the theft of the gates was so extreme that it required something extreme in order to meet it.

A gust of wind drew his attention outside. A freak thunder storm that had appeared without warning and raged for a half an hour was finally passing. He wondered what had caused it. All worlds were connected. When a storm raged on the surface of Earth there were scientific reasons for its origin and where it blew, but that was only the surface of it. There were deeper reasons—momentous events, both individual and collective, which reverberated from one world through the rest, manifesting in accordance with the laws of each. For a storm to wrack Renlock so violently, a place accustomed to storm, it had to have been something extraordinary.

Something's been opened, perhaps a door, releasing something powerful, he wondered, though he wasn't thinking of Pandora's Box, which was already open, but a person or beast. *An initiation? A dreadful act, maybe?* Whatever it was, the passing of the storm left Lawrence with an uneasy feeling.

'She's here,' said Geoffrey from his perch on the stairs, drawing Lawrence's attention back to office.

Several flights down the zig-zagging staircase, on top of the great wall, Goddess Luna was being welcomed by Wilderspin.

'She's here to test out the dream-screening device of that dreadful creep,' said Lawrence from the desk. 'Searching for a secret buried in the unconscious of a Surface soul.'

He closed his eyes for a moment and drew a deep breath. His presence at the demonstration would be expected. Lawrence got up, fastened his sword and cloak about him and joined Geoffrey at the top of the steps.

He had taken just a few steps down the staircase when he stopped and gasped. His heart sank. He gripped the wall to steady himself.

'What is it?' asked Geoffrey.

Lawrence said nothing. Eyes wide, he was studying Luna. Her appearance had changed dramatically since he last saw her. Even since her encounter with the angel in Pandora's Box it had changed. There was still something of the tree about her, most notably in her hands and feet, while her hair, though no longer twiggy, was a sumptuous mane of red leaves. The greater part, however, appeared more human than anything else. What had been a trunk was now feminine and shapely and what showed of her skin through a smattering of autumnal leaves glowed with the lustre of the moon. Most striking of all were her eyes. Emerald green and perfect ellipses, they shone with powerful allure.

'She's acquired a shadow,' remarked Geoffrey. 'Must be the sylph.'

'It's not the shadow,' muttered Lawrence, a dreadful feeling in the pit of his stomach.

'Then what?'

'It's her.'

'Who?' said Geoffrey.

'Rowena,' said Lawrence softly.

'The Goddess of Pride? Well, that makes sense. To leave the Core, Luna requires a body. Pride is the closest world. And by all accounts, Rowena is a pure soul and so is well-suited as cover for an innocent-seeming fertility goddess. But are you sure it's her?'

'Yes,' said Lawrence and released a heavy sigh. 'It's her and yet it isn't,' he added, noting how Rowena's graceful beauty had been transformed by Luna's energy into something smouldering.

Geoffrey studied him with a quizzical expression. 'This Goddess Rowena—please don't tell me you're in love with her,' he said in an exasperated tone. 'Things are difficult enough.'

His eyes fixed on Luna, Lawrence nodded.

With a roll of his eyes, it was Geoffrey's turn to release a despairing sigh.

'Well,' he continued, 'fortunately she doesn't think much of you, otherwise Luna would have felt something through her body.'

'Rowena's strong. She must be blocking her emotions,' said Lawrence. A rush of hope swept through him.

'Perhaps but it's highly improbable. Her place of power would have to be immense and something very inventive to conceal anything from someone like Luna.'

'Improbable, but possible,' said Lawrence.

He recalled his lesson with Geoffrey aimed at discovering his own place of power. The first place he had tried, a memory of a time he had shared with Rowena, had resulted in a great wave crashing against Renlock.

'The shark which leapt at me from the wave,' he said with a feeling of awe. 'Rowena must have sent it—a warning to not think of her with strong emotions for fear of alerting Luna. A part of her *is* independent of Luna's power.'

'You'd better hope so. You're already walking a fine enough tightrope. Now it's going to get a lot finer and you a lot heavier at a time when you need to be light.'

'We'll manage,' said Lawrence.

'Are you sure about that?' asked Geoffrey in a knowing tone.

Lawrence shot him a questioning look. His eyes widened as he realised what Geoffrey meant. 'The pinnacle!'

Having let his mind drift away from it, he immediately refocused. A moment later he was the wolf. Lawrence cursed. Having indulged in the thought of Rowena, his presence had weakened to such an extent that his place of power had completely faded. He was back in the dream room.

Geoffrey was also there, on the table gazing at a door. What before had been framed by the gaping jaw of a Siberian tiger was now an intricately carved homely-looking door framed in wild roses. It had merged with the part of Lawrence's psyche reserved for Rowena.

A chill ran through Lawrence. The door was wide open. Beyond it was an arbour of the same roses that led to a beautiful garden.

'This is precisely what Boreas is after. A weakness,' said Geoffrey. 'And oh, what a weakness. One which leads right to the very being he's so desperate to contact—Luna. He won't believe his luck.'

'I must close it,' said Lawrence.

He transformed into human form and leaped forward to do so.

'Don't touch the door!' commanded Geoffrey, stopping Lawrence just in time. 'It's different from when you stole Pandora's Box. That time Boreas had already found the dream room. But if you touch the door physically he'll find you even faster. Use your will power. But first you must empty your mind of Rowena.'

Lawrence closed his eyes. His brow furrowed as he bent his will to the task at hand.

At first nothing happened. Then things moved in the wrong direction. What had been a spring scene in the garden beyond the door blossomed into summer. Hatchlings took their first flights as bunnies sprang out from burrows and joined the rest of nature celebrating the gift of fertility.

'Your mind appears to be wandering,' remarked Geoffrey.

Lawrence opened his eyes and stared into the garden with concern. His feelings for Rowena were so strong that they were difficult to control.

'You've little time,' warned Geoffrey.

Eyes closed, Lawrence battled to empty his mind of her.

Several moments passed when the scene finally altered. Summer gave way to autumn as nature withdrew its life-force and birds took flight for warmer climes. A leafless vine reached out for the door handle in order to close the door.

Geoffrey nodded with approval when a freak gust of wind blasted the door open again.

Wide-eyed, Lawrence glanced at Geoffrey who was staring sternly into the garden.

When Lawrence looked back himself, terror shot through him like a bolt of lightning. An instant later his sword was drawn.

Standing at the garden's centre next to a cedar tree, poised to charge, was a Siberian tiger—Lord Boreas. His eyes flashed with fury. With another gust, what remained of the leaves on the trees were torn away and blasted into the dream room.

Winter spread out from the tiger's paws. In a matter of seconds the entire garden was covered in snow and ice. Lord Boreas bristled. He was about to charge.

But didn't.

Instead, he raised his nose and sniffed the air.

'Why's he not charging?' whispered Lawrence. 'The reality of Renlock is right before him.'

'He's tempted,' said Geoffrey. 'But he's no fool. It wouldn't be clean. You're armed and in the dream room whose power he can't fathom. He's thought of a better way.'

'What do you mean?'

'You've not only shown him the easiest way to enter the dream room, but by revealing your weak point, you've inspired him to send something else to do his work.'

'Meaning?'

'He knows which demons to send,' replied Geoffrey. 'Ones with the power to drag you off to a hell so deep that you'll not bother him or anyone else ever again. Demons with truths you're not yet ready to face.'

'Which demons would those be?'

'Yours,' said Geoffrey. 'Though they'll be from a past too distant for you to remember and so have power to ensnare you far more effectively than Boreas could himself. As the God of Greed, he has the keys to release them.'

A chilling laugh echoed from the tiger in confirmation and ran through Lawrence like ice. As a measure of the threat, Lord Boreas's presence bridged realities—his wintry laugh sent bitter gusts through Renlock's many portals and almost blew Wilderspin off the great wall.

'By the gods!' he cried as a cloud of pigeons righted his balance. 'I've never known such wild weather! Why, if I didn't know better, I'd say our God of the North Wind was having a party up there.'

Luna, who had been unaffected by the wind other than a ruffling of her leaves, glanced up the zig-zagging stairs.

Lawrence was descending towards her, doing his best to appear composed, while the other part of him watched the tiger-spirit of the real Lord Boreas saunter off smugly into the snow-covered bushes.

No words left Luna's lips. Yet such was the intensity of her stare that Lawrence feared the worst—she knew.

CHAPTER 18
ROOTS

UNABLE TO SLEEP, RANI HAD LEFT BIN IN THEIR HIDEOUT AND spent the small hours skulking about the fort, the atomic glove on her left hand just in case. Other than getting a feel for the place, she had been searching for the Tusk boy, hoping to observe him while he was resting. A troubled boy like him doubtless had nightmares and spoke in his sleep. In his dream state he might let something slip, some vital clue as to who he really was. Frustratingly, however, she had found no sign of him. Despite her long search, it was the jungle which beckoned her, not her bed, and so she stole down the outcrop and out across the savannah between the resting beasts.

The moment she passed inside the jungle she released a blissful yawn as the trees relieved her of her weighty mind and all its concerns.

'Ah, you're so beautiful!' she gasped as she moved through the shadows, dew glistening in the silver light of the moon. The trees rustled their leaves in greeting.

She inhaled the rich aromas summoned by the damp of night —the earth, the bark, the jasmine, the faintest hints of creatures nearby and many other smells. She let them fill her lungs and heart. As she passed each tree she ran her fingers across their broad trunks, sumptuously gnarled or smooth, and savoured the cushioned touch of the jungle floor and its gentle sounds.

Despite the peace of the trees, her chief preoccupation soon forced its way back into her thoughts—the Tusk boy. She didn't fight it, however. Rani had faith in instinct, which included what others called thought and imagination, for she had been spared an upbringing on the Surface and so what came to her was natural and undistorted.

'Beautiful trees, what are you telling me?' she whispered as she walked.

Another question returned to haunt her.

'Why did Braysheath call for me and not one of the more experienced panthers?'

The question had scarcely left her lips when she felt a weightiness in the pit of her stomach where it writhed about like a snake. Rani had never felt such a thing. It was highly disturbing. A Yakreth warrior had to be light like a bird, sometimes surrendering to the wind, at other times tilting one's wings to steer through the storm, though always at one with it, the senses projected to the horizon and beyond, ever alive to the in-between. But never within. For a panther, like all other creatures, there was no within. To focus within was to be separate, to become an obstacle, a target, out of synch with the flow of life.

She then recalled a talk she had once had with Ezram. He had been telling her the history of the Yakreth clan and how it had been formed in response to something which had happened during the retreat of the last Ice Age on the Surface. At that time a powerful goddess had corrupted a clan of trixies who created an apparatus to distort the Great Game. It was called the god gate. He had also told her that although she was a panther at heart, the rest of her body and the entirety of her soul were human and for a human the keys to truth could only be discovered within. A day would come, he had said, when she would feel something called emotion. And when it came she would have to strive for a middle way between the instinct of a panther and the free will of a human.

'Is this what Ezram meant by emotion?' she asked the jungle as she pondered the strange sensation in her stomach, which one moment felt almost pleasing, the next moment quite the opposite.

A solitary bird song gave a sweet confirmation through the softness of night.

Rani also recalled her questioning Ezram about what he meant by free will. He told her that for humans some of life's challenges were predetermined—obstacles specially selected to help one wake up to who they really were. How one reacted or responded to them, however, was entirely in one's own hands. This was free will. When ruled by emotions, one closed up and *re-acted* a past pattern of fighting the nature of things. When emotions were mastered, one *responded* to life's challenges with an open heart, surrendering their individual free will in exchange for the divine will of nature. The ability to respond was responsibility.

Rani took another deep breath of the jungle. From what little she had seen of the Surface, everyone appeared to be separate, fighting the nature of things and full of fear. Now she was being forced into contact with them.

'The clarity will come,' she consoled herself. 'I must be patient and trust in nature. She has put me here for a reason.'

As Rani spoke, she stopped to touch the petals of a flower. A light in her peripheral vision caused her to look up. She gasped. A little way ahead, someone else was walking through the woods, glowing like a moon.

Braysheath! The Ancient One!

Buzzing with excitement she followed him, keeping at a safe distance as he walked deeper into the jungle.

Surely he can sense my presence, she thought, still marvelling at the timing of his appearance.

In answer, a bat appeared, flitted about her for a magical moment before darting ahead and flying in circles in the mid-distance between her and Braysheath.

As it flew towards the undergrowth, a fox leapt up and playfully swiped at it, though wasn't quick enough to make contact. Rani delighted at the enchanting sight as the fox and the bat continued their playful dance in the silver radiance of Braysheath, while he himself wandered on, apparently oblivious to them.

He's doing this, she thought, for Rani had never heard of a fox play with a bat. Neither was the symbolism lost on her. Both were creatures of the night and both were highly perceptive. The Yakreth panthers referred to the bat as the guide of night. Because it was at home in darkness, it was, among other things, a symbol of initiation. The fox, meanwhile, was a great hunter, full of grace, wise and a master of concealment.

The fox Rani was watching was white. She had never seen one that wasn't red and was thinking how beautiful it was, especially in contrast to the dark bat, when the tempo of its play suddenly shifted and became hostile. With its next swipe it caught the bat.

Rani released a cry and gripped her heart as though it were her in the fox's clasp. She felt anger and then relief when somehow the bat escaped.

Immediately it took revenge on the fox and clung to the back of its neck. As the bat bit, the fox yelped and transformed into a cloud of moths to escape, flying deeper into the jungle, pursued by the feasting bat until they disappeared from sight.

Rani stood stunned.

Why did my heart hurt like that? And why moths?

She considered how moths transformed from caterpillars and how they were attracted to light, often fatally.

Like butterflies, they symbolise transformation and rebirth.

She looked up just in time to see Braysheath disappear into a granite boulder as though through a doorway. With a final glow of light, he too was gone.

Rani rushed forward to the boulder.

Where Braysheath had been just moments before was a vein of white quartz running through the granite.

'It's like frozen light,' she said in awe and put her hand close to it. The rock emitted a heat and she wondered whether she should touch it. Impulsively, she did.

In a flash, the quartz transformed from white to rose. A strange pulse shot through Rani's heart, somehow blissful, somehow not. It was so overwhelming that she almost fainted.

Panting, Rani tore her hand away from the quartz.

Her heartbeat calmed. Strangely, her breathing was still heavy—impossibly heavy. It was the depth of breath that could only come from a large creature.

A ghastly chill ran up her spine. The breathing wasn't coming from her but something behind her. Not stopping to wonder how such a large creature could have approached without making a noise, she spun round, knives drawn.

She needn't have bothered. Her knives were useless. Towering above her was the largest bull elephant she had ever seen, so large that it was otherworldly. Unbeknown to Rani, it was the same one that had charged towards Jake in the woods of his dream.

Its dark eyes shone with a fierce light and great power.

Rani looked into them for just an instant when a heavy darkness descended upon her.

A moment later, she fainted.

CHAPTER 19
TO DREAM OR NOT TO DREAM

RANI AWOKE WITH A START. SHE SUFFERED A MOMENT'S PANIC as she glanced about bleary eyed for points of reference.

She breathed a deep sigh of relief—she was in their hideout in the fort.

'Are you all right?' asked Bin from the orange tree, halfway through a trout.

Rani looked out the strange window over the savannah. It was first light. She had the vaguest recollection of a dream in which she had ridden on an elephant for what felt like forever, over mountains, across deserts, through ancient cities and even across oceans.

'Do you remember what time I got back?' she asked.

'No,' said Bin.

'But I did go out, right? You must have noticed.'

'Actually, I didn't. It's most unlike me, but I slept solidly the whole night,' replied Bin. 'But why are you confused? Did you have a dream? You don't normally have dreams.'

A chill ran through Rani. She opened her right hand to find an orange petal from the very same type of flower she had been admiring when Braysheath had appeared in the jungle the night before. Yet at the time she hadn't picked the petal. She never picked flowers but left them in peace.

'I'm not sure,' she replied. 'I thought I scouted the fort looking for the boy. Then I went across the savannah and into the jungle. But now I don't know. I don't remember returning.'

She sniffed the sweet fragrance of the petal and recalled what she had seen. *I had been thinking of the Tusk boy when I saw Braysheath. And then that fox appeared. Perhaps it's the boy's totem. Yes, cunning and good at camouflage, hiding his true na-*

ture, pretending to charm, yet ever-ready to pounce, she thought, in a less generous assessment of its symbolism than the night before.

When it came to the bat, however, and how she had shared its pain, Rani dismissed the whole thing as a dream. *I can't possibly have a bat as a totem! Of course I love all of nature. Of course! But still, it can't be a bat. I suspect it's a cat of some sort or perhaps an eagle. Braysheath must have a made a mistake. After all, no one's perfect, not even him.*

'What do you think about reincarnation?' she asked, recalling how the fox had transformed into moths.

'It's a human thing,' said Bin. 'The rest of creation is already aware that everything is one. When one life finishes we surrender our energy to whatever nature has in store for it. For humans it's different. Until they remember, they're reborn as humans on the Surface. Dreams are there to guide them.'

Was it a dream? wondered Rani. *The elephant must have been —the way it suddenly appeared without noise and how I fainted at the sight of it.*

'So if I was dreaming…' she started.

'Rani dear, you're no longer in Wrathlabad among panthers. You've been up to the Surface. You've mixed with other humans. Your soul is telling you that for now you're human and that you have a journey to make.'

Bin had confirmed Rani's own musings from the night before. She thought back to the fox and the bat. She realised that what Braysheath had shown her held deep meaning—she felt it in the pit of her stomach where she still sensed the snake.

Suddenly the symbolism made sense of her own doubts about Jake. *The bat was watching over the fox while it pranced about the woods. Yet, look how it turned on her! I must be careful.*

Ignoring any deeper meaning, of either the symbols or the strange sensation in the pit of her stomach, she sprang up and gathered her weapons and the atomic glove.

'Come on, Bin,' she said. 'We've got things to do.'

CHAPTER 20
RUFUS

JAKE AWOKE TO A SCREECH. FOR A MOMENT HE THOUGHT IT WAS one of the old hags beneath the tree and that he was still dreaming. With the second screech he recognised the sound.

Peacocks, he thought sleepily. *The farmhouse doesn't have any!*

With a rush of excitement his eyes shot open. *The House of Tusk!*

He sat up suddenly and spooked a nearby deer grazing on vines. An early morning mist hung in the air. He was in a hammock strung up beneath a trellis of grapes. To his left was a large airy room with arched windows and a fountain at its centre, decorated in a simple but sumptuous manner with carpets and cushions. To his right was a balustrade, the tops of trees beyond it.

'I'm still here! It wasn't all just a dream!' he said to himself. 'But am I awake?'

Jake sat there for several moments. There was something about the stillness that convinced him that he was indeed awake. As he dwelt on it, Jake not only felt awake, but more awake than he had ever felt before. Everything felt so real. His body tingled with the joy of being alive.

With a shudder he recalled the strange dream after he had fallen asleep in the spinney, especially the part with Nemesis and the amazing tree. Like all his dreams since returning from school, the details remained vivid as though they had actually happened. Awe and fear coursed through Jake in equal measure.

'It was a dream. But it was also real,' he said to himself, finally accepting what Frost had said of dreams.

For Jake it was a huge admission. Once made, however, it was as though a chest of treasure had sprung open and showered the world in magic—everything, every act, every thought suddenly held a secret meaning. Nothing in the universe went unnoticed.

Nemesis, he thought, *she must know everything about every human!*

The realisation was humbling and magnificent in the same moment.

Jake thought back to the spinney and the different paths he had to choose from. He came to the same conclusion as he had then—that it had been a test. *Braysheath and the others were testing me to see if I'm fit to replace Dad. The easy choice was back to the farmhouse. The one they probably hoped I'd take was the path leading to the fort. But the one I actually took…*

There was no doubt that it was the least appealing and so the most challenging path to have taken and yet Jake had a strange feeling that what his granddad said in the dream was true—that Jake wasn't meant to take it, nor ready to.

So why was it there? he wondered.

He thought of Nemesis and her role to restore balance. *Perhaps that includes dreams and if so then the path might have been her way to make contact.*

Jake couldn't help but feel pleased with himself. *I took the toughest path.* A strange thrill ran through him as he recalled the journey into the two woods, especially the first, and how it had been full of what felt like memories of great adventures. Until he recalled that all had involved violence. He shuddered at the memory of the gruesome sensation of cutting a throat and the dark intelligence of the man in the fog.

Could that really have been a memory of my soul? he dared to think. *Or was it symbolic of something deeper?*

He hoped the latter, though he couldn't escape the feeling that it was, in fact, a memory. Just as he did in his dream, he studied his hands, unable to believe that perhaps in a past life he could have killed someone in cold blood.

If it was a memory then it was only part *of a memory,* he reasoned.

He thought of how newspapers focused on the violent side of life without fairly presenting the context, the full story, or showing any of the beauty. Perhaps what he had witnessed was something like that. But then killing was killing. There was no excuse for it.

Whatever it means, it's the past, he decided. If he could no longer dismiss dreams as just dreams, at least he could dismiss the past.

The thought brought little peace. There had been the repeated appearance of the same ghost, along with three others, and the approach of the dreadful character from behind them, not to mention the strange prophecy of the Norns. The past, it seemed, was also his future, one which couldn't be escaped.

It was too early for such heavy thinking and Jake leaped up from the hammock to be free of it. Only then did he wonder how he had reached it.

Another mystery, he thought before letting it drift away with all the others.

He wandered up to the balustrade. At the sight of the courtyard below, his spirits soared. From the upper level it was even more impressive than it had been on his arrival. The lawn was so great that it made the turrets and ramparts appear squat—a far cry from the fort's imposing appearance from the outside. There were rose arbours, a pond and an orchard where a couple of ostriches were foraging for breakfast.

Jake's stomach released a rumble, reminding him that he hadn't had dinner the night before. He was ravenous.

'Good morning, Young Tusk!' came a cheery voice which startled Jake.

Standing before him was a human in all respects except in size. Despite being middle-aged he was half Jake's height, had dark curly hair, rosy cheeks and was so bursting with cheerfulness that there was something mischievous about him.

'Hello,' said Jake. 'Who are you?'

'That's no way to greet someone!' cried the little man in a broad Germanic accent. 'You would do well to remember that it is the manners that make the man. Now, allow me to demonstrate how to ask another's name. First you must introduce yourself thus…' said the little man and stooped in a low bow. 'I am Tancred, son of Goth of the sprites of Infincry, and butler to the House of Tusk.'

'Sprites?' said Jake, recalling the bustling storeroom beneath the courtyard.

'Of course sprites! You needn't look so surprised! We've often lived with humans. But during the epochs of the Great Game we and most of the fairies leave the Surface. Only the pixies and trixies remain.'

'Trixies?' exclaimed Jake, barely able to believe his ears. 'You mean they actually exist?'

Tancred threw back his head and guffawed. 'Of course they do! But they're not how you might imagine.'

Bill must have picked up the word from Granddad in a game of golf, reasoned Jake. 'So why have I never seen them?'

'You have but you're in too much of a rush to notice.'

'I think I would've realised if I'd seen a trixy,' said Jake.

Tancred released another guffaw though didn't share the joke.

'Well, Tancred, son of Goth,' said Jake, 'I'm starving. Any chance of breakfast?'

'Oh yes, always a chance, Young Tusk! Always a chance!' he said and sprang over the balustrade into the vines.

Jake peered over the balustrade waiting for more information, but none came. Tancred had disappeared.

Hoping he might pick up a scent of food as he went, Jake decided to revisit the spinney and inspect the pool.

THE SPINNEY WAS JUST AS IT HAD BEEN THE EVENING BEFORE, with a pool at its centre. Tentatively, Jake knelt down and studied its surface, though found nothing extraordinary. He touched it but nothing stirred.

'Hello there!' came a familiar bellow that made Jake jump. It was Braysheath. 'Looking for dragonflies?'

'Looking for breakfast,' replied Jake.

'Well you won't find it there. Have a nice time with Asclepius?'

'Oh yes, wonderful,' replied Jake dryly.

'Oh good,' said Braysheath. 'Splendid fellow, Asclepius.'

'Yes, he's a god, you know?'

'Yes, yes. Didn't I tell you?' replied Braysheath airily.

'No, you forgot to mention that.'

'Dear fellow, I've hardly had a chance, what with all your questions yesterday. Besides, gods are hardly worth mentioning,' said Braysheath whilst studying a leaf on a branch. 'They're a dime a dozen down here and all fall eventually. Then off they trot back to the Surface to start all over again, once more human, apart from those worthy of privileged positions in the inner-worlds—the noble gods, that is, who I'm afraid to say are much in the minority. Ti and Asclepius for example.'

Jake said nothing. Noble was far from the word he had in mind for Asclepius. He recalled the god's terse manner and how suitably he fitted the idea of a traitor suggested by his granddad's riddles. *And what better cover than a god of healing?* he thought.

'Fancy a stroll about the gardens?' said Braysheath and strode from the spinney, greeting the birds as he went.

Jake followed, emerging into the rose arbour running through the orchard.

'Did you sleep well?' enquired Braysheath, striking out from the arbour between some pomegranate and fig trees. He picked a fig and tossed it over his shoulder to Jake.

'I had a strange dream,' he said, catching the fig.

'Oh really—what happened?'

'That pool back there—can it become a gate?' asked Jake, almost tripping up over another sprite as it scurried along with a basket of fruit.

'A gate, you say? Humph. Well I've never known it to become one.'

'In my dream I saw Granddad, well, what looked like Granddad, and he said it was.'

'Oh really? How interesting.'

There was something in Braysheath's tone which suggested he knew all about the dream, which reaffirmed Jake's belief that it had indeed been a test of some sort.

'By the way, is anything being done to find Granddad?'

Braysheath turned and smiled kindly at Jake. 'Of course, dear boy, of course. Alas, wherever he is, he's well hidden.'

'But he is alive?' asked Jake, his heart in his mouth.

'I believe so. I've sensed his presence, though only briefly.'

'Where? Where did you sense his presence?' pressed Jake.

Braysheath's smile grew even warmer.

'He was in Egypt,' said Braysheath.

Egypt! exclaimed Jake in thought. *My dream of the Sphinx, the temple and the chamber beneath it!*

Given his recent acceptance of the reality of dreams, Jake's head reeled with the complexity of it all. There had also been the sword on the altar, along with the same wolf he had seen while dreaming on the train.

Now that he knew about his granddad and dad's secret lives as lords of the House of Tusk it cast the dream in a whole new light.

The dream was showing me what happened! But to whom? Granddad or Dad?

Jake felt it was his dad. His granddad must have gone to investigate then sent Jake the riddles before something had happened to him.

'Are you alright, dear boy?' asked Braysheath.

Jake looked up at Braysheath who was studying him with a curious expression. Since disembarking the train in Harkenmere,

Jake was growing used to hearing two voices in his head, though still wasn't sure which to listen to—the one which advised trusting and sharing or the other which remained suspicious.

He desperately wanted to confide in Braysheath, but Jake had to be sure that Asclepius was the insider suggested by the riddles and not Braysheath despite him seeming so trustworthy. In fact, to Jake's suspicious side, Braysheath was almost too trustworthy, too wonderful-seeming for someone so powerful.

Not yet, he thought to himself.

'I'm fine,' he replied finally.

Braysheath looked unconvinced but let it go.

'I suspect Nestor was kidnapped by something we call guardians,' he went on. 'They're beings made up of a destructive force, what those scientist fellows call radiation, which makes them rather tricky to track.'

'Radiation!' exclaimed Jake, his stomach squirming at the idea of his granddad in such company.

'Radiation is merely the side-effect of something much deeper, while destruction is actually rather useful. Life can't survive without it. Still, like all things, the dosage is critical and the guardians are a potent lot if one's not quite ready for them.'

'But why are these guardians interested in Granddad?' asked Jake, finding little comfort in Braysheath's words.

Braysheath regarded Jake with a weighty gaze. 'A powerful being who calls herself Luna has corrupted some of their company, just as she corrupted a certain tribe of the trixies. They work together.'

'What do guardians and trixies do?'

'Guardians are beings of inner-force, the force of the Inner-Peregrinus, where the soul is tested to the extreme,' explained Braysheath. 'Because the force is destructive, many fear it and think of guardians as evil. But they're a vital part of the whole. The force is destructive in the sense of destroying illusion—all those things humans have become so attached to, especially vanity and pride.'

'And trixies?'

'The trixies are the guardians' allies on the Surface. They're a demi-force—part force, part human. Think of them as the guardians' hands.'

'What about pixies then?' asked Jake.

'Pixies and the dryads, the tree people, are part of the Outer-Peregrinus. They're the outer-force equivalent of the trixies and guardians. They guide humans.'

Tree people! thought Jake, enchanted by the idea.

'It's like a smaller scale version of the Great Dance and the Great Game, played out on a daily basis,' continued Braysheath. 'Trixies create obstacles so that you learn the lessons of life properly. The pixies guide you through them. Though it seems like a battle in a given moment, through time it's a collaboration. Without them you wouldn't evolve.'

'Why do we even need such things? Surely one force is enough, such as gravity, the one that you said pulls us towards the Core.'

'These are sleepy times, Jake m'boy. Without pixies and trixies to give us a good kick in the pants, humans miss the signs.'

Jake remembered something Frost had said about unsubtle times and how the symbols and the meaning of things needed to be spelled out.

'And this Luna has corrupted some of these guardians and trixies?' asked Jake.

'Indeed. It's a very serious business.'

'And Luna—who is she?'

'The very same being who's been merrily chopping up my brother and sister shepherds all these years,' explained Braysheath.

'What? And now she has Granddad?' exclaimed Jake.

Braysheath placed a hand on Jake's shoulder. A blissful calm washed through him.

'I won't mislead you. Whoever this Luna is, she's the greatest challenge we've yet to face. But it's such challenges that bring out our best. She's like a trixy on a massive scale. Our duty is to stay calm and strive to understand what each challenge represents within ourselves. Like a seed in the soil, it first needs darkness and a bit of a struggle to reach the light. The most important thing is not to worry,' he said cheerily, releasing Jake's shoulder with a pat. 'Worry is the true enemy! You're here to become a warrior, not a worrier.'

'But Granddad?'

'Rest assured, dear Jake, we're doing all we can. Have faith. Nestor will spring up sooner or later and no doubt smelling of roses,' said Braysheath and strode on through the orchard.

Jake closed his eyes and drew a deep breath. *Faith*, he thought and knew at that moment that he had some, at least in Braysheath. He felt a tinge of shame for his earlier doubts. Jake couldn't imagine Braysheath seeking to harm anything. He opened his eyes and marvelled at how everything appeared to glow and buzz with life around the mysterious character. Colours became more vivid as he passed by. Trees seemed to lean towards him.

I must tell him—everything, he decided. *The ghosts, Granddad's riddles and especially about Frost.*

A great wave of relief swept through Jake. He sprang forward to catch up with Braysheath.

'Braysheath,' he said as he drew near.

'Yes, dear boy?'

'There's something I want to—' started Jake, but was interrupted by a finch fluttering about Braysheath's head, chirping excitedly.

'Ah, hello there!' said Braysheath to the finch. 'What's that? Oh, right you are. Jolly good. Thank you! I'm sorry, what were you saying, Jake?'

Jake made a second attempt. This time Braysheath was distracted by a branch of a tree, which moved its twigs in what looked like a dance.

'I see,' said Braysheath to the tree. 'Thank you, dear friend. I shall look into it.'

Braysheath turned to Jake. 'I'm terribly sorry, Jake, do carry on.'

Jake was about to open his mouth when he spotted a squirrel on another branch watching him intently, looking as though it was ready to pounce on Braysheath's shoulder and interrupt Jake a third time.

Strange, he thought. It was as though nature was telling him not to share such mysteries, at least not yet. The squirrel reminded him of the ones he had seen in the vines of Nemesis's hair. *Is she doing this? Or is Braysheath?* Jake preferred the latter idea because it maintained his new-found faith in the shepherd. Perhaps working out the mystery himself was also part of a test.

To be sure, Jake decided on a change of tack.

'The Norns,' he said. 'Do they exist?'

'What did you say?' said Braysheath, his tone suddenly serious.

'The Norns of Destiny,' repeated Jake, disconcerted by Braysheath's manner. 'One called Skuld told a prophecy.'

'And what did she say?'

As they continued their walk, Jake told Braysheath word for chilling word about a sinful eyrie, an ark in ice and a fiery gate, along with the warning to Jake about his behaviour in each place. Heeding the squirrel, he withheld how he had arrived in the Norns' cave or any details regarding Frost or the ghosts.

Braysheath had taken out his pipe and was filling it with tobacco. His eyes took on the distant look Jake had noted the day before.

'A prophecy is merely an opinion,' he said at last and took a puff on his pipe. 'And the future is nothing more than an idea created from belief. But a very powerful one all the same.'

'So these Norns actually exist?' asked Jake.

'Oh yes.'

'But how . . ?'

'As I said, dreams are interesting things. Especially down here,' replied Braysheath.

'You said a prophecy is just an opinion, but there are probabilities, aren't there?' said Jake, recalling what his granddad in the dream had said about the different paths of destiny leading away from the spinney.

'Indeed there are, though they're often traps. I prefer to focus on the possible and in so doing make it more probable. Focus on what you need and get on with it, that's what I say.'

Jake's stomach released another rumble. 'Well, if we're focusing on needs then how about breakfast?'

'You've just had it, you greedy devil.'

'What—a fig?' protested Jake. 'Tancred the sprite mentioned breakfast.'

'If you want a bigger breakfast you'll have to earn it.'

Jake and Braysheath had completed a circuit of the orchards and were back on the great lawn.

'On which note,' continued Braysheath, 'today we start your training.'

'Training?' asked Jake excitedly. 'In what?'

'Transport!' announced Braysheath. 'If you wish to find your dear old granddad you'll be needing transport.'

'Transport?' asked Jake in an uncertain tone. 'What sort?'

'Rufus!' bellowed Braysheath.

There was no response.

'The thing about carpets, this particular type being exceedingly rare, is that they don't like a change of master.'

'Carpet?' said Jake, thinking Braysheath had gone mad.

'It's a sort of code of conduct among carpets, you see. Out of respect for their old master they mustn't too readily accept a new one. You've heard of breaking in a horse, I assume?'

'Of course, why?'

'Well, trying to win over a carpet is rather like that. Etiquette won't help and neither will tantrums or tears. You simply have to get on it and stay on until it agrees to co-operate.'

'You don't mean a magic carpet, do you?' asked Jake, astonished that they really existed, despite all the wonders he had already seen. The thought of having his own magic carpet was too amazing to believe.

'Rufus!' bellowed Braysheath. 'I know he's around here somewhere. He likes the shade. A real character, Rufus. You'll love him. Eventually.'

Something shot out from the spinney, flew into the cloister and tore through it like a storm.

'Aha! Here he comes!' cried Braysheath.

It moved so quickly that Jake couldn't make out its details. There was only the chaos and curses left in its wake.

In no time at all it had reached the banyan-clad arch of the courtyard entrance, made a sharp turn and, after a final burst, came to a halt beside them.

'Wow!' gasped Jake as he beheld the rippling red carpet with flamboyant green patterning. It was worn with age, though no less marvellous because of it.

'This is Rufus,' proclaimed Braysheath.

'It has a name?'

'Of course! Just like you it contains a soul. There are some carpets whose souls have been entrapped against their will—very tricky customers those ones. In Rufus's case he volunteered.'

'Volunteered? Why would anyone volunteer to be a carpet?' laughed Jake.

'You can ask him yourself,' said Braysheath, his eyes glinting with amusement.

Jake studied the carpet more closely. For some reason one of its corners was singed. It was making strange noises, alternating between a growl and a maniacal wheezing snigger. Its surface quivered menacingly.

'How does it work?' asked Jake.

'Souls in carpets are advanced souls with a thorough understanding of the five forces. They utilise their opposing charges to great effect while understanding the subtleties of their potential union. But don't worry about that now. Just bear in mind that the confluence of the forces is particularly strong about the House of Tusk so Rufus can zip along at quite a pace. He's far niftier than a flying horse or any other creature for that matter. And once you two have got used to each other's company, you'll find him an indispensable companion. Not only is he a source of speed, but a veritable storehouse of invaluable information. There are few places he can't take you this side of the Orijinn Sea. He'll be your companion on many a great adventure.'

Braysheath clapped his hands with relish. 'Right, Rufus! You ready?'

'Ach aye I'm ready!' roared Rufus in a broad Scottish accent and broke into another fit of growling-sniggering.

'It's Scottish,' remarked Jake.

'Indeed he is,' said Braysheath. 'But we forgive him.'

'And appears to be mad,' added Jake.

'The two tend to go hand in hand. Come on, up you get,' encouraged Braysheath. 'No one can pick up your granddad's scent like Rufus,' said Braysheath.

'Aye!' cried Rufus, 'It's nae difficult! Yer can smell a Burton a mile off. Like a badger's arse!'

'I've never smelt a badger's arse,' said Jake as he wearily approached Rufus. He gave the carpet a gentle prod. Like a skittish thoroughbred it bristled with energy.

'Stop dallying!' cried Braysheath. 'Hop on!'

Jake wasn't quite sure how to get on the carpet. It wasn't like swinging a leg over a horse and so he scrambled on using his knees. Before he could make himself comfortable, Rufus gave a powerful buck and threw Jake off head first, followed by a roar of laughter.

'See, that wasn't so bad, was it?' said Braysheath. 'I think he likes you.'

'Likes me?' cursed Jake as he picked himself up. 'Do you have a whip or a stick or something?'

On hearing this, Rufus's laughter grew madder still.

'Have another go,' suggested Braysheath.

Resisting the urge to give Rufus a kick, Jake slowly circled the sniggering rug. When he had reached what he assumed was its behind, he leapt on and gripped as tightly as he could.

Rufus's sniggering ceased immediately. He roared as though for battle, reared up and tore off at breakneck speed.

'Enjoy!' cried out Braysheath as they shot through the great archway and across the drawbridge.

Rufus plunged down the steep outcrop, brushing the cypresses as they went, making it even more difficult for Jake to hold on.

Rather than flying out over the savannah he rocketed up in a gut-wrenching loop-the-loop.

'Wahey!' he cried. 'Lovely day for it!'

Thrilled, terrified, Jake struggled to hold on.

'Is that all you've got?' he shouted and immediately regretted it as Rufus plummeted towards the savannah. He tore about the animals—between the legs of elephants, woke resting lions, rocketed through the foliage of trees, just missing a python in one and a leopard in the other.

Trumpeting and roars erupted behind them so that when Rufus looped back for a second lap, laughing madly, tusks and claws swiped at them. The python struck out and almost caught Jake.

Heart racing, Jake cursed in thought. *He's mad!*

The breaking in was turning out to be much more serious than expected. One false move from Rufus and Jake could be dead, yet he refused to give the carpet the satisfaction of knowing his fear.

'Yer grip's gettin' weaker!' cried Rufus as he shot through a charging herd of buffalo, making them even wilder. 'You'll not last long now, yer scrawny little whippet!'

'Rubbish!' retorted Jake through clouds of dust. 'You're so slow I'm simply relaxing!'

'Oh aye, yer lordship? Then we'd better liven things up a little!'

Rufus sped for the great lake.

Jake dreaded to think what Rufus had in mind. He didn't have to wait long to find out. Following a couple of wild circuits over the lake's surface, Jake sensed movement beneath it—lithe shadows rising up from the depths and moving with chilling stealth.

'This is just a lake, isn't it?' asked Jake, doing his best to sound calm.

'Ach no, it's much more than that!' said Rufus. 'It's connected to oceans! Wanna see what we keep in it?'

Before Jake could answer, the gaping jaws of an enormous great white shark burst through the surface right in front of them.

'Wahey!' cried Rufus again, swerving just in time.

Jake was horrified. Worse still, there was more movement beneath the surface ahead of them. Though his arms ached terribly, he gripped the carpet even tighter.

'Relaxing enough for yer?' enquired Rufus.

Jake didn't answer.

A moment later, not just one, but several sharks exploded through the surface within split seconds of each other. As soon as

Rufus escaped a set of jaws from the left, another appeared from the right and so on in a deathly slalom across the lake.

'Ach, I do love nature, don't you?' cried Rufus amid the horror before rocketing back up into the air. 'I'd love to introduce yer to the crocs but I donnae think you'd make it. But before yer fall to yer miserable death, there's something else I'd like to show yer!'

He nosedived for the fort, spinning in a tight corkscrew. Jake wasn't sure how much longer he could hold on.

Rufus pulled out of the dive an instant before colliding with the lawn and sped for the colonnade. Jake's vision cleared just in time to see Braysheath by the spinney clapping his hands with delight and roaring with laughter.

The next moment Rufus was racing about a large kitchen causing chaos. Jake ducked between the giant pots and vegetables hanging from the ceiling and sprites flitting about preparing food.

Rufus made a quick circuit then veered off towards a large storeroom though not before thwacking the fulsome behind of a woman reaching into the oven.

'Never miss a bender especially when it's tender!' he cried.

'Rufus!' she shrieked and a wooden spoon whistled past Jake's ear.

'Right arm like a navvy!' bawled Rufus. 'Just how I like 'em!'

Showing no signs of tiring, Rufus headed for an especially large pot hanging at the far end of the storeroom. Compared to the other pots there was something different about it—a peculiar darkness within its bowl began to swirl.

A gate! thought Jake, dreading where it might lead.

Rufus accelerated. 'How's yer grip, laddie?' he cried.

Rufus's comment gave Jake an idea. In the instant before reaching the ominous pot he spun around, grabbed a handful of the carpet's decorative threads and gave them a firm twist.

'Ach m'tassels!' howled Rufus, arced back in pain, veered off course and crashed into yet more pots and pans.

Remarkably, Jake was unharmed. As he scrambled to his feet, his head spinning, a company of sprites pounced on Rufus, swiftly followed by the formidable-looking cook. Their combined force pinned him to the ground.

'Thank you!' said Jake, greatly relieved to be free of Rufus.

'You're most welcome, Jake, son of Lawrence,' said the cook who had a pleasant face and manner. 'Merrywisp at your service, pixy and chief cook to the House of Tusk.'

'Pixy? But aren't you a little, you know, *tall* for a pixy?' commented Jake, for she looked no different from a human.

'Oh no, they're all about my size, though some are a little skinnier.'

Rufus meanwhile released an agonised groan. 'Ach, yer evil, *evil*, brute.'

Merrywisp's eyes shot wide with indignation. 'With your permission?' she asked of Jake, her large wooden spoon raised above her head.

'Be my guest,' replied Jake cheerfully.

Merrywisp treated Rufus to three powerful wallops with her spoon.

Rufus released a cry, though whether it was in pain or delight Jake couldn't quite tell.

'Three is an excellent number,' said Merrywisp.

'When I said evil brute, I was referring to that little fff–' started Rufus, but was cut short by another wallop.

'Are you sure that's working?' enquired Jake. 'It's his tassels that seem to be his weak point.'

'Aye, you'll pay for that yer rotten bastard.'

'I'm sorry, what was that?' broke in Merrywisp, her wooden spoon at the ready.

'I said… yoppyfad-at-yewrot-timbers-tard, which is ancient Celt for *Ouch that hurt. A lot.*'

'Doesn't sound very Celtic,' remarked Jake.

'Aye, well it's ancient, ain't it?'

'Do you submit?' asked Jake.

'Submit? To *you*? Never!' cried Rufus.

Merrywisp shrugged her shoulders, more than accustomed to his incorrigible ways.

It was then that Jake noted a second pot which also looked a little different from the rest.

'These pots with the dark insides, are they gates?' he asked.

'Indeed they are, my lord,' beamed a male sprite and sprang atop the one Rufus had been heading for. 'This one is the gate to London.'

'London? Really?' enthused Jake, delighted to hear of an alternative portal to Thanador's backside.

'Precisely, my lord! And this one,' said the sprite and leapt to the other pot, 'is especially exciting! It'll take you to a city called Penumbra. It lies between here and the Core, right in the centre of the Orijinn Sea. Wildly wild and wonderful, it is. Sincerely wild. Sincerely passionate. Sincerely murderous. Sincerely everything.'

'I like the sound of it!' said Jake, feeling reckless. 'It sounds even better than this place.'

'Oh, it is!' enthused several of the sprites in unison.

Jake cast a glance at Rufus before taking a step closer to it.

'And where d'yer think you're goin'?' growled Rufus, making a vain attempt to fly.

'Somewhere sincere,' replied Jake.

A female sprite leapt to Jake's side and took hold of his hand. 'I'll come with you if you like?' she said. 'I can show you around!'

'A southern jessie wouldnae last a second in a place like that,' scoffed Rufus.

'Well then, it's a good job I'm not one,' retorted Jake, quietly confident that Rufus was on the verge of submitting, realising that throughout the wild ride across the savannah Rufus had actually been protecting him, even as they crashed into the pots. As such, he would never allow Jake to pass to such a wild-sounding place as Penumbra without him.

'Thank you, madam sprite,' said Jake. 'That would be lovely. Shall we?'

'Yes! Let's! First we must take a little run up and then we leap!'

'Great. Farewell, Rufus!' said Jake as he and the sprite prepared for a run up.

'Good luck with the famous flesh-eatin' nut-cracker fish,' said Rufus, his surface rippling beneath its load. 'They're said to be especially fond of really annoying, scrawny little English pansies who run away at the first wee whiff of trouble.'

'Ready?' said Jake to the sprite. 'After three. One, two...'

'Pansies just as annoying as their dad,' added Rufus.

'What? What do you know of my dad?' said Jake, totally thrown by the reference.

'What d'yer mean, what do I know of yer dad, yer daft brush? Who d'yer think was m'previous master?'

Jake did indeed feel daft. Amid the horror of riding on Rufus, it hadn't occurred to him who the carpet's previous master had been. He suddenly recalled tales his dad had told of flying carpets, ones which must have referred to Rufus.

'So who's your master now?' ventured Jake.

'When I say *master*, what I really mean is someone whom I've kindly offered to guide and protect in perilous adventure, with whom to share my inordinate wisdom and unrivalled speed and skill,' bragged Rufus.

'Well, that's wonderful,' teased Jake, again preparing to dive through the gate. 'But I really must dash. Teatime in Penumbra and all that.'

'All right, all right, keep yer bloody knickers on. What I'm tryin' to say, yer grisly little monster, is that, if you can improve upon those highly questionable manners of yours, not least that savage handshake, well, I might be willin' to cooperate ever so slightly. On a trial-run basis, that is.'

A great rush of delight swept through Jake, though he did his best to conceal it.

'Hmm, I don't know. What do you think?' he asked the others.

'Carpets are wily things, my lord. Especially that one,' said the sprite holding his hand, though she winked at Jake as she said so.

Jake stood for a moment, pretending to ponder.

'I've reached a decision,' he announced finally. 'The wonderful Merrywisp and sprites have restored my faith in the House of Tusk, sufficiently at least to give some of its less pleasant parts a second chance. And so it is that I accept your submission.'

Rufus snorted in response. 'Have yer nae heard of magnanimity?' he snarled.

'Never heard of him,' replied Jake.

'Heavens help me,' groaned Rufus.

'Merrywisp—I think we can now release Rufus,' said Jake. 'On a trial-run basis, that is.'

'Oh, there's no rush,' purred Rufus, his surface vibrating, at which point Merrywisp leapt up and dealt him another thwack with her wooden spoon. 'Ach, I deserved that,' groaned Rufus. 'How about another?'

'Incorrigible!' cried Merrywisp throwing up her arms and turned to Jake. 'Well, if you'll not be having teatime in Penumbra, what do you say to a hearty breakfast at the House of Tusk?'

'I say brilliant!' beamed Jake and for the first time since arriving at the fort, he finally felt welcome.

CHAPTER 21
OMINOUS GUST

IT WAS VIRTUALLY UNHEARD OF TO RIDE A HORSE UP IN THE mountains of northern England, at least not in modern times, not off the bridle paths. Strictly speaking it was illegal. It was also highly dangerous, especially in winter when the many rocks on which a horse could twist an ankle were covered in snow. Frost, however, cared for neither. Rules were for fools as far as he was concerned. All that mattered was intuition.

His black stallion galloped along ridges with such grace that its hooves barely seemed to touch the ground. Yet more impressive, Frost was riding bareback.

He was approaching the crags of the final summit before the valley of Snow Fell Farm when the caw of a raven caused him to rein in and slow to a walk.

'Ah, Silver!' cried Frost. 'How now? What news from Egypt?'

Silver landed on the withers of the horse facing Frost and proceeded to croak and gargle.

'Excellent, Silver! You found the gate records,' said Frost, referring to the god gate and the secret trixie records of who passed through it. 'And Nestor Tusk was in the chamber beneath the Sphinx! I thought as much. But investigating what? Ha! Lawrence was there before! On his own? What? With Lord Boreas?' exclaimed Frost, his face a picture of delight. 'What happened? No? Really? Mortally wounded, Lawrence leapt into the gate after Boreas? This is just too fantastic! In theory only one could survive, though I wonder, it would be unprecedented, but these are mysterious times, Silver! Wouldn't it be exciting? Exciting beyond words!'

Silver cawed enthusiastically.

Frost took out a dead rabbit from his shoulder bag and laid it in front of Silver.

'Well done, Silver. And no one saw you? It would've been too suspicious if I'd gone myself.'

Silver croaked between mouthfuls of fur.

'Good. And now I wish for you to return. Again, use our shortcut. I want you to destroy the records. It'll be our little secret.'

Silver released a sharp caw.

'Oh don't worry about Father finding out. Though he'd cut off the head of anyone else, he won't harm me. He'll commend me! After a little explanation, of course. Besides, isn't he always saying it's high time I assumed the great responsibilities I'm destined to assume? Well, taking the initiative is surely the sign of a true leader. So don't worry, Silver. I know what I'm doing. Besides, there's something about this Jake. I sense it. And you know my nose is better than any of the others in the tribe.'

Silver said nothing. His sharp beak had reached the rabbit flesh and he was busy tearing away. While he did so, Frost suddenly sat up in his saddle and sniffed the air. His eyes sparkled with intrigue. Silver started, flew up and gargled in alarm. The horse grew skittish.

'Company,' muttered Frost.

He coaxed the horse forward between the crags, making no attempt to avoid what was a perfect place for an ambush.

At the point where the crags were highest and most narrow, a man and a woman leapt down onto the track and blocked the way. The horse reared up.

Perfectly poised and grinning, Frost glanced about the rest of the company. Two more had blocked the way behind. Six others were dotted about the crags on either side while birds of prey kept a lookout from above. All looked lean and dangerous. Like Frost's, their eyes glinted with a bright wildness that was more animal than human and highly intelligent. While Frost's were full of mischief, theirs were grave and fierce. In each of their hands were lethal-looking knives.

'Eight pixies, is that all?' enquired Frost jovially. 'I see my vanity has got the better of me. I thought I was good for at least twice that number.'

'You're not even worth one of us,' spat the woman in front, stepping forward. 'Nor is anyone else in your corrupt tribe.'

Frost looked her up and down and snorted in amusement. 'You confuse quantity with quality.'

'We don't mistake the levels you'll stoop to,' said the woman, 'especially your father, your so-called leader. You think we don't know of his taking sides with this pretender-Goddess Luna?'

Frost smiled wryly.

'We've tolerated your flaunting of nature's laws for too long,' continued the same woman. 'But if you directly intervene in the destiny of Jake Burton any more than you already have…'

Again the horse grew skittish.

All eight pixies tensed. Fear flickered in their eyes, despite their greater number.

'Yes?' enquired Frost as he steadied the horse. 'What will you do?'

'You've been warned,' said the man beside the woman.

'It's not much of a warning,' remarked Frost and tittered. 'You lot need to move with the times and stop second-guessing nature's laws and destiny. After all, do not laws themselves evolve?'

'Not these ones,' said a man on the crags to Frost's right.

'Oh how you worship the Creator,' laughed Frost. 'The Great Mechanic who supposedly put these laws in place and was then content to simply sit back and let things unfold. Ha! What naivety! Have you ever met this Great Mechanic, this Great Lawmaker?'

None of the company said anything. All remained tense.

'Well,' said Frost, 'I've a feeling you're about to and soon. Just as I have a feeling that Jake Burton will shortly be calling upon me and asking my advice. And who am I to refuse one so prophetic?'

No sooner had Frost finished his sentence than a strong gust blew through the crags from behind him, whisked up the snow and buffeted all of them.

'Ah, an omen!' cried Frost. 'Mother Nature ushers me on!'

Heeding the call, Frost boldly rode forward and forced aside the two blocking his way. 'Farewell, little brothers, little sisters! To destiny!'

The woman readied to hurl her knife, but was checked by the man beside her.

Silver swept over them cawing and landed on Frost's shoulder.

'Not now,' muttered the man, glancing back in the direction the wind had blown from. 'That was unexpected. But we mustn't defy the wind. There must be more to this than we, or even he, realises. We must bide our time.'

The woman also glanced back before returning her gaze to Frost as he cockily rode away. Her eyes narrowed. 'There is no time, not for his kind. They must change or their world must come to an end.'

CHAPTER 22
ZARZANZAMIN

Following such an eventful morning, Jake had been allowed to spend the rest of the day exploring the fort. Rufus had taken him on a more civilised tour and had proven to be excellent company. By the end of the day they were almost friends. Jake was also exhausted. After a light supper beneath an apple tree on the ramparts, he went to bed early.

Sometime during the night he awoke to a huge explosion. He leapt from bed but immediately crashed to the floor with the aftershock.

Having just managed to jump into his jeans he tore out onto the balcony overlooking the courtyard. Others were scrambling across the lawn and heading for the spiral staircase. After another quake, Jake followed.

He had barely set foot on the stairs when he was swept up by Rufus who flew downwards at breakneck speed.

'What's happening?' shouted Jake.

'Somethin's broken into the fort!'

'Again? How's that possible?'

'I don't know but I've got a horrible feelin'…'

Rufus was cut short by another quake that almost sent them crashing into the stairwell wall.

'Where's it coming from?' asked Jake.

'Must be from the level of the gates.'

'Which gates?'

'The backdoor gates to the Peregrinus along with the holy-gates of the Scribes.'

'Scribes?'

'They work for Nemesis, monitoring every thought and action of every human,' replied Rufus, confirming Jake's earlier feeling.

A moment later Rufus swept from the stairwell, shot around a corner and flew in through a great arch to another courtyard. It was the same dimensions as the one above except instead of lawn there was flagstone, like that of a huge plaza. Each side contained a great arch leading to a hall. It was a scene of total chaos. They had scarcely entered when something large and brown and travelling at great speed just missed them and slammed into the wall.

'A grizzly!' exclaimed Jake, gawping at the unconscious bear.

There wasn't just one. The courtyard was full of them charging in all directions in the manner of guards. The shock of seeing a grizzly up close was nothing to what protruded from one of the shattered archways—a reptilian tail and a body the size of a large dinosaur.

'Just as I feared!' cried Rufus. 'One of the Zarzanzamin!'

'My God! Is it a dragon?' asked Jake.

'They look like them, but no. They ship rocks around the Peregrinus to maintain balance—a great responsibility. If there's one creature strong and wise enough to break in here so brazenly, its them. But it's unheard of. They're ancient creatures beyond corruption.

Another deafening crack shook the air, followed by a powerful quake.

A terrible nausea swept through Jake.

'Rufus, I feel... I think I'm going to be...'

'Of course! Inner-force! The creature is contaminated with rocks from the Inner-Peregrinus! Hang in there and keep yer head,' said Rufus and raced off with Jake towards the tail.

He hadn't gone half the distance when the enormous beast wrenched itself free of the hall and sent yet more of the archway hurtling through the air. A large chunk missed Jake's head by only inches.

The sight of the beast rearing up, its neck pressed up against the high-domed ceiling was so awesome that for a moment Jake quite forgot his nausea. Its primordial eyes bulged in their sockets. Smoke billowed from its mouth. The mighty beast seemed to be trying to digest something which was causing it great pain. Grizzlies and sprites dotted about the courtyard gazed on as dumb-struck as Jake.

Finally it released an ear-piercing shriek, plunged its head into the pool of the courtyard's fountain that caused a pulse of energy so powerful that everyone was floored.

By the time they recovered, the beast was gone.

'A hidden portal in the fountain!' gasped Rufus. 'I had no idea. And here of all places!'

'Isn't someone going to follow it?' Jake suggested.

'After you, your lordship,' said Rufus dryly and flew off with Jake to the damaged archway.

In the hall beyond it, apart from several injured grizzlies, were three smouldering holes, one in each wall.

'Ach bugger,' muttered Rufus.

'What?' asked Jake.

'It beggars belief, but it's somehow swallowed not only one but all three of the secret gates—to Leaf, Roar and Hunter, the three death dimensions of the Outer-Peregrinus.'

'What does it mean?'

'I dread to think,' groaned Rufus. 'But somethin' terrible.'

Another pulse burst from the courtyard and again sent everyone flying.

Having dragged himself to his feet, what Jake beheld was even more incredible than before. Another of the Zarzanzamin had arrived through the fountain. It released a harrowing shriek and stretched its wings that virtually filled the entire courtyard. Sitting behind its pointed ears was a man. Or rather, a god.

'Boreas! How the hell could he know that the fountain was a portal?' growled Rufus, not realising that it was Lawrence in disguise, carrying out Luna's orders to steal the gates that were key to her plan to topple Brock the Overlord.

Foe or not, he struck Jake as magnificent. He looked like a Viking. Lord Boreas inhaled deeply of the air as though it gifted him power. His piercing blue eyes surveyed the courtyard.

Reinforcements arrived in the courtyard. Grizzlies, sprites and other staff were poised for attack, though looked pathetic against such a creature. Their target, however, was Lord Boreas. Arrows, darts and spears flew through the air with lethal accuracy, yet he deflected them with effortless flashes of his Samurai-like blade.

At the sight of them, Lord Boreas roared with mocking laughter. 'Is that it? Is that the best you can do?' he bellowed in a powerful voice. 'Where's that *fool* Braysheath?'

At his command, the mighty beast roared out a fearsome jet of flame.

In an instant, Rufus had smothered Jake to protect him. What he couldn't protect Jake from was another noxious belch of inner-force that accompanied the flames. It was so powerful that Jake felt as though he were dissolving.

As Lord Boreas bellowed with laughter at all the confusion, Rufus shook Jake by the shoulders.

'Are yer all right, laddie? Christ that were a strong dose! Jake fella, come back to me!'

Jake didn't hear him. Rufus's pleas dissolved with everything else.

When Jake came round, his consciousness was somewhere else entirely—in the very place he least wished to be. He was back in the woods of his nightmare, the ones which had led him to Nemesis and the ghosts.

On his hands and knees, he felt the weight of other presences. Though the mist was too dense to see them, he could sense them moving closer, pressing in from every side, many more than before and much darker-feeling.

Suddenly the ghostly hands of those closest reached out through the mist. What little awareness was left to Jake threatened to dissolve completely.

There's no point in running, he thought, recalling what had happened the last time. *I must remember who I am! Must hold on! I'm Jake... the farmhouse, the House of Tusk, must get back...'*

Despite his efforts, as the hands moved closer and more phantoms pressed in from behind, Jake was losing his grip on the reality he knew. His mind clawed at anything to hold on to—a memory, a feeling, anything, but the darkness came too quickly.

Suddenly something stuck. It was a memory from the spinney, the same night of his nightmare—the memory of dad, granddad and Bill playing cricket. Imaginary or not, it didn't matter. It was like a bridge, a critical link to what he knew and loved. Above all, it was so bursting with genuine joy, so carefree and timeless, that it seemed to glow within his heart.

The more he focused on it, breathing life into it, so the glow grew brighter and brighter until Jake shone like a sun.

'Granddad!' he cried defiantly, rising up on one knee and stating his purpose. 'I'm here to save Granddad! I'm here to save Nestor Burton!'

The dark hands reaching out to take hold of him hesitated for a moment. A grim male face appeared, scrutinised Jake and, sensing a chink of weakness, was about to grasp him when his eyes suddenly widened. He recoiled back into the mist—not from Jake, but something behind him.

Jake spun around. A wan light shone through the mist. He recognised it immediately and his new-found spirit wavered. It was the light of a lantern.

The same ghost! He felt it in his bones.

The lantern grew in size until it was all Jake could see. A face loomed up behind it, a flicker of red in its beard. Its ghostly eyes widened as it inhaled then closed as it blew towards Jake through the eye of light in the lantern. Something dark shot forth from the underbelly of the flame.

Face and lantern suddenly retreated to their true distance as the darkness tore through the misted woods towards Jake. Phantoms scattered before it like birds to gunshot.

Jake knew there was nothing to do. His only choices in the split-second left to him were to close his eyes or watch on, to remain on one knee or to try and stand. Eyes open, he tried the latter.

His legs had barely straightened when the darkness struck him like a cannon ball.

Instead of flattened, his body went taut with power.

Back in the courtyard he leapt to his feet and cast Rufus aside.

'Whoa there, tiger, whoa there!' cried Rufus.

But Jake, or whatever it was that had possessed him, paid no attention.

Lord Boreas was on the verge of spurring the beast to action when, having sensed something, he spun around and locked gazes with Jake. His eyes widened with surprise and glinted with a complex light.

The awareness in Jake felt so detached, so lacking in emotion that it seemed alien. And yet, not entirely. There was also something familiar, though it was too distant to make sense of.

To Jake's eyes the courtyard had transformed. Though still the courtyard, it was delineated in light, the creatures included. He was seeing reality more deeply. Everything was alive, even the stones, and connected by particles of light. The connection between somethings was faint, as fine as dust in sunbeams. Others were denser, flowing like streams. It was like a strange three-dimensional ever-shifting web without a centre. The connection between Lord Boreas and Jake was particularly thick.

Suddenly, the web flickered. As Lord Boreas returned his attention to the task at hand, a powerful intention from somewhere above and to the right of him pulsed out through the web and struck Jake like a sting. Without flinching, he focused on a ventilation shaft. Concealed to all but him was someone hiding just inside, someone slight and strongly connected to himself.

With his special insight, he recognised her immediately. It was the warrior girl who had spied on him from the crags above the farmhouse. But that's not all she was. Jake recognised her soul and connected it with the same dangerous presence behind the many scenes of destruction in his woodland nightmare. This time she was holding a bow, fully drawn, the arrow pointing at Lord Boreas.

He felt her breathing as though it were his own, steady and composed. He felt her slightly shift her aim and knew the exact moment the aim was true, for the web of light not only flickered but almost went out.

As Lord Boreas commanded his beast to lunge at the arch through which all light was connected, the girl unleashed her arrow.

In that fateful moment Jake knew that if the arrow struck its target, more than Lord Boreas would fall. He felt it through the web. The connections were so complex, so intricate, so mysterious, especially between Lord Boreas, Rani and himself, that to remove one so abruptly would be catastrophic not just for themselves, but for many more. Perhaps for the entire cosmos.

'No!' commanded Jake as he struck out a hand in the direction of the arrow. The command had come from the pit of his belly. Imbued with great power, it rose up, flowed out along his arm and shot through the web like lightning.

The arrow was midway to its target when it suddenly slowed, glowed and disintegrated into particles of light that flowed into the restored web.

Rufus watched on astounded.

Lord Boreas was equally dumbstruck. As his beast lunged for the grand archway, he glanced at Jake.

Had Jake not been so focused on the storm of anger surging out from the ventilation shaft, he might have noticed a shift in the complexity of Lord Boreas's expression. Aside from surprise there were other emotions. One was concern. The other was pride, fleeting but clear—the pride of a father.

A moment later, the mighty beast tore a great chunk from the grand archway, revealing a remarkable octagonal hall. Six of its sides each contained a dazzling smaller archway encrusted with stars. They were the primary holygates which connected the worlds of the Peregrinus between the Surface and the Core—the soul portals of the cosmos. At the hall's centre was a Victorian-style rotunda. It too appeared to be some sort of gate, inside of which was the mosaic-like surface of a salt plain at whose centre, though out of sight, was the mystical woodland of Nemesis and the Scribes. Along with the light which streamed out from the rotunda were fairy-like creatures. They flitted over maps on tables pored over by sprites before darting off into one of the other gates.

None of the busy creatures gave more than a glance at the extraordinary intrusion. Not even the sprites closest to the archway who, using long sticks, shunted stars around the mapped-out cosmos that lined the walls of the hall. Their work, the allocation of souls, required total focus.

'What in the name of Odin's crows is goin' on?' exclaimed Rufus, thunderstruck by Jake's defence of Lord Boreas who was only a moment away from stealing a holygate.

Chaos erupted as the beast took another great bite from the archway. Grizzlies and sprites redoubled the attack.

Jake, however, was facing the other direction. He was staring into the shadows of the opposite arch, the one that he and Rufus had arrived through. The power which had gifted him insight and dissolved the arrow was receding back to its source via the rotunda. Jake's head grew light. Yet the effect was still strong enough for him to notice another detail. Someone was hiding through the entrance—a man in form but one with power. Jake felt the intensity of the man's interest in what was happening, along with his anxiety. Like everyone else he was connected to the web, to two people in particular. One was Jake. The other was Lord Boreas.

As Jake teetered on the verge of passing out, Rufus was about to sweep him up when a dreadful sound erupted from the other end of the courtyard. The mighty creature had ripped out one of the holygates. Another pulse of energy, more powerful than the others, sent everyone flying, Jake included.

The beast wrenched its head free from the battered hall. Like the one before it, it reared up as high as the hall permitted and released an agonised shriek—so ear-splitting that Jake's full awareness snapped back and the web of light disappeared.

Feeling faint, he looked up just in time to see the beast lunge forward for the gate in the fountain. In that moment he exchanged glances with Lord Boreas one more time.

The god was smiling yet there was nothing smug in it. The smile was one of gratitude.

With a final pulse, the god and the beast were gone.

Jake's consciousness slipped away though not before one final image imprinted itself upon his memory. The man hiding about the main entrance stepped from the shadows, except it wasn't man. It was another god—the very one Jake suspected of betraying the fort.

Asclepius.

CHAPTER 23
FATAL KISS

LAWRENCE WAS BACK IN HIS OFFICE AT THE TOP OF RENLOCK, gazing out at a grey, misty sky and a grey sea, a troubled light in his bright blue eyes. In front of him was a hot bowl of soup, but he didn't touch it. Despite the success of stealing the gates with minimal damage to the House of Tusk, he couldn't enjoy it for it only brought forward the next great challenge, one only moments away. Luna had just arrived for another visit. At least she hadn't seen through his cover as he feared she had on her last appearance at Renlock. If she had then she hadn't let on.

Wilderspin was currently leading her to one of Renlock's many secret vault-like halls—the one in which the stolen holygate had recently been placed. The three secret backdoor gates to Roar, Leaf and Hunter had been placed in another.

Just then a seagull swept between the clouds. It was the first time Lawrence had seen one on Renlock. In a world of grey—clouds, sea, granite, pigeons and more besides—it was like a ray of sun and summoned a tired smile.

Geoffrey was clinging to the wall on the lookout for a fly.

'I've a nasty feeling about this ceremony. You'd best be prepared for anything,' he said. 'When she releases the sylph into the holygate it's going to be interesting, to put it mildly.'

'I wonder how she'll get it into the gate,' said Lawrence, continuing to gaze out to sea. 'She can't risk going in herself. Her gravity is too great. It might collapse the gate. Though surely the sylph will need a host.'

'That's why I have a nasty feeling,' said Geoffrey.

Lawrence turned and stared at Geoffrey questioningly. His eyes widened slightly. 'You don't think?'

'You must be prepared for *anything*,' repeated Geoffrey. 'Any shocks will weaken you further. Remember, Boreas will not have wasted a moment since your last encounter in the dream room. He'll have been busy scouring the hells for your most troublesome demon. He's probably already found it. The slightest crack in your resolve and the demon will come crashing into your reality.'

Lawrence got up and paced the room. 'Whatever demon he's dug up, I shall embrace it. It's the only way. It must be integrated. To fight it will only give it strength.'

'That's the theory,' said Geoffrey. 'But as I've already explained, he'll have gone as deep into your unconscious as his keys will take him, to the very dregs of the sixth dimension. Have no doubt, he'll have found a horror—a truth too great for someone at your point in evolution. One you'll deny. If you try and embrace it too soon, you'll be in trouble.'

'I may not be able to embrace it, not at first, but I shall not deny it. Not taking responsibility will only make things worse. Little by little, I'll find the common ground.'

'I look forward to seeing it,' said Geoffrey in a doubtful tone. 'Remember, you'll not be dealing with it in isolation. Not only is there Luna to contend with, but also the young Lord Tusk.'

Lawrence stopped his pacing and stared into the fire which burned at the room's centre. It brought him little warmth. His brow furrowed. Something else he was unable to enjoy was Jake saving him from the arrow. It had been his son and yet it hadn't. Instead of the light and lively youth he loved, Jake had looked cold and hard as though in a trance.

Is all that I love to become possessed? he wondered as he squatted in front of the fire.

'That was an old power that flowed through Jake in the courtyard and saved your skin,' said Geoffrey.

'But to whom did the power belong?'

'To him of course,' replied Geoffrey. 'It couldn't have belonged to another, not whilst in the fort. Remember, we managed to break in not only because of the boldness of your plan to use the Zarzanzamin, but because we had insider knowledge. In other words, my knowledge of the fort and its loopholes and your right of passage as the previous Lord Tusk. It's the same with the new Lord Tusk—the fort will only allow passage to energy it recognises and accepts.'

Lawrence rubbed his chin, staggered that his own son had such power in his lightline.

'To do what was done to the arrow would require the power often associated with ghosts,' said Geoffrey.

'Ghosts?'

'The type who have disassociated from their lightline in order to investigate the great mysteries, primordial darkness especially, though they have the power to reconnect if they choose to.'

'Do you think Jake was in control of the ghost?' asked Lawrence.

'No. But to have been open to it and to have survived its passage proves he's strong. How strong remains to be seen.'

'Then...' started Lawrence, gazing deeper into the flames. 'Then whose skin was this ghost intent on saving? Do you think it knew who I really was?'

'The dream room is unique and powerful,' said Geoffrey, eyeing a moth fluttering close by. 'Whether such a ghost could see through the illusion is difficult to say. Such beings are difficult to gauge and unpredictable. Like your friend the charred angel in Pandora's Box, they often have their own vision of how the cosmos should be.'

While Geoffrey darted forward and caught the moth, Lawrence slowly shook his head, not knowing what to think. He closed his eyes, drew a deep breath and felt the wolf spirit inside of him. This was his new trick for maintaining presence in both Renlock and the dream room—visualising and feeling his every breath as that of the wolf's.

When he next opened his eyes he was the wolf in the dream room. Little had changed. The doors and doorframes continued to shift at varying speeds, reflecting his pre-occupied mind. All except one—the innocent seeming door that led to the garden paradise in which the real Lord Boreas had recently appeared. Though it was closed, Lawrence noticed something new in a corner of the doorframe—a spider was weaving a web. The symbolism was clear.

Boreas, he thought. *Geoffrey's right. He's not wasting a moment.*

Lawrence brought his focus back to Renlock, stood up from the fire and returned to the window.

'Given the timing of Jake becoming Lord Tusk, for these are desperate and momentous times, it makes sense that the Scribes would have chosen a soul which was...'

'Extreme?' offered Geoffrey. 'One whose past is steeped in power, along with its misuse. One whose destiny is so in the balance that his favour could swing in either direction? He has a great leap to make. Perhaps he'll have the courage to lead humans through their deepest fears at a time when they're most lost. Yet he might just as easily create chaos.'

'What sort of chaos?'

'What's the worse you can imagine?'

'Are you serious? Well, it can't get worse than Luna seeking a hidden exit from the cosmos and leaving with as much light as possible?'

'Can't it?'

Lawrence was about to take issue when he felt a sudden chill. He turned from the window in search of Geoffrey who had disappeared. Instead he found a dark-robed guardian of the inner-force.

'Goddess Luna expects you below. I shall escort you,' it said in the emotionless tone of the guardians, more a command than a request.

At the mention of Luna, Lawrence's heartbeat threatened to race. Maintaining a façade of haughtiness, he took a long and deep breath as the wolf, before finally gathering his sword and cloak and following the guardian down the steps.

MANY FLIGHTS DOWN THE STAIRWELL DEEP INSIDE RENLOCK'S great wall and after many twists and turns along dark passages, the guardian finally stopped in front of a granite wall. He placed his silvery hands against its surface. Following a strange vibration through rock and air, an archway appeared. They passed through it and the archway resealed itself.

Inside was a simple hall bereft of decoration. There was only a granite throne at the far end. Sitting upon it was Luna. She was flanked by both the guardian commander and Wilderspin who was busy describing something in his usual ingratiating manner. Luna's attention, however, was elsewhere. She was watching Lawrence. He was visibly taken aback at the sight of her, for yet again she had changed. This time her appearance was entirely human. Any sign of the tree she had used to transfer her immense presence into the body of Rowena had completely gone. Robed in purple, her fiery red hair wound up atop her head, she had the air of a witch. Above all, it was in her eyes. Though still green, there was something of the East in their shape and they shone with fierce allure.

A melancholy howl escaped the wolf in the dream room.

'Are you alright, Lord Boreas?' she said, bemused. 'You seem upset.'

Lawrence took a moment to collect himself, which wasn't helped by the sight of Luna's sylph-shadow. Paying no attention to the direction of the light cast by the torches on the wall, it moved about her at will, shifting its form between that of an eagle and that of a snake.

'My lady,' he said finally. 'I'm not upset. I am simply stunned.'

'By what?' she asked.

'By you, my lady,' he managed. 'Words fail me.'

'Words fail *you*, Lord Boreas?' she said delighted. 'The Lord of the Sirens whom I chose for his charm has *lost* his words?'

'Indeed, my lady.'

'Well, don't make a habit of it. You'll be needing them. I have work for you on the Surface.'

Lawrence bowed his head in acquiescence.

'Well I certainly haven't lost my words!' chimed in Wilderspin. 'My lady, you shine like a jewel! One so brilliant that it would take but the tiniest fraction of you to illumine an entire cosmos, as indeed it shortly will.'

Luna ignored Wilderspin as she continued to study Lawrence.

'Control yourself,' warned Geoffrey from beside the flickering candle on the table in the dream room. 'You've another shock coming your way. I've just learned how Luna plans to carry the sylph into the gate. My suspicions were correct.'

Fortunately the entrance to the hall reappeared, causing Luna to shift her gaze to the two guardians who entered.

Lawrence's respite was short-lived. The guardians were escorting the chosen host for the sylph.

Just as Geoffrey had suspected, it was Nestor, Lawrence's dad.

Lawrence's heart sank. He might have lost his balance completely were it not for Nestor's presence—far from appearing haggard by imprisonment, he strode in with his usual chirpy air.

Nestor was old-school, from his tweed sports jacket, club tie and deerstalker hat to his dignified countenance and the suave twinkle in his kind eyes.

Unabashed by the enormity of his company, Nestor slowly took in his surroundings with the eye of one who missed nothing. Having given Lawrence a long appraising look and unable to conceal a smile at the sight of Wilderspin, his gaze finally settled on Luna.

'Lovely,' he said at last. 'Quite lovely.'

Luna smiled enigmatically.

'I like the shadow,' added Nestor.

'I'm glad you like it,' said Luna 'because it's about to become yours.'

'I'd heard rumours,' said Nestor as though it were nothing.

'Rumours? Impossible!' interrupted Wilderspin. 'Simply impossible! Not here in Renlock.'

'The ants, Wheelspin, old boy,' said Nestor, deliberately mispronouncing Wilderspin's name. 'They're worse gossips than even the pigeons.'

'Nonsense!' scoffed Wilderspin. 'No one can talk Ant except the ants! And I should know. It took me a century to learn pigeon.'

'Morse code,' replied Nestor smiling. 'They're excellent at Morse code.'

'The sooner we silence him the better,' said Wilderspin. 'He's been a menace long enough. Shall we get on with it, my lady?'

Luna raised a hand to silence Wilderspin. 'We've chosen well in you, Nestor Tusk,' she said. 'I think the sylph will enjoy you. At least long enough to jam the gate a while.'

'I'm sure we'll get on famously,' remarked Nestor. 'In fact, I'm rather looking forward to it.'

'And so you should. If all goes to plan, you're about to become the cosmos's largest ever contraceptive.'

'Am I really? Ha-ha! What do you think of that, Lord Boreas?' said Nestor and gave Lawrence a wink.

Lawrence's expression remained impassive. Inside, however, his heart soared at his dad's humour.

'Well,' added Nestor, 'I suppose it's true what they say. What one sows one reaps.'

'In doing so,' continued Luna, ignoring the comment, 'you'll be playing a fundamental part in the downfall of your Surface god, Brock. It's a great honour.'

'Delighted to be of service. I expect Brock will also be delighted. I'm amazed he's lasted so long. What is it, two thousand years he's been up there now? Not bad when up against someone as tricky as you.'

'What are you talking about?' said Wilderspin. 'Goddess Luna has only just taken up residence.'

'As quick as ever I see, Wheelspin. But I assure you it's quite clear to the rest of us,' said Nestor glancing at the guardians and Lawrence, whose impassive expression shifted if only for a moment. 'Our delightful Luna here has been busy on the Surface since the retreat of the last Ice Age. She's simply shifting her strategy.'

Wilderspin glanced between Nestor and Luna in disbelief. 'Is this so, my lady?'

Luna didn't reply. Her smiling gaze was fixed on Nestor.

Though Nestor's manner was true to form, Lawrence was amazed his dad spoke so plainly in front of someone as powerful as Luna.

The boldness of age! he thought.

'We live in ironic times,' said Nestor in a tone that seemed to speak directly to Lawrence, and glanced down at the sylph shadow, which had remained quite still while he had spoken.

Lawrence also studied the shadow, wondering if his dad was making a hint. *Is there something we're missing—some deeper connection between the sylph and Luna?* he wondered.

'Well, enough with history. The present is much more fun, is it not?' added Nestor glancing back at Lawrence. 'Shall we do as our dear friend Wheelspin suggests and get on with it?'

At another reference to the head of Renlock as *Wheelspin,* Lawrence's eyes shone with amusement.

'Yes, let's,' agreed Luna and rose up from the throne.

'Brilliant!' enthused Wilderspin and clapped his hands together with relish. 'You do realise what you're about to absorb, don't you?'

'I have an idea, Wheelspin old boy. But it can't be half as bad as a mouthful of Bill's homemade gin,' said Nestor and almost caused Lawrence to bark with laughter.

'Bill?' enquired Wilderspin.

'Consider yourself lucky you've never met him,' said Nestor.

Luna crossed the hall and stopped short of Nestor. She reached up and removed his deerstalker hat to reveal his well-groomed gun-metal grey hair.

'There, that's much better. How handsome you look.'

'That's precisely why I wear it. One needs one's peace.'

Nestor's eyebrows suddenly rose as something emerged through Luna's cleavage. It was a lethal-looking red serpent. 'How novel,' he remarked.

Without a word, Luna took it in her hand, withdrew a knife from her robes and cut off its head. She then held its body above her head and drank down the blood.

'It'll soften the blow,' she said to Nestor once she had finished.

Two guardians appeared either side of Nestor and were about to take hold of his arms when Luna waved them away.

'I don't think that'll be necessary,' she said, gazing intently into Nestor's deep brown eyes. Her own flashed green. 'So, Nestor Tusk, are you ready for the kiss of your life?'

'I'm always ready for a good kiss,' replied Nestor, unruffled by the goddess's proximity. 'Though I should warn you, I was once set upon by Aphrodite, so it had better be good.'

'Oh, I think we can do better than that,' said Luna and gently touched Nestor's face.

Despite his cool, Nestor's body stiffened. The veins of his face suddenly surfaced and protruded grimly. He gasped as something of his light passed through Luna's hand.

Wracked with torment, it took great restraint for Lawrence not to leap forward and force them apart, even though such an act would be the end of him.

'With respect, my lady,' he interrupted instead. 'Are we sure this is the best way? I can't imagine how he could survive absorbing the entire sylph in one go. Perhaps...'

'It's not your imagination I value,' said Luna, maintaining her gaze on Nestor. 'Be silent.'

Lawrence nodded, closed his eyes and drew a deep inward breath.

Luna did the same as she prepared to transfer the sylph, which danced wildly about her feet like a caged beast sensing freedom.

Having taken her hand away from Nestor's cheek, her next inhale drew up the shadow.

Her body darkened as it progressed upwards. So too did the hall. The torches went out. The only source of light was Luna herself—it came from her aura. Suddenly visible, it blanketed Nestor like light from the moon.

In the half-light beyond, Wilderspin fidgeted with excitement.

The shadow fully absorbed, Luna held it in check at her throat. Her eyes blazed like infernos. Again she took hold of Nestor's face, this time with both hands. Again he stiffened.

A strange light flashed through his widened eyes as though he were seeing things beyond the scope of the room, beyond his comprehension.

Luna moved her blood-stained lips closer to Nestor's. The lights in her eyes took on a fascinated glint, apparently sharing what Nestor was seeing.

Her aura grew brighter.

A storm blew up and raged about Renlock.

Her lips moved closer still and parted slightly.

With a rumble of thunder, finally their lips met.

At first, nothing remarkable happened. The shadow remained at the level of her throat. She kissed him as a lover. The first kiss, the last kiss, tender and pregnant with mystery.

Luna withdrew a fraction, gazed into his eyes and smiled.

When she next kissed him, she released the shadow. It rushed up from her throat to her lips and passed to Nestor's.

Lightning and thunder shook Renlock.

Wilderspin's eyes shot wide with perverse relish, Lawrence's with shock. Even the guardians looked surprised.

Nestor was turning to stone.

Only his horror-struck eyes remained untouched.

The sylph inside him, Luna stepped back and watched on with fascination as his body underwent further transformation. One moment as solid as a statue, Nestor's body began to crack. Cracks spread through him like veins yet Nestor didn't crumble. Instead the cracks deepened and became like the bark of a tree, which immediately blackened and charred and changed again, this time to a reptilian type of skin, like that of a crocodile.

When Nestor's skin was finally his own again, his body was withered as though he had aged centuries in a matter of seconds. All but a corpse, the only sign of life remained in his eyes. They had grown misted, however, like those of a serpent before shedding its skin.

He teetered for a moment on shaky legs. His lips moved though no words escaped.

Before he collapsed completely, Lawrence dashed forward and caught him.

'I never thought I'd run to the rescue of this devil,' he said, glancing up at Luna. 'But now that he might finally be of use to us, we can't take risks.'

Nestor reached up a hand towards Lawrence.

Afraid of the effect it might have, Lawrence gently laid him on the ground and moved away.

Luna was watching Lawrence with intense curiosity.

'That will be all, Wilderspin,' she said.

Wilderspin looked hesitant, clearly not wishing to miss any excitement. 'My lady,' he said at last, before bowing and departing.

'Commander,' continued Luna, her gaze still fixed on Lawrence. 'Take Nestor into the gate.'

The commander picked up Nestor's frail body and with a flash of his dark cloak transformed into a magnificent silver lion. With Nestor slumped across his back, he shook his mane. Silver dust filled the air, a guardian magic which revealed the stolen holygate in the granite wall—an abyss within an arch of stars, just as it had been in the House of Tusk.

The commander focused on the gate. His sapphire-coloured eyes shone yet brighter. A leap later he was gone.

Remarkably, Luna hadn't watched any of it. Her attention had remained on Lawrence.

'That was brave, Lord Boreas,' she remarked. 'It's curious that you were unaffected by contact with the sylph. You're more powerful than I thought.'

Lawrence said nothing. He was focused on staying centred in both the hall, along with the dream room. Throughout the transfer of the sylph to Nestor, he had sensed the presence of the Siberian tiger and as Luna approached him it grew more intense as though it were right behind him.

The wolf spun around but the dream room was empty. The doors, though shifting at high speed, remained closed.

Regardless, as Luna approached Lawrence from the front, the invisible presence of the tiger moved closer from behind. When she finally stopped in front of Lawrence, he felt the tiger's breath upon his neck as though realities had already merged.

They hadn't, Lawrence knew that. It was a threat from Lord Boreas—that they could merge at any moment if he wanted them to, that the garden door could blast open and the tiger leap in. If not the tiger then something worse—one of Lawrence's darkest demons.

A base and rancid titter from over his shoulder reverberated through Lawrence in confirmation.

'Steady,' advised Geoffrey from the dream room table. 'Remember, if you feel trapped, observe yourself as though another person. Identify with the observer, not Lawrence, not your lower-self and all its fear. Identify with the sea, the sky, the air—infinity in other words. This is your advantage. And judge nothing.'

'What a dark one you are, Lord Boreas,' said Luna studying his eyes intently.

How tempting, said the tiger. *So close, hmm, so tempting.*

Battling to maintain his composure, Lawrence did his best to observe himself from the outside

'Well, I am the God of Greed, my lady,' he managed in as light a tone as possible. 'It goes with the job.'

Oh, if only she knew, purred the tiger, followed by a low growl. *But as your scaly friend has already guessed, I have something better in mind. In fact, there's someone I'd like you to meet.*

A chill dread shuddered through Lawrence.

'What is it I sense in you?' said Luna intrigued. 'A troubled soul? What is it you're battling, Lord Boreas? You haven't discovered a conscience have you? What a revelation that would be, not to mention a nuisance.'

Stay centred, warned Geoffrey.

'A conscience, my lady!' laughed Lawrence awkwardly. 'No, nothing like that.'

Instead of speaking, Luna gently touched her right hand to his left cheek.

The shock was too great. The intention and the power behind it was Luna's, but the hand belonged to Rowena—a hand whose touch he knew too well. A touch he craved. A touch he longed to feel as he once had in more innocent times—on summer days running through pastures and swimming in rivers, on winter nights wrapped up in blankets and all the moments she had taken him by surprise, wrapped herself about him as though nothing else mattered in the world. It was a touch that knew every pathway to Lawrence's pain and, in a matter of moments, reached it.

Lawrence was fully back within his lower-self as though Luna's hand had reached out through his pain and hauled the observer back inside of him.

Everything went dark—the hall, the dream room. Both floors gave way or so it seemed. Though he stood before Luna stony-faced, his soul was in freefall, into the abyss towards flames—an inferno shot through with the cruel laughter of Lord Boreas.

It lasted just moments but felt like eternity.

Remember the sky, came a familiar voice through the void. Lizard magic was powerful magic. Geoffrey's voice was like a hand that swept Lawrence up and placed him back in the re-formed dream room.

'Restore your place of power,' suggested Geoffrey from the table.

With great effort, Lawrence focused on one of the doors and bent his mind to the task.

Miraculously, the door opened and there it was—the pinnacle with the oak, connected to the dream room by a bridge across the sea.

It didn't last. Trapped between the crushing powers of Luna and Lord Boreas, the pressure was too great. The sky darkened and turned thunderous. A lightning bolt tore down, struck the oak and the entire pinnacle crumbled into the sea, dragging the bridge with it. Lawrence was back in the dream room.

A large green eye shone in the angry sky over the turgid ocean as Luna probed him—searching for whatever he was hiding. She was dangerously close to detecting the dream room.

An instant before she did, something stirred in the clouds. It was moving at great speed. In a flash of black and white it leapt forth, covered the distance of the ocean as though it were a puddle. It filled the doorframe and released a roar so powerful that everything shattered.

Once again, everything went dark.

A darkness without stars.

A darkness without moon.

A darkness complete, with no points of reference, no sense of flow. Not even the slightest sound—no dog bark, no bird song, no human voice, no wind in the trees, no reassurance whatsoever that life existed, not even a tremor through a ground Lawrence could scarcely feel.

It was not the darkness of night that brought peace, but the darkness of the abyss—the psychic darkness of deepest depression. Panic washed through him in a prickling heat.

Are you ready? taunted the tiger in a voice that reverberated through the void.

In the hall Lawrence's eyes were closed. He no longer sensed his presence there, unaware of the intensity of Luna's gaze.

'Where are you?' she whispered in his ear but he didn't hear. 'Who are you?'

You are the sun, came the voice of Geoffrey. *The sun in your heart. You must find it! Find a stronger memory, a stronger place of power to lead you to it. You are the sun!*

NO! boomed a giant voice. *I AM THE SUN!*

With a great crash, a door in the void was booted open. A terrific bolt of energy tore through the dream room.

In the hall, Luna stepped back, her eyes wide with surprise. Or rather, she was forced back by the pulse of energy from Lawrence's aura.

Something large and shadowy strode into the dream room. The door slammed closed and the void returned.

Laughter boomed through it. Grotesque, remorseless, it summoned Lawrence's deepest fears.

'Remember me?' came a playful whisper that crept up Lawrence's spine.

A black-bearded fulsome face emerged from the darkness, its every detail the epitome of greed. Its dark eyes had a feverish light—jovial yet murderous, intelligent yet depraved. A debauched sweat seeped from his pores.

Though he struggled to accept it, Lawrence knew what it meant. It was the face of his worst demon. Lord Boreas had unleashed it, just as Geoffrey had said he would.

The face boomed with laughter and sapped Lawrence of what little consciousness was left to him.

He was on the verge of passing out when another great roar jolted him back. The dreadful face was replaced by that of the tiger.

Time to play, he gloated before fading from Lawrence's vision.

Released from Lord Boreas's grip, Lawrence's awareness snapped back to Renlock. With a gasp, his eyes shot open. Luna was still in front of him.

'Where were you?' she asked, her tone a rich mix of intrigue and suspicion. 'You were far away.'

'My lady,' he said, recovering himself and mustering a charming smile.

'Yes?' said Luna, waiting for an explanation.

'Forgive me. I have a confession. The Goddess Rowena, I've always had a soft spot for her,' improvised Lawrence, at the same time confirming what Luna had already sensed. 'But with your spirit inside of her body, it's simply too much. You quite literally blew me away.'

Though his intention was to mislead, Lawrence had spoken the truth.

Luna studied him for a long moment, the glimmer of suspicion not leaving her eyes.

'Learn to control yourself,' she said at last, echoing the advice of Geoffrey. 'And no more surprises, Lord Boreas. No compassion. No infatuation or any other indulgence. Just presence. Total presence. Your energy depends upon it.'

CHAPTER 24
RAVENOUS

JAKE WAS SWIMMING UP THROUGH A MOST GLORIOUS SEA. He could hear singing, plaintive like whale song, filling him with a sense of peace.

He broke through the surface.

His vision cleared.

Yet he found not an ocean, but his bedroom in the fort. Everything was how he remembered it except for one thing—the presence of three of the strangest beings Jake had ever seen. They were seated about his bed. Half-tree, half-human, with skin as smooth and dark as hornbeam bark, Jake thought he was still dreaming.

On seeing he was awake they stood up, placed their hands together in a gesture of prayer and made to leave.

'Wait!' said Jake, wiping the sleep from his eyes. 'Who are you?'

'We're dryads,' said the one who was female in a serene voice. 'One from each of the death planets of the Outer-Peregrinus. Our combined song creates the outer-force, which on the Surface helps bring humans together. Alas, these days the inner-force is stronger.'

'Dryads?' muttered Jake, awestruck to see what Braysheath had mentioned just the day before. 'But why are you here?'

'To heal you. Last night you received an overdose of inner-force,' she replied.

With a chill, everything from the night before came flooding back.

'I trust you're feeling better,' said one of the male dryads.

'Yes, I do feel better. Much better, just...' said Jake.

The dryads repeated their prayer-like gesture and departed through a tree on the patio.

Jake would love to have spoken to the dryads for longer, especially about the break-in, though had the impression that it wasn't their place to comment.

He ran once more through what he remembered, this time more slowly—the inner-force transporting him back to the woodland of his nightmare, being struck by the darkness blown by the red-bearded ghost through his lantern, the courtyard depicted as a web of light.

A chill was followed by a flutter of excitement.

The girl who fired the arrow at Boreas was the same girl spying on me from the crags above the farmhouse! And she's in the fort! How the hell did she get in?

He remembered how Frost had referred to her as an assassin, but during the break-in she had aimed at Lord Boreas not Jake.

With thoughts of the arrow, the mystery of the girl was hurled aside by an even greater one—why had Jake dissolved the arrow and protected Lord Boreas?

'But it wasn't me,' he muttered. 'It was the ghost or whatever darkness it blew into me.'

Yet Jake couldn't escape the nagging feeling that the ghost had felt familiar—distant but familiar and in a way that went far beyond its appearance in his dreams as a child.

Confusion threatened to overwhelm him when he jumped with shock. A sprite had sprung onto his bed.

'Breakfast! The Banyan!' it cried joyfully and sprang off again, out onto the balcony and into the wisteria.

'The fort? Is everything okay?' called out Jake, thinking of the stolen gates, but the sprite was gone. The only answer came in the form of an image. Filling his mind's eye was the last thing he had seen before passing out the night before—Asclepius lurking in the shadows, watching on but not helping.

THE FORT'S DAY-TO-DAY DINING ROOM WAS IN THE UPPER PART of the mighty banyan. Once washed and dressed, Jake found the natural staircase that wound up through its vast trunk. Ordinarily, he would have marvelled at such a thing, but he was too preoccupied with everything that had happened.

At the top he passed into a room inside the tree's crown to find an incredible breakfast. Spread out on a large red carpet and tended to by a flit of sprites was a piping hot pot of porridge, bowls of fruit and all sorts of other delights. The delicious smells of fresh bread and coffee filled the air and summoned Jake back to the present.

Braysheath was also there. His back to Jake, he was standing in front of a bizarre-looking instrument that made up the entire part of the tree that faced the savannah. The grassland and creatures were partially visible through the many chinks in its great mechanism. It was like the insides of a fantastical clock. Its many parts were made up of images of trees, beasts, people, a sun, a moon, the various planets, even a comet. Some parts suddenly shifted, while other parts remained still.

'What is it?' asked Jake.

Braysheath spun around and stared at Jake with the glazed eyes of one whose mind was far away. A moment later they brightened and a great smile spread across his face.

'Hello there!' he hailed. 'Hello!'

'Hello!' replied Jake, remembering the importance of the greeting.

'Hello!' repeated Braysheath.

Fearing the greeting could go on for quite some time, Jake decided to sit down to breakfast.

'I don't know what it's called,' replied Braysheath, joining him. 'It's rather unique. Though a little tricky to read, it tells us a story.'

'About what?'

'The general health of the Outer-Peregrinus,' replied Braysheath, helping himself to some acorn bread.

Jake poured out some coffee for both of them and served himself some porridge.

'It must have shifted a bit after what happened last night,' he ventured, wondering what Braysheath would say about the break-in.

Braysheath studied Jake, his eyes sparkling with mystery. His gaze intensified and Jake had the strange sensation of being skimmed like a book by a skilful eye.

'You heard about everything that happened, right?' asked Jake.

'Everything?' replied Braysheath, his gaze becoming light again. 'It's difficult to know everything—not all at once. Now be a good fellow and pass me the marmalade.'

'You know what I mean,' said Jake as he passed the jar.

'If you're referring to the gates,' said Braysheath, smothering his bread in marmalade, 'yes, I heard.'

'You don't seem very shocked?'

'My dear fellow, it's terrible news! The cosmos could go pop at any moment or something even worse. But there's no point in getting one's knickers in a twist. In order to restore balance, one must be balanced.'

'I don't wear knickers,' said Jake.

You don't?' replied Braysheath, looking surprised. 'Personally, I find them remarkably comfortable. It's a testing place down here. Excellent underwear is paramount!'

'Can you be serious?' said Jake.

'I assure you, I'm being perfectly serious.'

'Where were you last night, anyway?' asked Jake, keen to shift the subject back to the break-in.

'Poking around the cosmos, looking for dear old Nestor. Alas, no luck. But fear not, Jake m'boy, we'll find him, just as we'll get our gates back.'

'But in what state?' asked Jake. 'And after how much damage has been done to the Surface?'

Braysheath gave Jake one of his warm smiles. 'Less porridge, more marmalade, that's the ticket for you. Keeps you light and zingy. Not all heavy and stodgy.'

Jake shook his head in bewilderment and took a mouthful of porridge, wondering how to approach the subject of what had happened to himself during the break-in. Following his attempt to tell Braysheath about Frost in the orchard, Jake was developing a sense that certain subjects were best broached less directly.

'One of the gates stolen was a holygate of the Scribes,' he started. 'How are they connected to Nemesis?'

'Nemesis is the original Tree of Life,' answered Braysheath. 'Each of her leaves represent each of the original souls, shed and re-sprouted with each new life. But with every shepherd sacrificed, a new tree sprouted up about her in order to track the behaviour of the new souls that were created. Thus there are now six trees in total. Connected to each tree are a group of beings called the Scribes. Together they weigh the thoughts and deeds of each soul at death and so help that soul determine the best place to start in the next life. That is to say, what starting point will best serve them in repairing their lightline. Of course, once born, how they respond to life is up to them.'

Jake's heartbeat began to race. He was getting close to what he needed to know.

'What do you mean by repairing our lightline?' he asked.

'A lightline is what connects all of your bloodlines, running through each life like a string through the pearls of necklace. But all lightlines of humans on the Surface have breaks in them. What we call ghosts,' explained Braysheath and caused Jake's heartbeat to skip a beat. 'They're past lives which, for whatever reason, usually a trauma, opt out of reincarnation and in so doing withhold both their own light and the light of all of their past lives. As such, they continue to exist independently.'

Jake drew a deep inward breath to calm himself. Whether he liked it or not, what Braysheath said rang true. It reaffirmed what Nemesis had said of the path into the fog that Jake wasn't ready to take. He could no longer pretend the ghost was nothing to do with him.

'But if there's no light, how can a soul be reborn? The part of a soul that wants to be.' he asked.

'Nature finds a way, usually after a long rest-up in the restorative worlds of death. Regardless, whether one is born with lots of light at their disposal or only a wisp, it's all of our duties to repair our lightlines and step by step gain full power. Once done, we're then fit to help others repair theirs.'

Jake took a pensive sip of coffee, looking out through the strange mechanism at a herd of elephants. 'But if lightlines have breaks, is it possible for a ghost to make contact?'

Braysheath beheld Jake with another weighty gaze.

'Under exceptional circumstances, yes. If a human were to choose a bold path, for example, or receive a rather large draft of inner-force, which has a tendency to blast open doors a trifle too early,' explained Braysheath with a knowing glint in his eye. 'In such cases, a spark of light can arc across the void.'

'Why?'

'Real contact can only take place through light and in the case of a ghost there must be a willingness to connect. It's very rare. Very rare indeed.'

A chill ran through Jake. It wasn't just the image of the ghosts which flooded his mind. He thought of the web of light in the courtyard and how thick the connection had been between himself and the warrior girl, along with Lord Boreas. The significance of what it might mean was overwhelming.

I must ask Braysheath directly, he decided.

Jake was about to do so when again he was interrupted. This time it was by Rufus.

'Ach aye!' he cried as he tore into the room and thwacked Jake on the head as he passed. 'How's fancy-pants this mornin'?

Made any pots o'porridge disappear with those dark arts of yours?'

'That's not funny,' said Jake. 'And they weren't *my* dark arts. In fact, I was just about to ask Braysheath—'

Before Jake could complete his sentence there was a terrible grating. The mechanism in the wall had suddenly shifted.

'Oh dear,' said Braysheath and jumped up to study it.

'What is it?' asked Jake.

'The stolen holygate from Hunter to the Surface—wherever it is, it's been jammed.'

Though none of them knew it, not even Braysheath, the gate had been blocked by the sylph using Nestor as host. His ravaged body was shot through with blinding light. The sylph's shriek, celebratory and threatening, wracked the cosmos in countless ways, in some places subtly, but violently in most.

'Bloody hell,' said Rufus.

Braysheath made to leave. At the doorway he stopped and turned back to Jake.

'By the way,' he said. 'As you have doubtless worked out, that dream you had in the spinney was a test. Though you somewhat overdid it, you passed with flying colours. As a reward, you've earned yourself a day's rest on the Surface.'

'I have?' said Jake, his spirits soaring. 'But shouldn't I stay here to help?'

'Freshen up above,' said Braysheath. 'That way, when you're back you'll be even more helpful. But make the most of it. Events will move quickly upon your return,' he said then disappeared down the staircase.

'I should go with him,' said Rufus.

'Hang on!' said Jake. 'How am I going to get to the Surface?'

'How else? Thanador!'

'On second thoughts, I think I'll stay here,' said Jake.

'Ach, don't be a pansy.'

It was then Jake remembered the portal in the kitchen storeroom. But it was too late. Rufus swept him up, shot from the room and tossed him out of the banyan—a three storey drop to the courtyard.

'Thanador!' he bellowed as he did so.

In the instant before Jake collided with the lawn, the horrific hound appeared beneath him. Tail whirring like a helicopter propeller and looking delighted, his bizarre mouth shot open.

Jake recoiled at the sight of it but there was nothing he could do.

In a rush of heat and darkness he was swallowed whole.

A MOMENT LATER, JAKE WAS FLAT ON HIS BACKSIDE IN THE farmhouse study. Tingling with bliss, it took him several moments to realise he was really there, whereupon he leapt to his feet and hurrahed. Despite all he knew of impending doom, it felt great to be back.

He literally sprang like a lamb to the kitchen and hurrahed again, this time at Trifle the cat, while the dogs leapt up about him.

'So, Trifle, since you no doubt understand every word I say, where's that drunkard Bill? Come on, speak up!'

Trifle, however, merely yawned.

'Suit yourself,' said Jake who turned his attention to the simple delight of making himself a cup of tea.

Once made, he put on a coat and took the tea with him out into the yard.

Given the time difference with Himassisi, which wasn't fixed, it was first light at the farm. Jake took a deep inhale of the cold still air.

So peaceful, he thought as he gazed up and about the shadows of the snow-covered fells and the fading stars.

There was no sign of Bill, though all seemed in order. Yet, just as Frost had predicted, it was different. Following Jake's trip through the inkwell the world of the Surface could never be the same again. He now knew, at least partially, that what Braysheath had said was true—that the planets in outer-space, though real on one level, were ultimately symbols of a vast inner-world where souls journeyed through many lives towards an inner-sun at the Earth's core. A journey now threatened by a being of untold power going by the name of Luna.

Jake shuddered at the scale of it. He recalled his nightmare where his granddad had given him a choice to turn back time. Like then, given another choice, Jake wouldn't change a thing. Ignorance was not bliss, he realised. He wanted to know the truth, something which, just like the inner-worlds, appeared to have many layers.

Perhaps how much of the truth we're able to see has something to do with how much responsibility we take, he thought.

Jake's chief responsibility was to find and save his granddad and find out what really happened to his dad. The best way to do that was through the fort, which meant fully embracing the role of Lord Tusk.

Fully, thought Jake, aware of a conflict within himself. The fort and all its wonders greatly appealed to Jake and now that he was on the Surface, part of him yearned to be back there. Yet, if he was sincere in his desire to know the truth of things, to become lord of himself, that also meant accepting the shadowy side.

A robin began to sing and brought Jake's attention back to the farmyard. As he surveyed the beautiful spot, he realised what a blessing it was to have been born to such a life in such a place.

'Did I really choose this?' he said to himself, recalling what Braysheath had said of the Scribes and how they guided a soul in choosing the next life. *Did I choose my parents? Did I really choose to become Lord Tusk at such a mad time?*

Again he thought of the red-bearded ghost and how it had saved Lord Boreas. *If I chose to be Lord Tusk, why would I defend someone who attacks the fort? It doesn't make sense.*

Again he thought of the warrior girl in the ventilation shaft.

Some mysteries Jake was happy to accept and embrace, but these two, unless resolved, would drive him crazy.

A raven released a caw from the copse beside the farmhouse and jarred the stillness. The interruption reminded him of Braysheath and how each time Jake tried to confide his secrets, something interfered.

No sooner had he thought so when something wonderful happened—like the time he was climbing the crags, a barn owl appeared. Time seemed to slow as the owl glided with the silence of falling snow, past Jake, disappearing into the twilight like a phantom.

Jake stood in awe.

I was thinking of Braysheath and it flew in the direction of Harkenmere! he thought and felt a tingle through his body as though it were agreeing with him.

Maybe this isn't a day off after all.

Either way, following the drama and excitement of the past few days, the idea of a silent four hour walk over the mountains to town appealed to Jake. Without further thought he returned to the farmhouse to put on his walking gear.

As Jake scaled the mountainside, the sun rose. By the time he reached the ridge, the summits were glowing like piles of gold.

Unlike his last ascent, this time his mind was blissfully blank. Upon the ridge, however, the great expanse invited thought. The first thought that came was regarding school and how it seemed like ages since he had been there when it was actually only a few days. Either way it didn't matter. In the grander scheme of things school seemed unimportant. Neither did he miss it. In light of everything that had happened, school didn't seem real and so he let any thought of it fall away and enjoyed the walk instead. He revelled in the way the wind blew up the snow and how the sun transformed it into gold dust, revelled in the touch of the wind on his face and all the other wonderful ways in which nature spoke.

FINALLY, THE SLATE-ROOFED TOWN DREW INTO SIGHT AND JAKE descended the ridge, down through the old woods which surrounded the lake. He delighted at the sight of them. Leafless and covered in snow, there was something haunting in their beauty.

He was halfway through the woods when a rush of sound shattered the peace. A black stallion leapt through the undergrowth onto the path, reared up and whinnied.

'We meet again!' came a familiar voice from atop the horse.

It was Frost.

Jake cursed. 'You frightened the life out of me!'

Frost barked with laughter. 'Frightened the life *into* you, more like!'

'Haven't you heard of a bridle path?' said Jake.

'Bridle path?' laughed Frost as he expertly pranced his horse about Jake. 'I don't have a bridle!'

Jake then realised that Frost was not only riding bareback but without any tack at all, something which required great confidence and skill.

'But I do have cake!' declared Frost. He reached into his shoulder bag and brandished a paper bag. 'Éclairs! Fresh from the baker! Six! One for you and five for me!'

Jake smiled, delighted to see Frost again.

'So, do you want yours or not?' said Frost.

'Where are you going with them?'

'To a secret cave. Jump up. If you can stay on I'll show you. And I've got freshly ground coffee. And there's no better place for coffee and éclairs than a secret cave!'

'Wait a second,' said Jake, his tone suddenly serious. 'I've have a question for you.'

'What? I need to pass a test to be graced with your company?' said Frost.

'When we first met in the street—why did you call me lord?'

Apparently without command, the horse ceased its prancing and stood completely still, adding to the tension created by Jake.

Frost smiled coolly. 'Because of your lordly ways, of course! Listen to yourself. Out of the goodness of my heart I offer you an éclair, invite you to a secret place and you get all high and mighty.'

'I'm not being high and mighty,' said Jake.

The only way to get closer to the truth was to ask Frost if he knew about the House of Tusk, but Jake wasn't ready to share such a secret. He held Frost in his gaze. A breeze stirred in the tree tops and a dusting of pure snow fell from their branches as though to say let go.

Am I being paranoid? wondered Jake, gazing up.

Frost held out his hand for Jake to mount up. 'This is your last chance for a free éclair, my lordly friend.'

There was something in his tone which told Jake that what Frost was really offering was friendship and friendship with someone like Frost could prove invaluable. He thought of the barn owl, which he associated with Braysheath, and how it had sent him in Frost's direction.

Could Braysheath already know about Frost? he wondered. *If so, is he telling me to make an ally out of him?*

The thought that he might be, assuaged Jake's doubts about someone he couldn't help but like.

What the hell, he thought. *Nothing ventured, nothing gained!*

Jake had barely raised a hand when, in a display of remarkable strength, Frost hauled him up onto the horse behind him.

A moment later they were galloping off around the lake.

Though Jake battled to stay on, he laughed joyfully. For a moment he felt guilty at being so happy when so much was as stake, including his granddad's life. He then realised that it was precisely because so much was at stake that moments of joy felt so intense. Just like Braysheath had said—amid the gloom, it was joy and laughter that kept one going.

Halfway round the lake the horse leapt off the path and tore through the woods.

'Do we have to gallop?' shouted Jake, ducking the branches.

'Yes!' came the sparing reply.

'Why?'

'Because there's not a moment to lose!' cried Frost as the horse leapt over a fallen tree and almost sent Jake flying.

'What are you talking about?'

'The éclairs of course! We must get them while they're fresh! Now stop asking such ridiculous questions!'

FINALLY THEY SLID TO A HALT.

'Follow me!' cried Frost, who leapt down with great aplomb and sprang up between crags and trees.

Jake followed, moments later arriving at a cave. Frost was standing imperiously in its entrance.

'Wow!' gasped Jake on turning to admire the view. Just above the canopy of the trees, the cave commanded a spectacular view of the lake and mountains. 'I can't believe I've never noticed this place before.'

'I can. You're blind,' announced Frost. 'You have to be able to see properly in order to find it.'

Without further explanation, Frost set about starting a fire just inside the cave while Jake observed the remarkable ease with which he did so. Everything he needed was already there—a pile of wood, some kindling, a pot, even a pool of water which was filled through a crack in the rocks.

In no time at all they were seated with piping hot mugs of coffee, a plate of éclairs between them, gazing out over the lake.

'You know,' said Frost, taking a large bite from an éclair, 'a chocolate éclair is quite possibly the king of cakes. It's so light and fluffy and yet there's something extremely powerful about it.'

Jake took a bite from what was indeed an extremely fresh and delicious éclair. 'I've never thought of kings as being light and fluffy,' he remarked.

'A fine king is always light and fluffy,' announced Frost.

Jake let the subject drop, too engrossed in the éclair.

'Where exactly do you live, by the way?' he asked Frost, between bites.

'Outside of town,' said Frost, already on his second éclair. 'But like this cave, I doubt you'd find it despite its size.'

'I'd like to see it,' said Jake, genuinely intrigued.

'You wouldn't like it. Very stuffy. Lots of servants, all terribly serious, not to mention Father's pet leopard. And the drive is so long it takes forever to reach it.'

Regardless of whether Frost was telling the truth or not, Jake smiled a secret smile as he thought about the fort and how wild creatures roamed freely about the place, not to mention the sharks in the lake. As for the drive, the one to the Frosts was surely nothing compared to the elephant ride through the oasis.

'What about your family?' enquired Frost airily. 'Any other houses? Somewhere nice and exotic perhaps?'

'Houses?' said Jake, for the fort hardly classified as a house. Neither did his family own it. 'No, just the farmhouse,' he replied and was about to take a second éclair when a raven swept past the mouth of the cave and released a loud caw. It landed in a nearby tree, the black of its plumage all the richer for the contrast with the snow.

'What is it with ravens this morning?' said Jake. 'That's the second one that's cawed out loud at a strange moment.'

'Don't you know anything?' exclaimed Frost. 'A raven is a very serious omen. It tells you that magic is in the air.'

'What sort of magic?' asked Jake.

'The magic of death,' said Frost. 'The auspicious appearance of a raven foretells death—the outcome of a great battle.'

'Mine, obviously,' said Jake dryly.

'Of course yours. It's a message from the spirit realm.'

At the mention of spirit, a chill ran through Jake. The image of the ghosts filled his mind. To make matters worse, the raven released another caw as though it were privy to his thoughts.

Jake gazed out over the woodland, aware of the intensity of Frost's attention.

'Have you noticed how ravens, rooks and crows always nest high up where they have the best views?' said Frost. 'They're sentinels. They watch. That's symbolic. And they're very smart. So smart, in fact, that in the early days of creation, it is said that the raven decided to remain a raven rather than evolve into something else. It was raven who retrieved the sun from someone who wanted to keep the world in darkness. What do you think of that?'

Another shiver ran through Jake. There was something in what Frost had said that seemed to fit the image of the ghosts in his nightmare, how the light in their lanterns lit up themselves and little else as though it were held captive. It also fitted with what Braysheath had said of ghosts withholding light from the evolving spirit.

'Who was it who wanted to keep the world in darkness?' he asked.

'Oneself of course,' replied Frost, adding to Jake's discomfort. 'One's little self. One's shadow.'

The raven released another caw.

'In myth, raven, like hare and coyote, is the trickster—the one who rocks your world until the illusion crumbles. Raven is also the symbol of alchemy.'

'Alchemy?' said Jake, his attention sharpening. Braysheath had referred to Jake's ancestor, Reggie Burton, as an alchemist.

'Alchemists are meddlers,' said Frost with his usual authority. 'They love to get involved in very dark stuff and often with disastrous effects.'

Although Frost's definition wasn't in conflict with Braysheath's, it was certainly darker.

The raven flew off, releasing another caw as it went.

'Meddling in what?'

'What else? Light! Life! Darkness and death,' said Frost. 'Evolution in other words.'

'What about owls? What do they symbolise?' asked Jake. 'One flew past me this morning, just after a crow cawed.'

'Really!' exclaimed Frost, halfway through another éclair. 'Well that's *very* interesting. As with all animals, when an owl appears in your life it's inviting you to embody its strengths—listening, seeing, stealthy hunting. And owls, like ravens, are associated with the mystery of magic, not to mention vision in darkness. There's hope for you yet.'

'And a barn owl in particular,' added Jake. 'Does it mean something?'

'Definitely. Tell me, what shape is a barn owl's face?'

'It's round-ish,' said Jake.

'It's flat and heart-shaped,' corrected Frost. 'What does that tell you?'

Jake shrugged.

'Oh, what ignorance!' exclaimed Frost. 'Oh, what unsubtle times! You see? People have forgotten the symbols, forgotten the wisdom of their ancestors. They only see the surface of things and even then they miss the clues. Too much maths, not enough myth. Everything must be spelt out.'

'But surely a symbol is an invention. It's a meaning placed on something which already exists.'

'Precisely! And wasn't the universe also invented?'

'Was it?' said Jake, for he had no idea.

'Symbols are a communication system with one's environment,' continued Frost, 'brilliantly designed in order to maintain balance. It's ancient! So ancient it's imprinted in our deepest psyche. It's how the universe communicates with us,' explained Frost.

'The universe?' said Jake doubtfully.

'Of course! The sub-conscious! The Universal Soul, God, Great Spirit, this vast living, breathing, beautiful thing called nature, of which, heavens help us, you're a part. It's through symbols that what is timeless and boundless can communicate with what is not—your conscious mind, in other words. Don't you see how incredible it is? Both in dreams and during daytime, the universe perfectly tailors the symbols to what your particular mind will understand, both common symbols, what some call archetypes, and the ones which have specific meaning to you based on your own experiences. And it does this for eight billion people in each and every moment. It's simply brilliant! You just have to make a little effort to understand the message.'

With the help of another sip of coffee, Jake attempted to digest what Frost had so eloquently said. It made sense. He beheld the striking landscape stretched out before them with a renewed sense of fascination.

'If that's the case,' he asked, 'why did the universe choose an owl if I don't know what it means?'

'Don't you see? Instead of your having to look up its meaning in a book, nature delivered you something far better—me! What greater blessing could you ask for?'

Jake snorted with laughter. 'So what does a barn owl symbolise?'

'Because its face is heart shaped it symbolises the union of heart and mind. Thinking through your heart. When you can do that, the world, the universe, is your oyster. Why? Because it's the same as saying the union of light and dark and every other opposite.'

As the symbol sank in, the second verse of Nestor's riddles popped into Jake's mind.

> *Go ladies to lotus to Greek god seek*
> *Imagining things of which none can speak*
> *They follow their hearts and know their minds*
> *Accepting in action is both the cruel and the kind.*

A rush of excitement swept through him.

They follow their hearts and know their minds! he thought. *I was thinking of Braysheath when the owl appeared.*

He wondered about Braysheath, that perhaps his role as a shepherd was more to guide than interfere too directly. Given how complicated everything was, Jake could see why.

His thoughts returned to the riddles.

Granddad passed on what he could before his investigation was cut short. That must be it. Maybe it's a riddle, not only because he feared his message might be intercepted, but because he couldn't be sure what had happened to Dad. He wanted a second opinion. He passed on the leads, passed on his suspicions but not the conclusions. Only suggestions!

'Interesting,' said Jake finally.

'It is, isn't it?' said Frost in a strange tone. 'Because of the barn owl's stealth and incredible hearing, it's known as the master hunter, a title it shares with the fox. When a barn owl appears in your life it's telling you to listen to your inner-voice.'

'Right,' said Jake, doing his best to dispel the image of the ghosts which once again wafted through his mind.

Frost was about to say something when he suddenly froze.

'What's the matter?' asked Jake as a chill ran through him.

Before Frost could respond, the sky darkened. The sun was eclipsed. A mesmerising green light danced across the sky as though the Northern Lights had lost their way. It was breathtakingly beautiful. There was something about it which made Jake think of spirits.

Following a moment that seemed both fleeting and timeless, the green light faded. Yet, as sunlight returned, the air was heavy with a sense of dread. Jake thought of the strange mechanism in the banyan and the awful grating it had made during breakfast.

The stolen holygate! he thought. He remembered how the movements of the planets outside of Earth were reflections of movements within, though why there was a time delay, if that's what it was, he couldn't say.

'Why is it,' said Frost in an ironic tone, 'I have a feeling that you know more than me about what just happened?'

'What?' said Jake. 'Me know more than you? Impossible, surely.'

'Spill the beans,' said Frost. 'You've been through the inkwell!'

'What are you on about?' said Jake.

'You're a hopeless liar,' said Frost. 'Besides, I knew the moment I saw you.'

'I don't see how.'

'Because you're not as blind as the first two times we met. So come on—what news of your granddad?'

Jake said nothing. He was studying Frost, staring into the intensity of his eyes. They were so bright and lively that there was something endearing in them. Yet the mischievous glint was ever-present.

Regardless, Jake was desperate to confide in someone, to help him navigate the great complexity that had forced itself upon him. He wasn't ready to trust anyone in the fort. Frost, however, had nothing to do with the fort, yet he knew so much about nature and myth that he was a much-needed bridge between two worlds.

Could the universe have really crossed our paths for this reason? he wondered.

Jake gazed out into nature, alert for a sign—a robin song or a gentle gust of wind, but found only stillness.

Is stillness a yes or a no?

Jake didn't know and so he closed his eyes and took a slow breath. *Trust*, came the calm answer from what felt like his heart. The message, however, was received by a mind that couldn't quite bring itself to trust Frost.

If Frost was a bridge then it was a peculiar one. It looked strong, but when stepped upon there was a sense of danger in the air as though a flash flood might suddenly sweep it away or an avalanche crush it to dust.

I don't need to trust him completely, Jake decided, *or any of the others in the fort. I don't have to tell any one person everything, just parts. I'll then take what rings true from each response and piece by piece I'll work out the riddles and find Granddad.*

'Come on you stuffy Brit,' said Frost. 'Loosen up and stop being so boring.'

'You're a Brit, too,' said Jake.

'I certainly am *not*!' protested Frost. 'I'll have nothing to do with this childish game of politics and drawing lines. I'm from the elements! But stop stalling. Tell me—what was it like jumping through the inkwell?'

There was a pause.

'Incredible!' said Jake at last and proceeded to recount the highlights of his adventure on Himassisi.

As he did so, he was surprised by what Frost found fascinating and what he dismissed. Most of the fantastical stuff washed over him. What intrigued Frost most were the details about Jake, his fascination so intense that it was powerfully contagious and before long Jake, despite his plan to be selective, had confided pretty much everything—Asclepius's suspicious manner, his journey through his nightmare to Nemesis, the fog, the ghosts and the giant of a man approaching from behind them. He mentioned the prophecy of the Norns, the theft of the gates by Lord Boreas and the bizarre incident with the arrow through the web of light. He also told him about the riddles.

'Having repeated the riddle,' said Jake excitedly, 'I'm now certain of what I suspected before—who the two lords in the riddle refer to. One refers Dad, Lord Tusk. The other must be Lord Boreas!'

'Spot on,' agreed Frost. 'Boreas has broken into the fort twice. It must be him. And you realise that the word *risen* in the third line of the first verse is an anagram of *siren*.'

'Inside the risen, the Muses' second kiss, followed by a question mark in brackets,' recalled Jake excitedly. 'Which now becomes—Inside the siren, the Muses' second kiss. Meaning?'

'Lord Boreas—he's a Greek God of the North Wind. Less well known is that he's also Lord of the Sirens.'

'Well done!' said Jake, delighted he had confided in Frost. 'Which reminds me—I had meant to research the Muses in relation to the sphinx.'

'No need,' said Frost. 'In Greek myth, it was the Muses who gave the sphinx a riddle with which to terrorise the people. Something which would create confusion.'

'What sort of riddle?'

'Well, that's the interesting thing. Most think it's a conventional riddle of words. But there are some who believe it's something else.'

Jake's excitement leapt even higher. 'The strange portal I saw in the chamber under the sphinx in my dream.'

'Exactly. To be kissed by the Muses is a poetic way of saying to pass through the portal,' said Frost, his eyes growing even brighter. 'Not any old portal, but one that creates gods.'

'Gods?' exclaimed Jake. 'How can gods be created?'

'It's to do with prematurely connecting the neutrons within a human body and permitting full memory of all of one's previous lives—'

'What do you mean?' interrupted Jake.

'Ever wondered why scientists haven't worked out what a neutron is, other than to label it and to say it's the part an atom with the highest mass? Ever wondered why neutrons are separated from one another by the dance of duality between protons and electrons? In other words, the path to union, to God, is through uniting the negatives and positives as they evolve through time.'

Jake hadn't, but it sounded incredible.

'And yet, those lunatic scientists fling them together at the speed of light in those ridiculous great machines of theirs. And why? To see if they can create a black hole without even knowing what a black hole is. Mad! They're completely mad!'

Jake agreed. *Who gave them permission to take such risks which threatened the entire planet and often doing it all in secret?* he wondered. It wasn't just mad, but reckless and irresponsible.

'But this god gate,' continued Frost, 'does understand such things. By prematurely connecting the neutrons in a human body it creates a shortcut to power. The downside is that it cuts one off from the potential to be even greater and so it's ultimately flawed. It's a wonderful great trap for idiots. Eventually the gods fall, though not before creating chaos. War and conquest, that sort of thing. All the modern gods who have ruled on the Surface were created by it. All except the current one.'

'If that's true,' said Jake, awed by Frost's knowledge, 'then who created this god gate?'

Frost smiled. His eyes shone with intrigue. 'It's a mystery,' he said.

'What? You mean you don't have a theory?' asked Jake, surprised.

'No, I don't, that's why it's a mystery.'

'Then how long has it been about?'

'Some say for ten thousand years or so—since the retreat of the last Ice Age, which makes sense because it's since that time that humans began warring.'

'Surely they warred before,' said Jake.

'They battled, occasionally, though only in order to maintain the balance of the whole. You know, when one tribe expanded too quickly, eating and drinking too much. War, however, is a childish thing. It's about destroying the other, though in doing so they ultimately destroy themselves.'

Jake looked up at the sky. Following the dramatic eclipse it looked strangely still.

The calm before the storm, he thought. *Whatever's coming, Luna or otherwise, things have to change.*

'So, getting back to the riddle,' said Frost, 'I would say that the line *Inside the siren the Muses' second kiss* refers to Lord Boreas having passed through the god gate twice.'

'Why would he do that?'

'To concentrate his power of course. Logically it could only be done at the expense of longevity, which is why few would do it. But if he's the henchman of this Luna then it makes sense.'

'Two lords a leaping, one known, one knot,' said Jake, repeating the first part of the first riddle, gripped by an ominous feeling. 'Untied or Titan'd, in Hades a plot. You don't think my dad could have leapt into the god gate with him do you?'

'I'm afraid,' said Frost, doing his best to look sympathetic, 'that's what the riddle suggests.'

A chilling breeze blew over the woods and gusted through the cave.

'It doesn't make sense. I'm certain Dad wouldn't be tempted to jump through such a gate. He didn't believe in shortcuts or power for the sake of power.'

'I've no idea what his motives might have been, but if he did leap through hit then I'd draw the same conclusion as your granddad. Only one could survive the gate and come out the other end. Given Boreas was already a god then your dad's spirit would either have been cast out into some sort of hell or…'

'Untied,' muttered Jake, doing his best to suppress a profound sadness. 'Whatever that means.'

'I imagine it means his energy would be stripped of its identity. Cleansed, some would call it.'

'Alright, I get the idea,' said Jake, not wanting to imagine such a thing. He thought of Nemesis and Braysheath. If his dad had survived in any shape or form, be it in a hell or otherwise, then surely they would have sensed his presence. But they hadn't. And so Jake drew the tragic conclusion that his dad was indeed gone. Forever. Never to be reborn.

As though to give voice to his feelings, a freak gust tore into the cave, more violent than the one before.

Neither Jake nor Frost said a word. The gust gone, they sat in silence until Frost finally broke it.

'Well, it looks like you've got your work cut out. Firstly, what's the connection between Boreas and the fate of your dad? And what's his connection to yours?'

'Mine?'

'Of course. Your saw it yourself through the web of light during the break-in. Your destinies are strongly connected. And was not Boreas's light also strongly connected to this Asclepius lurking in the shadows of the archway?'

Jake nodded.

'Tell me,' continued Frost, 'how did you feel when you had that vision of the web? In particular, how did you feel towards Boreas and Asclepius?'

Jake cast his mind back to the strange events of the night before and the sensation of great power that had flowed through him.

'I honestly don't know,' he said. 'It felt like I was possessed—'

'By yourself,' broke in Frost.

'By a ghost cut off from who I am today,' corrected Jake. 'Because of that, I don't think I was feeling anything. And yet I was aware of everything that was happening. I was simply observing it all without emotion.'

'And let's not forget the most interesting detail of all,' said Frost in an especially mischievous tone. 'The girl in the ventilation shaft! No special feelings there, might I enquire?'

Jake blushed. 'At dusk a few evenings ago—she was watching me in the mountains above the farmhouse. And you sensed her on the rooftops that evening in town, right?'

Frost nodded, looking delighted. 'Definitely an assassin. A very resourceful one. And she's in your fort.'

'But she fired at Lord Boreas, not me,' countered Jake.

'That doesn't mean that you're not next. Perhaps she's been hired by another player in the game to take out the competition.'

'Not another, surely,' groaned Jake. 'It's complicated enough!'

'I don't know what you're worried about, my dark and mysterious friend. You can dissolve arrows mid-flight!' said Frost.

'Look,' said Jake awkwardly, 'that wasn't—'

'Wasn't what? Wasn't you? It was. You know it, so stop denying it. Embrace your power!'

'Just like that?'

Frost shrugged. 'Give it a go.'

Jake looked out over the trees. The winter daylight seemed to be fading yet it was early afternoon. Instead of the snow, his worried mind saw only the patches of darkness—the bark of trees and the shadows between them.

'Well, Lord Tusk,' said Frost, gathering his things, 'I wish you good luck. It sounds like you're going to need it.'

'You believe in luck?' said Jake, remaining seated.

'Depends how you define it,' said Frost.

Without another word, he sprang down the way he came.

After the great relief of having shared his burden, with Frost's departure the woodland seemed to grow even darker. It blended with the memory of the strange eclipse. Frost had not only shed light on the riddles. In doing so, he had also shed light on the scale of Jake's task.

Free of Frost's company, Jake gave space to his sadness. It swept up from deep within, swirled about him, rushed out and smothered the woodland, which felt like an abyss.

What am I going to do? I can't do this all on my own.

Jake was at a loss when a sweet sound brought him back—a chirping from within the cave. Blinking away the mental darkness, he noticed a sparrow hopping about the spot where Frost had sat. It flew up and flitted over the path Frost had left on then shot back into the cave where it flew about Jake. Finally it flew off in the direction of the mountains and the farm.

With a rush of excitement, Jake realised what the sparrow was suggesting.

Frost! The inkwell! Invite him to the fort!

Jake stared out over the trees. It seemed too outlandish to even consider. *I barely know him and he's far too unpredictable. Imagine the chaos he could cause!*

And yet, the more Jake dwelt on the idea, the more he liked it. With so much going on, having a second opinion from someone like Frost would be invaluable. Daunting challenges would become great adventures.

But how was it possible? Assuming Jake could get him in, it would have to be in secret, which was justified by the riddle's suspicions of a plot.

But what if Braysheath found out? thought Jake, feeling a sense of loyalty to him despite the fact that he was, in theory, still a suspect. He then remembered his earlier feelings—that perhaps Braysheath was behind the meeting with Frost, perhaps even the behaviour of the sparrow.

He heard Frost whistle for his horse.

Again Jake closed his eyes, drew a calming breath and thought of the barn owl.

Heart in mind. I must listen to my inner-voice.

The answer was crystal clear. *My priority is to save Granddad. If Frost can help me, then I need him.*

He jumped to his feet at the very moment Frost's horse cantered off.

'Frost!' he cried. 'Wait!'

CHAPTER 25
THE INVITE

BY THE TIME JAKE REACHED THE BOTTOM OF THE CRAGS THERE was no sign of Frost, other than the imprints of horse hooves leading off into the woods.

'Balls,' muttered Jake, disappointed after the rush of excitement.

'You called?' came a voice from above, causing Jake to jump.

He glanced up to find Frost hanging upside down from a branch like a bat. Jake cursed. 'Do you always have to be so bloody shocking?'

'It's the only way to wake you up,' said Frost, remaining where he was. 'Anyway, what is it that you wanted?'

'I was wondering…' started Jake, battling to recover his resolution of just moments before, 'if you fancied visiting the fort. Of course it would have to be strictly secret and with the understanding that you'd be there to help unravel the riddles and help find Granddad and nothing else.'

As Jake had spoken, Frost had closed his eyes.

A great stillness fell over the woods as though everything within it were listening.

'Are you inviting me to the House of Tusk?' said Frost aloofly.

'It is not obvious?'

'If you're inviting me, in secret or otherwise, then kindly do it properly,' said Frost.

'Very well,' said Jake, amused by such formality. 'I, Jake Burton, as Lord Tusk do hereby invite Frost…'

'Frost the Great,' clarified Frost.

'Do hereby invite, in secret, Frost the Arse to the House of Tusk. There, how's that? Do you accept?'

Frost was silent.

'Well?' pressed Jake.

'I'm thinking about it,' said Frost. 'I'm terribly busy, you know.'

'Busy? You don't seem very busy,' scoffed Jake.

'How I seem and how I am are two entirely different things,' said Frost with an imperious air.

'What's that supposed to mean?'

'It means time is precious.'

'Then get on with it and make a decision,' said Jake.

There followed another silence.

'I've decided,' announced Frost at last.

'And?'

Frost's eyes flicked open and sparkled so brightly that Jake stepped back. With the skill of an acrobat, Frost swung down from the tree and grabbed Jake's right hand.

'You bloody betsky, comrade!' he cried.

'Brilliant!' cheered Jake.

'And to seal the deal,' said Frost who spun round and foraged for something on the ground.

'What are you looking for?' asked Jake when Frost spun back around with great speed and hurled something.

It was travelling too quick for Jake to dodge and exploded in his face.

'There!' said Frost. 'A snowball in the face. There's no better way of sealing a deal!'

Jake immediately scooped up some snow and returned the compliment. 'Done!' he cried.

'Excellent!' beamed Frost. 'Now what?'

'This is supposed to be my day off. I was hoping to visit town.'

'Day off?' exclaimed Frost. 'From assassins, urgent riddles and gods breaking into your fort? Have you told them?'

'It's not like that,' said Jake, half-laughing. 'Besides, there's Braysheath and Rufus and the others in the fort.'

'Ah yes, all of those who you trust with your life,' said Frost dryly. 'And I wonder where that girl is now,' he added as he looked about the woods.

'You think she could be back up here?' asked Jake.

'It's possible,' said Frost, sniffing the air like a fox.

'But how? She can't be using the fort's gates.'

'Who knows? But she's doing it somehow. She's clearly very sneaky.'

'Perhaps we should head back,' said Jake, scouring the woods for anything unusual though finding nothing.

Following a whistle from Frost, the stallion cantered into view.

A moment later they were mounted up and tearing off back through the woods.

'You wanted to see the town, right? Okay then, a quick tour!' cried Frost and raced around the lake towards it.

Once there, and much to Jake's embarrassment, Frost galloped straight up the middle of the high street, made the horse prance cockily around a group of girls, charged down some town bullies, forcing them to take cover in a shop for ladies underwear, insulted a policeman and tore off back to the lake.

'How was that?' he cried as they raced for the woods.

'Oh, perfect,' said Jake. 'Nice and relaxing, just what I wanted. Thank God for other worlds to escape to!'

'And off we go to them!'

With that they sped for the farmhouse, up the ridge and over the mountains.

BEFORE THE FINAL DESCENT TO THE FARM THEY DISMOUNTED amid the crags. Jake had spotted Bill in the fields. Fortunately it was one of the further fields from the farmhouse and his back was turned to them.

'It's that madman Bill,' said Jake.

'A madman and a reprobate,' added Frost, who was clearly aware of Bill's antics about town. 'But come on, we can sneak into the farmhouse without him seeing us.'

While the horse made its way back over the mountains to the Frost's mansion, Jake and Frost picked their way down the mountain side, stole through fields until they finally reached the farmhouse undetected.

SUFFERING A PANG OF GUILT, JAKE LEFT A NOTE FOR BILL ON THE kitchen table, saying that he was staying with friends and would see him around and about. He kept it nice and general and, generally speaking, true.

Finally he and Frost were standing in front of the inkwell.

'Hang on a sec,' said Jake. 'I've no idea where Thanador might be. What if he's with some of the others?'

Frost had a think. 'Why not try commanding him? Open the inkwell and speak into it. Tell him where you want him.'

'Do you think it'll work?'

'Try it.'

Jake took a deep breath, braced himself and flipped open the inkwell. Thankfully its pull was less chaotic than before. As Braysheath had said, the trick was not to resist it.

'Thanador!' commanded Jake. 'I want you to go to my bedroom straight away and wait for me. I have a guest. A very important one, but there's no need to tell the others. Tusk business.'

'Well done,' said Frost. 'That should do it.'

'Ready?'

Frost nodded. He seemed so excited that for the first time Jake sensed a hint of apprehension in his new friend.

'I'll go first,' said Jake, 'to make sure Thanador is where he's meant to be. Give me half a minute then follow.'

Here goes! he thought. He took another deep breath, a step backwards then leapt into the inkwell.

To Jake's great relief, Frost's idea had worked. Thanador deposited Jake in his bedroom. Fortunately it was dusk and the fort was quiet.

'Thank you, Thanador,' he said to the steaming hound before checking no one was out on the balcony.

By the time he returned, Thanador's tail was whirring madly. An instant later Frost flew out his backside. It was the most bizarre thing Jake had ever seen and he struggled to contain his mirth, doing his best to ignore the fact that he had arrived the same way.

Frost was less restrained and barked with laughter.

'Shhh,' hissed Jake. 'Keep it down!'

Fortunately Thanador didn't seem in the least bit bothered by Frost, but panted delightedly.

'Thank you, Thanador, that will be all,' said Jake.

Thanador was halfway to the doorway when he suddenly stopped. His tail whirled and something else shot out—a raven. Following an indignant caw, it flew out the window.

'That's strange,' said Jake as Thanador finally left.

Frost wasn't paying attention. He was leaping excitedly from window to window, feasting his eyes on all he saw.

'We should find you a hiding place,' said Jake, keen to get Frost out of sight.

'That shouldn't be too difficult. I bet this place is just like home—lots of secret passages behind the walls,' said Frost surveying the room. 'Aha! A fireplace! An excellent place to start.'

Jake watched as Frost climbed inside the large recessed fireplace which had seats on either side beneath the chimney. Frost sat on one while he tapped, pressed and pulled at various things until something clunked and he disappeared.

'Oh God, where did he go?' panicked Jake and rushed over.

By the time he got there, the seat and backrest swivelled round once more and Frost reappeared with a grin. 'Found it!'

Jake joined him on the seat and, a tumble later, found himself in something of a den, replete with cushions and a lantern, while a passageway led off into the shadows.

'It's perfect,' said Jake. 'But do you think someone already rests here?'

Frost sniffed about. 'No. It's here for your convenience, nothing else.'

'I'd better go and check in with the others,' said Jake. 'I'll come back as soon as I can with some food. In the meantime stay out of trouble, alright? And stay out of sight of the sprites. They're everywhere.'

'Of course, of course!' enthused Frost. 'Don't worry about a thing.'

CHAPTER 26
FORBIDDEN FRUIT

It was gone midnight and once again Rani was restless. What felt like a snake in the pit of her stomach refused to give her peace. When it stirred, everything prickled—her mind, her body, especially her joints and the only thing to do was to go for a walk.

Bin was out hunting, which suited Rani. She felt like being alone. So having collected her knives and the atomic glove, she set off along the secret passages of the fort.

Her chief concern was the Tusk boy. What she had seen from the ventilation shaft the night of the break-in had chilled her to the bone, leaving no doubt in her mind that he was in some way cursed. Confirming her intuition was the snake in her stomach. Whenever she thought of the boy it grew heavy. Sometimes it made her want to leap into his room, pin him down and confront him as to who he really was and what he was up to. At other times she simply wanted to put an arrow through him.

Rani would never forget his face the moment he had dissolved her arrow into light. Though impassive, his eyes had shone with what she could only describe as dark light. He had looked possessed. She had no idea by what, though it was obviously something with great power and, given it had defended the thief, something with dark intent. To be possessed by anything was, for Rani, a sign of great weakness.

My mission is to protect him, but how can I protect him from something like that?

As she wandered through the half-light of a passage, she was suddenly struck with an idea.

He must be sleeping by now. I want to observe him! Maybe he'll mumble something in his sleep. And there might be a tree or a plant in his room which might also give me a clue as to what he really is. Yes, it's an excellent idea!

Though Rani had yet to enter his bedroom, she knew the way.

In no time at all she was in the passage that led to the secret entrance into his room by the fireplace.

She was only a few paces away when she suddenly stiffened. Something was different. A lantern was lit, which was unnecessary, for the passageways were lit by torch light or moonlight which shone in through a clever arrangement of shafts. There were also cushions which had recently been sat on.

Rani sniffed the air. Her skin tingled with alarm. She sensed a presence, though nothing she recognised. Its energy had a destructive feel but not in the way of a typical predator. There was something subtle about it. Subtle but lethal.

When she sniffed the air a second time an image popped into her head.

No! she thought. *How could that be?* She had seen it twice before but couldn't believe it was actually in the fort.

The theft of the gates by a god was different. That was a surprise attack. But this new presence—his tribe were worse than gods. They were the ones behind the gods, the false gods, and had misused their gift as gatesmiths to create an abomination beneath the sphinx temple and started a war against humanity and Mother Nature.

How could one of his kind be here without being detected?

A chill ran up Rani's spine. She withdrew one of her knives and slowly approached.

Rani glanced about the shadows but sensed no movement. She made a quick appraisal of the area. There was still warmth in the cushion. He must be close.

Crumbs—bread, cheese and chocolate cake. Not a sprite, she deduced, for she had made a habit of listening in on the sprites in the kitchen, hoping to pick up gossip. Without exception, they couldn't stand chocolate. The grizzlies, however, loved it. So too did Rani.

The sample of crumbs fitted the image that had popped into her head. If she was right, then the confines of the passageway were a bad place to get caught. She quickly but warily made her way to the end of it, which she knew exited up some steps into the hollow of a tree and out onto a patio beneath the ramparts.

Once there, out in the open but in the shadows, she stopped. As still as a deer she waited for any movement. There was none.

She stole around to the first window into the boy's room and peered in.

He's asleep. Perfect! she thought, noting his shadowy form in the bed. Following a glance behind, she hopped inside.

The first thing she checked was the fireplace. Her heartbeat quickened as she approached the dense shadows gathered within it. Her breath was short. She stopped.

She recalled her training. *A Yakreth warrior must be at one with the rhythm of their surroundings. A racing heart is like a drum, a short breath like a gust of wind.* And yet, as she took a calming breath, neither would settle. *It's his presence. Their kind are different!*

She took the last few steps towards the fireplace, her empty hand forward in order to deflect, her knife-holding hand close to her body, ready to slash.

She reached the recess. Her heartbeat and breathing grew more erratic. She sensed him, but still there was no movement, not even a breath.

Taking a deep breath herself, she leapt into the recess and made a quick sweep with her hand, resisting the temptation to swipe blindly into the darkness with her knife, just in case she should harm something innocent.

There was nothing.

It's an energy trace! she realised with an inward sigh of relief. *He's been here recently.*

Regardless, she stayed alert as she crept towards the bed.

The boy Jake was lying on his back, his ribcage rising and falling with the rhythm of deep sleep.

Rani moved closer. Though her heartbeat and breathing had calmed, this time it was the snake in her stomach which disrupted her poise. With each step closer it grew heavier and began to writhe.

What's happening? she battled in thought and glanced about the shadows of the room. It was then she noticed a fruit tree in the corner, yet for the first time ever she couldn't sense its life force, at least not through its leaves. Its life force flowed from its roots, through the floor and into the bed.

It's gifting him energy! To keep him stable. Yes, that must be it! she reasoned. *Is that why I feel this weight? Is he taking my energy too?*

And yet, it didn't feel like that way. It was more like a door had been opened inside of her and something was flowing in and feeding the snake. Again she felt a great urge to leap on top of

Jake, grab his ears and wrestle the truth out of him. She resisted. Instead, she knelt gently on the bed and leaned over Jake to study his face.

He looks so innocent, she thought. He reminded Rani of a sleeping young lion. She reached a hand towards his face then quickly withdrew it. *Who would dare touch a sleeping lion?* she thought.

Rani leant further forward and sniffed the scent of his hair and skin, which, like his appearance, had something appealing about it. Out of instinct she almost licked his cheek. Again, she caught herself.

Rani remembered the fox from her strange walk through the woods at midnight, the night she had seen Braysheath a little ahead of her.

If his totem is the fox then it suggests that whatever possessed him was part of who he really because a fox is too cunning to be outsmarted, she reasoned, but that was getting into the business of past lives of which Rani knew nothing. Whatever had happened to him during the break-in, it wasn't natural. True power existed only where there was balance and it had to be earned, step by step.

Holding the tip of her razor-sharp knife just a fraction from his throat, she traced an arc about it, wondering if she would ever have to do it for real if he became too great a risk to nature.

My mission is to protect him but perhaps his greatest enemy is himself, she thought, taking a more liberal interpretation of protection.

The weight in her stomach became a nauseating ache. Keen to be rid of it, she gently rose and retreated from the bed.

There's nothing to discover here. Not now, she decided.

The ache immediately lessened. The air in the room lightened and she allowed herself to relax a little.

She turned and was about to stow her knife when, without warning, something vice-like gripped her wrist.

Her energy plummeted.

Her head swam.

The shadows of the room jumped to life and danced around her.

Only two things remained fixed: the vice-like grip and the devilish hazel eyes.

How could he sneak up on me without me sensing it? panicked Rani. It was as though he could control his presence. Now she was feeling its full force.

Except she wasn't. It grew even stronger.

With a rush of heat the room disappeared. A flash of visions raced before her mind's eye but they were too fleeting to make sense of. She felt herself being forced backwards rapidly across the room but hadn't the strength to do anything about it.

Rani had never experienced anything like it. She felt as though she were melting. The heat coursing through her was not like the heat of the sun, not life giving. It was taking it away.

Inner-force! she cried in thought. *Must find balance!*

Instead, however, she was hurled backwards through what felt like doors.

She landed hard onto a stone floor.

Released from his grip she recovered quickly. He had forced her through the secret door in the fireplace back into the passage, taking her knife in the process. She leapt to her feet and drew her second knife but he was nowhere to be seen or sensed.

Why hasn't he followed? she wondered, glancing in both directions along the passageway. *He's hunting. He wants a chase.*

Rani imagined him darting for another secret door, attempting to anticipate her moves. She glanced down at the atomic glove through her belt. It seemed dishonourable to use it in battle, but then *he* was dishonourable. Because of his nature, part force part human, he had an advantage she could never match without some help.

This just makes it fairer, she decided.

Rani put it on and felt it tingle with acceptance.

She quickly assessed her options. *Since he can manipulate his presence, I can't rely on that. And he knows my preference for space in which to fight so I must go deeper into the narrow passages. But then he probably knows I'll think this way!*

Rani's confusion was shortly followed by a flash of inspiration. *No plan. Just instinct.*

Thus decided, she stopped reasoning and headed back along the passage she had arrived through, moving at what she knew as a *warrior's walk*, which was like a jog but without the bounce. It allowed a warrior to move at a stealthy and efficient speed, always alert and poised for attack.

As she moved, she found herself tending towards the passageways which ran just inside the rampart walls. The sense of space beyond them, however, was a false comfort—it was a long drop to the moat and crags.

Suddenly she felt his presence. It rushed up from behind her. She spun around.

Nothing.

It's a trick!

She spun back round, blade outwards.

But he was too quick. He grabbed her wrists and forced her to the wall with his body. There was no way for her to knee or kick him. Unlike before, however, he wasn't sapping her energy. Her vision remained clear.

'Why do you struggle?' he asked and glanced at her atomic glove.

'What are you doing here?' she spat. 'It's bad enough that you're on the Surface.'

'That's not very nice,' he replied, feigning hurt. 'Besides, I might ask you the same thing.'

Rani raised her chin in a gesture of contempt and made a vain attempt to free herself from his powerful grip.

'My name's Frost. Can't we be friends?' he asked sweetly.

'Is that how you start a friendship? By sneaking up on people, grabbing them, stealing their property? Stealing their energy?'

'I didn't steal your energy,' he corrected. 'I took you closer to its source. And might I remind you that you were holding a blade to my friend's throat.'

'Friend?' scoffed Rani.

'We're becoming friends,' said Frost.

'Oh dear,' said Rani sarcastically. 'All this need of friendship. Are you lonely?

Frost cocked an eyebrow. 'The more the merrier. Besides, I like him. He's got potential. With a little help...'

'Your type don't make friends,' said Rani. 'You don't need them. Nor do you know how to help.'

'Then your understanding of the cosmos is disappointingly shallow. I expected more from you.'

'What could you possibly know of me?' said Rani.

'You're Yakreth, are you not?' said Frost.

How could he know? thought Rani, doing her best to disguise her surprise. *I'm the only human in the clan!*

He leant forward as though about to kiss her.

Rani made to head-butt him but he moved to the side. He wasn't trying to kiss her, but smell her hair, just as she had done to Jake. She turned away in disgust.

'I can still smell the woodlands of Wrathlabad,' he whispered in her ear. 'They're among the finest in the cosmos.'

'You've never been!' snapped Rani, amazed by his senses and thrown by his compliment of her home of homes.

'I've been to many places,' said Frost.

Rani turned to meet his gaze. For a fleeting moment something shifted—their lights seemed ancient and she wondered how old Frost really was. Physically he looked the same age as her but perhaps his type aged more slowly.

Suddenly she went weak again as Frost exerted his presence. 'Stop that! It's cheating! There's no honour in it! Can't you fight with skill alone?'

'I'm not doing anything,' he said, grinning. 'What you're feeling is attraction. What some call chemistry. It's your resistance to it that feels like you're losing energy.'

'Attraction!' hissed Rani. 'I find you repulsive! I see no beauty in you. It's inner-force, that's all.'

'What do you think inner-force is?'

Rani didn't answer. She knew what he would say—that without inner-force the cosmos would fall apart, that without its challenges no one would reach the source.

'You're proud,' continued Frost. 'But the process of attraction has already started. And if anyone's taking energy, it's you. Don't you feel it flowing into you?'

Infuriated at his arrogance and appalled by the idea, Rani did all that was left to her and spat in his face.

Frost barely seemed to notice. Again he studied her glove. 'As for honour...' he said dryly.

Just then, Rani felt the slightest tingle in the fingertips of her gloved hand.

A moment later, the sound of merry whistling came from further along the passageway.

Sprite! thought Rani.

As Frost turned in its direction, Rani tore free her gloved hand, grabbed him by the shirt and, trusting the glove would do as she intended, made to throw him through the wall and out over the crags.

Vibrating with power, the glove responded. It felt as though Frost weighed nothing and that the wall didn't exist.

In a flash it was over.

Rani gaped at the wall in astonishment. It was part of the rampart, metres thick, yet there was a hole clean through it. Frost was nowhere to be seen.

Wow! she thought.

Not taking any chances she quickly resealed it. Before the sprite bounded into sight, she ran a short distance in the other direction and made another hole, this time through the opposite wall.

It opened out onto a narrow stairwell up one of the turrets.

Up or down? Her instinct, which knew that Frost would somehow land on his feet, said down and back to her hideout to bide her time. Her curiosity said up. She wanted to look out over the ramparts and see what had become of him.

Her curiosity won out. Up she bounded.

She was close to the top. At the thought of seeing the sky, her spirits lifted when something pounced from the night through one of the windows.

Moonlight glinted on a blade she recognised as her own.

Rani didn't hesitate, didn't stop to wonder how Frost had managed it, but leapt to engage the shadow.

There was a blaze of blade strokes.

Both were highly-skilled in the art of knife-fighting and in the confines of the stairwell the clash was intense. Yet while Rani's face was gripped with concentration, Frost was smiling, as though it were just a game, his face lit up by the knife that glowed strangely in his clasp.

Rani combined her blade strokes with expert kicks but Frost simply blocked them. When a rare gap presented itself, she punched with her gloved hand but he ducked it. The glove seemed to have a mind of its own. For some reason it was withholding its magic.

'You know,' said Frost as he continued to toy with her, 'I've never found women of the Surface particularly interesting, not these days. But you…'

'You know nothing of beauty!' snapped Rani who, following a fierce flurry of blade strokes, finally managed to land a kick and knocked him down several steps.

Rani bolted upwards, desperate for the space of the turret's top, even though she knew it was a trap.

Frost's recovery was impossibly fast. She had only made half the distance when a fierce tug pulled her legs out from beneath her. An instant later Frost pinned her down. Both her hands were held fast above her head in just one of his.

Rani's chest heaved from the exertion.

Frost glanced down. He held the blade tip to the top of her leather bodice, toying with an idea.

'I know everything about beauty,' he said, eyes smouldering.

Rani said nothing. The tip of the blade against her skin felt like ice.

'I know where it comes from,' continued Frost. 'And it comes from the night as much as the day.'

'I know that! What do you take me for? An idiot?'

'A coward,' said Frost.

Fury swept through Rani at the irony in his words. There was no greater insult to a warrior of the Yakreth than to be called a coward. She writhed against his grip, wanting nothing more than to punch the grin clean off his face. But it was useless and only caused her blood to boil even more.

'I fear nothing!' she hissed. 'Least of all you!'

Frost's grin broadened. 'Maybe not me. Maybe not even a lion,' he said. 'But you're afraid of yourself.'

Frost's comment threw Rani completely off balance.

'You don't think of yourself as separate, do you?' said Frost. 'You were born on the Surface but not brought up there and so haven't been poisoned with their modern ways. For you the only beauty is balance.'

'Obviously,' said Rani haughtily.

'But you *are* separate,' said Frost.

'Of course I'm not! I'm Yakreth. I *am* balance,' she said, though felt the lack of conviction in her voice.

'You're human,' corrected Frost and drew the blade tip lightly over the skin of her shoulder as though to prove the point.

Rani didn't flinch as it cut her skin and a rivulet of blood rose up through the nick.

'Sometimes you're in balance. Sometimes you're not,' continued Frost. 'Because you were brought up Yakreth this realisation has been delayed. But now it's arrived. And until you accept this separation, this darkness, you'll never be able heal it and truly sustain balance. Never.'

Rani wanted to refute what Frost had said, but much to her annoyance it rang true and echoed what Ezram had said. She craved to be in balance all the time. It's what made a warrior great. In Wrathlabad, amid the peace of the ancient trees and their glorious shade, she managed it much of the time. But since receiving her mission she had never been further from it.

'And so,' said Frost, leaning so close that their faces almost touched, 'let's have look into those fierce eyes of yours and see what's going on.'

Again Rani went to head-butt Frost but he caught her by the chin.

'I merely wish to study your eye light,' said Frost, looking amused. 'To study your past. Don't you want to know?'

'Let go of me! Or I swear at the first opportunity I'll rip out your eyeballs and cut off your cursed tongue!' snarled Rani.

Again Frost exerted his presence. Rather than drain her, this time it was more like an anaesthetic, though just as alarming.

His eyes took on a mysterious light as he gazed deeply into Rani's. All she could see were his dilated pupils and the chink of light within them which merged and became like a tunnel. A prickling heat seared through her body. Within its fires something of herself seemed to separate from her body and was hauled into the tunnel of light.

Her consciousness flew through it at great speed in what became a kaleidoscope of images. They flashed past too quickly to see when suddenly one stuck.

It was a woman stealing through a dark corridor with a form of stealth Rani knew all too well. In her hand was a knife. In her heart was a deathly cold. Rani felt it as though it were her own. The woman arrived at a door beyond which two powerful-looking men held a conclave at a candle-lit table.

Before she could discover more, the image shifted and once again other images raced past or she passed them. Frost was clearly in control, apparently searching for something.

Rani could only guess at the depth of time through which they flew when, with another surge of prickling heat, a new image stuck.

It was a scene of a man and woman.

They were naked.

They clung to each other in a strange wrestle.

Rani had seen mating many times in the animal kingdom and had thought nothing of it. But it was somehow different with humans. Her head swam and stomach ached in synch with the woman's but she felt the same cold heart as the vision before—the same sense of power and control.

Again the image shifted and others raced past and so on through the kaleidoscope, the sensations growing stronger, the contrast more extreme, of passion and murder, of hot and cold, and secret meetings through leaps of time with the same person as though she were bound to him by contract—not Jake or Frost, but a presence of immense power, similar to Braysheath, though not him and always in the shadows.

The further back Frost carried her, so the sense of a pattern grew stronger when one image suddenly broke it.

A woman, who Rani reluctantly accepted as another of her past lives, was spying on a man through the trees. He was bathing in a lake at dusk, his broadsword and clothes left on the bank. She could see only his well-muscled back. Just like in the other images, the woman was armed and yet Rani sensed hesitation in her. Rani also sensed peace, the peace of mountains which shone from the man. It was so infectious that she stepped from the cover of the trees. The peace blossomed into blissful elation which washed through her and warmed her cold heart.

It was only then that she sensed a stirring in her stomach. Again it felt like a snake except this time it felt incredible as though there were two of them, coiling up her spine in a helix of exquisite-feeling energy.

No! It can't be! she cried out in thought, linking the sensation of the snakes to Jake, shocked at the implication that they might have known each other before and intimately. *There must be another explanation!*

The intensity of Frost's interest shot through the image like a scorching sun.

The man, meanwhile, sensing a presence, cocked his head, checking for movement in his peripheral vision.

The woman froze. Rani instinctively knew that were the man to turn completely, to see his eyes would be to know his light completely and unravel a powerful mystery spanning ages, one which involved her—the very mystery Frost burned to know.

Slowly the man turned.

The heat of Frost's interest burned hotter.

Suddenly Rani sensed another presence. It matched the powerful presence that connected all the other visions and belonged as much to the present as to the past. She felt its footsteps, heavy and portentous. She felt its breath tingle up her spine.

As the man had all but completed his turn, Rani spun around in the vision and gazed up.

Heart pounding, she gasped. Towering above her, just as it had in the woods of the fort, stood the mighty bull elephant. A shudder gripped Rani at the sight of the ancient light in its powerful eyes. This time she didn't faint but held its gaze. An instant of courage was all it took. In a flash she was through her fear. She and the elephant were on a vast white plain which shimmered with power. All she need do was accept it and it was hers to use, yet she feared the source of the power and the intent behind it. She was also desperate to be rid of Frost.

The bathing man's head had turned as far as his left shoulder. Still his head was cocked downwards so that his eyes were not quite in sight. Only a split second remained before they were visible.

Rani felt the leap in Frost's excitement.. Her fury returned. With a nod to the elephant she accepted the gift of raw power.

The rush of it was vast. So too was the sense of expansion in order to channel it. Rani didn't waste time in wondering at how such things were possible or why it felt so natural. She snatched free her wrists and booted Frost through a wall.

Released from the vision, unhurried yet lithe, she sprang up the remaining steps to the top of the turret. Under the stars she drew a deep breath and let the images of the past wash away. A breeze blew up and swept about her. She felt a profound sense of poise and as Frost leapt up to the turret, she shone with power.

At the sight of her, Frost eyes lit up. 'You're growing on me!' he declared.

'Well, you're not growing on me,' replied Rani calmly. 'Your type and mine don't mix. It's—'

'What?' interrupted Frost as he moved closer, tossing her knife up and catching it. 'Forbidden? Well, I'm not sure by whom, but oh dear, what a pity. We mustn't be naughty, must we? That would be far too exciting.'

Rani maintained her poise. The gift of power wouldn't last long. To make the most of it, she flicked her knife at Frost's heart.

She knew he would catch it. The moment he did, she was upon him. Helped by the intervention of a bat, which momentarily clung to his face, she disarmed him of one of the knives and kicked the back of his knee.

Frost went down but immediately sprang up, deftly deflecting the stroke to his throat, delivering a kick as he did so, which Rani deflected and countered in the same motion.

And so it went on.

They moved about the turret like an electric storm, each defence also an attack, executed at speed with great precision.

Releasing the idea that she was already fighting beyond her limits, Rani willed the elephant to gift her more power.

In the space created by her surrender came a series of blows so rapid that Frost was forced onto the back foot.

Finally one of her blows got through. It struck him in the chest. He was off balance for a split-second. It was enough for Rani to gash his chest and nick his chin. Both were expert cuts. One for revenge, one for good measure.

To his credit, Frost took them well. The shock was fleeting, swiftly followed by a grin.

'I shall treasure them forever,' he said.

Rani refrained from a fatal blow. She wasn't sure why. But in that moment's hesitation, the elephant withdrew its power and Frost knocked the knife from her hand, sending it flying over the ramparts.

Rani gasped as though it had been her hand and rushed to the edge to see where it fell.

Flushed and furious she spun round and glowered at Frost with daggered eyes.

'Oh, what a deliciously complex look,' purred Frost. 'It's just missing a touch more intensity,' he added and tossed her other knife over the side. 'There! Perfect!'

Without warning, a great exhaustion washed through Rani though she hid it well behind vengeful eyes.

'Leave me,' she said, part command, part appeal.

'Not until I have my reward for sharing so much,' said Frost, his eyes sparkling with suggestion.

'Reward?' she spat. 'You're lucky I only cut you.'

'If only you knew how much I've helped you.'

Rani snorted in contempt.

'I demand nothing more than a simple kiss,' said Frost.

As he took a step closer, Rani took a step backwards, her heels at the edge of the turret.

'There's nowhere to go,' said Frost. 'It's only a harmless kiss, after all.'

For the briefest instant, Rani felt another tingle in the fingertips of her gloved hand.

I must trust it, she thought, remembering who had left it for her.

She drew a deep inward breath, imagining she was standing at the top of her favourite waterfall on Wrathlabad, then stared hard into Frost's eyes.

'Never,' she said plainly and, without a moment's hesitation, dived majestically backwards off the turret.

Though the ramparts were vast, it would take just seconds for her to reach the moat, whose waters were too shallow to break her fall, all of which she knew.

Yet, in that timeless moment, in the face of death, she felt great calm. Three words escaped her lips as she thought of Mother Nature and all she held dear.

'I love you…'

Through the rush of air she could see the stars reflected in the rapidly approaching moat. It gave the impression of diving into infinity.

The stars grew larger. Only a millisecond remained before she smashed into the bottom of the moat.

The stars disappeared.

But she hadn't struck the water. Something had swept between them. Its soft plumage pressed against her chest. It was Bin. She swept up into the air just in time to avoid the moat and crags.

'Bin,' gasped Rani and all but passed out. 'Beloved Bin.'

CHAPTER 27
MARVELLOUS BATH

JAKE HAD AWOKEN IN A STRANGE MOOD. HE COULDN'T PUT HIS finger on what it was exactly, but he felt unsettled. It wasn't to do with Frost exactly or second thoughts about inviting him to the fort. Rather, it felt like something deep within him had been disturbed, a feeling he associated with the warrior girl, though he wasn't sure why.

His mood wasn't helped by the mirror he was looking into. It made combing his hair almost impossible. Although the mirror hung in his room, it reflected not only Jake but a jungle. If he gazed into it for more than a moment his reflection became part of it—his hair became vines which coiled up and around the branches. Birds flew in and out of his ears while a snake slithered out of a nostril.

At least it doesn't reflect the past, he thought.

Sudden screeches caused him to jump. They came from the mirror as birds took flight. In the depths of the reflected woodland a light appeared. A dreadful chill ran through Jake. The light was wan like a lantern and moving towards him.

Not again! he panicked, hoping it couldn't pass from the mirror into the room.

Tired of the strange terror he couldn't explain, part of Jake was tempted to strike out at the ghost through smashing the mirror. But he didn't. He recalled what happened the last time, when he lunged for the lantern in the fog and ended up in the Norns' well.

Instead, Jake stepped backwards.

Then leapt in shock. An icy hand had touched his shoulder.

He spun round, wishing he had some clothes on.

'Morning!' said Frost.

Jake cursed loudly and grabbed a towel. 'Will you stop bloody creeping up or leaping out on me! And your hands are freezing!'

'Why are you so jumpy? Did you see something in the mirror?'

'Didn't you?' asked Jake.

Frost stepped forward and stood in front of the mirror.

Jake peered over his shoulder, wondering if the ghost with the lantern was still there.

'What happened?' he gasped.

The mirror was completely blank. There was no reflection whatsoever—not of Frost, not of himself, not even the room. 'Before it was a woodland.'

Frost said nothing as he continued to gaze into the mirror.

As soon as Jake stood beside him, the woodland came back though nothing else, nothing of himself.

'Why isn't it reflecting us?' asked Jake.

'Watch,' said Frost. 'There's some movement in the trees.'

Jake stared into the woods, hoping it wasn't the ghost.

'I don't see...' started Jake.

An image filled the frame with such suddenness that he jumped.

It was the warrior girl. She was staring at them with fierce cat-like eyes. Jake was stunned. Though it was only an image in a mirror, her wild energy was overpowering.

'What's happening?' he said, unable to take his eyes off her. 'Why are we seeing her instead of our own reflections?'

'Because we're both standing in front of the mirror,' said Frost, also captivated.

'What do you mean?'

'Look,' said Frost.

Though the girl's expression remained fierce, Jake noticed a sadness in her eyes. A moment later, a single tear rolled from each of them.

'One for you,' said Frost, 'and one for me.'

The image faded and once again the mirror went blank.

'Why do you say that?' asked Jake.

'This mirror shows what it sees as truth,' explained Frost.

'Truth?'

'It reflects soul.'

'Then why did it show her?' asked Jake.

'Because all three of our destinies are interlinked—inextricably.'

'Why the tears?'

'Two handsome fellas and one girl…'

There was something in the way Frost was looking in the mirror that turned Jake's thoughts from the girl to Frost himself. He wondered if the mirror was also blank for Frost or whether he saw other things. If so, what?

Have I done the right thing by inviting him to the fort? he thought, realising how little he actually knew of him.

Frost turned to face Jake, his eyes alive with mystery.

'She'll love us both,' said Frost.

Jake cocked his head questioningly, both excited and disturbed by Frost's words. 'Like King Arthur, Guinevere and Lancelot, you mean?'

'Like Jake, Frost and whatever her name is,' said Frost, grinning. 'But don't worry. Nothing will come between our budding friendship!'

Jake wanted to laugh away Frost's comments, but the uneasy feeling in the pit of his stomach returned once more. For a moment, a wisp of a dream wafted through his thoughts, but was too ethereal to grasp. There was only vague awareness of himself bathing in a lake and someone watching him—what he felt was a woman.

'By the way,' said Frost, jolting Jake from his thoughts with a whack on the shoulder, 'I've just got back from Asclepius's secret laboratory.'

'He has a secret laboratory?'

'Yes! In the top of one of the towers. It's very interesting.'

'In what way?' asked Jake, reluctantly releasing his thoughts of the girl.

'He's up to something, just as the riddle suggests he is. I shall have to show you.'

'Definitely. And what else? Did you manage to stay out of trouble?'

'Of course. In fact, I saved your life.'

'What are you talking about? I've been in my room all night,' said Jake.

'Exactly. And while you were off with the fairies, your girlfriend was leaning over you with a knife to your throat.'

'You're joking, right?'

'I certainly am not. I suspect she was about to get you back for destroying her arrow,' said Frost. 'It's the sort of thing assassins get very upset about.'

Jake stared at Frost, waiting for a smile but none came.

'I thought you said she'd love us,' he said.

'Women are mysterious creatures.'

'So what happened?' asked Jake.

'I chased her off, of course.'

'You let her get away?' exclaimed Jake.

'She dived off one of the towers. It was rather impressive.'

They were interrupted by a familiar voice coming from the direction of the balcony.

'Wakey, wakey, Sleepin' Beauty! Rise'n shine!'

'Bugger, it's Rufus,' said Jake. 'Quick, into your lair! I'll meet you there around lunch time.'

With a mischievous nod, Frost disappeared through the fireplace the instant before Rufus flew into the room.

'Ah, good morning, Rufus,' said Jake breezily. 'Have you come to carry me to breakfast?'

Rufus suddenly stopped. One of his corners was upturned as he sniffed the air. 'Aye, there's a nasty whiff in here,' he growled.

'Well, it was all right until you arrived,' said Jake as he tugged on some clothes.

'I thought the dryads had cleansed the place.'

'Of what?'

'Inner-force,' said Rufus.

'Seems all right to me,' remarked Jake.

'Aye, well that's not sayin' much,' said Rufus. 'Which reminds me—when d'yer last have a bath?'

'None of your business.'

'It is if I have to carry you,' said Rufus who swept Jake up before he could protest, shot from the room and out over the ramparts.

Moments later Rufus deposited Jake next to steaming pool of crystalline water. Part of the outcrop just below the ramparts, it stood within a delightful copse of Scots pines and rhododendrons. Stretched out before it was a stunning view of the savannah, the lake and the distant mountains.

'Wow!' gasped Jake. 'Glorious!'

'The finest bath in the cosmos,' announced Rufus. 'Now do us all a favour and hop in.'

'It's a bit public,' said Jake feeling self-conscious.

'Ach, donnae be shy. Besides, you're the only one out here with clothes on,' said Rufus referring to himself and the creatures of the savannah.

Jake's thoughts turned to the girl, wondering if she was spying on him. The water, however, was irresistible and with a silent prayer the girl was elsewhere, he stripped off and hopped in.

'Oh wonderful!' he cried.

For a blissful moment everything in the cosmos was perfect.

The illusion was shattered with the arrival of a sprite. He was carrying a tray. On it was a fresh cup of coffee along with a newspaper.

'My Young Lord Tusk,' he said cheerily with a bow and deposited the tray.

'We don't usually allow these things into the fort,' he continued, referring to the newspaper, 'but it was agreed that you might like to know what humans call *news*.'

'I would, thank you,' said Jake and the sprite skipped off.

Jake took the paper in wet hands and studied the front page. Two headlines leapt out at him:

NOT A SINGLE CHILD BORN ALIVE IN LAST 24 HOURS THE WORLD OVER

METEOR SHOWERS HOLD WORLD AGASP

A shiver ran through Jake as he recalled the strange dancing green lights he and Frost had seen on the Surface.

'The holygate,' he muttered.

'Aye,' confirmed Rufus. 'God knows how, but Luna discovered a way to block it so that no souls can reach the Surface. It's only been twenty-four hours and already the panic is spreadin'. Stock markets are crashin' and governors are cryin' foul, claimin' some terrible international fugitive is to blame. Christ, if only they knew.'

'But isn't this good?' asked Jake. 'Isn't that the cause of all the problems on the Surface—too many people?'

'Aye, it is. But this is hardly the way to sort it out. The real cause is a lack of consciousness.'

'But how? I still don't understand how things have got so out of balance,' said Jake. 'I get the Humpty-Dumpty bit and how chopping up five of the shepherds has made getting him back into one piece even more difficult, while at the same time making humans more forgetful. And I understand that there are these alternating cycles of Great Dance and Great Game. But how is it that this latest Great Game has suddenly become such a great step backwards? Surely there's more to it.'

'Why, I canae tell yer. You'll have to ask Luna when you get the chance. As for the game and dance, in pre-history, or in other words pre-Luna, it were difficult to tell the cycles apart. The game was less a step back than a step down, like down a stairwell into the darkness for a game of what yer might call hide'n seek,' said Rufus, echoing what Braysheath had said. 'With yerself, that is, confronting yer fears and earning the right to see deeper into the sacredness of things. As such, both were about balance.'

'That makes sense, said Jake. 'And then?'

'Well, as though adding the shepherds to the mix wasnae bad enough, it was rocket fuelled by somethin' else.'

Jake thought for a moment. 'Inner-force,' he said, recalling his conversation with Braysheath about how inner-force was from the innermost worlds, creating obstacles and destroying illusion. But it was lethal if one wasn't ready for it.

'Spot on, laddie.'

'But you said inner-force was carried to the Surface in contaminated rocks by the Zarzanzamin.'

'Aye, I did. To the mid-oceanic ridges. But by the time those tectonic plates reach the continents, the inner-force has been tempered to just the right level to do its job. However, if you take a chest of jewels and precious metals straight from the Inner-Peregrinus and dump it bang in the middle of a nomadic encampment in a woodland called London, what d'yer think's gonna happen?'

'Are you saying eventually cities came about because Luna had chests of jewels and precious metals brought to the Surface at the end of the last Ice Age? But surely such things have always been on the surface.'

'Aye, the occasional lump found in a river and only by the person meant to find it. But no one collected such things. Why on earth would they? Everything was beautiful just the way it was. So was looking someone in the eye much more beautiful than gazing at a rock hanging around their neck. But stick a potent great chest of the stuff in front of a group who are already a wee bit shaky and you've got a recipe for disaster.'

'Greed,' said Jake.

'Aye, greed. The Great Game was no longer about hide'n seek but brutal competition. In other words—war. The oneness of life was suddenly forgotten despite death doing its best to restore it.'

'Death? Restoring oneness?' said Jake.

'Aye, that's what the worlds of death are all about. After the challenges of the Surface, you're first reborn on a world called Roar. There you're born as one of the animal kingdom. Which type depends on yer soul's requirements at the time, but whatever it is, the principal lesson is honesty, for if there's one thing a creature is, it's honest, even when it eats yer.'

'I remember Braysheath saying something about that.'

'And when yer ready to move on, off you pop to the world of Leaf to be reborn as tree or plant—'

'No! Really?' cried Jake.

'Aye, in your case a pansy. On Leaf you relearn compassion, offering refuge against the elements, offering yer branches for the nesting birds, holding the soil together for your burrowing friends, taking care of the rain and all that wonderful stuff.'

'My God,' muttered Jake, enchanted by the idea.

'And finally, there's Hunter. There you incarnate in human form to reacclimatise yourself pre-Surface and practise what you've learnt in a purer environment—to live as humans on the Surface did during the periods of the Great Dance. All life is part of yer family. No tribe stays in one place so long that they rot the land. On the contrary, the presence of humans brought light and diversity.'

'Why is it called Hunter?'

'Because ultimately your hunt yourself—your true self. Anyway, it's the gate from Hunter to the Surface which Luna's jammed.'

'So how long does that process of reincarnation go on for?' asked Jake.

'Ach, just a few thousand times in most cases. Until you've gained enough gravity to be hauled off to the Inner-Peregrinus, for what yer might call a more challengin' time.

They fell into a moment's silence as Jake absorbed what Rufus had said. He gazed out at all the creatures about the savannah and tried to imagine what it was like to be as a graceful as a deer, a leopard lounging in a tree or an eagle soaring high up in the sky.

'Anyway,' said Rufus, 'the trixies not only brought the chests of inner-force, but they showed humans how to tap the water table to irrigate crops and create surpluses, something which should never have been done. It allowed them to cheat the rain cycle and move out of balance with the rest of nature. And now that the water table of the Surface has almost run dry, following so much wastage and deforestation, what've you got?'

Jake was looking at the distant mountains when it suddenly clicked. He had been taught in school that there wasn't enough food in the world, but he now realised that it was the other way around. There was too much, otherwise the population could never have expanded so quickly. It was just that the food was unfairly distributed. Some countries were fat and wasteful, others were skinny, though still had too many children. While the sacrificing of the shepherds had created a surplus of souls, the trixies had shown humans—drugged by too much inner-force—how to feed the excesses which followed, even if many were often hungry.

'So before all this happened,' asked Jake, 'was there money?'

'No need. Almost everythin' was local, everythin' was shared. People trusted each other. And no poverty or any of that other modern stuff. No diseases created by cities, like cholera, because there weren't any cities.'

'What about crime?'

'Aye, there's always been a bad apple, even during the Great Dance, but it was rare. Why steal when yer see abundance all around you, yourself a part of it? And as for justice, it was corrective. One was booted into the desert or jungle where Mother Nature decides yer fate. If yer survived the allotted time, back yer came and all was forgiven.'

Suddenly the god gate sprang to Jake's mind. Frost had suggested it was a modern thing, but Jake wanted to double-check the information with Rufus. To mention it, however, would open a can of worms—the riddle and Frost, neither of which Rufus knew about. Jake pondered how to frame his question.

'Anything else?' he ventured.

'Aye, plenty. You need only study the structure of a city to work it out, especially the buildings which stand at its centre. But now that you mention it, there is one other thing the trixies did. They created something under an old temple.'

'Oh?' said Jake. 'What was that?'

'Somethin' called the god gate. It's under the sphinx in Egypt.'

Frost told the truth! cried Jake in thought as a great wave of relief swept through him.

'Why would they do that?' he asked.

'They were under the direction of Luna, who corrupted a group of them. The idea was to shatter the myth that created union—the myth of the *Mother Goddess of Many Names*. She who is in all things and whose centre is everywhere. By creating all these other so-called gods, demigods or tribal gods, mainly male, jealous and warring, each a champion of their chosen people, Luna succeeded in creating division.'

'And this one group who are corrupt…' he ventured.

'Are a very nasty business indeed,' said Rufus. 'Because forces and demi-forces are so powerful, ordinarily they can only operate within strict parameters—to influence but not intervene directly. So you can imagine what happens when one tribe decides to bend or break the rules. A demigod is nothing compared to a demiforce.'

'Demiforce,' muttered Jake, recalling that Braysheath had described trixies and pixies as half force, half human.

'They're physically powerful, live much longer lives than humans and are extremely intelligent,' said Rufus.

'And it's this tribe that made the god gate.'

'Aye, it's one of their many talents. They have a sixth sense for them, just as they do for anything secret. I'm not talkin' about the original holygates, or the secret backdoor ones created by Braysheath. Those ones are extremely sophisticated and subtle. But Luna's requirement to create the god gate was right up the trixies' alley. Destruction.'

'But they're false gods, right? They all fall.'

'Aye, they do. Most of the nasty buggers up on the Surface are fallen gods, thirsting after futile power until they finally learn their lesson. Which they all do. The hard way. Dragging everyone else down with them.'

'How come there are so many different types of gates and portals?'

'It's the nature of movement through the cosmos. In each and every moment on the surface of Earth you stand at a junction, even if you don't see it. You can lead an impoverished existence from your fearful mind, or live a full life from your trusting heart. Most choose the first and so evolve slowly. But for those who choose the second way, their soul moves quickly towards the source. Though you don't physically see the portal up there, except for in dreams, down here you see the deeper reality.'

'You're right. It is like that in dreams. Following an important decision the scene suddenly changes as though I've passed from one place to another.'

Jake was watching a herd of elephants pass across the savannah, whose size and magnificence reminded him of the Zarzanzamin and the break-in. 'What about the gate in the fountain?' he asked. 'Where did that come from and how come no one knew about it?'

Rufus released a heavy sigh. 'Aye, I know. It's incredible. But it hadnae been used in a long time. I can only imagine it was one of the first batch of gates brought into the fort for safe-keepin'. It was probably disguised as the fountain by one of the shepherds who have since been sacrificed. But like most gates it can only be used by certain members of fort staff, along with those with special invites.'

'Special invites?' asked Jake sitting up, his earlier restlessness returning.

'Aye—special deliveries from other parts of the inner-worlds or regular visitors. It's why you as Lord Tusk must be especially careful who you invite. And once inside, your invite acts like a sort of invisibility cloak in the sense that they blend in and aren't bothered by others.'

'Even if I invited Lord Boreas?'

'Aye—even him.'

The heat of panic rose up in Jake as he recalled how Frost had insisted on being *officially* invited and how it had been Frost who had befriended Jake—Frost who seemed to know everything. Jake drew a deep inward breath to calm himself.

Before such thoughts spiralled out of control, he reflected instead on his feelings about Frost. What he felt was genuine friendship. It was certainly a novel one—refreshingly honest and no-nonsense. Above all, in Frost's presence Jake felt alive. Surely that was the true measure of a healthy friendship.

Frost was just being eccentric, Jake decided. *Besides, he's been so helpful. As for knowing so much, it's possible to have special knowledge if you research such things. I'm being paranoid.*

Regardless, an unsettling feeling remained with Jake and he made a mental note to watch Frost more carefully.

'Anyway,' said Jake, keen to shift the subject, 'that doesn't explain how Boreas or the Zarzanzamin got in. Are you suggesting someone in the fort invited them? Someone like Asclepius?'

'What? Asclepius? Of course not! And what the Devil do you mean by accusing someone like him?' shot back Rufus.

Jake was silent, surprised at the passion of Rufus's reaction. *It's time to share the riddles with him,* he thought, recalling his earlier decision. He closed his eyes for a moment and took another deep breath.

'Rufus...' he started with as much gravity as possible.

'Aye,' said Rufus, his surface rippling ominously.

'I have a slight confession to make.'

Rufus said nothing, but continued to ripple.

'It's nothing to get overexcited about. Perhaps I might have mentioned this earlier, but given its nature I wasn't sure who I could trust, not to mention how rushed everything's been and...'

'Spit it out,' said Rufus.

'But if I do tell you, you must promise to keep it a secret, for now at least. You'll see why.'

'A secret, hey? They're funny things down here,' said Rufus. 'They stick out like a tart in church to the likes of Braysheath who, anyhow, have their own way of knowing.'

'All the same,' said Jake.

'Alright. If it makes yer feel better I promise not to *consciously* tell anyone,' conceded Rufus.

'Good,' said Jake. 'Granddad left me a letter in Dad's study. It's two verses—a sort of riddle that I think might tell us his whereabouts,' he said and braced himself.

'What?' exclaimed Rufus, stiffening. 'Yer bloody fool!'

Jake held his tongue, deciding it was better to let Rufus vent his anger.

Rufus, however, was silent, flying in agitated circles.

'Alright, let's hear them,' he said finally, his tone curt.

Jake recited them.

> *Two lords a leaping, one known, one knot*
> *Untied or Titan'd, in Hades a plot*
> *Inside the risen, the Muses' second kiss (?)*
> *In words, pain for some, for others perhaps bliss*
>
> *Go ladies to lotus to Greek god seek*
> *Imagining things of which none can speak*
> *They follow their hearts and know their minds*
> *Accepting in action is both the cruel and the kind*

He then explained what had been worked out so far, withholding the role Frost had played: how the two lords a leaping had to be Jake's dad and Lord Boreas, how they had for some reason leapt through the god gate together, resulting in Lawrence's energy becoming *untied* or being banished to a hell, and that there was a plot in Hades, in other words, The House of Tusk. He also explained that *inside the risen, the Muses' second kiss* (*risen* being an anagram of Siren, meaning Lord Boreas) was another way of saying that the god now had double power from passing through the gate a second time. The rest Jake wasn't sure about except that the Greek God was possibly Asclepius.

Rufus had flown in pensive circles as he listened.

'Well, Sherlock,' he said at last, 'I must say, that's quite an impressive bit of deduction for a wee fella who's been but two days in a brave new world.'

'Thank you,' said Jake, choosing to ignore the irony.

'And two thefts later, a wee bit late,' chided Rufus.

'I'm sorry,' said Jake, feeling foolish. 'But you have to realise—'

'Ach, donnae worry about it. You've had a lot on yer plate.'

'So what do you think?'

'We suspected your dad's fate had somethin' to do with the gate but we weren't sure of the circumstances. It was unlike him to go rushin' off without tellin' anyone, but there couldnae have been time. As for your conclusions about what happened to him, I'm afraid yer right.'

Jake put on a brave face.

'The rest of yer thinkin' is also pretty good. Are you sure you didnae have help?'

Jake shrugged innocently. 'Divine inspiration?'

'Humph,' said Rufus and was silent for a moment.

'Any other thoughts about the riddles?' prompted Jake.

'The first verse is the key one. As for the second, *Go ladies to lotus to Greek God seek*, well, I've no idea what *Go ladies* refers to, but *lotus* means Renlock. From the outside it looks like a human meditating in lotus position.'

'Renlock?'

'The biggest organisation of spies in the cosmos,' said Rufus. 'Pigeon spies.'

'Pigeon spies?' scoffed Jake.

'You might laugh, laddie, but pigeons are the best. Have you never wondered why they're always loitering on window sills of important buildings, gossiping like old maids? Brilliant linguists, they are. All that warbling, rife with devilish diphthongs and infinite inflections. Only the cuckoos understand it and when it comes to spying, they're the elite. One mere hoot of a cuckoo contains more subtleties than the entire works of Shakespeare.'

'Are all pigeons spies?' asked Jake, deeply disturbed at the idea.

'Pretty much. As for Renlock, it's hired out to second-rate gods up to no good—usurping other gods usually, especially those on the Surface.'

'Do you think that's where Granddad could be—in Renlock?' asked Jake excitedly.

'It's possible.'

'Then we must go!'

'Oh aye—yer just gonna waltz into the largest den of the most devious spies in the cosmos and make an enquiry are yer?'

'Of course not. I shall draw on the infinite wisdom of my dashing flying carpet who surely knows a way in,' said Jake silkily.

'Nice try but no chance. It's far too risky, even for someone as fearless and dashing as m'self.'

'So what are we going to do, just hang around while Granddad's strung up and tortured?'

'Calm down, lassie. I'll make enquiries. Yer not the only one who'd like to see him back in one piece, yer know.'

'I'm pleased to hear it,' said Jake. 'And what about this Greek god? If it's not Asclepius, then who is it?'

'There are quite a few of them still knockin' about down here. Lord Boreas for starters. He's Greek.'

'What? Boreas, Greek? He doesn't look Greek.'

'Aye, that's because he's also God of the North Wind, which must wreak havoc with his tan. He's even resident at Renlock— the Governor-General no less, and he's certainly one for the ladies.'

'But that's too obvious,' said Jake, clinging to his suspicion of Asclepius, the so-called god of healing.

'Maybe,' said Rufus. 'But donnae be so quick to assume.'

Having wallowed in the bath for quite long enough, Jake decided it was time to get out. 'Rufus, would you mind passing me my jeans?'

'Do I look like yer bloody wet nurse? Be a man! Leap out and stand proud. Roar like a lion! It's very liberatin', I assure yer.'

'How would you know?'

'I havenae always been a carpet,' said Rufus.

Realising Rufus wasn't going to help and having checked they were alone, Jake hopped out.

'Come on!' said Rufus as Jake was about to pick up his jeans. 'Stand proud! Look out over yer domain with pride! Go on, have a roar!'

'You're barking,' said Jake, when Rufus suddenly swiped his clothes. 'Hey! Give them back!'

'You cannae have 'em back until you face the savannah and roar!' he said.

'You're being very annoying,' said Jake doing his best to maintain what little dignity was left to him.

'Just a simple roar,' repeated Rufus. 'It'll help yer get in touch with yer wild side. Think of it as part of yer trainin'.'

'Bloody rug,' muttered Jake resigning himself to idiotic behaviour, wanting to get it over with as soon as possible.

Feeling extremely exposed, Jake turned to the savannah. 'Roar,' he said pathetically.

'Aye, you've gotta do better than that, laddie,' said Rufus. 'Put some heart in it!'

Following a dismayed shake of his head, he did another. It was a moderate improvement on the first.

'There,' he said, 'now give me my clothes.'

'Yer've got one last chance,' warned Rufus. 'If you fail to roar like a proper lion, yer makin' yer own way back to yer room. The long way and starkers.'

More out of frustration with Rufus than anything else, finally Jake raised his arms to the savannah and released such a roar that some animals glanced up at him.

'That's more like it!' cried Rufus. 'How d'yer feel?'

'Actually,' confessed Jake, 'pretty good.'

'Well, have another!'

'You know, I think I will!' said Jake and roared even louder.

'Hey-hey! That's the spirit!' celebrated Rufus and finally tossed Jake's clothes down.

After two roars, however, Jake was so at home in his own skin that he continued to stand proud, relishing the breeze about his body.

Until, that is, he heard a rustle of leaves. 'Oh God,' he muttered..

He glanced in the direction the rustle came from and, to his horror, spotted a face. It was staring at him through the foliage of a rhododendron bush directly in front of him. It wasn't the face of a sprite. Neither did it belong to any of the creatures of the savannah. Just as he had feared, the face was human. One he had seen just that morning in the mirror.

It was the warrior girl.

They locked eyes. Though it was only a moment, for Jake it felt like forever—time enough to see the tears of laughter in her eyes, her hand over her mouth to hold it in.

With the speed of lightning, he tore up a shrub to cover himself but it was hardly a fig leaf.

'Rufus! Quick!' he cried, in no mood to run after the girl himself. 'There's someone in the bushes!'

'Ach, it's just the monkeys.'

'It's not the bloody monkeys! It's a girl!'

'Ha! A couple of decent roars and listen to yer! Dream on, pal.'

By the time Jake glanced back at the bush she had already disappeared.

Jake closed his eyes, shook his head, swallowed his pride and finally laughed. *The embarrassment had been worth it to see her laugh.*

The image of her cat-like brown eyes glistening with laughter had imprinted themselves in his mind.

He looked down at himself, wishing the encounter had left more to the imagination.

'Rufus,' he said.

'Aye?'

'I wish to inform you that you're a bastard.'

'Ach, thank ye. Ye say the nicest things.'

CHAPTER 28
FURY ROSE

When Rani and Bin returned to their hideout, Rani was still stifling her hysterics. Bin had risked flying high into the sky so that Rani could release her screams of laughter without drawing attention.

'Oh, Bin,' sighed Rani with tears in her eyes. 'Have you ever seen anything so funny?'

Bin chortled. 'I must say, it was an unexpected treat. And just what you needed after last night's drama. There really is no better medicine than a good laugh.'

Rani had another fit of laughter.

'So what do you think of him now?' asked Bin.

'Even more dangerous than before,' said Rani between giggles. 'He's completely unstable. I mean it, Bin. He's liable to do absolutely anything!'

Bin was looking at her doubtfully.

Rani's laughter subsided. A smile still on her face, she closed her eyes. In the last few hours she had seen two males bathing, one from the back through a vision and—Rani giggled again—one from the front.

Could they really be the same soul? she dared to wonder, partly disturbed by the idea, partly fascinated.

Could the woman whose feelings she had shared in the vision through Frost really have been herself in a past life? She remembered how it had been the presence of the man in the lake that had brought the woman peace and thawed her cold heart.

Then why does this boy Jake unsettle me so much now? What's the darkness I sense in him?

The visions through Frost had been going backwards in time towards the bathing man. The darkness she now sensed in Jake somehow felt much older.

Perhaps Jake's ancient darkness is only rising up now. Perhaps there are ancient memories that I can't yet access though can still feel through intuition.

What they might be she couldn't imagine.

For some reason she thought of the powerful presence that appeared to her in the form of a bull elephant. She remembered her dream of riding it on a long journey through time.

Why do I think of that now? she wondered. *Does it also visit Jake? Is there a connection between the three of us?*

Rani placed her hands to her stomach. The snake inside of her was stirring again. *And what is this darkness I sense in me?*

On reflection, it wasn't just darkness. It was a confusion of feelings. She recalled the sight of Jake sleeping, the young lion, and the sensation felt surprisingly pleasant like a delicious ache. When she thought of the break-in and the cold power that had taken hold of him, the sensation felt heavy and nauseating.

Jake in the present, Jake in the distant past, she thought, distinguishing the two feelings. *But what happens if he embraces his past?*

She thought optimistically of the bathing man in her vision. The serpent flipped, writhed, began an ecstatic slithering up her spine and caused her heart to race.

With a gasp her eyes shot open.

'Are you alright?' asked Bin.

Rani was too flustered to answer.

The sensation subsided. Her heartbeat calmed.

Wishing the sensation would come back, her eyes fell to floor in front of the fountain.

Her heart leapt. This time it was nothing to do with Jake, but two items on the floor.

'My knives!' she cried.

At first light, she and Bin had searched for them tirelessly but found nothing. Rani had even slipped into the moat and searched about its bottom.

'But how?' she said.

Beside them was a red rose. Her blood boiled. First with anger and alarm that Frost had found and somehow managed to enter their hideout, but also with indignation.

'How dare he chop the head off a rose and offer it to me!' she exclaimed. 'Does he not know that there is no greater insult?'

'I suspect he does, Rani dear.'

'Then I shall do the same to him!'

They fell into a moment's silence while Rani closed her eyes and calmed down.

'We have to trap him,' she said at last. 'We've been charged with protecting the boy Jake, yet he himself is the greatest risk—a risk that becomes all the more real as long as this Frost is at his side. I'm certain his intention is to draw out this terrible darkness I sense in Jake.'

'How does one catch something as tricky as his kind?' asked Bin.

'That's what we need to work out, Bin. But catch him we will.'

CHAPTER 29
WAR ROOM

ONCE AGAIN, LORD BOREAS, WILDERSPIN AND THE COMMANDER, along with a select company of his guardians, were gathered in a secret hall in Renlock. Luna's plan to block the holygate from Hunter to the Surface had worked. With Nestor and the sylph inside the gate, no souls were reaching new-borns. It was time to up the pressure and move to the next phase of her plan.

Like the rest of Renlock, the hall was granite and devoid of any plant life. This one was particularly large with a ceiling of great height. Arranged in a broad-set triangle were three massive towering cone-shaped granite rocks known as menhirs, one of whose properties was to hold space for the discharge of great power. Masterfully deposited in each of them was one of the three secret backdoor gates Lawrence had stolen at the same time as the holygate. Their entrances, recalibrated for two-way movement, had been enlarged to cathedral size, each delineated by light: a lion's head mid-roar, a hollow tree and an arch formed by two peaceful-seeming hands which touched at the fingertips. They were the gates to Roar, Leaf and Hunter.

The three males were silent as they waited. That suited Lawrence just fine. Since Luna had touched his face at their last meeting and Lord Boreas had unleashed Lawrence's darkest demon, he had been struggling to sustain presence.

Using his wolf spirit, he was communicating telepathically with Geoffrey in the dream room.

You know how I hate to be negative, said Geoffrey, *but your chances of getting through this are extremely slim.*

Can you try to be little more encouraging, said Lawrence. *Just for once.*

That was encouraging. That was putting it very optimistically. You're about to the meet the Devil.

Lawrence looked unmoved.

Your own devil, continued Geoffrey, referring to the demon Lord Boreas had released. *The manifestation of your deepest darkest secrets which your conscious mind long ago buried and has no interest or desire to remember.*

The image of the repugnant black-bearded face fixed itself in Lawrence's mind.

Ordinarily, continued Geoffrey, *it would take centuries, perhaps millennia, for your conscious mind to come to terms with such things.*

The Commander, who as a being of inner-force had heightened senses, glanced at Lawrence with a curious light in his eyes, as though he perceived something unusual though didn't know what exactly.

It's alright, said Geoffrey. *He can't hear us. He simply senses a disturbance.*

Lawrence ignored the guardian. *Anything else?*

Just remember that by releasing the demon, Boreas is luring you into the Inner-Peregrinus before you're ready for it. Also remember that the only limit to what is possible is your imagination. But unlike your practice on the pinnacle in the sea, which was in the Outer-Peregrinus, in the oppressive air of the inner-realms your imagination will often fail you or lack strength. The weight of the unconscious is too heavy. At least until you've gained gravity. You'll feel pain, but healing by will-power will be difficult.

Understood, said Lawrence, glancing at Wilderspin who was looking jubilant with anticipation.

Sustaining presence in more than one dimension will also be difficult, continued Geoffrey. *I suggest you find a place to rest in one dimension while you focus your consciousness in the other. Needless to say, given your present company, that's going to be tricky.*

I have faith in my cause, said Lawrence. *The cosmos will help.*

You'd better hope so, said Geoffrey, *because once you've left the dream room, which is what a visit to the Inner-Peregrinus entails, I can't help you. We'll be out of contact until your consciousness returns here. It's the nature of the journey. One must battle one's demons alone.*

Lawrence's eyes met the Commander's. Feeling vulnerable, he closed them.

So you see, concluded Geoffrey, *I was being quite optimistic before because, actually, you're well and truly stuffed.*

I really should have chosen one of the other lizards, said Lawrence.

One last thing, added Geoffrey, *If you're struggling to sustain presence, ask questions—of your surroundings and the characters within it, remembering that everything is real, but also symbolic, reflecting yourself. Questions are tool for remembering that you actually know nothing while the unconscious knows everything. Humility is powerful. So is self-honesty and gratitude.* Geoffrey suddenly sat up. *Luna's approaching the hall. Prepare yourself.*

A moment later, wisps of purple-tinged smoke appeared high up in the hall.

Wilderspin gasped on spotting it. His ever-watchful eyes brightened with relish. Guardians gazed up impassively while Lawrence did his best to stay calm.

The smoke spiralled down to a point at the very centre of the menhirs. A ball of light appeared at its centre. It pulsed with such intensity that all but the guardians were forced to shield their eyes.

When Lawrence and Wilderspin looked out again, standing before them in purple robes was Luna.

'My lady!' exclaimed Wilderspin. 'Each time we're blessed with your presence you grow evermore captivating! I thought it impossible but it's true! How *do* you do it?'

'The usual way—light,' said Luna. 'And it's time to collect more. Are you ready for war?'

'We certainly are!' beamed Wilderspin. 'Blocking the holygate was a masterstroke, my lady. A masterstroke! Not only will humans waver in their faith, assuring Brock's fall from the Surface, but it traps souls in death. Each day their number swells. They're ripe for the picking! Ripe to become lost to the Peregrinus!'

'And their energy used for a more worthy cause,' added Luna.

'May I ask, my lady, where the light will be stored?' asked Lawrence.

Luna studied her henchman for a moment. 'In an ark, Lord Boreas. Concealed in a place where not even meddlers like Braysheath can find it.'

'The Eye of the Orijinn Sea!' gasped Wilderspin, eyes wide with awe. It was the mother ocean, located midway between the Surface and the Core, caused by the clash of the inner and outer forces. 'If there's a place to hide something, it's there!'

'That's none of your business,' chided Luna.

Though Wilderspin bowed in feigned deference, his eyes twinkled with what he took to be a confirmation.

Luna slowly circled the menhirs, running her fingers across the menhirs. 'I'm pleased with this war room. Never before has there been such a place. Surface souls trapped in the worlds of death. Restful worlds, yes. But not for long. I'm about to open up free movement between them, something that's in direct conflict with Universal Law. The confusion will create war, right here in this room, and such a trauma that souls will become lost.'

'Ripe for the picking!' repeated Wilderspin. 'It's genius, my lady! Pure genius!'

Lawrence's eyes rolled.

'Once on my ark,' continued Luna, 'I shall extract and cleanse the light from their soul vessels.'

'How will you transport them to your ark, my lady?' he asked.

'With this,' said Luna. She opened a hand and a stream of silvery butterflies flowed from it. They became a cloud that magically coalesced to form a unicorn so white that it glowed.

'Oh marvellous!' cheered Wilderspin. 'Delightful! The purest of creatures!'

Lawrence cursed in thought at Wilderspin's incessant creeping. *I know where I'd like to shove that bloody horn.*

The guardians looked as though they were having the same thought.

Geoffrey tittered.

Guided by Luna's hand, the entranced creature rose up into the air and was carried to the upper part of the back wall. A portion of the wall disintegrated and became shadowy, enough to accommodate the unicorn's body so that, like a trophy, only its head was showing. It then returned to granite, the unicorn included. Only its pearly horn continued to shine.

'A lightning conductor,' she said merrily.

'My lady!' declared Wilderspin. 'You never cease to amaze me with the immense mastery of your power. What purer conductor than a unicorn horn? What a wonder you are!'

Ignoring Wilderspin, Luna withdrew the glass flask of light from inside of her cloak. Its uncorking left an exquisite ringing in the air and a look of longing on the Pigeon Lord's face. She closed her eyes while she drained the flask.

A shiver later, her tresses transformed into serpents—bright orange, writhing like flames with green eyes. Their other-worldly hissing sent a shiver down Lawrence's spine.

Wilderspin was beside himself, but Luna raised a hand to silence him. She reclosed her eyes and began an eerie-sounding chant. Her hands moved in a mysterious choreography as she pulled at the essence of each of the three gates embedded in the menhirs and weaved them through one another.

The air vibrated.

The guardians took up positions about the edge of the hall.

Wilderspin made a hasty exit to the safer vantage point of the gallery above.

A momentary uneasiness showed itself in Lawrence's expression. His right hand moved to the hilt of his sword.

As Luna's movements grew more rapid, the vibration mounted to a higher frequency. The air grew charged. Shadow seeped from each gate as though from a wound and gave expression to her work, lacing about her and merging.

The strange dance grew more intense, more frenzied. Skies rumbled. Lighting forked down. Thunder cracked throughout the cosmos so terrifyingly that even the least conscious of beings cowered, wondering what it meant.

The sense of perversion was so great, the shadowy air so suffocating, that Lawrence felt sick. He was on the verge of vomiting when Luna struck out her hands. Energy pulsed through every atom in the entire cosmos, especially in the war room.

Luna stood motionless. The shadow subsided. The air rang.

Her eyes shot open and flashed with delight. She was looking directly at Lawrence. Though he hadn't vomited, the threat remained and he battled not to show it.

With a sense of great purpose Luna clicked her fingers, dissolved into smoke and reappeared besides a spellbound Wilderspin, her hair back to normal.

The stillness, the sense of expectation, was immense.

An ominous breeze issued from each gate. Leaves blew from Leaf. The wind from Roar carried the screech of peacock. From Hunter spilled the fading light of dusk and filled the hall with an eerie air.

The weight of it showed on Lawrence's brow. He remained beside one of the menhirs, just beyond the fray of the fateful space between all three.

Finally there was movement. A man popped through the gate from Hunter. He was dressed in pre-historic garb of leather and furs and armed with a bow. He studied his new surroundings, looking confused. It wasn't long before his gaze was drawn to Luna, whose eyes shone with anticipation.

The man was looking at her as though trying to recall where he had seen her before, when his eyes suddenly widened in terror. He was distracted, however, by the arrival of three wolves from Roar.

Tension crackled through the hall. Confusion transformed to anger. Hackles up, the wolves snarled. The man reached for his knife.

Others popped on to the scene—a man and two women, a lion, a boar and a python.

The tension multiplied to breaking point.

It was delayed for a moment when an oak tree burst through from Leaf. Leaves rattled. A plaintive groan resounded about the hall. Starting deep it rose to the pitch of an agonised wail and coursed through the others like electricity, their tortured expressions perfect mirrors of the oak's anguish.

The breaking point rose to a higher threshold.

At last the wailing stopped. With a final rustle the oak stiffened, contained itself until it no longer could, then released a roar that shook Renlock.

An elephant burst forth from Roar, trumpeted in fury and charged at the oak.

The impact made a dreadful crack but the oak held, gripped the elephant with its branches and hurled it against a menhir. A horrendous cry pierced the air as the elephant shattered into light.

Luna alone stood enlivened as the light arced into the unicorn's horn and produced a deafening crack.

Every being and beast gazed in astonishment as the unicorn's eyes glowed in response.

Luna clapped in delight.

The instant its eyes dimmed, all hell broke loose.

Fuelled by new arrivals through the gates, every manner of beast leapt through trees and hunters in brutal combat.

My God, muttered Lawrence as a tree was felled with a mighty sword stroke.

It's intent that matters, not size, said Geoffrey as another tree wailed in horror. A lion had sunk its claws into its trunk before it was torn apart by the tree's roots.

The bursts of light grew so intense that the atmosphere of the hall was like that of a storm, the air ringing with the terrible cries of lost souls arcing into the unicorn horn. From there, lost souls raced through the cosmos towards the unicorn's twin. Its horn had been enlarged to form the mast of a special ship—Luna's ark, moored on an arctic shore in a secret world in the Eye of the Orijinn sea, what Lawrence had glimpsed on their first visit to

Renlock. The souls shot down the mast into a large spherical turquoise vault below deck, one cut off from the rest of the cosmos.

The arrival of the souls into the vault had a clear impact on Luna. She arched back and released an ecstatic scream so powerful that it cut through the mounting din of war and gale of leaves.

In no time at all the battle had become so dense that in-fighting broke out and soul upon soul disappeared through the horn in a constant stream.

As she acclimatised to the flow, Luna shone like a sun.

When the battle spread back through the gates and on to the three worlds of Death, she released yet more silvery butterflies, a cloud of them for each gate.

'Go, my wondrous unicorns!' she cried. 'Gather my light!'

While Lawrence watched them with a sense of despair, he was distracted by a particularly fearsome-looking hunter. Their gazes locked. Having nodded to two of his tribe, the three hunters marched towards Lawrence.

This is it, warned Geoffrey from the dream room. *If they manage to breach the threshold of the menhirs, you'll know Boreas is behind it. He's taking advantage of the situation—Luna, the tension of war, you can't escape. He means to drag you off to the Inner-Peregrinus. Get ready.*

One of the men had two swords and rushed forward swirling them with great skill.

Now that the moment was upon him, Lawrence felt calm. He coolly unsheathed the powerful sword that belonged to Lord Boreas.

As the hunter breached the fray unharmed, roaring his battle cry, in one powerful stroke Lawrence sliced clean through both blades and took off his head.

The other two hunters flinched with the crack as he turned into light. His soul, however, didn't arc to the unicorn horn, but into the tip of Lord Boreas's sword. It had been designed by dwarf-smiths to absorb the souls of whoever it slew in order to enhance its power.

Taking note, the guardians glanced up at Luna. She was watching Lawrence with great interest.

Watch your intent, said Geoffrey. *To slay a soul already in death will taint your own.*

Its better off in this sword than Luna's vault, said Lawrence as the other two raced forward. *And the power will help!*

Each you slay will be followed by more, said Geoffrey. *Luna's watching. You must do something. Don't delay the inevitable.*

Like the one before, both hunters breached the fray. Rather than slay them, however, Lawrence parried their strokes, biding for time.

I have an idea, he said and punched one of the hunters unconscious as another arrived. *If I'm to be dragged off by Boreas and I only have enough energy to focus in one dimension at time, then I need a hiding place. What if I take refuge in one of the worlds through the gates? Leaf, for example.*

You're alive and Leaf is a place of death. In theory it's not possible, said Geoffrey. *But the dream room might allow it. Boreas might allow it. Do it!*

In a sign of confirmation, one of the Bengal tigers in the thick of battle broke free and circled behind Lawrence. Fighting the hunters with great skill, he made a convincing show of being forced by the beast towards the menhirs.

'Lord Boreas!' rang out Luna's voice, her gaze fixed on Lawrence. 'Your duty is to monitor the battle, not partake in it. This light is not for you.'

Lawrence upped the intensity of his blades strokes and pretended not to hear.

'The battle's gone to his head, my lady,' remarked Wilderspin. 'Are you sure you've chosen well in Lord Boreas? Not that for *one moment* I wish to doubt you, of course, but one does wonder…'

Luna said nothing. Rather than intervene, she watched on, intrigued.

Lawrence was just an inch from crossing the battle line. Death's chilly clasp reached out for him. His life flashed before his eyes. *It's just fear!* he cried in thought to reassure himself.

Braced for anything, he took the fateful step.

An almighty pulse of energy shook the hall.

The menhirs rocked.

Lawrence felt as though he were about to be torn apart—suspended in time, his fate in the balance while the cosmos made a decision.

Real time snapped back. He had survived.

His step had not only taken him across the battle line but somewhere else—the dream room. The two dimensions had merged. Dream room doors filled the gaps between the menhirs in a perfect circle.

Adding to the confusion of battle, one of the dream room doors exploded open. A man strode forth—one of such presence and such vitality that he appeared twice the size of everyone else. Dressed in the garb of a pirate, with bright red clothes and broad-brimmed hat, a cutlass through his thick leather belt and with large gold earrings, he was fulsome in every respect. From black beard to rosy cheeks, he couldn't have looked more imposing. Bursting with life, he surveyed the battle as though it were a bountiful port.

A sailor, remarked Geoffrey sardonically from the table. *Good luck!*

Lawrence immediately recognised his debauched face. Despite appearances, he was standing before his worst demon.

Taking a ferocious swipe at him, Lawrence tried to slay the pirate. Instead he beheaded two hunters as though the man were nothing more than a phantom.

The pirate tossed back his head with a bellow of thunderous laughter.

That's denial for you, remarked Geoffrey from the wall. *You don't really believe he exists. See how it strengthens him? It's not like gods. Some need belief to exist. Unconscious entities need denial.*

Fortunately for Lawrence, who was under great strain to avoid injury amid the chaos of trees and beasts, the man was content to simply watch on, his dark eyes bulging with exuberance. As Lawrence fought his way back towards the gate of Leaf, slaying for power as he went, the pirate beamed with delight.

Hands on hips and visible only to Lawrence and Geoffrey, his presence was like that of a giant beacon—a bright red lighthouse, though one which misled rather than saved. In contrast to the pirate everything paled, even Luna, despite her green eyes shining with so much stolen light.

Consumed by his presence, Lawrence was almost trampled on by a tree. He sliced off one of its roots, only to be leapt upon by a leopard from its branches. He impaled it in the chest and in the same movement wrenched free his blade, reversed it and did the same to a hunter attacking from behind.

The pirate bellowed with joy.

See how Lord Boreas toys with you, remarked Geoffrey. *Using the pirate he could drag you from the dream room right now if he wanted. But he has other plans in store. Stop wasting time and take the initiative. Pass onto Leaf.*

With a final burst of fight, and in a display of great swordsmanship, his blade glowing with power, Lawrence hacked and thrust his way to the threshold of the gate to Leaf.

Bloody hell, these trees! he cursed, doing his best to avoid them as they crashed through the gate like an army of giants. The trees were getting larger, but only became visible once they leapt through the shadowy entrance of the gate.

Luna's still watching, warned Geoffrey. *Make it look convincing.*

A banyan burst through the gate, swinging its aerial roots wildly.

Let it take you, said Geoffrey.

What? barked Lawrence.

Let the tree take you. A Siberian tiger is in its branches. It's a sign. For now you must trust it.

Trusting Geoffrey, Lawrence relaxed his guard for just a moment. He used it to glance up at Luna. Her eyes shone with curiosity.

This will be difficult to explain, he thought

One step at a time, said Geoffrey.

The next moment Lawrence was swept up by an aerial root and hurled back through the gate.

LAWRENCE CRASHED THROUGH THE FOLIAGE OF A TROPICAL TREE, luckily avoiding the trunk. Finally he gained his balance and swung down through the branches.

He stopped for a moment to catch his breath in the node of a redwood on the march—the final branch before the great descent down its vast trunk.

Stretched before him, all the way to the horizon, were trees on the move—an army. Their mighty trunks were like towers. Their plaintive groans and wails jarred the air and Lawrence with it.

The redwood was nearing the gate. In no mood to return so soon, Lawrence ran out along a branch and leapt.

His fall was broken by a willow whose yielding branches carried him to the ground where he met a yet greater challenge—avoiding the multitude of moving roots.

Use your imagination, said Geoffrey, still able to communicate. *You're still in the Outer-Peregrinus. Forget the laws of the Surface.*

As the roots of a yew threatened to crush him, Lawrence leapt.

The first leap was just enough to clear the immediate danger. The second was like a gazelle's. By the third he was leaping like a flea across the sea of roots.

Ahead to the right, said Geoffrey. *A cave in the outcrop of rock. The Siberian tiger is standing in front of it. There you can rest in this dimension and focus your attention elsewhere. And stop wasting time with leaping. Arrive where you need to be.*

Where's the pirate? asked Lawrence.

You'll seen him soon enough.

Lawrence spotted the tiger as it passed into the darkness of the cave and he willed himself to join it.

A moment later he arrived, grateful for the respite from the trees as they stomped around the outcrop of rock.

You've only a moment, said Geoffrey. *Make the most of it.*

Lawrence placed his hands and forehead against the cool granite and took a deep breath.

'Father Sky, Mother Earth... Mother Sky and Father Earth,' he whispered, addressing the four key gods of the old world, 'whatever fate awaits me, give me the strength and grace to embrace it.'

He took a final glance at the trees, scarcely able to believe what was happening—Luna's horrific war siphoning light from the Peregrinus, himself on Leaf, a planet of Death, about to be dragged off by his darkest demon to depths of the cosmos his soul was far from prepared for. All the while, Lord Boreas waited on the side lines for the auspicious moment to pounce.

The chances of his survival were close to zero. And so he brushed them aside and thought of Jake, Rowena and Nestor instead.

'For you, my loves,' he said to himself and stepped into the cave.

The moment his foot touched the insides, he blacked out.

CHAPTER 30
LOYALTY'S LIMITS

SITTING CROSS-LEGGED ON THE CUSHIONS OF HIS LAIR AND SMILING smugly was Frost.

'You know, Silver,' he said, addressing his companion the raven which was preening itself on the bench of the secret fireplace, 'I'm having tremendous fun. Oh, what mischief I could weave, what wonderfully poetic mischief, if only I could allow myself to really let loose! But something holds me back. Me, holding back? It's a first! Do you think I'm developing a conscience?'

The raven released a dubious-sounding gurgle.

'Imagine what Father would say!' cried Frost. 'And yet, neither can I wholly ignore my nature. After all, I am what I am, Silver.'

Frost took up a walnut from a dish beside him, tossed it in the air and caught it on the tip of his tongue before munching it down.

'And so, Silver, a plan. Since we're growing fond of new-friend Jake, we shall help him as much as mischief permits. No need to tell Father of course. He *instructed* me to simply *observe* the new Lord Tusk in order to gauge whether he's a threat or not. But where's the fun in that?' exclaimed Frost, his eyes glistening in the torch light. 'What sort of agent simply observes? Once on the ground one must improvise. Especially when the plot unfolding is so intricate—one in which we too have a role to play.'

Silver cawed in agreement.

'And oh, what a role, Silver! For who knows more than us? Who else has intelligence from both sides of the fence? Not Braysheath. Not even Luna! And not any old intel, but top quality intel direct from the source, like getting a peek at the god gate records. Of course such powerful beings as Braysheath and Luna can see on deeper levels, but deeper levels remain a mystery unless the surface can be cracked. Why, we even know the real identity of Luna. It's so obvious! Obvious and beyond belief! That's the beauty of big truths—they're too big to believe. And Jake's riddles of course—apart from that tedious *Go ladies* bit, we've already sussed it. *Imagining things of which none can speak.* Oh, how excruciatingly I understand it!'

The raven released an excited caw.

'Of course, Silver. Don't you worry. We certainly can't tell Jake that. That would spoil all the fun. Timing is everything. Spontaneity is the key. We shall have to be very careful in how we guide him through this ever-shifting labyrinth. Very careful indeed. If he works things out too quickly that could prove fatal—for him, for everyone. A red herring here and there to throw him off the scent, that's what's needed.'

Silver gurgled with approval.

'And one thing in which I shall remain steadfast, Silver—I shall always be honest-ish! It's one thing I'm extremely principled about.'

Frost took up a perfect-looking peach from his stash of food and bit into it.

'And this Rani,' he said between bites. 'I must confess, Silver, I haven't quite worked her out. She's as mysterious as Jake. And here she is in this very fort. I wonder what the fates have in store.'

Frost finished the juicy peach, a secret smile in his eyes.

'By the way, Silver, you did destroy those records, didn't you?' said Frost, referring to Lawrence and Lord Boreas's passage through the god gate, along with something especially secret that had happened there sixteen years earlier. Frost scarcely dared think about it, let alone voice it, in case his thoughts were heard.

Silver cawed.

'I'm pretty sure none of our clan have seen the recent records. I know it's breaking the rules, but that's what rules are for, are they not? Especially when there are bigger fish to catch. I can't have someone in the clan spilling the beans to Father before they're cooked.'

With no more sound than a flap of wings, Silver took sudden flight into the darkness.

Taking note, Frost sat alert.

A moment later the bench spun around and Jake appeared.

Without a word, hands on hips, Jake stood tall, like a king before his court. No longer was he wearing his clothes of the Surface, but a kilt, a musketeer-like khaki shirt and a black turban, tied about his neck and head in the manner of a Bedouin.

'Wow!' exclaimed Frost. 'Look at you!'

'The colours of the House of Tusk,' announced Jake proudly.

'Very fetching!' proclaimed Frost.

'It is, isn't it? It's also easier to jump into,' said Jake, fresh from the adventures of his bath. 'By the way, I was thinking, this girl in the fort…'

'What about her?' said Frost, his eyes brightening.

'Well, apart from the fact I've no idea what she's up to, she's trespassing,' said Jake. 'I was thinking of asking Glabrous the thorsror to track her down and bring her to me.'

'Were you indeed? Ha!' cried Frost. 'You're certainly settling into this lord of the fort business. And a thorsror! What a brilliant idea. I must say, I'm impressed.'

'You are?'

'Of course. You can't have an imp like her skulking about and causing trouble.'

'You don't think sending a thorsror is too much?' asked Jake. He had been battling with the idea. Since the bath, he couldn't stop thinking about her. By having her brought to him, he both fulfilled his responsibilities as lord and also got to talk to her, even if the manner of the summons might start their relationship on a slightly tense note.

'Certainly not. She's exceptionally tricky. In fact, thinking about it, I'd send two.'

'I think one should be enough,' decided Jake. 'Glabrous is bloody scary.'

Frost nodded, looking delighted. 'So what else has his lordship been up to?'

'God, don't call me that.'

'Alright, his *dark* lordship.'

'I told you—stop that rubbish. Anyway, I decided to tell Rufus about the riddles.'

'Another excellent idea,' said Frost. 'You can trust him. What did he say?'

'That the word *lotus* relates to a place called Renlock. By the way, did you realise that pigeons are spies?'

'Are they really?' said Frost. 'Makes sense now that I think about it.'

'This place Renlock is apparently full of them and it's where Granddad is possibly being held prisoner. Rufus said it's too dangerous for me to go, but I have to. I need to find out how to get there.'

'Leave it to me.'

'You think you can do it?'

'Just you wait and see,' said Frost.

'Good,' said Jake. 'He also thinks Asclepius is loyal.'

'Oh does he? Well then, it's time to show you his secret laboratory. Follow me!' said Frost who sprang from the cushions and into the gloom of the passageway.

A SHORT WHILE LATER, FROST'S HEAD EMERGED FROM A CABINET—the exit from a secret passageway into Asclepius's laboratory, situated not in the hospital below, but in the top of one of the towers.

'All clear,' he whispered and sprang out.

Jake followed, immediately struck by an aromatic smell of burning leaves.

'Voila!' said Frost

They had arrived into a bizarre-looking high-domed circular room. Standing in the centre were cluttered work benches arranged in a cross, each distinct though overflowing with a peculiar brand of wild science. It was as though a mad professor and a witch had got together for a great experiment.

At first glance it was simply too much to take in. Especially strange was the mature oak tree which stood in the space at the centre of the cross of benches as though it were the experiment's heart. Clematis and other vines reached out from its branches and wove about the profusion of tubes and other apparatus, apparently lending a hand.

'What is it?' said Jake.

'Don't you see?' exclaimed Frost. 'It's not boring old chemistry. It's alchemy!'

'It is?'

'Look!' said Frost, pointing to the floor and trains of ants which led out in all directions from the oak. There were scores of lizards too, clinging to the walls and the bark of the oak. At any given moment, one would dart off looking purposeful.

'And the birds,' added Frost pointing up at a shaft of light that beamed in through a small window in the dome.

As Jake looked up, a couple of birds arrived and flew down into the oak while another left.

'It's funny,' he said. 'It almost feels like an observatory.'

'It is. A fantastical one. Rather than look outwards at the stars, it looks inwards.'

'You mean all these creatures are observing something?' asked Jake, delighted by the idea.

'Of course. It's an experiment—a *real* one, alive and connected to the very thing it's investigating. Do you see anything dead, chopped up, isolated from the very whole which gives it life and meaning?'

Jake didn't. A rat scurried over one of his feet as though to prove the point.

Careful not to tread on any ants or the red-capped mushrooms sprouting up between the stone slabs of the floor, Jake walked about the experiment.

He had only gone a quarter of the way round when he stopped and gasped. Resting in the oak's lowest branch as though it were a leopard was a large wolf, so white that it glowed.

The vision on the train! The dream of the chamber beneath the sphinx! He shook his head in shock, wondering what it meant. *It's the same wolf.* Jake simply knew it and his body tingled in confirmation.

Though powerful-looking, it had a fatigued air. While its eyes were closed, Jake had the sense that it was very much awake.

Once his own eyes had adjusted to the glow, Jake noticed that there were turquoise butterflies dotted over its coat, slowly opening and closing their wings. One of them flew up and landed on Jake's right hand.

To his surprise, the tingle became a swell of emotion. Tears threatened to break free and he battled in confusion to keep them down. The butterfly opened and closed its wings three times before returning to the wolf.

'The experiment's heart,' said Frost, who had appeared at Jake's side, referring to the wolf. 'Tricky colour, white. Oh, how people flock to it, hide in it. Oh, how they misunderstand.'

'Why is there a haze of light around the wolf?' managed Jake. 'Is that its aura?'

'No. It's light leaking from the wolf. Whatever the wolf represents, its soul is fractured,' explained Frost.

With a blissful whir of purple wingbeats, a flock of hummingbirds flew in and hovered about the wolf for an iridescent moment then flew off again.

'Part of the function of this experiment is medicinal, like a giant bandage,' said Frost pointing at the small fire of leaves on the floor. 'All these plants in the fire and the flasks—yarrow, vervain, wormwood and henbane, juniper, broom and mandrake, stone fungus and snow fungus, they're medicinal and very powerful in the right hands.'

'And mistletoe,' said Jake, spotting clumps of it in the branches about the wolf. 'Wasn't that something to do with druids?'

'Precisely. Their most sacred plant!' enthused Frost. 'Each fruit is like a moon, connected to rebirth.'

Jake's gaze remained on the wolf. 'How can a soul become fractured?' he asked.

For the briefest instant, too fleeting for Jake to notice, Frost's eyes flashed brighter. He knew the true purpose of the experiment. He had observed Asclepius enough to know his connection to Lawrence and that Jake's dad lived. The fracture was caused when he had leapt, mortally wounded, into the god gate. Though Frost didn't know of the dream room, he knew the wolf in the tree represented the wounded aspect of Lawrence's soul. But it was too early for Jake to know such things. As Frost had said to Silver just moments before, timing was everything, especially as far as decoding the riddles was concerned. It was time for one of Frost's red herrings—to bend the truth and throw Jake off the scent for a while.

'Well, that's what I've been wondering,' said Frost, 'because it must be something very rare, perhaps only possible through some terrible perversion of nature.'

'Like what?'

'Maybe a wound inflicted by a magical weapon in some battle between gods and hellish things,' said Frost excitedly.

'You think the wolf could represent something hellish?' said Jake doubtfully.

'Don't be fooled by appearances,' warned Frost. 'We all look pitiful when we're injured. And remember this is Asclepius's experiment. My guess is that this whole contraption is designed for healing and reviving a demon of some sort so it can be set free for some wicked purpose.'

Is that why I felt so sad a moment ago? wondered Jake.

Just then, a gazelle trotted up to the tree, gently pressed its forehead to the trunk and closed its eyes.

Jake cast his mind back to the time of the break-in and Asclepius lurking in the shadows of the archway. Four important gates had been stolen that night, yet the god of healing had stood by and watched.

'If that's what all this is really for, do you think he's planning to release it here?'

'Possibly,' said Frost. 'It's clear Asclepius is in cahoots with Lord Boreas, Luna's henchman. But I have a feeling a deeper intrigue is afoot, that while she plans to topple the god of the Surface, Boreas and Asclepius plan to topple her.'

'And using the fort to do so?'

'Why not? It's a powerful place. Who knows what it can do, or guess at its ultimate purpose?'

Jake shook his head in wonder at Frost's idea, which though fantastical, was credible.

'What about the rest of this?' he asked, focusing back on the experiment. 'What else does it do?'

'As far as I can tell, it's a sort of broadcaster-receiver to whatever hell this beast is located in,' said Frost.

'Broadcasting what?'

'The healing of course. But the best part of it,' said Frost bounding to the other side, 'is this!'

Jake joined him. 'Wow!' he gasped.

Taking up a whole bench and over-spilling its sides was a turtle, its head hidden inside its great shell.

'The projector!' announced Frost.

'Projector? Of what?'

'Of whatever info Asclepius needs to receive from the demon. With a bit of luck we'll see. We need an acorn to fall into that flask,' said Frost, indicating a flask full of a liquid which looked like blood. 'The acorn contains a concentration of all the intel brought by all the ants, lizard, birds and whatnot—translated and filtered through the wisdom of the tree. The rest of the apparatus acts like a transformer, reducing the intel's intensity to the wavelength of humans and gods.'

Jake ran a hand over the smooth shell of the turtle. 'Incredible.'

'The Primal Mother,' said Frost, referring to the turtle as totem, 'and full of myth. To some, the top part of the shell symbolises heaven, the under part, earth, the two unified through the creature inside. Only if it's alive of course. It also shows us how we need to withdraw inwards now and again.'

Their fascination was suddenly cut short. A powerful quake shook the room. Jake gripped the bench to stay on his feet. Bats and birds flew out from the oak which suddenly turned orange with autumn. Alarm calls of creatures rang out across the savannah.

Once the quake subsided, Jake and Frost dashed to the window. From the tower they could see out over much of the oasis. Every tree, even the evergreens, had turned autumnal, just like the oak.

'It looks so beautiful!' said Jake.

'Autumn marks the start of a hero's journey,' said Frost, 'into the darkness of winter. Don't be fooled!'

The quake had not only hit the fort, but every world in the cosmos as the impact of events in Luna's war room rippled outwards. In worlds less balanced than Himassisi, the shock was much more violent. Three volcanoes erupted on the Surface, spewing lava, and a fearsome cyclone gathered in the Pacific.

'What caused this?' said Jake, his heart racing. 'Something to do with the gates?'

'Maybe,' said Frost. 'Or perhaps to do with everything in this room. Perhaps both!'

Jake looked back at the wolf. A chill ran up his spine.

Its eyes were open and fixed on him. They were blue, the right one brighter than the left and shining with a terrible light.

'Whatever's happened, we'd better hide,' said Frost. 'This is Asclepius's most cherished thing. He'll be up here any moment.'

Frost dragged Jake to a cedar tree in an adjoining hallway of the rampart, one of whose giant branches reached into the laboratory. With astonishing agility Frost leapt up the trunk and hauled Jake up behind him.

They had barely settled in a well-concealed node of the branch in the laboratory when something large and dark swept in through an open window—a vulture.

Before its feet touched the ground it transformed. Its wings became the robes of a dark cloak.

Asclepius! thought Jake. *How fitting that he can shift shape into a scavenger.*

His expression tense, Asclepius marched between the benches up to the tree.

Aftershocks reverberated through the oasis as he studied the wolf.

With a wave of his hand the oak released an acorn into the very flask Frost had indicated. The red fluid released a great hiss and was shot through with light as the acorn dissolved—light which raced through the monstrosity of glass tubes, stopping here and there and sending arcs of light to other parts of the apparatus before a mesmerised Jake and Frost.

The contraption burst to life too rapidly for Jake to follow—the clematis shed its leaves, bats flew up in a purple hue shot through with golden glowing bees and much else besides.

Finally everything settled. With a puff of light particles from the final flask, a dragonfly flew up and landed on the back of the turtle.

Frost gripped Jake's arm in excitement.

The moment its delicate legs landed, the light flowed from them and lit up the turtle's shell into an amazing grid of swirls.

With another wave of Asclepius's hand, the turtle's head emerged. He clicked his fingers. The turtle's eyes flicked open and light shot out through its amber eyes.

To Jake's astonishment, just as Frost had said it would, the turtle acted as a projector. An image like a hologram appeared before them. It was shadowy and unclear. Something chaotic was taking place—a ferocious battle involving not only humans, but trees and animals.

A terrible sense of foreboding swept through Jake.

Frost watched on, enthralled.

My God, thought Jake, tearing his gaze away from the ill-omened scene to glance at Frost. *He's really enjoying this! As though it were a game. Yet he knows so much. Above all he knows what's at stake. Why isn't he nervous?*

In the space created by Jake's suspicion, something Rufus had said popped into his thoughts. He recalled Frost's incredible strength—pulling Jake up the tree with just one arm. Jake was strong but nothing compared to Frost. He also dwelt on Frost's sixth sense for anything secret and his intuition about gates—how he had known to call through the inkwell to instruct Thanador.

A dreadful feeling rose up from the pit of Jake's stomach, like it had during the marvellous bath but much worse. The logical conclusion was almost too chilling to draw.

Could he be a trixy?

Jake became nauseous.

I invited him into the fort! But surely if he was a trixy then the invite wouldn't work.

He then remembered how Rufus had said that Jake could even invite Lord Boreas if he wanted.

But I sense goodness in Frost. He's bloody weird, but I like him.

As Jake reasoned with himself he felt a pang of cowardice, of self-deceit and guilt. He determined to straighten his thinking but was cut short by a horrific roar of laughter that echoed through the laboratory.

Jake looked down into the shadowy image cast by the turtle to see a huge man, rotund and dressed in red. His great dark-bearded head was thrown back in cruel laughter. He looked like a pirate.

Frost glanced at Jake, his eyes wide and excited. 'Demon!' he whispered.

He certainly looked like one and if Jake had any doubts, as the image shifted to one of a cave, the wolf leapt up on the branch and released a haunting howl.

CHAPTER 31
THE PIRATE AND THE DAGGER

HAVING BOOTED HIS WAY INTO THE DREAM ROOM, THE PIRATE grabbed the wolf by the scruff of the neck. An instant later it transformed into Lawrence, hauling his entire presence from the cave in the world of Leaf.

'You want to embrace me?' bellowed the pirate, mocking Lawrence with his own words about embracing his shadow. 'How touching!'

Lawrence said nothing. He was too weak with shock.

'Plenty of time for that later!' cheered the pirate. 'First, fun! But where to go?'

The pirate focused on one of the dream room's twelve portals. A series of doors raced before his eyes.

'Aha! That'll do!' he cried, fixing on one. 'Now let me show you something of my world! Or should I say, *ours*?'

'Farewell,' said Geoffrey, with characteristic calm and a crooked smile. He was on the table beside the candle which flickered with the fragility of Lawrence's light.

Before Lawrence could answer, he was hurled through the doorway and halfway across the cosmos.

WHEREVER LAWRENCE AND THE PIRATE HAD ARRIVED, IT WAS NIGHT time. Remarkably, Lawrence was standing upright and looking well. Not only that, but he was in his own body, the body of Jake's dad. Lord Boreas's had been left behind in the shallower realities of the Outer-Peregrinus.

Tall, lean and tanned from work abroad, with a fulsome beard, his thick brown hair tied back, he looked fitting company for the pirate, even his clothes. He was dressed in a kilt and khaki shirt, a sword across his back.

Lawrence took a deep breath of the salty air. The shrewd light in his brown eyes brightened. It felt good to be back in his own skin.

He took in their surroundings. They were standing outside a lively tavern on a medieval-looking quay.

'Welcome to the unconscious!' said the pirate.

'How can it be that I feel fine?' asked Lawrence.

The pirate, who was a little taller than Lawrence, though greater in bulk and presence, regarded him with humorous eyes. 'You have a benefactor,' he said, clearly referring to Lord Boreas.

'I don't need a benefactor,' said Lawrence curtly, but immediately slumped and would have collapsed entirely had not the pirate grabbed him with one hand and held him up.

'I'm afraid you do, my friend,' he said.

'The minimum to follow my will,' muttered Lawrence, for he knew that to borrow power from Lord Boreas was false power and would hasten his own downfall. It was just as Geoffrey had said—Lord Boreas would play Lawrence like a fish, gifting him energy when he needed it, in order to lure him into a deeper grave.

'So be it,' said the pirate and Lawrence recovered though looked less robust than before.

'There's my ship,' announced the pirate proudly, indicating a fine wooden vessel moored in the harbour. A large lantern lit the deck in a mysterious light. 'We should go on a voyage! A voyage of discovery!'

'One from which there's no return,' said Lawrence dryly.

'Naturally. Why return?' said the pirate. 'That would be boring! Haven't you done enough returning up there on the Surface?'

'One returns in order to complete.'

'We can do all that here. We can do everything here!' declared the pirate.

'Except reach the Core.'

'And what would you do once you got there?' exclaimed the pirate. 'By thunder you're dull! We'd better brighten you up. And what better place to start?'

The pirate clamped a great hand on Lawrence's shoulder and turned to the tavern.

'The Conclusion,' said Lawrence, reading the tavern's sign.

'Indeed. Get to the point, it's more honest. No preamble, no excuses and none of that tricky politeness. So take care!'

'Honest?' queried Lawrence. 'We're on Greed, are we not?'

'Most definitely. In its heart, no less! You'll not find a more honest place in the cosmos. Try wearing a mask and it'll be ripped off and your head with it. As for hypocrisy, you'll be skewered alive. But enough talking. Let's drink!'

Music and cheer erupted from the tavern. The moment Lawrence and the pirate stepped in, however, it ceased. A deathly silence hung in the air as every set of wild eyes bored accusingly into Lawrence. He didn't belong there and they sensed it.

To his credit, Lawrence stood tall and looked across them with a dispassionate air.

Unabashed, the pirate swept up the nearest pint of ale, drained the glass and punched unconscious its protesting owner.

'It's alright!' he bellowed to the tavern, beaming with festive cheer. 'He's with me!'

The imposter accounted for, the tavern burst back to debauched life.

As the two of them squeezed through the crush of people, the pirate walloped the backside of a voluptuous blonde and cheered heartily.

She swung round, belted him in the face, considered a head butt, kissed him passionately instead then belted him a second time before returning to her business as though nothing extraordinary had happened.

'Ha-ha!' cried the pirate. 'How's that for fair trade?'

Lawrence looked unimpressed, feeling more out of place with each moment.

Women eyed him salaciously.

'There's something for everyone here!' said the pirate and grabbed another woman—an Eastern beauty who obviously knew him well.

As they reacquainted themselves in no uncertain terms, a woman stepped in front of Lawrence and blocked his way. An amazon of a woman with hungry eyes, her skin the colour of ebony, she grabbed him by the shirt, but he pushed her away.

Her eyes widened in fury. 'Liar!' she hissed and swiped at his face.

Lawrence blocked it.

Bountifully built, she followed up with a combination of quick and powerful blows.

Again Lawrence fended them off, but didn't know how to deal with her.

Though it was just another fracas in a fracas-ridden inn, its whiff of deceit roused mounting interest.

Whether out of jealousy or something else, a man leapt up to attack Lawrence. With his spare fist Lawrence knocked him to the ground.

The show of strength provoked an attack from two other men. They flew at him at the same time, the one behind him armed with a knife.

Booting the amazon back, Lawrence sidestepped the attack, grabbed the knife-held hand and sliced the shoulder of the man in front then elbowed the one behind and broke his nose. Following another blow to each of them, they collapsed.

No sooner had he done this, he was set upon by three women. They forced him backwards and off balance. With the help of the amazon, they bundled him into a backroom.

LAWRENCE LANDED FLAT ON HIS BACK IN A DIM-LIT, STALE-SMELLING room.

The amazon sprang atop him, straddled his midriff while the others pinned down his hands and legs.

Each of the four women was wildly distinct, as though the earth had selected its finest specimen from each of its corners—intelligent, ample and exotic.

'Not tempted?' asked the amazon with a suggestive shift of her weight.

An amused light in his eyes, Lawrence studied the women in turn. Each smouldered in their own way, eyes alive with play along with something darker.

'No,' he said plainly.

Immediately their presence grew more powerful.

'Oh, the self-denial. The control, the morality, how tragic!' said the amazon in dismay. 'Will the pattern ever break?'

She surveyed his lean body. 'Shall we liberate him, sisters?'

'It's the humane thing to do,' said the Turkic beauty holding down one of his arms.

The other two nodded in agreement.

'She's right,' said one of them, her eyes twinkling. 'It's our duty. He *must* be healed.'

'Then we shall heal him,' concluded the amazon with a sly smile.

She leaned forward, took hold of his head and was about to kiss him when the door swung open. Filling its frame was the pirate.

'Not today, my lovelies!' he said. 'The heart of the matter beckons! I'll make it up to you later.'

The amazon was furious. 'Not until we've had our fun!'

The pirate rumbled with laughter. 'You're wasting your time with that one,' he said. 'Now be off with you.'

The amazon looked ready to kill the pirate, then turned to Lawrence, glowered, slapped him hard across the face and finally got up.

Again the pirate laughed.

The other women giggled, each in turn planting an intense kiss upon Lawrence's lips.

The women gone, the pirate closed the door.

Somewhat disorientated, Lawrence got up, dusted himself off and straightened his clothes.

When he looked up again, he found a table where moments before there had been nothing. On it were two objects: a beautifully crafted dagger with a ruby set in the end of its silver hilt, along with a silver chalice containing a poisonous-looking dark fluid.

'You have a choice to make,' announced the pirate, as he strode over to the table and laid down his hat as a third object. 'You must choose one of these objects,' he said. 'The hat is obvious.'

'Your ship and the voyage I'm not ready to take,' deduced Lawrence.

'The voyage,' confirmed the pirate, refraining from saying more.

'The dagger?'

'A unique weapon with the power to slay something with a single stab which ordinarily would take much longer—lifetimes longer in your case.'

'A ghost?' said Lawrence

'Not yet. But if left undealt with, it'll become one. It's your deepest secret from yourself in your current life and thus very powerful.'

Lawrence stepped closer to inspect the contents of the chalice. 'Poison?'

'Ignorance. The same thing,' said the pirate. 'Drink half and you return to your friend the lizard and we continue our game of cat and mouse. A game you'll ultimately lose. Drink it all and you'll be swept off to death and again the tiger wins.'

'Rebirth these days means Luna's ark,' said Lawrence as he took a closer look at the dagger, though didn't touch it.

'Once you've chosen an object, a door will appear in the far wall,' added the pirate. 'It's the only way to leave this room.'

Lawrence looked in the direction of the door to the tavern, but it had vanished.

'I have little choice,' he said.

'You have three choices,' corrected the pirate. 'Besides, have you not heard the expression that real freedom is having no choice at all?'

'Let's get on with it,' said Lawrence and swept up the dagger.

Just as the pirate had said, a plain wooden door appeared in the wall.

'A fine choice!' commended the pirate. 'After you...'

Without further ado, Lawrence opened the door and a blaze of light filled the room.

Bracing himself, he stepped into it.

IT WAS A FALSE LIGHT. BEFORE HIS FOOT TOUCHED THE GROUND he was sucked into a vacuum of darkness. He almost passed out. He thought he had been tricked when whatever gripped him suddenly let go and he stumbled into a deeper part of Greed—the middle of a desert in midday sun with no trace of the door through which he had arrived.

'Ah, how wonderfully symbolic!' said the pirate. 'Just your sort of place. Rather barren. Rather boring!'

With the dagger through his belt, Lawrence glanced about the landscape. There was nothing but rocky desert in every direction. 'Now what?' he asked.

'We wait,' said the pirate who sat down on one of two seats which appeared beside them.

'For what?'

'For you to work out what you're raging about,' said the pirate.

'Raging?' laughed Lawrence who remained standing. 'I'm not raging!'

As soon as he said so the sun grew hotter. Perspiration broke out on his forehead.

'If you're here, my friend, there's rage,' said the pirate as a parasol appeared in one of his hands, a cool beer in the other.

'Ultimately the rage is with yourself. But you'll never accept that until you discover where you've heaped the blame.'

'You speak as though you were my guide,' said Lawrence.

'But I am!' beamed the pirate.

Lawrence looked at him doubtfully.

'Ah, trust,' sighed the pirate. 'And after showing you what an honest place this is. You'll have to give up some control if you wish to get anywhere here.'

'I understand what you are—'

'Not completely,' broke in the pirate, noting how a mosaic of cracks appeared about Lawrence's feet.

'How do you expect me to trust you when you have no desire to leave this place?' continued Lawrence unperturbed.

'You misunderstand me,' said the pirate. 'Your past is my present and because I'm present I already have infinity.'

'This is your idea of eternal bliss?' cried Lawrence glancing about the desert.

'No. This is yours. Mine's the inn!'

'Fleeting pleasures.'

'Dear brother, thanks to your eternal rage and self-denial, my fleeting pleasures are never ending! Why, I must thank you! What blissful beauties you send me! Not to mention the occasional brawl.'

A smile escaped Lawrence and he actually laughed. The pirate joined him.

'While you serve in your idea of heaven,' added the pirate, 'I rule in your idea of hell, though there's irony in both. And it's the irony you must come to terms with if you're to sail a steady course. It's *Irony* I sail for, if only you'd join me on the voyage.'

As the pirate spoke, an inlet of sea appeared in the desert, the ship moored in its glorious turquoise waters. A cool breeze glanced off its surface, a brief respite from the tortuous heat.

'We can leave whenever you want,' he said, his eyes brightening at the thought of adventure.

'Now I know why Geoffrey called you the devil,' said Lawrence dryly.

'You flatter me!' said the pirate. 'But devil is such a confusing term. We can do better! Let's see, how about Dionysus? How about two of them? One for you and one for me. An inner and an outer, a frolicker and a sage. Who's who, I wonder?'

A silence fell between them.

As the pirate sipped his cold beer, Lawrence stood as though waiting for a bus, gazing into the horizon.

He turned to address the pirate, but the pirate had disappeared. So had the vessel and chairs. There was only a red parrot flying off into the distance.

Lawrence remained where he was, apparently calm, yet in his eyes were the glints of contrast—of hope and despair, of courage and fear and everything else that came with staring eternity in the face, but not knowing how to grasp it.

How long he stood like that was impossible to gauge for the sun remained at its zenith. At some point, however, a dark speck appeared from the shimmer of the horizon and slowly grew larger. Someone was approaching.

As the figure drew closer, it swayed with the gait of a woman, graceful and unhurried.

Captivated, Lawrence watched on.

When close enough to see her features, his eyes widened and his heart leapt. He stood tall as strength returned to him.

It was Rowena, though as he knew her before Luna had possessed her body. Like an English rose midwinter, she appeared like a dream, swathed in a red robe with a smile to melt the coldest heart.

Lawrence was spellbound as she approached in silence, reached up and placed a hand lovingly against his left cheek.

His eyes closed in peace.

They opened again. He was about to say something, but she placed a gentle finger to his lips.

'Shh, don't say my name,' she said softly.

'Is this real?'

'As real as anything,' she replied.

Lawrence took her hands in his and gave them a loving squeeze.

'You're not that bloody pirate in a dress, are you?'

Rowena pulled his head closer and placed a soft kiss on his lips.

A glorious warmth flowed through him.

'God, I hope not,' he said at the end of the kiss.

'It's hot,' she said, leading him by the hand. 'Let us take shelter.'

A short way off, a cave had appeared in an outcrop of rock.

'But wait,' said Lawrence remaining where he was.

'Now is not the time for questions, love,' she said with the subtlest suggestion in her smile.

Still Lawrence resisted.

Rowena looked questioningly into his eyes, gently pulling at his hand. When he failed to yield, her hand slipped through his to the point where only their fingertips touched.

Confusion gripped Lawrence. His emotions wrestled with reason. Not only was Rowena slipping from his grasp, but all the wisdom Geoffrey had shared.

Finally the contact broke.

Thunder rolled from far off. The sky darkened.

Rowena's expression suddenly shifted, from one of searching to one of someone betrayed. Still she walked for the cave, glancing back at Lawrence who was unable to disguise his torment.

The thunder grew louder. This time it was the thunder of galloping hooves.

Lawrence swung around to find four dark riders galloping across the desert like Knights of the Apocalypse. Wearing black turbans, they tore past him, swarthy faced and fierce eyed. They tore past Rowena.

The last to pass her reached down, swept her up and slung her across the horse.

'No!' cried Lawrence.

Rowena offered no resistance.

As they galloped for the cave she looked back, maintaining her gaze on Lawrence—a complex expression, reflecting back at him his own anguish.

'Recognise that look?' said the pirate who had reappeared at Lawrence's side.

Lawrence cast him a quick glance but was too preoccupied with what was happening.

'It's disappointment. She thinks you're a coward.'

'What are you talking about?' barked Lawrence.

'A violent coward. Who do you think those riders represent?'

Lawrence shot the pirate an incredulous look. 'No?'

'Of course! Remember where you are. Here your deceit is writ large, especially deceit of yourself. Fear, jealousy, anger and hatred. They're different faces of the same thing—your ignorance and distorted love.'

'And Rowena?' asked Lawrence, watching the riders arrive at the cave, dismount and drag her into it.

'The female aspect of your soul. Your ability to receive higher wisdom, to read the signs and be spontaneous. Your ability to feel. Your compassion. But your male aspect has become twisted and paranoid and seeks to control—to *subdue*. To *take* but give nothing in return.'

Though the riders and Rowena were out of sight, the sounds of their movement were amplified through the desert: hurried footsteps, the rip of clothing, ragged breath, a body thrown to the floor.

'Then this is all just symbolic,' said Lawrence, his voice tense. 'It's not actually happening as it appears.'

'Oh, I assure you it is.'

'But it's symbolic!' insisted Lawrence.

'And life on the Surface isn't?' said the pirate. 'It's the same, it's just that here the effects are immediate. No time is wasted. Nothing is hidden. Except of course your soul. A bit here, a bit there. All that power scattered about, which takes almost forever to find.'

The sounds from the cave caused Lawrence to wince. He reached for the dagger.

Still he hesitated and a sapling sprouted up beside them. It matured before their very eyes and blossomed into a tree.

Suddenly it was beset by vines. In a matter of moments they had coiled themselves about its branches. Their grip tightened, they swelled in size. The creaking sounds merged with the discordant sounds from the cave as the vines throttled the trunk.

'I see you're finally using your imagination,' said the pirate, observing the tree.

'This is a trap,' said Lawrence, a tremor in his voice. 'Just a trap. Surely.'

'Whatever it is, it requires action. Engage or walk away. Indifference will cost you dearly,' advised the pirate and gazed about the desert.

The storm clouds grew darker and the air more oppressive. If the symbol of the tree wasn't enough, a white deer streaked past them pursued by a pride of lions. They were gathering speed, spreading out in a pincer.

'White,' said the pirate as his gaze followed it. 'The symbol of purity, while the deer is...'

'Grace,' said Lawrence, the tension in his eyes mounting with the storm.

'It's interesting how she hasn't cried for help, isn't it?'

'What are you saying?' snapped Lawrence.

'What does it do to one's sense of self-worth, I wonder? To be so easily detached from by someone who once loved you—that someone would submit to such violence rather than cry out.'

Lawrence snatched the dagger from his belt. 'If you represent the greater part of my unconscious then perhaps it's you I should slay.'

'Be my guest!' said the pirate cheerily and opened his arms in a gesture of offering his heart. 'It's my duty to warn you, however, that you lack the gravity. The very act will send you straight to my ship, though with considerably less power had you chosen my hat. As is often the case, what seems the shortest route is often the longest.'

'I can't walk away,' said Lawrence, unable to take much more. The lions were at full speed and gaining on the deer.

'Then I recommend you start by slaying the riders. With a bit of luck you might get one, perhaps two.'

The ambivalence in Lawrence's eyes sharpened and hardened to resolution. A white stallion appeared from thin air, reared up beside him and whinnied. He leapt upon it. The horse reared up and whinnied once more then tore off at a full gallop for the cave.

'Ah,' sighed the pirate as he watched Lawrence blaze off, casting up clouds of dust. 'The saviour. How impressive it looks. The ultimate self-delusion.'

Halfway to the cave, Lawrence glanced over his shoulder. The lions were closing in on the deer. In a desperate last attempt to evade them the deer was zigzagging but losing valuable speed. Only seconds remained. Vultures circled in the sky above.

'Faster,' hissed Lawrence to the horse. 'Faster!'

The horse sped across the desert like a dart.

At the cave Lawrence leapt from the horse and bounded up to the cave mouth. Before crossing the threshold he took a last glance back. The leading lion put in a final burst of acceleration. Dread filled Lawrence's eyes and as the lion leapt, so did he—into the shadows of the cave.

THE MOMENT HE LANDED IN THE CAVE, A TORCH OF FLAME appeared on the wall, yet it revealed nothing but emptiness. There was no sign, no sound of Rowena or the riders, not even a breath. Everything was still.

Lawrence looked out the cave at the very moment a bolt of lightning pierced the now-night sky and struck the ravaged tree.

'Rowena!' roared Lawrence helplessly into the desert. 'Rowena!'

But there was nothing, not even an echo, not even the half-light cast by a solitary star. Once the lightning had struck, total darkness covered the desert.

'It's symbolic. Above all, it's symbolic,' he said, trying to reassure himself, though it only heightened the sense that something terrible had taken place.

The hairs on his neck suddenly rose.

He spun around.

One of the riders had emerged from the shadows of the torch-lit cave.

'Where is she?' demanded Lawrence as he stowed the dagger and drew his sword.

The rider said nothing. Only his eyes showed through his turban and they creased with a grin.

Lawrence pointed his sword toward the rider's neck and repeated his question.

The rider raised his sabre.

When the blades touched, the sabre glowed a bright green. Lawrence visibly weakened as though it were sapping his energy or contaminating him with something lethal.

He stepped back to break contact but it made little difference.

Time was of the essence.

Realising there was nothing to do except fight, Lawrence made a thrust at the rider's throat

The rider effortlessly knocked it aside.

Lawrence drove forward with a devastating combination of strokes yet, while he held his sword with two hands, the rider used just one. Neither did the rider adopt a defensive stance. He simply stood his ground and parried the strokes with rolls of his wrist which held great power.

Lawrence managed only five or six clashes of their blades before the rider nicked his shoulder.

Ignoring it, Lawrence drove back with all he had.

After a few strokes more, the rider inflicted a second wound—this time to the other shoulder, and deeper.

Lawrence disengaged a moment to check it. His brow was perspiring heavily. Frustration showed in his eyes. He glanced about the cave, reviewing his options. He was outclassed.

'I demand to see the creator of this world!' he called out, trying something Geoffrey had suggested.

The flame of the torch flickered for a moment, but that was all.

The rider tittered. '*You're* the creator of this world,' he said in a hard and dispassionate voice.

'Then I demand this scene to change,' he said. 'I demand you to be gone. I demand to see Rowena. Now!'

'Those are just words,' said the rider. 'Everything you really want is already happening. You want to be rid of her and so she's gone. You want to fight. So fight.'

He was right and Lawrence knew it. Regardless of his conscious wishes, they were overwhelmed by those of his unconscious—a saboteur inside of him.

'What other choices do I have?' asked Lawrence feeling desperate, remembering Geoffrey's advice to ask questions rather than making assumptions and reacting.

'You can fight or you can die,' said the rider plainly. 'In here or out there. You don't have the power for anything else.'

'And if I die?'

'Back in your other world you will have lost power,' replied the rider and with a flash of his blade he widened the gash in Lawrence's left shoulder.

Lawrence winced with the pain, knowing full well what a loss of power in Luna's reality would mean—his cover as Lord Boreas would be blown.

'So I suggest you fight like a man,' added the rider. 'And stop being a coward.'

Blood flowed from Lawrence's wounds. Anger flashed in his eyes. The arrival of his anger created passage for the arrival something else, something he didn't notice.

Behind him, in the mid-distance of the desert, moving stealthily closer, shone an ice-blue pair of eyes. When they flashed brighter, so too did Lawrence's until they shone with the same light, no longer brown but a cold, piercing, lethal blue.

Too desperate for a way out, too arrogant to wonder at the source of power, not realising he had received a gift, Lawrence raised his blade. His eyes narrowed.

The rider tittered as he raised his sword to meet it. It continued to glow green, only marginally brighter than the brightening blue light in Lawrence's eyes, a margin which was rapidly closing.

Lawrence no longer felt his wounds. When he attacked it was with such power that for the first time the rider was forced backwards.

He was quick to counter.

The clash of blades was intense as they parried about the cave. The rider still had the initiative, but as the bright eyes in the desert darkness drew closer to the cave, so Lawrence's eyes grew even brighter until he rivalled the rider in both power and skill.

Lawrence's brow relaxed.

The rider's furrowed and began to perspire. The intensity of the duel mounted. Lawrence managed to nick the shoulder of the rider's free arm.

The rider's blade dimmed. Drawing on hidden reserves, he came back at Lawrence with astounding skill and forced him back towards the cave mouth.

As Lawrence approached its threshold, so too did the creature of the desert. Finally it drew into the half-light cast by the torch.

Still, Lawrence was unaware of its presence despite its size, despite its eyes burning with the same ferocious light which burned in his own. It was the Siberian tiger—Lord Boreas.

If he wished, in a single leap he could be on Lawrence, tearing him to shreds before reclaiming his body in Luna's reality. Instead, he deeply inhaled the cave air. As Geoffrey had warned, Lord Boreas had more concrete plans for Lawrence.

By simply being close, Lord Boreas gifted Lawrence yet greater power. For the first time his blade and the rider's locked in stalemate. Both grabbed the other by the robes, their eyes as locked as their swords.

The tiger reached the end of its long inhale. Following a fateful pause, it released a roar which shook the cave and desert.

Lawrence didn't hear it. He felt only its power. Still he didn't question its origin. He was on the planet Greed and he greedily claimed it as his own.

With the presence of a giant, his blade glowing with the same intense blue as his and the tiger's eyes, he hurled back the rider as though he were merely a child. Following a moment's hesitation, the rider attacked with all his strength.

The first contact shattered the rider's blade. The second took off his head.

On pure instinct, Lawrence rushed into the shadows as though intent on leaping through the rock. He swung his blade. At its point of maximum strength, a rider leapt from a concealed fissure but was cut clean in half at the midriff.

With a deft swirl of the arms, Lawrence repeated the stroke except higher.

The third rider had scarcely appeared when his head was severed from his shoulders.

The fourth, however, didn't reveal himself.

Lawrence stood poised. The shadows cleared to reveal a passageway through the fissure in the rock.

He was about to pass inside when the fourth rider finally stepped into sight. He didn't attack. His expression was strained. He staggered along the passageway and collapsed in front of Lawrence, a knife lodged in his back.

With the challenge over, the immense power coursing through Lawrence subsided. His eyes returned to brown, a glimmer of hope in their lights.

Another figure stepped into the passage. It was Rowena.

To Lawrence's great relief she looked unharmed. Despite the brutal symbolism of the lightning-struck tree, her dress was intact and yet its bright shade of red had dulled to the burgundy of wine. In fact, everything about her seemed to have lost its sparkle. And when she smiled, it was less a smile to melt a heart than one to boil the blood—with lust, jealousy and anger.

'Hello, my love,' she said coyly as she moved along the passage, trailing a hand against the rock. 'You've been busy.'

Lawrence looked down at the figure at his feet and recoiled in shock. It was no longer the fourth rider but a slain young boy, his face the epitome of innocence.

Lawrence spun round to face the cave. The same had happened to each of the other riders, though all still bore horrific wounds.

In horror and disgust, Lawrence cast aside his sword and knelt down next to the upper part of the one he had chopped in half.

'My God!' he groaned as he gently cupped the boy's head in his hands. 'What have I done? What in the name of God…'

Just then the pirate strode in from the desert darkness. The tiger had disappeared.

'How are we getting on in here?' he said breezily. 'Oh. Whoopsy daisy. A little anger perhaps?' he added as he surveyed the carnage before him. 'I suppose I should have warned you to control your anger. It's a channel to the tiger's power and to slay with borrowed power is, well, not helpful as far as you're concerned.'

'What does it mean?' appealed Lawrence, still gazing hopelessly at the slain boy.

'It means that your hidden power, which you so desperately seek, is now even more deeply hidden. You slayed with rage, unconscious of your actions. Had you controlled your imagination and used the special dagger, you might have won some of that power. Alas…'

Rowena knelt down beside Lawrence and put an arm around his shoulder. 'Never mind, darling,' she said in a condescending tone. 'It was an awful lot to expect of you.'

Lawrence shot her a fierce glance and recoiled a second time.

Her beauty had vanished. In its place was the face of an old crone.

'What happened to her?' he asked the pirate.

'Distorted. What was beautiful has become bitter and vengeful. I'm afraid you've missed your chance to merge with something pure. As a result of your hesitation, followed by rashness, all you've managed to save is your image. The very thing you need to release.'

'Ooh, how beautiful!' cooed the crone as she reached for the special dagger stowed in Lawrence's belt.

He caught her by the wrist, stood up and withdrew the dagger.

The pirate was smiling wryly. 'It's a good idea, my friend. It'll unravel the mess you've made here. But have you got the balls to do it?'

'It's not that simple,' said Lawrence, the dagger shaking in his hand with rage and fear. 'If she symbolises Rowena, who in another world is possessed by Luna, then I've no idea what could happen. It's too big a risk.'

'What's really at risk?' questioned the pirate. 'Your heroic role to save your damsel in distress? To save the world? We've already seen where that gets you. And you forget the power of the dagger.'

'It's more complicated than that,' insisted Lawrence.

'You want it to be more complicated,' said the pirate. 'You slay the crone, you destroy the distortion and you set free the woman you claim to love. In so doing, you gift her power. Or perhaps you like slavery. You enslave yourself. You enslave others for company. Solidarity, is that what they call it?'

Lawrence looked into the crone's beady eyes.

'Why don't you try kissing me instead?' she suggested with a gruesome smile. 'I might turn into a princess.'

Kissing her was the last thing on Lawrence's mind. He studied the knife instead, took a deep inhale and gazed out into the darkness of the desert. He closed his eyes, opened them, looked back at the knife and the crone, desperate for clarity.

He grabbed her robes even tighter and placed the tip of the dagger under her chin.

The crone simply cackled, her eyes dancing.

He pressed it to the point of drawing blood.

His temples pounded with confusion. Everything the pirate said rang true, yet Geoffrey had called him the Devil. Lawrence scrutinised all he had heard from the pirate for any deceit but found none, then scoured his mind for another way, a higher logic, but again found nothing.

His body tensed. A rivulet of blood flowed along the blade as he pressed harder.

'Nice-n-quick, or nice-n-slow, my lover,' said the old crone, enjoying the moment. 'Makes no difference to me.'

Lawrence closed his eyes, took another deep breath and braced himself before the kill.

But his heart wasn't in it. With a heavy sigh, his shoulders slumped. He lowered the dagger and cursed. 'I can't do it. The risks are too high.'

No sooner had he said so than the crone dissolved before his eyes.

The slain boys also disappeared.

A door appeared in the rock, for Lawrence was in the unconscious where every decision closed one door and opened others.

'So be it,' said the pirate, moving towards it. 'Shall we?'

CHAPTER 32
SEA-ING SPHERE

WHILE JAKE AND FROST SNUCK AWAY FROM ASCLEPIUS'S LABORATORY, Rani, with Bin on her shoulder, was searching the fort for a suitable place to lay a trap. She was determined to capture Frost. Though she had no idea about the outbreak of Luna's war and had yet to see the woods outside, she sensed something terrible had happened. She and Bin had been creeping along a corridor lined with beech trees when the quake had struck. In the blink of an eye, all of them had shed their leaves, which were suddenly red, orange and yellow.

They were several levels down from the great lawn. The deeper one ventured down through the outcrop and into the bedrock, so the grandeur above gave way to something less refined. Stairwells, passageways and halls grew increasingly rugged and wild, the sources of light laws unto themselves. There were streams, cascades and even lakes. Such symbolism wasn't lost on Rani. As she and Bin moved ever deeper, so it seemed to reflect her own inner-voyage—inescapable, chaotic and, as much as Rani hated to admit it, highly disturbing.

Nevertheless, she remained focused on her task, repeating her intention in silence, asking for guidance.

'Rani dear,' said Bin at last, 'don't you think we're straying a little too far if you wish to lay a trap?'

'All the better,' said Rani. 'That revolting thing will easily pick up our scent and the more mysterious the journey, the more intrigued he'll be.'

Just then they drew level with another corridor, except this one was different. It continued for several paces then abruptly ended.

'Strange,' said Rani and ventured cautiously along it.

She ran her hands over the walls as she went, sensing for signs of a secret passageway, but found none. Having arrived at the dead-end, she put on the atomic glove and gently placed it against the wall.

At first nothing happened. But something told Rani to be patient. As she waited, she repeated her intention—how she wanted an appropriate place to lay a trap, one that would work.

Suddenly, her heart leapt. The glove vibrated. It took an unusually long time to have an effect when, finally, part of the granite wall became a mass of whirling particles.

'Wait here, Bin,' she whispered excitedly and poked her head through.

Rani gasped in awe. She was staring into a great stone shaft that defied the dimensions of the fort and was so deep that it disappeared into total darkness. The source of light came through the open doorway of a spherical room floating at the shaft's centre, but there was no way to reach it.

Following her intuition, Rani poked a leg through and placed it into the void. To her delight, the start of a narrow stone bridge appeared beneath her foot. She carefully climbed through the portal and placed another foot forward. The bridge extended to meet it.

Ecstatic, she spun around and beckoned Bin who flew through and landed on her shoulder.

For several moments they stood in silence, taking in the vast chilly space.

'It must be one of those secret parts of the fort that you mentioned!' said Rani. 'One that only powerful beings can find. Like Braysheath!'

'If the glove allowed you in,' said Bin, 'one wonders if Braysheath already knows of Frost's presence in the fort. In which case, why are we laying a trap?'

'That doesn't make total sense, Bin. I realise he *ought* to know, but he might not. After all, he's spending a lot of time away from the fort. Either way, here we are and we need to lay a trap. And what better place than somewhere only Braysheath maybe visits? Perhaps the glove will let us set the portal so Frost can enter but not leave. Then once we've caught and interrogated him, we can leave him for Braysheath to deal with.'

Rani beamed with the brilliance of the idea.

Bin shivered and ruffled her feathers. 'The air in here feels strange.'

'It's stale, that's all,' said Rani and took a tentative step forward to see if the bridge continued to unfold towards the sphere. It did. Her heart raced with excitement. 'I wonder how far it goes?' she said, peering down into the gloom.

'And to what?' said Bin.

'Have faith, Bin. The glove has led us here.'

'Reluctantly,' said Bin, reminding Rani of how long the glove had taken to decide.

'Come on!' said Rani. 'Let's investigate that interesting-looking room.'

While Bin flew a circuit around the outside of the spherical room, Rani advanced towards it, moving slowly just in case the bridge suddenly stopped forming and sent her plummeting. She loaded her bow.

Having reached the doorway without event, Bin landed on her shoulder. Rani peered inside the room.

At first glance it looked like an ordinary room except full of old junk—cast aside pictures, furniture, cases, mirrors and all sorts of other things you might find in a curiosity shop.

Rani took a step inside and slowly crossed to the centre.

'Be careful,' warned Bin. 'These things may look ordinary, but consider where they're kept.'

Rani looked up at a painting on the wall. It appeared to be of the House of Tusk oasis, but as she studied its details it came to life. Sea flowed over the dunes until the desert was completely submerged. Rani gasped. The oasis was flooded and sea water washed across the room's floor and over her feet.

She stared at them in astonishment. When she looked up again, she and Bin were no longer in a room, but on a beautiful tropical beach.

It lasted just a moment before the room returned.

'Wow!' she whispered. 'What just happened?'

'I don't know,' said Bin, clearly disturbed. 'But this room is full of objects of power—more subtle than the weapons I've heard are locked up in that strange red vault we saw the other day.'

Rani looked about the room at the various objects. Similar to what had happened with the painting, if she looked anywhere for more than a moment, the imagery shifted, revealing something of its power. Instead, she looked between things and saw through the many layers of what appeared to be never-ending piles of objects. The deeper she looked, the more mysterious and ancient-looking the objects became.

'Are you seeing what I'm seeing?' she asked.

'I don't know, but I'm seeing a lot.'

'There's got to be something here to trap Frost,' said Rani. 'First we need an object to tempt him, some sort of bait, and then something to imprison him.'

Rani put on the atomic glove, certain it would help them find what they needed.

'Right, Bin,' she said, 'let's get searching.'

CHAPTER 33

SIFTING FOR SECRETS

MOORED OFF A LAND OF SNOW-COVERED MOUNTAINS, AMID THE drift ice, was Luna's ark. The flow of lost souls into the unicorn horn mast was now continuous and the gauge on the turquoise vault below deck was rapidly rising.

'One tenth of human light,' said Luna, looking radiant. 'It's progressing better than I had expected.'

The Commander standing beside her said nothing.

'And now to see if any of those we've already captured have the secret I'm looking for,' continued Luna. 'I've given up with that device of Wilderspin's for screening Surface dreams. It's yielded nothing.'

'Their dreams are shallow,' said the Commander in a cold monotone. 'Their guilt and shame, in which secrets lie, are buried deep.'

'And so we shall search the next level down,' said Luna referring to the Outer-Peregrinus where the war she had so skilfully engineered was now raging. 'A way out of this abysmal cosmos exists. Each day I feel it more strongly. Whether it's a type of temple or a simple door, a human soul contains the map and key. We must find it.'

'Then you'll need to search deeper than this,' said the Commander referring to the vault.

'All the same, no stone must be left unturned. Open it.'

The Commander approached a tap on the outside of the vault. Inside was divided into three parts. There was the main chamber into which all lost souls arrived. In this part the souls were prized open and the light cleansed, the pure light siphoned off to another part, while what Luna referred to as *the scum* went to a third chamber. It was the third chamber the Commander was about to open.

With a nod from Luna he did so.

Phantoms burst out and filled the hall-like lower deck of the ark. Trees, creatures and humans swirled about groaning and wailing in a dreadful cacophony—last gasps of what they once had been, a seething ferment of regret and sorrow.

Though they were little more than memory, each contained a flicker of colour like stellar dust. In the humans and creatures it swirled in a space between the brows known as the third eye. In the trees it was just down from their crowns.

'What a pitiful din!' exclaimed Luna from the centre.

'Self-pitiful,' said the Commander.

In no time at all they were surrounded by layer upon swirling layer of phantoms, like never-ending curtains to a grand theatre.

Luna stood eyes half-closed as though in a trance.

'I sense nothing of value,' she said finally, the gravity of her voice cutting through the clamour.

The Commander scrutinised the thickening swirl, his nose raised like a hound.

'Nothing,' he confirmed.

He raised a hand and clenched his fingers as though gripping the air. His sapphire-like eyes shone brighter. It was as though a plug had been pulled in the centre of his palm as every phantom was sucked through it.

In just seconds it was over.

As the ringing in the air subsided, he opened his clenched fist to reveal a gem—not an emerald or a ruby but a dull brown one that was completely occluded.

He tossed it to Luna.

On landing in her hands it disintegrated into a puff of dust.

'Flawed,' he said.

Luna sighed though didn't look surprised. 'There's more to come,' she said, looking at the gauge on the vault.

The Commander shook his head. 'Don't hold your breath.'

Regardless, Luna drew one, closed her eyes and clicked her fingers.

A moment later, Wilderspin appeared looking thoroughly confused.

'I say! What, where? My lady! My word, haw-haw, what mastery!' he cried, unable to disguise his irritation at being summoned in such a way.

It soon disappeared, however, on noting the novelty of his surroundings. 'Your ark, my lady!' he exclaimed and bound over to a portal to peer out at the arctic landscape. 'Are we in the Eye of the Orijinn Sea? I say!'

'I have a job for you,' said Luna.

'Of course, my lady, of course,' said Wilderspin, tearing himself away from the view and bowing deeply.

'Find me a way to plumb Nestor Tusk's mind.'

'But he's in the holygate, my lady, and in the grips of the sylph.'

'Which is precisely why he's of use. To find what I search for we must go deeper,' said Luna. 'He's linked to the House of Tusk—the home of the shepherds, a place full of the cosmos's deepest secrets. It may contain something to help us find the one I seek. Through Nestor's connection we can scour the fort. And the sylph will be curious. With its power behind our enquiry, I'm certain something will come of it.'

'The end of Nestor Tusk, I should imagine,' chuckled Wilderspin.

'Life is fraught with risk,' said Luna.

'Quite, my lady, quite. And, naturally, I shall do my best. I'm just wondering with what to start.'

'Your imagination,' said Luna. 'And this…'

Again she closed her eyes and inhaled.

What remained of her shadow, the small portion she had withheld from Nestor, shrank from sight as it was drawn up through her feet. A moment later it reappeared, contained in a small glass flask in her extended hand.

'A residual of the sylph,' she said. 'Use this to establish the connection. The details I leave up to you.'

Eyes wide with awe, Wilderspin reverently took the flask in both hands.

'That will be all,' said Luna and was about to click her fingers when Wilderspin raised a hand in question.

'My lady, permit me one question.'

Luna nodded in assent.

'The door you seek—what makes you so certain that an exit from the cosmos exists?'

Luna closed her bright green eyes.

She drew a deep breath.

The arctic landscape suddenly darkened. With loud cracks the drift ice froze into a single sheet.

Wilderspin glanced through the porthole, his expression a mix of excitement and fear.

Finally Luna calmly exhaled.

Light returned and the cracking subsided.

'Because,' she said, a dangerous inflexion in her voice, 'if *I* were the Creator, that's what I would have done. Shepherds are all good and well and faith is a nice idea, but great plans can go awry. It's wise to have a back-up.'

'Yes, I see what you mean, my lady,' said Wilderspin, clearly humbled by the display of power. 'A door, I imagine, which allows the one who finds it to leave this tired old cosmos behind and create something else. And given that a Creator must be a playful spirit—for why else create such a grand experiment as the cosmos?—so the door will be well hidden.'

'Indeed,' said Luna.

'Thank you, my lady' said Wilderspin with another bow. 'What you have so gracefully shared will help me greatly in aiding your search. Yes indeed, a door! And, just as important, someone to lead you to it. A guide! Though, naturally, one who doesn't know it. Ah, how ingenious!'

Luna slowly nodded. 'At least, not until he or she has enough power.'

'Yes!' cried Wilderspin. 'But which way will the power lean?'

Luna nodded. 'That's the game.'

CHAPTER 34
DOORS OF HELL

WHEN LAWRENCE PASSED THROUGH THE DOOR WHICH HAD appeared in the back of the desert cave, he suffered the same smothering sensation as he had leaving the inn, except this time he was ready for it.

He arrived with the pirate into a rough-hewn room of the same stone as the cave. The atmosphere was dank and Lawrence felt bleak and heavy. There were three other doors and nothing else.

The pirate sniffed the pungent air. 'A little fruity,' he remarked. 'Death and sewerage. Recognise the smell?'

Lawrence said nothing. His mind was still in turmoil following the events of the cave.

'Everything here is you, including the smell,' said the pirate. 'Isn't that heartening? We're going deeper!'

'I must choose a door?' asked Lawrence.

'Indeed you must. The first I need not explain,' said the pirate and booted open a plain oak door.

Fresh sea air, a warm breeze and the sound of gulls wafted into the room and would have lifted Lawrence's spirits had he not known what it meant. Up a gangplank was the pirate's vessel. It was being made ready for a voyage—one Lawrence was far from ready to take.

'Ah, fresh sea air!' cried the pirate. 'Nothing like it!'

'And the other two doors?'

'Different paths to the same place—the roots of your rage and enslavement. Strong paths. The strongest!'

Lawrence studied the first door. It was made of yew. Engraved in its surface was the image of Christ on the cross, a sun over his right shoulder, a moon over his left.

'The Path of the Puritan,' said the pirate.

He kicked it open and a foul belch of air escaped the darkness. All that could be seen were the first few steps of a narrow stairwell leading steeply downwards.

'Or should I say, The Path of the Zealot?' said the pirate.

'What can I expect if I take that one?'

'Surprises,' said the pirate with a grin.

The last choice was composed of two towering solid doors of imposing metal, like those of a vault.

'The Path of the Banker,' said the pirate.

He placed his hands against the doors and, employing the entirety of his great bulk, slowly forced them open.

They led to another stairwell except this one was grand, made of marble and lit by finely-crafted lanterns.

Once more the pirate sniffed the air. 'Stale, though no less deathly. Subtle, though no less sinister.'

Lawrence studied them in silence.

'If it's the truth you seek,' said the pirate, 'these three paths are the most direct. What you might call the doors to hell.'

'How much time do I have?'

The pirate shrugged. 'Who knows?'

'Can I at least have some time alone to think?'

'Of course!' said the pirate. He clicked his fingers and a silver tray with tea and cake appeared on an ornate wooden table. 'And if you're up for a game of hide and seek,' he added as though reading Lawrence's mind, 'so am I! It's my favourite game and I'm *very* good at it.'

The pirate transformed into a red parrot and flew through the doorway which led to the quayside and the nearest inn.

The parrot out of sight, Lawrence turned to a wall where there was no door. He placed his hands and forehead against it. He took several calming breaths. His presence grew.

'I must first return to Geoffrey and the dream room. I must return to Renlock before Luna and Wilderspin get suspicious,' he said, for though time worked differently in the unconscious, he didn't want to take the risk. 'As creator of this world, I summon a place to rest in—long enough to tend to matters before returning here to choose a door.'

At first nothing happened.

A moment later a dragonfly appeared, a symbol of brightness in the dark. It landed on the wall between his hands and dissolved into light which flowed into the rock.

Lawrence's spirits leapt. The outlines of a door grew visible. Within seconds its reality was complete—the sort of door one might find in a country cottage. There were even daffodils beside it.

For the first time since arriving on Greed, Lawrence smiled. Following a quick glance for any sign of the pirate, he opened the door and stole inside.

It did indeed lead to a cottage. Lawrence placed his hands against the closed door. 'May this doorway remain invisible to the pirate until it's the...' Lawrence thought for a moment, recalling what Geoffrey had explained about the importance of choosing one's words with great care. 'Until the *constructive* time to return,' he said at last.

Lawrence strode passed all the comforts of the cottage—the cosy fire, the kitchen with all its temptations—and out the backdoor into the charming garden and the woodland beyond.

With each step, his presence grew with the sense of peace gifted by the trees. He walked until he was well into the thick of the wood and stopped at an old trunk of a fallen tree.

'This will do,' he said with another smile.

Following another deep breath, he transformed into an adder, slithered beneath the trunk and coiled up to rest.

CHAPTER 35
NET OF LIGHT

IT WAS MIDNIGHT WHEN RANI AWOKE WITH A START. HER HEAD was vibrating. Or rather, the atomic glove was. She had gone to sleep with it under her head in case it alerted her about the trap.

'Bin!' she hissed as she leapt to her feet and gathered her weapons. 'The trap—it's been sprung!'

Rani's heart pounded as they stole along the passages down through the fort, but not only with excitement. To her disgust, she also felt fear. Frost, for all his swagger, was a lethal opponent. If he got bored with play he could kill her in an instant.

They reached the dead-end of the mysterious corridor. Rani placed her gloved hand against the wall, waited for the appearance of the portal and crept through.

As before, the narrow bridge materialised to meet her feet. With Bin on her shoulder, she waited a moment.

'Mist,' she whispered and a chill ran through her.

The shaft was full of it. Though she could see a haze of light in the direction of the spherical room, she couldn't see inside.

'Where has it come from?' she asked.

'I don't know, but I don't like it,' said Bin.

Rani loaded her bow and drew it taut. As she advanced along the bridge, she strained her senses for any movement, her eyes fixed on the haze of light.

Is he doing this? she wondered, thinking of Frost. *But he doesn't have the power to command the elements. Braysheath, yes, but not Frost.*

But Rani didn't know what Frost was capable of. Though she had little experience with his kind, what she had so far seen of him broke the mould. He was different—more extreme, less predictable.

Halfway across the bridge Rani had a terrible feeling that it was she and Bin who were walking into a trap, that Frost had sensed the one she had set for him and had turned the tables.

Her grip tightened on her bow—too tight, too tense for a warrior to be fluid in movement. She made a conscious effort to relax, but it made little difference.

Finally she arrived at the door. Mist also obscured the insides. Rani and Bin listened for any movement but heard nothing.

There was no tingling of warning from the atomic glove. She remembered how in her fight with Frost there were times when its protection seemed to leave her. She couldn't rely on it.

Then why did it wake me from sleep?

There was only one way to find out. She dropped all thought, re-inhabited her senses, inhaled softly, harmonised herself with the chill mist as best she could and slipped into the room.

The mist was inside as well. Rani felt her own tension mirrored in Bin, whose talons pressed into her shoulder.

Almost at the room's centre, where she had laid her trap, her heart skipped a beat. She sensed a presence and pulled her bow fully taut.

A sudden gust blew through the room. Like a mighty breath, it blew out the mist in a single puff.

Rani's eyes shot wide. The trap had been sprung.

'You!' she cried accusingly.

Relief, confusion, followed by fury swept through Rani. She had set her trap so carefully. It had taken her and Bin ages to find the mysterious net of light which perfectly camouflaged itself until it was touched, before sweeping up its prey to hang from the rafter. The bait had been even more difficult to find in the cluttered room. Many objects had been cast aside which at first she thought might work—strange mirrors, a beautiful knife and many other things—but Frost, she realised, was only interested in knowledge and knowledge he could use.

After much searching, she had finally found a peculiar orb, a bit like a crystal ball except it showed Earth. All the other planets of the cosmos were inside of it, depicted in the manner of an atom with an outer and inner ring of orbs. In particular it showed the Core as a ball of light, along with smaller specks of the same light which moved about the orb, a few on the Surface and a few dotted throughout the rest of the cosmos—advanced beings from the Core.

Bound up in the net of light, however, was not Frost.

It was Jake.

Yet more frustrating, until Rani had startled him, he had been asleep.

'What are you doing here?' she hissed.

It took Jake a few moments to fully wake up. On finding himself caught in a strange net, he was even more confused than Rani.

'Well?' pressed Rani, aiming her loaded bow at him.

'I'm dreaming,' he said with relief, for the symbolism made perfect sense—he was caught in the net of his own desire for a beautiful girl who actually wanted to kill him. That the net was made of light was perhaps a symbol of truth.

'Don't treat me like an idiot,' threatened Rani and pulled the bow taut.

'I'm not,' said Jake, his confusion returning. 'You mean this is actually happening?'

Rani's eyes narrowed.

Jake felt the net of light. It felt very real. The more he focused on it, the more he became aware of a subtle tingling sensation that ran through it.

Rani was losing patience when the snake in her stomach suddenly stirred, reminding her of an inner-conflict—attraction, fear, innocence, darkness and many other things.

'How did you find this place?' she pressed.

Jake looked into her striking eyes. 'I promise you, I've no idea. After supper I went to bed. I was dreaming. I can't remember of what exactly, only that I vaguely remember Braysheath being around.'

Braysheath! thought Rani, her turn to be thrown. That he was capable of merging dreams with reality didn't bother her. What did, is why he might lead both her and Jake to the same place. Her thoughts were cast back to the vision of the bathing male warrior. Her cheeks flushed.

'I was also dreaming of you,' admitted Jake and his heart fluttered.

If Rani could have pulled her bow more taut she would have done. She was sorely tempted to release the arrow.

'How dare you dream of me!' she snarled, casting aside any ideas that Braysheath was behind their meeting. 'That you're full of darkness is bad enough, but you're totally out of control! You dream of me and here you are without the slightest idea of how. I can't believe you're lord of this place. You're a liability! I should shoot you now!'

Rani's words struck a raw nerve in Jake. His mind was besieged by images of the ghosts and the strange web of light he had seen the night the gates were stolen.

'It was you in the ventilation shaft, wasn't it?' he said.

He saw me! she cried in thought. Her sense of alarm shot higher.

Frost was right, thought Jake. *She is an assassin. But not on the side of something evil. It's me she thinks that's evil! And how the hell did I arrive in this room?*

Rani's eyes bored into him.

Bin shifted on her perch on the rafter, looking uncomfortable amid the tension.

Jake closed his eyes for a moment and took a deep breath to calm himself.

'I'm not evil,' he said, looking at Rani straight in the eyes. 'I've no idea about past lives, what I may have done or why I was selected to be in this fort at this time, but I'm not evil.'

Rani looked unconvinced.

The longer Jake spent in her presence, the deeper became his fascination with Rani. She was so enchanting, even in her fierceness, that he found himself letting go of all his doubts and confusion. Everything was perfect. He had wished to meet her and there she was before him, closer than ever before. Jake smiled.

'What?' growled Rani.

'Have you any idea how beautiful you are?' said Jake.

The snake in Rani's stomach flipped with such suddenness that her body jolted. The arrow shot from her bow, shaved Jake's left ear and buried itself in the wall.

The loss of control appalled Rani. A warrior must never lose their composure.

'That was a warning shot!' she lied, but was so annoyed with herself that she threw aside her bow and took it out on Jake. She whisked out a knife, grabbed his shirt through the net and pressed the blade tip to his throat.

Bloody hell! thought Jake.

Blood thumped through both their temples—Jake's in fear and fascination, Rani's in total confusion.

Before either could say anything, something strange happened. They were touching—not just physically, but also through the mysterious net of light. It began to tingle again. Both felt it. Both their eyes widened.

To Jake's eyes, Rani's face suddenly shifted and continued to do so at great speed as scores, perhaps hundreds of different faces sped past. He was seeing her past lives in a matter of seconds.

A great heat washed through him. He sensed the same presence he had in his woodland nightmare—the dangerous woman behind the scenes, behind the chaos. Her energy was intoxicating. But that wasn't all. Jake sensed something behind her, like a shadow. It was the elephant—the huge bull that had charged at him. This time, however, he made the link. The elephant and the woman were in some way connected.

Rani's confusion was just as great. Bin flew up and about her in panic, but there was nothing she could do. The scale of Jake's shadow was even worse than Rani had thought. Behind him was the image of a giant man exuding immense power, so dark that his presence eclipsed the sun—the same presence Jake himself had seen behind the ghosts in the fog. But in the Jake before her she saw a king—a noble king with a lion's heart. Acknowledging his grace, the snake in her stomach spiralled up her spine. Rani flushed and gasped in ecstasy. Yet it came with a tinge of pain as though the snake were rattling its tail in her stomach, overly stretched between fantasy and reality, torn between shadow and a trick of its making, or so it seemed to Rani.

HIDING BEHIND A TALL MIRROR AMID THE PILES OF FURNITURE and other objects was Frost. He couldn't have looked more thrilled. Just as Rani had planned, Frost had followed her trail to the strange room. She had chosen the bait well. The sphere and what it showed had immediately caught his attention. Suspecting a trap, he had approached it with great caution for though he hadn't seen the net of light, he had sensed its power. Frost had been sniffing around it when the trap had suddenly sprung. But rather than himself being caught in the suddenly visible net, Jake was, sleeping like a baby.

Given Frost's heightened perception, he was able to see everything the net was showing Jake and Rani of each other.

Incredible! he thought, wondering at the net's origin. *It's not only showing truth, but also potential! It's amplifying the small but critical changes. It's showing exactly what I myself have sensed in Jake! His potential to be something noble and great, but also something terrible!*

Frost delighted in seeing Rani's confusion and how her and Jake's destinies were interwoven though with the finest of threads.

THROUGH THE BLITZ OF IMAGES, THROUGH AN EXQUISITE TORMENT similar to Rani's, Jake searched for the girl and a way back to the reality of the room.

But the elephant's shadow wouldn't let him go. Its breathing engulfed him—heavy, dense, inescapable as though to say that Jake couldn't find the girl without the elephant. The two were inseparable.

Yet, in that suffocating space Jake also sensed light. In the dangerous presence of the woman he also sensed something queenly—just a hint, but so graceful, so perfect, that like a tulip on a mass grave, it shone as a beacon of hope.

Rani was close to passing out. The conflict of suffering and ecstasy was growing more extreme. She fought to release Jake yet craved to grip him tighter, yearned to kiss him but then slice his throat, until finally, summoning all her strength and awareness, she tore herself from Jake and the net.

Both their eyes were wide with shock. Both were as flustered as the other, gasping for air when Jake noticed the peculiar orb Rani had used as bait.

'What's that?' he stammered. 'Why is it glowing?'

Rani turned sharply. The core of the orb was no longer a soft yellow light but pulsing a bright green.

EXCITEMENT COURSED THROUGH FROST. *LUNA! I KNEW IT!*

The orb, like many of the objects in the room, was ancient. Given the nature of what it measured—wise light and its whereabouts—the orb could also send messages in the other direction. The connection between Jake and Rani was so powerful that the powerful souls the orb tracked had sensed it, one above all—Luna.

The mist, symbolic of emotion, was the effect of Jake's and Rani's powerful chemistry, he deduced. *Now comes the flood! I'll bet this shaft is connected to the Orijinn Sea. Perhaps Luna has a secret base there in one of the many shadow-worlds! She wouldn't be the first. It's a perfect hiding place. Braysheath must use this room to scan it. But like the orb, if used unsubtly, others can see in. Perhaps even enter!*

Frost was suddenly gripped by an extraordinary idea. *Maybe the real trap has been set by Braysheath in order to flush out Luna, using Jake and Rani as bait! Perhaps me too!*

A CHILL RAN THROUGH RANI. THERE WAS SOMETHING ABOUT the nature of the green light that left her cold. It wasn't the hopeful green of nature, but the green of envy and disease.

'You hear that?' said Jake. 'It sounds like water.'

An ominous-feeling wind blew up the shaft and through the room. Rani dashed to the entrance. The shaft was filling with water and fast, surging towards the bridge.

She turned to Jake in the net. She had no idea how to release him. Her plan had been to capture Frost and leave him dangling for Braysheath to discover. Regardless of whatever she thought of Jake, she couldn't let him drown.

She dashed back to the net and tried to cut through it while Jake stretched it taut. But it was useless. The net was unbreakable. It was why she had chosen it.

'Try the knot,' suggested Jake, doing his best to remain calm, referring to how the net was fastened to the rest of the trap.

'It won't budge!' said Rani.

Water rushed into the room. Cold and dark, in seconds it was at her waist and rising.

'Find something, Bin!' she cried.

Bin flew about frantically in the diminishing space of the room, joining Rani in the search for an object that might help, but most of them were already submerged.

'You and your friend must leave,' said Jake. 'I arrived here through a dream. Maybe I can leave that way.'

Rani ignored the suggestion. He didn't realise that her secret mission was to protect him. And she had yet to tell him the truth about Frost. Now was not the time. The water was at her chest. She spotted the orb bobbing on the surface and thought of trying to break it, hoping that might reverse the flow of water, but something told her that to try would be fatal.

PEERING THROUGH THE FLOATING MASS OF OBJECTS, FROST COULD see that there was no escape for Jake, and that Rani and Bin were likely to die trying to save him. It was then he spotted something flash through the water. He sank beneath the surface to find electric eels racing excitedly into the room from the shaft—bright orange with green eyes.

Luna! Her awareness is closing in!

He noted that their eyes were misted. *She doesn't see clearly. She only senses power. But her vision could clear at any moment and what would she see of me? Can I disguise myself against one so powerful? Can I disguise my true self from the net and them,* he wondered, looking at Jake and Rani.

Rani was having to swim to stay above the water.

'Bin! Leave while you can!' she commanded as what remained of the open doorway disappeared beneath the water.

'Not without you!' said Bin and landed on the top of the net.

'What can we do?' appealed Rani.

Jake closed his eyes and called out in his thoughts to Rufus and Braysheath, hoping they might hear, but he had the feeling that he was in a place cut off from the world above.

Rani cried out in shock. Something had stung her.

'Electric eels!' noted Bin. 'Lots of them!'

Jake and Rani gazed on in horror as the bright orange eels swarmed about the mysterious net, trying to get in.

Rani wasn't so lucky. The water was soon boiling with them and each time they brushed past her they gave her a shock.

The water had reached Jake's neck. He was already at the highest part of the net. Rani tugged in desperation at its cords of light, doing her best to ignore the shocks from the eels. She appealed to the atomic glove for help, but none came.

In that moment of great stress, an inexplicable calm came over Jake. All that mattered, as the water rose to the ceiling and Rani remained with him beneath its surface, was that they held each other.

As Rani continued her vain wrestle with the net, he reached out and held of her hands.

Yet again their eyes shot wide. Energy pulsed out from Jake and Rani and shook the room. The net glowed. Yet more eels swarmed in from the shaft—so many that it was almost impossible to see anything else, but now Rani was immune to their touch.

The hint of the queen Jake had seen in Rani now shone before him like a rising sun. Time stood still. The crown of his head, along with his heart, felt like they were opening up in a blissful yawn.

Rani, however, felt and saw nothing. It was as though a great void had opened before her, yet in it was everything.

I must be running out of air! she panicked, trying to understand what was happening.

As soon as she thought of air, her awareness left the subtlety of the void. The pressure in her lungs was mounting. She struggled to free her hands from Jake's but he appeared to be in a trance.

With a great jolt something shifted.

Another presence had arrived.

The image of the graceful queen suddenly flickered and went out. Jake's presence returned to the net, along with his desperate need for air, yet all he saw was a great darkness—not the liberating void which Rani had felt, but a dense terrible place which prickled like hell.

Rani also felt a great shock. She turned to find Frost's face appear amid the turmoil of eels, except it wasn't Frost exactly—through the shadow of what she knew and detested in him, she saw something of great beauty, something princely from a vast and distant unknown kingdom. In his hand was a golden key. Vision or real, it shone with immense significance.

It's a trick! she cried out through her failing consciousness and the key became a knife.

With a single stroke, Frost slashed through the mysterious net. Its light flickered. In the instant before it faded completely, Jake had one last vision. The graceful beauty he had seen in Rani shone through the darkness. Not as a queen but as something divine. A mermaid, in fact. Beside her was a merman. The golden light of fish reflected in their scales.

Frost! thought Jake.

As Frost reached into the net and took hold of him, Jake felt a flood of warmth, of friendship, which cast back the chill of the water and dissolved the lingering fear about what Frost really was.

Free of the net, which had partially protected them, reality returned ice cold. Their lungs about to burst, both Rani and Jake were on the verge of passing out.

Holding each by the hand, Frost swam effortlessly for the shaft.

Bin, who had been surviving on a last gasp of air about the ceiling, swam down and followed them, expanding her size in the shaft to make the swim to its other side less of a strain.

As Frost swam through the doorway of the room, both Jake and Rani felt themselves revive a little. Frost was gifting them life-force. Ordinarily, Rani would rather have died than accept it, but she was too confused, too weak, to be anything but grateful.

Despite their already desperate state, the sight that greeted them as they entered the shaft was horrifying. It seemed endless, a green light blazing from far off that shot through the orange serpents and lent them the appearance of writhing flames.

Just like in the room, the number of eels was growing so thick that were it not for Frost, Rani and Jake would have struggled to swim, like Bin behind them. Jake noticed how some of the eels had misty eyes. The eyes of others, however, were clearing. One glanced at Jake with such intensity that he felt a shock—not to his skin, but inside of him, like a pin prick to the heart.

Who are you? he heard in an eerie female voice.

Though the voice was soft, there was something terrible in it.

Who are you? it repeated.

Jake was tempted to return the question but remained silent, fearing that were he to answer, it would be like opening a door even wider.

Luna probed him with greater power. His head grew light. He battled to stay awake.

Finally Frost reached the other side of the shaft. The eels were so dense about Rani's portal that they were like a knot. With a slash of Frost's knife they dispersed, just long enough for him to haul Jake and Rani through into the corridor, along with Bin who reduced in size.

With what little energy Rani had left, she sealed the portal with her gloved hand. Her head spinning with confusion and fatigue, she collapsed to her knees.

Bin nestled her head against Rani's cheek.

'Bin,' she gasped with relief, 'are you okay?'

'Are *you* okay?' asked Jake, between pants of breath, placing a hand softly on her shoulder.

Rani recoiled from his touch. She had had enough shocks for one night. She looked between Frost and Jake, her mind a whirl amid all she had seen, not knowing what to believe—the extremes were too great.

She had nothing to say to either of them. Exhausted, she craved to be alone and hauled herself up to leave.

Where the mysterious corridor met the main one, she glanced back at them. Jake's eyes were full of concern. Frost's eyes were twinkling. He smiled. But who was smiling, she couldn't tell—devil, prince, or master illusionist.

CHAPTER 36
BATTLE OF BEAUTY

A CHEERFUL WHISTLING COULD BE HEARD AS SOMEONE APPROACHED the north gate from inside the oasis. It was Braysheath.

'Hello there, Glabrous!' he cried to the Commander of the Gate.

Now that the oasis was orange with autumn, the thorsror was almost perfectly camouflaged. Once seen, there he was as though he had appeared from thin air—vast and lethal, eyes blazing.

'Just taking an afternoon stroll!' said Braysheath.

Glabrous bowed his head as Braysheath strode past.

'Look after this for me, will you?' A staff like a wizard's appeared in his left hand. He planted it in the earth where it glowed for a moment as though something of his energy had passed inside it. Coiled about its top was the cobra. With a shriek, his eagle flew down and landed on a nearby branch.

'One likes to travel light!' he said and strode out into the baking heat of the dunes.

Glabrous watched him as he went.

Braysheath's whistling became a song—strange, ancient-sounding and wonderful.

Only moments passed before he was a mere speck on the horizon, singing his song, the landscape answering, clouds scudding across the sky as though time had been sped up.

A stride later, it was night time, the sky full of stars.

Following three more strides, the desert sand began to glow. Its grains coalesced and shone so that the sky and desert were indistinguishable. Braysheath appeared as though he were walking through the Milky Way.

A sun loomed up and blazed. Braysheath gazed right at it without squinting. With another stride he stood in its fiery core and glanced about as if it were no more than an intersection of roads.

Still he sang.

He took a turn and passed through the sun.

Another sun sped towards him. Again he stepped inside, took a turn and passed from the second sun to a third where he finally stopped singing and gazed up. As he did so, the sun retreated to a setting orbit and Braysheath was once more on the ground.

'Oh dear,' he said as he glanced about. 'Not quite as I remember it.'

He was standing in a wasteland of smouldering tree stumps in the world of Pride. Famed for its beguiling beauty, the only sign of it was a golden woodland in the distance.

Braysheath reached down, picked up a handful of ash and sniffed it. 'Ah...' he said. 'I see. Yes, I was afraid of that. Still, one mustn't jump to conclusions. Best to keep an open mind, though there's no doubt that gravity at the Core grows weaker.'

He sniffed the air. For a moment his eyes grew misty.

'And which probably means...'

Before he could complete his sentence, the ground shook with the movement of many hooves.

A moment later, two great armies lined the ridges either side of the wasteland. Mounted on horses, stags and other magnificent creatures, the riders bristled with weapons, their armour glistening in the orange sunlight.

'One tries to reduce one's gravity,' he sighed, for it was Braysheath's energy the armies were drawn to. 'Alas, in such times, in such places...'

The armies had formed in less than a day, jolted from their journey towards to the Core by Luna's war which, though raging in the Outer-Peregrinus, reverberated throughout the entire cosmos. Neither side knew why it fought. They had lost their centre. Emotions were in flux, chief among them fear. Lacking the imagination to do anything else, they did what they had done for thousands of years—fight. It mattered not who.

With a trumpeting of horns and cry of beasts, the armies charged.

Just the thunder of hooves and the ringing of steel would have tested the resolve of the most battle-hardened warrior, let alone the awesome sight of the two armies racing towards one another, intent on total destruction. And yet, as they closed in from either side, Braysheath simply gazed out towards the golden woodland with an almost bored air.

Ash billowed up. Lances levelled as the armies reached full-gallop.

Only seconds from engagement, arrows whined through the air.

Braysheath stood calmly.

An instant from contact, the arrows transformed to a sheet of rain.

Finally the two front lines crashed through one another. Those closest to Braysheath slashed and thrust at him as they raced past, desperate to win his gravity but, like the arrows, they couldn't harm him.

The entire plain smothered in war, each vanguard a good way through the other's army, Braysheath's aloof expression finally shifted. A subtle smile broke across his face—one which held great power.

With a tremendous creak and rustling of leaves, the armies transformed. Warriors became trees, plants or creatures of the wood. In a matter of seconds, not a single sign of war remained. The air was filled with the scent of flowers and the buzzing of bees. Even the smouldering tree stumps had gone.

'That's better!' cheered Braysheath. 'Much better! It would be such a waste to see you all fall back to the Surface, especially having come so far.'

A breeze blew up and soughed through the trees.

'Trees are so agreeable,' continued Braysheath. 'Whenever I find myself getting a bit hot and bothered, becoming a tree is the perfect remedy, sinking your roots into the cool earth and creating your own shade. Yielding to the wind rather than fighting it. I usually go for a yew myself. There's nothing quite like it!'

Braysheath inhaled a satisfied breath of air.

'Yes,' he said. 'Humility and compassion, my dear friends. They are the only paths through Pride and there are no better teachers than trees. However, you're looking a little too green compared to that other woodland. Best not to stand out. Let's see…'

In little more than a blink of Braysheath's eyes, four seasons swept through the wood, coming to rest in a golden autumn just as vivid as the other.

'There, that should get rid of any traces. I expect she'll think it's a reflection of her growing power,' he said referring to Luna. 'I take it this is one of her bases?'

A badger poked its head out from a burrow and glanced at Braysheath before disappearing inside again.

'Thank you!' said Braysheath, before turning to a chirping finch. 'Yes, I imagine she has left a few traps.'

He looked about the woodland with a twinkle in his eyes. 'Perhaps we've created one of our own. With a bit of luck she'll take a stroll through here on one of her trips back to the Core. I don't suppose any of you would recognise her?'

The wood fell deathly silent. Not even an insect was heard.

The silence was broken, not by Braysheath, but by the sound of approaching riders.

A company of ten rode into view, a mixture of men and women. They were dressed like monks in maroon robes though armed like warriors. Half were on horses, four on stags, one mounted on a rhino. Not one of them looked friendly.

'Oh, hello!' beamed Braysheath.

'Who are you?' barked the male leader.

'Oh, no one of consequence,' replied Braysheath airily.

'Why aren't you armed?' he barked again.

'Since when has it been necessary to carry a weapon on Pride?' asked Braysheath.

'It is these days,' said a woman gruffly. 'In which case, *what* are you exactly and *what* are you doing here?'

'The same as you, my dear. I'm searching.'

'Maybe he's an alchemist,' she said to the leader with a flicker of fear in her eyes. 'Or something even worse.'

At the mention of *alchemist*, two women with loaded bows aimed and pulled them taught. The others drew swords.

'An alchemist?' cried Braysheath. 'Why, you flatter me!'

'Hey!' barked the leader. 'Where did the others go?'

Suddenly there were only five riders.

'And that boulder wasn't there before!' he noted, staring at where only moments before had been the mounted rhino. On top of the boulder was a lizard.

An owl took flight and three squirrels darted about the branches of four newly arrived trees.

'And these trees! What's going on?' growled the leader, a tremor in his voice. He rode a step closer to Braysheath, his sword pointed forward.

'I've no idea,' said Braysheath, shrugging innocently. 'But you ought to know that here on Pride evolution is rather snappy.'

No sooner had he said so than a great trumpeting shook the air as two horses became elephants. Hornbills flew up from their backs.

All that remained was the leader and the two women armed with bows. One was in front of Braysheath and one behind. In the same moment, both released their arrows.

'Oh, how lovely!' cried Braysheath as a robin appeared on top of his head and a ladybird on his robe in the region of his heart. The arrows were nowhere to be seen. Neither were the archers. As their stags leapt away, so also did two toads.

Conquering his fear, the leader drove his horse forward and swung his sword for Braysheath's neck.

As his horse disappeared from beneath him, he fell to his knees. His sword had transformed into a bunch of roses.

'Why, this is too much!' exclaimed Braysheath. 'You shouldn't have!'

Braysheath took the roses from the astounded leader, buried his nose in them and sniffed heartily. 'Delightful! Quite delightful!'

The leader looked about for his horse as a grass snake slithered away into the undergrowth.

'Who are you?' he asked of Braysheath, he stammered in fear and awe.

Braysheath looked down at him with a gentle smile. 'Part of you, dear fellow. And if you adopt the same attitude, you'll do just fine down here,' he said. 'In the meantime, I'm going to do you a favour.'

Before the man could protest, he transformed into a boar.

'There! Perfect!' proclaimed Braysheath. 'And don't go believing any of that new world nonsense about pigs being unclean, just because the Egyptian god Set caused a rumpus in the form of a pig. Oh, how Ra has cursed you!'

The boar released a disgruntled snort at the sight of its tail.

'Now, now, don't be like that. Think of the Celts. They worshipped you for your courage, strength and your powers of healing, not to mention your remarkable ability to sniff out hidden treasures. Why, Ceridwen, their Goddess of Inspiration, was a snow white sow! Yes, it's perfect for you.'

The boar released an unconvinced-sounding snort.

'Don't worry, it won't last forever,' reassured Braysheath. 'Like this woodland and everything in it, at the auspicious moment you'll be able to become whatever you wish. For now, however, you could all help me out. If you spot Luna wandering around these parts, give me a shout. You only need think of me and I'll be here in a tinkle. You think you could do that?'

The boar snorted.

'Splendid fellow,' said Braysheath, who tossed him an apple and disappeared.

CHAPTER 37
TRICKY FRIENDSHIP

IT WAS IN THE SMALL HOURS OF MORNING WHEN JAKE AND FROST arrived back in Jake's room.

'I'll raid the kitchens for a midnight refreshment. Back in a moment!' said Frost and disappeared through the fireplace.

Having changed into some dry clothes, Jake passed onto the patio and climbed the steps onto the ramparts. The sight of the night sky and the savannah was a welcome one, embracing Jake in its stillness. He needed it. Like Rani's, his mind was a whirl of confusion.

In order to create some mental space, he put aside the big questions he couldn't yet answer—the identity of the voice in the flooded shaft and the identity of the demon connected to Asclepius's contraption. Though both threats seemed dangerously close, neither were in the fort, at least not in a way Jake could understand. More pressing were the mysteries which *were* in the fort, namely the girl and Frost and the strange connection between the three of them.

That evening, Jake had gone to bed with a heavy burden.

Frost was a trixy.

Viewed from a distance, it was so obvious that Jake kicked himself that he hadn't realised it before. Rufus's warning to take great care who he invited had echoed through his tortured mind.

Jake closed his eyes and drew a deep breath.

He saved me. And the girl.

He recalled the warmth he had felt when Frost had appeared at the net. Whatever Frost was, Jake sensed the bond of friendship even stronger than before.

Rufus said that trixies were as vital as pixies on the journey to truth, he remembered. *Perhaps I shouldn't judge too quickly.*

Maybe there's a deeper reason why our paths have crossed. Besides, if I had to choose between a pixy or a trixy as a guide on a mission to Renlock, a place of spies, then I'd choose a trixy. As long as I could trust it. I just need to remember that Frost's truths are tricky truths.

Another aspect of the burden cast its shadow upon his newfound clarity—what Braysheath had said of a powerful tribe of trixies that had been corrupted by Luna.

Jake sighed. He had no way of gauging such things.

It's possible that Frost is part of the corrupted tribe, he accepted with a wince. *To deny it would only make matters worse. If he is, then I must keep him close, perhaps not confronting him quite yet, even though I'd prefer to have it all out in the open. I'll watch him for a while just to be sure. And at the first opportunity, I'll share this with Braysheath and Rufus.*

Jake recalled his earlier attempts to confide in Braysheath and how each time something had interrupted him. *Surely he knows. If he's so powerful how could he not know? Yes, there must be a deeper mystery to all this.*

The more Jake thought of having a trixy as a friend, the more he warmed to the idea. If used properly, he could turn out to be a great ally.

And how the hell did I get from my bed to that weird net if it wasn't through the intervention of someone like Braysheath or Nemesis?

Despite the scale of the mystery, the force of the girl was greater. Having found some peace with the idea of Frost as a trixy, Jake welcomed her into his thoughts.

No sooner had the image of her bewitching eyes filled his mind than Frost appeared with a tray. Reluctantly, Jake tore himself away from her.

'Stew, cake and ginger ale!' enthused Frost.

'Great!' said Jake and helped himself to a bowl. After the cold water in the shaft he was famished.

Though it was the small hours of night, Frost took the precaution of sitting between the roots of a tree which was standing on the ramparts.

Both tucked into the food.

'Thank you,' said Jake between mouthfuls. 'For saving us.'

'Of course! What are friends for?' said Frost and glugged down some ale.

'How did you know we were there?' asked Jake as innocently as possible.

Frost grinned at Jake. 'The girl. She laid the trap to capture me! It was a good one too, but I still smelt it a mile off. And so I waited for her return, when all of a sudden you popped in.'

Makes sense, thought Jake and took another mouthful of stew.

'And the net,' he continued. 'Things looked strange through it. What was it?'

'An amazing thing! One of a kind. That room was full of powerful objects, but that net was especially powerful—too old for its origin to be remembered. But my guess is that it showed you things which ordinarily you'd struggle to see.'

'What sort of things?'

'Things others wish to hide,' said Frost, bending the truth, for he knew all too well that what it really did was magnify small but critical changes taking place within someone.

Jake reflected on what he had seen of the girl, how her beauty had been consumed by a sense of great danger and darkness, how it had reminded him of the female presence in the woods of his nightmare, and that the only explanation which made sense was that he and she had somehow known each other in a previous life, perhaps many lives. It was an incredible idea—exciting and alarming, which cast her presence in the fort in an entirely new light.

Jake recalled his earlier idea that perhaps she thought of herself as good, an assassin of dark things, just as he thought of himself as honest.

It fitted his feeling that there was a deeper level to the mystery that neither of them could currently grasp, though would ultimately make sense of all the madness. A lightness filled Jake. It was an empowering thought. He wasn't the only one who was confused and lost in a strange new world. She was too.

Regardless, the responsible thing to do, given his position, was to have her brought to him—not in the manner of a lord, but as someone who wished to talk to her in order to discover truth.

Frost was studying Jake as he drank his ale.

'I wonder what she saw of me?' asked Jake.

'Something extremely unpleasant,' said Frost and caused Jake to laugh.

With his laughter came other images of the girl, the ones which emerged from behind the darkness.

'You know what I saw?' he said, curious what Frost would say.

His mouth full of stew, Frost raised a questioning eyebrow.

'When you touched the net she looked divine. A bit like Nemesis in my dream. Beautiful beyond words! A mermaid, in fact, and you…'

Jake laughed at the recollection.

Frost's expression became a light-hearted frown and Jake enjoyed the novelty of knowing something that he didn't.

'You were a merman.'

Frost barked with laughter though it lacked its usual gusto. The comment had thrown him off balance. His eyes probed Jake's to see if he was joking.

'It was strange,' said Jake, 'as though the net were showing me that both you and she are somehow the same.'

Frost scoffed.

'I mean at a deeper level,' clarified Jake, 'in the sense of becoming my friends—'

'Ha! Of course I'm your friend, but her? Good luck!' cried Frost and glugged back more ale.

'And,' continued Jake, unabashed, 'friends to each other. Perhaps in a romantic way.'

Frost almost spat out his ale. 'She's all yours!' he laughed. 'Anyway, I'd take what the net showed you with a pinch of salt. You must be very careful with an object of power. You need to know who made it and for what purpose—to tell the truth, to deceive or something of both.'

Jake studied Frost. 'Be honest. You don't fancy her?'

'Fancy?' cried Frost.

'Come on, let your guard down.'

Frost smiled, part-mocking, but not completely. Jake caught a glimpse of the deeper Frost—a softness, a vulnerability, a conflict, something real, something on which to build a genuine friendship. A moment later the shields were up, but Jake wouldn't forget that look. It matched the warmth he had seen in Frost in the spherical room and he knew that the net had showed something of the truth. He also remembered how the queenly image of Rani had suddenly become a hellish darkness.

Was that when Frost made contact with the net? he wondered. *The mermaid and merman had come a moment later. If that was the case, what does it mean? That Frost first brings chaos, but from the chaos comes beauty?*

'She's interesting,' admitted Frost vaguely.

'An understatement,' said Jake. 'Go on.'

'At first glance she's hot to look at, sure, but without inner light to shine through her outer-appearance and bring it to life, she's dull.'

'She can't be dull and interesting at the same time.'

'She's got potential, but she refuses to embrace her darkness in order to find her real light,' said Frost.

'You know that already?' exclaimed Jake, delighted to hear that he and the girl had something else in common.

Frost nodded and took a bite of chocolate cake. 'It's obvious.'

'Is that what the net showed you?'

'More or less, but I was too busy trying to save you.'

They fell into a silence as Jake finished his stew. He had the sense that Frost was withholding what he had really seen—an insight into the deeper mystery which so far eluded Jake. He also wondered what the girl had seen in each of them and why it was, really, that the three of them were in the fort together and especially in that mysterious room floating in the shaft. Jake had no idea what the girl thought of Frost, but he could tell that Frost was more interested in her than he was letting on. If she embraced her darkness, things would change. Frost would become fascinated by her. Jake felt it.

The image of fireworks and terrific explosions filled his mind.

Complicated, he thought, battling to bring his mind back to more immediate concerns. Yet he couldn't escape a lingering feeling that some great intrigue lay in store between the three of them.

Despite Frost's withholding, Jake felt much better about his strange friend's presence in the fort. Whether or not their emerging friendship withstood the great tests that were doubtless ahead of them, at least Jake was now playing the game—he knew what Frost was, but was playing it cool.

'It's funny,' he said. 'Despite the danger of drowning in the net, that ghost I told you about, the one with the lantern, he didn't appear.'

'Perhaps because someone more powerful was present,' said Frost, with a mysterious light in his eyes.

Jake cocked his head questioningly.

'Luna,' said Frost.

The words *Who are you?* ran through Jake like ice. 'The green light!'

'The light of her eyes.'

'Was she actually in the fort?' asked Jake, horrified at the thought.

'I don't think so,' said Frost. 'The light and the eels represented her attention reaching out.'

'To what?'

'Something powerful,' said Frost.

Jake studied the light in Frost's eyes and recognised that, yet again, he knew much more than he was willing to say. Tempted to push the point, Jake refrained. To do so would only invite a deception. What Frost had said so far rang true.

He thought back to his time in the net. He had heard the rush of water up through the shaft when Rani had touched the net, connecting her to Jake. Frost's contact seemed to amplify that connection.

'How much do you think Luna sensed?' he asked.

'Difficult to say,' said Frost, 'but she certainly would have sensed something of great interest to her within the fort. You can expect her to pay closer attention.'

'Hasn't she taken enough?' said Jake. 'Pandora's Box, the gates...'

'Those things are only tools to help find what it is she really seeks,' explained Frost.

'Which is?'

'Apart from power, in other words light, I don't know,' said Frost. 'But I feel there's something else.'

'I thought you knew everything,' said Jake dryly.

'Want to find out?'

'Meaning?'

'Renlock! I've found a way in!' declared Frost. 'In searching for your granddad we might also discover what Luna's up to.'

'Where *do* you find the time?' exclaimed Jake, amazed by Frost, trixy or not.

'Unlike you, I don't spend half my life sleeping.'

Jake was delighted. The thought of finding his granddad gifted him energy.

'Of course you're suggesting we leave right away?' said Jake.

'Of course!'

Jake thought of Rufus and suddenly felt guilty, but if he told anyone, he might not be allowed to go and any delay could prove fatal for Nestor.

'Give me a second,' said Jake. 'Before we go I need to speak to Glabrous. I want to ask him to find the girl. If there was more time I'd try to find her myself, but there isn't.'

Frost's eyes lit up like torches. 'Excellent!' he hissed and sprang off for his secret den.

Jake descended the ramparts to the patio. He recalled how during his capture in the net of light he had tried to summon Braysheath and Rufus through thought. It hadn't worked in the shaft, but he wondered if it would work with Glabrous from his room.

Glabrous, Commander of the North Gate, this is Jake, he said in his head. *Please come to me on the patio outside my room. I need you.*

Jake waited, but nothing happened.

He tried again except this time he first closed his eyes and spoke through his heart with full presence, visualising his words speaking to the heart of Glabrous.

A moment passed.

A powerful charge prickled the air. Jake opened his eyes to find the mighty Glabrous towering before him, peering haughtily down his nose.

His mesmerising eyes fixed on Jake as he drew a long deep omniscient breath.

Like the first time they had met, Jake felt himself being weighed and measured. The sensation of Glabrous's breath passing through him reminded Jake of the girl—how her shadow through the net had appeared like an elephant. The thorsror's eyes widened. His gaze grew more intense. A heat rose up in Jake. He battled to clear his mind of all thoughts about his recent adventure, especially relating to Frost.

Taking control, Jake closed his eyes. 'Glabrous,' he said calmly, before reopening them.

'My lord,' said Glabrous in his lofty manner and made a cursory bow.

'What do you see?' asked Jake spontaneously, his curiosity overwhelming his caution.

Though Glabrous's proud face remained impassive, for a moment his eyes grew misted.

'Challenges,' he said at last.

'Anything in particular?' ventured Jake.

'Everything in particular,' replied Glabrous without elaborating.

Sounds about right, thought Jake.

'Well, starting with one of them,' he said, 'do you realise that there's a human warrior girl in the fort along with her sometimes-*giant* osprey?'

'Not until a moment ago,' said Glabrous imperiously, referring to what he had sensed through Jake. 'And you didn't *invite* them?'

Another heat rose up in Jake, but he did his best to remain calm.

'If I had invited them, Glabrous,' he said plainly, 'then we wouldn't be talking about this.'

Again, Glabrous's chilling gaze bore into Jake, but he stood firm, keeping his mind as blank as possible.

'They shall be found,' said Glabrous at last.

'Thank you, Glabrous. Please bring them to me. I wish to talk with them.'

Following another cursory bow, Glabrous leapt clean over Jake and the ramparts.

His heart racing, Jake exhaled with relief then made his way to Frost's den.

CHAPTER 38
SPYING ON THE SPIES

FROST BEAMED AT JAKE WHEN HE ARRIVED THROUGH THE FIREPLACE.
'All done? Set the beast upon her?'
'I hope she doesn't take it too badly,' said Jake.
'She'll take it terribly,' said Frost, rubbing his hands together with glee. 'You'd better hope the thorsror makes a clean sweep of it, otherwise you'll wake one morning without your balls.'
'Which way to Renlock?' said Jake, keen to get moving.
'This way!' said Frost and sprang off along the passageway.
Many twists and turns later and after scaling dozens of steps, they finally arrived at the top of one of the turrets.
'It's almost first light,' said Frost. 'We'd better get moving!'
'Where?' said Jake.
Instead of answering, Frost put his hands about his mouth and made a braying sound which carried eerily over the savannah. He did it twice.
Jake glanced about when a sudden rushing sound of large wings made him jump.
Landing gracefully on the turret was an incredible creature—a large antelope with wings, just like the one he had seen in the healing hall on his first night in the fort.
'A zorlop!' announced Frost and leapt upon its back. 'Hop aboard!'
'Isn't Renlock another world?' asked Jake. 'Isn't there a gate we can take to save time?'
'Sort of. But it's not in the fort,' said Frost, who leaned down and hauled Jake up.
'Aloft!' he whispered in the zorlop's ear and it leapt to flight.
'Wow!' cried Jake as the zorlop soared upwards towards a majestic crescent moon.'

'Not bad, hey?'

Jake shook his head in wonder as he looked down at the shrinking image of the fort and out across the oasis and the desert beyond.

'Life! One must find the joy in every moment!' cried Frost. 'Don't worry about the future, dear friend Jake. Just live and everything will fall into place!'

Jake said nothing. He simply nodded, warming to the celebration in Frost's tone.

The moon re-caught his attention. 'This goddess Luna,' he asked, 'is she really a goddess of the moon?'

'I doubt it,' said Frost. 'But someone as mysterious and as powerful as her would choose a name which, though a cover, also held a clue as to her true identity.'

'Why?'

'Because every so-called baddie thinks they're a goodie in pursuit of their own twisted view of truth. They want people to know who they are,' explained Frost. 'Or at least, who they think they are.'

'So what's the clue?' asked Jake as the zorlop flew out over the lake.

'The moon is a rock reflecting the sun, like the relationship between body and spirit. It's a symbol of fertility, ultimately fertility of the mind—the transformed mind. The moon sheds its shadow like the snake its skin to be born again. It represents the power of life caught in time until it throws off its shadow once and for all and unites with the sun which has no shadow.'

'Are you saying she represents mind?'

'I'm saying she's from the sun, which some say is a symbol for truth, reflecting the Core of Earth. Heaven in other words.'

Jake's mind was cast back into the shaft and the chilling green light shining up from beneath them.

'In order to make an appearance outside of the Core she must take on a shadow. That is, she must use a body. It's the same as saying that something perfect must adopt an imperfection.'

'But how can Luna be from truth?' asked Jake. 'She's causing chaos.'

'Chaos from your perspective,' clarified Frost, 'which, either way, is critical to truth and perfection.'

Jake was reminded of his earlier thought—that the beauty in Rani, symbolised by the mermaid, perhaps also the beauty in himself, would be brought about by the trixy's chaos.

'Then what is perfection?' he asked.

'Perfection is conscious change—a process, not a destination.'

Jake looked down, half-expecting to see Luna's bright green eye blazing up at them. Instead he saw the lake which was so big it appeared more like a sea.

'This should do it,' said Frost

'Do what?' asked Jake.

'The dropping off point. Ready?'

'You don't mean into the lake?' exclaimed Jake.

'I do,' said Frost who, without any further explanation, shoved Jake off the zorlop.

Jake couldn't believe it. He was plunging what felt like miles towards a shark-infested lake. All thoughts of friendship were tossed out the window, replaced by curses and thoughts of murder.

Finally he struck the dark surface of the lake and plunged deep beneath it.

It seemed to take forever to swim back up, despite his panicked strokes.

With a deep gasp, at last he made it. Frost was already there treading water, a broad grin on his face.

'You've been eating too many pies!' he cried.

Jake expressed himself clearly and colourfully and might have attempted strangling Frost were he not so preoccupied about the other inhabitants of the lake.

'We're one step closer,' said Frost, laughing at Jake's temper. 'Now we wait for our next taxi.'

Jake dreaded to think what Frost had in mind.

Within moments, ominous swirls in the water heralded the arrival of something large. Something *very* large.

'That better not be a shark!' exclaimed Jake, gripped with fear.

'You're going to love it!' cried Frost. 'And so am I! I've never travelled by...'

Frost was cut short by something smooth and shiny like a wet boulder rising up through the surface beside them. A dark eye appeared within it, as large as Jake's head. It studied them for a solemn moment before sinking back beneath the surface.

'A whale!' gasped Jake, his heart racing.

'Pretty cool hey, Jonah?' said Frost.

'Jonah?' said Jake. 'You're not suggesting...'

Frost's grin broadened.

A moment of agonising stillness followed.

Then it came—a rush of movement from beneath. A bow wave lifted them up. Frost cried out in delight. The wave collapsed as the whale burst through the surface, its cavernous mouth wide open.

There was only a horrified moment for a last glimpse at the stars before the whale swallowed them whole.

Down they tumbled through the rush of water. Jake counted three complete rolls head over heels then struck something solid—solid and surprisingly comfortable.

When he finally got his bearings, he found himself in an armchair and completely dry. Frost was beside him looking ecstatic. He too was in a chair, though one very different from his own. In fact, they appeared to be in a room whose design was split in two.

Jake's half was a strange mix of his dad's study along with something grander, almost regal, while Frost's was like a spooky-looking forest, his chair woven from blackthorn. It lasted only a moment before undergoing a sudden transformation. The spooky appearance became more homely, like a treehouse, inhabited by various creatures of the wood, including an owl, an adder and a raven.

'Brilliant!' declared Frost. 'It's a reflection of who we are. Mine shows my love of nature while yours shows what a lazy and pretentious toad you are.'

He altered his own half, thought Jake, taking it as another confirmation that Frost was indeed a trixy.

Frost was studying Jake with a curious glint in his eyes and a wry smile. 'I wondered how long it would take you.'

'How long what would take me?'

'You've worked out that I'm a pixy,' lied Frost.

'Pixy?' said Jake, feeling both relieved, but also a little disappointed.

Frost barked with laughter. 'Don't tell me you thought I was a trixy! Ha! How generous of you!'

'Prove to me that you're not one,' challenged Jake.

Frost put his hands together in thought.

'Alright. You've doubtless heard that trixies are associated with the inner-force and precious stones and metals while pixies are connected with the outer-force and thus the dryads in the trees.'

Jake nodded.

'Well, while a trixy could turn a rock into a diamond, they couldn't make a flower sprout up from the ground because that would require assistance from the trees and dryads. It's a very basic example but true.'

'Go on then,' said Jake.

With a twinkle of Frost's eyes, a branch of blackthorn extended in through the window in his treehouse room and miraculously blossomed, its white flowers releasing a delightful musky scent.

'Some of nature's greatest gifts are protected by thorns and poison,' said Frost somewhat cryptically.

'What about your knowledge of gates and anything secret?' asked Jake.

'Any pixy worth its salt has a sixth sense for such things,' countered Frost. 'Besides, both pixies and trixies are different sides of the same coin. We both seek wholeness, trixies through trickiness and pixies through kindness. Neither gets far without the other.'

'Given we're off to Renlock, I was hoping you *were* a trixy,' admitted Jake.

Again Frost barked with laughter. 'As you will soon discover, I am no ordinary pixy,' he boasted.

'But won't you stick out like a sore thumb?'

'Not if I'm focused,' said Frost. 'Ultimately all forces are in union. And so a skilled pixy, like a skilled anything else, has the ability to blend.'

A pixy, thought Jake, getting used to the idea. *At least I now know he's not from the corrupted trixy tribe.*

'You'd never have believed me if I had told you when we first met,' said Frost. 'It's also why I had to make sure you officially invited me to the fort. Strictly speaking, it's forbidden for a pixy or a trixy to enter. We're bound to the Surface. The cook is an exception.'

'By the way, are we still inside the whale?' asked Jake.

'In its stomach! But as you've no doubt gathered, just as I'm no ordinary pixy, this is no ordinary whale. His name is Deuteronomy. He's Lord of the Blue Whales and has special powers. He's a bit like a gate, able to take us anywhere where there's sea within the Outer-Peregrinus.'

'Can he take us to Renlock?'

'If that is your wish,' resounded the deepest voice Jake had ever heard.

Jake's eyes lit up as bright as Frost's.

'There is a hidden cave within the headland beneath the cliff of Renlock,' said Deuteronomy. 'With care, I can deposit you there.'

'That's it!' cried Frost. 'That's what I heard! Odin had the dwarf-smiths create it so he could spy on the spies—other gods who sought to topple him when he was Overlord of the Outer-Peregrinus.'

'Odin?' said Jake, the name vaguely familiar.

'A Norse god,' explained Frost. 'He was a wise god, so when his reign on the Surface came to an end he never completely fell. Like the gods in the fort, he has privileged power in the inner-worlds. He rules an estate called Valhalla. Rufus used to work for him.'

'He did?' asked Jake.

'Before he became a carpet he was Odin's head of intelligence.'

'Really?' said Jake, impressed. 'How long will it take to get to Renlock?'

'Renlock is worlds away but it won't take long,' said Deuteronomy.

'Each stroke of his fins are quantum strokes,' explained Frost excitedly. 'It's like swimming the entire breadth of the Pacific in a single stroke.'

Jake was about to pour out some tea when he noticed a door at the far end of the peculiar room.

'Where does that door lead?' he asked.

'The cockpit!' said Frost. 'If you pass inside, you experience our journey as Deuteronomy.'

'Seriously?' exclaimed Jake, unable to believe his ears.

'Try it,' said Frost.

'Be my guest,' said Deuteronomy. 'You can return to the room whenever you wish.'

'You mean that I will feel as though I were a whale?'

'You'll feel as I feel,' responded Deuteronomy.

'No way!' exclaimed Jake and bounded up to the door. Following a final glance back at Frost, Jake opened it.

THE MOMENT JAKE OPENED THE DOOR HE WAS SWEPT OFF HIS feet. The next, he was a whale and the ocean exploded to life—a great oceanic symphony resounding through his every fibre, above all, the cries of whales echoing from near and far, as joyful as they were plaintive, guiding him like a tribal song-line.

It was even more amazing than diving through a holygate. For a start, it lasted longer. Similar to a gate, he felt connected to everything, felt the same life-force running through all creation, including himself.

He was swimming through the trenches of an ocean floor. It was like nothing Jake had ever imagined, like swimming between mountains at night with plankton for stars. Giant squid, stingray and other mysterious creatures of the ocean depths swept past as fleeting images. In and out of caves they swam, into new trenches, each another world.

JAKE HAD NO IDEA HOW MUCH TIME HAD LAPSED WHEN SUDDENLY he was swimming upwards. He breached the surface of a grey sea into a grey day, a great dark cliff before them. A wan light shone from countless portals within it. Together they created the image of a human sitting in the lotus position of meditation.

Go ladies to lotus! thought Jake recalling the riddles and Rufus's description of Renlock.

Streams of pigeons flew in and out of its many portals, bringing it to life with what looked like many arms. They reminded Jake of images of Hindu gods and goddesses.

Pigeons. Spies! Definitely Renlock.

He dived sharply down then sharply up and arrived in a cave within the cliff.

Jake felt an ache in his stomach he knew to be Frost. He opened his whale mouth. A moment later Frost was standing before him on a narrow vein of rose quartz that ran through the granite like a path.

Finally, Jake closed his eyes and drew a long deep breath.

When he reopened them he was himself once more, standing on the tip of Deuteronomy's giant tongue, feeling a great sense of peace.

'Careful,' warned Frost in whisper. 'You've got human legs again. Give them a shake. And whatever you do, don't touch the granite. It'll set off alarm bells. You must stay on the quartz. It's the work of the dwarf-smiths.'

Jake walked an uncertain circle on the whale's tongue, reacquainting himself with his legs before daring to pass onto the start of the rose quartz path.

'Thank you, Deuteronomy,' he said turning to face the blue whale and bowing his head. 'That was amazing.'

Just call me in thought if you need me, he said inside Jake's head. *If you're in or near a sea, I'll come as soon as I can.*

With that, Deuteronomy sank beneath the surface and disappeared.

'So, Jonah,' said Frost, 'feeling resurrected?'

There weren't the words. Jake simply shook his head in wonder, wishing he was still swimming through the serene oceans.

Frost smiled at Jake's bliss. 'Time to become Jake again. We're beneath Renlock. Keep that sense of peace, but sharpen your wits. And only whisper and only if absolutely necessary. Got it?'

Jake nodded.

'Follow me,' said Frost, who proceeded to pick his way through the half-light of the cave.

The mysterious path gave off the faintest glow. It was just enough for Jake to appreciate that they were moving up through an ever-changing passageway, sometimes cavernous, sometimes no more than a fissure.

Bit by bit the path grew steeper.

After a while, a soft orange light glowed through a small hole ahead. It led to a vast dome-shaped cavern where a multitude of quartz veins streaked down from its centre, glowing like rivulets of fire.

Yet more spectacular, Jake and Frost had emerged from the hole half-way up the dome. The rose quartz path was brilliantly disguised in a spiralling recess just large enough for one person at a time to scale an otherwise impossible convex climb. From the ground, the recess would be impossible to make out through the chaos of orange glowing veins.

With a nod, Frost climbed the staircase, Jake following close behind.

After what seemed an age of dizzying progress, they reached a hidden hole just short of the highest point of the dome.

Once through it, the quartz stairwell became a tight spiral that led directly up into the shadows. His calves aching, Jake followed as Frost continued upwards. As he did so, Jake realised that the entire staircase had been carved from a single vein of quartz. He could touch wherever he wished without fear of setting off alarms. He was marvelling at how long it must have taken to chisel out when a dim glow of light lit up the quartz a little way ahead.

A moment later they were peering through the rock at the distorted image of a hall.

'It's all right, they can't see us,' whispered Frost. 'The quartz is specially treated so that we can see them and listen, but they can't see or hear us. It will appear like granite from their side. Still, it's best to whisper, just in case.'

'Do all pixies know this stuff?' asked Jake, astonished by how Frost knew so much.'

'Unlikely,' scoffed Frost. 'I only know it because I've always had a secret desire to pass myself off as a trixy without a trixy or guardian suspecting it. And what better testing ground than Renlock?'

Jake took a closer look through the strange rock-window. The hall was long and a clamour of pigeons flew in and out of a small opening at its far end. Each pigeon joined one of many queues, like lines leading to cashiers at an old-fashioned bank. Once at the front, they gave their report to another pigeon before flying back out the way they came.

'It's just one of many departments,' explained Frost, before leaving the window and proceeding upwards.

The stairwell within the vein of quartz continued to wind its way up past the many other departments that gathered intelligence from a different area of the cosmos. All were on the side facing out to sea. Suddenly, however, light spilled in from the other side.

Both gasped. They were level with the top of a great wall, beyond which was a vast chasm. The instant they focused on it, the scene shifted. It became a back alley, grim yet filled with a golden light, which seemed strangely paradoxical until Jake noticed that the light shone from a giant bottle of whisky on a rooftop. A tube ran from the bottle down into the alley. He gasped again. It led into the right arm of a giant tramp.

'The Hollow-gram of Brock,' whispered Frost, truly awestruck. 'I've only heard of it. But to see it! To see Brock—'

'Brock,' muttered Jake, recalling what Asclepius had said in the healing hall. 'You mean God Almighty?' A great thrill coursed through Jake. 'But where is he?'

'The tramp,' said Frost. 'He represents Brock's true state on the Surface.'

Jake thought Frost was joking. But as he paid closer attention to the tramp slumped against the wall, the image zooming in and out to suit Jake's focus, a great sadness swept through him. It made perfect sense. God, in other words the awareness of how sacred life was, had been forgotten on the Surface, except by a few. Many claimed to worship him. But much of what Jake saw on Earth was war—inside homes, outside homes, war between couples, war between countries, war between companies. If people really worshipped the sacredness of life there would be no war at all.

'The bottle of whisky,' said Jake, noting the cloud of pigeons about its top. 'It's almost full. Does that mean something?'

'When it's full, Brock will fall from being Overlord of the Surface and the rest of the Outer-Peregrinus,' said Frost.

Just then, a peculiar-looking group appeared on top of the great wall and moved in their direction.

At the front was a bald, portly man in a pinstriped suit talking about something with great enthusiasm. About him were three chilling-looking male characters in dark robes with silver-coloured skin and eyes that glinted like sapphires. By far the most chilling was the woman at their centre. Strikingly beautiful, she radiated a sense of immense power, but it was her eyes which left Jake cold—they were bright green, the same shade of light which had shone up through the water in the mysterious shaft earlier that night.

Luna! he cried out in thought.

Jake glanced at Frost and for the first time noted a flicker of fear in his friend's eyes as though the protection of the quartz didn't exist. Confirming his fear, Frost grabbed his arm. A tingling of energy flowed from Frost to Jake. Maintaining his grip, Frost put a finger to his mouth and gestured silence.

Who are you? The memory of her voice echoed through Jake's mind.

Her eyes reminded him of Braysheath the first time Jake had seen them, that were he to gaze into them for more than a moment they would somehow consume him. The difference was that Braysheath would never allow that, Jake simply knew it. Luna, however, would. Her pupils were like collapsed universes—concentrated, singular and utterly heartless.

As though she had heard his thoughts, Luna stopped. All that separated her from them was the quartz and a few feet of granite. Despite the draw of the hollow-gram, she turned to the wall.

Jake's heart thumped so hard that it reverberated throughout his entire body. Frost's grip tightened. The flow of energy grew stronger. Hoping it might help, Jake closed his eyes and did his best to breathe calmly.

'Is something the matter, my lady?' enquired the portly man.

Through the special properties of the rose quartz, Jake and Frost could hear their conversation.

Luna said nothing. With a curious glint in her eyes, she raised her head slightly and inhaled the air.

Bewildered, the portly man glanced about the atrium. The guardians, meanwhile, closed their eyes and angled their heads in concentration.

His curiosity getting the better of him, Jake opened his eyes and looked at Luna.

The very act seemed to draw her attention. She shifted her head so that she appeared to be gazing right at him. Her eyes brightened.

Jake clamped his eyes shut again. Frost's grip grew even tighter and a terrible nausea swept through Jake—whether from Frost or Luna, he couldn't tell. It grew so intense it prickled. The sensation felt like an army of ants scurrying through him, picking away at his atoms and carrying them off in separate directions until he no longer existed as himself.

An unusual panic rose up within him. He wanted to tear himself free of Frost and bolt back down the stairs, when another image came to his rescue—of himself as Deuteronomy. The ants suddenly became urchins which fell peacefully to the rocks of the seabed. His atoms glowed like plankton—a non-existence of a different kind offered by the ants, constructive and inclusive. He drew a deep breath. He pictured himself swimming peacefully through the ocean of his inner-depths where everything was him, connected and whole.

The lessening of Frost's grip drew his attention from the ocean back to the tension of the stairwell.

'This rock is strange,' he heard Luna say. To be on the safe side, Jake kept his eyes closed and remained focused on his breath.

'It has a high concentration of inner-force,' said a steely voice, which Jake took to be one of the silver-skinned beings.

'Impossible!' exclaimed the portly man. 'These rocks have been here ages!'

'And yet,' continued the steely voice, 'it's mixed with something else, something I can't quite place.'

'Are these rocks from a burial ground?' asked Luna.

'Certainly not, my lady!' refuted the portly man. 'Renlock was created from the headland itself and scoured thoroughly beforehand.'

'Well, I suggest you scour it again,' said Luna before finally moving on.

'Of course, my lady, of course…'

Jake opened his eyes in time to see the group descend a stairwell.

He looked at Frost and noted another emotion he hadn't seen in him before—relief.

'Luna,' whispered Jake.

Frost nodded. 'I've heard her power is to take people deep within themselves, door after door, far deeper than they're ready to go. She shows them the extremes of their past lives, the blood on their hands, and creates such trauma that they become lost. And that's when she takes their light.'

Frost's words not only made sense of the surprisingly deep fear Jake had just felt, but reminded him of the blood he had seen on his own hands during his nightmare in the woods.

'I can believe it,' he said with a heavy exhale.

'She almost had us then,' said Frost.

'That silver-skinned ones...'

'Guardians of the inner-force,' explained Frost.

'He detected inner-force in the rock. Are you sure you're not a trixy?'

'Oh ye of little faith. I was focused on that place where the forces are in union. Naturally the guardian sensed the force he was most familiar with, but he might have sensed any of the other four. But this is not the place to chat. Let's get moving,' said Frost and sprang up the stairs.

Jake took a final glance back at Brock. The god's weak appearance caused him of think of his granddad and how he might be in similar or even worse state. There wasn't a moment to lose. Following a deep breath, he leapt after Frost.

CHAPTER 39
THE TELL-US-SCOPE

LAWRENCE WAS BACK IN HIS OFFICE IN RENLOCK. HE HAD A WILD air about him. Only moments before he had returned from the cave, back through the wrathful trees who were marching for the gate in ever-greater number, back through the war room, all without raising suspicion.

He was standing at the window looking out over the ocean, hoping it would bring him calm.

'I feel this *terrible* anger!' he cursed and thumped the stone. 'Where the hell does it come from?'

Geoffrey was on the wall. 'You know where it comes from. Hell. Your hell. Because you've left your dream body in your unconscious,' he said, referring to the snake hiding under the log, 'you have a direct line to fury.'

'But this can't be me!' insisted Lawrence.

Geoffrey sighed and shook his head. 'Have a cup of tea and calm yourself down.'

With heavy exhale, Lawrence sat down at the table. He winced with pain. As Geoffrey had warned him, because Lawrence was plumbing depths he wasn't prepared for, the wounds he sustained in his dream body remained with him in the reality of his conscious world. With a shaky hand he poured out a saucer of tea for Geoffrey and a cup for himself.

'I suggest you have some sugar,' said Geoffrey, who joined him at the table.

Lawrence stirred two heaped teaspoons into his cup. Following several sips the tension in his brow softened a little.

'I told you this wouldn't be easy,' said Geoffrey. 'And it's going to get a lot harder.'

Lawrence continued to sip his tea.

'You might be a man of integrity on the Surface,' explained Geoffrey. 'But you have a past—one which reaches back millions of years. You're trying to redress it in a matter of days.'

'But is it not true that all karmic debts and patterns of past lives are imprinted in this life?' asked Lawrence. 'If we make peace in this one then we also make peace with the ancient past, both through lightlines as well as our bloodlines.'

'If that is your destiny in this life and you fulfil it, yes, but often it's not,' said Geoffrey.

'Either way, I haven't made a very good start,' said Lawrence and appraised Geoffrey of his journey with the pirate and the slaughter in the desert cave.

'Don't judge yourself so harshly,' said Geoffrey once Lawrence had finished. 'Despite your performance, you're going deeper. Whether you take the Path of the Puritan or the Path of the Banker, you've changed stairwells for a steeper, more perilous one. The rewards are greater, but the steps more tricky. And doubly tricky because the tiger is feeding you its power in order to take you as deep as possible, so that when he finally makes his move they'll be no coming back for you. What you're now suffering from is cold turkey.'

'I feel like a turkey,' said Lawrence.

'You look like one, too,' said Geoffrey and summoned in Lawrence a much-needed chuckle. 'You should have a shave, by the way. Never under-estimate the value of such seemingly small things—a cup of tea, a shave and so on. They keep you grounded.'

'You're right, old friend,' said Lawrence who, having found his appetite, helped himself to a sandwich from a plate.

They fell into silence. The simple pleasures of cheese and pickle on fresh bread brought Lawrence back to the present.

'By the way,' he said, 'before Luna transferred the sylph to Nestor he saw through my disguise as Lord Boreas and knew that I was his son. He looked down at her shadow and said that we live in ironic times. I felt he was trying to communicate something to me. With all that's happened since I haven't had a chance to think about it. What do you suppose he meant?'

WHILE GEOFFREY AND LAWRENCE WERE TALKING, FROST AND JAKE made their way up the final part of the quartz staircase. They stopped one floor from the top at an office that caught Frost's attention. It was large though had little in it. There was a grand desk at one end and a surprisingly small window, along with a few mysterious objects both on the desk and scattered about the floor and walls.

'This must belong to the fat one called Wilderspin,' said Frost. 'Even though he has rented the place out to Luna and Lord Boreas, he's the real boss at Renlock.'

'What about the office above?' asked Jake, glancing up at the final light spilling into the stairwell.

'Lord Boreas's, though you can be sure that little happens without Wilderspin knowing about it. Come on, let's investigate.'

'What? I thought we couldn't leave the safety of the quartz.'

'The risk of alarm is mainly on the outskirts of Renlock where there are fewer guards. As long as we're not seen or heard we'll be fine. If you want to find your granddad, Wilderspin's office is the best place to start.'

'What about all the pigeons?' asked Jake, keen to investigate but struggling to believe they wouldn't be detected.

'In the atrium, yes, but not in the office. Besides, look, there's an exit here,' said Frost, indicating another vein of quartz.

To Frost's delight, he had only to place his hands against the wall and a door of thin rock appeared and opened without sound.

'These dwarf-smiths are amazing,' he whispered.

They passed onto a quiet landing just around the corner from the entrance to Wilderspin's office, whereupon the secret door closed silently without leaving the slightest sign of its existence.

Frost stood marvelling at where the door had been.

'Let's get a move on,' said Jake.

They crept to the corner and peered around it. To get to the office meant being exposed to the main staircase and thus the atrium for two or three paces.

'What do you think?' whispered Jake.

Frost's reply was a finger to his lips. Once more he grabbed Jake's wrist. Again Jake felt a subtle flow of energy pass from Frost to himself.

Frost's grip tightened to signal the go-ahead. Not daring to hesitate, they stole across the landing. They were almost at the office when a pigeon flew out of the office doorway. Frost wrenched Jake into a recess in the wall. Sensing movement, the pigeon hovered in the hallway, scouring the passageways. Frost's grip tightened. Jake grew nauseous with the prickling flow of energy. The pigeon moved closer. Jake steadied his breath and once again thought of whales.

The pigeon was studying the shadows of the recess when a strong gust blew it away. Much to Jake's relief it didn't return. With another sharp tug from Frost they leapt into the office.

'Phew! That was close!' whispered Frost and immediately set about appraising the office. 'Don't close the door. It'll look suspicious. And don't touch anything you're not sure of. Remember—this is a spy master's office.'

Jake had barely begun to study a strange map on the wall when Frost hissed at him.

'Here, look at this!' he said.

Frost was looking through a brass telescope, except rather than pointing it out at the sky, he was aiming it within Renlock.

'Incredible!' he said, popping an earplug into his left ear. 'It allows you to see into every room and hear what's being said. Here, stick this into your ear.'

Jake took the second earplug. The scope had two eye sockets like binoculars that allowed them to look at the same time.

Frost scoured Renlock with his sixth sense for secret things. He moved too quickly for Jake to see anything until, with a delighted gasp, Frost finally stopped. The scope was pointing at the office above.

Jake moved his eye closer to the scope.

'Lord Boreas!' he gasped, recognising the striking figure from the break-in.

'And he's talking to a lizard!' said Frost. 'They're one of the sacred keepers of wisdom. And why, might I ask, is a macho god like Lord Boreas delving into the ancient mysteries? One would've thought he'd be too arrogant to think they'd be of any use to him. Humph. Interesting!'

'Do you think Wilderspin spies on Lord Boreas?'

'Definitely, but he'll not hear anything of use while the lizard is about—it would sense him and warn Lord Boreas. Lizards are brilliant!'

'Then how come we can listen in?'

'Because we're not Wilderspin and the cosmos is a mysterious place,' said Frost.

'Shh!' said Jake. 'They mentioned Granddad's name. Something about transferring a sylph into him, whatever that means.'

'A sylph!' exclaimed Frost.

'Shh!'

Struggling to contain his excitement, Frost kept quiet and listened in to the conversation.

'With all that's happened since,' said Lord Boreas, 'I haven't had a chance to think about it. What do you suppose he meant?'

The lizard took a thoughtful sip from its saucer.

'The obvious suggestion Nestor was making is that it's ironic that Luna is using the sylph as part of her plan to capture light from the Outer-Peregrinus.'

Lord Boreas's eyes brightened with inspiration. 'She referred to humans of the Surface as *the walking dead*. The majority of the Surface population has come from the sacrificed shepherds. Tell me, Geoffrey—what do you perceive in the sylph?'

'It's extremely powerful, its essence is ancient and yet its form is no more than a few thousand years old.'

'And if you had to guess at its origin, what would you say?' pressed Lord Boreas, the excitement rising in his voice.

'A ghost, I suppose.'

'Exactly! But powerful beings aren't easily shocked. So what type of shock could create bitterness so powerful that it's capable of destroying energy?'

Geoffrey smiled wryly as the penny dropped. 'An original sin. A sin against the origin of things. The sylph is the combined consciousness of the sacrificed shepherds, of their ghosts.'

Frost was quaking with excitement. Again Jake silenced him, trying to digest what the horror they had described meant for his granddad.

'It's why in the vault of Pandora's Box there were five voices in that strange wind!' continued Lord Boreas. 'It explains why the angel, the *arch*angel, had charred wings. He symbolises all five of them.'

'I'm impressed,' said Geoffrey. 'You see, there are benefits to waking up your unconscious.'

'Unconscious...' muttered Lord Boreas. 'That's just it. My God, the irony! The natural order of things is for a human soul to be born on Earth into forgetfulness of its true origin then spend the rest of its life remembering. But for the human souls that came from the sacrificed shepherds, the majority of souls, it's much harder. The sylph is too bitter to release their consciousness. Nothing short of epic heroics on a grand scale would cause it to do so. It enjoys its bitterness too much!'

Lawrence shook his head in amazement.

'Humans meanwhile have no idea of this,' he continued. 'They strive to convince themselves that they're content with life, but they never can be. Not until they slow down and connect with each other, realise their origin then do something about it. To unite across all boundaries and effectively reform the shepherds.'

'If I was a betting lizard, I'd bet against it.'

'I certainly wouldn't bet in favour, as much as I'd like to. As humans repeatedly fail to unite, the sylph destroys their energy one by one. Destroys itself! And knowingly! Why, it's tantamount to suicide and yet the sylph is beyond the Scribes and so such sacrilege goes unchecked. It simply sits there observing, solitary in the aisles while the audience is on stage, a new galaxy formed as each one disappears, the cosmos expanding at an accelerating rate towards a critical point where it can no longer regather itself. Potential moves beyond reach. *Dark energy* science labels it without the slightest idea of what it really is. My God, Geoffrey, it's all so damned twisted!'

'Sounds a bit like Brock,' said Jake as he thought of the god slumped in the alley with whisky flowing into his arm.

'Very different,' said Frost. 'The bum in the alley is symbolic of Brock's wretched state as his number of followers drops and humans become more separate than they already are. Regardless, Brock is still on the Surface doing his best, watching over humans, trying to inspire them to wake up and unite.'

Lord Boreas stood up from the table and paced the office.

Jake observed Lord Boreas with great interest. It was the very god who had murdered his dad. His blood ought to be boiling. He ought to be tearing upstairs to seek revenge regardless of the odds. But he wasn't. Jake couldn't explain it, but there was something about Lord Boreas that he actually found endearing.

Perhaps it's part of his power, he reasoned. *After all, he's a god from the Inner-Peregrinus and Lord of the Sirens.*

'Surely Luna realises,' said Lord Boreas.

'Don't count on it,' said Geoffrey.

'But she said herself that a sylph contained more than one soul. How could she fail to see it?'

'Pride, arrogance. They're powerful masks. To her the sylph is simply a mysterious being of power. She cares not for how it came about. She assumes herself to be more powerful. The irony Nestor alluded to was deeper than the simple irony of her plan backfiring.'

Pride, thought Jake. *That's her weakness. Arrogance and pride.*

Lord Boreas stopped at the window and pensively rubbed his stubbly chin. 'She can't be more powerful than the sylph.'

'Can't she?' challenged Geoffrey.

'The shepherds have lived since the origin. Together they represent half the cosmos's energy.'

'That still leaves the other half,' remarked Geoffrey.

'What are you suggesting?'

Again the scope quaked with Frost's excitement.

'I'm not suggesting anything,' said Geoffrey. 'I'm simply pointing out the facts.'

Lord Boreas stared at Geoffrey, his eyes glazing as though entertaining an idea too vast to grasp.

With a shake of his head, he looked back out to sea. 'Whoever she is, perhaps she's playing a game of bluff. Regardless of the motives of the sylph, she intends to upstage it. If she finds this door she thinks exists, she'll be off in her ark, having cheated it yet again.'

'What door?' pondered Jake out loud.

'No idea,' said Frost, 'but it must be a cracker!'

Geoffrey said nothing and took another slurp of tea.

'And yet,' continued Lord Boreas, 'what are the motives of the sylph in playing along with her plans? Surely revenge. A revenge that could be even more destructive than Luna's.'

'Or simply morbid curiosity. Just another part of the play,' offered Geoffrey.

'Perhaps both,' pondered Lord Boreas. 'She's offered it a different seat from which to watch. And what a seat! A holygate and with Nestor for company!'

'What? Granddad in a holygate?' exclaimed Jake, as if a sylph for company wasn't enough. 'I thought that was impossible!'

'Stay calm,' said Frost. 'It sounds like he's alright.'

Jake looked back at Lord Boreas whose eyes widened, suddenly struck by an idea.

'What if *I* could get into the holygate?'

'The way things are headed, you'll end up there anyway,' said Geoffrey.

'The odds are as absurd as the variables are mindboggling,' said Lord Boreas, his excitement feverish, 'and yet, with so much power in play, the potential for even the remotest thing is possible if the will behind it is strong enough.'

Lord Boreas resumed his pacing about the office.

'The sylph has been starved of hope for so long that it's surely forgotten what it feels like,' he continued. 'Just imagine if it can be won over and its power can be redirected.'

'As you've already said, to penetrate such bitterness would require heroics of mythic proportions,' said Geoffrey in a doubtful tone.

'Of course! A burst of hope as intense as the sun! One which untwists the twisted myth. A sacrifice. But unlike those of the shepherds this one will be pure. The young Lord Tusk! We must find a way to get both of us into the gate!'

Frost and Jake looked up from the scope and stared at each other in disbelief. Any sense of endearment Jake had felt for Lord Boreas vanished and was replaced by dread.

'And what of the pirate and tiger?' asked Geoffrey in a dry tone.

'Pirate and tiger?' muttered Frost, returning his attention to the scope.

'As vital as my fractured soul,' said Lord Boreas. 'They make the act all the less likely and so all the more heroic.'

Geoffrey looked unconvinced.

'Timing will be critical,' continued Lord Boreas. 'But with Asclepius's help, it might just work. As Luna attempts to pull a fast one on the sylph, we'll do the same to her!'

'Asclepius! See?' exclaimed Frost. 'We got it right.'

Despite the revelation of Asclepius's treachery, there was so much new information that Jake was struggling to keep up—a mysterious door which Luna sought, a pirate, along with a tiger.

Inspired by his plan, Lord Boreas looked like a man renewed. Until he suffered a sudden chill as though struck by a bout of malaria. He grabbed the sill of the window and clutched the bridge of his nose. 'Damn it!' he cursed.

'What's wrong with him?' asked Jake

'Must be the effect of going through a god gate a second time,' said Frost. 'He said his soul was fractured.'

'Sit down,' suggested Geoffrey. 'You're over-stretching yourself.'

As Lord Boreas remained where he was, battling to remain present, battling to contain a rage, Jake was suddenly wrenched away from the scope and hauled by Frost beneath the desk. Someone was coming up the steps.

It was Wilderspin.

He swept into the office, whistling as he approached his desk, fortunately the opposite side to Jake and Frost, apparently checking something.

'That's funny,' said Wilderspin, 'I don't recall leaving my scope like that.'

Jake's heartbeat raced as he and Frost shrank into the scarce shadow beneath the desk.

Wilderspin walked up to the scope. Jake could see his legs. His feet, however, were not pointing in the direction of the scope but towards them as he surveyed the rest of his office.

There was a dreadful moment of silence.

Finally his feet turned the other way.

'Ah, excellent,' he said, peering through the scope. 'The bastard's back.'

With that, Wilderspin left the office whistling.

As Jake breathed a deep sigh of relief, Frost sprang back up to the scope, gesturing for Jake to do the same.

By the time he looked back through it, Wilderspin had arrived up the stairs into the top office.

'Ah, dear Lord Boreas, you're back!' he hailed.

Lord Boreas, who was still battling with his rage, swung around to face him, his eyes blazing. 'What do you want?' he barked.

Wilderspin was so taken aback he almost lost his balance and fell down the stairs.

Jake was also shocked by the sudden change in the god's mood. With a rush of excitement he recalled the two books in his dad's library which had twice caught his attention—The Tibetan Book of the Dead and one on Janus.

Is that what the cosmos was trying to show me? he wondered. *That Boreas has two faces like Janus because he went through the god gate twice and that Dad is dead. Truly dead?* It made sense. Awful sense.

'My dear Lord Boreas, there's no need to be like that!' said Wilderspin recovering himself. 'I realise you've probably had quite an adventure through the gate, but we're all friends here.'

'What do you want?' repeated Lord Boreas icily.

'I've come to inform you that today is a *great* day! Luna commissioned me to create something rather marvellous and, as a mark of honour to yourself and your own knack of leaping into gates, Luna has *suggested* that you test it out.'

'What are you talking about?' growled Lord Boreas. 'What has she asked you to create?'

'As you know, she searches for a secret.'

An exit from the cosmos, thought Lawrence.

'However,' continued Wilderspin, 'since scouring Surface dreams and the memories of lost souls has yielded nothing, she plans to look deeply into the House of Tusk—to see if *it* has anything that might help.'

'The House of Tusk?' snapped Lord Boreas. 'What nonsense is this?'

Wilderspin smiled with great satisfaction. He was enjoying the moment.

'See?' said Frost. 'See how protective he is of the fort. With the help of Asclepius, he has his own plans for it!'

Jake said nothing. His mind and heartbeat were racing.

'It's far from nonsense, my esteemed tenant,' continued Wilderspin. 'It's brilliant! What I've created establishes a connection with the sylph. Using it we're going to mine Nestor's mind and all that he knows of that cursed House of Tusk. With the sylph's power behind it, just imagine! We'll see into its deepest secrets!'

This time it was Lord Boreas's turn to be taken aback. He glanced at the table, but Geoffrey had already taken to the walls.

Jake's heart sank as dreadful images filled his mind of his granddad being tortured.

'So, when you're ready, Lord Boreas, we'll see you downstairs. Goddess Luna is waiting. It's the same hall where you last saw Nestor,' said Wilderspin with a mischievous smile and disappeared down the stairs.

'Well, it looks like you get to test your theory sooner than you thought,' said Geoffrey from the wall, referring to the sylph and whether it could be won over.

Lord Boreas looked pale.

'I've no idea what he's created,' said Geoffrey, 'but if it connects with the sylph then it promises to be far livelier than even the dream room. While you were in the vault taking Pandora's box, the sylph saw right through you—your plans, both conscious *and* unconscious. What it chooses to show Luna and Wilderspin will depend on its humour.'

'It's a gift,' said Lord Boreas, though his voice lacked conviction.

'Yes, for the tiger. With the sylph's power behind it, doors will be unearthed from the darkest depths of your unconscious—ones you don't have the strength to open, not even with the tiger's power. The sylph's power, however, is quite another matter. If your curiosity gets the better of you, the sylph might just oblige and open them for you. And if that happens, you'll be sucked off somewhere far beyond the tiger's wildest dreams. He'll leap into Renlock in an instant.'

CHAPTER 40
EMOTIONAL WHIRL

DESPITE THE TRAUMA OF THE FLOODED SHAFT, RANI FELT THE NEED to be back in water but on her own terms. Going up to the lake was too risky. What drew her more was to go even deeper into the womb-like depths of the fort.

Following their instincts, she and Bin finally found an underground lake. Bathed in the silver light of the chasm's own moon, the lake was an enchanting sight, fringed with moss-covered oaks, beech and ash trees. A delightful breeze glanced off its surface. At its far end was a cascade.

Without a word, Rani cast aside her bow and arrows and dived in. Its touch was bliss. She swam underwater all the way to the lake's centre where she floated on her back.

Beloved Mother Nature, help me find peace. Help me see through all deception, she implored and finally opened herself up to all that had taken place in the shaft.

Rani scarcely knew where to start, or what to believe in all she had seen in the spherical room, mistrusting both the darkness in Jake and especially in Frost.

Except it wasn't that simple. The clarity of her earlier mistrusts had become hugely muddied by an unexpected deluge of emotion. First was her pride. It infuriated Rani that Frost had saved her from a trap that had been meant for him—saved her only in order to deceive the Tusk boy into believing that the trixy was something good.

He cut a powerful net I didn't think could be cut. Even if he were from the corrupt tribe of trixies, which I'm certain he is, that still couldn't account for how he managed it.

She closed her eyes and tried to release her tension into the gentle rhythm of the water.

How did he do it? I don't believe it was the knife, which is what he'll doubtless tell the Tusk boy. It's something to do with him. Tell me, Great Mother... please.

Before it had become a knife it had been a key of gold that now shone in Rani's mind just as it had in Frost's hand.

Why was it first a key? Did it simply mean that he had the key to the Tusk boy's release from the net? Or did it mean something bigger? The release of Tusk's darkness? Yes, that must be it!

But that wasn't it and Rani knew it. The conflict between what she felt and what she believed was too great. Once again, she saw Frost as she had seen him holding the key. She struggled to admit it, but he had looked beautiful—a shining prince amid the eels. His eyes had been strong but gentle, not full of devilry as they usually were.

Why had he appeared like that? It happened when he touched the net, when all three of us were connected. What does it mean?

For a moment, Rani dared to put aside her suspicion that dark arts had been at play and opened her mind to other explanations.

Could it mean that he somehow holds the key to something the three of us must do together, unlocking our potential perhaps, that there's much more to Frost than meets the eye?

She imagined him like a gemstone of unknown origin—multifaceted, flawed and yet still beautiful, perhaps all the more so because of his flaws. It was a huge idea. In the moment she surrendered to it, a great heat swept through her. She gasped. It spread up from the pit of her stomach. Unlike the serpent she associated with Jake, this time it felt as though she were a forest set ablaze, the oxygen sucked from the air, the fire inescapable, scorching, seducing her lushness with the promise of renewal though ultimately leaving her hollow.

Rani's body tensed. She sank beneath the surface, panicked, righted herself, spun away from the image of Frost only to find herself in the arms of Jake—lion-hearted and kingly.

Just as it had in the spherical room, the serpent stirred and slithered ecstatically up her spine, adding to the heat of her confusion. Jake's fire, however, was a slower, deeper-feeling burn than that of Frost. All the while, a great cloud of shadow loomed up behind Jake, threatening to overwhelm the promise of great good with great evil, made all the more probable by the presence of Frost. Worst of all, it made Jake fascinating.

No! It's trickery! she cried in thought as her mind fought back her feelings. *There is more to Frost than meets the eye—more to his power to deceive!*

The images shifted. Jake was consumed by his shadow. Frost lost his princely glow and became a sparkly-eyed devil once more. Suddenly the lake became a threatening place. She sensed dangerous beasts stirring within its depths, reminding her of the darkness which Frost had revealed within herself and wondered what he and Jake had seen of her through the net of light.

It's a lie! she cried and swam quickly for the shore. *My love for nature is pure! How can there be this darkness in me?*

As she swam, her mind was awash with imagery: the peaceful warrior bathing in the lake, warming her cold heart as she watched on captivated, the powerful dark eyes of the mysterious bull elephant, the chilling green light which had shot through the cold waters of the shaft and now seemed to light up the water beneath her as she swam more frantically. All the while Frost's lies echoed about her—*I didn't steal your energy. I took you closer to its source. What you're feeling now is attraction. If only you knew how much I've helped you...*

Rani leapt from the lake ready to kill him, if only he were there.

'What's the matter, Rani love?' said Bin.

Chest heaving, Rani stared back at the lake, expecting to see a giant serpent burst through its surface.

Gradually the ripples caused by her distraught swim settled back into stillness.

'We need a new plan, Bin,' she said as her calm returned.

'What do you suggest?'

'I don't know,' admitted Rani. 'Our mission is to protect the Tusk boy even though that cursed trixy is making it seem the other way round.'

'What happened with the trap didn't help,' said Bin.

Rani's blood began to boil again as she reflected on how wrong it had gone. She wondered how the Tusk boy had managed to dream his way into the trap, if that's what really happened.

'Do you still feel that the greatest risk to Jake Tusk is himself?' asked Bin.

'I do,' said Rani. 'A risk made all the more real by his being so ignorant and having a trixy as a friend.'

'And yet, things are no longer quite so clear,' suggested Bin.

Rani stared at Bin with a vacant expression. 'No.'

She picked up her bow and arrows. 'Part of me wants to find a way to destroy this fort and be done with it. It feels cursed,' she said. 'But even if that were possible, there's something about this place. It's as though it were the heart of something much greater —the rooms which are hidden, the ones that appear, the potential hidden behind deception and intrigue. Everything seems so finely balanced.'

'I feel the same about it,' said Bin. 'When things are so finely balanced and the sides unclear, then it's wise to withhold our judgements and to simply observe until things become clearer.'

Rani nodded gravely. 'In the meantime we need to discover Frost's weakness.'

'Trixies aren't like other species,' said Bin. 'Because they're part force, you'd think the opposite force, outer-force, would weaken them. But I'm not sure it's as simple as that.'

'He must have a weakness,' insisted Rani. 'Everything has. It's just a matter of finding out.'

'There's always an exception,' said Bin.

Bin had barely completed her sentence when a chill ran through Rani. She sensed a powerful presence. Both she and Bin glanced back into the shadows of the trees.

Rani was about to leap up onto Bin when a terrific roar shook the air. She collapsed to one knee and almost fainted. A cloud of dust exploded over them as the nearest trees disintegrated before reforming elsewhere.

Recovering her wits, Rani jumped onto Bin who launched into flight and swept from the chasm.

'Thorsror!' hissed Bin as she raced with great agility along the dimly-lit passageways. 'We've little chance of losing it.'

Another roar shook the air followed by the eerie rustle and creak of destruction and re-creation.

'Hurry, Bin!' cried Rani. 'It mustn't catch us!'

Bin flew down some stairs and veered off to the right which fortunately opened up into a great cavern. A fast-flowing river ran through it over a cliff into darkness.

'Over the waterfall and down!' barked Rani. 'It'll buy us some time!'

As Bin swept over the river and prepared to dive, Rani glanced back just in time to see the thorsror bound into the cavern. She had never seen eyes so frightful—the certainty of death seen in a serpent's, reinforced by the fury of a tiger. They fixed on her, seemed to question her very existence and blazed with such power that Rani almost fainted a second time.

Bin tucked in her wings and dived down the face of the fall. The rush of cool spray helped restore Rani.

They were soon back in the confines of passageways, halls and stairwells. It slowed them terribly.

'What about a thorsror's weakness?' she shouted over the clamour caused by another roar.

'They're the exception I spoke of!' cried Bin. 'Supreme in perception, they can leap through walls. Your arrows won't touch it. It's to do with harmonics and has a similar effect to that glove of yours.'

Another barrel-chested growl reverberated through the air. It was only a hall or two away. The thorsror was closing in fast.

'I wish I could use the glove now!' cursed Rani, 'but I can't touch the walls while I'm on your back.'

No sooner had Rani completed her wish when the familiar vibration coursed through the glove. A moment later, a portal appeared in the wall ahead.

'Bin!' she cried.

Bin flew through it, whereupon the portal immediately closed up.

Rani's spirits leapt as another portal appeared in the wall in front of them. And so it continued.

Despite the mysterious assistance of the glove, the thorsror was more than equal to their frantic flight. Rani glanced back. As the last portal resealed she glimpsed the thorsror leap clean through the preceding wall as though it didn't exist.

She was worried the glove's power might suddenly run out when again it came to their rescue. Instead of creating portals which Rani willed open, the glove took control. Rather than swooping down stairs and through halls, a hole appeared in the floor and they were hauled sharply downwards.

'What's happening?' gasped Bin, wings pinned back as floor after floor opened up before them in perfect synchrony.

'I don't know but don't resist it!' shouted Rani.

As Bin surrendered to the glove's guidance, Rani looked back. The floors had resealed. She couldn't see the thorsror, though sensed it wasn't far behind.

Over the rush of air, Rani could hear deep booms. 'We must be close to the fort's furnaces of the dwarf-smiths!'

She felt a flicker of excitement. Few in the inner-worlds were privileged enough to have dwarf-smiths work with them. She had never seen one, only heard of the amazing things they were capable of.

Several floors later they burst into the vast chasm-like hall of the dwarf-smiths, the ceiling so high that it was like arriving into the sky of a new world. The sight was so marvellous that for a moment Rani completely forgot the thorsror. In each side of the hall were doors to vaults, large enough for giants. Light beamed from each. They were the storerooms of light of every kind. Rani gasped at the sight of them. Covering the floor between were many pools, each a different colour—bright red, turquoise, yellow, green, black, white, to name a few. At the centre of the hall stood a large anvil. Standing about it were several normal sized men and women in leather aprons full of tools.

Bright-eyed, they glanced up at Rani as Bin hovered in the air for a moment.

'Where are the dwarfs?' asked Rani.

'That's them,' said Bin. 'They're not called dwarfs because they're small, but because their art is to condense great power into small things.'

Just then something large and orange bound into the hall.

'The thorsror!' cried Rani.

Furious-looking, the thorsror locked eyes with Rani and released its lethal roar.

Had it not been for the protection of the glove, Rani and Bin would have been stunned, fallen from the air and been caught in the thorsror's mighty jaws. Instead, the air crackled with the clash of power.

'There, Bin!' cried Rani. 'The red pool—it's whirling. Fly into it!'

'But these pools could be fatal,' said Bin.

'We must trust the glove! Dive for it, now!' commanded Rani.

Bin did so.

Rani held her breath as the thorsror bound towards the same pool. Fortunately it was in the farthest corner of the hall. It was going to be close.

As Bin shot for the whirlpool, the thorsror leapt over the final pool. A flash of orange. A flash of red. Rani braced herself for the impact of the beast's claws.

They just made it. Bin swept into the whirlpool and was guided perfectly through its swirling spout by the glove.

'It hasn't followed!' cheered Rani.

They spiralled down through the spout for what felt ages though was only seconds.

Suddenly the spout turned upwards. The next moment they popped into a small cave where Rani slid from Bin panting.

'Phew! That was close!' she cried, exhilarated by the adventure. It was just what she needed to rid herself of so much thought—thoughts which returned in an entirely new light.

'That Tusk boy set it on us! How dare he! A thorsror!'

'Can you blame him?' said Bin, catching her breath. 'We're in the fort unannounced and you caught him in a net of light which almost cost him his life, not to mention ours.'

'That's beside the point! That hardly justifies sending something like a thorsror! Were he a man he would use his initiative and come and find us himself.'

'Perhaps he's busy with other things.'

'Next time I'll leave him to drown,' said Rani.

Following several fantasies of different ways to torture Jake, finally Rani took a closer look at the cave. The waterspout had closed up, leaving a pool of red. There were no doorways leading out of the cave, only another pool, one which was pitch black.

'What do you think?'

'We can't go back the way we came. The glove must have brought us here for a reason.'

Rani dipped a finger into the black pool. It stank of swamp. 'Not a very appealing option,' she said.

'But the only real one. We can't stay here.'

Rani placed her gloved hand close to the surface of the pool. It tingled. She thought of Braysheath, how Jake had arrived in the net of light, of Frost with the golden key. For a moment she felt like a puppet in a play.

No, it's not like that, she corrected. *I'm being guided, but it's I and Bin who decide whether to follow the signs or not.*

'I don't know where it leads, Bin, but I trust it'll take us where we need to go,' she said.

Bin shrank down in size and hopped onto Rani's outstretched arm.

Black water, she thought with a chill, realising how deep down in the fort they had to be. By jumping into the dark pool she would be plunging deeper into her own darkness.

It's the only way, she thought bravely.

She drew a deep breath, covered her nose and mouth and jumped into the pool.

CHAPTER 41
WILDERSPIN'S WIZARDRY

WHILE LAWRENCE, DISGUISED AS LORD BOREAS, MADE HIS WAY down the stairwell, Frost was still busy with the scope, nosing around other parts of Renlock.

Jake's heart was still racing from their near encounter with Wilderspin and the news that some dreadful experiment was about to take place involving his granddad, not to mention Lord Boreas's plan to sacrifice Jake in the stolen holygate.

'What do you think the lizard meant when it said this sylph-thing will see through Lord Boreas's plans?' he asked.

'His plan to use the House of Tusk to betray Luna of course,' said Frost, continuing to twist the truth. 'With the help of the devious Asclepius.'

Jake recalled how suddenly Lord Boreas had lost his temper. *It's possible*, he thought. 'That's his conscious plan. But the lizard also mentioned his *un*conscious plans.'.

'Things even darker. In other words, the logical extension of his conscious plans, such as the domination of all worlds and mass suffering,' explained Frost.

'The lizard also spoke of the sylph's power to open a door, that if it did, Lord Boreas would be sucked off somewhere and a tiger would leap back into Renlock. What do you make of that?'

Frost turned from the scope and looked at Jake, his eyes alive with great excitement.

'It sounds like Lord Boreas is being stalked in another dimension by something powerful in the form of tiger! Perhaps some old enemy who knows what Boreas is up to. What intrigue! While Luna seeks to topple Brock with the help of Boreas, Boreas seeks to topple her with the help of Asclepius and a demon, while this tiger seeks to topple Boreas!'

Jake looked nervously in the direction of the door, grateful the scope was in a far corner of the office. 'You really think we'll be able to watch this experiment through the scope? It might make things a lot clearer.'

'We'll soon find out. Look, Boreas is outside the hall now,' said Frost. 'Hang on! He's ducked into the shadows.'

Jake leapt up to the scope, stuck the earplug back in and peered through.

The lizard had hissed at Lord Boreas from the wall, having followed him down.

'A further thought,' it said, 'because once you're inside that thing of Wilderspin's, we won't be able to communicate. Whatever happens, Luna must *not* step into the contraption while you're inside of it. If we're right about Rowena having hidden the greater part of her light in an object of power, then this will expose her and possibly destroy her if Luna decides to hunt it down.'

Lord Boreas nodded gravely.

'Rowena?' said Jake. 'Isn't that the Goddess of Pride whose body Luna has possessed?'

'Yes!' said Frost excitedly. 'It sounds like she and Boreas are lovers. This just gets better and better!'

Lord Boreas reached inside of his robes and withdrew a tiny bottle. 'Maybe it's time for this.'

'What is it?' asked Geoffrey.

'All that remains of Medusa's blood. This sample came from the part of her which is said to gift immortality. It won't in my case because of the fracture to my soul. But it might plug it for a while and give me the strength to endure whatever awaits me. There are only two drops. It was all Asclepius had left.'

'Asclepius again!' said Frost and gave Jake a nudge in the ribs.

Jake said nothing. He watched on as Lord Boreas uncorked the flask.

'One drop now, one for later,' he said.

One for the holygate, thought Jake, dwelling for a moment on his own impending doom.

Lord Boreas carefully let one drop fall on a fingertip before licking it off.

Geoffrey watched on. 'Any effect?' he asked after a moment.

'Not that I can tell,' said Lord Boreas. 'How does my hair look? Any snakes?'

'I can't work this Boreas out,' said Jake. 'One moment he seems on edge, the next he makes jokes. I suppose it's to do with this fracture he mentioned.'

'Probably,' said Frost. 'He's very interesting!'

Jake remembered something else the lizard had said. 'What do you suppose the lizard meant when it spoke about the benefits to waking Boreas's unconscious?'

'The greater part of a human's power is hidden in the unconscious. I expect he's trying to unlock as much as possible ahead of doing the dirty on Luna, especially if he's looking to take control of the fort as well as the sylph. Just imagine how powerful he'll be if he succeeds!'

'I would've thought a god already had access to their total power,' said Jake.

'Weren't you listening when I told you about the god gate? It's a short cut to power, for those who don't have the patience or courage to face their shadow.'

'If his soul is fractured, what's the point of searching for power? Surely his days are numbered.'

'I imagine the sylph could help him out with that. It's what he was hinting at when he said the sylph might be tempted in another way.'

'What do you mean?' asked Jake.

'The way they spoke of your granddad, it sounds like this sylph needs a body in order to move beyond where it's from, just like Luna does.'

'He also mentioned a pirate.'

'That bit sounded so out of place with this reality that it must be a symbol—part of this business to do with his unconscious,' explained Frost.'

'Maybe the pirate is searching for more demons to help Boreas and Asclepius, in addition to the one symbolised by the wolf in the tree,' said Jake.

'Yes! Maybe!'

'Do you think it could be searching for one of Boreas's demons?' asked Jake, his own ghosts in his forethoughts.

Frost's eyes shot wide open. 'Brilliant, Jake! Of course it is! What better way to find power than to integrate one's darkest demon? A god looking to master its shadow—how unusual! Perhaps the pirate is the demon itself!'

Frost was about to say more but his attention was hauled back to the scope. 'He's about to enter the hall.'

A door had appeared in the rock in front of Lord Boreas where a guardian permitted him entrance. As he stepped through and the door closed, Jake crossed his fingers that the scope would allow them to see through to the other side.

The view through the scope went blank.

'Bugger,' cursed Jake.

'Wait a moment,' said Frost as he experimented with the focus. 'Got it!'

'Well done!' said Jake as an image filled the scope.

They had a perfect view of a large hall. It contained the same group they had seen on the great wall.

Jake realised that the perspective of the scope appeared to be driven by the user's curiosity. Like the hologram of Brock, he and Frost could focus on different things at the same time. When Jake thought of Lord Boreas, his face filled the scope.

'My God, what's happened to him?' said Jake. 'Look how fierce his eyes are.'

'Medusa's blood must have kicked in,' said Frost.

Frost wasn't the only one who seemed delighted by Lord Boreas's appearance.

'How wild you look, Lord Boreas! It just goes to show how the company of trees does a man good,' said Luna, referring to his adventure through the gate to Leaf.

'It's true, my lady,' said Lord Boreas in a powerful voice and bowed his head in greeting.

'And *why* did you decide to join the fight in the War Room, Lord Boreas, then leap through the gate to Leaf?' she asked in a light but dangerous-sounding tone.

'Forgive me, my lady. When those hunters came at me I lost control of myself. They brought out a demon in me I hadn't realised existed,' said Lord Boreas, sticking loosely to the truth. 'The only way I could come to terms with it and avoid taking any more light from the War Room was to pass on to the world of Leaf.'

Luna studied him for a penetrating moment until finally she looked satisfied.

'Well, Lord Boreas, now is your chance to make up for it. Only this evening I had a powerful premonition that something very secret and very powerful exists within the House of Tusk. It's made up of three parts, which if combined, if harmonised, will provide the key to what I seek.'

Jake and Frost stared at each other wide-eyed.

'You were right!' said Jake. 'The green light in the shaft—it was her!'

'And the three parts,' added Frost. 'You, me—'

'And the girl!' *Just as I thought*, reflected Jake privately and his heart skipped a beat. It was followed by a dreadful chill as Luna's words sank in. Though she didn't appear to know what the three parts were, she knew of their existence and was determined to have them.

Their attention was hauled back to the scope by Lord Boreas speaking.

'And this is your *great* creation?' he said to Wilderspin, noting the only object in the hall other than themselves—a simple-looking arch composed of ice.

'Certainly, Lord Boreas! But what you see is merely the entrance. Once you pass inside what lies beyond will spring to life! It's what I like to call *mad mansion*, for is not the mind like a mad mansion, full of secret passageways and cellars we've yet to discover?'

'What are you talking about?' asked Lord Boreas. 'Some sort of device for revealing the contents of a person's mind?'

'Indeed! Yours and Nestor's! For in true science the subject and the observer can never be separated. Thus, *our* job,' said Wilderspin, with a courteous bow towards Luna, 'is to interpret what you so boldly reveal.'

Lord Boreas looked uncertainly at the arch. 'Well let's get on with it,' he said curtly.

'I should point out,' said Wilderspin, unable to disguise his relish, 'that there is the *slightest* chance of your being incinerated as you approach the arch. Alas, such things are beyond my control. It's all down to the sylph and what it makes of you. Needless to say, we all have great faith in you, my dear Lord Boreas, so try not to worry.'

Despite Wilderspin's warning, Lord Boreas took a step closer to the arch before glancing back at Luna.

Looking magnificently composed and smiling subtly, she raised an eyebrow to signal the go-ahead.

Only two paces remained between Lord Boreas and the arch. The god collected himself. The tension was so palpable that Jake felt it as his own.

'When you're ready,' said Wilderspin unhelpfully.

Ignoring him, Lord Boreas waited a moment before taking a step forward. There was no reaction from the arch. He took a second step. Still nothing. His third step took him over the threshold. It was halfway complete when a giant eye filled the archway and blazed like a sun.

It filled the scope. Jake started back in shock. Frost gasped with delight.

Orange and reptilian, it was so powerful that all in the hall, save Luna, were forced to shield their eyes.

Lord Boreas appeared to be frozen mid-step as the gaze of the sylph bore into him.

'If I didn't know better,' said Frost, 'I'd say that was a dragon's eye! It's deciding whether to let him enter or send him up in flames!'

The sylph's eye was so intense that, unlike Frost, Jake could only behold it for an instant at a time.

When he next looked back he gasped in horror. The image in the scope was no longer the eye, but that of his granddad held in the clasp of a giant talon. His body was limp. His were eyes closed. The veins in his face protruded grimly. Light shot through the entire scene as though he was held at the brink of death.

'The light!' said Frost. 'It must be the souls from Hunter trying to reach the Surface. The sylph is sitting on the gate like a hen on eggs!'

'Granddad...' muttered Jake in anguish. 'Is he—?'

'He's alive,' reassured Frost. 'I'm sure of it.'

'Barely,' said Jake.

The image shifted back to the eye in the arch. It blazed for a moment longer then finally relented. A blink later it was gone.

Released from its grip, Lord Boreas's third step finally touched the ground on the other side of the arch.

Wilderspin could scarcely contain his excitement in the stillness which followed. 'Watch!' he cried. 'My lady, watch!'

Whether it was the effect of Medusa's blood or not, Lord Boreas was quick to recover from the shock. With his next step a peculiar light flickered in the air of the otherwise vacant space beyond the arch.

'You see?' gasped Wilderspin. 'You see?'

The flickering began to create something—vaults of intricate geometry.

At the end of Lord Boreas's next step the network of light grew more complete and flexed with power. Again Jake was forced to turn away. When he looked back, the scene had changed dramatically. Filling the entire space beyond the arch was a grand gothic mansion, except there was something strange about it—it existed, but not completely. Parts of the building continually shifted, especially the outside, while elsewhere the insides were visible. For example, Jake could see Lord Boreas standing in the reception hall as well as seeing the drive.

The mansion had seen better days. Much of it had fallen into disrepair and the garden was wild and overgrown. It was also mid-winter. Icicles hung from wherever possible and snow had blown into the reception hall.

'Mad mansion!' exclaimed Wilderspin with a clap of his hands.

Luna looked impressed. The guardians watched on with curious expressions.

Lord Boreas wrapped his cloak tighter about him and ventured another step. Immediately the image shifted. Instead of seeing the greater part of the mansion, it zoomed in on the reception hall.

'Ah, excellent!' said Wilderspin. 'You see, my lady, what's visible is what the sylph decides to focus on, though perhaps we don't see as deeply. It's in control, you see. It reveals to us as much as it wishes. It's a bit tricky like that. But it has to show something because it can't resist it. After all, it's the theatre of life that the sylph exists for.'

'And this mansion,' said Luna. 'Are we seeing the minds of both Lord Boreas *and* Nestor?'

'I believe it's just Lord Boreas's for the moment, my lady. And I must say, it certainly makes one wonder. What a wreck! Look at the state of the roof! There's a great hole in it!'

'The fracture,' said Frost to Jake. 'The mansion is not only revealing his mind, but also his soul.'

'Yes, it is rather in a state,' agreed Luna. 'But you have to admit it's got potential.'

Wilderspin looked like he wished to disagree, though thought better of it. Instead he focused back on Lord Boreas who was confronted with a choice. To his left was one hallway, to his right another.

'Note all that snow on the floor in the left hallway and the flickering lights,' said Wilderspin. 'That must be Lord Boreas's mind. But I'll bet the hallway to the right is the way into Nestor's.'

Jake's heart skipped a beat as he peered into the right hallway, desperate for signs of life.

To his great relief, Lord Boreas chose the right hall. In contrast to the other, it was as though he had passed into springtime in a single step. Birds flitted and sang. Joyous laughter and music spilled from rooms into the hallway. As Lord Boreas ventured along it, Jake caught glimpses of great festivity—in bars, in streets, on yachts.

A great warmth flowed through him. 'This is *definitely* Granddad's hallway,' he whispered.

'Was this your granddad in his youth?' asked Frost.

'Probably just a few weeks ago,' said Jake with a smile.

No sooner had he said so than a voluptuous woman burst from a room just ahead of Lord Boreas and ran off down the hallway giggling between screams. She was shortly followed by a merry man on a bicycle.

'Come here, you little beauty!' cried an image of Nestor as he wobbled after her and almost crashed into the wall.

Fortunately for Nestor the hall opened out into a grove of olive trees which the woman ran into. As the man did his best to cycle after her, the sylph's focus shifted away from them. It raced through the grove in another direction apparently in search of something.

To Lawrence it appeared as though the grove were racing past him. The sylph's attention brought him to a grand driveway lined by trees. There were just five, each of them less a tree than a smouldering trunk. Regardless, they were vast and each distinct from the other.

The sky darkened and thunder rumbled so menacingly that it prickled Jake's skin.

'The sylph, it's angry,' remarked Frost.

In a wondrous whir of violet wingbeats, a flock of humming-birds hovered about the trees. Daffodils and bluebells sprouted about the trunks.

They had scarcely blossomed when they turned to ash. The birds were blown away by a fierce gust. Yet still they came back and the flowers re-bloomed.

'Your granddad—he's trying to console the sylph!' remarked Frost in awe. 'He's caught in the talons of the sylph yet here we see the compassion of his soul at work. He's quite something, you know.'

Jake looked up from the scope at Frost, who remained fixed on the scene. It was the first time Frost had said something complimentary and in a tone that was humane. For Jake it was defining a moment. Their tentative and strange friendship was deepening.

'Yes, he is,' said Jake, who gazed at Frost a moment longer before returning his attention to the scope.

Lord Boreas stood in the drive, apparently deciding whether to proceed or not.

'Five smouldering trees, each from a different region of the world,' said Frost.

'How can you tell?' asked Jake.

'Because I know trees. And there's no tree to represent either the Middle East or, let me think—the Americas.'

'Do the trees symbolise something?'

'Of course! They're trees of life, each for a different root race of humans. They represent the five sacrificed shepherds. It's why the sylph is angered at the sight of them. It's like looking at its own gravestone.'

'Braysheath looks Arabic. It's why there's no tree from the Middle East, because he hasn't been sacrificed,' realised Jake.

'Exactly,' confirmed Frost.

Wilderspin was not as quick as Frost. He simply watched on with great interest, along with the others. Whether Luna understood or not was difficult to tell—her enigmatic expression remained unchanged.

'Then the oldest member of the shepherds,' started Jake, but was cut short by the appearance of a bright light. It shone from the distance and cast back the livid clouds, a light that was both intense yet gentle and so pure that, unlike the blazing eye of the sylph, Jake was able to behold it.

It dimmed a little to reveal the form of a heron-like bird. Wings outstretched, its neck craned towards the heavens, clutched in its feet was a turquoise sphere. The heron hung in the air above a mountain of the same brand of light.

'Nashoba,' purred Luna.

'You're right, my lady!' enthused Wilderspin. 'The phoenix of rebirth! And the mountain must be Braysheath! And what light! I'm sure you wouldn't mind that in your ark.'

'Their day will come,' said Luna with a calm conviction that left Jake cold, extinguishing his delight at finally seeing the symbolic form of the oldest shepherd.

'The mountain,' he said, 'it reminds me of the one near the House of Tusk.'

'And the sphere clasped in Nashoba's feet represents the cosmos,' added Frost. 'Infinite light inside the planet Earth. Turquoise is the best mineral for containing light. What we're seeing is the sylph's deeper understanding of Nestor's memories concerning the House of Tusk.'

'Does that mean Nashoba is inside the fort?'

'Only the portion of his energy that went into its formation,' said Frost. 'I expect he resides elsewhere. Look how he siphons the dark clouds into his wingtips. It's as though he's drawing off excess darkness and recycling it.'

'By darkness do you mean evil?'

'Ignorance is a better word than evil,' clarified Frost.

'But the clouds have come from the sylph, haven't they? The sylph isn't ignorant.'

'No. But what it represents is,' said Frost. 'Humans. Most of them anyway.'

Whether bored, disgusted or otherwise, the sylph shifted away from the phoenix and swept through eerie-looking woods where the trees were twisted and gnarly in a way that seemed pained. Moss hung from their branches in great sheets.

Lord Boreas ventured into them. A twig cracked under his footstep and echoed through the stillness.

'My lady,' said Wilderspin, 'shouldn't we try and direct Lord Boreas into the House of Tusk?'

'No,' said Luna, looking enthralled. 'Let's not interfere. Perhaps it's taking us into Nestor's unconscious.'

'Of course! The dark and tangled forest! Yes, doubtless you're right, my lady,' agreed Wilderspin.

'Regardless,' said Luna, 'the sylph will be attracted to hidden power. Our interests are aligned.'

'Oh look!' said Wilderspin. 'Something of the mansion has returned. He must have some more decisions to make.'

Lord Boreas was once more in a hallway as gloomy as the forest, which partially faded into the background. A suit of armour and a moose head, which hung from the wall, did little to improve it.

Some way along the corridor, Lord Boreas reached an open door on his left. It was a circular room with many doors lining its walls. Inside were two chairs and a table. Upon its surface burned a single candle, its flame weak. On the far side of the room one of the doors was open and seemed to lead down to a cellar of sorts.

Lord Boreas tried to walk past it, but the sylph took control. Without Lord Boreas needing to take a step, its curiosity took them rapidly through both doors and down, each step of the stairwell triggering an image. They were fleeting. Jake caught sight of a harbour, an inn, a desert and a cave when another hallway formed.

Lord Boreas seemed reluctant to advance.

'This is not your granddad's unconscious,' remarked Frost. 'It's Boreas's. The lizard mentioned something about a dream room. I've never heard of such a thing, but I'll bet it was the room the sylph just took us through.'

Jake said nothing. He had a feeling Frost was right.

Realising he had no choice, Lord Boreas set off slowly along the hallway. As he approached the first door on the left it swung open to reveal a marsh. A chill-looking mist hung over it. Going nowhere on one of the larger pools of the marsh, and looking very out of place, was a large wooden ship. Unlike the rest of the marsh, the pool was frozen. The ship's sails were covered in frost and icicles.

'An ark perhaps?' ventured Wilderspin.

Luna said nothing, though the ark wasn't hers.

'The pirate,' said Frost. 'The ship could be his.'

'But the ship is stuck,' said Jake.

'It means Boreas has some work to do—treasures to find, energy to release, that sort of thing. The ice symbolises frozen emotions. In other words, the ones he's denying. He needs to accept them and then pass through them.'

The stillness of the marsh was shattered by the enchanting singing of women. Four bewitching beauties flew up and about the deck of the ship like phantoms, their wanton eyes fixed on Lord Boreas who was undergoing a great struggle to resist their call. While his eyes feasted on the sirens, he gripped the door frame with both hands.

'How curious,' said Wilderspin. 'The Lord of Sirens of Greed resisting their call? I wonder what it could mean?'

Still Luna said nothing. The lights of her eyes danced with fascination.

This time the sylph didn't force Lord Boreas into the room. Perhaps it helped him, for he suddenly tore himself away from the seduction of the sirens and slammed shut the door.

Eyes closed and breathing deeply, Lord Boreas took a moment to recover himself. He looked back through the arch of ice into the hall and locked eyes with Luna. Her expression remained one of intrigue.

Returning his attention to the hallway, he stepped back in shock when a brown and black patterned snake slithered passed him from a doorway a little ahead to his right.

'It's just a common adder,' said Frost, 'yet he looks shocked. It must mean something important to him. Death and rebirth, of course, but something else, something more personal. A fear. Perhaps something sexual.'

The same door swung fully open and a great black bird swept into the hall.

'A vulture!' said Jake. 'Asclepius!'

It swooped down, picked up the adder and deposited it about the hilt of the sword on the suit of armour then flew back the way it came.

'Yes, it must be Asclepius,' agreed Frost. 'A serpent coiled about a sword. Though it's just one snake rather than two, it looks like a caduceus, the symbol of healing. But I have a feeling that's just the surface of it.'

The image of the snake loomed large within the scope.

'The sylph wants Boreas to make a choice—the adder or the sword,' said Jake.

Lord Boreas came to the same conclusion, though was reluctant to do so. Tentatively he reached towards the hilt.

His hand had only made half the distance when the adder transformed into a bright red cobra. It reared, flared its hood and hissed venomously.

Lord Boreas lunged forward to grasp its neck.

The snake was quicker. As it struck forward its mouth expanded at great speed. Magnified further by the sylph's attention, its fangs filled the entire view through the scope. Jake leapt back. So did Frost.

'Wow!' he gasped then leapt back up to the scope. 'Look! The cobra's mouth has become a door!'

Jake rushed back to the scope. Lord Boreas was standing at a door whose frame was the gaping mouth of the cobra. What lay beyond was forming before their eyes through a fading dawn. A golden sun was rising behind a mountain. Sitting on its summit, facing the sun, was a woman—silhouetted, naked, youthful yet radiating a sense of maturity that filled Jake with a longing to know who she was.

He wasn't the only one. Everyone in the hall, even the guardians, looked mesmerised. Lord Boreas gazed on from the doorway, a peculiar conflict in his eyes, part longing, part fear.

The sun continued to rise then stopped so that the silhouette of the woman was fixed at its centre, creating the effect of a giant aura.

'The epitome of peace,' said Frost. 'It's her. The serpent turned red because it represented Lord Boreas's passion.'

The penny dropped. 'Rowena!' gasped Jake, recalling Geoffrey's warning to Lord Boreas. Whatever the adder and the sword represented individually, together they revealed the greater part of her energy beyond Luna's grasp. 'Do you think Luna realises?'

The image in the scope shifted to Luna's face. She was so fascinated that she took a step closer to the archway of ice. Jake recalled the lizard's warning that she mustn't enter the experiment.

'Not yet,' said Frost. 'But she's desperate to know.'

Wilderspin also took a step forward, his eyes shining. 'My lady, I wonder, are we seeing into the future? I can't quite put my finger on it but something's shifted'

Luna was too absorbed to answer.

'It's not the future exactly,' said Frost. 'It's a possibility. The sylph is way ahead of us. Though the vulture symbolised Asclepius, its appearance was the sylph's doing. As the lizard said, it sees deep into the unconscious of Boreas and is shifting around the symbols in the manner of cracking a code. It's searching for something.'

In the stillness that followed, Jake looked away from the scope and about the office, suddenly feeling exposed, wondering how long their luck could last.

'Don't worry,' said Frost as he continued to gaze through the scope. 'I'll hear if anything comes. Besides, I suspect the sylph is controlling events beyond the hall. It knows we're here.'

'What makes you think it will protect us?'

'Because we too have a role to play in all this,' said Frost.

Less than reassured, Jake looked back through the scope, just in time to hear Luna speak.

'Step into the room, Lord Boreas. Approach her,' she commanded, her voice carrying as though she were right beside him.

Lord Boreas, however, tore his gaze away from the meditative woman on the mountain. He looked to the far end of the hallway, in the opposite direction to the arch. Another door had formed—composed entirely of steel, it was just like the door of a vault.

'You don't think?' started Jake.

'The lizard's other warning,' said Frost. 'The sylph's found a door to his darkest demon! One Boreas hasn't the power to confront. It's presenting him with a choice, though actually he doesn't have one. Just the sight of the demon will destroy him!'

As Lord Boreas beheld it, his grave expression confirmed Frost's thought. He looked back at Luna and nodded his acknowledgement to pass through the doorway leading to the woman.

'This will be interesting,' said Frost.

Lord Boreas beheld Rowena's back. He lowered his head as though making a prayer.

Then took a step.

Similar to his fateful step through the arch of ice, before his foot even touched the ground the sun shone powerfully. Its beams shot through the mansion and out over the entire hall.

A great shift took place.

It was almost too quick and too dazzling to follow. All rooms appeared to combine into one. The sun became the flame of the candle from the dream room, which merged with the sword that now stood tip down in the pool of ice. It shone with such power that the ice melted.

Before Lord Boreas knew what was happening the hull of the great ship was surging down the hallway about to run him down. There was only time for him to turn his back on a bow wave so mighty that Wilderspin did the same.

Several moments passed before both realised the ship had vanished before it struck.

'I say!' exclaimed Wilderspin. 'My invention has surpassed my wildest dreams!'

Though she didn't express it, Luna shared his euphoria. It showed in her glistening eyes as she beheld the scene before her. In the wake of the ship another hallway had appeared, one which looked even more rundown than the one before. Cobwebs hung everywhere. Hanging from the walls were four tattered hunting trophies—a white wolf, an elephant, a walrus and, strangest of all, what appeared to be the head of a black unicorn. There were many doors, though all were closed.

The one that held Luna's interest was at the hallway's end. Unlike the vault-like door at the end of Lord Boreas's hallway, it looked quite ordinary, wooden and arch-shaped, like a door to a church sacristy. There were two oddities—a lantern that hung above it and a blackthorn bush which framed it, both lending the door the appearance of being outside.

'This hallway belongs to someone else,' said Luna, her smile becoming less subtle.

'Quite possibly, my lady,' said Wilderspin, without offering a suggestion.

'She's right. Any ideas?' said Frost in a knowing tone.

A chill ran through Jake. *A lantern!* He turned to Frost who was grinning at him. 'No—not me?'

Frost nodded.

'Why would a door relating to me be in the mad mansion?' questioned Jake before recalling the strong connection between Lord Boreas and himself through the web of light during the break-in. 'Besides, there's blackthorn, like your chair inside Deuteronomy. Maybe it's yours!'

'The blackthorn does represent me, but the door is yours. As I said before, our destinies are intertwined. We're soul brothers!'

Jake said nothing. With a shiver, he looked back into the scope.

Luna moved closer to the ice archway until she was just a few steps short of it.

Lord Boreas, meanwhile, tried to open the doors closest to him, but all were locked.

'Call me your crown of thorns if you like,' continued Frost, 'but my role is one of protection. It's Saturn and Mars who rule the blackthorn and thus it's my destiny to help you face your shadow.'

Jake remained silent. Frost's words had a disturbing ring of truth to them. Jake, however, was more focused on Luna and whether she intended to cross into the experiment.

'Isn't that the same sword?' said Wilderspin, referring to a sword which stood tip down, no longer in ice, but in front of the door that Frost had said was Jake's. 'Yes, it must be! I must say, this is most fascinating! How richly symbolic it is, despite being in need of a jolly good dusting.'

'You realise what you're seeing here, don't you?' said Frost. 'The sylph's been moving through the threads of power. It's effectively showing us a story—not so much the surface of it, but the subtext, both the conscious and the *un*conscious goals. In other words, the hero's journey. And not just yours, but several—'

'Yours, too,' said Jake.

'Maybe. Who knows? But the important point is that all paths meet on yours.'

Luna had taken another step closer. 'The cobwebs are the most telling symbol of all,' she said, in response to Wilderspin's suggestion of dusting them off. 'Webs of fate. Whoever this hallway represents, they have the power, or *potential* power, to write the fates and on a grand scale.'

'She can't be talking about me,' said Jake. 'I know I'm supposed to be Lord Tusk but—'

'That's just the surface of a story that's still unfolding,' interjected Frost. 'There are probabilities and possibilities, just as there are gaps between them. And there are powers, perhaps just one or two, that can bridge the two.'

'Lord Boreas,' said Luna. 'I want you to open the door at the end.'

Jake's heart was in his mouth as he watched on.

Lord Boreas proceeded slowly down the hallway, glancing up at the trophies as though expecting them to burst to life.

He was just a step or so from reaching the sword when a great crack appeared in the floor. He made to leap over it, but the crack tore open into an abyss as the hallway split in two.

Lord Boreas disappeared between them.

'Where's he gone?' gasped Jake.

Wilderspin couldn't have looked more delighted. Or more disappointed when a hand appeared and Lord Boreas clawed his way back into the half of the hallway he had leapt from.

'Fascinating,' purred Luna, her gaze fixed on the door now on the other side of the abyss. The sword remained sentinel-like in front of it, along with the heads of the elephant and walrus. The heads of the wolf and unicorn remained in the half with Lord Boreas.

'Such blackness,' delighted Frost as he marvelled at the abyss. 'As black as a panther's coat.'

'Why do you say that?' asked Jake, noting Frost's suggestive tone.

'The assassin in the fort—she was raised by a tribe of panthers called the Yakreth.'

'So what if she was?' said Jake. 'That hardly means she's symbolised by the abyss.'

'Not only her. There are many factors in play. But she has to be symbolised somewhere,' said Frost.

'We don't even know if this corridor is definitely mine,' said Jake.

His hopes were shattered by the arrival of someone on the far side of the abyss.

The ghost.

This time, however, there was a key difference. He wasn't a phantom. He looked real, of flesh and blood. Neither was he holding a lantern—it was already fixed above the door.

Jake watched on mortified yet fascinated to see more of the mysterious character's grizzled features. His beard was less red than orange, faded with age, while his eyes were a fierce blue—not the fierceness of a warrior, more like the fierce intelligence of a scholar interrupted during study.

'Druid!' cried Frost, noting the man's white robes.

The druid had arrived through a new door to the side of the one with the lantern. Once passed through, it disappeared. Completely ignoring Lord Boreas and the others, with a wave of his hand the abyss widened to twice its width.

Wilderspin was so captivated that for once he was lost for words.

When a table and two chairs appeared in front of Jake's door, Luna's eyes flashed with great power hungry for more. The druid sat down and the light of the lantern went out.

Jake's stomach turned with dread. The hall *was* his. Frost was right. Worse still, the last people in the cosmos he wished to see it were staring at it with intense interest.

'Someone else has appeared and sat opposite the druid!' said Frost, zooming into the shadows in front of the door.

Jake strained his eyes, trying to make sense of the subtle variations in shade. 'Yes, I see something. But it's a strange shape. Has it got something on its back?'

'Wings!' gasped Frost, whose vision was superior to Jake's. 'But they're a darker shade than its human body as though burnt. Like the trees! It must be the sylph in a different form. The form of an angel with burned wings. Lord Boreas mentioned it. Yes, it fits. Amazing!'

'How can the sylph be both creating this reality as well as stepping into it?' asked Jake.

'Because it can. It's massively powerful. Don't waste your energy trying to understand it. More importantly, who's that druid it's meeting with?' said Frost, his tone mischievous.

'Someone who possibly, just maybe, might have something to do with me,' admitted Jake.

Though the scope permitted Frost and Jake a closer view than those in the hall, they heard nothing of what was discussed between the druid and the sylph. No one did—not even Lord Boreas who was closest, though unable to cross the abyss. Not even Luna heard.

'Oh to be able to hear their words!' cried Frost in frustration. 'Imagine the level on which they're talking! Perhaps they're making an agreement!'

'Maybe to release Granddad,' said Jake hopefully.

'Oh I think they're talking far beyond the fate of your dear old granddad,' said Frost.

He's right, thought Jake, wishing it wasn't so. *Then what are they discussing? If the druid is part of me, ghost or not, wouldn't I have some sense of what he thought and felt?*

It was a daring thought, especially in Renlock, where momentous thoughts drew attention, especially since Jake had until that point denied any connection with the ghost. But seeing it there with the sylph, the powerful being which held his granddad captive, Jake was willing to take a risk.

Druid, he said in thought, maintaining his focus on the druid through the scope, *what will happen to Nestor, my granddad? What happened to Dad? What will happen to Brock and the Surface?*

Through the shadow, Jake sensed a subtle movement—the turn of a head. A terrible heat engulfed him. It was worse than the effect of Frost's grip in the stairwell. Much worse. His indulgent questions had upset the druid. Now he felt his anger—like a warning from a father to a child not to interfere in something of great importance.

'What is it?' asked Frost.

'Nothing,' said Jake, steadying himself as the heat relented.

'Luna just glanced in our direction,' remarked Frost. 'She sensed something. Whatever it was, she's now even more keen to enter the mad mansion.'

Jake focused on Luna. She took a step closer to the archway of ice. Only two paces remained to its threshold.

'Rowena,' he muttered, fearful for the woman on the mountain—the part of the goddess's energy hidden from Luna. He thought he saw the sword glow as though it too sensed danger. The woman and the sword were somehow linked. Jake felt it.

'Luna's dying to know what they're discussing,' said Frost.

Without warning, he shifted the scope to another part of the mansion.

'What are you doing?' asked Jake.

'There's someone else skulking around. I sense something,' he said and scoured the basements.

'There! Look!' he cried. 'The pirate!'

Creeping through the cellar as though looking for something was a striking character—swarthy skinned, bushy-bearded with a chest the size of a beer barrel, he looked like a classic pirate. He seemed to be enjoying himself, as though playing a game of hide and seek.

'Isn't it him that we saw projected from the turtle in Asclepius's lab?' said Jake.

'Yes, you're right! It's strange that Luna doesn't seem to have sensed him. I'm sure the sylph and druid have, just as they've sensed us. Because this is your corridor, they must be permitting us extra insight.'

'You really think this pirate is one of Lord Boreas's demons?'

'Possibly,' said Frost. 'Or something to do with them. And I have a feeling that it wouldn't fare well for Lord Boreas if the pirate appears in the hallway.'

As Jake wondered what it might mean, not only for Lord Boreas but also for himself, frustration was starting to show on Luna's face.

'Wilderspin, if your invention is so brilliant, can you not adjust something to allow us to hear their conversation?'

'Not if the sylph doesn't wish it, my lady, much as it pains me to say so.'

'It will pain you if you don't come up with something,' she threatened, eyeing the arch.

'Right, my lady, right. Of course!' said Wilderspin in a fluster.

'The pirate's coming up the staircase!' said Jake, as he watched the delighted-looking pirate approach the door at the top of the staircase that entered the hallway just behind Lord Boreas.

Luna looked back for Wilderspin but he was gone. 'There's nothing for it,' she said as she withdrew a flask of light from her robes.

Jake cursed. 'She's going to enter!'

As she and the pirate closed in on the hallway, the knotting in Jake's stomach doubled.

Luna uncorked her flask of light.

The pirate's hand tightened about the door handle.

Fear gripped Jake.

Excitement gripped Frost.

Lord Boreas appeared unaware of the imminent danger as he continued to gaze across the abyss into the shadows of the mysterious meeting.

Finally the pirate opened the door—just enough to peer through. On spotting Lord Boreas so close, his eyes widened with joy.

Finally Lord Boreas sensed him. He swung around. His eyes also widened—with horror. The sylph was merging realities, linking the hallway with the pirate's search for Lawrence deep within his unconscious where he still hid under a log as an adder.

The pirate made to step into the hall.

Luna hadn't yet seen the pirate, though would do any moment.

Jake's heart skipped a beat.

Before the pirate completed his step, a subtle movement showed in the shadow of the druid—the wave of a hand.

The pirate was thrown back through the door. Instead of striking the staircase, his body dissolved into thin air.

Yet another mystery was too much for Luna. She gulped down the light and strode the final step into the arch.

'No!' cried Jake.

The druid sprang from the shadow. His eyes fixed on Luna. His gaze was so fierce that it stilled Jake's heart. It had as similar effect on Luna's step, slowing down its movement.

The druid raised his left hand. His lips moved rapidly as though chanting a spell. Then stopped. Time stopped too, or so it seemed to Jake. All attention was on the druid. All breath was held. The druid's gaze fixed on Luna with yet greater intensity. Her step was only an instant from completion. Then, as though he held the fate of the cosmos within his fingers, he clicked them.

A pulse of energy exploded from the air above the abyss. Lord Boreas was hurled back through the arch like a ball from a cannon, smashing Luna back into the hall and landing on top of her.

Both looked back just in time to see a wall of black fire tear down the hallway and consume the arch of ice.

An instant later, it was gone. Not the slightest trace of the mansion remained—not the druid, not the sylph, not the sword, nor anything else.

'Wow!' gasped Frost.

Jake felt great relief, though couldn't fully surrender to it.

Black fire, he muttered in thought. The only time he had seen or heard of it was in his nightmares as a child, when the druid ghost had appeared and Jake had plummeted into an abyss filled with black flames.

Luna looked up at Lord Boreas who was sitting astride her. His eyes were wild, not from Medusa's blood, which had worn off, but from shock.

'Boreas will be pleased,' said Frost. 'The sylph let him survive. It must sense something heroic in him. It means his mad plan in the holygate has a chance, that the sylph might permit him entrance, perhaps even support his cause.'

'Wonderful,' said Jake dryly. Lord Boreas's plan meant the sacrifice of Jake.

'And look at Luna's eyes,' added Frost.

They were just as wild as Lord Boreas's—wild with delight.

'Black fire,' she muttered. 'Where there's a paradox, there's a mystery. And what greater paradox than black flames? Now I'm certain—I've found what I'm looking for. A gate of black fire!'

She looked at Lord Boreas and raised an eyebrow. 'Lord Boreas, if you please.'

'My lady, forgive me,' he said, coming to his senses and dragged himself up.

'Are you injured?' she said, as he helped her to her feet.

'Nothing serious, my lady.'

'Good. You and I have business on the Surface, so prepare yourself.'

Lord Boreas bowed his head in acquiescence, looking ready to collapse.

'Time also draws near for relieving the sylph,' she added.

Lord Boreas stiffened. 'But, my lady, souls will reach the Surface. If you intend to topple Brock, doesn't the gate need to remain blocked?'

'Once the war in the War Room reaches full steam, few souls will be free to return to the Surface. Just enough to ensure human faith in me as their new Overlord—their Goddess of Fertility. After I've performed a little miracle for them, that is. Don't you love the irony?'

Luna studied Lord Boreas. 'I would've thought that after your latest experience, Lord Boreas, you'd be pleased to see the back of the sylph. It can no longer be trusted.'

'And what of Nestor Tusk, my lady?' asked Lord Boreas, articulating Jake's concern.

'He too will shortly have served his purpose. Naturally the way to relieve the sylph is to slay its host.'

'No!' gasped Jake.

Shock and horror turned to anger. Goddess or not, Jake determined there and then to do whatever it took, not only to save his granddad, but to thoroughly ruin her plans.

Luna looked back to where the hallway had been and smiled. 'Well done, Lord Boreas,' she said, too blinded by the idea of a gate of black fire to wonder at the events that led to its revelation, or to wonder at what the mansion had shown of the being she assumed was Lord Boreas.

'My lady,' he said with another bow.

'I might have guessed,' she continued, 'that the very door I seek to complete my plan is not only in the House of Tusk, but connected to the lord himself. The new lord.'

'What?' exclaimed Jake, as another wave of dread swept through him. 'What's she talking about?'

'I told you!' said Frost excitedly. 'All paths cross on yours. Your destiny is not only intertwined with Lord Boreas's but also Luna's!'

Jake couldn't believe what he was hearing. It was bad enough that Lord Boreas had his secret plan to sacrifice Jake, but now Luna was after him too, along with three powerful objects in the fort, having not yet realised that Jake was one of them—that perhaps Jake, Frost and Rani were somehow the key that opened the fateful door.

'Lord Boreas, Commander,' said Luna addressing her henchmen, 'bring me Lord Tusk. I don't care what it takes, just make sure he's alive. I need his light. I doubt it currently has the power to reveal what I need, but with a bit of tweaking I think I can save some time.'

Jake had heard enough. It was time to leave.

'Well, well, well,' came a familiar voice from behind him that caused Jake to jump.

He spun around to find Wilderspin entering the office.

'We haven't yet had the pleasure,' said Wilderspin to a horror-struck Jake, 'but given what I've just witnessed I feel like I already know you. The new Lord Tusk, I presume.'

Jake was about to pretend he had never heard of Lord Tusk when he realised something else was wrong.

Frost had gone.

CHAPTER 42
LIGHT INTERROGATION

As Wilderspin stepped deeper into his office, the door closed with a fateful thud.

Jake resisted the temptation to glance about for Frost. *There's no point in both of us getting caught,* he reasoned, fighting back a sense of betrayal. *And this Wilderspin is clearly sneakier than he lets on. Perhaps Frost only sensed him at the last moment.*

'You knew I was here before, didn't you?' said Jake, trying to discover if Wilderspin had also sensed Frost.

'Patience is a great virtue,' said Wilderspin. 'Please, take a seat.'

Wilderspin gestured to a sturdy wooden chair facing the desk.

Sitting down in Wilderspin's presence was the last thing Jake wanted to do, but he had little choice. *Perhaps I can discover something that'll help Granddad and find out more about Luna,* he thought, sensing Wilderspin's loyalty was to himself alone and that he might let something slip.

Reluctantly, Jake sat down. The moment he did so, cords of light appeared from nowhere and bound his wrists and ankles to the chair. His energy plunged. His head swam. He couldn't believe it. Only earlier that evening he had narrowly escaped a net of light, his interrogator an assassin. Now he was trapped by a spymaster.

'They're made of inner-force,' explained Wilderspin, noting Jake's alarm. 'Marvellous stuff. It destroys all sources of false strength—false hope, false anger, false fight, you name it.'

'Then it replaces it with real strength,' countered Jake, struggling against their grip despite what Wilderspin had said.

'Eventually. But not until you've been destroyed yourself. Or rather, the idea of who you think you are and that's a long journey indeed, my dear Lord Tusk. So I'd give up struggling if I were you. Not even Hercules could break those cords.'

They also had the effect of summoning Jake's fears, especially of the druid—fears of such depth that he still battled to make sense of them.

I'm here to save Granddad, he reminded himself in an attempt to fight it back. *Whatever it takes.*

Perched on the front of his desk, Wilderspin chuckled. He took something black and shiny from a bowl, popped it his mouth and chomped through it.

'Cockroach?' he said, offering one to Jake. 'They're roasted—extremely good for you, especially for stamina, something you're going to need. No? Suit yourself.'

Having had his fill of cockroaches, Wilderspin lit a cigar. In no hurry, he took several slow puffs, all the while regarding Jake through the smoke.

'You're in rather a tight spot, aren't you?' he said at last.

'What's the worst Luna can do?' said Jake as casually as possible. 'Take my light and erase my identity? If so, then what would be left of me to worry?'

'I'm afraid it's a little more subtle than that,' said Wilderspin. 'You see, though Luna *could* take all of your light, she much prefers to leave a tiny shard of consciousness to each soul. Perhaps just one per cent, perhaps less, though still more than the paltry percentage most humans currently use.'

'Why would she do that?' asked Jake.

'Because, my dear Lord Tusk, like all true tyrants, she's merciless. She wants to inflict maximum pain, maximum suffering without feeling the slightest remorse herself. She considers humans vermin.'

'If the consciousness she leaves is more than humans currently use then it doesn't sound much like suffering to me,' said Jake.

Wilderspin indulged in another chuckle. 'That's because you don't understand *real* fear. Like most humans, you feel fear when something you held to be true and dependable is suddenly not so—your view of a person, your view of the world and how it works. But that's not real fear. That's simply ignorance. Real fear is not a loss of grip on what you thought you knew. It's being *stuck* with your impoverished view of reality, being conscious of the fact and without the slightest hope of it ever changing—like never-ending rain, you bound to your room like a prisoner. Or floating in the middle of an ocean with nothing but sun, not the slightest breath of wind, not the even the wispiest wisp of a cloud or any other suggestion that things might change. It's being aware of the consequences of all your misdeeds, but never able to make amends. *That*, my dear Lord Tusk, is fear, despair, depression and everything else that goes with it.'

'But why wouldn't it change?' asked Jake.

'Because you've lost your potential—the ninety nine per cent of your light that's with Luna. And without your potential you can never master what little consciousness is left to you. Hope, inspiration and all the other links to your potential—gone! All that would be left to you is the imagination of a pauper, tortured fantasies impossible to fulfil.

Wilderspin took another contented puff on his cigar.

What he had said made sense to Jake. He imagined what it would be like to be stuck in the chair in Wilderspin's office for the rest of his life, his hands bound, without any hope of escape.

His thoughts drifted back to Frost, not only where he had disappeared to so quickly, but a darker thought behind it—that perhaps he was a trixy after all. A corrupted trixy.

But if Frost was a trixy, he reasoned, *then surely he would have exposed me himself and taken the credit. The test will be if he tries to save me. If he does, then he's a pixy. If not...*

'But if I know Luna,' continued Wilderspin, 'in your case, Lord Tusk, she'll make an extra effort. Before taking your light, she'll open your memory to your past lives, for what greater torment can there be than to know you have been great without hope of restoring such greatness or even exceeding it?'

'Great?' said Jake doubtfully.

'Oh yes, without a doubt! Greatly good, greatly evil, it matters not which. Either is better than being dull,' enthused Wilderspin. 'Yes, I'm certain that's what she'll do. However, I can't be certain which method she'll use, but rest assured, Lord Tusk, it'll be the most painful—the light equivalent of a disembowelment. Yes, something like that, something *truly* torturous.'

Despite Wilderspin's flare for drama, Jake didn't doubt his words. All the same, he did his best not to get caught up in them, but the cords of inner-force continued to sap his energy and summon his fears. Frightful images flashed through his mind.

'And especially after that druid of yours cast her through the arch! My stars, that was brazen!' added Wilderspin, having clearly understood more than he had let on in the hall.

'How could a druid have done that to someone as powerful as Luna?' asked Jake, fighting to stay focused.

'The perfect alignment of thought, word and will force,' he explained. 'Such magic was commonplace on the Surface during what academics so casually dismiss as *Pre-history*, but it's non-existent these days. The sincerity must be *one hundred* per cent whether creating or destroying.'

'The druid was guarding a door,' said Jake, sticking with the facts.

Wilderspin took another puff on his cigar as he studied Jake. 'Yes, he was, wasn't he,' was his sparing reply.

'What's Luna looking for?' pressed Jake, deciding to go for the direct approach, hoping that Wilderspin would find it difficult to resist showing off how much he knew. 'That door with the lantern above it?'

An unpleasant smile formed on Wilderspin's lips. He chuckled.

'I shall tell you,' he said at last, 'what I have so brilliantly deduced of Luna's plans for no other reason than the sheer enjoyment of observing your reaction. Besides, I shall wipe your memory of our encounter once I'm finished with you, before handing you over to Luna.'

Jake said nothing, refusing to give Wilderspin the satisfaction of seeing his fear.

'Oh, how very Tusk,' remarked Wilderspin. 'Steady under fire. Your father would be proud, that is, if there was anything left of him to be proud.'

Fists clenched, weakened by inner-force, Jake battled to contain his emotions, this time fury, which shot from his eyes like daggers.

'Good job we've got those cords, hey?' remarked Wilderspin with another chuckle.

A puff of his cigar later, he finally answered the question. 'Luna wishes to leave,' he said.

'Leave where?'

'The cosmos,' replied Wilderspin plainly, as though it were the simple matter of catching a bus.

'That's not possible,' scoffed Jake.

'I agree,' said Wilderspin. 'But Luna is more powerful than either of us and soon more powerful than your bothersome friend Braysheath, if not already. And thus, one must wonder why she thinks such a thing.'

'Why would she want to leave?'

'Ah, the ignorance of youth, the false hope,' sighed Wilderspin.

Jake waited for further explanation.

'Luna is fed up with humans. Let me ask you—if you were stuck in a house full of brats would you not want to leave?'

Jake wished to counter such a negative view of the world, but the cords of inner-force sapped him of hope, all save his fiercely guarded determination to save his granddad—a man whose cheer and optimism was so authentic that nothing could touch it.

'And if there is a way to leave?' he said instead.

'Then I for one don't intend to be left behind!' declared Wilderspin. 'Can you imagine what it would be like? No light. Just shadow. Just billions and billions of pitiful human entities, no longer pretending everything is fine, but moping about in despair, raging, looting, searching in vain for potential, wailing and groaning, unable to die, unable to live. Dreadful! Whatever would I do? What of worth would be left to spy on?'

'And that door in the mad mansion, the one the druid sat in front of—is that the exit she's after?' asked Jake, dreading the answer.

'I doubt it,' said Wilderspin. 'But it's through that door that she'll find the way.'

Jake closed his eyes, continuing to battle against the extraordinary fear summoned by the cords.

'One must also wonder,' continued Wilderspin, 'why it is you who are destined to be her guide. You and your light-line.'

Jake's eyes flashed open. 'What? Guide? What are you on about?'

'Oh yes,' delighted Wilderspin. 'Map, compass, guide and key! All in one!'

'But if she's so powerful, why would she need one?'

'It's precisely because she *is* so powerful that she, or anyone else for that matter, can't find it alone. It's part of the cosmos's design—like an insurance policy. There must be challenges and tests and dreadful traps.'

'This is ridiculous,' said Jake, reasserting his reason. 'It just *doesn't* make sense.'

'Not yet. You don't have the power to unlock the knowledge, let alone understand it. But that druid of yours is another matter.'

'Then I'll refuse to have anything to do with the past,' said Jake.

Wilderspin chuckled. 'Which will only serve to make you more present and presence is the key to accessing and integrating the past. So you see, my valiant little friend, you can't escape your destiny.'

THE STAGNANT POOL RANI AND BIN HAD LEAPT INTO THROUGH the cave was an illusion. The moment her feet breached its surface, Rani felt a great tug. A terrific heat engulfed her.

A gate! she thought.

It was, but not one to a specific place. Rather, it spat them out into a dark void.

For a timeless moment they hung suspended in the air, waiting for something when a giant face appeared before them. Delineated in blue light, it tossed back its head and bellowed in laughter.

Rani gasped. She knew the face though not what it meant.

It was the face of Braysheath.

The laughter subsided. His eyes fixed on Rani and Bin. They glowed with delight. With a sharp intake of breath, he inhaled them whole.

JAKE MADE ANOTHER VAIN ATTEMPT TO BREAK FREE FROM THE strange cords which bound his wrists. The very act drained yet more of his energy and so he gave up trying.

'Know what this is?' said Wilderspin, withdrawing from his jacket what looked like a silver cigarette case. 'No? I'll show you.'

Wilderspin opened the silver case and held it in front of Jake. Inside were two objects. In one half was a small fresh-looking leaf whose stem was fused with the metal of the case. In the other half was an opaque stone.

'I designed it myself,' beamed Wilderspin as he approached Jake. 'All I need do is pop a drop of your blood on this here leaf and, well you'll see. Shall we try it out?'

Before Jake could protest, Wilderspin had pricked his finger and taken a drop of blood. 'Ever heard of an oracle?' he asked as he returned to his desk.

Jake had, but said nothing.

'They're very crafty, the good ones,' said Wilderspin, taking a seat behind the desk, placing the silver case in front of him. 'They make excellent interrogators. It's to do with the way they question. They never ask too directly. Rather, they ask your unconscious dozens of questions all at once and through a process of triangulation they find out just what they're after. Quite brilliant. And especially this one!'

Jake was watching the leaf in the peculiar case. It appeared to be waking, straining for the drop of blood that Wilderspin carefully balanced on the needle just above it.

'And so, dear Lord Tusk,' said Wilderspin, 'let us plumb the depths of your dark and mysterious past and see what we can discover! Not only why your light is tied to that door Luna's after, but why Nemesis and the Scribes selected your soul to be the son of Lawrence and heir to the House of Tusk!'

Jake's throat went dry as Wilderspin let the droplet of blood fall onto the leaf.

For a tremulous moment, nothing stirred from the strange case. Peering forward, Jake could just see the drop of blood.

The leaf suddenly sucked it in. It shivered. It glowed. The light then passed through the silver case to the stone.

Jake watched on intently, part-horrified, part-fascinated as the stone grew in brightness until a halo formed above it. He gasped. A blinding light pulsed out from the space in between. It was so bright, Jake was forced to look away.

When he looked back, a head had appeared between the stone and halo—that of an old woman composed entirely of light.

It was the oracle.

Following a sharp inhale, her eyes flicked open and fixed on Jake with a terrible intensity.

Wilderspin leapt up ecstatically from his desk and planted himself between them.

'Great oracle!' he cried. 'You've tasted the blood of this mortal being. From its liquid decrypt the light. From the soil find the root. Find it and trace it back! Tell me what you see!'

The oracle closed her eyes. She took a slow, deep inhale and went into a trance. Jake's innards felt as though they had turned to ice. His head grew dizzy.

'G-h-o-s-t...' gasped the oracle. 'I see a ghost.'

'Excellent!' enthused Wilderspin. 'How far back?'

'Recent. The most recent past life.'

'What sort of ghost,' quizzed Wilderspin. 'A weak or strong one?'

'Strong. Bitter...'

'Oh, this is very exciting!' said Wilderspin to Jake. 'Tell me, oracle, what did it do?'

As the oracle intensified her enquiry, Jake struggled to remain conscious. He suffered the strange sensation of his mind and body being swum through by a knot of snakes, dispersing and regrouping as they searched for secrets.

'Difficult, difficult to see…' struggled the oracle, whose head remained between the halo and stone. 'Something at the heart. Something hidden…'

'At the heart? A broken heart? No, too common,' decided Wilderspin. 'The heart of the system, perhaps. Yes! Something secret!'

'Perhaps…' said the oracle.

Jake's mind was cast back to the chilling images he had seen of himself on passing through the woods of his nightmare.

'You see,' said Wilderspin, turning back to Jake as though he were giving a lesson, 'ghosts are quite common along a lightline, but they're usually a sign of a weakness—a life too easily traumatised by the ups and downs we all go through. Too weak, too lost, too dull to see beneath the surface of things. But sometimes, though it's very rare, the opposite is true! That is to say, an old and powerful soul is putting itself to the test. With the help of the Scribes, those mysterious beings who determine the circumstances of each soul's birth, it places itself into an especially challenging life on Earth which, if mastered, will make it yet more powerful.'

Making a great effort against the draining effect of the cords and the oracle's probing, Jake fought to stay alert. 'A strong ghost doesn't sound like a very positive thing to me,' he said.

'Oh, it is, it is! It's a sure sign of high quality light.'

'Light has different qualities?'

'Oh yes,' replied Wilderspin with the sagacity of a connoisseur. 'And this is only the start of it, because one must ask what sort of soul is testing itself in such a strong way. Usually it's a saintly type, either in a hurry to get to the Core or returning from the Core to the Surface to help out its kin, and though the quality of light in such cases is high, they're actually rather boring. But once in a while, once in an aeon or so, it's not.'

'Then what is it?' asked Jake, unnerved by Wilderspin's zeal.

'A prize worth pursuing,' replied Wilderspin and licked his lips. 'But let us proceed, for we already know your lightline is rare!' said Wilderspin 'To the druid, great oracle! Tell me its age!'

As the oracle plumbed deeper, again Jake almost passed out.

'Foggy, very foggy…' said the oracle. 'So much cloud. So much darkness…'

'Try, great oracle! You must try!' commanded Wilderspin.

The light of the oracle's face grew brighter. Jake's nausea worsened. Despite his best efforts to express no pain, an agonised groan escaped him.

'Y-e-s...' gasped the oracle. 'Y-e-s. I see the white one.'

'How old? Does it predate the last Ice Age?' pressed Wilderspin. 'For that's where the real power is,' he said to Jake.

'T-h-r-e-s-h-o-l-d...' said the oracle. 'It stands at the threshold. Not one, but four lanterns...'

Wilderspin was beside himself with excitement. 'Four! Four lantern-bearers! A powerful number of powerful beings! Sentinels! Guarding something even more powerful!'

With the little consciousness left to him, Jake's mind reached back to his journey to Nemesis's tree and the four phantoms with lanterns in the mist.

'What are they guarding? Is it a door?' continued Wilderspin.

'Y-e-s... d-o-o-r...'

'Take us through it!' demanded Wilderspin. 'What lies beyond?'

Jake felt something violently take hold of him—not from the outside. It took place inside. The snakes of light he had felt slithering through his memory tightened into a suffocating knot, dragging his consciousness into the depths of time. Nemesis's tree, Wilderspin's office, everything merged in a swirl of darkness. An abyss lay before him. Beyond it was the same door he had seen in the hall just moments before. Jake resisted. The oracle flickered. The cords tightened. With the loss of energy, Jake was hauled into the abyss.

Rather than fall, he swam. The abyss had become like a dark lake, the serpents ushering him through its murky depths.

In a warp of time the abyss was crossed. Imprisoned within the knot of snakes, Jake was ushered to the fateful door.

Wilderspin's voice echoed across the abyss. 'Take him into the keyhole!'

Again the serpents tightened about Jake. He fought against them but in his weakened state there was little he could do. He braced himself for the worst when a familiar light shot through the water and dispelled the serpents. It was the light of a lantern.

Floating between Jake and the door was the druid, his long red hair and beard lending him the appearance of an octopus. His penetrating blue eyes bore into Jake's, both threatening and yet somehow questioning as though awaiting a command.

Despite the druid having apparently come to his rescue, the same old fear rose up in Jake.

Part of Jake resisted the fear. Desperate to be rid of Wilderspin he was sorely tempted to enlist the help of the druid. But he didn't. He had no idea at what cost the help would come.

I don't want your help, said Jake in thought to the druid. *Leave me.*

The druid held up the lamp closer to Jake's face. His gaze grew harder. *Are you sure about that?* he said slowly in thought.

His words flowed through Jake like molten lava.

Jake nodded.

The druid beheld Jake for a moment longer before fading into the shadows of the water.

Wilderspin's laughter echoed from across the abyss. 'Into the keyhole!' he cried.

The serpents returned with a vengeance. They bound him so tightly that he thought he would be crushed when, with a jolt like an electric shock, something shifted. It felt as though he had dissolved, though still existed. Unsure of his form and feeling utterly helpless, the serpents swept Jake into the keyhole.

The door didn't open. Jake's awareness remained in the keyhole, looking through to what lay beyond. Wilderspin's excitement willed him onwards, but there was nowhere to go except into a cave, inside of which slept a full-grown grizzly bear.

'Wake it! Wake it up!' commanded Wilderspin.

Jake felt so weak that he was almost beyond caring. Yet so great was the sense of danger that he remained alert. He didn't have the strength, however, to resist the oracle. Instead of snakes, the force of her enquiry swept through him as an army of spiders.

I've got to act! thought Jake, as the spiders closed in on the bear. There was something about the sleeping beast that filled Jake with a dread even greater than his dread of the druid. *But what can I do?*

Jake didn't have a body. All he had was awareness and that was rapidly fading. The oracle was using him as a key to access the depths of his unconscious. All he could do, it seemed, was watch on as a witness.

The spiders swept through the bear's coat and set about its skin, biting, injecting their poison—a prickling Jake shared even though he was without a body.

His thoughts returned to his nightmare at Nemesis's tree, to the fog beyond the clearing, the four lantern-bearing ghosts and to the powerful footsteps approaching behind them.

The bear! panicked Jake as he recalled the great silhouetted man with the sun-eclipsing shadow. *It symbolises the man whose presence almost consumed me!*

Wilderspin's laughter rang out over the abyss. 'Bite harder!' he cried feverishly to the Oracle's ants. 'Wake it up! I must know who it is! Who it *really* is and the secrets is hides!'

No, you mustn't! You don't know what you're doing! warned Jake, even though he himself wasn't sure what would happen if the bear awoke, though he was certain it wouldn't be good.

'Use something bigger than ants!' commanded Wilderspin, but Jake knew that the oracle couldn't—she too was at her limits.

Jake felt a shudder.

The bear's coat had quivered—once, twice, then a third time as it stirred from its slumber. A sleepy growl escaped its mouth, followed by another quiver. Still the spiders attacked. It frowned. An eyelid twitched.

Jake gasped as one eye opened slightly, attempted to focus, then gave up as sleep hauled the bear back.

While Wilderspin barked at the oracle to try harder, Jake stopped worrying about what would happen if the bear did wake and wondered instead what would happen if it didn't. Wilderspin would probably give up and hand him over Luna even sooner. The oracle and her ants were tiring.

'Wake it up!' screamed Wilderspin with mounting desperation.

Jake was at his wits end, especially with Wilderspin. He had to do something. The one thing he felt he could do was wake the bear, hoping that waking it didn't mean accepting its power.

Jake took a deep inward breath.

You want it awake? he said through thought. *So be it.*

Jake calmed his mind and focused everything he had on the bear.

Wake up, he said calmly but firmly, sensing Wilderspin's euphoria.

The bear's eyebrows twitched. It growled sleepily. An eye threatened to open, did open and was about to close again.

The connection between them was so deep and the bear's sleep so heavy that Jake was almost swept up in it. His eyelids grew heavy.

He just caught himself before they closed, shook his awareness awake, focused on all he held dear, dug into his deepest reserves of strength and fixed on the bear with total focus.

Wake up! he roared. *Wake up!*

The bear's eyes shot open. They blazed with terrible intelligence. The bear, the man it symbolised, understood everything in a single moment yet cared for nothing—not for Jake, not for anyone. He was separate, wanting no part in creation. Jake felt it. His fury and the power behind it was so clear and resolute that he seemed more dreadful than even Luna.

The bear leapt up on all fours and released a roar to shatter mountains.

But it was more than a roar. It was a command, a spell, power itself, and cast out the intruders with the force of an erupting volcano.

In less than moment, the ants had reformed back into the horror-struck head of the oracle which shot through Jake in the keyhole, hauling his awareness back into the office.

The oracle's head shook above the silver case as though it were about to explode. Her eyes blazed with the same ferocity as the bear's.

Wilderspin stood electrified by the desk. What hair he had was standing on end. 'Back into the cave!' he commanded the oracle. 'I *must* know what the bear's hiding!'

The oracle didn't hear. Her head of light blazed brighter, shaking violently.

'Oracle! I command you!'

Whatever had infected the oracle had also taken hold of Jake. In his case, it took the form of rage. It tore through him like a tsunami rising up through his legs. The room darkened. It shook. But Wilderspin was in too much of a frenzy to pay it attention.

As he barked his orders yet again, the rage erupted from Jake with the same force as it had from the bear.

'Enough!' he thundered.

The thick granite cracked with shock. Wind whistled in.

For the oracle, the surge of power was the final straw. Following a moment's stillness, she widened her eyes and exploded like a bomb.

With a flash of red, Jake thought his moment had come.

Remarkably, he was merely blown over backwards in the chair.

The cracked wall, however, was blasted out to sea while Wilderspin was hurled the entire length of the office, crashing into the granite. In a display of astounding resilience he bounced back almost immediately, just in time to see what appeared to be a guardian rush in to unfasten the light cords which bound Jake to the chair.

A dazed Jake recognised the face concealed within a hooded cloak.

Frost!

Freed from one of the cords, his senses came flooding back. So also came great relief—his friend had returned. Not only was there a chance of escape, without Wilderspin wiping his memory of Luna's plans, but Frost had passed Jake's test. If he was trixy then surely he wouldn't have returned.

For one so portly, Wilderspin moved with astonishing speed. A glowing dagger clasped in his hand, he sprang off the desk and leapt for Frost's back.

'Watch out!' cried Jake to Frost who was busy untying the second cord.

He tried to drag Frost aside, confused that he did nothing to protect himself.

Frost was smiling, a knowing glint in his eyes.

The air whined.

Wilderspin howled in pain.

He glanced off Frost and rolled out of the office, the door opening at his approach. The dagger lay on the ground. It had been shot from his clasp by an arrow.

Finally free of both cords, Jake and Frost spun around at the same time to discover the identity of the archer, only to find a mysterious portal in the wall—fuzzy as though the granite had been turned to dust.

'The girl? The assassin?' muttered Jake, delighted, confused, concerned. 'But how?'

A company of guardians burst into the room

The appearance of the girl as she leapt through the portal was like a dream. Jake was spellbound. Before her feet had touched the ground she released two arrows, each striking the guardians square in the heart. They exploded in a blaze of blue light which, though not strong enough to knock the others over, had an affect just as lethal—the light released was pure inner-force.

The result was immediate. While the girl's fighting grew more aggressive, the effect on Jake, who was already suffering from an overdose, was quite the opposite. The additional dose swept his spirit into passion.

Oblivious to the danger, Jake stood in a heated stupor, marvelling at the girl, not paying the slightest attention to the osprey that burst through the portal, expanded to giant size and knocked back the guardian reinforcements with its mighty wings.

'No time for that, my friend!' said Frost who, with a mere touch of his hand, restored Jake's balance.

'More guardians are coming!' cried the osprey. 'We must escape!'

The girl glanced back at the wall but the portal had closed.

Jake noted the peculiar glove on her bow-holding hand. She was about to touch the wall with it, though appeared to have second thoughts.

'This way!' barked Frost who dashed to the large hole in the wall caused by the exploding oracle. Far below, through moonlit wisps of mist, the ocean crashed up against the craggy cliff.

It was only then that Jake noticed a familiar looking carpet on the floor, which hadn't been there when he entered the office.

'Rufus!' he cried, realising as he said so that the flash of red just moments before had been Rufus protecting him from the exploding oracle. *How did he know I was here?*

'Hurry!' cried the osprey. The girl was already on its back, releasing arrows at new arrivals in the doorway.

Rufus merely groaned.

'Follow me!' cried Frost. He winked at the girl, whose own expression revealed nothing but contempt, and dived dashingly from the tower.

'Frost!' shouted Jake and was about to race to the edge, but Wilderspin reappeared with yet more guardians and a cloud of pigeons.

'Grab them!' he barked.

With nothing else at hand, Jake grabbed an apple from a spilled bowl of fruit and hurled it with all his might at the spymaster. A fine throw, it struck Wilderspin in the left eye.

'My eye! My eye!' he shrieked and ran off again.

'Good shot,' groaned Rufus, partially revived.

'Can you fly?' asked Jake as he beat back the vicious pigeons.

'I cannae. The blast, the forces, I cannae harness them.'

'Come on!' ordered the girl, dismissing another guardian. 'Just dive!'

Another company of guardians swept into the office.

'Time to go,' said Rani.

With a mischievous wave, she and Bin followed Frost.

Jake was about to follow when, with a great fluttering and warbling, the hole was filled by a mass of pigeons.

The guardians were about to attack, but were forced aside by towering figure of someone else—Lord Boreas.

'Nice of you to pop in,' he said, an amused light in his eyes.

'And now I'm popping off,' said Jake.

With Rufus rolled up under his arm, he dashed for the wall of pigeons and threw himself into them with all his strength. It was the strangest sensation. The wall of pigeons was so dense that having dived into it he almost stopped until an explosion of blue light sent from the guardians loosened them up.

Jake cursed as he slipped through the cloud of pigeons.

He gathered momentum. The flashes of blue grew more violent. It felt as though he were falling through a thunder cloud.

'Rufus!' cried Jake through a mouthful of feathers. 'Come on! Now's the time to show me how brave and powerful you are!'

'I just did that,' groaned Rufus.

The cloud of pigeons came to an end. The sight that greeted Jake—the distant rocks, the seething sea—left only one thing to do. Curse. And so Jake did, loudly.

They plunged through an explosion of blue flak. Guardians mounted on winged silver lions were diving after them.

'Guardians!' shouted Jake as they shot past the girl on the osprey.

Four arrows later the guardians were gone.

'What an idiot I look!' cried Jake, realising how absurd he must have appeared plummeting past the girl with a carpet under his arm.

'I've been tryin' to tell yer that since the first day I met yer,' said Rufus.

'Bugger! The rocks!' cried Jake. 'We're going to hit them!'

'Aha!' cried Rufus. 'The forces! They're comin' back to me!'

'About bloody time!'

'Ach, I was only messin' around back there. It would take more than an exploding oracle to knock me out.'

'Rufus, you fff—fly!'

Just moments from crashing into the crags, Rufus shot out from under Jake's arm and swept him up.

Relief and anger coursed through Jake as they broke out of the dive and skimmed over the surface of the choppy sea.

'What do you mean you were messing around?'

'Let that be a lesson to yer for going against my advice. You're a bloody fool for entering Renlock on your own, although I find it a wee bit difficult to believe you were.'

Frost! panicked Jake, grateful Rufus hadn't noticed him in the office. *Where is he?*

He scoured the rocks and the sea, suddenly not so sure if it was wise to tell Rufus of his secret friend.

He's a pixy. He'll be fine, Jake reassured himself, feeling a pang of guilt.

'Lost somethin'?' asked Rufus.

'No,' said Jake and looked back at the tower the very moment more guardians flew out on winged lions—too many to fight off. 'We've got company.'

'We certainly have,' said Rufus in a cheeky tone.

Jake looked to his left to see the girl on the osprey flying level with them, though too far off to talk. He gave a wave.

To his delight, she waved back though there was something menacing in her expression. The strange glove she wore sparkled. In a flash of light she and the osprey vanished.

'Where did they go?' gasped Jake.

'Get used to it, laddie.'

Jake glanced back at the company of guardians closing in.

'More in front,' said Rufus.

Jake turned back to see another company on winged lions closing in just as fast. Only seconds remained to collision.

'Time to head for the skies,' said Rufus, 'and find a way back to Himassissi.'

'No!' said Jake as a burst of blue flak exploded about them. 'Stay at sea level.'

'Are yer mad? Have yer nae had enough excitement for one day?'

'Not quite,' he said with a secret smile.

The explosions of inner-force grew more intense, only narrowly missing them.

'Are you sure about this?' cried Rufus.

Less than a hundred metres separated them from the guardians racing in from the front. They drew their swords.

Jake closed his eyes for a moment. 'Yes, I'm sure,' he said confidently.

Blades arched back, the company was so close that Jake could see their sapphire-like eyes burning with wrath. One sped forward directly for Jake. He swung his blade. Jake didn't flinch.

The stroke went uncompleted. Something burst through the surface of the sea and cast the guardians aside.

It was Deuteronomy the whale, answering Jake's call.

'You bloody beauty!' cried Rufus.

In the fateful moment before being swallowed whole and plunging for the ocean trenches, Jake glanced back. Not at the guardians. Guided by a strange feeling he looked back at the cliff of Renlock. Someone was on one of the landings. Despite the distance it was impossible to miss. It was the aura Jake saw more than a body—the same shade of green as the owner's eyes.

It was Luna.

The full weight of her attention bore down on him, though far from her anger, he felt something even worse—her joy.

Anon, Lord Tusk, she said in his mind. *Anon.*

CHAPTER 43
ASCLEPIUS'S HUNT

AFTER ALL THAT HAD HAPPENED, AS SOON AS JAKE SAT DOWN inside Deuteronomy's stomach he fell into a deep sleep and didn't stir until they arrived back at the fort's lake.

Having thanked the great whale, he and Rufus stood on the shore in the stillness of dusk.

'Do you mind if we walk back to the fort?' asked Jake. 'I've had enough flying for one day.'

'You walk, I'll fly,' said Rufus and off they set.

'No offence, of course. And thank you, Rufus. Thank you for saving me from the exploding oracle.'

'Ach, think nothing of it, laddie.'

'I shall think everything of it,' said Jake as they skirted past resting elephants. 'How did you know I was there, by the way?'

'I didnae. As *promised*, I was doin' some sniffin' around for yer. However, I suspect yer found out more than I, for I'd only just arrived when I spotted yer.'

'From the quartz staircase?' asked Jake.

'Aye. And yer might wanna tell me how yer managed to find it.'

Jake found himself caught in a conflict. Despite his earlier decision to confide in Rufus, his intuition told him to not yet mention Frost—that the pixy's influence would make sense in time, but to mention him now would create confusion and jeopardise something subtle. It grated terribly, however, with his sense of honesty.

'Deuteronomy showed me,' began Jake, playing for time.

'And...'

I must tell him, decided Jake, battling with his conscience. *I must trust Rufus. He saved me.*

'And there's something else,' started Jake, but just like the times he had tried to tell Braysheath, he was interrupted. A nearby elephant trumpeted so loudly that Jake jumped.

To be sure it wasn't a coincidence, Jake tried again. This time a lion's roar cut him short. Both interruptions had burst so suddenly from the stillness that, with great relief, Jake took it as a sign.

'Aye, what else?' pressed Rufus.

'A zorlop,' improvised Jake, staying with the truth, albeit a selective version. 'It was a zorlop which took me to Deuteronomy.'

'Right,' said Rufus in a dubious tone. 'And I assume yer were caught the moment you strayed off the rose quartz path.'

'No, actually. I was caught in Wilderspin's office. I was spying on a secret meeting held by Luna where Lord Boreas entered a strange mansion to make contact with the sylph and Granddad,' said Jake, hoping so much juicy information would skip over any mention of Frost.

Rufus stopped. 'Did you say *sylph*?'

'It's how Luna's blocking the holygate. Along with Granddad.'

'Tell me everythin',' said Rufus in a grave tone. 'Everythin'.'

NIGHT HAD FALLEN BY THE TIME THEY REACHED THE GREAT courtyard of the fort. Jake had recounted all he could remember, including the part about the druid whose power Rufus had already witnessed during the break-in.

'So you see,' said Jake, keeping his voice down, 'there's no doubt that Granddad's suspicions of Asclepius were right. He's up to something with Boreas. They're planning to topple Luna using the fort.'

'Oh, just like that, hey?'

'No, not just like that. The pirate represents a terrible demon, perhaps one of Boreas's,' explained Jake and thought of the white wolf leaking light, symbolic of the god's fractured soul. 'They plan to use it to take control of the fort and then use its power against Luna.'

'Listen pal,' said Rufus, 'if there is an insider in the fort, the one person it's not, is Asclepius.'

'Then what's he up to in that secret laboratory of his in the top of one of the towers?'

'That's not a secret laboratory! He's a healer. It's where he does his experiments.'

Jake was unconvinced.

'Look, you've had a long day,' said Rufus. 'Get some rest. Besides, that's a lot of intel you gathered in Renlock and none of it's simple. It needs some thought. And we must share it with Braysheath as soon as he's back. It's too risky to send by message.'

Jake nodded.

'And fella,' said Rufus before leaving. 'Well done. I cannae condone your recklessness, you risked too much. But now that you're safe, very well done.'

Jake beamed.

'By the way, who was that lassie?'

'I don't know her name, but she's the one I saw in the bushes while having a bath. She sneaked into the fort to spy on me,' said Jake matter-of-factly.

'Oh aye?' said Rufus. 'Keep dreamin', pal.'

With that, Rufus flew off.

Alone on the lawn, Jake smiled. *They saved me*, he thought, thinking of Frost and the girl, wishing he knew her name. *But why did she save us, when Frost claimed she was an assassin?*

Jake recalled her playful wave and his heart skipped a beat. He also dwelt on her fierceness, which he found equally attractive. She had about her a wild grace he had never seen in a girl before. It captivated Jake entirely and in a way that felt free. She couldn't be owned, nor would he want to own her, for it was her wildness and freedom that made her so beautiful.

He was heading for bed when his thoughts returned to Asclepius. Despite Jake's physical tiredness, his mind wouldn't let go of the matter.

I wonder if he's in his laboratory now. After everything Boreas just went through, there's a good chance.

Jake looked at the fireplace, recalling the secret passages Frost had led him through to reach the lab. *I'm sure I can remember the way.*

Realising he wouldn't be able to rest until he paid the laboratory a visit, Jake made for the fireplace, sat on the bench, pulled the lever and disappeared.

JAKE HAD SERIOUSLY UNDERESTIMATED THE MANY TWISTS AND turns in the passageways. As he wandered along feeling lost, he thought of Frost and the turgid sea raging about Renlock and suffered another pang of guilt.

How will he get back? I should have whispered to Deuteronomy to return and search for him.

He imagined Frost bound up in cords he couldn't escape from and wondered what dreadful things the guardians would do if they caught a pixy.

Tired of such wild imaginings, Jake stopped for a moment. *I must trust my intuition*, he thought and closed his eyes. He recalled how Frost had not only evaded Wilderspin, but while saving Jake he had sensed the presence of the warrior girl, knowing that she would save them. *His perceptions are incredible. He'll be fine.* And Jake really felt it. Any heroics on his part to go searching for Frost would only create complications. In fact, he could almost feel Frost urging him on towards Asclepius's lab.

Feeling better, Jake continued his journey and soon stumbled upon a junction in the passageways he thought he recognised. There was a narrow stairwell off to the right. *Yes, this is it!*

He crept as quietly as possible up the stairs until he finally reached the recess which led to the cupboard. Jake put an ear to the door. At first he heard nothing. As his breathing calmed, he heard mutterings on the other side.

He's there! But what's he saying?

Jake gently turned the latch of the door and eased it open.

After an inch or so it creaked. Jake froze. He listened for any reaction from Asclepius. There was only silence.

To Jake's great relief, a moment later the mutterings continued.

Jake eased the door open a little wider and peered through the gap.

His next challenge was not to gasp. Sinister or not, what he saw was mind-blowing.

The cross of benches about the oak and the chaos of apparatus were just as they had been on Jake's earlier visit. The context of the room, however, had completely changed. It was as though the entire cosmos was somehow contained within the high-domed ceiling. Asclepius stood beneath it, shifting planets, even galaxies, with the simple wave of a hand. He appeared to Jake like a great magician searching for something in the heavens.

The white wolf was resting within the oak tree and still leaking light—it streamed out like a Milky Way and merged with the stardust above. Despite it, the wolf was sitting upright, looking up in a state of wonder.

The wolf looks stronger, thought Jake. *If Frost is right about it representing a demon, perhaps Asclepius's treatment is starting to work. Or it senses what Boreas achieved in the mad mansion—that the sylph might allow him to enter the holygate, perhaps even help him.*

The other thing which caught Jake's attention were the amber-coloured eyes of the turtle. They glowed like jewels.

Frost's idea makes sense, thought Jake, *but could there be another explanation?*

He wracked his brain for an alternative, but the events so far were so intricate that Frost's explanation was the only one which fitted.

'Must find a way in,' muttered Asclepius, a hint of desperation in his voice. 'But mustn't be seen. Especially not by Luna. Especially not by Braysheath.'

Frost was right! He is searching for a way to get a demon into the fort!

Jake looked up. His eyes shot wide. Faces faded in and out of stardust amid the planets, which caused Asclepius to shift hurriedly to other parts of the universe. They struck Jake as powerful-looking faces belonging to those who could perceive what Asclepius was doing.

'There's little time,' continued Asclepius. 'A demon, the deepest, the darkest, a destroyer. The pirate will find it.'

I wish Rufus was here to witness this! lamented Jake.

He then spotted something which almost caused him to bang his head against the cupboard in shock. Specks of light, like stardust, had started to flow from his own body. They flowed out through the cupboard and joined the cosmos in the lab.

Jake ducked back into the stairwell and patted his body, trying to find where it was coming from. But it wasn't coming from a hole or a wound like the wolf's leak. It came from every part of him. He thought of the birds and ants and all the other creatures he had seen before and what Frost had said of real science.

Maybe by observing I'm contributing to the experiment.

The sensible thing was to close the cupboard and return to his room, but he couldn't. He was driven by a force deep within him that had to know what Asclepius was up to.

He peeped his head back in. Fortunately Asclepius was so absorbed in what he was doing that he didn't seem to have noticed the subtle input from Jake. It was then Jake noticed a similar flow from Asclepius, though in his case it came from the area of his navel.

As Jake watched on, he shook his head in wonder at all he had witnessed in just one evening—the complex insight into Frost and the girl through the net of light, the insight into Lord Boreas, Rowena and himself through Wilderspin's mad mansion, the chilling confirmation of his own dark past through the oracle, and now this, the confirmation of his granddad's suspicion that Asclepius was indeed betraying the House of Tusk.

Suddenly Jake jumped. Asclepius too. A new galaxy burst through a black hole, swiftly followed by one after the other in a catastrophic-feeling chain reaction.

Asclepius stepped back in shock.

The strange expansion was heading directly for Jake. Still he couldn't tear himself away. Something else burst forth—a face, one Jake had seen just hours before in Wilderspin's strange invention.

It was the pirate. His eyes shone with a sinister delight and his face expanded to the exclusion of all else. He reached out a hand intending to grasp Jake.

Asclepius's head turned towards him.

Horrified, Jake ducked inside the cupboard. In the rush, the door slammed shut. He cursed.

Jake leapt up, conflicted. Part of him wanted to confront Asclepius, yet his wiser side advised patience. Now was not the time.

He sensed Asclepius approaching the cupboard.

Reluctantly, Jake fled down the stairwell and bolted along the passageways, chiding himself as he went—it had been the contribution of his light which had aided Asclepius in his search for the demon.

When Jake reached Frost's deserted lair, he leapt onto the bench, ready to pull the lever. Before he did, he strained his hearing for any sound of Asclepius's pursuit.

Other than his own heartbeat thumping about his temples, he heard nothing.

Jake sighed with relief, pulled the lever and tumbled into his room.

As he lay on his bed, despite his physical fatigue his mind was in even more of a whirl than before. He closed his eyes and let the vivid images of the day race before his mind's eye. One stood out. It was neither the pirate nor Asclepius. Nor was it the image of the girl. He wished that it was. It was the image of the door with the lantern above it accompanied by the voice of Luna. A chill ran through him. Her words were not a memory. They were real time.

Rest, Lord Tusk, she said and Jake immediately felt sleepy. *Conserve your energy. You and I have a door to open.*

Despite his alarm at hearing her voice, Jake released a giant yawn. An instant later he was fast asleep.

CHAPTER 44
DEVIL IN THE DETAIL

FOLLOWING HIS ENCOUNTER WITH THE SYLPH, AT THE FIRST opportunity to get away, Lawrence flew off on his winged horse with Geoffrey concealed in his cloak. Some distance along the headland of Renlock, away from the pigeons, they found a cave.

'Perfect,' said Lawrence as they landed.

The cave was within the headland, halfway up the sheer cliff and commanded an excellent view of the sea and sky.

While Geoffrey checked out the cave, Lawrence sent the horse back up into the clouds to keep watch.

'Are we alone?' he asked.

'Just a few spiders and some lizard friends,' said Geoffrey. 'It's safe.'

Lawrence closed his eyes and drew a deep breath of sea air. 'At last,' he sighed.

He ventured a little way into the cave and found a sheltered spot away from the gusts. Taking a seat he withdrew a flask and, having poured a little tea on the rock for Geoffrey, he poured a cup for himself. As he took a sip, a smile spread across his face.

'So, the young Lord Tusk found his way into Renlock. Impressive,' he said as fatherly pride warmed his heart.

'He had help,' said Geoffrey. 'The quartz stairwell is unknown to the pigeons, but not to the lizards who saw what happened.'

'You mean that good-for-nothing carpet?'

'No. He came later. He has, let us say, an *interesting friend*.'

'Oh?'

'What I would call a *wildcard*—the mythical trickster.'

'We already have a wildcard. The sylph!' said Lawrence. 'Not to mention Luna.'

'This one could be just as wild. Who knows, perhaps wilder.'

'But not as powerful as the sylph, surely?'

Geoffrey gazed out to sea. 'This one's power is more subtle because of what he is and what he's becoming. Among his kind he's something of an anomaly, though none of them realise it yet. His own awareness of the fact is only just emerging.'

'How do you mean?'

'He's a trixy.'

'What?' exclaimed Lawrence. 'You're joking?'

'That's not all. He's Count Frost's son,' said Geoffrey, referring to the chief of the clan corrupted by Luna.

Lawrence cursed in astonishment. 'Why is he an anomaly? What's he becoming?'

'He's developing a conscience.'

'A trixy with a conscience?' laughed Lawrence. 'They have their nature and that's it!'

'This one is different. Of course his trixy nature is extremely strong, perhaps even stronger than his father's, but that's the test —the fine thread on which destiny hangs. Regardless of that, perhaps because of it, he has all the makings of a great hero. He's the fastest, most skilful and brightest in his tribe. And being close to the key players on both sides, namely his father and your son, he has more practical knowledge than anyone else. But his key strength lies in his quick wits, his charm and his keen sense of timing. When great powers come to a head, it's his sleight of hand that'll make the difference—a whisper here, a decoy there. He has the power to outfox fates. He'll either make all the difference in the world, or destroy everything.'

Lawrence was both disturbed and excited by what Geoffrey had said. 'I suppose it all comes down to whether his conscience can develop at a quicker pace than the already lightning speed at which events are unfolding.'

'Precisely. The key is his growing friendship with Jake. It's no coincidence that each of them has been born to a great legacy, one to rule an underworld, the other to rule the Surface, for Count Frost, despite his understated title, rules it like a hidden king.'

'They each have something to teach the other,' mused Lawrence. 'Jake will teach the trixy heir what it means to be noble. The trixy will help Jake outfox the great challenges ahead of him—navigating his darkness and especially Luna's.'

Lawrence's mind was cast back to the hallway in the mad mansion. Though he had intuitively felt the last hallway was

Jake's, it had come as a shock, not least the abyss which had opened up and the appearance of a powerful druid.

'Assuming, that is, their friendship holds,' added Geoffrey.

Lawrence cocked his head questioningly until he recalled the young warrior on the giant osprey. He had glimpsed her just before she flew from Wilderspin's office, but a glimpse had been enough.

'I see,' he sighed. 'They'll both fall for her and perhaps she for them. A love triangle. The cause of many wars.'

'Perhaps a love triumvirate, something with enough power to conquer Luna, though the odds are against it,' said Geoffrey. 'Either way, the fate of the cosmos is in their hands—a trixy dark prince, the daughter of a Yakreth chief and a young lord, the depth of whose history can only be guessed at, but from what we've seen so far...'

Lawrence recalled how the arrow fired at him during the theft of the gates had been dissolved—something he now realised had been the druid's power, a conscious ghost from Jake's past. The druid must have known Lawrence's true identity during the break-in and so protected him. It was an incredible revelation. *It must be confusing the hell out of poor old Jake*, he thought.

Lawrence took another sip of tea. 'At least there's one advantage of Jake being friends with this trixy,' he said. 'If Jake can get into Renlock, there's hope he can get into the holygate, without which our plan comes to nothing.'

'Your concern is how *you* get in,' said Geoffrey. 'Your son will make it into the holygate because a sufficient amount of the cosmos's awareness, in particular the sylph's, already knows of his intention to save Nestor. Thus, it will conspire to make it possible. The sylph will find such heroics irresistible while Luna couldn't have asked for more. She wants his light. What better place to take it than inside a holygate?'

'After my exploits in Wilderspin's mad mansion, the sylph will also know of my intentions in the holygate,' said Lawrence. 'Will not such a sacrifice be even more heroic?'

'If you fail to integrate your demon, allowing yourself to be overwhelmed by its rage, then your plan to reverse the long history of father-son betrayal will backfire. You will become your own tyrant, perhaps even worse than Lord Boreas himself. And yes, foreseeing this, the sylph may permit you entry to the gate all the same and delight in the chaos that follows.'

'I won't let that happen,' said Lawrence resolutely. 'Whatever it takes, I shall sacrifice what's left of my life-force to my son while in the gate and with full awareness of my actions, with full awareness of my intention—to break the bonds of custom, of control, and sever the legacy of ignorance and fear. I shall then offer my soul to the sylph. It may use it as a vehicle in whichever way it wishes.'

'Very noble,' said Geoffrey, 'but will your son be fully aware of *his* actions? Because if he slays you thinking you're the real Lord Boreas and so slays in anger, unaware of the symbolism, then nothing changes. Any chance of igniting a flicker of hope in the bitter heart of the sylph will be wasted.'

'Then we must ensure Asclepius makes him aware at the right moment.'

'No,' said Geoffrey. 'The sylph sees all. To convince it that humans are a worthwhile enterprise the heroics must be total. Your son, the people's champion, must work it out himself. I have a feeling the sylph will permit him entry into the gate only if he has already seen through your disguise, realised what he must do and do it out of mercy. If he tries to enter with a vengeful mind, the gate will destroy him and probably the entirety of his lightline.'

'How can you be so sure of the sylph's mind?'

'It's easy. Think of the longest odds, the all-but-impossible, and that's what it wants. It's not interested in the probable.'

Lawrence looked out to sea. 'The odds,' he sighed. 'So many variables...'

'That's why it will permit you entry only if you've already opened that steel door you saw in the mansion and freed what lurks behind it.'

The image of the vault-like door filled Lawrence's mind. He closed his eyes and shifted his focus to the serene woman meditating on the mountain. *Ah, Rowena, my love.*

Geoffrey shot him a sharp glance. 'Don't indulge. It weakens you.'

'It feels like strength to me.'

'To your outer-self, but it's the inner-part you must identify with,' chided Geoffrey.

The two of them fell into silence.

Lawrence smiled at the memory of Jake's leap from the tower. *He's becoming a man*, he thought. *Oh, how I wish I'd spent more time with him.* Again he dwelt on the druid and its incredible display of power, casting back even Luna.

'Jake's lightline...' he started.

'Is a lot older and a lot darker than yours,' said Geoffrey. 'Perhaps history's darkest.'

Lawrence recalled what Geoffrey had said following the display of power during the break-in of the fort, that the Scribes had placed Jake as heir to the House of Tusk in history's darkest hour. A great leap was required to restore universal balance. Though ultimately all humans had to make the leap, the first would be made by a soul whose lightline was immensely dark. It was symbolic of the almost impossible made probable—a heroic transformation, a heroic example for others to follow.

'History's darkest?' muttered Lawrence, struggling to believe such an idea.

'Yes. One who stood at the threshold of pre-history's power, the true power of united hearts, and history's false idea of individual power and thus destruction. One who must have consciously done something of such importance that his light has the power to communicate with beings like the sylph and Luna. And for that to be possible there must be common ground, perhaps even a common cause, though coming from different angles,' pondered Geoffrey. 'As I said before, Nemesis and the Scribes who decide such things have taken a big gamble.'

'Jake's lightline has common ground with Luna?'

'There's alchemical wisdom in both Jake's bloodline and his lightline, especially the latter. I suspect that during the retreat of the last Ice Age, in the hinterland between pre-history and history, he was experimenting with something. It's not unheard of for alchemists to meddle with something as grand as evolution itself—to redirect it, to collapse all energy and start again, to seek hidden doors that allow such things, daring to believe themselves creator-destroyers rather than simply co-creators.'

Lawrence slowly shook his head in disbelief. 'So the druid is not the full story of Jake's lightline.'

'Something in between the two extremes of who Jake has been and who he is now. A messenger of sorts.'

'What do you think the druid and the sylph discussed? I couldn't hear a word from across the abyss.'

Geoffrey took a slurp of tea and looked out to sea.

'I wish I knew.'

WHILE LAWRENCE AND GEOFFREY DISCUSSED HEAVY MATTERS IN the cave, the pirate was wandering through a charming garden, singing to himself.

'Oh dreams, dreams, wonderful dreams, what wonderful plans we have. But without a little house-cleaning, oh how they come to nothing…'

The garden path wound into a wood. A little way in he stopped. He looked down at a fallen tree trunk and beamed with delight.

'Lift a stone and thou shalt find me,' he said drawing his cutlass. 'Cleave the wood and I am there.'

He had found Lawrence's hiding place. With a powerful blow he cleaved the tree trunk in two.

Feeling the weight of his task, Lawrence got up and walked to the cave mouth for a breath of sea air.

'Faith. You must have faith, based on the miracles in life that you've already experienced,' said Geoffrey. 'Despite the odds, this is your most powerful weapon. Faith and courage.'

Lawrence turned to face Geoffrey. He was about to the say something when he felt a sudden blow between his shoulders and collapsed in a heap.

CHAPTER 45
FROST MANOR

Frost was back in Harkenmere, both his and Jake's hometown. Following his dive from Wilderspin's office, he had bobbed in the sea, watching to ensure Jake managed to escape. Once he had, Frost had snuck back into Renlock and used its gates to return to the Surface.

With Silver perched on his shoulder, he was walking across the snow-covered fields of the Frost family estate. He preferred the fields to the grand drive, especially at dawn. Oak-peppered, rolling and full of crows, they were wonderfully irregular. There were the woods too. Untouched for millennia, for that's how long the Frosts had been there, the trees were so vast that they looked as though they had come from another world. But then, the Frost's estate was like another world, or rather, an old world. It was a vast place, a sanctuary even, where wolves and boars still roamed, along with other species long since extinct in the hostile world beyond the perimeter wall.

There was a spring in Frost's stride and a broad smile upon his face.

'Exciting times, Silver!' he cried.

Silver released a joyful caw.

'There's so much to look forward to that it's hard to contain myself! Though contain myself I must. Father will of course know where I've been, but there are certain things which, for now at least, must remain secret.'

Silver gurgled in agreement.

'Jake's dad for example and his heroic struggle against Lord Boreas. It's incredible. Not even Luna knows! She soon will, however, as she grows stronger and Jake's dad weakens. And all the while the *real* Lord Boreas craftily waits in the shadows for the perfect moment to strike and reclaim his place in this reality. But can Jake's dad last long enough? Will Jake work it out in time? And not just about his dad, but what his dad intends to do in the gate, for dear Jake has got the wrong end of the stick. I wonder how?' said Frost with a twinkle in his eyes.

'We've done well there, Silver, for he mustn't work it out too soon—before he enters the gate, yes, but no more than a day or so before, otherwise other variables will interfere, especially doubt. The heroics must come hard and fast with powerful resolution. As always, spontaneity is key!'

Silver cawed loudly.

'It's true, Silver. He must work it out himself. It's critical,' agreed Frost, echoing what Geoffrey had said to Lawrence.

Frost revelled in his self-appointed role to ensure that the timing of Jake's realisation was perfect—throwing him off the scent when he advanced too quickly and giving helpful hints when he lagged behind.

They crested a hill. Spread before them was less a manor than a palace—an immense gothic mansion with gardens to match which, despite it being winter, were as exquisite and shameless as in the heyday of the British empire, for the Frost's fortunes never dwindled. Come depression, come war, come whatever, they only grew.

As for Frost, he didn't much like it. He preferred his treehouse in the woods. The mansion was kept more for show, to impress impressionable humans, those with whom Count Frost, his father, had dealings.

As Frost and Silver gazed upon the familiar view, a herd of deer wandered past them, unperturbed by Frost's presence. He waited until they were a distance off before continuing their conversation.

'Neither shall I divulge to Father all we know of Jake. It could create unnecessary complications. He'll discover the truth soon enough, but for now we don't want any additional orders. We must remain footloose and fancy free.'

Frost surveyed the distant mountains. 'Ah, but Silver, has not Jake exceeded our wildest expectations?'

Silver gurgled.

'It was obvious that the new Lord Tusk would have a strong and interesting lightline, but this talk of writing fate at the threshold of an Ice Age and me his crown of thorns—what a prize! Though prize doesn't quite seem the right word.'

For a moment Frost was lost in thought. His eyes took on a distant light. 'I see many things ahead, Silver, too many things to be clear. And this Rani—I have a feeling she's going to complicate matters brilliantly.'

Silver released a strained-sounding gurgle.

'But enough, Silver!' cried Frost, snapping back. 'Fly off, dear comrade, and speak with friends while I speak with Father!'

As Silver took flight with a caw, Frost spotted a second stag walking towards them. He looked at it in a certain way, communicating in thought. Though wild, the stag allowed him to approach it and leap upon its back.

'To the manor, my friend!' he cried. 'To the manor!'

The stag leapt forward and sped down the hill towards the mansion, kicking up snow as it went.

As Frost galloped impressively across the lawn, workers in the garden and about the house bowed their heads. They were all trixies of the same tribe, for no outsiders lived on the estate. Regardless, there were ranks based on merit and everyone knew their place. The bows were sincere.

As Frost approached the mansion's entrance, he leapt down from the stag.

'Thank you!' he cried as it sped off.

A butler appeared at the top of the steps

'Welcome home, Master Byzin,' said the butler, referring to Frost by his first name.

'Morning, Petherwin!' said Frost. 'How goes it?'

'It goes, Master Byzin. It goes.'

'Father in his cave?'

'If you're referring to his office, yes, he is.'

'Splendid!' said Frost, bounding up the steps.

Count Frost's office was more like an Eastern durbar—a large hall where he held court. Since the mansion was located on a bluff, it commanded a glorious view of Harkenmere lake and the surrounding mountains. The hall inside was virtually bare. There were no paintings or objects of curiosity to distract attention, not that anyone would dare look away from the Count whose presence was like a magnet. There was simply a large old desk on a Persian carpet and a fire burning in an impressive fireplace. Sprawled upon it, just as Frost had bragged to Jake, was a real leopard while perched with dignity on the corner of the desk, its eyes wide and alert, was an eagle owl.

Finally there was the Count himself. Though seated at his desk, he was clearly a tall man, his deceptive strength well concealed in lengthy limbs. Immaculately turned out in tweed and tie, his dark hair oiled back, he looked the part. His eyes, however, told a different tale. They were hazel like his son's, though while Frost's sparked with mischief, his father's glimmered with raw power. It was not false power which hid behind guns, hired thugs and every other protection that money could buy, but real power—wild, intelligent and self-sufficient, a power that gave him an ancient air.

He was talking with two of his lieutenants when Frost bounded in.

'Hello Father!' he interrupted.

The Count looked unimpressed.

'Have you missed me?' added Frost. 'Does your love for your son still flow like a mighty river, pure and full of bounty?'

With an imperious wave, the Count dismissed the two trixies who, with subtle smiles, bowed to Frost as they left.

'You test my patience, Byzin,' said the Count in a refined and unhurried voice which resonated with the same power as his eyes.

'And you pass the test with flying colours, Father!' said Frost as he wandered about the great room as though he owned it. 'Which is excellent, for as you've oft told me, patience is paramount.'

The Count's expression gave little away as he regarded Frost —his only offspring, for the tribe managed their number with care, the chief included.

Most would have shrunk beneath such an intense appraisal from the Count, but Frost simply stood looking jubilant.

'So,' said the Count at last, 'what do you have to tell me?'

'What can I say to one who knows all, oh great Father and ruler of all that glitters,' said Frost and stooped in a deep bow which verged on mockery.

Finally, the corners of the Count's lips curled into a smile, though it lacked warmth.

'And what, dear Father, have you to tell me?' said Frost, turning the tables, 'for am I not heir to your mighty empire?'

'I tell you most things,' said the Count. 'To what are you referring?'

'To the things you don't tell me, dear Father! Luna for starters,' said Frost and caused the Count to raise an eyebrow. 'You know who she is, don't you? Who she *really* is?'

Initially the Count said nothing. His already intense gaze bore into his son. 'You've been spying on her?' he said in a tone which, though calm, caused the owl to take flight and the leopard to sit up and whine.

'Our paths happened to cross,' said Frost unabashed.

'In Renlock,' fathomed the Count, his tone turning icier.

'Indeed, Father,' said Frost as though it were nothing. 'Of course, no one saw me. But the point is that she seeks a special door—one which she believes is an exit from the cosmos.'

At the mention of this the Count's eyes widened slightly.

'And so,' continued Frost, 'one must ask *who* exactly would seek such a thing? And one must also answer and so I shall...'

The Count raised a finger.

Though Frost stopped talking, his expression remained bright.

'I've read your thoughts,' said the Count.

His failure to say anything else was all the confirmation Frost needed.

'That slippery toad Wilderspin is already making plans,' said Frost. 'But what about our tribe? What becomes of us?'

The Count exhaled heavily. 'These matters are work in progress, Byzin. The Bank and all it represents will transform and manifest into something else. These things I will share in due course, but not now.'

'Ah, The Bank!' said Frost. 'The new temple, the new god! And yet, it would seem its demise will accompany Brock's.'

The Count smiled wryly. 'Brock as Overlord was doomed from the outset. His imminent fall is *because* of The Bank...'

'And its sponsor,' interjected Frost, referring to Luna.

'Modern humans believe in what they can see and count,' continued the Count. 'The Bank will change in name. Its appearance will also change but the force behind it will remain the same. Have patience.'

'Of course, Father. But while patience is one thing, timing is everything, is it not?'

'You're suggesting there is little time based on something you're withholding from me,' intuited the Count, for he could not read all of his son's thoughts and memories, only the ones Byzin permitted.

'Me, Father? Holding back from you?' said Frost, a picture of innocence.

'I taught you too well,' said the Count. 'Despite your age, you have more talent than the rest of the tribe combined. If only you weren't so disobedient. Your mother has much to answer for.'

Frost stepped back in feigned horror. 'Father!'

'I am well aware of what's going on,' said the Count without elaborating, 'and I'm quite confident that things will not unfold as quickly as *some* might hope.'

Frost's eyes lit up with intrigue.

'And you can stop pretending to be concerned about The Bank and the tribe,' added the Count.

Head high and still beaming, Frost held his tongue.

'You've grown fond of the Tusk boy, but your nature is too strong for the two of you to be anything more than fleeting friends. One day you will duel Lord Tusk. It's written in the stars.'

'And I look forward to it, Father!' declared Frost, playing along. 'In the meantime, it's friends close and enemies closer, so fear not.'

'You have your leash for now. As before, just observe the new Lord Tusk,' said the Count. 'And do not disappoint me, Byzin. Blood may be thicker than water, but light has more value.'

'Quite right, Father. Quite right.'

'Now get out,' concluded the Count, shaking his head.

With another deep bow and flourish of the hand, Frost departed.

BOLDLY HIDING IN THE BUSHES OUTSIDE THE COUNT'S OFFICE, wrapped in a fur, was Rani with Bin. What Rani hadn't heard, Bin had.

'Not only is he from the corrupt tribe but his father is chief of it!' hissed Rani. 'I ought to have known. It explains why he's so arrogant.'

'But notice how he speaks to his father and how much important information he withheld about Jake. He's up to something,' whispered Bin. 'Perhaps things aren't as bad as you think.'

'I wouldn't be surprised if he cheats his father. But there's something else...'

'Something that doesn't quite make sense?' enquired Bin.

Rani nodded.

'He likes Jake,' said Bin. 'That's what it is. He's busy plotting, playing both sides, but he's growing fond of the enemy.'

'That's true, Bin, but someone like Frost will never let friendship get in the way of ambition—not when the crunch comes. But come on, let's get out of here. It was hard enough getting in.'

Using all their skill, Rani and Bin stole away from the mansion and made for the woods.

AFTER HALF AN HOUR OR SO OF SNEAKING THROUGH THE ANCIENT woodland, Bin felt enough at ease to expand to her full size and fly up with Rani.

They had barely breached the canopy when they were set upon by a flock of ravens. Like a black cloud, they mocked in such number that Bin, despite her giant size, struggled to fly and was forced back into the woods.

'These ravens must be cursed!' cried Rani amid the wild flapping of wings, swinging her bow though not wanting to hurt them, wondering why they mocked in silence.

'It's no use,' struggled Bin, as yet more ravens joined the mocking. 'We have to land!'

As soon as Bin landed and Rani hopped down, the ravens dispersed, leaving behind them a winter silence so complete that it put Rani yet more on edge. The only movement was her breath in the chill air.

In an instant, her bow was loaded and ready to fire. She scanned the area between the trees, though found nothing out of place.

Bin reduced in size and kept watch from a branch.

Rani was lowering her bow when a voice spoke from right over her shoulder, taking even Bin by surprise.

'Welcome to my home,' it said softly.

Heart pounding, Rani spun around and aimed her arrow at his throat.

It was Frost.

Yet there was something different about him that left Rani feeling disarmed—there was a warmth and openness in his presence and a searching look in his eyes.

Not forgetting what he was, mistrusting what she saw, Rani flexed the bow fully taut.

'Your home?' she spat. 'You don't own this land any more than anyone else up here. You hoard nature's beauty behind high walls, while impoverishing the land outside them.'

'Own? I own nothing. Even this life is just a gift,' corrected an unruffled Frost. 'As for nature, I *protect* her beauty from the outside world. However, for those humans who visit Father, your accusation is true, though ultimately everyone is to blame—the so-called rich, the so-called poor and the really boring ones in-between.'

To Rani's surprise several owls swept past them and took up perches in the nearby trees, one beside Bin, as though to lend weight to what Frost had said.

Rani took a step back from Frost, though maintained her aim. His manner was confusing her.

'Won't you join me for something to eat in a nearby tree-house?' he said, gesturing the direction.

'Not a chance,' said Rani, sensing a trap. 'I'm not falling for all this.'

'Falling for what?' said Frost and strolled about the great trunk of an oak. 'For me?' he said, playfully poking his head out the other side.

'That's not what I meant,' retorted Rani. 'Unlike the Tusk boy, I'm not falling for your manipulative games.'

'The Tusk boy?' said Frost, continuing his stroll about the trees, looking at Rani with the same searching look in his eyes and the same gentle smile. 'His name is Jake.'

'I know what his name is. He's just a boy.'

Frost's smile expanded. There was something sympathetic about it, which only added to Rani's irritation.

'*Manipulating* is a strong word,' said Frost. 'I prefer *guiding* him.'

Rani scoffed. 'Guiding him towards what? What is it that you want? To do in your father and take his power? To lead Jake astray, *manipulate* him to the point of finding this hidden door out of the cosmos so that you can outdo this crazy Luna? And if such a door exists, what would you do when you reached it? What would you wish for?'

Frost was halfway around his aloof circuit of Rani, skirting the trees, her still-flexed bow following his course.

'What do I want?' he mused. 'I want what my father doesn't have, what you almost have, though not quite, what Jake could have in great abundance if forged in a high enough heat, and what Luna will scour the cosmos for, but never find, not on her own.'

Rani looked at Frost questioningly.

'If such a door exists and I feel it does,' continued Frost, 'I wouldn't open it. Maybe it offers a wish. Maybe it's a trap—another idea to become lost in, like the god gate, except much worse. Maybe it's both. But what more could I wish for than this?' said Frost, with a celebratory twirl, his arms held out to nature, a gesture which included Rani.

'Then?' pressed Rani, curious to know what it was she didn't quite have.

Frost slowly skirted behind Rani who this time didn't turn, letting him move from the arrow's aim, though she watched him from the corners of her eyes.

'I seek the hunt, though not for the hunt's sake, but for those magical moments of intensity along the way—when all hope seems spent, when death is close, when you finally appreciate what it is you're about to lose, when you truly value each breath as possibly your last,' said Frost from right behind Rani, causing a shiver down her spine.

Rani almost spun around and re-aimed her arrow. Instead she slightly lowered her bow.

'Presence,' said Frost softly into Rani's ear, finally answering her question. 'Life. There is only one door worth opening—the one into this very moment. It's the only thing that's real in this great cosmos and it must be honoured and explored to the fullest extent, no stone left unturned, no postponing into the future what can be fulfilled, enjoyed, right now. Everything I need, everything you need, is right here.'

An even stronger shiver ran along Rani's spine. She spun round and took aim. Her eyes bored into his, searching for the slightest hint of deception, but she found none.

Rani remembered all too well the last time Frost had accused her of not being present.

Despite the closeness of the arrow, Frost hadn't flinched. He looked amused. 'Look at yourself,' he said. 'Despite the fact that you were spared an upbringing on the Surface, your defences are up. You can only be fully present, fully alive, if they're down—to have the courage to be vulnerable, to be open, where your true strength lies. Trusting, not fearful and controlling.'

'Stop all this talking!' cried Rani, her heart fluttering strangely. 'What you say makes sense, but you're just saying it. Like everything else about you, it's a trick, a deception.'

'Do you know what the most attractive, most thrilling thing is?' said Frost, only encouraged by Rani's mood. 'It's honesty. It's spontaneity. So dare to be honest now. What does your heart want? What does your body want?'

'I want you to shut up,' said Rani.

Much to her anguish, a robin appeared, hovered for a moment close to her heart, moved reluctantly towards Frost and flew off again, giving voice to feelings she refused to express.

Frost laughed. 'That's your mind talking. As for the robin...'

'This wood is cursed!'

He took a step closer to Rani until the arrow tip touched his throat.

'Don't you feel the electricity of this moment?' he said. 'You and me in the woods with an infinite number of possibilities to choose from?'

Rani did feel an electricity. It tingled through her, shortened her breath and caused her great alarm.

'Why is it,' continued Frost, 'that humans, in each and every moment, when given the chance to create, they choose violence instead?'

'This is a necessary defence, not violence,' countered Rani.

Frost cocked an eyebrow. 'It looks violent from where I'm standing. I'm not armed.'

'You're made up of inner-force,' said Rani, referring to his great strength and agility and many things besides. 'Of course you're armed!'

'And you're made up of limitless potential,' countered Frost. 'In theory you have more power. You just don't know how to tap it. Perhaps you're afraid to tap it.'

Rani jilted her chin in defiance at Frost's smooth talking.

'Next you'll be telling me that your feelings are indifferent towards me,' said Frost.

'They are,' said Rani, unsure how she really felt.

'If that were true then you'd be guilty of the worst types of violence of all.'

'Nonsense!' cursed Rani.

'You would leave me to suffer in bleak silence rather than love or hate me honestly.'

Maintaining her flexed bow, Rani took a few steps back from Frost. His presence was suffocating her. She needed perspective and was tempted to leave with Bin there and then, but she didn't. Instead, she tried to separate herself from her emotions. She asked herself what was it she needed from their meeting.

I need to know if he really is different from other trixies, but how can I tell? she thought. Her intuition had become too muddled with her emotions. Only time would answer her question.

'You said that Jake, if forged in a high enough heat, would have an abundance of...'

'Presence, life, light,' replied Frost.

'What do you mean by high enough heat?'

'I mean us,' said Frost.

Rani glanced about the trees. A light breeze rustled their leaves. Their trunks seemed to lean closer, as though listening.

'You and me?' said Rani in a doubtful tone.

'The three of us,' corrected Frost. 'Our fates are interwoven.'

Rani wished to dispute the idea, but hesitated.

'Jake is the key to the door Luna seeks, but only if he has enough power,' said Frost. An owl hooted in agreement. 'Without him realising it, Luna will seek to guide him secretly along paths to power. If he follows that subtle guidance he'll be hers to use.'

'And if he follows one you guide him along, he'll be yours to use,' countered Rani, not convinced that Frost wouldn't be tempted to open the mysterious door himself.

'One *we* guide him along,' corrected Frost. 'Won't you lower your bow? You're in no danger here.'

'Aren't I?' said Rani sceptically.

'Only from your own mistrust,' said Frost.

In her own time, Rani lowered her bow, suspecting that even an arrow fired point-blank wouldn't touch Frost.

'Like that bow of yours,' said Frost, 'for the arrow to fly and reach its target, both the aim and the tautness must be perfect. So it is with Jake. Our relationship to Jake, to each other, with ourselves, is a vital part of creating that tension, so that his release, his eventual surrender, is perfect.'

'Surrender to what?'

'To something greater,' said Frost. 'Not forgetting your own surrender.'

Rani refused to give Frost the satisfaction of explaining what he meant by her surrender. Doubtless he meant to himself.

'Your father said that you're destined to fight Jake, that it's written in the stars,' said Rani.

'The stars are doubtless right. But the word *fight* can be interpreted in many ways. Perhaps we'll fight over you,' said Frost and something of his mischief returned to his smile.

'That's ridiculous. Why would you fight over me?'

Frost said nothing, but there was something in his expression that reminded her of the princely Frost she had seen through the net of light holding a golden key.

Is that what it meant? she wondered for the second time, though strongly resisted the idea. *That together we hold the key to*

Jake's destiny, to all three of our destinies and perhaps the destinies of others?

Rani looked to one of the owls for conformation of her thought, but all it did was blink its eyes which, if a message, was far from clear.

'If what you say is true then why me?' she asked.

Frost hopped up and sat on a low hanging bough of a tree. 'I've already shown you,' he said.

The serpent stirred in Rani's stomach as she recalled the vision of the bathing warrior.

'You and Jake have an intense connection through many past lives,' said Frost. 'None of them are by chance. They've been building up to your fateful encounter in this life.'

'And why you?' she asked.

'Is it not obvious?' said Frost with a grin.

Rani snorted and glanced at Bin whose expression remained impassive.

'Whether you like it or not,' continued Frost, 'the three of us have a great and grave responsibility, to each other and to the cosmos. It's like a bond, though one without guarantees—only life, death and the journey between them. Naturally, I have a vision of what lies ahead, but to divulge it would spoil the fun. Besides, it's best to keep things open. I'm simply sharing this with you now so that you're aware.'

'Of your twisted view of the world,' said Rani.

'You feel the truth in this, I know it. And yet there is so much in this mystery you've yet to work out.'

'Like what?'

'I can't tell you. Not yet. The timing must be perfect,' said Frost.

Rani cursed in Yakreth which, roughly translated, equated to *bollocks*.

Frost barked with laughter.

'You don't speak Yakreth!' she cried.

'I like you more every time I meet you,' he replied in perfect Yakreth, leaving Rani speechless, not to mention furious that he could speak it.

'But rest assured,' he continued in English, 'when the time comes, you'll know.'

Rani was feeling like shooting him again, but resisted the temptation.

'All you need to understand now is that the three of us are set on a course through shadow—yours, Jake's, the collective shadow—'

'Not your own?' interjected Rani.

'Sometimes we'll walk separate paths, but at fateful moments they'll cross,' said Frost, ignoring Rani's comment. 'Just like in Renlock when you saved me.'

'Saved? I was simply—'

'What was that, if not an act of love?' teased Frost.

'Love? You've got to be joking!'

'You can't help yourself. Like a typical woman, you've seen darkness in both Jake and I and now you wish to save us when it's yourself you need to save. The act was symbolic of what you feel unconsciously. Why else would you have saved Jake after the oracle had confirmed your worst fears about him?'

Rani's temper was rising.

'At the very least,' said Frost, 'you were paying me back for saving you from that charming trap you set for me.'

'It's time to leave, Bin,' said Rani. Yet, when she turned, a great stag appeared next to the tree in which Bin was perched. It was so large, so magical to see so close, staring at her with such fierce grace beneath its mighty antlers, that Rani was stilled.

Why does nature come to him like this? A pure trixy, fine, but not a corrupted one! thought Rani, not willing to accept that he might really be different.

'What do you think of me?' asked Frost, putting Rani on the spot.

'There aren't the words,' she replied, though the fierceness in her eyes spoke plenty.

Frost laughed with genuine delight. 'I see much more than you realise.'

'You've already spoken too much about what you see.'

'All right then, let's try something from another source which you might trust more,' started Frost. 'Want to know what Jake and I saw of you through the net?'

Rani turned away from Frost, feigning disinterest, knowing her eyes would betray her fascination. She said nothing.

Reading her body language like a book, Frost answered anyway.

'Jake was able to see through your darkness.'

Rani's heart skipped a beat.

'First he saw something queenly, something noble, then he saw you as a mermaid, full of grace and divine beauty,' he went on and caused Rani's heart to soar. Mermaids existed in the world of Wrathlabad. She adored them.

Only the owls saw Rani's face light up in a beautiful great smile. Without her fully realising it, she smiled not only for the compliment itself, but because it had come from Jake—someone she wasn't ready to admit was handsome like a lion, and definitely not ready to admit that he was intensely interesting, as much for his darkness as his light, for his connection to the druid and the striking warrior bathing in the lake.

She waited to hear what Frost had seen of her through the net.

Frost, who had noticed the sudden relaxation in her shoulders and knew she was smiling and waiting, said nothing.

'And you,' said Rani finally, doing her best to sound only mildly interested, her back still turned to him, 'what did you see?'

Rani felt the intense silence in the woods as Frost played out the moment. Not a single leaf stirred. The only movement which caught her eye were two rabbits in the distance, the female coy, feigning disinterest in the male's advances.

Growing impatient, Rani was about to turn to leave when finally Frost spoke.

'There aren't the words,' he said gently.

The smile fell from Rani's face. She flushed. Confusion washed through her in a sizzling warmth. Frost had thrown her yet again.

Inner-force! she thought.

She was right—it was inner-force, but it hadn't come from Frost, not directly. It had come from within herself through a process that was entirely natural. Otherwise known as passion, it flowed through her deliciously, riling the serpent in the pit of her stomach, creating an ache her body longed to explore. Her mind, however, wouldn't permit it. She couldn't surrender to what she didn't trust. She wasn't fooled by Frost's striking outer appearance, his incredible skills as a warrior, nor his silver tongue—it wasn't enough.

The ache threw her yet more off balance at a time when she needed focus. Rani brought her awareness back to her head. She was in the woods on the estate of the most devious tribe in the cosmos being seduced by the tribe's heir, the most devious of them all.

'Bin!' she commanded, walking away from Frost without facing him. 'We're leaving!'

Bin expanded to full size, swept her up and headed for the skies, leaving Frost with a smile as bright as Rani's had been just moments before.

CHAPTER 46
THE THREE-PART KEY

LUNA STOOD ON THE DECK OF HER HIDDEN ARK ACCOMPANIED by the guardian Commander. Flashes of light lit up the night sky and the mosaic of drift ice as the ever-increasing flow of lost souls streamed in through the unicorn horn mast.

'Tell me, Commander,' said Luna, 'when we were standing on the wall in Renlock you sensed a high-concentration of inner-force in a certain spot in the rock. What was it?'

'It was almost imperceptible, but it came from a life-form with a much higher frequency than rock.'

'Yet it was part of the rock?' asked Luna.

'Between the rock,' said the Commander. 'There must be a secret tunnel within Renlock.'

'Really? How interesting,' said Luna. 'So what was inside the tunnel?'

'A trixy,' said the Commander.

The wry smile on Luna's face lengthened. 'I did wonder,' she said. 'What a delicious intrigue. And did you sense anything else?'

'A shadow.'

'A human,' clarified Luna. 'But to have sensed shadow through rock...'

'Dwarf-smith rock,' interjected the Commander.

'Then the shadow must've been a very powerful one,' deduced Luna and closed her eyes for a moment.

'And yet you didn't say anything,' she said calmly.

'It was wiser to leave them—in order to reveal their business in Renlock.'

Luna nodded her agreement.

'A human in the inner-worlds with the audacity to spy on Renlock,' she continued. 'After what we saw through the mad mansion, who else could it be than the new Lord Tusk? One with sufficient gravity to attract a trixy for a guide.'

When Luna opened her eyes they shone even brighter.

'It makes sense,' she said. 'The premonition I had of a powerful energy in the House of Tusk was composed of three parts—I thought it might relate to objects of power, a map of some sort, a key and something else. But perhaps the objects are living objects. A male human, a trixy and a female energy, I believe, which must unite in order to unlock their potential, perhaps to reveal some hidden mystery.'

The silvery lion-like face of the Commander remained without expression as he gazed into the darkness of the horizon.

'We shall have to pay close attention to movements in and around the House of Tusk, Commander, though not to the exclusion of other signs. For now it's just a feeling, but a strong one. With each moment the new Lord Tusk grows more fascinating.'

'Shall I make enquiries as to the identity of the trixy?'

'No, Commander. Let's not interfere prematurely. Rather, let the trixy do our work for us and when the time is right we'll make our move. For now, all we need do is gather as much light as possible.'

Luna raised her head and sniffed the air.

'I sense the hand of a shepherd in all this,' she said.

'Braysheath?'

'Yes. He's never been one for convention. First, he allows a human to become a lord in Himassisi all those years ago, and now he permits access to a trixy too. This has the flavour of Braysheath's taste for irony. What he has yet to realise, however, is that it was I who created irony. He cannot win.'

'A shepherd does not seek to win,' commented the Commander. 'It seeks balance.'

'I know, Commander. But he shall not have it.'

CHAPTER 47
HIDE AND SEEK

THE PIRATE LAUGHED JOYOUSLY AS THE ADDER TRANSFORMED BACK into Lawrence in his own body, dressed in a kilt.

'The Gospel of St. Thomas,' said the pirate as Lawrence got to his feet, referring to his Biblical quote of cleaving the wood. 'Telling us how God is in all things, under a stone, within wood and yet look! Just when you might think there's no need for one, a chapel has appeared!'

It took Lawrence a few moments to adjust to being back in the depths of his unconscious. He gazed deeper into the woods where a chapel had indeed appeared. His place of refuge from the pirate had somehow merged with the Path of the Puritan, one of the three paths he had yet to choose.

Thank God I was in the cave again when I collapsed and not in Renlock, he thought. He scanned the woods for any sign of the tiger, though found none.

'What a wonderful run around you've given me!' declared the pirate. 'I must say, you're an excellent player of hide and seek.'

'What now?' said Lawrence, keen to get on with matters.

'Time to confront that self-image of yours.'

'I wasn't aware of having one.'

'Of course not!' laughed the pirate. 'That's the idea. You sneakily created it long ago to hide all sorts of nasty things you wanted to forget and have indeed forgotten. Remember, this is the unconscious.'

Lawrence frowned. He had always considered himself open.

'Guilt, my friend. Guilt and shame. And what better place to start than the chapel? Shall we?' said the pirate and gestured the way forward.

As they walked along the path, the woodland grew dark and twisted.

'Why the chapel?' asked Lawrence

'Like everything down here, it's a symbol. Morality. Control. Sound familiar?'

'Not in my life, no.'

'Oh, I know, it's painful to admit,' teased the pirate, 'but let me put it another way—the white knight? The oh-so-pure and holy saviour? Why, it wasn't so long ago I saw one galloping across a desert.'

Lawrence was about to take issue, but the pirate tutted. 'It's all a façade, dear friend. You're hiding something very dark. Something you're deeply ashamed of. And unless you pass through it you'll never have the power to be a true saviour.'

'What the hell could I be so ashamed of?' muttered Lawrence.

'We're about to find out!'

CHAPTER 48
VAULT OF THE NAGA

JAKE AWOKE TO THE CLINKING OF CHINA. THE SUN WAS UP AND Tancred the butler was standing beside his bed with a tray of tea, a broad smile on his ruddy face.

'Ah, Young Tusk, it looks like you've been dreaming with the angels!'

'Definitely not,' said Jake squinting through bleary eyes. He had had a fitful night's sleep, haunted by images of his grand-dad's suffering in the clutches of the sylph. With a chill he recalled how it had been Luna who had sent him to sleep.

'Here,' said Tancred. 'A cup of tea will do you good!'

'Thanks,' said Jake, sitting up and taking it. 'Is Braysheath back?'

'Not yet.'

'Did he not say when he might be?' asked Jake, keen to share all he had learned in Renlock.

'You can never tell with Braysheath,' said Tancred. 'He pops off when you least suspect it, then pops back in the same way! But if you need to speak to him, try walking around with a jar of marmalade. Two, if it's urgent.'

'Are you serious?'

'It's worth a try,' said Tancred.

Jake shook his head in dismay and took a sip of tea.

'On which note, breakfast is served in the Banyan. Afterwards, you have a lesson with Ti.'

'I do? What's the lesson?'

'I'd hate to spoil the surprise,' said Tancred with an unnerving light in his eyes.

'After yesterday, I could do with a day off,' said Jake.

'Good luck!' said Tancred as he bounded from the room and leapt over the balustrade into the vines.

As Jake swigged his tea, Frost popped into his thoughts. 'I wonder…'

He leapt from the bed and over to the fireplace, hopped on the bench and pulled the lever.

But Frost's lair was still empty with no sign of his having returned.

Jake spun back into his own room, reassuring himself that Frost was fine.

WASHED AND DRESSED IN A CLEAN KILT, JAKE ARRIVED IN THE banyan. Breakfast was laid out on the carpet as usual, though no one else was there, not even Rufus. Ordinarily Jake was more than happy in his own company, especially at breakfast, but these were heavy times when light-hearted company was a blessing.

'Hello love,' said Merrywisp as she entered with a couple of sprites.

'Hello, hello!' replied Jake as they added a few more treats to the spread. 'No one else joining?'

'Who knows, dear? But you tuck in and make the most of the peace.'

'Right,' said Jake and helped himself to some scrambled eggs and toast.

Once Merrywisp and the sprites had left it was difficult to find peace, especially each time the strange clock-like mechanism within the wall suddenly shifted, portending some ominous event somewhere in the cosmos.

'Hello Jake,' said Ti as he passed into the room.

'Morning Ti! Where you have been? I haven't seen you around.'

'China. I still have some worshippers there.'

'But, with respect, I thought you were a *fallen* god,' said Jake.

'*Officially*, yes,' said Ti.

'Ah, right,' said Jake. 'Well, are you going to join me for breakfast?'

'No. You're going to join me for a lesson in duelling.'

'Duelling?' said Jake. 'But breakfast…'

'Follow me,' said Ti and left down the natural stairs which wound around and through the banyan's trunk.

'Duelling?' muttered Jake, not quite sure what he thought about such a thing. It sounded exciting enough, though the reality was probably something altogether different. The idea of stabbing someone was far from appealing. But then he thought of his granddad and the need to save him from the holygate where he might meet Lord Boreas who had his own plans for Jake. Though Jake had little hope of rivalling the god in swordsmanship, he might learn a trick or two in order to win some critical time. Thus resigned to the path of heroics, Jake took a mouthful of porridge, grabbed some toast and followed Ti.

He found him walking about the balcony of the second level.

'Where are we going?' asked Jake.

'To the vault.'

At the mention of the word *vault*, the image of the steel door in the mad mansion concealing Lord Boreas's darkest demon flashed through Jake's mind.

'The vault is a place where we keep powerful objects,' explained Ti, 'which over the years have been either collected or confiscated.'

Powerful objects, mused Jake. He had heard that expression twice recently. 'Is this the only place in the fort where powerful objects are kept?' he asked, thinking of the strange room in the shaft and his capture in the net of light.

'Yes,' said Ti, studying Jake for a moment. 'Why do you ask?'

'Just a question,' said Jake looking as innocent as possible, realising that he, Frost and the girl had been in a secret part of the fort that not even Ti knew about.

'So what sort of objects are kept in the vault?' he asked, struggling to recall the other reference to powerful objects.

'There are many,' said Ti. 'For example, there's Hades' helmet of darkness, Dagda's season-summoning harp, the four talismans of the Children of Danu, Mo-li Hung's storm umbrella. Many things, which in the wrong hands can become a serious nuisance.'

'And swords, I expect.'

'Many swords.'

The hall they passed into was a bizarre sight. Consuming the greater part of it and apparently floating was a vast rectangle of roughly hewn red rock. Stranger still, its surface appeared to be moving.

'Snakes!' exclaimed Jake.

Virtually the entire surface was covered in them—all red, including their eyes.

'The vault,' said Ti.

'But it's floating!'

'The dwarf-smiths made it. It's safer afloat, held in the air by the clash of gravity and time, which are subtler longer wave forces than the outer and inner forces. The vault is forged of tiger iron and garnet. It deflects negativity. In theory, anyone wishing to enter the vault with ignoble motives will fail. The snakes, meanwhile, are the Naga—their venom and beauty is lethal to all, if they so choose.'

'Was this the vault that was broken into when Pandora's Box was stolen?' asked Jake.

Ti nodded.

'But how?' asked Jake.

Ti paused. 'With wisdom.'

'And the snakes didn't see anything?'

'No. To have eluded both the Naga and special properties of the vault took great power,' said Ti.

Without warning, a red cobra reared up in front of them.

Jake stepped back in shock. Not only did it rival him in height but its face transformed to an Indian lady of striking beauty, similar to the one he had seen in Asclepius's hospital.

'My lady,' said Ti bowing. 'With your permission we wish to enter the vault.'

She regarded them for a haughty moment before nodding her assent and making way.

As they stepped forward, a knot of snakes interlocked to form a remarkable staircase that led up to the vault.

Ti went first, followed by an astonished Jake.

At the top of the steps, Ti placed his hands against the rock of the vault. Two giant doors appeared in its surface, unlocked themselves with heavy clunks, and slowly opened inwards.

Jake's face lit up with a golden glow. He gasped in disbelief. It was as though he stood before Aladdin's cave where the space inside was miraculously greater than its outer dimensions. There were stairs and corridors and even a ship marooned amid heap upon heap of shimmering weapons.

'Don't touch anything unless I say so. To touch some of the objects will bring immediate death. But there are worse fates than death,' warned Ti, echoing something Braysheath had once said with reference to Jake's dad.

'You mean they're *magic*?'

'I mean they contain a soul. In some cases several.'

'Like Rufus?'

'Yes, like Rufus. Sometimes the soul volunteers to inhabit an object like a sword, sometimes they're forced, absorbed when the weapon strikes.'

Ti and Jake crossed the threshold into the vault.

A great commotion broke out—jeering, cheering, growling, laughing and a general hurling of insults, some in foreign tongues and some in English. Some objects took flight.

'Hey-hey! Looky here! We've got us a new Tusk!'

'Nice and thin n'all! Could chop 'im in two with a single blow!'

'That head would come off nicely!'

'Bet he couldn't even lift me off the ground! C'mon Tusk, I dare you to try and lift me, you scrawny wretch!'

'Ignore them,' said Ti calmly to a bewildered Jake as a golden helmet whizzed about his head, sniggering before flying off again.

'Mercury's winged helmet,' explained Ti. 'Useful, but quite harmless on its own.'

As Jake took in the scale of the raucous arsenal, his attention was drawn to a single sword at the far end of the vault. Its blade glimmered strangely, but it was so fleeting that Jake couldn't be sure if he imagined it or not. It was propped up against the wall and stood a little separate from everything else. It was as though it wished to be on its own, or perhaps the other weapons preferred to keep their distance. At first glance it looked quite plain. And yet there was something about its elegant simplicity which set it apart.

'What's that sword over there?' asked Jake.

'That sword?' replied Ti, with a hint of unease. 'Very little is known about that one except that it's probably the oldest in the vault. Braysheath himself brought it here a few years ago. It's not been touched since. The blade is believed to be the work of Sindri, once the master of the Norse dwarf-smiths who are generally regarded as the best.'

'Did he make many swords like that one?'

'The legend goes that he made just the one of that quality. He was well over seven hundred years old at the time—which is old for a dwarf-smith. It's the last weapon he made. Sindri was the only smith who knew how to forge the six rocks of the Peregrinus, the six rocks of Death. Three from the outer part—Roar, Leaf and Hunter. And the three from the Inner—Fear, Greed and Pride.'

'You mean the sword is made of rock?'

'No, only the eye-like circle in the hilt,' replied Ti.'

Jake strained his eyes and noticed in the cruciform part of the hilt a misted gemstone about the size of a large coin. He also noticed how exquisite the blade was.

'That alone would make the sword extremely powerful, not to mention highly unpredictable,' explained Ti.

'If Sindri managed to forge those six rocks then isn't the stone a symbol of union,' asked Jake.

'Only if the wielder of the sword is also a symbol of union,' said Ti. 'If not, the sword could be used to wreak great destruction.'

A shiver ran up Jake's spine as he beheld the sword. 'So it's unique?'

'To prevent Sindri from making another, the person for whom he made the sword slew him by it. For this reason the sword is considered cursed.'

'Was his soul absorbed into the blade?'

'Apparently not. Yet his soul was somehow banished from the Peregrinus.'

'For whom was the sword made?' asked Jake.

'I expect only Sindri knew that, but it was clearly someone both ruthless yet sophisticated, otherwise why else seek to unite the six stones?'

With a shiver, Jake recalled the cold intelligence of the dreadful character from his nightmare in the woods. The description fitted him perfectly. But he dismissed it as paranoia. History had to be full of such characters.

'Then whose soul is inside the blade?' he asked.

'Our smiths say it's that of a lady—one of great power though nothing is known of her history.'

With a thrilled jolt, Jake suddenly remembered why the expression *powerful objects* sounded familiar. *Objects of power! Of course! The lizard's warning to Lord Boreas before he entered the hall in Renlock. He suggested Rowena had hidden the greater part of her light in an object of power, that if Luna stepped into Wilderspin's mad mansion it would expose her and perhaps destroy her if Luna found the object.*

Ti seemed equally lost in thought as they beheld the sword.

Jake's heartbeat raced as he remembered the sword in the mad mansion. He also recalled the snake coiled about its hilt, how its mouth had expanded to create the room where Rowena sat on a mountain. He thought how amazing it would be if that sword was the same as the one he was currently looking at, that it might be the hiding place of Rowena's light. Unfortunately, Jake couldn't recall the exact details of the other sword.

It could be one of countless swords scattered across the cosmos, he realised with a tinge of disappointment.

'So no one knows anything about her?' he asked. 'Not even Braysheath.'

'If he does, he hasn't said so,' said Ti. 'Either way, our smiths refuse to handle it and the fort has the finest smiths in the cosmos. To have such a soul in such a blade makes it too dangerous.'

'So how does someone ever use such a sword?' asked Jake.

'To wield a powerful sword, your own soul must be equal to it or win its respect somehow and, in turn, its cooperation. That usually means that the sword must recognise your potential to be great. Swords tend to be proud, however, and have their own ideas of greatness—often far from noble, thirsting after blood.'

'But how do you know whether it's safe to even touch such a sword?'

'One never knows for sure. This is why weapons rarely change hands and are often buried with the remains of their wielders. In some cases a powerful warrior pours secrets into their weapon that they would rather not share with Nemesis and the Scribes at the moment of death. In time you'll develop an instinct for such things.'

'And if I picked up a powerful one ignoring such instincts?'

'If you're absorbed into a sword, you're effectively removed from the Peregrinus—from rebirth and evolution. Worse still, it might possess you and force you to carry out its own wicked acts, tainting your soul, perhaps setting you back hundreds, maybe thousands, even millions of years.'

Despite Ti's warning, Jake couldn't take his eyes from the sword. The longer he stared at it, the more it drew him. The din made by the other weapons seemed to fade until there was complete silence. It lasted for a moment when it was broken by a song. At first it was faint. It appeared to be coming from far off. It grew louder, appeared to come from the sword and rang with such beauty that its pull on Jake grew even stronger. The voice was a woman's, the chant foreign. Unlike the bewitching song of the sirens in the mad mansion, this one sounded pure.

'That song—it's beautiful!' declared Jake moving towards it.

Ti placed a hand on Jake's shoulder and gently held him back.

'Forget that sword, Jake,' he cautioned.

'But can't you hear that singing?'

Ti looked at Jake quizzically.

'No, I cannot. Ignore it. And remember, appearances this far into the inner-worlds can be extremely deceptive. The more beautiful something seems, the sweeter its song, the more wary you must be. But come—we'll find you another sword with which to practise.'

For a moment or two the singing grew louder and its pull more powerful. Making a great effort, finally Jake tore himself away and followed Ti. He glanced back, but the song faded and finally stopped, leaving him feeling empty.

'Here,' said Ti, holding out a battered-looking sword. 'This will do for your training today.'

As Jake reached for it, the blade grumbled and cursed in a foreign tongue. 'Are you sure?' he asked.

Ti nodded.

Jake cautiously took hold of the hilt and almost dropped it. It writhed in his clasp and was far heavier than it looked.

'Ha! Look at the blade Tusk's got! What a wuss!' shouted another sword. The other weapons bellowed with laughter.

'What's the matter, Tusk? Afraid of handling something more manly?' bawled one.

'Don't worry if it feels heavy,' said Ti, paying no attention to the heckling. 'It's just being lazy. It'll get lighter. And for me I think I'll take, yes, Caladcholg—a good all-rounder.'

Ti expertly rotated the blade about his wrist and gave it a nod of approval. 'To the Celts, this is the sword that inspired the tale of Excalibur,' he said.

'Excalibur! The magical sword of King Arthur!' exclaimed Jake, both thrilled and daunted at the same time.

'Let us begin,' said Ti and strode from the vault.

Jake took a final glance at the exquisite sword at the far end of the vault and had a powerful feeling that one day it would be his.

CHAPTER 49
TAINTED SAINT AND THE PURITAN

As Lawrence and the pirate approached the chapel, the dark and twisted wood became delightful again, except rather than spring it was autumn.

'Ah, autumn!' sighed the pirate as he marvelled at the blaze of orange and red on the trees and ground. 'The shedding of the old to make way for the new!'

He glanced at Lawrence. 'How about you, my friend? Are you ready to do the same? Ready to release what you hold most sacred?'

Lawrence dwelt on the images of Rowena and Jake and his heart ached.

The pirate rumbled with laughter. 'This is going to be fun!'

'Fun?'

'You're way off the mark—still stuck on the surface of things,' said the pirate as he opened the gate to the graveyard and gestured for Lawrence to enter. 'Tell me—who are you?'

'You know who I am,' said Lawrence as he passed into the small cemetery.

'Yes I do. But you don't.'

'At the surface level, I'm Lawrence Burton, Lord of the House of Tusk—'

'Ex-Lord,' corrected the pirate.

'And I realise I have a lightline—'

'Indeed, but you can't access its power until you drop the adopted roles. The self-image.'

Lawrence pondered what the pirate had said before about white knights and saviours.

'Whoever you think you are,' said the pirate, 'here your name is *Denial*.'

As they approached the chapel entrance, a striking woman wandered gracefully out. Parasol in hand, she was dressed in the manner of a Victorian lady with the face and bearing of an English rose. As she passed them, she cast a coy glance in the direction of Lawrence.

'Ah, the Victorian age,' sighed the pirate. 'How wonderful it was! So much forbidden fruit! And oh, how rich the flavour!'

Paying her no attention as she walked away, Lawrence stopped at the entrance. He stroked the cool surface of its stone.

Symbols, he thought. *They have many layers of meaning. On one level this chapel might just as well be a bank, a barracks, or a university laboratory. All are in the same boat—control. A boat that's sinking.*

He took an inhale of the church, of damp parchment and polished pews, and found peace in the familiar aroma.

On a deeper level this church represents me—my inner-temple of self-deceit.

'Churches,' remarked the pirate looking up. 'I've always thought they look a bit like castles.'

'I like them,' said Lawrence.

'So would I if they still served their purpose. But the priests have long forgotten the mysteries behind the religious symbols—too busy fighting amongst themselves and defending their institutions. A bit like those oh-so-proper English manners of yours—a façade to hide behind.'

'A façade covering what?'

'Fear of course! Sharpened into hatred and rage but dressed in the clothes of charity.'

'That's nonsense,' said Lawrence.

'I assure you it isn't, my friend. Ashamed of one's emotional numbness at the suffering of others, instead of having the courage to confront one's demons to understand why, one overcompensates with false sentimentality. Like those spineless missionaries, one marches out into the world trampling over all that's beautiful, all that's sacred and harmonious, polluting it with insecurity and weakness. Pseudo-charity, my friend. It's a terrible thing! One must clean one's own house before attempting to help others clean theirs. And clean it completely!'

The pirate was right. It was simply that Lawrence, while content with the pirate's description for the world at large, didn't like to think of himself in such a way.

He studied the pirate in silence. He was somehow even more impressive than Braysheath—he was less accepting and more outspoken. His words were hard to swallow, but they rang true.

Geoffrey said he represents the hidden energy in my unconscious. But does he really want me to retrieve it, for what would happen to him if I did? Does he not fear his death? If he has any sense of loyalty it can only be to himself. After all, his appearance is that of a pirate—a looter.

'Numbness,' repeated the pirate. 'If you want to know what evil is, it's that, and all that stems from it—the defences built against feeling again, fearing the pain of a forgotten childhood—'

'But I consider my childhood blessed.'

'As do most! Because they've buried the pain in shame and guilt, and banished the memory of it. But in shutting out pain, you shut out joy, shut out feeling the raw and glorious extremes of life. Why, humans even enjoy their numbness! Secretly of course. They're addicted to it. All they wish to hear and read about is suffering of others, because it makes them feel better off. Remarkable, isn't it? It's the same as worshipping the Devil! Worshipping evil, believing in it and so sustaining it. For ten thousand years or more, while claiming to worship God, humans have unconsciously worshipped the Devil. Can you believe it? He's an invention, of course, but very real.'

Lawrence was about to take issue but the pirate raised a hand.

'Remember!' he said. 'This is the unconscious. The greater the denial, the stronger the case against you.'

'Who are you, really?' asked Lawrence, curious to know what the pirate would say in his current state of mind.

'I am the flames of hell through which you must pass, my friend. Assuming you wish to reach heaven.'

'If I wish to have the power to live as the person I truly am, you mean?'

'Indeed! It's time to burn off the illusory husks, to cast off the armour you no longer need, nor have needed for quite some time. But enough talk! Let us pass inside! Though before you do, I offer you this one warning—make no attempt to defend your self-image. It's the quickest way to lose energy when you have precious little as it is.'

As Lawrence passed inside ahead of the pirate, he once more ran his fingertips over the stone of the chapel, once more reassured by its cool and solid touch.

This is real. I must remain objective and not identify with anything. I must simply observe without judgement.

He passed down the aisle. The chapel appeared to be empty. There was only the echo of their footsteps.

Half way in, he turned and faced the smiling pirate, looking for guidance.

The pirate's smile broadened as he gestured towards a confession box.

What on earth am I to confess? wondered Lawrence as he studied the box for any trickery though found none.

'Go on,' coaxed the pirate. 'It's the way.'

Lawrence approached the confession box. As he took hold of the handle he instinctively took hold of the hilt of his sword.

'You've no need for that,' said the pirate. 'Besides, it has no power down here.'

Objective observation, Lawrence reminded himself as he released the sword. Following a deep breath, he opened the door.

The box was empty except for a seat.

He passed inside, closed the door and sat down.

'Hello, my son,' came a priestly voice through the wicker netting.

Lawrence scrutinised the figure on the other side, though could see little more than the shadowy head of an old man.

'What is your confession?' asked the priest.

'What is yours?' countered Lawrence.

'Ah, my son, I hide nothing from you. What would you like to know?'

'Who are you?'

'I am what you might call a tainted saint. I offer you lies that work, not truths that don't.'

'What do you mean by that?' asked Lawrence.

'There's no point in telling you the truth, my son. The truths down here are too big for you as you currently stand. They'll consume you. A lie, however, or shall we say a *half-truth*, will serve you well.'

'Such as?'

The priest released a heavy sigh.

'My son, one cannot walk on water until one is weightless, until one has drunk fully from the cup of life, one's thirst thoroughly quenched and no longer left wanting. Before you can walk on water you must first be able to truly walk on earth. Only when one's ego has become healthy, mastered, free of all distortion, can it be surrendered to the divine. This was the path of Dionysus. It is the path for all.'

Dionysus, thought Lawrence. *The Greek God of the grape harvest and general debauchery.* He recalled the pirate's earlier reference to the god, how there had been an outer and an inner-Dionysus. Only when Dionysus had finally tired of wine and orgies was he ready to journey inwards to become a sage.

'That sounds like a truth to me,' remarked Lawrence.

'Then it serves you well.'

As the priest had spoken, the young Victorian lady had returned to the chapel and taken a seat in a pew outside the confession box.

'It doesn't serve me at all. I have loved and loved fully. And I continue to love,' said Lawrence, his family in his heart. 'It's quality I'm interested in, not quantity.'

'So you say, my son,' said the priest. 'But I sense a deep hatred in you.'

'Hatred?' cried Lawrence.

'It pains me to say so and it will be difficult for you to hear, but those you say you love, you unconsciously hate.'

Once again, Lawrence's hand intuitively moved to the hilt of his sword.

'Make peace with the past, my son, by being honest with yourself in the present. Forgive those whom you incarcerate in hatred. Go out into the world and worship God through the abundance he has blessed us with. Love again and love truly.'

'I have no need to love again,' said Lawrence, doing his best to control his anger. 'My love is pure.'

'Go in peace, my son,' said the priest, calling an end to the confession.

Lawrence stared at the shadowy profile through the screen.

Stay calm, he said to himself. *This is about self-image—the white knight not ready to save is the same as the tainted saint. The saint, the priest, he represents my self-image. His half-truth suggests that I'm ready to go deeper.*

Lawrence stood up. *I won't attempt to defend him,* he thought, recalling the pirate's advice. *I'll symbolically slay him instead.*

As Lawrence barged open the door of the confession box, he was taken aback by the sight of the lady.

Startled from her prayer she stared intensely at Lawrence. Their gazes locked. Colour rose in her cheeks. Despite her demure appearance, her energy struck Lawrence like a force ten gale, enveloping him with her true intent.

'My word! What a shock you gave me!' she gasped in a dulcet voice. As she took off her bonnet to fan herself, her luxurious brown hair cascaded about her shoulders.

'As if it wasn't hot enough already,' she went on. 'Don't you think it's hot for autumn?'

Her presence was so powerful that Lawrence battled to stay focused on his intention to slay the priest.

'Oh, but I do love autumn, don't you?' she continued, her brown eyes lighting up and adding to her powerful allure. 'I love the red leaves. Such a beautiful colour red. It's so, how would you describe it?'

Lawrence said nothing. He couldn't break free from the woman's spell. Each moment longer he spent in her presence, so his mission slipped further from his grasp.

'It's such a powerful colour,' continued the lady, unabashed by Lawrence's silence. 'It's life, it's blood, it's so rich. There's a wildness about it. Like a rose! Ah, roses! They're so beautiful. I love watching their petals unfold, don't you? There's something about them, their shape and colour. What is it, do you think?'

As she talked, the light in her eyes grew wilder. They fixed on Lawrence with increasing intensity. Her passionate presence pressed in about him, challenged his resolution, fired an imagination which dived wholeheartedly into the metaphor she tantalisingly offered.

The lady got up. Lawrence couldn't help but appraise her young and fulsome form. She gazed out longingly at the trees.

'Sometimes I just want to cast everything aside and run through the leaves,' she said. 'Run and run, feel my heart beating faster and faster, crying out for joy, run until I run out of breath!'

God she's beautiful! thought Lawrence and cursed himself for stealing another eyeful of her form.

She turned back to Lawrence, her eyes yet more enchanting, as though by gazing at the trees, nature had gifted her yet more beauty.

'But I like churches too,' she said with a hint of mischief.

She moved out from the pews, her cheeks growing more flushed.

'I really shouldn't say this,' she said glancing around to make sure they were alone, 'but I have this... this fantasy... '

She reached for Lawrence's arm.

The electricity of her touch summoned craving. It surged through him in a great wave. For a moment her face became Rowena's. Longing burned in his eyes and loins. Unable to restrain himself a moment longer, he clutched her shoulders, lunged forward but, at the last moment changed his mind and instead of kissing her fulsome lips he cast her to the ground.

'No!' he roared and spun around to the confession box. Not daring to hesitate, he drew his sword and yanked at the door with such force that he tore it off its hinges.

Seated inside was the old priest, smiling angelically.

'Why do you suppress your nature, my son?' he said calmly, glancing down at the lady on the floor who burned with all the more passion for Lawrence's show of strength.

'I don't suppress this!' growled Lawrence and thrust his sword into the priest's heart.

Still the priest smiled, apparently unharmed.

Why is he not bleeding? panicked Lawrence. He wrenched free the blade. There was no blood, no wound or any other sign of it having entered the priest's body.

'My dear boy,' said the priest standing up. 'You don't have the power to slay me.'

'This can't be!' muttered Lawrence.

As the priest stepped from the confession box. Lawrence swung the blade at the old man's neck. The blade passed clean through it, again without leaving a mark.

The priest tittered as he walked towards the altar.

'It is you who lack reality, not me,' he said.

To Lawrence's astonishment, the sword in his hand dissolved into thin air.

Unbeknown to Lawrence, the real Lord Boreas in the form of the Siberian tiger had emerged from the woods. Just like he had outside the cave in the desert, he sensed the kill. He entered the cemetery and sat on his haunches, a satisfied smile playing on his lips.

Having arrived at the altar, the priest turned to face Lawrence. His gentle features had darkened into something sinister.

'You had your chance,' he said, his tone unpleasant. 'Now on your knees.'

'On my knees? To what?' asked Lawrence.

'To me,' said the priest.

Not only had his voice become more powerful, but his presence too. As it grew so also did his body until he towered as high as the ceiling. A terrible darkness spread out from the priest towards Lawrence.

The demonic priest released a gruesome laugh and the darkness grew heavier.

Lawrence's head swam with a fear that he battled with all his will power.

'Kneel!' boomed the priest with a voice like thunder.

I lack the power to kill him. Why? I've got this far, thought Lawrence as he struggled for a way out.

'Kneel!'

To kneel before the priest meant Lawrence's surrender to his self-denial and thus being ensnared by it for a whole lot longer. Yet his resolve was weakening. His legs also, as though willing him to obey. He almost did when the tendrils of a memory reached into his mind. It was something the pirate had said in the desert about an object which allowed him to slay something which would otherwise take much longer. *What was it?*

Within the dreadful darkness, Rowena appeared like an angel.

'Kneel, love,' she said in a voice which melted his heart. 'It's the only way out.'

'Love!' he sighed and almost knelt to her, yet still he resisted.

The darkness threatened to consume Lawrence. It weighed upon him with such force that his knees began to buckle.

'My love, my heart,' he muttered to Rowena, as though it were his last word. If so, then it was the perfect word for it lifted the mist hiding the memory. *Heart! Red! Ruby! The dagger!* he cried out in thought. *I didn't use it! Thank God! Could I still?*

'Kneel!' boomed the priest once more, his patience at an end.

'Love! Kneel now before it's too late, I beg you!' implored Rowena and though Lawrence knew it wasn't really her but a trick, still her voice carried power.

His knees almost at the ground, Lawrence placed a shaky hand against the flag-stoned floor. Its touch brought him a moment's calm. He focused his mind on the farmhouse, the mountains, his family and all he held dear.

I summon, with all my heart and with the purity of my love for the Great Spirit in all its forms, he thought and felt his skin tingle. *I summon that knife—in my right hand. Now!*

'Kneel!' boomed the priest a final time. A giant hand reached down to grab Lawrence and slam him to the floor.

'If he touches you, love, you're doomed!' cried Rowena. 'Kneel!'

The priest's giant hand was almost upon Lawrence when the tingling crescendoed into a rush of power. Something materialised in his right hand. It was the special dagger with the ruby in its hilt—the one he had selected from the table at the inn, unused and still charged with power. Lawrence's heart leapt.

'Priest!' he roared with such strength that the priest stopped just short of grasping Lawrence. 'I accept you! I created you! But now it's time for a change!'

The tiger outside sensed the shift. He leapt to the chapel entrance and roared.

But it made no difference. As the priest lunged, Lawrence sprang up with all his strength and thrust the dagger into the giant hand.

Lightning exploded from the tip of the dagger. The priest wailed in pain as it tore through him and battled with the darkness.

He teetered, shook violently as the light took hold.

Releasing the dagger, Lawrence stepped back, his eyes as wide as those of the priest.

The priest's lips quivered. A word was forming. If it was spoken, it went unheard. In a blaze of light, he exploded.

CHAPTER 50

THE ART OF DUELLING

BY THE TIME JAKE STEPPED OUT ONTO THE LAWN, TI WAS NOWHERE to be seen. What he found instead caused him to drop the sword.

Standing before him, shimmering silver-white, was a unicorn.

'Take my sword for me, Jake, and jump on,' it said in the voice of Ti.

'Ti?' said Jake. 'Is that really you?'

'I'm able to shift my shape into any one of the four benevolent creatures of Taoism,' explained Ti.

'Taoism?' questioned Jake as he marvelled at such a magnificent creature which was larger than those depicted in fairy tales. Ti was the size of a thoroughbred horse.

'It means being in harmony with nature, simplicity, patience. You might call it a religion. A true one—one which takes you within, not around in circles.'

'And the other three?'

'The tortoise, the phoenix, while the fourth is not the dragon, which is a popular misconception, but the badger.'

'Because dragons don't exist, right?' said Jake. 'Only symbolically.'

'Dragons are extremely rare,' corrected Ti. 'Only seven have ever existed. But come, let us start the lesson.'

Seven, thought Jake with a shiver as he picked up the swords. Unlike the cantankerous sword Ti had given him, Caladcholg was surprisingly calm, though weighed even more. As he beheld the weapon there was something about it that looked familiar. An image popped into his mind. It was from his strange dream he had in the farmhouse—of the sword on the altar in the Temple of the Sphinx. But like the sword in the vault and the one in the mad mansion, he couldn't be sure if they were the same. *It could have been any sword*, he thought.

Gripping both swords in one hand, he mounted the unicorn.

Ti leapt to a smooth canter, descended the outcrop, crossed the savannah and leapt into the jungle.

A SHORT WHILE LATER, THE JUNGLE WAS INTERRUPTED BY A DEEP ravine.

'We're here, Jake. You may dismount.'

'Why here?'

'This place is ideal for honing the skills of duelling. Balance and timing,' said Ti. 'Skills which are far more important than brute force.'

Jake slid down and Ti returned to his human form. He strode over to a great cedar tree, one of whose mighty branches reached out halfway across the ravine.

He touched his hand gently to the trunk. 'With your permission,' he said softly to the cedar.

A moment later he hopped up onto the branch. Halfway along it he stopped and faced Jake.

'Come,' he said.

A skilled rock climber, Jake had a head for heights. What he wasn't prepared for was the loud creak released by the thick branch as he set foot upon it.

'What's happening?' he asked, noting the river running through the ravine—it was so distant it appeared no more than a silver thread.

'You're heavy,' said Ti. 'A warrior must be light.'

'I'm lighter than you!'

'In body perhaps, but your mind is weighed down with fear. I'm not referring to fear about the lesson. There are many types of fear. It's nothing to be ashamed of. You've been brought up on it without realising.'

'But I thought a bit of fear is a useful thing. It keeps you alert.'

'That's fright you're talking about. It's instinctive. The fright of a deer when a lion is near keeps it alive. Once the lion is gone, the deer relaxes. Fear, however, is something learned, instilled from the outside which does precisely the opposite. It leaves you in a state of constant anxiety that you grow used to and prevents you from living out your full potential. It keeps you locked in the past and future when power is found in the present. On the positive side, you attract what you fear until you finally confront it. It's the same with beliefs, which is what fears hide behind. Once you've passed through one layer of fear, you learn to see it as a valued ally for fear will always reveal the surest path to truth.'

Jake nodded. He recalled his dad having said something similar. *March towards your fears, Jake. Always.*

He moved further along the branch towards Ti, the branch creaking a little less than before.

'You must unlearn what you have learned,' continued Ti. 'Even though you were brought up with the positive influence of your dad and granddad, who knew better, you've been to school, been among society, among your friends' parents, and so you've unconsciously absorbed lots of fear.'

'I've never thought of myself as full of fear,' said Jake, who had always stood his ground and when it came to mountains he could climb almost anything.

'Few do. In fact, those who deny it most fiercely are usually the ones suppressing the most fear. Their false bravado is simply a mask.'

Makes sense, thought Jake, recalling some arrogant boys from school.

'You must unlearn the programme that confines you to a restricted world,' said Ti, echoing Frost, 'where an infinite number of possible futures has been collapsed into the very one your heart seeks least. True nature, however, has no limits. If you can tap into that then neither will you. This is wisdom—to be willing to let go of everything in order to have an encounter with what is real.'

Jake looked down at the grumbling sword in his hand then back at Ti, whose posture remained poised.

'But Ti, why am I learning to fight at all?'

Jake recalled what Braysheath had said about the absurdity of *holy* wars, that to fight anything changed nothing, no matter how righteous-sounding the cause. All types of fight belonged to the same story—one of separation, of them against us when real change could only come from being inclusive.

'Surely to take a life is a terrible thing,' added Jake.

'On the Surface, of course, and one pays dearly for it through the Scribes and where they place you in the next life. But you're currently beneath the Surface where you're effectively slaying what stands between you and your true identity. It's critical you're aware of this, otherwise slaying here is no different from killing up there.'

'I don't understand,' said Jake.

'Everything you sense in the world is a reflection of either your inner-beauty or your inner-ugliness. When you smile, others smile. When you frown, others frown. Thus, your opponent's greed and aggression is a reflection of your own. You must recognise this. Your sword is a symbol of clarity—it cuts through illusion.'

'Illusion?'

'An outer distortion of the truth within. Take greed for example. Behind greed is a want of attention. Behind that is a cry for love. In slaying the reflection, the distortion, you get closer to your true nature. You're cutting down the defences built from hatred so that love can shine out. The slaying is symbolic, but your intention is not to destroy. It's to pass through the fear to the pain it's hiding, and so free up the energy used to sustain the illusion.

Jake looked out over the lush jungle on either side of the ravine to gain some perspective.

'It sounds too convenient,' he said. 'Anyone could kill and claim it was all in the name of getting closer to the truth.'

'Man refers to nature as chaos because his definition-dependent mind can't grasp the boundless scale of her intelligence or the extreme intricacy of her order. Everything is part of this evolving intelligence. Nothing is left to chance. Who you meet, the warriors who cross your path, it's all for a very specific reason. Nature's aim is balance and wholeness. Always. Every thought, word and act is accounted for. The Hindus call it karma. And when it comes to harming another being, self-deceit is no excuse. Ignorance is no excuse, especially if carrying out the orders of someone else. The Scribes judge such things very harshly.'

Jake had heard of the word *karma* in school. He had liked the idea of a divine and flawless system of justice when so many crooks, suited or otherwise, seemed to escape it in reality.

'One's aim in life is not to suffer and watch others suffer as some take karma to mean. Your mission is to realise that you are fully responsible for where you stand at a given point in time, to evolve, helping others as you go, aware of your limits on a journey towards none.'

'Are we still talking about duelling?' asked Jake dryly.

'Duelling, like any other activity, can be transformed into something sacred. The fight is simply the surface of things, but deep down it becomes a prayer,' said Ti. 'This is why your intent during the duel, and especially at the moment of slaying, is critical to that soul's onward journey. If you slay in anger, you not only curse the other's soul but curse yourself too. Sooner or later you pay a price.'

Jake took a moment to try to take in all of what Ti had said.

So one must never kill another being on the Surface, while down here the intention in slaying an opponent is to cut through illusion to get closer to your true self.

He still wasn't comfortable with the idea.

'Enough talking, let us begin,' said Ti and took some practice strokes. His blade made powerful sounds as it sliced through the air.

'Hang on,' said Jake. 'You haven't taught me anything yet! How do you expect me to duel you? You're a god!'

'Like I said, Jake, you already have too much learning crammed inside of you—'

'Not in duelling!'

'Yes you have. In your past lives you have duelled many times. It's just a case of remembering.'

'Oh, why didn't you say so?' said Jake in mock relief.

'As a god my power has limits. As a human, if you can harmonise with your surroundings, you have access to the infinite power of the cosmos. The power of a creator.'

'Of course! How silly of me to have forgotten!' said Jake and laughed at how ridiculous the situation was.

Ti suddenly swept forward and swung Caladcholg at Jake's neck, intent on severing his head.

Jake couldn't believe his eyes. His sword roared in protest as he swung it up and just managed to block the stroke in time. The power in the clash of blades jarred him to the bone and he almost fell from the branch.

Jake cursed loudly, adding to the curses of his blade. He tried to cast it aside, but it refused to leave his hand and tried to pull him off balance.

CONCEALED IN A NEARBY TREE, RANI AND BIN WERE WATCHING Jake's lesson, except Rani wasn't paying much attention. Since her visit to Frost's estate, she had found it hard to focus on anything. Everything was confused.

She pondered the trap she had laid using the net of light. In a way, it hadn't backfired. By capturing Jake she had also captured Frost, but in a manner she hadn't expected. She wondered—of all the things she might have chosen to lay a trap from, she chose the net of light, the mysterious object that had revealed something hidden within each of them.

Part of Rani wanted to believe in what she had seen, but that meant unleashing a storm of feelings, ones she wasn't yet ready to admit, especially about Frost—his insight into her psyche, his poise, his wildness, his sense of rebellion, how the trees and creatures felt warm about him and how these things made Rani feel not so deep down beneath the surface of her fierce pride. There was also the fact that Frost seemed much older than he looked. For there to be any attraction between the two of them felt strange. But then, since entering the fort and gaining insight into some of her past lives, Rani also felt much older than she had before.

Either way, for now it was easier, safer, to mistrust. After all, how could she be sure what the net had shown was true? A prince with a key? A noble king with a dark past? A mermaid?

The mermaid, yes, she thought with a little smile. *I can trust that. Frost, still no. And Jake...*

Ti took a few steps back from his engagement with Jake. 'Remember,' he said, 'no fear.'

'That's easy for you to say!' said Jake and cursed again.

'Your chief challenge is to win the co-operation of your sword,' explained Ti. 'The souls inside swords respond to displays of courage, regardless of your level of skill. Their five senses have been combined into a sixth. If they choose, they can lead your moves, anticipating your opponent's strokes.'

'I just can't see it, Ti,' said an exasperated Jake.

'It's not about seeing, but feeling. You have two brilliant tools at your disposal—a body and a mind, both equally remarkable as a soul. Empty your mind so that your heart can fill it,' said Ti, reminding Jake of the barn owl he had seen at the farm and its heart-shaped face. 'That's how to unlock its power. That's where you fight from. The body, meanwhile, remembers everything. It releases memory through intuition and reflexes which are much safer than trying to access a ghost-ridden and volatile lightline. One must be strong before trying to access the past.'

Jake thought of the druid and the even darker person symbolised by the bear in the cave. The idea of either of them appearing on the branch chilled him to the bone. Jake had no control over either.

'So,' he said, 'I must try to be present.'

'Exactly. Let the beauty of nature still you, for that's her gift,' said Ti, his voice suddenly hypnotic. 'Feel your gratitude for all she gives us tingle through your body. Connect to her. Inhale her. Imagine the sap of the tree as the blood in your veins. Search for her beauty in your opponent regardless of their appearance. Hear in their battle-cry their cry for help. See their potential for beauty and leave the rest to your blade.'

Jake looked back out over the jungle. It truly was a beautiful sight. He imagined it as Ti had described—one great intelligence in constant communication with all its constituent parts. His skin tingled in awe.

Without warning, Ti came at Jake like lightning. His mind was elsewhere, yet Jake deflected the blinding blade strokes without a thought—five, six, they were too quick to count when his fear suddenly returned and broke the flow. The next stroke saw Jake disarmed, both blades held criss-cross about his neck.

His heart was racing.

Ti's expression remained impassive, though there was a hint of a smile in the light of his eyes.

'One day, one lifetime, your faith will become sincere. When it does, your willpower unites with nature. You'll see everything as part of yourself, your opponent included. Everything becomes a projection of your inner-landscape, you the creator of all that takes place in your life. You make no attempt to fix the outer-world. All change takes place within, which the outer-world then reflects. This being the case, there's nothing to fear. Without fear, you'll feel no anger, only compassion for all you see, because all you see is beauty. Thus surrendered to the divine, in duelling you let nature decide whose cause is most holy. To her all is energy. And you trust in her wisdom as to where it's needed.'

Ti lowered the swords.

'When someone reaches that stage, do they fight with a sword?' asked Jake, fascinated by the idea.

'There's no need. Such a being has learned duelling to the point of perfection. And then unlearnt duelling. Only then is one sufficiently powerful to engage without a weapon. It is the power to transform atoms, for the true warrior never tries to kill. The warrior knows that all is energy, that ultimately nothing can be killed. To try to do so is a trap.'

'Is that how someone like Braysheath fights?' asked Jake.

Ti thought for a moment before answering. 'Yes.'

'Why did you hesitate?'

'Braysheath is a shepherd. He has special powers. But your question caused me to realise that ultimately he is a symbol of what all humans can and must become.'

What Ti suggested was a huge idea for Jake to digest, but he liked it, for it gave him hope that behind all his darkness, perhaps concealed within it, was the light of wisdom.

'What about wands and staffs?' asked Jake excitedly. 'Are they like a stage in between using a sword and being like Braysheath?'

'You could say that. Though such objects may contain their own power. Like a sword, they're ultimately instruments for focusing one's intention.'

Ti returned Jake's sword. 'Let us try again. Stay present and do your best to be relaxed, but alert. And have faith in what I said. Faith and courage. These are a warrior's greatest companions.'

As Ti rotated Caladcholg about his wrists, Jake attempted to do the same, but his sword was determined to do precisely the opposite and continued to curse and complain. Trying to ignore it, Jake focused on Ti. He tried to imagine the god's face as a reflection of his own fear and anger, though it seemed impossible in someone so serene.

'Now come forward and strike me as hard as you can,' instructed Ti.

Not worried there was the slightest chance of hitting Ti, let alone hurting him, Jake gave it his best shot.

He took a step forward and attempted a feint stroke.

Before he had the chance to commit to the real one, Ti moved like a phantom. All Jake saw was the swish of dark robe and a flash of blade. A searing pain shot through his right arm. His sword was gone.

Jake spun around to find Ti behind him, having pirouetted with great aplomb. Yet again he had both swords.

'Still too heavy,' said Ti and the branch creaked in confirmation. 'You're thinking too much.'

Jake glanced down at a nick in the skin of his right arm.

'I thought this was supposed to be a lesson,' he said as calmly as his anger allowed.

'It is a lesson. Were it not, you'd be missing a limb,' said Ti plainly. 'You must get used to such pain and learn to use it to sharpen your focus, not take it away.'

'And what if you had chopped off an arm?' shot back Jake.

'Then it would have grown back.'

'Grown back?' exclaimed Jake.

'Yes. Eventually. Assuming you behaved well in death, you'd be reborn with two arms,' said Ti, without a hint of irony.

Jake was lost for words.

Ti held out Jake's sniggering sword. 'Duelling is more like a dance. Stay light on your feet.'

They tried the same exercise twice more with the same result. Ordinarily, Jake was a quick learner, but Ti's lesson was too advanced. Jake was growing frustrated.

'Let's try something else,' suggested Ti. 'Take off your shoes.'

His granddad in mind and determined not to give up, Jake did as Ti said. The bark against his feet felt good and helped calm him.

'Now, vent your anger.'

'What do you mean?' asked Jake.

'It's better to release pure anger, or rather frustration, than bottle it up and create poison. Have a roar.'

'A roar? Have you been speaking to Rufus?' said Jake.

The memory of the marvellous bath and how Rufus had told Jake to roar while naked came flooding back. So also did the memory of the warrior girl hiding in the bushes. He almost smiled.

So almost did Ti. 'He did mention something. But it's an excellent exercise. Let it out. Roar at the jungle like a lion.'

Jake glanced about, wondering if the warrior girl was once again watching.

Feeling self-conscious, Jake made a half-hearted attempt.

'Again,' instructed Ti.

Jake made more of an effort and this time enjoyed it.

'Once more. Roar as loud as you can.'

Emboldened by his last effort, Jake roared with all he had. The frustration left him. He felt light and fantastic. His body tingled all over.

RANI WAS SMILING. 'HE'S ROARING AGAIN,' SHE SAID.

'He makes a good lion,' said Bin.

Rani glanced at Bin, whose tone had been suggestive, then looked back at Jake without comment. Her smile remained. The serpent stirred in the pit of her stomach though this time it was calm as though it were stretching.

He does look like a lion, she thought, remembering her impression of him as he lay in bed asleep.

Ti nodded with approval. 'Good. Now hold your blade against mine.'

Jake did so. The resistance of the sword was less and the branch remained quiet. The only sound was an eerie whine of the blades as though they were talking.

'Now focus on my eyes,' said Ti.

Jake looked into Ti's placid eyes. On top of the lingering sensation from his roar, he felt something else—like a flow of energy.

He's helping me, thought Jake. *Finally!*

Time seemed to slow. In the periphery of his vision things started to merge—leaves were like birds which appeared to fly up and carry the tree into the sky. Wing beats fused with the beat of his heart, which in Jake mind's eye became a rose, slowly opening its petals, releasing its perfume to the world, surrendering its essence to the wind.

As the first petal reached the ground, the jungle exploded to life. A twig cracked under the hoof of a deer. A lion exhaled. A bird of paradise pranced and flapped before its mate. Jake shared the sensations, near and far, as though they were his own. The buzzing of bees merged with the tingling in his body, amplifying it to a higher frequency. The earthy mulch, the musk of glands, rustling leaves, claws in bark, the taste of nectar—it all blended into a single sense, so intoxicating that for a moment Jake quite forgot himself.

Then something shifted. Something which didn't feel right.

Ti felt it too. His eyes widened.

The harmony of the jungle was interrupted by a strange wail yet it came not from nature. It came from the swords.

As the wail grew louder, Jake tried to pull his free but it wouldn't move. It was as though Caladcholg was holding on to it.

Ti also tried but it made no difference.

My God! thought Jake as the realisation suddenly hit him. *It is the same sword! The sword from the Temple of the Sphinx!*

Once again Jake was beset with the sword's memory, this time the full version. Just like in his dream, he lived it as though he had been the bearer of the sword in the chamber beneath the sphinx, someone who Jake now knew had been his dad.

The air in the chamber was heavy as though a mighty storm were about to break. In the half-light he perceived sudden movement. With a swirl of cloaks and a blaze blade strokes an almighty duel broke loose—the clash of steel, powerful punches and a roar of fury.

His dad's skills were dazzling but against a god they weren't enough. Following an admirable effort, he collapsed to his knees, blood gushing from his wounds.

'Look at you. How pathetic,' spat Lord Boreas.

Jake's stomach knotted with dread as he recalled what came next.

'You're time is over, Tusk,' continued Lord Boreas. 'The time for all humans is over.'

He glanced over his shoulder at the vortex of the god gate. 'Destiny awaits. I would wish you farewell, but that would be pointless.'

With lightning speed he swung his blade. This time the memory wasn't cut short. Jake saw it all. There was a blinding flash and a crack like lightning swiftly followed by a horrendous sound —that of a sword being thrust through flesh, a deathly groan, a victorious cackle.

Fortunately Jake no longer experienced the memory first hand, but as an observer. The first thing he saw was a gruesome wound—Lord Boreas's sword lodged through a chest in the area of the heart.

A terrible nausea swept through Jake. What he saw next almost caused him to fall from the branch. It was the face of the fallen man, a face he loved with all his heart—his dad's.

Though Lawrence's eyes welled with the shock and blood spilled from the corners of his mouth, his expression was one of dignity.

Jake's eyes also welled.

The image shifted to the face of the murderer. Sneering with sadistic relish, Lord Boreas kicked Lawrence free of his blade and, following a final cackle, leapt through the god gate.

Jake watched on incredulous as his dad made a heroic effort to get to his feet. He managed to stagger three steps forward, just enough so that when he fell forward the god gate whisked him up and sucked him through it.

Though the memory was over, Jake's consciousness remained in the chamber. In the stillness that followed, he reflected on what Rufus had said, that his dad couldn't have survived such a thing. He was right. Any lingering hope Jake had that his dad might have survived evaporated there and then. So too did his nausea. The vacuum it left was swiftly filled by something else.

A rage of hellish proportions.

It rose in Jake like magma bursting up through a volcano's throat. With it came something else—the power to control it. At the point of eruption, Jake held the fury in check.

On the branch, he bristled with power.

Ti watched on with deep concern as their still connected blades whined and wailed yet louder.

Still Jake kept his fury in check. Still the pressure mounted. He battled inside with what to do when someone else appeared in the chamber, where part of Jake's awareness remained.

The druid.

His presence was separate from the memory. Jake's tapping it had somehow summoned him. As before, he held a lantern. With a wave of his hand across its flame its dark underpart transformed into a portal. His expression stern, he gestured for Jake to enter.

The pull of its power was huge. It was the power to direct his anger.

No! thought Jake, remembering it was the druid who, using Jake's body, had protected Lord Boreas during the gate theft— the same druid who had met with the bitter sylph in Wilderspin's mad mansion. *I can't trust him. I must draw on nature's power in the present!*

But he couldn't. The greater part of his awareness was in the chamber and full of rage. He could no longer sense the tree bark beneath his feet or anything else of the jungle. Apart from the druid's portal there was only one other choice.

Jake turned to the god gate. It was still there.

Perhaps I can save Dad, he thought desperately. *Perhaps I can offer my life for his. Somehow, symbolically through the gate...*

The longer he hesitated, the more powerful became the Druid's portal.

Standing between the two portals, Jake glanced between them.

The druid's face remained grave, without any further suggestion of what Jake should do. He simply stood there beside the dark portal.

Battling to keep the rage in check, Jake closed his eyes and did as Ti had said—thought from his heart.

The decision was easy.

Without hesitation he leapt for the god gate.

But didn't reach it.

Again there was a shift and Jake was fully back on the branch, as though it had been a test—that in order to win power, one must first refuse it. And though Jake couldn't help his dad, not in the way he had tried to, what mattered was his selfless intention.

He shone with power. So did his sword that now as felt as natural as the hand that held it. With a fearsome roar it broke free from Caladcholg's grip. Surrendering to the moment, Jake forced Ti back with a lightning-fast kick. Driven by instinct he adopted a sideways stance. He held the sword above his head, its tip pointing directly at the anxious eyes of Ti.

An explosion of sword strokes followed. To Jake it was like a dream, rapid yet slow, fatal yet enchanting. Like a conductor directing a magnificent concerto, he knew each and every note before it was played, he and his sword in perfect harmony. He sensed Ti's mastery. It was child's play, however, compared to the power and wisdom which flowed through Jake.

He was night and Ti was day, but behind the night was something else. In Jake's mind's eye, stars became gulls who swooped down on the clumsy crows of daytime, carrying the dance-like duel to the sky in a display of exquisite chaos. With the gulls came the power of the sea, a reserve of power far beyond the reach of Ti, who competed with Jake for the jungle.

All Ti saw of Jake's vision, all Rani and Bin saw of it, were storm clouds. They appeared from nowhere, gathered over the oasis, as Jake turned the energy of Ti's every stroke back upon him, effortlessly driving him along the thinning branch, their movement so perfect it was more like a ballet than a duel—a lethal dance in a whirlwind of contrast.

Rani watched on in awe, shock, fear and something else—a deep stirring as though the serpent had become an electric eel, gifting her energy with its stinging touch. The image merged with the fiery eels in the shaft, water surging upwards, emotion surging along her spine.

The gulls grew in number. The crows began to flee. Exertion showed in Ti's brow. As the branch groaned beneath him, so also did Caladcholg groan, the blade glowing orange with strain.

Cool and collected, Jake was focused on Ti's left eye, observing its light, waiting for a sign.

It suddenly flickered. The moment had come. With a quantum leap in speed and skill, Jake made his move.

With a terrible wail, Caladcholg shattered.

A moment later, Ti was flat on his back. His arm was nicked. His chest was heaving. The tip of Jake's blade was just a millimetre from his shocked left eyeball.

The duel had been timed to perfection. The power faded from Jake and rain broke from the livid clouds in great sheets.

The cool touch of the rain grounded Jake. He glanced at the sword in his hand, which once again felt alien. He noted the wound to Ti's arm. Confusion gripped him. His head grew light. He dropped the blade and staggered backwards, gripping his forehead. His legs faltered.

Jake fell from the branch.

As he plunged, his consciousness fading, a final thought passed through his mind. It was the last line of the first riddle: *In words pain for some, for others perhaps bliss.* *Words* he realised was an anagram for *sword*. The pain had been his dad's. Now it was Jake's.

CHAPTER 51
OCEAN OF EDEN

The explosion of the priest had felt to Lawrence like the end of the world. Effectively it was—the end of *a* world that needed to end so that something new could rise up.

His actions had resulted in a particularly beautiful sunrise over the British Isles, while an otherwise devastating forest fire was averted in Arizona, not to mention many other less obvious, though no less significant effects throughout the cosmos.

Still kneeling, Lawrence slowly lowered his arms from about his head and took stock. The first thing he noticed was that he was no longer in the chapel but a cathedral.

Slowly he stood up. He checked himself for injury, but the explosion had been symbolic and he was fine. In fact, he was more than fine. In slaying the tainted saint he had won energy.

'Bravo! Bravo!' hailed the pirate as he strode in through the main entrance. 'Sincerely bravo! Brilliantly done!'

He stopped short of Lawrence and beamed with delight.

'Why are you so happy?' asked Lawrence. 'Isn't my gain your loss?'

'Indeed, but it was well worth it. Besides, such a feat this far in merely sets you up for a greater fall, hence the cathedral. The stakes have been raised, dear friend!'

It was then Lawrence noted there was another person in the otherwise empty cathedral. Half-way back, sitting on one of the many pews, was a lady. Unlike the Victorian lady in the chapel, this one couldn't have looked more ordinary. She was dressed in modern clothes, was slight in build, middle-aged and had nothing remarkable about her other than her humble presence. She was looking at Lawrence with a shy but curious light in her eyes.

'Who's she?' he asked.

As the pirate studied her, she got up and scurried out of the cathedral.

'Why, I've no idea,' he said as he watched her leave.

He's withholding something. It's the first time, noted Lawrence. *I wonder? Could it be? Has my ego splintered?*

Lawrence recalled something Geoffrey had said—how there comes a point during one's journeys inwards when the ego splits. Its purer part escapes the grip of the part that's poisoned and shows an interest in the soul.

It fits! he thought excitedly. *She looks so delicate, afraid and humble, as the ego should be in front of the soul. And female—receptive to higher wisdom. Yes! Surely yes!*

'Shall we?' said the pirate, gesturing to some steps further back in the cathedral. 'You have another choice to make.'

Greatly encouraged by what he had seen, Lawrence followed the pirate down into the crypt.

There, in the far wall behind the tombs of kings, bishops and poets, were three archways. The pirate was silent as Lawrence studied each in turn.

Through the first was a sight which beckoned every aching limb in Lawrence's body. It was a grand dining hall. The long oak table brimmed with a feast fit for a king while beside the sumptuous-looking fire was an inviting chair.

By God, how I'd love to step through there, he thought. *But I fear it'll only take me backwards. Back to Greed and all that comes with it—sloth, lust and everything else. I've had enough of cursed sirens! No, I must go forward.*

Through the next archway was a full-length mirror. There was nothing special about it. The reflection was of himself. He smiled, reassured to see that he still existed as he remembered.

Vanity! he thought. *And self-image. Aspects of Pride. Heading in the right direction, but what about the third?*

Through the final archway was a walled garden full of flowers, vegetables and fruit trees, all beautifully cared for. The sound of birdsong lifted his heart. Standing at its centre was a woman. Dressed in turquoise silks she looked like a woman from the East. Though her back was to Lawrence, her head was half-turned, just enough to see the profile of an attractive young woman. Lawrence noted how the colours through the arch were especially rich and vivid.

Walled orchard, thought Lawrence. *Apiri-daeza—Persian for Paradise. A trick of course. This looks promising.*

The pirate's eyes shone with excitement as Lawrence took a couple of steps back and surveyed the arches a second time.

'There are, of course, the steps we came down,' said the pirate. 'If you care not for the arches, they'll take you back to your miserable reality above.'

Lawrence said nothing. Something was missing.

What is it? he wondered. *Yes! Of course! The ship! It's always been visible, but why not here? Perhaps because I now have a chance, slim though it may be, of surviving the arduous journey, it's been hidden. It must be moored through one of the arches. And I must take it. I must make the most of the energy won before it leaks through my fractured soul.*

Lawrence walked up to the third archway, wondering if the woman would give anything away.

'Hello!' he cried. 'Hello there!'

Slowly the young lady turned. She walked slowly towards the archway. Her head was slightly bowed so that he couldn't see her eyes.

When she finally looked up, Lawrence stepped back in shock. Her irises were almost entirely white, flecked with a hint of bright green. On second glance there was something captivating about them and the way she looked into Lawrence's eyes as though searching for something. Their coy lights beckoned powerfully.

'Your eyes,' said Lawrence. 'They're…'

'Too strong for most,' she replied and continued to look deeply into his.

What is too strong to look at? thought Lawrence. *Something we refuse to confront. Something we hide and then forget we've hidden it.*

Lawrence studied the strange green flecks in her eyes.

The green of envy—dragging others down to one's own level by gossiping behind their backs. But why? Because we lack the courage to face our shadow. Because we're afraid to reveal our guilt and shame. Because we're too proud, afraid of what others might think.

He smiled.

Through this arch is the quickest way to Pride. The ship's through here. This is the way to the steel vault door that I must open.

Lawrence looked back at the pirate.

'Decided?' he asked.

'Yes,' said Lawrence and held out his hand towards the lady.

As she gently took hold of it, the pirate's face lit even brighter.

Lawrence stepped over the threshold.

The instant he did so, the garden transformed into a busy dock and the woman into a pirate deckhand—a beast of a man who hurled Lawrence forward into a net which swept him up and dropped him below decks.

'Ahoy there, m'hearties!' cried the pirate captain as he stepped through the arch to join them. 'Prepare to set sail!'

'Where to Cap'n?' cried the pirate on deck.

'To Eden, my lovely! To Eden!'

CHAPTER 52
VICAR'S TEA

WHEN JAKE CAME ROUND FROM PASSING OUT, HE WAS LYING ON leaves in a wood—a wood, he was surprised to discover, that was inside Ti's vast study. A medicinal leaf had been fastened to his arm, covering his wound.

Noting he was awake, Ti approached.

'Here—take this,' he said and held out a cup of something hot and exotic-smelling. 'It's eyebright, juniper and spruce. It'll help with the shock.'

Jake took a sip and felt a pleasant warmth spreading through his body.

'I fell from the branch…'

'And I caught you,' replied Ti.

Jake raised his eyebrows questioningly.

'I transformed into a phoenix.'

'Thank you,' said Jake and closed his eyes.

He remembered everything from the lesson, above all the image of his dad, a sword through his heart. Painful though it was to recall, he didn't try to block it. At least he knew the truth. Knowing something made it easier to accept and eventually let go of.

Tears gathered in each of his eyes. He defiantly wiped them away. *I've cried my tears*, he thought to himself, recalling the day he heard the news of his dad's death.

He held the image of his dad in his mind. Instead of the wound, he focused on his dad's face and a great swell of admiration for his courage and strength welled up within Jake.

Ti sat opposite him on the back of a resting tortoise. He gestured for Jake to do the same. Spotting another beside him, Jake did so.

'I too shared Caladcholg's memory,' said Ti. 'I'm sorry, Jake. I hadn't realised your dad had taken that sword. Neither do I know how it found its way back into the vault.'

'Caladcholg wasn't Dad's usual sword?'

'No. His old sword had been broken in a duel. He must've taken Caladcholg as a replacement.'

Jake drew a calming breath.

'It's okay,' he said. 'I'm glad you chose it.'

Ti nodded, maintaining his appraising look.

'But I sensed that you saw more than me,' he continued gently. 'For me the memory ended with your dad's fall through the gate.'

Jake dwelt on the image of the druid. He still couldn't work him out. His actions seemed dark, yet each time he approached Jake his presence was patient. *Actions speak louder than words*, he thought and felt it was right to refuse whatever it was the druid offered.

'The manner in which you fought,' said Ti, 'I've never seen it before and I've fought many duels in my time. I've rarely lost. Which means the style you used was ancient. And as a general rule, the more ancient the skills, the more lethal, learned in times when duelling was high-art, when the smiths forged swords of untold power like the one you saw in the vault.'

'I don't know where the power came from,' said Jake, still confused by what had happened when he leapt for the god gate, and where the power had come from.

'Jake, we all have darkness in our past. At various points among so many past lives we have all done terrible things. But we've also done things of great beauty. It's important to remember that the two are connected.'

Jake sipped his drink in silence.

'However it happened, the fact that you managed to connect to something so ancient is remarkable. That you managed to resist it, for I sensed you did, is even more remarkable. Though something of the power remained with you for a while, you also managed to control it.'

'Did I control it? It didn't feel like that.'

'You didn't slay me,' said Ti. 'Had it been purely destructive darkness you would have.'

Jake was unconvinced.

'We must all eventually embrace our pasts, Jake. Perhaps it is your destiny to do so sooner than most,' said Ti, reminding Jake of something similar that Nemesis had said. 'But for now, do as we discussed today—do your best to stay present and draw on the power of nature. Ultimately the past and the present combine, but only by maintaining presence.'

Ti got up and placed a hand on Jake's shoulder. 'If you need me I'll be in the herb garden,' he said and left.

Jake walked over to a window. The study took up a corner of the fort and commanded a spectacular view of the savannah. He took a deep breath and sighed.

'No self-pity,' he muttered. 'I must focus on Granddad.'

Sensing a presence behind him, Jake turned to find Rufus hovering in the doorway.

'I heard you had quite an eventful lesson this mornin'.'

Jake said nothing, though Rufus's presence was a welcome one.

'C'mon, laddie—you need to get away from the fort for a while. And I know just the place.'

'No gates,' said Jake, in no mood for adventure.

'No gates,' confirmed Rufus.

'No branches, no swords, no quartz stairwells and no roaring naked.'

'Just a rather handsome flyin' carpet for company, if yer can cope with that,' replied Rufus as he flew over.

'Just about,' said Jake and climbed aboard.

MUCH TO JAKE'S RELIEF, RUFUS FLEW CALMLY AS THEY SET OUT over the ramparts and headed for the mountains. The sun was setting and the sight of the savannah and the dunes beyond was a soothing one. Graceful cranes descended towards the oasis after a long mountain journey, weaving between the wheeling kites and other birds of prey.

Half-way up the ridge, Rufus stopped at a magical spot—a small bluff with a grove of Scot's pines, a pool with daffodils around it, along with a few boulders. It was as though a chunk of Scotland had gone astray.

Jake hopped down from Rufus. Finches were singing and flitting between the pool and the branches.

'Beautiful, Rufus,' he said, feeling a little less heavy.

'Aye, I s'pose I am,' sighed Rufus.

'You really are an idiot of a carpet,' said Jake and managed a laugh.

'Coming from an idiot, I'll take that as a compliment.'

Jake inhaled a deep breath of the fresh and fragrant air.

'This was your dad's favourite spot,' said Rufus.

'I'm not surprised,' said Jake warmly. 'He loved places like this. And so do I.'

'I'll be back in a jiffy,' said Rufus. 'You start a fire.'

By the time Rufus returned with some plump fish and a collection of exotic-looking coconut-sized fruit, dusk had descended and Jake had started a camp fire.

'How does a carpet catch fish?' he asked.

'With a damn slight more skill than those lazy bloody humans,' replied Rufus.

'What are those?' asked Jake, referring to the fruit.

Rufus belched. 'Whoopsy. Vicar's Tea, I call it—a refreshing, tingly sort of beverage that's guaranteed to lift even the gloomiest of spirits. Poke a hole in one and try.'

Jake did so. 'Tastes fermented. Is it alcoholic?'

'Ach, I donnae know about that. Possibly.'

Smiling, Jake prepared the fish on sticks and left them to cook over some embers.

'Aye, lad!' celebrated Rufus. 'This is the life, ain't it?'

'This bit is, yes,' agreed Jake. 'I'm not sure about some of the other stuff.'

'These are auspicious times, laddie. Naturally, one would expect Nemesis and the Scribes to have scoured the cosmos for a fittin' soul to become heir to the House of Tusk. You know—powerful, courageous and full of charm.'

'Yes,' agreed Jake. 'I suppose so.'

'Aye, but they chose you instead and yer just gonna have to accept it.'

Jake laughed.

'By the way,' said Rufus, flipping something small over to Jake. 'A prezzie for yer.'

Lying in Jake's hands was a strange-looking though beautifully made small leather pouch on a neck cord. 'What is it?'

'Protection. An amulet. Inside are a set of three stones from each of the six dimensions of the Peregrinus—amethyst of Roar, malachite of Leaf, and amber of Hunter. From the Inner-Peregrinus you've got emeralds of Fear, gold from Greed, and pearls of Pride. The inside of the pouch is lined with turquoise to protect you from their properties, though if ever you find yourself in one of those dimensions, then take out the opposing stone—one, two or three depending on the strength required—and pop it in the smaller pouch on the front, which isn't lined.'

Jake marvelled at the amulet, surprised at how light it was.

'Each stone is extremely powerful so use them with great care. This is art as much as science, but with practice you'll get the feel for it.'

'Where did you get this?' asked Jake.

'It was your dad's.'

Jake closed his eyes, gently squeezed the pouch and thought how brilliant Rufus was.

'Thank you, Rufus,' he said.

'Ach, donnae mention it. Now, very carefully take out one of the emeralds—fear being the closest opposite to hope—and pop it in the front.

'What about rubies, sapphires and diamonds?' asked Jake.

'Aye, they're also from the world of Fear, but emeralds work best.'

On loosening the cord about the pouch, Jake's head swam with the potent stew of energies.

'Easy there, lad. You need to pluck one out and quickly.'

Not daring to marvel at the blaze of colours, Jake plucked out an emerald. No sooner had he grabbed one than his mind was beset with the horrific recollection of his lesson with Ti.

His head spinning, Jake received a thwack across the back from Rufus and the stone was knocked from his hand. His head cleared a moment later.

'See what I mean?' said Rufus. 'Now, pop it back in and take out an amethyst to see how it compares.'

The moment Jake touched an amethyst his spirits soared to such a height that he was about to spring up and skip about the pool when he received another thwack and dropped the stone.

'Demonstration over. There are other ways of using the stones when not in the various dimensions of death, but only in extremely special circumstances and with great care. And remember—too much hope can kill yer when it's out of balance, just as quickly as too much fear.'

Restoring the stone to the amulet, Jake fastened it and with great pride hung it about his neck. 'Much better than a sword,' he said.

'Aye, well you'll be needin' one of those too.'

'I'd rather not,' said Jake. 'Despite everything Ti said about the symbolism of duelling, it just doesn't feel right.'

As he turned the cooking fish, he relayed all he could remember of his lesson.

By the time he had finished, the fish was ready and they ate in contented silence.

At the end of the meal Jake helped himself to another Vicar's Tea. He realised that each time he did so, Rufus disappeared into the bushes and each time he returned, he belched.

'Where have you been?' asked Jake.

'Just stretchin' m'legs.'

'You don't have legs,' remarked Jake.

'Oh aye, that's right. But I used to have 'em. They're difficult things to let go of. Especially Merrywisp's.'

Jake shook his head and smiled.

'Tell me about Dad,' he said, changing the subject. 'Was it as tough for him to become Lord Tusk as it is for me?'

'Yer dad, hey? Well, you know, I think it might well have been. Perhaps even tougher, though for different reasons.'

'How so?' asked Jake, intrigued.

'Times weren't quite as desperate as they are now of course, though yer dad was goin' through a rough time of his own when he started out here. Yer mother had only recently passed on and you were just a nipper. But there was somethin' else goin' on,' said Rufus mysteriously.

'What?'

'That's the thing. I never knew what it was exactly. It was between him and Braysheath and no one else. Lawrence simply said that he was in Braysheath's bad books.'

'You must know something!' pressed Jake, dying to know.

'Nope, afraid not. Not even Nestor knew. But it must have been one hell of a stunt.'

Jake's mind boggled at the scale of the misdemeanour that would upset Braysheath, and from his dad of all people, someone who had always struck Jake as so measured and never reckless.

'Did you know my mum?' he asked.

'No, unfortunately not. And yer dad never spoke of her. Not, I donnae think because she didnae mean the world to him. Quite the opposite, in fact. I think it was because she was somethin' so sacred that followin' her passin' he could barely speak her name.'

Such a definition of sacred struck Jake as sublime.

'He rarely spoke of her,' he said. 'Do you think he might have tried to track her down in her new life?'

'Oh, I doubt that. It's best to let go. Let things take their natural course. Yer dad knew that.'

Jake sipped at his drink, wishing he could remember his mum. He remembered something his granddad had once said: that she was beautiful beyond words—like a Celtic queen, the most gorgeous thing he had ever seen.

'Anyway, laddie,' said Rufus interrupting Jake's reverie, 'never forget—your family's always growin'. You've got us now!'

'Yes!' said Jake and smiled warmly. 'Thank you, Rufus. You're a fine friend.'

'A brother!' hailed Rufus.

'A brother!' agreed Jake and raised his Vicar's Tea.

'Ach aye! To the vicar!' cried Rufus.

'To the vicar!'

FINALLY RUFUS PASSED OUT, BUT JAKE WASN'T TIRED. THE NIGHT was simply too beautiful and, apart from Rufus's snoring, was blissfully silent. The moon reflected in the pool.

Jake got up and walked to the edge of the bluff and looked out over the oasis. He recalled how Ti had described nature as one vast intelligence and how every thought, word and action was accounted for. Jake was starting to feel it.

He bent down and picked up a fallen rose petal from the ground. He placed it in the palm of his hand and blew it over the edge of the bluff.

'Farewell, Dad,' he said. 'I'm not going to think of god gates or cleansed light. No. I'm going to think of you, your spirit, somewhere far away but always close, doing something great, and have faith that one day, in some shape or form, we'll meet again.'

No sooner had he said so than a star shot across the sky.

CHAPTER 53
PAIN AND POTENTIAL

LUNA WAS BACK ON PRIDE ON HER WAY TO THE CORE. EVERYTHING was going perfectly—the ark was filling with light, Brock was close to falling, while the House of Tusk, through Jake and his two friends, had even more to offer her. Much more. With a little prodding here and there in his dreams, Jake was certain to enter the holygate in his attempt to rescue Nestor. Once there in that special place she could mine his light for information. She would then decide whether to take his light or nurture it.

All that remained was her planned miracle on the Surface and the launch of a new religion. That, however, would be left to spontaneity. Thus, there was little to do except have a bath and there was no better bath than one of light.

Luna could reach the Core from any point on Pride. This time she chose a wood which had mysteriously reappeared not far from the Goddess of Pride's tree—the one where she had opened Pandora's Box. The yellow of the new wood's leaves was so perfect that she couldn't resist it.

'Curious,' she said to herself as she entered the wood. 'Priders had burned this the last time I saw it.'

Luna ran a hand over the bark of one of the trees as though testing its reality. The wood remained.

'Beautiful,' she murmured, assuming it was a reflection of her increased power.

As she wandered through the wood, one tree in particular caught her attention. It was an old yew. A boar was snuffling about its roots. The gap between them was the perfect shape for resting. At the sight of her, the boar released a squeal and bolted.

'Yes,' she said. 'This will do just fine.'

She placed a hand on its thick trunk. 'Fair yew,' she said, 'would you be so kind as to guard this body while I visit the Core?'

After a moment's pause, the yew rustled in reply.

'Most kind,' she said, sat down between two of its mighty roots and closed her eyes.

Luna appeared to be in meditation when she suddenly inhaled. A pulse of light shot through the wood. Rowena's body went limp. Standing beside her was a being in a cloak of light.

She held an outstretched palm away from the yew. All before her transformed to light. Tree roots mirrored branches which formed a grand avenue with creatures of light between them as though the whole of creation was watching on, waiting for a queen. The avenue, however, led not to a palace, but to the swirling darkness of a portal.

As Luna took a step towards it, a breeze blew from behind her. It took her by surprise, for Pride was her domain, where all elements were under her command. She turned. As the breeze swept by, her appearance changed. Her cloak vanished. It revealed a body of light, more human than anything else.

Free of the cloak her presence grew. Dark veins rose up and ran through her sinewy body like poisoned rivers. Her lank hair streamed out in all directions in the manner of a floating corpse while the sockets of her sunken eyes had the appearance of mines in a ravaged earth.

She glanced back in the direction the wind had blown from, smiled with grim intrigue, suspecting something though unable to name it.

The avenue had also changed. As she resumed her walk, it was through a gutter of human famine and pestilence, of desperate faces and clawing hands, though none could touch her. Flies of light filled the stagnant air.

The rank gutter gave way to a deathly desert leading to the portal. Before she reached it, another wind blew. Again she turned. The gutter remained but the breeze became a gale. Luna let the wind wash over her, eyes closed as though remembering.

As the wind grew stronger, for the most fleeting moment her appearance shifted. Whether male or female it was difficult to tell, yet standing before the portal, the light of her body now golden, was a being of Elfin beauty.

A moment later it was gone. The grim Luna turned her back on the wind and stepped through the portal. With a final pulse of light she and the portal were gone.

Though the woodland returned to its autumn glory, not a single sound stirred.

The stillness was broken by creaking and rustling as Braysheath emerged from the old yew. He stared in the direction of where the portal had been, his expression grave. The lights of his eyes glinted with disbelief and a flicker of sadness. Both the breeze and the gale had been his doing.

Though the portal had closed, a darkness remained where it had been. Suddenly something shot out of it at great speed. Iridescent, it headed straight for Braysheath, who made no attempt to move.

Rather than strike him, it hovered an arms-length short. It was a hummingbird, shimmering green and violet in the sun.

Braysheath sighed—something between awe and recognition and the shock in his eyes faded.

Following its burst of vitality the hummingbird died. Its whir of wingbeats simply stopped. Braysheath held out a hand to catch it, but the hummingbird became a shower of light which slipped through his fingers.

He closed his eyes, slowly nodded his head and released a heavy exhale.

'All is accounted for,' he said to himself in a wistful tone as he gazed upon the slumbering Rowena.

Braysheath crouched down in front of her. He gently kissed her brow.

'Braysheath,' she muttered as though in fever.

'Dear One,' he said softly and stroked her cheek.

Her eyes slowly opened. Free of Luna's wintry light, Rowena's eyes were as soft as spring.

'How wonderful you are,' said Braysheath. 'Be patient. Everything will be fine. I promise. Now rest.'

Rowena managed a weak smile before she closed her eyes and fell into an exhausted sleep.

CHAPTER 54
THE PROPHET

It was dawn. Jake had just arrived back from the bluff with Rufus. Once alone, the first thing he did was head for the fireplace, sit on the bench and pull the secret lever.

'You're back!' cried Jake, delighted to see Frost sitting on the cushions.

'With fresh éclairs from Harkenmere bakery!' declared Frost, gesturing to a cardboard box. 'Cup of tea?'

'That would be grand.'

'One cup of tea coming up!' said Frost and poured out a cup.

'Where have you been?'

'Harkenmere of course. I had to make an appearance—keep the old man happy, you know,' said Frost, referring to his dad.

'You mean you're not *assigned* to me?' asked Jake, not sure how these things worked. 'Not my own personal pixy?'

'Your personal pixy?' exclaimed Frost and barked with laughter. 'Certainly not. We're friends, Jake. And befriending humans is extremely irregular among my kind. In fact, it's unheard of.'

Jake took a sip of tea. 'It's good to see you,' he said, greatly relieved that Frost was in one piece. 'How did you get back from Renlock?'

'I bobbed around in the sea, watched your epic leap from Wilderspin's office then snuck back into Renlock and returned to the Surface through one of their gates. And what have you been up to?'

Jake told Frost what he had seen on his second visit to Asclepius's lab and of his traumatic duelling lesson. They then went over all they had seen and heard in Renlock, though their conclusions remained the same—Boreas and Asclepius were planning to take the fort with the help of a demon then usurping Luna with help from the sylph.

They also went through Nestor's riddles once more, Jake explaining that *words* was an anagram of sword.

'So, the first verse of the riddles is clear. There's a plot in the fort. And Dad...' said Jake and took a deep breath, 'Dad was stabbed by Boreas then leapt through the god gate.'

Frost nodded gravely, before recounting the second riddle:

> *Go ladies to lotus to Greek god seek*
> *Imagining things of which none can speak*
> *They follow their hearts and know their minds*
> *Accepting in action is both the cruel and the kind*

'The Greek God and imagining things of which none can speak—we know that relates to Asclepius's plot,' said Jake, 'but what the hell does *Go ladies to* mean? I've tried anagrams, but came up with nothing.'

'It's a tough one that,' admitted Frost. 'But at least the last two sentences now make more sense. They're intended to prepare you for something you must do in the holygate.'

A chill ran through Jake. 'God, I hope it doesn't mean I have to put Granddad out of his misery. And to think that he would have foreseen it.'

'That doesn't sound right,' said Frost. 'I have a feeling that your tough old granddad will make it.'

'I hope so,' said Jake, taking an éclair. 'Perhaps it refers to my own sacrifice at the hands of Boreas.'

'Don't worry about that. Things rarely work out as planned, especially with so many factors in play. Besides, you've got a druid on your side!'

'A dark druid,' corrected Jake.

'You said he appeared in the chamber beneath the sphinx. Did you speak to him—ask him who he was and what he wanted?'

Jake shook his head. 'There wasn't exactly time for a chat.'

Frost took a pensive bite of an éclair. 'If I were you, I would pluck up the courage and talk to him. That's the problem with humans these days—full of judgement, they assume they know everything when actually they know nothing. That's why they miss the signs.'

Jake took sip of tea.

'Any news from Harkenmere?' he asked, changing the subject.

'Not really,' said Frost, withholding his encounter with Rani. 'However, I overheard the sprites saying that Braysheath is back and that you and he are off to London.'

'What?' said Jake, delighted to hear of his return. 'Why London?'

Frost tossed over a newspaper from town.

Amid a whole collection of alarming headlines, one stood out:

PROPHET TO APPEAR IN TRAFALGAR SQUARE

'Boreas?' asked Jake. 'The miracle Luna spoke of?'

Frost nodded excitedly. 'It's been over a week since a baby was born on the Surface. Can you imagine? People are either going mad or moping around in utter despair while the idiots among them fight and steal. All the stock markets have crashed. And no one up there has the slightest clue what's really going on —not the scientists, not the priests, while all the idiot politicians say is, *Spend more money! Everything will be fine!*'

Jake glanced back at the front page. It made for grim reading. There was also an article on yet more strange events in the skies —meteor showers and comets, along with a rise in earthquakes, tsunamis and volcanic eruptions.

'Bloody hell,' he muttered, 'Luna's plan really is rising up to the Surface.'

'It's been up there for ages.'

'But now she and Boreas are making an appearance,' said Jake, trying to imagine such a thing. 'And the people actually believe a prophet will really appear?'

'My dear Jake, they're so desperate for hope they'll believe anything. Luna has timed it perfectly.'

CHAPTER 55
RAGE

DESPITE THE ROUGH MANNER IN WHICH LAWRENCE HAD ENTERED the pirate's ship, he had been given a private cabin below deck. It was night time and the ship was rising and falling through large swells. A storm was brewing.

Lawrence was sitting in the chair at his desk, a blanket about his shoulders. He looked dreadful. It wasn't because of the sea. He was feverish. Having outsmarted Lord Boreas in the chapel, Lawrence was going far too deep far too quickly. Though he was at sea and the air smelt fresh, inside his lungs it felt like poison. Whether it was his own shadow or Lord Boreas secretly feeding him power, perhaps both, Lawrence could feel himself filling with darkness.

He was thinking of going above deck to see if it made a difference when a mouse appeared on the desk.

'Lawrence?' it said in a small voice.

Hearing his name was like a tonic and on spotting the mouse he managed a smile.

'Yes. And who are you?' he asked.

'That's not important. A seagull has just passed me a message from a lizard called Geoffrey.'

'Really?' said Lawrence, his spirits lifting. 'Please go on.'

'The message has been passed through many creatures to get here, so I hope it's still correct,' said the mouse. 'Anyway, here it is. *Get back to the cave immediately. Luna's miracle beckons.* Does that make sense?'

'Unfortunately yes,' said Lawrence with another shiver, wondering how on earth he could perform what Luna expected of him. 'Can I get back from here?' he thought out loud.

He was much deeper into the unconscious than the time he had hidden as a snake under the log. The return to the cave was equivalent to travelling through multiple galaxies.

'Of course you can,' said the mouse. 'It's simply a question of tension.'

'You mean I'll be stretching myself very far?' said Lawrence, referring to the distance between his dream body, which would remain on the ship, and the body of flesh in the cave.

'Precisely,' said the mouse. 'You might find yourself a little touchy.'

'Is there time?' wondered Lawrence. 'Do you have any idea how long this sea voyage is?'

'That's probably up to you.'

Lawrence nodded. *Besides,* he thought, *it makes no difference to Lord Boreas where I am when I run out of energy. And the pirate knows I'll do my best to get back to the ship.*

'I must try,' he said. 'Should I change into another form in order to protect myself here?'

'Why not a mouse?' suggested the mouse. 'There are no cats on board and I can show you a good hiding place. I can even watch over your body until you return.'

'Thank you, my friend,' said Lawrence after a moment's thought. 'It's an excellent idea.'

He then drew a deep breath, closed his eyes, focused his mind and willed himself to transform.

Despite his wretched state, thanks to the power he had won in the chapel he managed it first time. A moment later he was scurrying across the floorboards with his new friend, heading for a hole in the wall.

When Lawrence repossessed the body in the cave, what he had understood as *stretched* he now felt. He was at snapping point.

His eyes flicked open and bulged like a madman's.

Geoffrey's crest shot up in alarm and he leapt back. 'Take it easy,' he said.

On hands and knees, his every limb as tense as a wild cat about to pounce, Lawrence looked ready to murder. Instead, he leapt up, turned to the mouth of the cave and released a crazed roar to the sea.

Mist cleared. Storm clouds gathered. Lightning forked down into the sea and pigeons fell from the sky.

Finally it came to an end, though when he turned back to the cave he looked just as deranged as before.

'Drink the last drop of Medusa's blood,' advised Geoffrey. 'Forget the holygate for now. If you don't survive this you'll never get there. Drink it now. It's your only hope.'

Eyes blazing, Lawrence stared at Geoffrey. He clutched his head in his left hand. With the other he struck the cave wall and a large chunk fell away and plummeted to the sea.

'Drink it!' commanded Geoffrey. 'You're Lawrence Burton, father of Jake! You have work to do!'

At the mention of Jake's name, the mists in Lawrence's mind cleared a little, enough for a moment of clarity.

'Yes. Yes, you're right...' he stammered, before screeching a curse as he swung back into a state of madness and smashed another chunk from the wall.

'Control yourself!' barked Geoffrey.

Still Lawrence raved. A blizzard tore through the cave.

Geoffrey's expression was pensive, as though battling with his next words, unsure whether to voice them.

'Just this once,' he shouted over the blizzard, 'think of Rowena.'

At the mention of her name, Lawrence stopped.

The blizzard ceased.

All was still save Lawrence's panting.

'Rowena...' he gasped. 'My love...'

'Drink the last drop of Medusa's blood, now, for her sake. For Rowena.'

Lawrence slowly withdrew the tiny glass flask from a pocket and held it up to study. He glanced back at Geoffrey. His gaze hardened as though distrustful and the madness threatened to return.

'Just bloody drink it, Lawrence,' said Geoffrey. 'And stop being an arse.'

Lawrence muttered his own name and his tension relented. 'Yes. Yes, that's my name. I'm Lawrence...'

Finally he uncorked the flask, gazed at the final drop of blood and drank it down.

CHAPTER 56
A MIRACLE

JAKE WAS ON THE ROOF OF THE NATIONAL PORTRAIT GALLERY overlooking Trafalgar Square. On seeing him back at the fort, Braysheath had simply cried *Hello!* and held out his hand. The moment Jake had taken hold of it, following a blaze of light, they were suddenly in London on a roof top in Trafalgar Square, Rufus included.

They were the only ones up there. Everywhere else, however, was a sea of people. The streets were filled in every direction, balconies were bursting while heads poked out of thousands of windows. The police were out in force as were the army. TV cameras were mounted on cranes. A giant screen covered an entire building.

It was night time. A light snow was falling. It was bitterly cold. The tension in the air was palpable despite the wintry conditions.

'Why here?' asked Jake as he looked down upon a scene of empire past—the grand fountain at the centre of the square, Nelson's column and four giant statues of lions guarding it all.

'London is an important place,' said Braysheath as a sparrow landed on his shoulder. 'The British Isles are on a spot where the forces flux in a particularly potent manner, especially in London. Temple upon temple have been built in such places, the latest of which is St. Paul's. Old temples have been smashed down the world over, rebuilt in different shapes and sizes, but the energy flowing through them is always the same.'

'Even the Bank of England,' added Rufus.

'The Bank is a temple?' asked Jake.

'Aye, of a different sort,' replied Rufus, though didn't elaborate.

'There hasn't always been a city here,' said Braysheath, reminding Jake of what Rufus had said. 'London, like all cities, is modern.'

As Jake looked out over London with new eyes, he had the strange sense of watching himself. So much had changed in just two weeks that it seemed like a dream. He had lost his dad, possibly his granddad too, but gained Braysheath and Rufus, amongst others. And though it wasn't a question of trade, it felt good to have such a family.

Again Jake wondered about Frost and the warrior girl. Each time he had tried to tell either Braysheath or Rufus about them he had been interrupted by nature.

I'll try one last time, he thought. *If I'm interrupted again then I'll accept the message—that now is not the time.*

'Braysheath,' he said.

'Humph? Yes, m'boy?' said Braysheath, not taking his gaze from the scene before them.

'There's quite a bit I need to tell you. Aside from everything I saw in Renlock...'

Braysheath turned to Jake and beheld him with an intense gaze. 'Ah, yes!' he said, his gaze relenting. 'Rufus said you'd been a busy bee.'

'Yes, but there's also—'

Yet again, Jake was interrupted, this time by Big Ben striking nine o'clock.

So be it, he thought, not entirely relieved, for he would have liked Braysheath's perspective. *It's something I have to work through myself, or rather, the three of us have to—myself, Frost and her. It's like a test. Besides, Braysheath must know or at least suspect what's really going on. And he must be content with how things are unfolding. Were it not for Frost, I wouldn't have got into Renlock. Were it not for the warrior girl, I wouldn't have escaped it.*

An air of expectancy fell over the murmuring crowd. A portion near the square parted to make way for someone who was walking through. His image appeared on the big screen.

'Boreas,' growled Rufus. 'Old fancy-pants himself.'

Yet there was nothing fancy in either his appearance or the manner of his arrival. If anything it was understated. He wore a regular dark winter coat with the collar up and walked as though he were on his own, paying no attention to the crowd. He couldn't, however, conceal his presence. Lord Boreas was almost seven feet tall and though he wore normal clothes he still looked like a Viking.

As he walked up the steps to the fountain the snow stopped. Clouds cleared and stars shone. The crowd fell silent.

Lord Boreas looked out over the gathering, a slight frown upon his face as though his mind were elsewhere. He drew a calm breath and as he exhaled a breeze blew through the crowd.

There were no microphones nearby, but when he spoke his voice carried to one and all, along with the billions watching the live broadcast—deep and calm, he was the embodiment of true authority.

'Your god has left you,' he said plainly and a murmur rippled through the crowd. Lord Boreas waited for it to die down.

'I'll tell you why. You've forgotten how to worship, forgotten the wisdom and beauty of your ancestors who had no need for belief in gods because they felt the sacredness in all things. They had no need to search for meaning because they created it in all they did—great meaning in the smallest acts of kinship.'

Yet again, Jake was thrown by Lord Boreas. His tone sounded so sincere. He couldn't have been more different from the cruel god he had seen in his vision through Caladcholg.

'His voice...' he said.

'Aye, you're listenin' to Boreas, Lord of the Sirens. A right smoothie and a far cry from the chilly God of the North Wind,' said Rufus. 'Though I must say, even I'm surprised by this performance.'

Jake looked up at Braysheath whose eyes were closed as he listened.

'You have lost your faith,' continued Lord Boreas. 'And for those of you who have it, it's blind. You pray in your temples. You pray for yourselves. You make promises of peace then step outside and make war. Worse still, you're not even aware of it.'

Despite his strong words, the crowd was silent.

'You insult creation at every turn. You take and you take and you take, but give nothing in return. All you've created is yet more of your number, more people who grow more destructive with each generation. And so your god, like a pied piper, has left with your future children, because through so much taking you've already robbed them of their future. You've drunk it. You've chopped it down and left a desert. You've turned a blind eye and done nothing. You've watched on as though it were a show in the so-called comfort of your tomb-like homes.'

Jake watched Lord Boreas's powerful eyes on the big screen, as captivated as everyone else.

He's right, he thought. *He's telling the truth.*

As Lord Boreas let his words sink in, finally someone broke the silence.

'Who are you to say God has left us?' bellowed a middle-aged man from the bottom of the steps.

Lord Boreas held the man in his gaze before answering, a look of compassion in his eyes. 'I am just a messenger,' he replied.

'For who?' bellowed back the man.

Lord Boreas closed his eyes for a moment before looking up to the sky.

Thunder rumbled.

Clouds gathered and blocked out the stars.

Every light across London went out.

The thunder grew louder as it closed in. A fierce peal cracked directly overhead, so loud it was as though the sky were being torn apart. The crowd cowered beneath it.

They shrieked when a bolt of lightning exploded from the sky and struck down directly into the water of the fountain.

When the crowd looked up, it gasped. Not only had the square transformed into a lush oasis, but floating above the fountain in an aura of light, the single source in the entire city, was what looked like an angel.

It was Luna. She was back from her bath of light at the Core, back in Rowena's body, which Braysheath had had to leave on Pride. Taking it wouldn't have addressed the cause of the problem. Luna would have simply found another victim. What he had gained was a deep insight into who Luna really was—a revelation few were strong enough to bear. For now he kept it to himself.

As Luna gazed across the crowd, she was the epitome of fertility. Her luxurious red hair flowed as though in a breeze. The lustre of her skin was as soft as moonlight. Her gentle smile was all-knowing yet somehow innocent at the same time, exuding motherly love. Such was her gravity that it felt like the world leaned towards her—the trees, the crowd, the clouds, even the buildings.

The phones and cameras of those who dared take a picture disintegrated in their hands. Only the TV cameras remained intact.

Lord Boreas knelt before her, his head bowed.

'Blimey,' muttered Rufus. 'Brock's buggered.'

'Where is Brock?' asked Jake when, to his surprise, the sparrow hopped from Braysheath's shoulder onto his.

'At the brink of falling,' replied Rufus. 'He's too weak, too wise to do anything about this. Were he to try, he would fall more quickly.'

'Children,' said Luna, her ethereal voice washing through the spellbound crowd. 'You have heard my prophet speak. I understand the pain of your god. But I cannot condone his deserting you.'

The sparrow on Jake's shoulder released a chirp and another landed on Braysheath. Jake glanced at his grave expression, before gazing down at the oasis. Its stark contrast with wintry London made it all the more surreal. What had been the stagnant and littered pool of the fountain now sparkled aquamarine.

'Because your god has turned his back, I, Luna, have come. Though fear not, my children, I will not desert you,' she promised and gazed across the silent crowd.

'I offer you no sacred book,' she continued, 'and let no priest preach in my name.'

She gestured towards the large mysterious covered building Jake had seen on the TV news report. With a wave of her hand the scaffolding and covers disappeared, revealing a giant statue of a seated cat carved entirely of jade. It reached high into the sky, higher than any of the surrounding buildings.

The crowd gasped.

'You have my temples,' said Luna, 'one in every city. Worship me, and me alone and I shall bless your children with life.'

Part of the crowd cheered. The rest was a mix of consternation and disbelief.

And then she'll take their light, thought Jake.

A desperate woman bravely mounted the lower step of the fountain. 'Prove it!' she cried.

Still floating, Luna's gaze fell upon her. She noticed the woman was clutching something to her chest. Swaddled in blankets, it was her recently stillborn baby. Luna floated down to the flagstones where Lord Boreas still knelt.

'Come here, my child,' she said to the woman.

With a glimmer of hope in her otherwise petrified eyes, the woman climbed the final step and knelt before Luna, unable to look the goddess in the eyes.

Luna reached down, took the dead baby in her glowing arms and closed her eyes.

Jake was watching the big screen, for Luna's back was turned to him. To his horror, while she held the baby, he heard her voice in his head, just as he had when escaping Renlock.

Jake Tusk, she said in the same enchanting voice. *Will you worship me? When your grandfather is gone, and go he must, will you understand?*

No! said Jake defiantly in thought. *I will not. I will not understand. And I will not worship you! Ever!*

You will. Once you realise who you really are, she said gently and an image filled his mind's eye—that of the blackthorn-framed door he had seen in Wilderspin's mad mansion. *You and I are not so different. You will see. You will understand.*

Jake was growing nauseous when he felt Braysheath place a hand on his shoulder. Her voice and the image of the door disappeared.

Luna still held the baby in her arms. The crowd remained silent. Then a cry rang out: first a cry from the baby, next the mother, swiftly followed by the entire crowd.

The mother held out her arms to take the child back. 'Thank you!' she sobbed. 'Thank you!'

'This is an ancient gift,' said Luna to everyone before she returned it.

'Yes, yes!' cried the mother, desperate to hold her child.

'It is delivered through you, not of you. It's perfect, like all newborns. Cleansed of custom, purged of judgment and delivered from duplicitous ways, it's yours to cherish, though not to own. It does not belong to you.'

'Of course!' cried the mother, straining her arms towards the child. 'I promise to cherish her!'

'Do not fill it with your own fears and weakness. Draw out its strengths. Draw out its gifts. Cherish its innocence and sense of wonder and rediscover your own. And if you ask me for another, I will know you have not.'

The mother nodded frantically.

Finally Luna returned the child to the ecstatic mother and again the crowd cheered.

Luna floated up a little and silence returned.

'As an act of faith in all of you gathered here, for those of you with child, it shall be born with life. That is my promise.'

The crowd roared with euphoria, while pregnant women shrieked with joy as they felt their children move within their wombs.

'All I ask for in return is worship, true worship, from you and your child and their children also. If none of you can keep this promise then life will be taken away.'

A solemn murmur carried through the crowd. Many were on their knees.

Smiling benevolently, Luna's image faded. Her aura gone, for a moment there was total darkness.

The first light came from the moon as clouds retreated. It was followed by the stars.

When the lights of London finally returned, Lord Boreas had also disappeared. The temple, however, remained, as did the oasis, along with a festive cheer.

'What now?' asked Jake, both shaken and awed.

'Exactly what she wants to happen,' replied Braysheath. 'Imagination will continue to fail the people of the Surface and out of desperation they'll worship her.'

'But will people really change religion just like that?' asked Jake.

'You bet they bloody will,' said Rufus.

'And so…' said Jake.

'The Overlord Brock will fall. Won't he, my friends?' said Braysheath to the sparrows who were chirping about him.

'God, you mean? God Almighty?' asked Jake, trying to imagine such a thing.

'Yes, Jake. God.'

CHAPTER 57
COUNCIL OF SHADOWS

As soon as Luna and Lord Boreas had disappeared from Trafalgar Square, Braysheath had transported Jake and Rufus straight back to the great lawn of the fort where it was already dusk.

'I believe you wish to tell me about your adventure in Renlock,' said Braysheath.

'Yes,' said Jake, following Braysheath as he strode for the spinney.

'Well, you can tell some excellent friends of ours at the same time.'

'Friends? Who?' asked Jake, noting that grizzly bears were standing on guard about the spinney.

Braysheath was already greeting them.

'The Council of Shadows,' said Rufus as something large and dark swept over them and landed in one of the trees—one of the council, perhaps bird, perhaps something else. 'A very select group of gods and other powerful beings. Some are still worshipped on the Surface, others have post-fall positions in the inner-worlds.'

As they passed inside the spinney the air was so charged with power that Jake shuddered. The lamps which usually hung in the branches were unlit. Instead, a fire burned by the pool casting wild shadows among those gathered and who, bereft of pomp, looked more like bandits than anything else. Chief among them was a large character sitting in front of the fire. Two wolves at his feet and a raven perched on each shoulder, he was dressed in wolf skins and looked like a Viking chief. As Jake entered, he felt the intensity of the man's gaze. There was something odd about his eyes. While his left one sparkled with humour, the other seemed oddly distant as though he were looking deeply into the future.

'Odin dear fellow!' cried Braysheath and embraced him heartily. 'Meet Jake Tusk—our intrepid new addition to the fort.'

'An honour!' boomed Odin in a sonorous voice.

A great warmth flowed from his mighty hand as it enveloped Jake's in a handshake.

'The honour is mine,' said Jake, awestruck to meet a god he had recently heard about.

Odin's distant-looking eye hardened, widened, as it bore into Jake, while his humourful one grew brighter. It was the strangest thing. Jake grew dizzy.

Odin finally released his hand and belted him heartily on the shoulder. 'Sit next to me, Lord Tusk!' he bellowed and gestured to the boulder beside him.

Jake sat, grateful to be accepted by Odin.

The rest of the council Jake could barely make out. They were standing back from the fire among the shadows of the trees, or sitting up in the branches, their faces fleetingly lit up by the fire.

There were creatures, too—owls, a lion, even a dryad, some sprites, of course, while Ti was in his preferred form of the unicorn.

'Dear friends!' hailed Braysheath with a clap of his hands, 'I believe we're all here save one, who if I'm not mistaken...'

There was a disturbance in the waters of the pool. A moment later a remarkable-looking god appeared who instead of skin had scales which glistened in the fire light.

'Poseidon dear fellow, welcome! Hello!'

'Hello, Braysheath. Excuse my tardiness,' rasped the grave-looking god, his voice reminding Jake of a retreating tide through a pebbly shore. 'The forces move strangely through the seas these days.'

He stepped from the pool in a smattering of seaweed and took a seat on a boulder beside the fire.

'Indeed they do,' said Braysheath and looked slowly around the gathering before continuing.

'It's been a long time since we last convened and for that we must be grateful. But Brock's fall is imminent and though it is not our business to interfere with his destiny, if it's our collective belief that his replacement as Overlord threatens the very stability of the cosmos then, my friends, we have reason for action. And we must prepare to take it.'

Braysheath fell silent for a few moments. Jake tingled with awe at what he was part of.

'Am I correct in saying that this is, indeed, our collective view?' asked Braysheath.

'It is,' said Odin.

'Very well,' replied Braysheath. 'Very well.'

'Are we to raise armies?' came a rich female voice from the branches above that made Jake think of Africa.

'Not yet,' said Braysheath. 'There may come a day when a decisive battle is necessary. For now, until we know more of what we're up against, our strength lies in being light and nimble.'

Odin nodded with approval.

'First we must discover where Luna is storing all the light she's stealing from the Outer-Peregrinus,' said Braysheath. 'I myself have discovered nothing.'

'Alas,' sighed Odin, 'my ravens and wolves have scoured the cosmos—the parts they're able to visit. They also have found nothing. I fear she is hiding it in one of an infinite number of shadow worlds in the Eye of the Orijinn Sea.'

'A needle in the proverbial haystack,' said Braysheath.

Rufus gave Jake a prod.

Jake plucked up his courage. 'She's using an ark,' he said.

Everyone's head swung in his direction. The weight of their attention grew so strong that Jake felt like he was shrinking. He focused his attention on Braysheath and Odin, the only ones who appeared delighted at hearing him speak.

'She's planning on leaving the cosmos,' Jake continued.

'Leave the cosmos? That's impossible,' mocked a male voice from the shadows.

'Nothing's impossible, is it Braysheath?' said Jake, refusing to be intimidated. 'With a sprinkle of time and an occasional stir.'

Braysheath's eyes glistened with pride.

'Quite right, Jake m'boy. Quite right.'

'How could it be possible?' asked a gentle-sounding Chinese goddess, her face just visible in the half-light.

Jake hesitated as he recalled all he had seen in the mad mansion.

'She believes there's a hidden gate or door,' he said, withholding the fact that the door was somehow related to himself, for Jake wasn't familiar with most of the gathering, even though Braysheath had called them friends. He dared not look at Braysheath, though felt the intensity of the shepherd's attention.

'And how do you know this?' came an old male voice from one of the silhouettes leaning against the trees.

'I was spying on Lord Boreas in Renlock—'

'Rubbish,' hissed a python that appeared about a branch above Jake's head. 'He's making it up.'

'Rufus was there too,' replied Jake calmly.

'Aye,' said Rufus, shrewdly refraining from adding any more.

An uncomfortable silence hung in the air

'Well done, Lord Tusk!' encouraged Odin. 'What else did you discover?'

'She's blocking the holygate from Hunter to the Surface using something called a sylph,' said Jake.

'A sylph?' said Odin and shot a look at Braysheath. 'This is a thing of legend. It has never been seen.'

Braysheath was looking at Jake with yet greater intensity.

'Do *you* know what it is?' he asked Jake.

'You mean you don't?' said Jake, suddenly nervous that he should be the one to break the news to Braysheath.

'No, but I have a feeling. Tell us,' he said, his tone as distant as his gaze.

Jake glanced at Odin, who was looking at Jake with equal intensity, especially his left eye.

He then looked at Rufus.

'Go on,' he encouraged.

'Well,' said Jake, 'according to Lord Boreas, the sylph is a ghost, but not just one ghost, but erm…'

'Yes, Jake?' coaxed Braysheath. 'There's no need to be nervous. You can say what you want here.'

'It a combination of five ghosts. Almost five.'

'Almost five in one entity?' came another female voice from the shadows. 'How can this be? And ghosts of whom?'

Jake looked back at Braysheath. 'The ghosts of the shepherds.'

A heavy silence fell over the gathering. This time all heads turned to Braysheath. His gaze had lengthened even further, as though he were plumbing the deepest depths of the cosmos.

Finally his attention returned.

'Of course,' he muttered. 'I can't believe it didn't occur to me before. Well done, Jake. And well done for saving it until now.'

'Really?' said Jake, even though he had tried to tell Braysheath before.

'Yes. Perfect timing and quite appropriate.'

'That's not all. Granddad, Nestor, is also in the gate,' said Jake, expecting another interruption, but this time everyone remained silent. 'The sylph is using him as a host.'

'Yes, yes, I understand,' said Braysheath. 'An ingenious idea. Reckless, but ingenious.'

'You've given us much to reflect upon, Lord Tusk,' said Odin and for the first time Jake appreciated the title, for it seemed that Odin used it as a title of honour rather than something that was simply inherited. 'Our priority is to devise a way to staunch the flow of souls through this war room of Luna's. We must also discover a way onto this ark.'

'And Granddad of course,' said Jake. 'We must find a way to release him from the sylph. Right, Braysheath?'

'I'm afraid,' said Braysheath, 'that's even trickier than tracing the ark. You see, to step into a holygate is lethal for god and mortal alike. And especially lethal for me. It's to do with gravity.'

'But Luna must have done so. How else did she get the sylph into the gate?' countered Jake, astounded that his granddad was so far down on the list of priorities.

'I suspect that she didn't go herself,' said Braysheath. 'She probably used a guardian, in other words a force.'

'Nestor will have to take care of himself,' came a familiar gravelly voice that added fuel to the anger rising in Jake.

It was Asclepius, standing in the shadows beside a tree. Jake caught a glimpse of his cold eyes.

'There are only so many of us,' added Asclepius, 'and we must focus those resources as *efficiently* as possible.'

'Efficiently!' growled Jake. 'And how *efficiently* have you been using your time?'

A deathly silence hung in the air.

Asclepius's eyes glinted with a complex mix of amusement and something dangerous.

Jake battled to hold his tongue, sensing that it was neither the time nor the place to reveal what he and Frost had seen of his alchemical experiment.

A warning jab from Rufus brought Jake down a step of two from the heights of his anger.

It was followed by a reassuring pat on the shoulder from Odin.

'Don't lose hope, dear Lord Tusk,' he said kindly. 'Much remains to be discussed, though thanks to your good self we've covered much in a short time. Let us break for refreshments!'

'Lord Tusk,' beckoned the Chinese goddess who had spoken earlier, as other members of the council also approached Jake, all with questions on their lips.

Jake, however, needed to be on his own. He made as polite a withdrawal as his dark mood permitted and slipped into the shadows with one clear thought as he went—if his granddad was to be saved, it would be down to him and him alone.

CHAPTER 58
PARADISE

AS SOON AS THE MIRACLE WAS OVER, LAWRENCE HEADED straight for the cave in the headland of Renlock. He only just made it. The effect of Medusa's blood was rapidly wearing off. His winged horse had barely landed when Lawrence leapt down and fell to his knees.

'God help me!' he cried as the darkness returned

'God help me!' he roared and caused a great crack in the back wall of the cave.

'You must find power,' said Geoffrey calmly from the horse's withers. 'The ship on which your subtle body travels represents your mind. There'll be power hidden somewhere on board. Find it.'

Still on his knees, Lawrence's hands were curled into fists, his body knotted with tension.

'Always follow the darkest path,' added Geoffrey. 'Kiss the crone, embrace the beast, quality over quantity always. These are your guides. Remain conscious of the symbols along with the distortions. And when the shit hits the fan, if you remember just one thing, let it be this—that everything is you. See the drama, the divine play, through the lens of death. In other words, with the objectivity of one looking back on one's life. From there the decisions are clear.'

Lawrence's bloodshot eyes fixed on Geoffrey, though he said nothing.

'In the moment of crisis, then is the time you must turn the other cheek and love your so-called enemy,' said Geoffrey. 'And if you've won enough power, if you've sufficient grace, if your faith is authentic then you might just survive.'

Geoffrey waited a moment before adding dryly, 'But I don't fancy your chances.'

For the briefest moment, a flicker of humour showed in Lawrence's eyes.

'Good luck, Lawrence,' said Geoffrey with uncharacteristic warmth. 'Now go. Time is of the essence.'

Lawrence tried to smile and say thank you, but the sentiments were consumed in the tempest of fury which raged inside of him. Instead he closed his eyes.

A moment later his consciousness was gone and the body of Lord Boreas slumped to the ground.

UNLIKE IN THE CAVE, WHEN LAWRENCE ARRIVED BACK ON THE ship his rage was reflected not in his behaviour, but in the conditions of the sea. Lightning streaked through a thunderous night sky. Sheets of rain lashed the decks and promised ruin. The ship seemed tiny as it rose and fell through mighty swells.

He was scarcely aware of transforming from a mouse back into human form. Feverish, gripped by a terrible chill, Lawrence gazed down at his navel. As though he had been stabbed, light leaked out like a plume of smoke.

'P-power, energy, m-must find some,' he stammered.

He turned to his cabin and desperately tore things from the shelves, upturned his bed and desk.

'No, not here!' he panted, his brow heavy with perspiration. 'Of course not! Too obvious!'

He staggered out of his cabin and almost fell down the stairs to the lower deck in the ship's hull.

Once there, all he found were great bales of cargo piled so high that they reached the ceiling. Tightly packed, Lawrence could hardly move between them. He then realised that each was labelled.

As he read them, he shook his head in despair. They were all labelled with one of three words—GUILT, VANITY or PRIDE.

Lawrence dragged himself back up the stairs. He fell twice as he made his way down the corridor to the exit onto the deck. At the porthole in the door he gazed out at the storm.

'Courage and faith,' he muttered, repeating Geoffrey's advice. 'My greatest weapons. Maybe the power I need is not on the ship, but in the sea. Yes, the symbol for the Great Mother! If I dive overboard, if I unite with Her, then something must happen!'

Lawrence barged open the door. The gale wrenched him from the corridor and hurled him across the waterlogged deck. He caught hold of a rope just in time as the ship scaled wave so large it defied belief. Lawrence couldn't just slip into the sea by accident. His entry had to be strong and purposeful.

My God! thought Lawrence, wondering how he would survive the storm if he didn't soon find power.

Though Lawrence couldn't see him, the pirate was at the helm, singing heartily, his powerful voice defying the storm.

What Lawrence could see, which was far worse, was the back of something sitting on the roof of the cabins from which he had just emerged.

It was the back of a tiger, the back of Lord Boreas, looking as much at ease as the pirate sounded.

Feeling exposed, Lawrence glanced up at the crow's nest. To his horror, he discovered someone looking directly down at him. Through the driving rain he could just make out the face of what looked no more than a boy of ten or so. The boy, however, didn't raise the alarm. He simply stared at Lawrence, his expression mirroring Lawrence's own feelings—a mix of fascination and horror.

Lawrence's attention was torn away by a sight which left him cold. His leaking light was being whisked up by the wind and was eddying close to the tiger.

Sensing it, the tiger sniffed the air. Its ears pricked up. Lawrence watched on as its head partially turned and sniffed again.

Its bow pointing skyward, the ship was almost at the crest of the vast wave. In a moment it would be too late to dive off the back without being noticed.

It's now or never!

He glanced up at the boy who was still watching him and, as the tiger shifted to turn, Lawrence leapt over the stern of the ship.

A clap of thunder exploded overhead. The world turned white with lightning. Lawrence felt a terrific jolt, so powerful that he must have been struck. Whatever had happened, it hadn't gifted power.

Lawrence's attempt to leap into the sea had taken him someplace else. As his senses returned, he discovered himself not in the sea but face down in one of the cabins, gripped by a terrible tension. A great threat was upon him—he could feel it.

When a hand reached through the darkness and touched his shoulder, in one swift move he spun around and thrust his dagger straight through the heart of whoever it belonged to.

The tension vanished. A flash of lightning lit the room and lit up a face. To Lawrence's horror it was the face of the boy from the crow's nest. Except it wasn't a boy, but a girl in disguise. Immediately he thought of the shy woman in the pews in the cathedral and his only hope of survival. Their energy was the same. They were the same symbol—the humble, positive aspect of a warring mind, curious to know the soul. A valuable companion and guide. A source of energy.

'Oh God, what have I done?' he groaned as the girl looked down in disbelief at the dagger through her heart. Her eyes welled with tears.

Feeling a terrible loss, Lawrence gazed down at this navel. What had been a leak was now haemorrhaging.

'No! Don't go!' appealed Lawrence as the girl backed out of the cabin with a look of betrayal that tore him apart.

Before she left, she glanced at something in the corner of the cabin.

Growing weaker by the moment, Lawrence followed her line of sight through the shadows to what looked like a treasure chest.

I'm in the captain's cabin! Of course! It's why I stabbed the girl. The tension in the air—a defence mechanism of some sort...

He turned back, but the girl was gone. With no time for remorse he focused on the chest. *It could be a trap*, he thought. Yet with no other option, his head growing light, he tore it open.

A golden light lit up his face and the cabin.

Rather than gold he found four bottles. Each was labelled: *Rum, Water, A Medicine to Cure All Ills.* The last bottle was marked with a skull and cross bones and labelled *Poison*.

In his feverish condition, Lawrence craved the water, so too a miracle medicine. Mistrusting appearances, he resisted both. *Poison for whom?* he wondered. *Nothing can be as it seems, not here.*

As Lawrence reached for the bottle labelled Poison, he heard footsteps approaching the cabin—stealthy, yet such was their weight that the floorboards creaked. A chilling growl reverberated through the air.

It was the tiger—Lord Boreas.

On the verge of passing out, light gushing from his navel, Lawrence tore the cork from the bottle and gulped down the lethal-looking contents.

It felt like liquid fire. The spinning in his head grew worse. It was so bad that it appeared the ship was also spinning—so much so that he didn't see the door pushed open.

He crawled to a porthole and gazed out.

The ship was spinning.

'Whirlpool!' he gasped and passed out.

LAWRENCE CAME ROUND TO THE CRY OF LAND AHOY! THE STORM was over. He was back in his cabin lying on the bed.

Feeling remarkably well, he leapt up and peered out of the porthole. It couldn't have been fairer weather. Nor could the tropical island they were approaching have looked more idyllic. He glanced down at his navel, amazed to find he was no longer leaking light.

The poison, he thought. As he had hoped, it had been the opposite. *But surely it wouldn't have cured me completely. Perhaps it bought me just a little more time.*

Lawrence looked out at the island. It was then that he noticed cannon fortifications above the otherwise tranquil-looking harbour.

'What is this place?' he muttered, though had little doubt that what appeared to be paradise was only the surface of it.

He ran the journey over in his mind.

The girl, he thought, certain she was a symbol of the promising split in his ego he had first noticed in the older woman in the cathedral—a tentative rebel against the pirate.

Could she have survived the stab? he wondered. *If she's a rebel then she's searching for real power beyond the pirate, searching for God. Could the force of her enquiry alone have gifted her immortality, or at least the power to survive a mortal wound?*

Lawrence's spirits sank. She had been symbolised as a child, innocent but vulnerable. *The connection with immortality couldn't have been established. A child could not have survived such a wound.*

He realised something else: the reason he hadn't been able to dive into the sea was because he wasn't ready for such a leap. He wasn't pure enough to merge with what the sea represented. His courage, however, had been rewarded by his landing in the Captain's cabin.

'Ahoy there!' boomed the pirate as he strode into Lawrence's cabin and interrupted his musings. 'Enjoy the voyage?'

'Wonderful,' replied Lawrence dryly. 'Where are we?'

'Come! I'll show you!'

Without further explanation, the pirate led him above deck.

To Lawrence's surprise, the ship had become something far grander—more like a Spanish galleon. Not only that, but a great crowd had gathered to greet them. At the sight of the pirate and Lawrence there were thunderous cheers and hats were tossed into the air.

They passed from the vessel to the dock and proceeded along a street that grew grander with every step. It dawned on Lawrence that the reception they were receiving was fit for a hero.

The pirate's the hero, he thought. *I'm the prize.*

'Welcome, Lawrence!' cheered the pirate as they walked like royalty along an impressive promenade lined with palms and yet greater crowds of cheering citizens. 'You are my guest of honour!'

Lawrence could barely believe his eyes. The more he gazed about the city, the more splendour it revealed—majestic libraries and temples, a city of terracotta roofs and balconies festooned in grapevine, to say nothing of the palace they were approaching, a masterpiece of domes and arches.

A façade of leisure and learning. Like Babylon, he thought. *And doubtless just as corrupt.*

As they passed through the palace gates, the crowds gave way to a great army pristinely drilled in the parade ground. In full battle regalia and glittering with weapons, it looked as impressive as any of the ancient world.

'One can't be too careful,' said the pirate to Lawrence as he saluted the commanding officer. 'One must protect what one values, is it not so?'

Lawrence said nothing. With each step he felt more trapped.

They walked up the steps to the palace and crossed into a vast hall where a full king's court was assembled. It was completely silent as Lawrence followed the pirate along a red carpet towards a throne on a raised platform. If the pirate was to receive a hero's medal, there was no king to present it. The throne was empty.

Lawrence gaped as the pirate boldly ascended the platform's steps, turned to the court and plonked himself down in the throne.

The instant he did so, his pirate clothing transformed into that of a king. His hat became a magnificent gold crown encrusted with jewels.

Standing at the bottom of the steps, Lawrence gazed up in amazement at what was less a king than an emperor, not sure if he should kneel or run, not that he would get very far if he tried.

'General!' boomed the Emperor. 'What news of the threat?'

A powerful-looking man stepped forward and knelt before the Emperor.

'Your Majesty, it is the same as before. The scouts and assassins we sent have not returned.'

The Emperor leaned forward to address Lawrence. 'Alas, we have troubles on our borders. The usual—a terrible darkness threatens the beauty we have striven to create. But fear not. It's simply a question of time.'

Your borders are the sea, thought Lawrence, the symbolism not lost on him.

The Emperor looked back at the General. 'Go yourself, General, with a collection of your best. Hunt it down and kill it.'

The General rose, bowed and marched from the court.

'I have a feeling that with our esteemed guest of honour present in the palace,' said the Emperor to the departing General, referring to Lawrence, 'you'll have more luck. He's our lucky charm!'

Lawrence looked about the court. Many of its faces were fixed on his, their expressions stern, some even threatening. He looked for any sign of Lord Boreas, but he was nowhere to be seen.

'Why don't you take a tour of the palace, Lawrence,' suggested the Emperor. 'I have some dull matters of state to attend to. I would, of course, offer you the delights of my harem, but I know how principled you are. Perhaps the rose gardens will be more to your liking.'

Regardless of the pirate's sudden elevation to emperor, his eyes still shone with the same humour of the quayside inn.

Lawrence, meanwhile, was doing his best to play the part of the objective observer, keeping in check a mounting sense of dread.

With a bow of the head, Lawrence departed.

He was wandering along one of the corridors when a woman approached him. She was dressed in simple white robes and moved with grace. Lawrence studied her, unable to fathom her station—servant girl or member of a royal house, she seemed to defy all labels and had about her an understated air. She was also difficult to age, for though her tanned skin and rich brown hair were youthful, the lights in her brown eyes seemed older and exuded great strength.

When they met with Lawrence's, they withheld everything, all save a cursory respect. They were neither cold nor coy.

She stopped short of Lawrence. 'Would my lord like to be shown to his quarters?' she asked, her voice, like her eyes, suggesting nothing.

Lawrence nodded and proceeded to follow her along another corridor, a beautiful courtyard with fountains visible through the arches.

'Where are we?' he asked.

'We're here,' she answered plainly without turning.

'But what does it represent?' he asked more specifically.

'It is what you make of it.'

'It feels like a prison to me,' remarked Lawrence.

'Then that's what it will become.'

They shortly arrived at sumptuous quarters.

'If you have need of anything, you may send for me,' she said and with a tilt of the head, departed.

Lawrence watched her leave, only then realising that he had forgotten to ask her name. Though she had been respectful, there had been something in her manner that suggested she was in the palace against her will and in a position far beneath her.

Lawrence turned his attention to his room which reminded him of the House of Tusk. He walked to the balcony.

The view was perfect—the meticulous grounds, the turquoise sea beyond the harbour, the bazaars in between, their bustle made gentle by distance.

'Too perfect,' he muttered and inhaled deeply of the pleasant air, again impressed by how healthy he felt. *It's this island that gifts health. But I wonder what would happen if I tried to leave.*

As an experiment Lawrence closed his eyes and attempted to transform into a mouse. Nothing happened. He tried a cat, then a fly or leaving his body directly. Still nothing.

As I suspected, he sighed inwardly. *I'm beyond the point of no return. I'm trapped in paradise, my captor a pirate-emperor, the honest thief no longer quite so honest.*

He studied his hands and recognised the scars that he had accumulated over the years.

This is my body, but where is the rest of me? Where's my soul? he wondered. *Like Geoffrey and the pirate have both said, it's concealed within a hidden fear. But how am I to find this buried trea-*

sure while locked up here where, each day, each moment, I grow more fearful, clouding the picture yet further?

He thought of his dad, Nestor, trapped in the holygate.

'*He too will shortly have served his purpose.*' Luna's words echoed through his mind and weighed on his heart.

Somehow I must get back. It must be me Luna sends to slay him. If I'm stuck here she'll send the Commander and I'll miss my chance to save Dad, protect Jake and impress the sylph. Christ, so much depends on it!

Suddenly Lawrence looked up. Two swans were flying past. It was a divine sight when another sound caused him to glance to his left—also the sound of flight but much faster.

A young prince was standing on a roof top with a bow he had just fired.

Lawrence watched on with disgust as the arrow whined through the air and struck the female swan in the chest.

There was something surreal in her silent acceptance as she fell from the sky.

Given where he was, where everything was symbolic, Lawrence knew it was a sign. And it wasn't good.

CHAPTER 59
GLABROUS

Rani and Bin were lying low on part of the fort's roof where the vines were thick. Much to Rani's frustration they couldn't risk being any closer to the secret meeting in the spinney, even with the atomic glove—there weren't only the gods to worry about, but also the thorsror whose pursuit of them was making movement about the fort extremely difficult. Bin was only catching snippets of what was being discussed.

Before the meeting had started, Rani had been gazing down at the lawn, contemplating Jake when, in that very spot, he had popped out from nowhere, accompanied by Braysheath and Rufus. They had returned from the miracle that she and Bin hadn't risked attending.

As he had walked towards the spinney, the electric eel in the depths of her soul roused once more, danced through her waters and stirred up the ocean floor. Like Frost, Jake was growing more mysterious.

Despite how disturbing his dark arts in duelling had been, when he had fallen from the branch, she and Bin had been poised to save him. Fortunately Ti had beaten them to it. That night she had watched Jake and Rufus about their camp fire on the enchanting mountain bluff. She had been deeply touched when Jake had blown a fallen petal into the wind in prayer, unlike Frost who tore the heads off roses.

It didn't change the fact that Jake was a great liability. He appeared to have no control over his darkness. Like a dangerous weapon, were he to fall into the wrong hands it could prove fatal, perhaps for everyone.

Rani released an exasperated sigh at all the uncertainties. Part of her longed to step out into the open and stride right into the secret meeting. After all, it was Braysheath who had brought her to the fort. But she had to have faith in the reason why he had done so in secret. Which raised another question that continued to gnaw away at her: had Frost also been secreted into the fort by Braysheath? Not directly perhaps, for it was Jake who had idiotically invited him. But Braysheath must have allowed it. Nothing could happen in the fort, secret or otherwise, without him knowing. A portion of his own soul had gone into its making.

Assuming Braysheath had allowed Frost in, once again Rani wondered why. What Frost had said in the woods on his family estate refused to give her peace: that he, she and Jake were destined to unite in some way. She still couldn't trust him. His change of mood had been too sudden and smacked of high-trixiness.

Rani felt trapped—harassed by Frost, pursued by thorsrors and unable to think of a new plan. She thought back to her training. When trapped, a good warrior shifts their perception and transforms the threat into an opportunity.

But how? she battled in thought.

She closed her eyes and tried an old trick of hers. Having asked a question, she let her heart ponder peaceful things—the jungle, the waterfalls of Wrathlabad and other such wonders—and permitted the answer to come in its own time.

It worked. She was floating in an imaginary sea when, like a bolt of lightning, she was struck with an idea.

'Bin!' she hissed, suddenly sitting up. 'I've had a brilliant idea!'

'What?'

'If I can't decide what to do about Frost then we'll let the thorsrors decide for us!'

'How do you mean?'

'They can't know about Frost being in the fort otherwise he'd have been caught. He has the added protection of Jake's invite.'

'Jake? Not the *Tusk boy?*' teased Bin.

'Shut up, Bin, and pay attention,' chided Rani. 'It's risky and going to take a lot of skill, but using ourselves as bait, we'll lead the thorsror to Frost's lair. Brilliant, isn't it? It was probably Frost who encouraged Jake to set the thorsror on us in the first place. Now we set it on him!'

Rani rubbed her hands together with excitement at the thought of Frost's face confronted by a thorsror.

Bin was quiet while she thought it through.

'What if they fight and the thorsrors destroy him?' said Bin. 'If Frost is right about the three of you being a key—'

'Frost cannot be trusted, Bin,' interrupted Rani firmly. 'I can't see a problem with the plan. If thorsrors are as perceptive as everyone says they are, then the one hunting us will sift truth from deception and know exactly what to do. And since we would've helped it find the real threat, it might give us a break and allow us to get on with things.'

'And if we're caught?'

'Though we're here in secret, we have nothing to hide. We're Yakreth! Come on, let's do it now. Frost must be back from the miracle and there's a good chance he'll be in the lair behind the fireplace. He couldn't risk being anywhere near the meeting,' said Rani, for even if Braysheath knew Frost was in the fort, she was certain the gods didn't.

Rani put on the atomic glove and spun around to the roof.

'The glove will help us reach Frost's lair before the thorsror catches up with us,' she said excitedly and made a portal through the roof. 'Oh, to see his face!'

She glanced down into the attic room, checked it was all clear, and leapt down.

When Rani landed, she froze in horror.

Towering in front of her, where only moments before had been nothing but air, was a thorsror.

Awe and terror shot through her. Wide-eyed, open mouthed, she gasped. Its fearsome eyes and powerful muscles, accentuated by its sleek tiger-patterned serpentine skin made it the most impressive creature she had ever seen.

Bin bravely landed on Rani's shoulder and restored her dignity.

'I am Rani, daughter of—'

'I know *who* you are,' interrupted the thorsror in an unhurried and cavernous growl.

Rani did well to conceal her umbrage at being cut short.

'I am Yakreth—'

'I know *what* you are,' broke in the thorsror once more and proceeded to slowly circle Rani and Bin, which he only just managed, for though the attic was large, it was small for the thorsror. It inhaled deeply as it went—powerful breaths whose heat sent a dreadful shiver along Rani's spine.

'What I do *not* know,' it continued, 'is what business you have here.'

Having reached Rani's side, he sniffed at the atomic glove.

'Where did you get this?' it asked.

'For a thorsror, about which I have heard many great things,' said Rani haughtily, 'you strike me as remarkably... unperceptive.'

The thorsror, whose nose was still at the glove, glanced up. Its eyes were the size of Rani's hands and glinted with raw power. He laughed dryly. The very act electrified the air, as though to say, *My roar will kill you, let alone my bite.*

'Do you not know what the Yakreth represent?' quizzed Rani, refusing to stand trial.

'Every tribe has its rogue,' replied the thorsror airily, pre-empting her point.

'Perhaps among thorsrors, but not the Yakreth,' countered Rani.

The thorsror sat back in front of Rani with a look of wearing patience.

'You know full well that I am no rogue,' said Rani. 'Thorsrors are famed for their sense of sincerity. And you must also know that the Yakreth may go wherever they choose. So don't question my motives. Rather, have the courage to introduce yourself as all honourable creatures should.'

The thorsror exhaled heavily, as though deciding whether to eat her or not.

'I am Glabrous, Commander of the North Gate,' he said at last. 'And I have orders from my lord to take you to him.'

'Your *lord*?' shot back Rani. Glabrous had touched a raw nerve. 'You mean that *boy*? *He* ordered *you* to fetch *me*?'

Glabrous said nothing as he studied the feisty young warrior before him.

'You'll do no such thing!' said Rani as her hand instinctively moved to the hilt of one of her knives. 'How dare he? If you do so much as take me within a hundred feet of him, I'll put an arrow through his heart.'

Bin craned her neck and glanced at Rani, clearly shocked by her brazenness.

'Unless, that is,' continued Rani, 'you can tell me, with total honesty, that his heart is pure.'

The lights in Glabrous's eyes grew suddenly mysterious. As he gazed at Rani she felt as though she were being drawn into them, or rather, they were probing into her, so deeply that she grew lightheaded.

It lasted a few moments when he finally relented.

'If I didn't have faith in my master,' he said, 'then I would not be following his orders.'

'Well, I have less faith,' replied Rani curtly.

'Hmm, I imagine you do,' said Glabrous in a knowing tone.

'What's that supposed to mean?' she shot back. Everything she knew of Jake flashed through her mind, especially the visions.

Glabrous glanced back at the glove and again his eyes grew misty.

An awkward silence hung in the air as Glabrous journeyed through his sixth sense and Rani wondered about her plan to lead the thorsror to Frost.

I'll go ahead with it, she decided when a fly flew into her left ear. It was a disagreeable feeling. Suspecting it was a sign she left it. *All right then, I won't show him Frost*, she experimented and the fly left.

She repeated the two thoughts and the same thing happened. It was a sure sign. Rani was deeply disappointed, not only because she was looking forward to executing her plan, but it lent credibility to what Frost had said about their destinies.

'It means,' answered Glabrous at last, as his eyes cleared, 'that I know of Chief Ezram and will pay him the courtesy of helping you,' he replied at last.

'Help us?' said Rani, taken aback.

'I will delay in taking you to Lord Tusk. Perhaps a day, perhaps two. In that time you have the chance to prove your point.'

To prove Jake's heart is not pure? Why would Glabrous do this? she wondered, knowing better than to question such a mysterious creature. *Because he has faith in Jake, but it's not complete. He has doubts just like me. And because he must perceive Braysheath's presence through the glove and perceive Frost and Jake through me, sensing something of this deep mystery. It's so strange and complex that not even a thorsror can see clearly! He must, however, see further than me, perhaps realising that I'm more useful to Jake and the fort if left free. He knows I'll meet Jake soon enough, at the auspicious moment, whether he takes me or not.*

Rani nodded, maintaining her haughty manner. Inside, however, she was overjoyed.

'Rest assured,' added Glabrous, 'I will know exactly where you are at all times.'

Glabrous allowed the raw power in his eyes to glint once more in warning before turning his back. The air became electrified with his soft growl. In a single bound, he leapt clean through the wall.

CHAPTER 60
GO LADIES TO...

HAVING BEEN AMONGST GREATNESS, SOMETHING OF IT RUBBED off on Jake. Though Odin's Council had angered him for its lack of sensitivity towards his grandfather's suffering, he focused that anger constructively—it became fuel to his fire and his determination to enter the holygate and do what was required. But fire needs air and so did Jake—air and silence.

Having slipped from the spinney he found himself at the top of one of the spiral staircases which led down through the many levels of the fort. As promising as anywhere for peace and quiet, he proceeded down into its depths.

As he descended, he couldn't help but feel disappointed in Braysheath, whom he had grown fond of. From someone who had claimed that all was possible, Jake had expected Braysheath to have been more decisive. Jake also understood that big decisions required thought. As for Asclepius—the world *efficiently* still rankled.

If Jake was to enter the gate, he needed to crack the rest of the riddles to improve his chances of survival. He thought of Frost and wondered where he might be.

Probably spying on the meeting in the spinney, he thought with a smile.

Jake glanced back into the shadows cast by the torches in the wall, but saw nothing, relieved to be on his own. He could consult Frost later.

In the meantime, as he passed through floor after floor, he had a go at the riddles on his own.

Go ladies to lotus to Greek god seek. It was the key part which neither he nor Frost could work out. The one sentence contained three separate clues - *lotus* referred to Renlock, *Greek god* to Asclepius, and *Go ladies to* something else.

But what? he wondered.

Jake had been lost in thought for quite some time when he suddenly stopped. He had gone far deeper into the fort than he had been before, even deeper than the mysterious corridor which led to the shaft. Most of the levels above had a courtyard, though with different functions. The one Jake was currently on didn't. There was simply a rugged stone corridor.

Jake turned to the part of the wall where on other levels stood an arched entrance. He ran his hand over the smooth rock. It began to tingle. Thrilled, fascinated, he caressed the rock when the outlines of an archway began to form.

Jake's eyes lit up with excitement.

When the outline of the archway was formed, the process suddenly stopped—like a sketch but with no way through it.

Strange, thought Jake.

He waited a while.

When nothing further happened he sat down with his back against the wall and took a rest.

His mind returned to the riddle. 'Go ladies to…' he muttered. 'What the bloody hell does it refer to?'

Without any warning, Jake rolled backwards. The rest of the archway had suddenly formed without a sound.

Heartbeat racing, he jumped to his feet. 'I was thinking of the clue when it opened! Maybe the fort is helping!'

He was in another courtyard-hall except this one was different. In each of its corners was a cave-like chamber, each glowing with a different colour, while at the centre of the otherwise nondescript hall were two megaliths. Joined on top by a capstone they reminded Jake of Stonehenge, all the more so for an eerie mist which hung about them.

Jake took a tentative step inside. The megaliths drew him most. He had only taken a few steps towards them when he was gripped by a terrible dread. Heart thumping and hot around the neck, he backed off.

What is this level? he wondered.

He recalled being told how there were many parts of the fort which remained unseen until one was ready. And yet, though the main entrance had opened, he clearly wasn't ready to approach the megaliths.

He turned his attention to the chambers instead and made a slow circuit of the hall. Of the four chambers, the one that felt most pleasant was the one which glowed a soft blue.

Jake stopped in front of it. Over its entrance was etched something in runes. Though Jake had no idea what they meant, he had a feeling that he was meant to enter the chamber.

For Granddad, he thought and holding the unresolved clue in his mind, he stepped inside.

As his foot touched the ground, a blissful peace washed through him. Intuitively he lay down on his back at the chamber's centre and closed his eyes.

His thoughts drifted back to fond memories of the farmhouse, of himself with his dad and Bill gathered about the kitchen fire, laughing hysterically as his granddad recounted one of his tales. He recalled spring walks up in the mountains about the farm, finally settling on the image of a grove of trees nestled in a bowl between two mountain peaks—a place he considered especially sacred.

Something shifted. Everything was so vivid that Jake felt he was actually there. Yet there was a difference. There was something about it that reminded him of his nightmarish journey to Nemesis's tree. He almost sat up in panic. But didn't. Trusting that the chamber was trying to show him something, he kept his attention in the woods where he was standing, gazing about the trees. All was still. He took a step forward, half-expecting something terrible to happen. The woods remained still and so he walked slowly between the trees, moving as silently as possible.

After some time, the woods too quiet for comfort, Jake froze. He spotted a lizard clinging to the trunk of a nearby tree, reminding him of the one he had seen with Lord Boreas. Sensing his attention, it darted off.

Doubly alert, on he ventured, deeper into the woods.

ODIN'S COUNCIL WERE STILL TAKING REFRESHMENTS. FROST, WHO was indeed hiding in the shadows, listening in on conversations, wondered where Jake had got to. Picking up his scent, he followed it all the way down to the blue-glowing chamber. There he found Jake resting, eyes closed, on an inner-journey of some sort.

Frost read the runes, studied the stone and smiled.

'Go *ladies-to*, not *Go-ladies*! Now I understand! It's an anagram of sodalite! Brilliant!' said Frost, touching the blue sodalite rock in which the cave was formed. 'Just as I suspected, Nestor made the riddle especially cryptic because he didn't want it unravelled too quickly. The timing is critical. Jake must only work out the hidden meaning just before he enters the gate. If he doesn't work it out before entering the gate, then his mission is not heroic enough and will lack power. True heroism is the only language that has a chance of touching the sylph.'

As he studied Jake's body, Frost shook his head in amazement.

'Could Nestor have seen that far ahead? Could he have foreseen that I would play my part in ensuring the timing is perfect, or did he just trust in the cosmos?'

He recalled the image of Nestor in the mad mansion, cycling tipsy after the playful woman.

'Either way, I like him! Possibly even more than Jake! So bright, so light and yet so profound. Just my cup of tea!'

Frost closed his eyes and ran his left hand over the runes of the arch. He muttered something in the same archaic tongue and with a slow wave of his right hand he magically revealed Jake's inner journey so that he, and he alone, could see it.

JAKE HADN'T GONE FAR THROUGH THE WOOD WHEN AGAIN HE froze. He had spotted another creature. It was moving through the undergrowth a little way ahead—something much larger than a lizard.

The white wolf!

Jake recalled how Frost had said that it symbolised the demon Asclepius was searching for.

A child was riding on its back. It couldn't have been more than five years old. Stranger still, it was dressed for battle.

Jake dared not move. His heart leapt when the wolf stopped and glanced over its shoulder. It looked Jake straight in the eye. So did the warrior child, though where the child's expression was angry, the wolf's was gentle and searching. Finally they looked away and resumed their journey deeper into the wood.

The wolf's challenging me to follow it, thought Jake, fear and excitement coursing through him. He was aware that his physical body was in the cave, though kept his awareness with the journey.

The wolf was already out of sight. Jake was wondering whether to follow or not when something caused him to duck for cover. A large bird swooped down through the trees. It was a vulture. As it landed it transformed into Asclepius, who proceeded to follow the trail of the wolf.

Jake could scarcely believe his eyes. *Am I seeing the other side of Asclepius's strange experiment?*

He knew he had to follow. Yet he was held back by a powerful fear.

I must follow! he repeated, worried he would lose them.

At that moment a dove of the purest white appeared and hovered where the wolf and Asclepius had been. It beheld Jake for an auspicious moment before it flew off in the same direction as the others.

The very sight of it gifted Jake the courage he needed to follow.

Fortunately he found a slight track. The effort to follow it, however, seemed immense, as though he were wading through treacle.

A short while later he arrived exhausted at the top of a cliff. The path had come to an abrupt end. From the cliff Jake had a fine view of a bay belonging to a tropical island, yet there was no sign of the others. Instead, his attention was drawn to a large ship moored in the harbour.

Could that be the same one we saw in the mad mansion? he wondered. *Has Boreas taken a journey in search of the demon?*

Jake surveyed the beach. It appeared empty. Then he spotted someone.

'Boreas!' he gasped.

Though the god was some distance off, he looked peaceful as he wandered down to the sea. He stopped at the shoreline and gazed out at the horizon for a while.

Then something extraordinary happened. Having taken a step into the sea, he threw up his hands to the sky and released an awful wail. The sky darkened. Thunder rumbled. The calm sea transformed to something stormy.

An aura of light shone from Lord Boreas. When he wailed a second time lightning forked down over the sea. It was a display of great power. But it was maniacal and summoned from some place deep within Jake an equally powerful reaction.

'Why did you kill my dad?' he seethed.

Rage welled up in Jake, as alien a feeling as the fear of just moments before. He was deep in the unconscious where everything was more extreme. There and then he swore to avenge his dad's death.

The dark intent in Jake's thoughts was so potent that they carried like arrows from a bow.

Lord Boreas spun around. He stared directly at Jake with blazing eyes. Lightning which had raged over the sea streaked down through the trees about Jake. Some caught fire.

The god's presence multiplied. He appeared like a giant. His eyes bored into Jake with murderous hatred.

'Get out of my fort!' he roared in a voice so powerful that it tore through Jake like a blizzard. 'You imposter! It is *I* who shall have *my* revenge!'

Frost was ecstatic as he watched on.

Oh, how perfect! Jake will think it's Lord Boreas when it's really his dad. Lawrence must be deep down in his psyche. Too deep! He's been overrun, driven mad by a hatred he buried away and has refused to admit. Jake's mother, thought Frost, who knew Jake's history, *she died during his birth. Unconsciously Lawrence blames Jake though he doesn't realise it—doesn't realise it's just a projection of an ancestral wound far older. It's totally natural! Totally unreasonable! Consciously he loves Jake. Unconsciously he hates him and wants revenge.*

All this Frost already knew. He had seen the now-destroyed god gate records, not only of Lawrence's recent journey through the gate, but of what Lawrence had done sixteen years before, which had so upset Braysheath.

Frost tore his attention from the drama in the chamber. Someone was coming. A knowing smile spread across his face and he darted for the mist of the megaliths.

So powerful was Lord Boreas's wrath that it shook Jake free from the anger that had taken hold of him.

The god's rage grew even worse. The scene shifted. Lord Boreas was no longer standing on the beach but seated on a throne surrounded by an army which reached to the horizon. He stood up and roared to the sky with such fury that he appeared in pain.

A chill ran through Jake, not only at the sight of Lord Boreas: he sensed a presence in the woods. Something of great darkness was moving towards him.

Lord Boreas's demon! he panicked and spun around. *The one he and Asclepius are searching for!*

Jake stared into the dark wood, dreading what would emerge.

And the chamber! Not only have I helped them find the demon, he worried, recalling his second visit to Asclepius's lab, *but now I've opened a portal into the fort! It's time to wake up and get out of the chamber!*

Yet when Jake willed himself to sit up, he no longer had any sense of being in the chamber. He tried again and willed with all his might. Still it made no difference. He took a few steps back along the path, thinking it might help return to the chamber, but the darkness heralding the demon was like an impenetrable wall. As it got closer, Jake edged backwards towards the cliff until there was nowhere to go except over the edge to the distant crags below.

Still Lord Boreas roared to the sky, willing the demon on.

A shape began to take form within the darkness.

Jake battled against a terrible fear, battled to think of something intelligent to do, but there only appeared to be one option—to dive off the cliff.

Or maybe I should confront the demon, he thought. Yet the darkness was so dreadful that it seemed to portend the end of everything.

No. I must confront the source—Boreas. Diving off the cliff takes me towards him, he bravely decided.

With not a moment to lose Jake prepared to dive but was prevented by a terrific jolt. For a moment he feared that the demon had him.

Recovered from the shock, he found a woman holding his wrist. She was unlike any woman he had ever seen, more remarkable than even Nemesis or the serene woman on the mountain in the mad mansion. She was a warrior. Her beauty and origin defied description while the mature light in her striking brown eyes exuded great power. Behind her stood a huge bull elephant. She shone like a star. Through her contact, so did Jake.

For a moment they simply stood there. She looked as puzzled as Jake by the powerful energy coursing between them—not dark exactly, nor purely light, but powerful enough to hold off the demon for a critical moment.

She tugged on Jake's arm to leave. He turned to look back at Lord Boreas who, dazzled by their light, had ceased his roaring to the skies. Their light, however, was starting to dim. The initial burst had been spontaneous, fuelled by body contact alone. Jake's thoughts, however, were starting to interfere, draining light from the present and into the past and future.

Noting it, Lord Boreas shrieked his summons louder than ever. The wall of darkness reasserted itself. It shimmered, quaked, was about to open.

A nightmarish roar shook the woods as though it had echoed up from the deepest hell, from a giant and ancient beast. The demon was about to step into the reality of the fort.

Jake was spellbound, trapped between fear and fascination.

The darkness opened. The silhouette of something beastly arose from a place of great destruction.

In the moment its attention fixed on Jake and promised ruin, the warrior woman wrenched Jake's arm with such force that she hauled him completely clear of that world.

With a sudden gasp and heart racing, Jake sat bolt upright. He was back in the chamber.

'You!' he gasped.

Rani's only response was to drag him to his feet and haul him out of the chamber before anything else happened.

Finally free of it, Jake glanced back just in time to see a strange vision. It was the white wolf, except that this time the child on its back was naked and smiling. The wolf stood calmly within a peculiar gateway of black fire while the white dove hovered above its head. The wolf was looking directly at Jake, a curious look in its intelligent eyes. A moment later the image faded and the chamber returned to its former appearance.

Rani, who shared the vision, shuddered. *Was that the gate Frost mentioned Luna was after?* she wondered. The idea of leaving the cosmos, along with a gate of black fire, seemed equally strange and so she put the two together. Worse still, if that's what it was, it meant that Frost had been telling the truth.

Black fire, thought Jake with a chill as he recalled the wall of flame that consumed Wilderspin's mad mansion, along with his nightmares as a child. *But why here and again with Boreas? What's he got to do with a door that's supposed to be part of my lightline?*

When Jake turned from the chamber, the sight of the girl standing so close was the best tonic he could have wished for.

'That's the second time you've saved me,' he said with a grateful smile.

'It wasn't me,' said the girl flatly and glanced down at her mysterious glove.

After her meeting with Glabrous, Rani had used her new-found freedom to take a secret wander down through the quieter parts of the fort. As she had approached the floor of the chambers, the glove had vibrated violently, leading her through an archway she hadn't noticed before, only to find Jake in the chamber having a seizure of some sort.

'What is that?' he asked, studying the glove.

Rani flicked up her chin in a defiant gesture.

'Won't you at least tell me your name?' said Jake, mystified by her manner.

'Mind your own business,' said Rani, conveniently forgetting the etiquette she had demanded of Glabrous only that evening.

Far from taking offence, Jake found her haughtiness endearing.

'What are you smiling at?' growled Rani.

'You.'

'Why?'

'You looked different in there,' said Jake, avoiding the question.

Rani recalled what Frost had said about Jake seeing her as a mermaid through the net of light.

'How so?' she asked, feigning boredom.

'Equally impressive as you look now,' said Jake. 'But different. Older.'

Rani gave Jake an imperious toss of her head, which made her even more attractive.

'Did I look any different?' he asked.

'Nothing special,' said Rani, concealing her inner turmoil.

Despite the protection of the glove, when she had taken hold of Jake's wrist she also had felt a great jolt. She had seen nothing of the bay or the approaching demon in the woods. She had simply seen him—not as he looked now nor as the man in the lake, though she had felt his energy. The wrist she had gripped had belonged to a man, great in size, lordly in bearing, fiercely intelligent, but dark as hell. The chamber had revealed what she had only glimpsed through the net of light, before it had revealed Jake as a noble king—his shadow, one powerful enough to eclipse the sun.

Any defrosting in her feelings towards Jake had immediately refrozen. Any sympathy for his plight had fled for those who might stand in his way. And yet, for the briefest moment, the dreadful image of the dark man had been lost in a beautiful light. In that moment she had seen Jake as she saw him now.

It was the memory of that light mixed with the shadow that threw Rani back into confusion.

'You do realise there was an elephant behind you,' said Jake.

'Elephant?' said Rani, her haughtiness shattered. Despite the number of times it had now appeared to her in visions and dreams, it remained a mystery to her.

'A bull elephant. The largest I've ever seen.'

'Rubbish,' said Rani, regathering her composure. 'Anyway, I have to go. I have things to do.'

'Go where and do what?' exclaimed Jake. 'You're not even a guest here!'

'I'm more a guest than you!' shot back Rani, glancing again at her glove.

'I don't need to be a guest,' said Jake laughing. 'I'm supposed to be the lord of this place.'

Rani treated Jake to another toss of the head. 'Supposed to be.'

'You still haven't answered what it is you have to do.'

'House cleaning,' said Rani.

Jake got the gist of what she was implying. 'Frost says you're an assassin,' he ventured.

'Then I shall assassinate him,' said Rani matter-of-factly.

God, she's gorgeous! thought Jake.

'By the way,' he asked. 'What do you think of pre-determined meetings? You know, like you and me. Perhaps we've met before and were destined to meet again in this life for some important reason.'

Jake had touched a raw nerve in Rani. She wasn't in the mood to explore Frost's idea about the three of them having some great mission together.

'What do you think of predetermined departures?' she replied and made to leave.

'Wait!' said Jake. 'Do you know what these runes say?' he asked.

'No,' said Rani, turning back for a moment. 'But I know the rock is sodalite.'

'Sodalite? What does it do?'

'It's a powerful rock. It's used to banish confusion and summon truth,' she said, realising the irony, for she was more confused than ever. 'To control it requires great power and wisdom. Which is why I had to come and drag you out.'

'Sodalite,' muttered Jake as he recalled all he had seen and how it seemed another confirmation of Frost's theory that Asclepius and Lord Boreas were conspiring to take the fort using a demon.

'Rocks see very far,' continued Rani. 'But they are less forgiving teachers than plants and can take you to places from which you might never return.'

Jake then recalled how he had been mulling over the riddle when the arch had partially appeared. *Perhaps it was her presence nearby which allowed the arch to form completely. It took a girl, a lady.*

It struck Jake like a thunderbolt.

It's not 'Go ladies'! he cried in thought, coming to the same conclusion as Frost. *It's 'ladies-to'! It's an anagram of sodalite! Go to sodalite—go to the chamber to see the truth!'*

While Jake was lost in revelation, Rani slipped into the shadows.

CHAPTER 61
THE ONLY WAY OUT

ONCE MORE LAWRENCE WAS ON HIS HANDS AND KNEES, THIS time on the beach.

'God help me,' he muttered, having cried to the sky three times. On the third cry something incredible had happened. A pure and powerful sensation had coursed through his body as though God were actually answering. For a few moments it had outshone the appalling darkness. It was the darkest he had felt so far, darker than the god gate, darker than the voyage on the ship, darker than anything he could imagine. It had been triggered by his setting foot in the sea, making escape impossible. Whether it had been the full force of the Emperor's darkness or just a fraction, it was too much for Lawrence. For a dreadful moment he had felt the tiger's breath upon his neck.

'I can't believe it,' he despaired. 'The Emperor, the pirate, he was right. There *is* a hatred in me. And oh, what hatred! Unconscious but real. I felt it! An abyss of hatred so great that the Emperor almost had me.'

Lawrence thumped a fist into the sand. 'A hatred of...' He could barely say the word. 'Of Jake for heaven's sake! And when, consciously, I love him more than the life itself.'

Lawrence sat back on his heels and gazed out at the turgid sea. *But where does it come from? From a past life, from this life? When Gwendolyn died at his birth?*

He released a heavy sigh.

It's possible. And with all the guilt and shame at feeling such a thing for my only son, it's been buried and forgotten. Buried oh so very deep, here in this cursed place so close to the glorious sea.

Lawrence ran a weary hand over his face. 'Gwendolyn,' he sighed. *I thought I had righted that. Did my unconscious not take note?*

As Lawrence buried his head in his hands, the world closed in about him. 'How will I ever manage? How can I surrender my soul to the sylph through my son if I feel this uncontrollable hatred for him? I'm more likely to kill him!'

He shook his head.

In a holygate, in front of the sylph, already bitter with despair, my God, I dread to think. By entering the gate, I could make things even worse. An act intended to save the cosmos could end up doing precisely the opposite.

The world closed in yet tighter. He almost couldn't breathe when a glimmer of light came to his rescue.

'Jake!' he gasped as he recalled what he had seen up on the cliff—not Jake as a sixteen year old, but as a man, a warrior, later joined by a warrior woman, who together had created a light so bright that it had cast back the darkness.

Just the memory of it cast back the darkness once more. Light filled Lawrence's heart and the world reopened for him.

The uncanny appearance of Jake had initially almost destroyed Lawrence. Instead, however, it had gifted him vital insight into the truth of his own demons ahead of entering the holygate. Forewarned was forearmed.

'Ah, my son,' sighed Lawrence with a glow of pride. *He must have found a way into one of the more powerful parts of the fort. Perhaps the chambers. I wonder how he managed it?* Lawrence had heard of them, though never seen them himself.

He recalled the powerful symbols of Jake's corridor in Wilderspin's mad mansion.

My God, this cosmos! And the Scribes! Surely Nemesis foresaw all of this. She knows our lightlines. And surely it was written in the fates that Gwendolyn would die that day Jake was born—for a reason that's vital to this mighty test of courage. This great test of faith. For Jake, for myself, for all of us. We are all part of what Jake must become, for all our sakes, perhaps even for Luna's, who knows?

Again, Lawrence shook his head, this time in awe. 'It's all so damn subtle! Oh, how we miss the point and blame others instead.'

The more Lawrence reasoned it through, the more his strength returned.

'Yes, by God!' he cried and leapt to his feet. 'I love my son! And my conscious love will conquer my unconscious hate! And I shall enter the holygate! And as God is my witness, as I stand before you, Great Mother of all creation, I do solemnly swear to pass through this dark, dark night, to fight what I must fight and offer my soul, such as it is, to you, My One True Love in all your forms!'

Lawrence took a few steps forward and fell to his knees. He dared to place his hands into the sea of his imprisonment which just moments before had caused him such torment. This time, as he scooped up some water and cleansed his face with it, he suffered no pain. And though shark fins rose up through the sea's surface, a ray of sun broke through the still stormy sky and shone down upon him.

'My Love,' he repeated softly and reverently bowed his head. 'Guide me. I am your servant. Show me how to leave this cursed place so that I may prove my love.'

The ray of sun brightened and shone upon Lawrence for a moment longer before once again disappearing behind the clouds.

Full of hope, his faith restored, Lawrence stood up, placed his hands together in prayer to the sea and finally departed the beach and made his way back to the palace.

It was dusk by the time Lawrence entered the palace gates. He decided to wander through the royal gardens with their glorious array of trees, shrubs and flowers.

He was passing through an avenue of rhododendrons, his mind far away, when he was ambushed and hauled into the bushes.

His attacker, though strong, was no warrior. Following a frenzied struggle, Lawrence pinned the person down. The moon was up. Just enough light filtered through the foliage to reveal a face.

'Well, well,' said Lawrence as he gazed down at the very same mysterious woman who had shown him to his quarters. Part of her robes had been torn in the scuffle. His eyes widened with shock when he noticed a scar on her left breast—a recently healed dagger wound.

'How did you get this?' he quizzed.

'Do you not recognise the work of your own hand?' she replied curtly.

'Then you live!' cried Lawrence.

His sense of hope grew stronger still. Though her appearance had changed, she had the same energy as the girl on the ship who he had stabbed in panic. 'Oh, what joy!' he cried. 'Forgive me! Please forgive me. That cabin, that ship, there was something—'

'I know,' she said.

'It was you in the cathedral too, wasn't it?' said Lawrence as he released her.

She nodded.

Lawrence's spirits soared. 'Then I'm right in thinking that you are—'

The lady put a finger to his lips. 'Control your emotions. Keep your feelings light. Nothing goes unnoticed here.'

She survived! thought Lawrence, referring to the pure aspect of his ego. At this point in the journey she was an inner-guide he could trust.

She survived a mortal blow! She's getting stronger, more mature. I must have done something right. And she's beautiful!

You must leave this place,' she said. 'The demon they fear is moving closer. They cannot risk it entering the city. Lord Boreas will make his move before it does.'

'His move against me?'

'Yes. And if he strikes you in this place where you're weak despite the illusion of health, he will effectively destroy you. You will remain here forever and he'll repossess his body and rejoin Luna.'

'This demon…' asked Lawrence.

'Let us speak no more of it. It's too risky. You'll recognise it when you see it.'

'I'm going to see it?'

'You have to,' she said without elaborating.

Lawrence nodded, doing his best not to dwell on what it meant. Instead he gazed at the woman in complete awe at what he saw.

A gentle smile graced her face. Its effect on Lawrence was like spring sun following the bitterest of winters.

'You must leave,' she repeated as her troubled expression returned.

'But how? We're on an island. The sea is cursed.'

'There's a way,' she said and took his hand. 'There always is.'

'I leave now?'

'There's not a moment to lose,' she said. 'Follow me.'

Staying close to the cover of the trees and bushes, she led him to a pond.

'Where now?' whispered Lawrence.

'The only way out is in,' she said. 'In and through.'

'The pond?'

'The darkness. Come,' she said and led him quietly into the water.

Lawrence was about to ask her where they were going when she turned and put a finger to her lips. 'Have faith.'

Still holding Lawrence's hand, she sank beneath the surface.

Taking a deep breath, Lawrence followed.

As they swam down through what was a surprisingly deep and murky pond, Lawrence was amazed to discover that he didn't need to breathe. *It's her contact!* he realised.

Towards the bottom they swam past a boulder and through some dense reeds. They entered a downward slanting tunnel, just wide enough to swim through.

Down and down they went through a tunnel that seemed to go on forever when, finally, it came to an end and they swam up through a hole. They emerged into a narrow cave.

Again the woman put a finger to her lips. Still holding his hand she slipped through a crack at the end of the cave.

As they advanced through a fissure, the air grew cooler. A great torrent could be heard ahead.

A short while later the woman stopped. The fissure had reached what seemed like the back of a cavern, though was in fact a broad ledge of a waterfall.

Staying in the shadows of the fissure, the woman indicated two male guards standing either side of the waterfall. Lawrence studied them. Armoured in leather like Mongols of old, they bristled with weapons—sabres, knives, with bows and arrows an arm's length away leaning against rocks. Lawrence had no weapons. Ordinarily, it would be possible to materialise weapons using his imagination. As Geoffrey had warned, however, Lawrence was out of his depth. To try would either result in nothing or backfire disastrously.

Any fighting would be back to basics.

With her right hand over her heart, she drew the finger of her left hand across her throat.

Kill with compassionate intent. Understanding the symbolism, he nodded, nourished by her strength.

Lawrence slipped from the fissure. Both guards were looking out over the mighty chasm beyond the waterfall. Keeping to the edge of the rock wall where the shadow was thickest, aided by the roar of the waterfall, Lawrence crept round to the guard on his side of the river.

Within two paces of reaching him, just as Lawrence had expected of an elite warrior, the guard sensed his presence. Lawrence sprang forward. In an instant, the guard reached over his shoulders for his sabres. As he swung round with both blades, Lawrence was already sweeping behind him. He grabbed a dagger from the guard's belt and, with a prayer on his lips, drove it up through the ribs and into the heart.

The guard collapsed to the ground.

The other one swept up his bow and deftly loaded an arrow.

Lawrence grabbed both sword hilts of the slain guard as he kicked his body over the ledge.

The other guard released his arrow.

Lawrence didn't waver. His movement fluid, he deflected the missile with one blade and hurled the other across the river.

It spun like a propeller over the water. As the guard stretched his bow a second time, the sword slashed it clean in two and gashed his cheek.

The guard ran a hand over the wound. His eyes narrowed as he studied his attacker.

Lawrence bowed his head. *Hello brother*, he said in thought. *I surrender to the cosmos. Let it decide the fate of our dance.*

The guard made a cursory bow, drew one of his swords and rushed forward.

Equally spaced across the river were three stepping stones. The warrior's feet scarcely touched them as he swept across.

Hardly a second had passed before their blades clashed.

Lawrence stepped back to absorb the blow of energy before turning it back on the guard in what did indeed become a dance. A dance with Death. A dance with fate.

His mind empty, Lawrence surrendered to the flow of existence—the river, the air, the rock, the fire of the lanterns, everything flowed. Definition dissolved. Time lost its meaning. Their bodies had form and yet were formless. They became like concentrations of coloured particles, the colours of their robes like dust shot through with light, swirling with and through everything else, the sword nothing more than a channel for a willforce superior to his own.

There in the extreme of his existence, his life hanging on the finest of threads, energised by the presence of his guide, Lawrence danced with creation in all its forms.

Tears welled in his eyes.

In the very moment he forgot he was even duelling, the moment he was completely empty, a surge of energy flowed through him and out along the blade. Following a series of strokes—impossibly fast, impossibly skilful—the duel was over.

Dust settled. Definition and time returned. The guard was on his back, a blade through his heart.

Lawrence knelt down, placed a hand gently over the guard's face and made a prayer—asked forgiveness, gave forgiveness and fared him well for the onward journey.

He stood up and turned to the woman. A glorious smile lit up her face. She ran over to him. As she wiped the tear from his cheek, her eyes shone into his.

Without a word, she once more took his hand and ran forward. Together they leapt over the waterfall.

The drop was far, but there was nothing to fear. They dived through the spray with the grace of ospreys, plunged to the bottom of the deep pool and swam up to the shore.

'Hurry,' she said, as she led him up the crags. 'Your battle will have been sensed. And they'll definitely notice when we open the door. There's little time.'

Having scaled a portion of the crags, she led Lawrence along a thin ledge behind the cascade. It opened out into a cave. At the back of it was a smooth wall of granite.

From behind a boulder she collected a bundle. 'Here,' she said. 'You'll need these.'

Wrapped within a bundle of winter clothes was a rifle, a pistol, an ammunition belt, another sword to add to the one he had taken from the guard along with a knife.

'This deep into your unconscious, you're going to feel the cold,' she said.

'Guns?' said Lawrence, surprised, for guns were the weapons of cowards—death dealt out from a safe distance.

'These were all I could find. Besides, they'll be pursuing you with guns and it's your intention that counts.'

'And the door?'

'Do as I do,' she said. While kneeling, she placed the palms of her hands against the granite wall.

Lawrence followed. He sensed her prayer, though didn't hear the words. A flow of energy coursed through him. The surface of the rock vibrated. The sensation grew more intense, crescendoed, when a blast of light shot through them from the rock.

It was followed by a blast of snow. A hole had appeared in the wall.

To Lawrence's astonishment, the portal led to a snow covered mountain pass and a treacherous-looking ridge leading up to a summit obscured by clouds.

'Hurry, put these on,' she said, handing him a pair of mountain boots.

'Where does the ridge lead?' he asked as he changed shoes.

'To liberation, to damnation, the choice is yours. Remember what I said. The only way out is in and through. You must pass through all obstacles that stand in your way. If you try to avoid them you will slip and fall straight into the jaws of the tiger.'

Harsh voices echoed throughout the chasm as orders were barked from the top of the waterfall, their grave portent penetrating the thunder of crashing water.

'If you flee your fear,' continued the woman, 'you'll only empower it. You must listen to the sorrow behind it. Only when you experience that sorrow, experience it objectively, can you understand it then give it new meaning in order to release its power.'

Lawrence finished tying up his boots. 'These challenges—are they from past lives, just this one or both?'

'It's all the same. The pattern repeats until it's resolved. If you atone for this life, you atone for all,' she said, confirming Lawrence's own feelings.

He tugged on the jumper and Arctic coat, stowed the weapons, slung the belt of ammunition around him and checked the rifle.

The woman placed a hand gently against his cheek.

'You must become a *true* king,' she said. 'Not like that emperor up there. That one's a spoilt child, compensating for his deep insecurity with over-confidence, but he's extremely dangerous all the same. You must become the king of yourself. Only then can you fully surrender to infinite grace and true power.'

Lawrence placed a hand against her cheek and smiled.

The woman leaned forward and placed a soft kiss on Lawrence's lips. A flow of unimaginable warmth washed through him and boosted his spirits.

'I love you,' she said, her eyes welling with tears.

'And I love you,' said Lawrence, his heart overflowing, almost forgetting that she was simply part of himself.

The moment was broken by voices from below. Warriors had already dived into the pool and were scaling the crags.

'Go!' she whispered.

'Will you be alright?'

'That's up to you,' she said and pushed him towards the pass.

Lawrence cocked the bolt of the rifle, stepped through the hole in the wall and looked back a final time. He gave the woman a grave nod.

As he disappeared into the blizzard, she slipped into the shadows of the cave. The portal remained open—once opened, it couldn't be closed.

CHAPTER 62
POWER OF ACCEPTANCE

CLOAKED IN A WORLD OF PIGEONS, ONE WHICH COVERED VIRTUALLY every patch of Renlock's inner walls, was the Pigeon Lord himself—Wilderspin. He stood on the great wall, his eyes bulging with anticipation.

The pigeons were beside themselves with excitement. The din of cooing would have been intolerable to all but Wilderspin as they fluttered about the almost full giant bottle of whisky, fluttered about the slumped form of Brock in the alley, fluttered everywhere, forever shifting their roosts.

The cooing suddenly rose to a feverish pitch.

With a wave of Wilderspin's hand, it stopped. Fluttering pigeons parted like waves to make way for one pigeon in particular that flew gravely to the top of the whisky bottle.

There, as countless pigeons had done for hundreds of years, and with great ceremony, it cried a single golden tear into the bottle—the last selfish human prayer that Brock would receive from the Surface. It tallied perfectly with his flock of worshippers falling below the critical level required to sustain him as God of the Surface and Overlord of the Outer-Peregrinus. The Threshold of Belief had been crossed.

A powerful quake shook the atrium

Pigeons flew up in frenzy.

Wilderspin clapped his hands together in delight and cheered.

The ancient valve hidden within the walls had clamped shut, cutting off the energy which flowed up through Renlock, up to the sacred sites beneath the Surface temples and gifted an Overlord omnipotence.

The bottle shone powerfully. No longer the sickly gold of whisky, for a glorious moment it blazed like a sun.

Then it dimmed completely—to the colour of bog. The dark fluid flowed down through the intravenous tube like the poison it was, towards the right arm of Brock who still hadn't stirred.

Finally the fluid flowed through the needle into his body.

The pigeons quietened. Wilderspin watched on enthralled.

Moments passed until finally there was movement.

Contrary to Wilderspin's expectations for something more dramatic, the image of Brock slowly raised his head, stretched his arms and released a giant blissful yawn as though he yawned for all humans, releasing them, through himself, of part of their burden—a farewell gift. It was reflected in the movement of dark fluid. As he stretched and yawned, the entire bottle was drained through his system, yet appeared to have no effect on him.

He got to his feet and stretched again. As he did so, the filthy alley and the rest of the insides of Renlock transformed into a jungle paradise, bursting with life. A crystalline waterfall cascaded behind Brock. Deer and other woodland creatures frolicked about while tropical birds astonished the pigeons with their sweet songs and dazzling flight.

Brock's rags were gone. Simple and radiant, his body painted in the symbols of the land, he stood as an Aboriginal tribesman, a beautiful smile upon his face.

All that remained of the alley was the now-empty bottle of whisky, perched on a cliff, the tube from its bottom still connected to Brock's arm.

He beheld the confounded Wilderspin. Eyes shining and with an expression of pure compassion, Brock placed his hands together in prayer.

Wilderspin rubbed his hands together awkwardly for want of something to do with them—anything but Namaste back.

Unperturbed, Brock glowed. His aura became so bright that the magnificent light surged from his right arm, up through the tube and filled the giant bottle.

In less than a second, it was glowing once more. This time, not like the sun, but a star. As Overlord, Brock had never relied on the energy of Renlock. His power had come from presence.

Wilderspin licked his lips at the sight of so much pure light.

Then the bottle began to crack.

His greed became panic.

Pigeons flew up in shock.

Seeing Wilderspin's fear, Brock shone even brighter. So too the bottle. The cracks were spreading.

There remained an exquisite moment of suspense. Cracks united. Light flexed. Bodies braced themselves.

The bottle exploded.

Wilderspin threw up his arms to protect himself from the shards of glass cast out like missiles by the blaze of light.

He needn't have bothered. Following a moment's silence, he peeped out through his arms, then checked himself for wounds. There were none. He looked about Renlock to check his pigeons—though stunned, none of them had been harmed in the blast. The shards had become butterflies of light which flitted about them.

Finally he looked for Brock but he was nowhere to be seen. Paradise had gone. The alley had gone. There was simply the granite atrium, a mature oak standing resplendently at its centre—a departing gift from Brock to an institution mistrusting of plants.

'Well, I'll be dammed,' muttered Wilderspin. 'They do say, that in order to change one must first accept one's plight. Alas, dear Brock, your time is up! You'll have to wait till the next life!'

CHAPTER 63
THE FALL

AS JAKE MADE HIS WAY FROM THE CHAMBER BACK UP TO HIS room, he felt like a bird flying through the eye of a storm. By saving him from the chamber's truths, the warrior girl had gifted him wings—his heart soared and he with it. But saving him from the chamber couldn't save Jake, or anyone else, from the unavoidable—darkness. Darkness from Lord Boreas. Darkness from the sylph. Darkness from himself. From everyone.

Beneath it all was the uneasy feeling Jake had about the riddles. Though he had cracked the final clue relating to the sodalite chamber, he felt no sense of completion. On the contrary, he felt that he and Frost were missing something, that there was another layer to the riddles. Two sentences in particular bothered him: *Imagining things of which none can speak* and *Accepting in action is both the cruel and the kind.*

In one respect he marvelled at his granddad's cleverness. Not only was *Ladies-to* an anagram of sodalite, but it implied a female was required to open the way. And perhaps not just any female. That the girl had turned up when she did was incredible.

The riddles, however, seemed too clever, though Jake quickly realised that their real genius was that they weren't supposed to be conclusive. The riddles were leads. Only by following his heart and knowing his mind, as the riddle suggested, would Jake work it out.

By the time he reached the lawn, a great exhaustion swept through him. It had been another incredibly long day. His mind simply gave up pondering all the mysteries or worrying about whether he had made matters worse by entering the chamber. Neither had he the energy to confide in Frost. Jake simply trudged up to his room, collapsed onto his bed and fell into a deep asleep.

SOME HOURS LATER, JAKE AWOKE IN A COLD SWEAT TO THE haunting howl of a wolf followed by the screech of an owl
　He opened his eyes. A chill ran through him.
　Something moved in the shadows next to the bed.
　'Mornin' Sleepin' Beauty,' said the voice of Rufus.
　Jake cursed. 'What are you doing here? What time is it?' he asked.
　'It's bloody early, but it's time to get up.'
　'Why? What's happened?'
　'Get yer skirt on, hop aboard and I'll show yer,' said Rufus.
　'Skirt? I thought you were Scottish. It's a kilt.'
　'Not if it's worn by a southern Jessie. Now get movin'. We'll breakfast at the farmhouse.'
　'The farmhouse!' exclaimed Jake, brightening up. 'We're going to the farmhouse?'

HAVING LEAPT THROUGH THANADOR, RUFUS AND JAKE ARRIVED in the study. Though inner-time worked differently to time on the Surface they occasionally overlapped. Just like on Himassisi, it was pre-dawn at the farmhouse.
　Jake took a deep inhale of the familiar smell of books and smiled.
　'I'll go and put the kettle on,' said Rufus realising Jake wanted a moment or two alone in the study.
　'I don't suppose you can butter toast as well?' said Jake, giving up on wondering how a carpet could do such things.
　'If I can create flight by harnessing the subtle magic of the five forces, I think I can handle a bloody knife,' said Rufus and disappeared.
　While Rufus was in the kitchen, Jake searched the shelves for a book on animal symbols. Despite what he had heard from Frost, he wanted to know more about wolves. There were a number of things which bothered him—inconsistencies between what the riddles suggested, what he himself had seen and Frost's theory of a demonic threat to the fort. Though he had felt the horror of the demon through the chamber, something didn't quite make sense. It was just a feeling and had something to do with the wolf.

He spotted a book titled *Animal Speak*. Having checked it covered the wolf, he popped it in a shoulder bag he took from the back of a chair, intent on reading it later. Before he left the study, he took a final glance around it.

Two butterflies appeared.

Butterflies in winter!

The sight of them reminded Jake of those he had seen resting on the coat of the white wolf in the tree of the lab. They each landed on a different book.

To Jake's amazement they were the very same books he had noted in his dream—one titled *Janus*, the other, *The Tibetan Book of the Dead*.

This time Jake wasn't so quick to dismiss them. First he picked the book on Janus and turned to the first chapter.

Janus is the God of Beginnings and Ends, God of the Journey and all its transitions. He is sometimes also called the God of Gates, sometimes the God of Chaos and Deception.

Gates! thought Jake, before realising it was probably a general reference rather than relating to anything specific.

He went on to read how Janus presides over the start and finish of any conflict. The rest of the text became heavy and academic, stating how Jana, Yana, Gnana or Gnosis were all the science of Janus or the science of initiatic knowledge. He leafed through the remainder of the book though nothing caught is attention.

It was the same with the Tibetan Book of the Dead.

'Perhaps it's just the title I'm supposed to notice,' he muttered.

He studied the cover picture of the two-faced Janus. The first image that popped into his mind was of Lord Boreas ranting on the beach, which was in stark contrast to his smooth performance in Trafalgar Square. The word *dead* in the title of the second book reminded Jake of his dad. He knew little about *The Tibetan Book of the Dead* except that it was something to do with guiding the soul on the journey through death to rebirth. In other words, physical death was just the surface of things. What seemed dead, wasn't really. Both books were in his dad's study.

Jake's heart leapt as he dared to imagine once more that his dad had survived the leap through the gate with Lord Boreas, that the conflict Janus presided over was between Lord Boreas and his dad.

It lasted only a moment. The evidence against it was too strong: the mortal wound through the chest, the opinions of Rufus and Braysheath that he couldn't have survived, along with what Lord Boreas had roared at Jake from the beach—*Get out of my fort! You imposter! It is I who shall have my revenge!* His dad would never say such things. It was clear to Jake that Lord Boreas was what he seemed and intended to take the fort. To think otherwise achieved nothing but torment.

'Then what does it mean?' he asked the butterflies.

They flew up, danced about each other—an erratic flight that became increasingly graceful, ending with a pop as they disappeared through the inkwell, just as the moth had done before.

Maybe Lord Boreas has become two-faced like Janus as result of passing through the gate with Dad. And the Book of the Dead— perhaps the message is that he can be defeated and sent back to the Surface to be reborn as a fallen god, mused Jake.

Given Jake's destiny to enter the holygate, it was an encouraging thought. His deductions, however, still didn't feel quite right. Regardless, with a final glance at the room he loved, he made for the kitchen.

Just as he had promised, Rufus had prepared both tea and toast. Jake sat down to breakfast.

'I was wondering,' he said. 'In passing through the god gate twice, would that make Boreas a little mad at times?'

'I suppose so. That sort of power goes to the head. Why?'

'I'm trying to account for his mood swings,' explained Jake.

'Aye, well a god like him is especially touchy. God of the North Wind, Lord of the Sirens. Not like Brock, the current Overlord. Well, I say current...'

Something shadowy swept past the kitchen window. It was promptly followed by another then a whole group.

'Are those owls?' asked Jake, having never seen more than one at time.

'It's started,' said Rufus gravely.

'What has?'

'Brock's fall.'

'You mean his fall from being Overlord—the god of the Surface and Outer-Peregrinus? Luna's replaced him?' asked Jake as a chill ran through him.

'Aye.'

'Granddad,' muttered Jake. 'If she's Overlord then she has less need of the sylph, less need of Granddad. Time is running out!'

'Bring yer tea and toast, grab a coat and hop up, lad,' said Rufus in a kind tone. 'Let's first say our farewells to Brock.'

Jake did so and they flew out into the fading night.

He gasped. The sky was full not only of owls but sparrows too, all flying in the same direction as though a great migration were underway, their wings silvered by the moon.

Jake studied the glowing orb. *Luna*, he thought, noting the irony in her choice of name.

It started to snow. The flakes seemed to fall unnaturally slowly and added to the solemn poetry of the flying birds who made no sound save that of their flight.

One owl flew so close that Jake noticed that it was carrying something writhing in its talons—a snake. It wasn't the only one. Straining his eyes, he realised many others were also carrying them.

Rufus flew higher.

Soon they were over the coast and flying out to sea. The birds were coming from all directions, merging like rivers that had taken to the skies in search of their source. The owls, sparrows and snakes were joined by another type of bird. Its white wings were vast.

'Albatrosses!' gasped Jake.

At first the migration had seemed to Jake like a funeral. It was too magnificent for that, however. His skin tingled with wonder.

'My God,' he muttered.

'Not anymore,' said Rufus sardonically.

'This is all Brock, isn't it?'

'Aye. He's regathering himself. Most Overlords prefer to appear in the form of a single god and frighten the crap out of everyone. But Brock split himself up—many of the owls, sparrows, albatrosses and grass snakes the world over are Brock, along with many other creatures. In all places at once, as it were, watching over humankind night and day, whether on land or at sea. You cannae see them from here, but most of the snakes will be swimming through the oceans.'

Jake was dumbfounded. A wave of great affection washed through him. He reflected how each morning it was the chirpy sparrow who gently awoke him to the blessing of a new day, while the call to sleep came from the owl. He was grateful that all of them weren't leaving, though wondered at the impact on the food chain from those that were.

'Where are they going?' asked Jake looking out over the astonishing flock.

'Wanna see?'

'Yes I do.'

As they flew, Jake felt a great sense of peace, despite what the event portended.

'Why is there an Overlord?' he asked. 'Surely nature takes care of itself.'

'There didnae used to be,' said Rufus. 'But when the god gate appeared, a succession of gods—mainly gods of war—took control.'

'What about Brock? Surely he isn't a god of war.'

'Far from it. In fact, he was on the verge of passing from Pride to the Core when Braysheath asked him to compete for the role. It was an attempt to restore balance. Brock refused at first. He foresaw the scale of ignorance and how believers would fight over him, claim him for themselves. But Braysheath is a persuasive fella and Brock eventually agreed. Even though it meant that one day he would fall and have to return to the Surface and start all over.'

'What? He can't continue where he left off?'

'Nope. Such are the rules of the god gate. But souls like Brock advance quickly. They die aware of who they really are. It's the same when they're reborn. Why, the likes of Brock could reach the Core in a day if they chose to.'

'I don't mean to be disrespectful, but in the end, given what a mess everything is up here, what did Brock really do?'

'All any of us can do, laddie. He did his best. He lived his message of peace. Look at the beauty in all the creatures about us. Those that aren't Brock are here to pay their respects.'

As Jake once more marvelled at the creatures, he thought of the wars now raging on Roar, Leaf and Hunter. The peace that Brock so deserved in the worlds of Death would be hard to find.

'The truth is,' continued Rufus, 'we'll never really know how much shadow he absorbed on behalf of humans and how much light he gave out, but he played his part in bringin' us to this critical point. Humans prayed for a saviour and that's what they got. Now that he's fallen, humans must recognise the mistakes they've made. Their entire system is based on fear, along with the hatred and selfishness born of it. Starting from this fateful day that has to change. They must save themselves.'

As Jake drank down his lukewarm tea, his mind turned to the shepherds and what he had seen in the mad mansion, in particular the white phoenix.

'What about the oldest of the shepherds?' he asked. 'Why have I never met him?'

'Yer might do one day. He has little time to spare.'

'Why, what does he do?'

'He's the only one strong enough to absorb all the excess darkness created by humans and transform it back into light. What Brock couldn't absorb, he took, and every day the darkness increases. Each time it almost destroys him.'

'Absorb?' asked Jake.

'Aye. Every dusk of every day, for ten thousand years or so, toiling the whole night and collapsing at dawn.'

'Where does he do this?' asked Jake, aghast at such an image.

'Some place where he won't overheat,' said Rufus. 'The North Pole. Of course, up there it's dark all winter and light all summer, but the dawn and dusk I spoke of are symbolic of the whole world, one that only he sees. Only the most powerful souls are able to see him unless he wants to be seen. He exists on a very subtle plane. All humans see of his work is what they call the northern lights.'

The thought of such a being living in such a place, doing such a thing, was almost too fantastic for Jake to believe.

'But if he's so powerful, why doesn't he sort out Luna?'

'Because he cannae risk leaving his post. He quite literally holds the cosmos together. And with so great a task, he hasn't the energy to spare.'

Jake shook his head in wonder, unable to imagine what it would be like to meet such a being. The idea kept him occupied for quite some time.

Eventually it stopped snowing. With the arrival of first light, Jake could just make out the ghostly coastline of France. On looking up, one bird in particular caught his attention.

'Isn't that Braysheath's eagle?' he said.

Rufus had barely answered in the affirmative when the eagle banked in their direction, expanded in size and swept them up so that Rufus became Jake's saddle.

'Wow!' he cried. 'How—?'

'Quite simple,' said the eagle in a familiar voice.

'Braysheath? Is that you?' exclaimed Jake.

'Part of me. So too is the cobra. But he and my human form are elsewhere right now. Just thought I'd pop up here and wish dear old Brock *Bon voyage!*'

Though Braysheath's wing beats were unhurried, he was covering the Surface at astonishing speed, just like Deuteronomy had through the sea. Soon Jake could see the Mediterranean Sea and the Atlas Mountains of Morocco beyond.

'Oh look!' cried Braysheath. 'Whales!'

Jake looked down to see the majestic sight of a huge pod of whales, flanked by dolphins leaping in and out of the sea. As the whales glided through the surface they blasted water through their blowholes and kicked up their mighty tails.

'Ha! They too have come to say farewell!' said Braysheath. 'How wonderful!'

Next arrived a vast flock of starlings. Thousands of them burst up through the gaps between the other birds in a dazzling dance of perfect synchrony, the entire flock moving as though operated by a single brain, expanding and contracting, twisting and turning as they spiralled up.

All three of them released cries of delight.

As they passed over Africa, Jake fell into silence, too absorbed by the miraculous sight below as great herds of wildebeest, elephants and other magnificent creatures galloped and charged in farewell to Brock.

By the time they reached the Great Rift Valley of East Africa, the gathering of Brock had become so dense that Jake could scarcely see the land beneath them.

He looked on spellbound as the migration merged into a mighty swirl over a broad-lipped crater, imagining the carpet of snakes slithering up its sides between all the mammals.

Despite their vast number, still the birds remained in silence. Not a single chirp escaped them as they spiralled down into the crater.

'Where are they all going?' asked Jake.

'At the bottom of the crater is a portal that opens only at this special time of Fall,' explained Braysheath. 'It leads to what's called a gene pool—a large lake. A true wonder! The portion of the mammals and reptiles that make up the Overlord enter it from one end, the birds landing on its surface, whereupon it becomes a magnificent lake of glowing light as their energy unites. What emerges from the other end is a single being. In this case Brock. Oh, for you to see it! Alas, it's a private affair. Spectators are forbidden.'

'What about the Brock I saw in Renlock?' asked Jake.

'The hollow-gram?' said Rufus. 'Already gone. 'It was an image of his inner-reality. What we're seeing now is the outer-reality following suit, freed from human pollution.'

'Is there any end to the wonders of this cosmos?' muttered Jake.

'I hope not,' said Braysheath.

Finally the sun's rays reached out from the east and all Jake could see in every direction was a mottled sea of birds.

Though the three of them were soaring well above the birds, something fluttered about Jake. One of the sparrows had broken away. Jake instinctively held out a hand. His heart leapt when it landed on his palm. It was a timeless moment. The sparrow's glistening eyes gazed at Jake with such warmth that his own welled with bliss. It was then he realised that the real miracle had not taken place that ominous night in Trafalgar Square, but on each and every day and every night outside of the event. Every chirp, every hoot, every joyous leap of every fish, it was all a miracle.

Thank you, Brock, said Jake in prayer. *May you journey in peace.*

THE HOLYGATE
OF HUNTER

CHAPTER 64
STONE CIRCLE

WHILE JAKE WAS ON THE SURFACE WITH RUFUS AND BRAYSHEATH, Rani also felt the need for a change of scenery. But it was the desert that drew her, not the Surface.

As the sun rose, so did she and Bin. They soared high above the oasis before flying over its perimeter and heading for the sand.

Seeing so much space without trees unnerved Rani. She felt exposed and vulnerable. And yet there was a certain thrill in it. It also mirrored a longing she felt inside. The completeness of the desert's silence was precisely the medicine she needed.

Neither could she deny the enchantment of the desert's sensuous lines. Windswept to perfection, they were powerfully feminine and full of life despite appearances.

They had been flying for a while, the oasis long out of sight, when Rani spotted a landmark amid the sea of sand. It stood on top of one of the dunes.

'Over there, Bin. Some stones. Let's take a closer look.'

Bin flew closer.

'A stone circle!' said Rani excitedly, noting the oblong stones.

'Menhirs,' remarked Bin. 'It's a place of ceremony.'

Bin circled above, careful not to breach the area inside the menhirs.

'It feels peaceful,' said Rani.

'I'm not so sure,' said Bin. 'Such places are difficult to gauge.'

'Land, Bin. I like it here.'

Reluctantly, Bin landed just outside of the circle.

Rani dismounted and approached one of the menhirs. She stroked its surface before placing her forehead against its cool surface. 'With your permission,' she said softly and kissed it.

She glanced back at a concerned-looking Bin and smiled. With a fateful step she crossed the circle's threshold and passed inside. Other than a slight tingle through her body, nothing unusual happened.

'Go for a fly, Bin. Have a proper stretch of your wings and come back for me later.'

'I'd rather stay,' said Bin. 'You don't have the protection here that you have in the oasis. And you didn't bring the glove.'

'I don't want the glove right now or the protection of the oasis. I just want to be with nature. That's all the protection I need. You understand, Bin, I know you do. I'll be fine.'

Bin closed her eyes in resignation and nodded. 'If you need me, cry out for me.'

'Thank you, Bin.'

Rani watched Bin fly up and off over the dunes. *Dear Bin*, she thought.

Having slowly completed a reverent circuit of the stone circle, running a hand over each stone in turn, she laid down her bow and arrows and sat cross-legged at its centre.

She closed her eyes and took a deep breath. 'No more thinking,' she thought, tired of all the confusion. She placed her hands together in prayer.

'Beloved Mother Earth, beloved Father Sun,' she said softly. 'Thank you for your beauty. Thank you for everything. Thank you for this life even though there's so much I don't understand. But I have faith that you know exactly what I need and that all I need is right here, within me and around me. I pray that I may play my part in restoring balance to the cosmos.'

At the end of her prayer she bowed her head and sat in meditation, distancing herself from her busy mind.

With inner-silence her senses awoke. She could smell the trees of the distant oasis, hear the footprints of a lizard to her left, while on a dune to her right she could feel the slithering of a snake through the sand. A gentle breeze embraced her. All sensations merged into one and the memory of the desert filled her heart, pining for the sea. The breeze picked up. Her connection to the elements intensified. A powerful tingling coursed through her body until the separateness of things vanished from her awareness.

The sensation crescendoed. Following a blissful pulse, Rani was in the void, a place of union. It wasn't the first time it had happened to Rani and she surrendered to it without fear.

What should have been timeless, however, lasted for just a moment. A terrible jarring shook the void. Rani's consciousness was hauled back to the dune.

Her eyes flicked open. She leapt to her feet, both knives drawn.

Three others had appeared at the circle's threshold, spaced out to surround her. Silver-skinned, dark robed and with lion-like humanoid faces, Rani recognised them immediately.

They were guardians of the inner-force—two male and one female. In fact, they were more than that. They were three of the Commander's special troop.

'Your presence has not gone unnoticed,' said the female guardian. 'Someone wants to see you.'

'That weasel Wilderspin?' said Rani, battling to master her fear.

'Someone far more important.'

'Luna?' guessed Rani. 'Well if she wants to see me, then she can come here.'

The guardians shared a wry smile.

'She's a little busy,' continued the female guardian. 'And so she sent us to collect you.'

Rani glanced down at her bow. So did the guardian, whereupon it dissolved into blue light and disappeared, along with the knives.

'You can't fight us without your weapons,' warned the female guardian. 'We're a force and you're merely human.'

Bin! cried Rani in thought. *Come back! Quick! I need you!*

'Just *one* force,' scoffed Rani boldly, playing for time. 'I am *nature* and thus all five forces and much, much more. I shall fight you just as I did at Renlock. And I shall win.'

'I admire your courage, young warrior,' said the female guardian as she and the two others passed inside the circle. 'But I sense the gap between your words and what you're capable of.'

As they closed in on Rani, she adopted a fighting stance. Though the guardian's assessment was correct, Rani refused to believe it—belief cuts one off from greatness. She focused her mind. Guardians couldn't be killed exactly, but they had bodies. If the encasing was punctured the force escaped but to touch them barehanded could be fatal. Without weapons, however, Rani had little choice.

One of the male guardians withdrew a cord of silver light from his robe just like the one Wilderspin had used to restrain Jake. He dashed forward.

Rani brushed his hands aside and delivered a punch to his neck. He started back in surprise. Rani, however, staggered backwards, her head spinning. Despite the speed of contact, her energy was almost depleted.

The guardian smiled and once more advanced.

Her legs wobbly, Rani swiped at his face, hoping her nails might tear into his skin. Her moves were so slow that the guardian ducked to the side and kicked her legs away. As she collapsed face first in the sand he bound her wrists.

At the draining touch of the cord, Rani was spent. She struggled to remain conscious. *Bin*, she murmured in thought. *The guardians blocked my call.*

'Good,' said the female guardian. 'Let's go.'

One of the males transformed into a winged lion which the female mounted. The other, with Rani slumped over his shoulder, was about to do the same when something flashed through the stone circle and took the guardian with it.

At the point of impact, Rani had spilled from his grip. She was still in the circle, still conscious. As she struck the ground, a burst of blue light shone from beyond the circle. The guardian had been slain.

The female leapt off the lion, which immediately transformed back to its former shape. Their eyes shone a fierce blue as they stood alert.

Rani's energy slowly returned. Whoever had ambushed the guardian had somehow cut the cord about her wrists.

The eyes of the female guardian narrowed. 'What is this?' she growled noting the cut cord. 'Only inner-force could break that.'

The guardians moved to the centre of the circle, back to back, and waited for the attacker to reveal itself.

When it did, Rani was just as shocked as the guardians.

It was Frost. He stepped into the circle with his usual swagger.

The female guardian threw out her hand in his direction and a bolt of inner-force struck Frost in the chest.

Instead of being flattened, he merely absorbed it and thanked her, his eyes shining with the additional energy.

'This is forbidden!' seethed the female guardian, realising what he was.

'Which is why I like it,' said Frost airily.

'You'll pay dearly for this betrayal,' threatened the other guardian.

'Nothing of worth is gained cheaply,' countered Frost.

'Are you referring to *that*?' spat the female guardian, glancing at Rani.

Frost looked at Rani but said nothing. He simply smiled his cocky smile and winked.

Ordinarily Rani would have hurled a knife at him had there been one at hand, but she was too confused by Frost's behaviour to know what to do. Words were cheap in the safety of his estate, but this was action against his own kind. He was taking a huge risk.

Her mistrust was quick to return. It was no different to his helping Jake. Frost played a high stakes game. To gain what he wanted, he bent the rules or broke them completely.

'Then let us see just how much she's worth to you,' said the female guardian and both she and the other one swept toward Frost at the same time.

Despite her mistrust and desperately low energy, Rani staggered to her feet to help, but was immediately booted down again by one of the guardians and left more drained than before. She called again for Bin in thought but it was no use. All she could do was watch on in anguish.

Yet to watch Frost fight two elite guardians barehanded left the warrior in her astounded. At close quarters, at lightning speed, his martial arts were those of a master and Rani realised just how much he had been toying with her during their fight in the fort.

As he and the guardians moved about the circle with fierce grace, it was clear that two guardians against Frost was an equal match. Rani observed the eyes of the female guardian. In their focused lights was disbelief. Guardians were meant to be more powerful than Frost's kind—they were closer to the Source, a pure force, while trixies were part-force, part human. Frost's eyes retained their cool light, twinkling with play.

To break the stalemate both guardians leapt back, drew their swords and tore into Frost.

He didn't falter. He simply slipped between the blaze of blade strokes, turning each upon the other, occasionally throwing them together as though it were nothing more than a barn dance. Their speed of recovery, however, was staggering.

During one such move, Frost tried to snatch the male guardian's sword but was too hasty. The guardian whipped out a dagger and thrust it between Frost's ribs.

Rani gasped as the dagger sank in—to the hilt.

Frost barely flinched. His eyes widened and shone. The playful light vanished in a flash, replaced by fire. As the female guardian delivered a killer stroke aimed at his head, Frost spun the male guardian at the sword instead.

As his head spun off beyond the menhirs in a blue blaze, Frost turned to the remaining female guardian. She grinned grimly. A moment later Rani understood why.

Six guardians appeared from thin air, three female, three male. Frost was surrounded.

A brief communication passed silently between them. With a nod of the head, they attacked as one.

Frost showed no fear. His presence was total. This time he was armed with the sword of the fallen guardian. As before, he danced through their lightning attack. To his credit he managed to slay one, gaining a second sword, using both blades together with immense skill. But it was only a matter of time before he was overwhelmed. Rani sensed it.

The guardians drew daggers as well as swords. Between the slashes they delivered stabs and before long Frost was bleeding from multiple wounds. He was receiving the death of a traitor—a slow one. Frost, however, refused them the satisfaction of seeing his pain. He remained completely focused, continuing to parry the majority of the strokes with great strength.

Watching on without being able to help was torture for Rani. She wracked her brain for an idea when it suddenly struck her. Unarmed and still exhausted—these were her weaknesses. She would turn them to her advantage. Sitting up in prayer as she had done before, she closed her eyes and did her best to find silence.

Beloved Mother Earth and Father Sun, my body is your tool. When my day comes I will give it up willingly. But please, my great loves, help me make it an offering worthy of your beauty. I cannot watch this unfair fight and do nothing. If it be in accordance with your divine will and... Rani thought for moment, deciding to add something to help with her confusion... *if it's true that Frost, Jake and myself have some great destiny together, then... then save Frost.*

Covered in blood, Frost was slowing, though still fighting, his eyes alive with the great adventure of life in all its shades. The death blow was just moments away.

Suddenly five guardians disengaged from the fight, leaving the original female guardian.

'You're a disgrace,' she sneered.

'You're too kind,' panted Frost, managing a smile. 'All my life I've aspired to be one. You make me very happy.'

'Your father will be ashamed,' added the guardian, readying her blade.

'I certainly hope so,' said Frost. 'For one so shameful to be ashamed, that's something to be proud of.'

'Enough of this!' she hissed. 'It's unprecedented that a guardian slays a trixy, treacherous or otherwise, so I've no idea what fate awaits you. But I trust it's a hellish one.'

Rani had been listening with her eyes closed. A powerful tingling rose in her body. Suddenly there was silence. She sensed the guardian draw back her sword, sensed her relish in the split second before she swung it.

As the stroke was made, the tingling in Rani became a storm.

Her eyes shot open. The earth shook. The menhirs blazed like suns and caused the slaying guardian to hesitate mid-stroke. The other guardians swung round in shock at the very moment lightning streaked out from the twelve menhirs, tore through them and into Frost.

An explosion of blue light filled the stone circle as the guardians' life force was released. Lightning continued to streak into Frost. Held up by its power, he shook uncontrollably.

Finally it stopped. The menhirs returned to normal and Frost collapsed.

Rani was unharmed. In fact, her energy hadn't only been restored, she felt stronger than ever.

After so much drama, the silence was immense.

Frost lay motionless.

Her heart racing, Rani leapt up and knelt beside him. He didn't appear to be breathing. The tingling she had felt just moments before returned to her right hand. From pure intuition, Rani did something she had never done before—she gently pressed a thumb to his forehead and slowly drew it down to the point between his brows, praying for his life to be restored.

Energy flowed through her and into Frost, though didn't deplete her—it was coming from the earth, using her as a channel.

With a rush of wings, Bin landed beside her.

'I saw the first explosion of blue, but I couldn't reach you!' said Bin hurriedly. 'A force field was up. Are you okay? Is he okay?'

'I'm fine, Bin, but he...'

Frost's eyes slowly opened. They took a moment to focus. A grateful smile spread across his face.

He's alive! thought Rani, greatly relieved.

She gazed at one of the menhirs. *Nature answered my prayer*, she realised, wishing she had been more specific with the final bit. *A great destiny together* could mean anything, creative or destructive.

It didn't occur to her that perhaps the reason that she had left the question so open was because deeper down she wanted to save him. To have narrowed down her question might have left him dead.

Rani studied his body. There was no sign of any wounds while his clothes were as good as new.

Frost sat up. 'Are you okay?' he asked.

Rani nodded. 'You?'

'Thanks to you, yes. That was quite something. This circle of stones is ancient. Such places are usually stubborn. They won't answer to anyone—only to those with a strong connection to ancient power and sincere intent. You could've fried me alive if you'd wanted.'

'If only I'd known,' said Rani with a wry smile.

Frost laughed.

'Why did you save me?' she asked.

'Why did you save me?' countered Frost.

Rani waited for his answer.

'You still don't trust me,' laughed Frost, getting to his feet as though nothing had happened. 'Regardless, I shall keep answering your call until you do.'

'I didn't call you?' retorted Rani.

Frost smiled—not smugly, but warmly. 'Didn't you?' he asked.

A mini-whirlwind of sand blew in unexpectedly and swept about Frost. For a moment he was lost to sight. When the whirlwind swept from the circle Frost was nowhere to be seen. Like a desert jinn, he had disappeared.

CHAPTER 65
THE WOLF

Following the fall of Brock, Jake and Rufus returned to the fort. It was late afternoon. Jake had about him a serene air. Everything seemed brighter—the red sandstone of the fort, the autumn colours of the trees, the blue of the lake, the flowers, everything was amazingly vivid. Even the smells seemed richer.

'Does the fort seem brighter?' he asked as Rufus put him down on the courtyard lawn.

'Looks the same to me, laddie,' said Rufus. 'Anyway, I'll catch yer later. I've got some things to tend to.'

Following a moment of marvelling at how incredibly beautiful the courtyard was, Jake headed for his room.

While having a wash in his basin he had the strange sensation of being watched. He turned to find Glabrous filling the doorway, his large green eyes studying him with a curious glint.

The girl! thought Jake. In all the excitement, he had forgotten that he had sent Glabrous after her.

'My Lord,' said Glabrous and tilted his head in a bow.

'Hello, Glabrous,' said Jake as he put a fresh shirt on.

'Glabrous raised his nose and sniffed the air. 'There's a strange smell in here,' he said.

'I've been with Rufus,' explained Jake, hoping it wasn't Frost the thorsror sensed. 'Did you find her?' he added, changing the topic.

'I did.'

'Where is she?'

'I let her go,' said Glabrous.

Jake was disappointed and relieved at the same time—relieved because, since sending Glabrous after her, she had saved him from the chamber. *No wonder she was so cold towards me!*

'Why?' he asked.

'My lord, I am a thorsror. As such, my nature is to use my initiative. On encountering the Yakreth warrior—'

'Yakreth?' he queried, recalling that Frost had mentioned the word in passing.

'Nature's warrior. They fight for balance.'

'Not an assassin?' asked Jake.

'If someone is the cause of imbalance the Yakreth might be considered assassins.'

'Am I a cause of imbalance?' asked Jake plainly.

Glabrous drew an unhurried breath and the air tingled. 'She thinks you are.'

Jake couldn't help but smile.

'And what do you think, Glabrous?'

Glabrous's powerful eyes bore into Jake. His head grew light. The thorsror appraised Jake for a good while before finally answering.

'She's right,' he said.

Jake's smile broadened and he actually laughed. Though he knew Glabrous wasn't joking, it was a relief to hear such honesty.

'But then,' added Glabrous, 'all humans are out of balance. And like all humans, you have in you a seed to restore it. It has started to sprout. Whether it prefers the sun or the moon only time will tell.'

Jake's smile faded.

'Are you suggesting that I might side with Luna? Because I assure you, Glabrous, that will never happen.'

Glabrous took another unhurried breath.

'You're not as different from her as you might think,' he said, echoing what Luna herself had said in Jake's head at Trafalgar Square.

The image of the fateful door in the mad mansion flashed through Jake's mind.

'But I am different,' he insisted. 'I feel it strongly.'

'Consciously, yes,' said Glabrous. 'But it's the not-so-deep-down that you must watch.'

Jake closed his eyes a moment. He thought of the druid and the grizzly bear in the cave. *I am different from Luna*, he repeated. *Nothing will change that, least of all her.*

'How did the warrior girl get into the fort?' he said, shifting the subject away from himself.

Glabrous's gaze weighed on Jake a moment longer before answering.

'It's a mystery,' he said. 'I imagine she has a powerful accomplice in the fort. She has a peculiar glove I've not seen before. It holds great and ancient power.'

The glove she held my wrist with in the chamber, Jake remembered. At the word accomplice, his thoughts turned to Asclepius, but that didn't make sense. During the theft of the gates she had fired an arrow at Asclepius's ally, Lord Boreas, and had not Glabrous called her nature's warrior?

'Is there anyone you suspect?' he asked.

Glabrous closed his eyes for a moment.

'No,' he replied.

'Is that why you let her go free, to find out who it is?' asked Jake.

'I released her because she's more useful to you free than captured.'

'Why? Because she also has darkness?' asked Jake, recalling what he had seen of her through the net of light. 'Because perhaps we've met in previous lives?'

A flicker of surprise showed in the thorsror's eyes.

'Time will tell,' he replied sparingly.

Jake nodded slowly. Glabrous was right.

'Any advice on how to... approach her?' he asked, keen to get to know her better.

Again Glabrous closed his eyes, this time for longer.

'Courage,' he said dryly and caused Jake to smile.

'Thank you, Glabrous. Is there anything else?'

'No.'

Jake smiled and bowed his head.

Glabrous did the same and departed.

Jake was about to sit down at his desk to study the wolf in the book on totems when he heard a hissing. He turned to find Frost's jubilant face in the fireplace.

'Feast!' he whispered and disappeared back into his lair.

Postponing his studies, Jake passed through the fireplace and joined Frost.

'Hungry?' asked Frost. He was sitting amid a delicious-looking picnic including fresh bread, cheese, salad, even lobster, not to mention a dish of blackberry and apple crumble with cream.

'My God!' exclaimed Jake. 'How did you manage to pilfer all of this?'

'With practice,' said Frost and tucked in.

Jake sat down and poured out some lemonade. After such a day, it tasted sublime.

'It seems like an age since we last spoke,' said Frost. 'Lots has happened, hey?'

'Were you at the miracle?' asked Jake.

'Wouldn't have missed it for the world!' said Frost, his mouth half-full.

'The fall of Brock?'

'Felt it, but went for a stroll in the desert instead.'

'That's hardly a place for a stroll,' remarked Jake with a frown. 'What about the Council of Shadows?'

'Heard every word.'

'And so—it's down to me to save Granddad,' said Jake stoically.

'Maybe,' said Frost in a mysterious tone.

'Are you saying you can come?' asked Jake, delighted at the idea.

'Not me, I'm afraid,' confessed Frost. 'Trust me, my fine friend, I'd love to. But my chances of entering and surviving are even slimmer than yours. It's in the pixy contract. I'm not even supposed to be here. On which note, tonight I must return for a spell on the Surface.'

'Really?' said Jake, disappointed, more in need of clarity than ever. 'So soon?'

'Remember what I am. Remember I have my nature,' said Frost and looked at Jake with a peculiar intensity. 'And I must answer it! I've been extremely negligent since meeting you.'

The comment struck Jake as strange, as though it contained hidden meaning, but he let it pass.

'So what do you mean by *maybe*?' he said, getting back to the holygate.

'The girl.'

'The girl?' said Jake, at first baffled until he remembered that it had probably been her presence, combined with his own, which opened the way to the chamber, not to mention the effect of her contact when she had saved him. 'Were you there? When I entered the chamber?'

'A chamber? Sounds exciting!' said Frost, his eyes lighting up as he grabbed some lobster. 'This you must tell me!'

Jake did so.

'You see?' exclaimed Frost once Jake had finished. 'It confirms my feelings. There's a mysterious connection between the two of you. I expect it goes back aeons. You have something to unlock in one another.'

'Well,' said Jake, recalling her taciturn manner, 'if it's a connection then it's very one-sided.'

'Like I said before, don't be fooled,' said Frost. 'A woman like that is not easily won. Her outward manners cannot be trusted. If she punches you in the face, she likes you. If she stabs you, you're in there!'

'She shaved my ear with an arrow fired point-blank,' said Jake.

'That's fantastic! She definitely fancies you.'

Jake laughed.

Resisting the temptation to dwell on the girl, Jake's thoughts returned to the mystery of the chamber. 'So what do you think about Boreas's behaviour? The more I think about it, the more I feel that something doesn't quite fit. His cry to the sky seemed furious, but also pained.'

'Pain is fury's root. It's a cry for attention. A cry for exclusive love.'

'Then... ?'

'Let me ask you,' said Frost, the peculiar intensity returning to his eyes as though he wished Jake to pay extra attention. 'Was the *sun* shining?'

'What do you mean? It was before the storm came.'

'Yes, but how about during the storm?'

'Of course not,' said Jake.

'Really?' said Frost. 'Sometimes it does.'

Jake studied him with a quizzical expression while Frost helped himself to crumble. He was growing accustomed to Frost's strange ways. Frost knew too much, so when he was vague he was getting at something, which perhaps his nature prevented him from saying outright.

'By the way,' added Frost, 'I overheard the sprites say that one of the lizards was taken from the library about the same time Pandora's Box was stolen.'

'A lizard? From what library?'

'From the fort's lizard library.'

'Lizard library?' exclaimed Jake. 'What are you talking about?'

'You don't even know your own fort! What sort of lord are you? It's a special library. Lizards have long memories. Anyway, the one stolen was the most skilled in dreaming.'

'You think it could be the same lizard we saw with Boreas?' asked Jake, also recalling the one he had seen on the tree through the chamber.

'Something to think about,' said Frost. 'Dreaming can take you anywhere. Anywhere in the entire cosmos. Even to the most secure of places. It's what you might call a loophole.'

Jake felt something shift in the deepest recesses of his thoughts, something at the heart of the riddles, yet he couldn't quite grasp it.

'Have you still not got a weapon?' asked Frost, shifting topics.

'No. Not that I'm in any great hurry to have one.'

'You'll need one if you're to enter the holygate and do anything about it. And a good one too.'

Jake took a sip of lemonade. He thought back to the powerful sword in the vault that had caught his eye and how Ti had explained that a sword choses the wielder, not the other way around.

Was the singing I heard the sword calling me? he wondered excitedly, for if he had to have a sword and it was his choice, it would be that one, regardless of Ti's warning.

'Right, my courageous friend,' said Frost and sprang to his feet. 'I must fly!'

'What—already?' exclaimed Jake and got to his feet. 'You said tonight!'

'It *is* tonight.'

'Yes, but...'

'Places to visit! People to meet!'

'Well, will I see you before entering the holygate?' asked Jake.

'Depends when you enter it,' said Frost unhelpfully while stuffing his pockets with food. 'But I suspect not, for the day draws near and I have much to catch up with on the Surface.'

'But the riddles and everything else. There's still something to work out. Something big! I can't put my finger on it, but...'

'Follow your heart and know your mind,' reminded Frost, gazing at Jake intently. 'These riddles were meant for you. For your mind and your heart.'

'But you've been so helpful,' said Jake, desperate to run through all his latest thoughts with someone who understood so much.

'Let's hope so,' said Frost. He ruffled Jake's hair and gripped him by the shoulders. 'We'll meet again! Fear not!'

Following a cheeky wink, Frost leapt into the shadows and was gone.

In something of a daze at the suddenness of Frost's departure, Jake took what remained of the food back to his room.

He sat at his desk, made a sandwich then opened up the book on totems to the pages on the wolf.

The very first paragraph almost caused him to drop his sandwich.

The wolf is one of the most misunderstood of all animals. Demonised in the western world as savage, to the tribespeople of the ancient world it was sacred and epitomised the spirit of freedom.

'My God,' muttered Jake. *Frost's very first comment regarding the wolf was that it was misunderstood, but then he went on to demonise the one in Asclepius's lab!*

Jake read on.

A necessary predator, the fate of the wolf also epitomises everything man has done wrong in reshaping nature in his preferred image... To some Native American tribes the wolf guarded the path walked by the dead and cleansed souls in the river to make them sacred again... The wolf is also associated with rebirth.

'Rebirth,' muttered Jake. It reminded him of one of the sentences in the riddle—*Inside the risen, the Muse' second kiss.* 'Risen is an anagram of siren, but perhaps it also simply means *risen*.'

The image of the *Tibetan Book of the Dead* flashed through his mind.

Jake read some more.

As a totem, the wolf is a symbol of stamina, extreme intelligence, loyalty to its pack, co-operation and courage. Though it is fierce in attack, its personality is shy and it will go out of its way to avoid a fight.

Reading such admirable traits, Jake's mind wandered away from the subject to his dad—they seemed to fit him perfectly.

He focused back on the book.

When a wolf shows up in one's life it signals a time to access one's truth. As pathfinder, the wolf appears to those who have lost their way and are in need of warrior skills to survive. It teaches endurance in the face of obstacles while its depth of perception is critical in a world of shadow... Only complete exhaustion, utter futility or death will divert the wolf from its prey.

Jake put the book down, leant back in his chair and thought over what he had read.

It doesn't seem like an appropriate symbol for a demon, he reflected. He took a sip of lemonade, looked out of the window and up at the moon.

Suddenly Jake was struck by an idea.

'What if the wolf doesn't represent a demon with an ancient wound, but Boreas himself!' he thought out loud. 'After all, he said his soul was fractured, hence the leaking light from the wolf in the tree. And I suppose the positive traits of the wolf can be twisted to fit Boreas.'

But then, he thought, *Boreas is hardly shy. And is he lost?* Jake thought of Lord Boreas's pained cry to the sky. *If he's losing light then in a way, yes he is. And if something of Dad's strong character washed off on him then that would explain his varied moods.*

Jake took a bite of his sandwich.

And so perhaps Asclepius is simply helping to heal Boreas, not searching for a demon as Frost thought. Boreas meanwhile still plans to use his fractured soul to his advantage by trying to win the allegiance of the sylph—by offering me as sacrifice in the holygate.

Not dwelling on what that might involve, he took another bite of his sandwich.

But what's so mythical about sacrificing me in the gate? he wondered, recalling what he had overheard between Lord Boreas and the lizard. *Regardless of what others have said about my lightline, if I haven't connected to it, if I resist it as I do then surely my sacrifice doesn't count for much.*

Once Jake had discovered one inconsistency, others followed. If Boreas wasn't searching for a demon then what was the dark presence in the woods of the chamber? And Jake still didn't understand what the pirate and the tiger were all about. There was also the wolf itself. Each time Jake had seen it, the wolf had seemed so peaceful, especially in the chamber when it wasn't leaking light.

Why was there that child in armour riding on its back? Maybe that symbolised the fighter character of Boreas. After all, to fight and to be greedy is very childish.

'God, this is too complicated,' he sighed then remembered something his granddad had once said. *If something is too complicated then something is amiss.*

Jake leant back, took a deep breath and dared to look at it all from a different angle.

'If the wolf is not the demon and not Lord Boreas then who does it represent?' he wondered.

He also wondered at the timing of Frost's departure and remembered his earlier thought that the riddles were intentionally complex so they couldn't be deciphered too quickly, like a long fuse to a bomb—the bomb being some great revelation at the heart of the riddles. There was no doubt Frost had been a great help. But maybe he had been deceptive at times in order to throw Jake off the scent, at least until Frost left as he had just moments before.

Jake thought back to Frost's strange mood. It seemed to fit this latest idea.

'If that's the case, then why? What is it I mustn't know before... before what? Before entering the holygate?'

Another great tiredness descended upon Jake as though it too wished to slow him down.

'So many mysteries,' he sighed

With a great yawn, deciding it wiser to revisit the riddles after a good night's sleep, finally Jake headed for bed.

RANI, ALSO TIRED AFTER A LONG DAY, HAD BEEN SPYING ON Jake through a tiny portal she had made in the wall with the glove. She had been paying less attention to Jake's mutterings about wolves and demons than to her own feelings.

She couldn't explain it, but though Jake and Frost were so distinct on the Surface, deeper down they were starting to merge.

Rani had once likened Frost to a forest fire that scorched the earth. Now he felt more like a bolt of lightning exploding from the sky and penetrating the earth with its white heat, electrifying some place deep within where spirit danced wildly and ran naked through woods as Rani had often done on Wrathlabad.

As one heat moved inwards another rose up from the cold ocean depths. Jake. There too a change was taking place. A flow of warmth had broken free from somewhere deep within and found a way through the ocean trenches—a warm current snaking its way towards the surface.

The outer reaches of the two sources of heat danced through the tides of Rani's being, awakening a force so powerful that it held the promise of new and great growth. And equally, the promise of death.

CHAPTER 66
THIN AIR

LAWRENCE HAD ONLY TAKEN A FEW STEPS ALONG THE RIDGE WHEN he collapsed to his knees. Having escaped the island he had also fled its peculiar healing powers. The fracture to his soul returned even worse than before. He tried to stem the flow from his navel with a hand. The light not only passed through it, but streamed out in the form of bright red butterflies. They managed a short distance of flight before dropping dead to the snow, leaving a trail like blood.

'Damn it!' he cursed.

Lawrence glanced back, though could barely make out the portal through the blizzard. In the other direction it cleared just enough to reveal the precipitous ridge of snow and rock towering upwards.

He desperately needed to put some distance between himself and his pursuers, whose sharp voices he could hear through the howling wind.

The wolf, he thought. *I need its stamina.* He also had to be as efficient as possible with what little light he had left. Anything fancy, such as shapeshifting, could prove fatal.

Despite his haemorrhaging light he still felt the power gifted by the woman's kiss.

I must try, he decided. *It's a gamble I must take.*

Lawrence focused his mind on how it had felt to be a wolf when he had used the totem in the dream room. He cleared his mind of all other thought. Following a deep breath, he willed himself to become one with all his heart.

A powerful gust blasted through him as the blizzard grew stronger. His body shivered.

The pursuers had reached the portal but were blown back into the cave by a fierce wind. It lasted just long enough for Lawrence to gaze down at his white paws before leaping forward and bounding up the ridge.

Though the transformation had cost him light, the decision had been wise. Energy shifted from his mind to his body. Intuition took over. Despite the ongoing drain of energy, as he loped through the snow, over and between the crags, he felt light, almost strong.

It wasn't long, however, before puffs of snow exploded about him shortly followed by the crack of gun fire. The wolf's white coat was perfect camouflage. But in a place where energy was easily perceived, it counted for little, especially light which leaked and fluttered red.

The bullets of the eight pursuers homed in on the wolf with increasing accuracy. Butterflies exploded in red puffs as the bullets raced down the line which led to Lawrence. When they were only a butterfly away from striking his body, Lawrence leapt behind a crag for cover.

Bullets ricocheted off the rock. In order to defend himself Lawrence had to transform back. It cost him dearly. Suddenly freezing, he pulled his coat tight about him. His teeth chattered. He panted for breath as he tried to adjust his exhausted body to the thin air. The pursuers were less than a hundred metres away. Lawrence had to act.

He took the rifle, checked the magazine was full, re-cocked the bolt, made a guess at the distance and set the sights.

The eight pursuers moved with the speed of commandos while maintaining a lethal accuracy of gunfire.

Following a deep and calming breath, Lawrence suddenly rolled to the side. He had barely pointed his rifle through a small crack when the bullets rained in about him, forcing him to duck back in.

He was trapped. There was no way up or down the ridge without exposing himself, while the drop to either side was sheer. Neither was there any way of crawling away without the butterflies betraying his position.

Suddenly Lawrence was struck with an idea. *I must use the butterflies to my advantage!*

While the commandos narrowed the distance with alarming speed, Lawrence focused his attention on his navel. He willed the direction of his leaking light to the boulders behind him and to not become butterflies until it reached them.

To his great relief it worked and the direction of the bullets immediately shifted.

Lawrence peeped round the rock, checked the distance, readjusted his sights and aimed at the first commando. He hesitated. His finger was ready to squeeze the trigger. He could pick off four of them in quick succession, but something stopped him.

'I can't! It's cowardice!' he hissed, unable to convince himself that the bullets were somehow symbolic.

Lawrence rolled back behind the rock. *This is all me*, he reminded himself. *Any attempt at integration must be hand to hand.*

With a curse he emptied the barrel and tossed away the magazine of rounds along with the rifle. His trick with the butterflies faded and the stream returned to his navel. The commandos' fire returned with a vengeance, hammering into the crags about him.

Lawrence was about to cast away the pistol as well when something miraculous happened. It transformed into a small glass of light—a reward for his intelligence and courage.

Astonished, delighted, he downed it in one. His body and soul sighed with bliss. The leak at his navel remained, however. The boost wouldn't last long. He had to use it to get free from the commandos.

A smile spread across his cold face. He had a brilliant idea.

The commandos were less than fifty paces from Lawrence, continuing to fire as they moved, anticipation glinting murderously in their eyes.

There was a sudden shriek of women's voices. It came from the crags just below Lawrence. The firing stopped instantly. Weapons lowered, the commandos stood bewildered. Their mothers were charging through the snow towards them, arms wide, shrieking with delight as though they hadn't seen their sons in years.

Powerful women, they descended upon their sons like an avalanche, cast aside their weapons, hugged them like bears and showered them in love. The effect on the commandos was like a spell. They completely forgot about Lawrence. An inviting-looking hut appeared beside them, smoke issuing from its chimney. As the mothers bundled their sons towards it for a hearty meal, Lawrence made a break for the higher crags.

He arrived panting and freezing. The illusion he had created with the mothers and the hut had cost him all the light he had won through the pistol, but he still managed a chuckle.

A cry drew his attention to the sky. Four eagles were flying together.

Eagles don't usually fly in flocks, he thought, sensing that they signified something else. *Four tests perhaps, which if passed gift flight. If failed, I'll be torn apart between talon and beak.*

The eagles flew up the ridge beyond Lawrence and out of sight.

He studied the crags above and found a fissure. He didn't like the look of it. Though it appeared to lead through the crags, providing shelter from the blizzard, it was perfect for an ambush. But there was no alternative. The ridge was sheer in all directions except down.

Lawrence looked back at the trail of fallen red butterflies which, glowing brightly, seemed to defy the blizzard. He strained his hearing for pursuit though heard nothing but the wind. Keen to get moving before any more commandos appeared, Lawrence stepped into the darkness of the fissure.

He cursed. The light leaking from his navel announced his arrival to anyone hiding in the shadows, though cast too little light to see by.

Lawrence placed a frozen hand about the cold hilt of his drawn sword, braced himself for attack and advanced silently through what became a narrow cavern. As he moved, he dwelt on the eagles.

Whatever tests they represent, surely one is in this cave.

A few steps later the hairs on his neck shot up. He sensed a presence. A light glowed to his left. Lawrence swung round, ready to strike.

All he found was a recess in the cave with a simple but cosy-looking chair. Yet more tantalising, next to it burned a glorious-looking fire.

Frozen stiff, Lawrence craved its warmth.

Surely a trap, he groaned in thought.

He waited for a movement.

When nothing stirred, he slowly approached the fire, poised to fight.

On reaching it, sensing no immediate threat, he crouched and placed the sword down in order to warm his hands. Yet when he put his hands close to the fire he felt no warmth.

'You must sit in the chair to feel the fire's warmth,' came a soft woman's voice that made him jump.

In an instant, the sword was back in Lawrence's hand. He spun around to find what looked like a servant girl. Pretty, sweet-natured and holding a tray with hot food and drink, she knelt between the chair and the fire.

'It *is* a trap,' sighed Lawrence.

In his freezing condition the sight of a fire that gave no heat was torture. His stomach rumbled at the sight of the food and drink.

'A trap?' queried the girl. 'I don't think of life as a trap. My mother says that our job is to embrace our earthly duties, that it doesn't matter what we do as long as we're present when we do it, always doing our best. That way everything always works out.'

'The chair is the emperor's throne in disguise,' said Lawrence, not to be fooled. 'If I sit in it then I'll be trapped forever on the island hell and all its distorted beauty.'

The girl reached out and touched Lawrence's free hand. Her touch gifted warmth though only to his hand. The rest of his body felt even colder.

'If you were emperor you could change everything,' she said. 'You would make a great and noble emperor, I know it! I can see it in your kind face. You could free us all and turn the island into a true paradise.'

'If I sat on the throne now I'd become a tyrant. Only by reaching the top of this mountain can I become an authentic master,' said Lawrence, realising that the girl, along with the fire and chair, had indeed been one of the eagles. The other three lay in wait higher up the ridge.

'Won't you at least have some nice hot pie and warm ale?' she asked sweetly. 'It's hard to think straight when you're cold and hungry. Everything will be much clearer after a nice warm meal and a rest.'

With great reluctance, Lawrence withdrew his hand from the warmth of hers.

Tears welled in her eyes. 'Why? Why won't you help us?'

Lawrence closed his eyes and drew a deep breath.

When he opened them, the image of the girl and the chair faded and the temperature dropped to even lower than before.

He looked down at his navel. The flow of leaking light was growing weaker, not because the wound was healing, but because he had little light left to leak.

'How on earth will I make it?' he muttered through chattering teeth.

Regardless, Lawrence stoically pushed on through the cave, trying not to fantasise about warm fires and hot food or losing himself in what horrors lay in store.

With the drop in energy he was growing light-headed. He stumbled on the rocky path, fell and bashed his head. Too tired even to curse, he stayed down on his hands and knees for some time, teetering on the edge of delirium when a voice stirred him. Female, with a gentle strength, it sounded familiar.

'Lawrence,' she said. 'Get up.'

Lawrence dismissed it as imagination and didn't move.

'Get up, Lawrence,' she repeated. 'You're wanted back on the Surface. Luna has summoned you to her temple.'

This time he lifted his head. A woman stood before him. Blinking away his bleary vision he realised it was his secret helper from the palace and his spirits lifted.

'Is that really you?' he mumbled.

'I've come to you in spirit. My body is in the palace. But you must get up and get to Luna's temple in London.'

Lawrence could hardly believe his ears. 'What? I can barely move here!'

'You must try. You have to try. You can do it, I know you can. You have more strength than you realise.'

'I wish I had your faith,' he gasped and managed to sit up a little. 'Besides, I can't afford to rest here while my awareness travels to London. I'll be too weak and exposed on the ridge. And God only knows how I can maintain my cover in front of Luna.'

'A little further through the cave, before it returns to the ridge, are some yeti cubs. You can rest with them if you need warmth.'

'Yetis? Yetis exist?' exclaimed Lawrence, for though he had seen many extraordinary creatures in his life, he had never seen a yeti.

'Everything imaginable exists,' she replied.

'What about the mother!' exclaimed Lawrence.

'She's out hunting. If you conclude your business with Luna quickly, you can return here before the she-yeti returns.'

'Can it get any worse?' said Lawrence and managed a weak laugh.

'It'll get a lot worse,' said the woman plainly. 'Now get up. You've little time to waste.'

'I don't suppose you could give me another one of those kisses?' he asked, fondly recalling not only the sensation, but the energy it had gifted.

'I'm not here physically,' she said with a smile. 'Neither can I intervene too directly.'

'Pity,' he sighed.

'I must go,' said the woman, looking suddenly concerned. 'Someone is coming.'

'No, wait!' said Lawrence, but her image had already gone.

In the dim light cast by his navel he noticed something steaming. He gasped with delight at the sight of it. Though she hadn't been able to give him a kiss, instead she had left him the next best thing—a steaming hot cup of tea.

How she had managed it didn't matter. Lawrence warmed his hands about the hot cup and sighed with joy. Following a glorious sip of its sweet taste he managed to sit up properly and sip some more.

'Ah, the healing powers of a hot cuppa!' he gasped.

After a few more sips he hauled himself to his feet. Taking his tea he slowly made his way deeper into the cave, careful not to spill it.

After a short while, just as the woman had said, he heard the soft sounds of cubs shifting in their sleep, searching for their mother's teats.

Lawrence arrived at the yeti cave. His heartbeat sped. He waited at the threshold just to be sure the mother wasn't there. Nothing stirred. Greatly relieved though still alert, he crept in and eased himself into the soft bedding among the three bear-like cubs. Thinking he was their mother they called out excitedly and nestled up to him. Lawrence held his breath. Despite their disappointment they seemed to accept him and snuggled up closer.

Lawrence relaxed. The cave was cold, but he hoped that the warmth of the cubs and the bedding, combined with the tea, might just be enough for his body to survive while the greater part of his awareness left for London.

He smiled at the image of himself sipping a cup of tea among the cubs whose simple company was welcome. He was reminded of his duelling lesson with Geoffrey, one part of him pouring tea in Renlock while the rest of him duelled on the pinnacle.

Now I must put that lesson into practice, he thought, *staying alert here, in case the mother returns while trying to convince Luna I'm Lord Boreas. Though how the hell am I going to get back to Luna's world?*

Lawrence swigged back the last of the tea, savouring its warmth.

He closed his eyes and drew a deep breath. 'Great spirit, I don't have the strength to travel back to Renlock. If may call upon you just once in this lifetime then let it be now. Help me. Please.'

Almost immediately, Lawrence felt himself slip into sleep. 'Renlock,' he muttered as he drifted off, not sure if his prayer was being answered or his body was giving up. 'I must get to...'

CHAPTER 67
SONG OF AN ANCIENT BLADE

JAKE SAT BOLT UPRIGHT IN BED IN A COLD SWEAT. HE HAD AWOKEN from his worst nightmare yet. Following several deep breaths he sighed with relief. Unlike his other dreams he could only recall scraps.

It had started wonderfully. A Celtic-sounding enchanting song had drawn him to the top of a green hill. Her voice had been vaguely familiar. There he had found an old oak as white as the dove perched on one of its branches, reminding him of the dove he had seen in the sodalite chamber. It had been a peaceful scene.

Then a raven had landed in the tree and cawed with such violence that it had jarred Jake to the bone. The sky had darkened. A bolt of lightning had struck the tree, so close that he felt as though it had struck him too—that something deep within him had been blasted open, releasing a fear of demonic proportions.

Jake—you must die...

The druid's voice had echoed through Jake.

When another bolt of lightning tore into the tree, the dove and the raven had taken flight directly for Jake. Almost upon him, talons outstretched, the raven had cawed a final time—so loud and deathly that it had forced Jake awake.

Jake muttered a curse. 'What the bloody hell was all that about?'

His mind was too groggy to make any sense of it. Remembering his first strange dream in the farmhouse, Jake got up and rinsed his face in the basin just to make sure he was properly awake, rather than waking up into another dream.

The water refreshed him and quenched his dry throat.

'I'm awake,' he realised.

Before heading back to bed he stepped out onto the balcony overlooking the courtyard. It was still dark. He deeply inhaled the cool air.

His mind had finally calmed when he heard something that sent it straight back into shock—singing. It was the very same song from his dream.

Then it clicked.

It's the same voice I heard from the sword in the vault!

The song exerted its powerful pull. Jake's heartbeat raced. He stood there half in fear, half ecstatic. Frost's words of just the evening before filled his mind—*You'll need a sword if you're to enter the gate. A good one.*

Good? thought Jake. The word hardly fitted Ti's description of a sword that he had said was cursed and powerful beyond words.

In need of clarity, Jake closed his eyes and thought of his granddad.

I must go to the vault, he decided. *I don't have to touch the sword, but I should at least go, otherwise the real curse will be not knowing if the sword is meant for me or not.*

Jake put on his kilt and shirt and headed barefoot down to the hall that contained the strange floating vault. With each step the song grew louder. He worried it might wake others in the fort when he remembered how Ti had been unable to hear the song.

It's calling me, he realised. *No one else.*

Jake reached the entrance to the hall and peered in. To his surprise the hall was quiet—the serpents covering the vault's surface seemed to be sleeping, something that wasn't supposed to happen. He took a step inside and braced himself for a shock.

Much to his relief, the female Naga didn't appear. Stranger still, the doors to the vault were open and the serpentine stairs already formed.

Jake passed to the base of the steps. The power of the song was so strong it literally pulled him inside.

At the top of the steps Jake resisted it for a moment in order to study the vault. It appeared different. All the weapons, which had been so dazzling the first time he had entered, now seemed dim. Not one of them made a sound.

He cautiously stepped inside. The weapons remained silent, but he felt their attention. It was a brooding silence, one that felt like fear.

Jake's gaze fell upon the same sword that had caught his attention the first time. Like then, its blade gave off a subtle iridescent glow.

As Jake walked slowly towards the magnificent-looking sword, Ti's warning rang out in his mind: *the sword is cursed... ill-fated... not even the dwarf-smiths will touch it... nothing is known of the powerful soul inside...*

His eyes locked on the peculiar gemstone in its hilt—the six stones of the Peregrinus, stones of Death, forged together by the master-smith Sindri, which made the sword extremely powerful, but highly unpredictable.

Jake stopped just short of the sword and knelt before it. He tingled with fear and awe. He was just inches away from the most powerful weapon in the vault.

The singing stopped.

In the silence that followed, Jake realised just how much the song had nourished him. It had made him feel more complete, just like in his dream.

The dream, he thought. *One which had become a nightmare.*

There was no denying that the song linked the dream with the sword, but the song had seemed to come from the white oak tree, which had struck Jake as peaceful.

He thought back to the chamber. *That dove encouraged me to follow Asclepius and the wolf,* he remembered. The path had proved traumatic, but he had survived the ordeal and come away with great insight even if he hadn't fully worked out its meaning.

The truth is traumatic, made up of both light and dark, he decided, putting the dove and raven together. He wondered if the raven represented Frost and that the jarring caw was in some way telling him to get on with it and take the sword. Perhaps the lightning bolt was a symbol of waking up.

Jake—you must die...

The druid's words returned to haunt him.

Was he trying to prevent me from taking the sword?

He drew a defiant breath.

I must take this sword—for Granddad's sake if no one else's. As Ti said, the sword chooses its wielder.

Casting aside the idea of his soul being sucked into the blade or becoming possessed, Jake steadied his nerves and slowly reached for its hilt.

The tingling in his fingers intensified.

Energy surged up his arm.

'Don't do it!' cried someone from behind and caused him to jump. Jake spun around to see who it was, though found no one.

'Why not?' he asked, realising that it had been one of the other objects.

There was no answer.

The interruption summoned doubt.

The song, he thought. *It sounded so beautiful, so wholesome. But what if the soul inside is some kind of siren? The Queen of the Sirens!*

Again, Ti's words rang through his mind about how the more beautiful something seemed, the more wary one should be.

Tired of so many doubts he closed his eyes.

Follow your heart and know your mind, he thought, recalling the advice of the riddle. *My heart is set on saving Granddad and my mind is fully behind it.*

Before further doubts could stop him, eyes closed, he reached forward.

A collective gasp escaped the vault.

A bolt of energy shot up his arm and through his shoulders.

His hand only an inch from the hilt, he hesitated for just a moment then finally clasped it.

The jolt of power almost bowled him over.

He went white with shock.

His eyes shot open.

In his outstretched arm was the sword. Beams of light shone from its blade and filled the vault. A wild-feeling energy coursed through him. He felt giant.

For the briefest instant light flickered in the misted stone of the hilt.

Jake braced himself for something terrible.

Instead, the wild energy subsided and the beams of light were sucked back into the blade.

Jake could scarcely believe what he had done. He got up from his knees, turned to the rest of the vault and held up the sword to marvel at it. In his hands it looked even more glorious.

He took a practice stroke through the air. It felt incredibly light, though carried a profound sense of power, while the ringing it left in the air was nothing short of exquisite.

Jake had never thought he would be proud to own a weapon, but this one was different. Rather than shame, he felt elation.

'Thank you,' he said reverently to the sword and bravely placed a kiss on the mysterious stone in the hilt. His lips tingled in a further sign of the sword's acceptance.

To win the co-operation of the sword is the greatest challenge in duelling, he thought, recalling what Ti had also said.

It had almost been too easy. His doubts threatened to return until he reflected on the legend of King Arthur. When so many knights had failed to pull Excalibur from the stone—a sword whose power was a small fraction of the one he held in his hand—it had been a simple peasant boy who had managed it so effortlessly. Of course it later turned out that Arthur's bloodline had been one of kings.

Jake thought of his own bloodline that reached back to and beyond the first Lord Tusk, the alchemist Reginald Burton. Jake suspected that it was less his bloodline that had allowed him to hold the sword than his lightline. He thought of the druid and the dark and powerful man further back in the fog about Nemesis's tree, who was somehow associated with the door in Wilderspin's mad mansion that had fascinated Luna. Jake once again wondered whether it had been this forbidding man who had commissioned the making of the sword then slayed the maker.

Despite so much uncertainty, the sword felt right in his hand as though it were meant for him. Jake noted the conflict in how he felt about the sword and how he felt about his lightline. *Perhaps the sword is a way of making good on a dark past*, he thought. *Maybe it somehow connects the two.*

'As long as the sword accepts me, I shall carry it,' he decided and picked up the plain leather scabbard from the floor. Following a final marvelling at its blade, he sheathed it.

Rather than returning to bed, Jake sat on the lower steps of the gilded staircase. Completely awake, he decided to pick up his ponderings from the night before and was surprised by how clear his mind felt, as though the sword resting across his knees were gifting him clarity.

'The white wolf,' he said to himself, voicing his main concern. 'It doesn't fit. Frost said white was a tricky colour...'

'White, not light!' cried out a voice that made Jake jump. It was a male voice and hadn't come from the sword.

A golden helmet with wings flew up and about Jake. It was Mercury's helmet which he had seen on his first visit.

'An obsession with white is for those who impersonate light, caught in a dream of appearance. But light is reality! It can only be found through shadow!'

Jake was delighted that another object from the vault was helping him as though his courage in grasping the sword had won him the respect of the other weapons.

'If a god who had been through the god gate was leaking light, would it be bright and pure-looking?' asked Jake, recalling how clear the light from the wolf had been.

'Oh no! It would look dirty - tainted and shadowy, veiled in delusion and false ideas of power. Force not power! There's a difference. Force is for fools, but real power belongs to wise souls united through the heart,' said Mercury's helmet before flying off again.

The subject of light reminded Jake of something Frost had said the night before. *Was the 'sun' shining?* he had asked in a knowing tone as though he had been watching Jake in the chamber and had seen something Jake had missed.

The only thing shining, thought Jake as he cast his mind back to watching Lord Boreas on the beach from the cliff, *was myself and the girl when she took my wrist... me, Jake Burton... son of Lawrence...*

There followed a moment of total silence, especially within Jake. It wasn't the peaceful silence of the night or the imposed silence of a library: it was the brand of silence which heralds a great event. It was a mental stillness where all conflict and confusion disappears because something vital, a missing link, is tantalisingly within reach.

During that moment Jake's face went blank. His eyes took on a distant light as though he were seeing something too great or too strange to comprehend.

With an almighty jolt, the missing link clicked into place.

His eyes widened.

The blood drained from his face.

'My God!' he gasped.

The weight of the revelation was too great. The floor gave way beneath him. He plunged into an abyss of disbelief where the only light was the one that lit the scale of his enormous error.

His mind scrambled to understand how it happened and what it meant, desperate to bridge a gap that only seemed to widen. The threads, however, were too many to make sense of all at once, and it was the vibration of the sword that brought him back—a flow of energy that shone a light on what really mattered, regardless of how it happened.

DAD'S ALIVE!

He longed to cry it out aloud, leap about the vault and give voice to his immense relief and joy, but he just caught himself. There were too many souls in the vault, many of dubious origin. Something told Jake not say a word—not there.

Still, his eyes shone. His heart soared. He could barely believe it.

The sun shining was not the sun in the sky. There was no sun visible during the storm. It was a play on the word 'sun'. Frost was hinting at the 'son'! Me, son of Lawrence! He was suggesting Dad was present, otherwise why refer to me as son? Boreas on the beach was Dad, symbolised by the wolf! The wolf whose characteristics in the book fit Dad so well. The gentle-seeming wolf which led me to the cliff. The same wolf leaking pure and clean light in the tree. It's why he was crying out in pain! He's suffering.

Jake's heart raced as he pieced it all together.

Everything is possible, he thought, echoing Braysheath. *Everyone said Dad couldn't possibly have survived, even Braysheath himself. Yet he was strong enough to leap into the gate despite a fatal wound. Two at once leaping through the god gate must've caused something unusual to happen. It's what my dream on the train was showing me. The wolf was Dad's spirit was calling out to me!*

As the realisation sank in, an immense pride swept through Jake.

But his soul is fractured, he remembered, suddenly weighed down with sadness. *Lost his way... in the shadow, Titan'd not untied. His soul is trapped in a hell, not cleansed of identity.*

Everything started to slot into place.

Was that island some sort of hell? Then who is the Boreas in Renlock?

Another part of the riddle suddenly came back to him—Inside the risen the Muse's second kiss. *Only one body could emerge from the god gate, but with two souls battling for possession of it! The grace and courage of Dad against the vanity of Boreas.*

The two books that had caught his attention in his dad's study blazed in his mind and confirmed his intuition.

Janus—two faces, or rather two minds battling for possession of one body. The Tibetan Book of the Dead—a journey through hells.

Jake suddenly realised that each time he had seen the body of Boreas, the soul inside of it had been his dad's. It explained why Jake had been unable to feel anger at the sight of him.

Amid so much thinking, Jake took a mental step back. Was there a better explanation? Had he misunderstood Frost's clue?

No. Jake knew Frost's mannerisms well enough—when he said too little, when he said too much, when something important was suggested by a shift in his tone.

The words sun-son are key. He has probably known for some time that who I assumed to be Lord Boreas was really Dad. He even fuelled the idea!

How Jake felt about Frost's behaviour was pushed aside for the moment while he remained focused on the mystery of his dad.

The lizard's reference to a tiger flashed through his thoughts.

I bet it symbolises Boreas's soul, thought Jake. Its sleek and grand appearance fitted the image of a God of Greed and Lord of the Sirens. *The pirate is probably someone working for him. And the ship in the bay—it must have been the same one we saw in the mad mansion. Maybe Dad had taken the ship in order to find something… something he needs for his plans.*

His plans!

With a chill, the word *sacrifice* echoed through Jake's mind. For a moment Jake doubted everything he had just deduced for surely it had been the real Lord Boreas who had planned to sacrifice him in the gate.

Jake tried to remember what he had heard in Renlock.

To penetrate the sylph's bitterness, the lizard had said, *would require heroics of mythic proportions.*

Jake recalled the boyish excitement of what must have been his dad. '*Of course, of course!*' he had cried. '*A burst of hope! One which untwists the twist! A sacrifice! But unlike those of the shepherds this one will be pure! The young Lord Tusk! We must find a way to get both of us into the gate.*'

Another momentous click resounded through Jake as a further piece of the puzzle slotted into place. He remembered his conversation with Frost by the inkwell about how modern myth was full of fathers and sons slaying one another for the sake of power.

Jake's heart sank. He felt nauseous.

Dad wasn't planning to sacrifice me. He's planning to sacrifice himself!

It all made appalling sense. To untwist the myth meant an heroic act of selflessness, one that might stir the sylph to side against Luna. This way his dad's fractured soul was an asset. Its offering was not only heroic, but the fracture created an opening for the sylph to enter, providing the vessel it required to take action. Once inside, the sylph's power would heal the soul while his dad's energy would be destroyed.

So why does he need me in the gate? Jake wondered.

With another dreadful realisation the abyss yawned wide. Jake plunged yet deeper.

He means for ME to slay him! he cried out in thought.

His mind reeled in confusion.

Though he plunged in his mind, in the vault he leapt to his feet and walked in circles in a vain attempt to escape the grim deepening of reality.

But why? I could never do it! And even if I did then it would be just another twisted myth!

He thumped the bannister of the stairs.

Why must it be me?

'Because you're his son. And you must do it not in anger, not in lust for power, but fully aware and in mercy.'

The ethereal voice of a woman had rung out through the void with such warmth and strength that just the sound of it seemed to catch Jake. It had come from the sword in his hand.

He was stunned. *You can hear my thoughts?* he asked.

'I hear many things,' she replied as though she had spoken out loud though she was communicating in thought.

While the tiniest fraction of Jake understood the logic of what she had said, the rest of him rejected it outright: to have just discovered that his dad was alive, but destined to die by Jake's own hand was simply too cruel a twist of fate.

'Your father's soul is fractured. It can only be healed through death.'

Or destroyed, thought Jake.

'The ship you saw in the harbour,' continued the sword, 'was a voyage your father was not ready to take, though had to take if he is to make it into the holygate.'

Jake released a heavy sigh as he tried to re-engage his brain.

What sort of voyage? he asked.

'One to the darkest depths of his being. There he battles his shadow.'

With a shudder Jake recalled the chamber. The dreadful darkness moving through the wood suddenly made sense.

What if the demon wins? he asked.

'Your father will be possessed by it and Lord Boreas, who is trapped in the void, will be free to re-enter his own body.'

Jake closed his eyes for a moment, battling back the gruesome images that threatened to consume him.

Frost's theory wasn't so wrong after all, he reflected. *Lord Boreas was searching for a demon—one of Dad's. Which still might invade the fort.*

Jake recalled his dad's shriek at him from the beach. It now took on a more sinister meaning—*Get out of my fort!*

Frost's theories reminded Jake of something else.

'My God, Asclepius!' he exclaimed out loud.

'An exemplary god!' cried out one of the other weapons. 'The finest of healers!'

Jake saw Asclepius's laboratory in an entirely new light, along with the god's mutterings about his need to find a way in. *He hadn't been referring to a way into the fort, but a way into Dad's unconscious in order to try and help him!* realised Jake.

Another part of the riddle flashed through his mind—'Imagining things of which none can speak'.

Things of which Asclepius couldn't speak. Not even to Braysheath. Walls have ears, especially in this place. If Luna found out Dad was spying on her...

Jake dreaded to think.

He also realised that when his granddad wrote of a plot in Hades it must have been a more general reference to the underworlds rather than specifically the House of Tusk that guards them. The plot was Luna's, who had since created war in the worlds of death.

I must speak to Asclepius as soon as possible! decided Jake, greatly relieved he wasn't Lord Boreas's insider.

The insider was Dad! he realised, connecting what Frost had once said about lizards and dreaming and how dreaming was a loophole into the fort. *And to think—he stole not only Pandora's Box but the gates, too!*

Jake sat back down on the stairs.

She probably would've got the objects anyway and caused a lot more chaos than Dad did when he broke in.

The theft reminded Jake of Asclepius lurking in the shadows. *He was watching out for Dad.*

Another mystery from that same night caught Jake's attention. It lurked in the shadowy wings of his mind though refused to come onto the already crowded stage—something important, a critical link, something huge but elusive. He thought hard. Then stopped thinking altogether, creating space for it to emerge.

It was almost within reach when something large and dark swept in and caused it to fade from his grasp. A vulture filled Jake's mind. It carried his thoughts elsewhere, to the sword in the mad mansion. Again he found himself wondering if it was the same one as the sword resting across his legs—the very object of power the lizard had referred to. Jake shivered in awe at the implication, that the soul inside the sword was the greater part of Rowena's power, the Goddess of Pride, something that had happened relatively recently.

Another chill ran through him. *What if the sword was somehow connected to Luna through Rowena's body?*

Having quite forgotten that the sword was privy to his thoughts, he suddenly stopped them and waited for any response.

None came.

The silhouetted woman on the mountain—she seemed so peaceful, he thought, wishing he could have seen her eyes. He reflected on her image and how well it fitted the voice from the sword. He dwelt on all he had seen in the mad mansion including Luna and Wilderspin's reactions.

No, he decided. *They had no idea who she was. The room was completely cut off and separate from Luna. It was in the corridor relating to Dad. It only appeared when Asclepius placed the snake on its hilt and could only be opened by Dad when he reached for the hilt.*

He remembered Frost's reference to the lady being Lord Boreas's lover. Jake shuddered at what that suggested—that she was his dad's lover.

'No,' he muttered out loud, shaking his head. *There was only one woman for Dad and that was Mum.* Even though she had died when he was a baby, Jake simply knew it.

Frost said that a snake around a sword was a symbol of healing. Perhaps the room it opened represented healing Dad's pain regarding Mum's death. Or perhaps the woman on the mountain was the Goddess of Pride, meaning that his pride needed to be tested before he could advance further along the hallway.

That his dad would revere such a goddess was natural. It didn't mean the woman was his lover as Frost had fancifully thought.

Jake put his hand gently on the hilt.

Are you Rowena? he asked softly.

The sword remained silent.

Perhaps her attention has been drawn elsewhere, he thought as he ran a thumb over the mysterious stone in the hilt. *Of course the soul inside could be any number of other wise souls.*

Jake realised that he wanted the soul inside the sword to be the woman on the mountain, whoever she was. He loved mountains. They were solid, dependable and always brought him peace. Those at peace in their company were also full of peace.

Jake thought he felt a tingle come from the sword, though it was so faint he couldn't be sure.

Overwhelmed with sudden tiredness, finally Jake got up to leave.

'I hope this isn't a dream,' he said as he looked about the vault before leaving.

'Life is but a short dream!' cried out one of the other weapons. 'So said the Romans!'

Jake smiled. 'Yes, I suppose you're right. Good night,' he said and made for the exit.

'Good night, Lord Tusk,' said the weapon in a respectful tone.

The other objects glowed brighter—not in a way that dazzled, but with a hazy sort of warmth.

As Jake stepped down the snake stairs, the doors clamped shut. By the time he reached the dawn-drenched lawn the chilling sound of the Naga could be heard once more, apparently oblivious to what had taken place just moments before. He shivered with awe. It was a demonstration of the sword's power.

CHAPTER 68
JADED ENDURANCE

LAWRENCE BROKE INTO A FIT OF COUGHING. ONCE AGAIN IN THE body of Lord Boreas, he was halfway up the jade staircase which spiralled through the spine of Luna's cat temple in Trafalgar Square.

'Put your hands against the wall,' instructed Geoffrey from inside his cloak. 'Jade is a stone which brings calm amid the storm. It also helps to heal guilt.'

'Guilt? Still?' said Lawrence between feverish coughs, his brow perspiring.

'Yes, guilt. It runs deep,' said Geoffrey. 'You're thirteen levels into your unconscious. The level of transformation. The level of make or break. You're very open to the healing powers of jade.'

Lawrence placed his hands along with his forehead against the cool of the stone. He took several long deep breaths. It brought some calm, but not enough. Battling to maintain presence in two dimensions at once was taking its toll. While he stood on the stairs, the other part of him had roused from his sleep and was trying to warm himself amongst the yeti cubs, desperately trying to stay awake in case their mother returned.

'It's no good,' he said. 'I'm too weak. How the hell am I going to face her like this?' he said, referring to Luna.

Geoffrey released a heavy sigh and climbed out on Lawrence's right arm. 'Open your mouth,' he said. 'I've got some medicine for you.'

'What are you talking about?'

'I'm giving you my light.'

'What?' exclaimed Lawrence. 'Certainly not!'

'Strictly speaking it's not allowed, not for lizards, but since everyone appears to be breaking the rules I may as well join them.'

'But Geoffrey, you offer too much!' said Lawrence, deeply touched. 'I can't accept it. I simply can't.'

'Your need is greater than mine so shut up. And realise that you'll not have access to my wisdom, just the energy of the light. But it should keep you going long enough until you find some more.'

Lawrence was shaking his head.

An amused light glinted in Geoffrey's heavy-lidded eyes. 'I'm ancient. Look at the state of my skin. And it's been an age since my crest stood proud. It's time for a change. Besides, I have faith in you, Lawrence,' he said. 'And you must have faith in yourself. Remember—faith is your lifeline.'

Lawrence was about to object when Geoffrey simply closed his eyes and transformed to light. As Lawrence's mouth gaped open in astonishment, the light flowed in.

The effect on him was immediate. He stood tall and bristled with health. Lawrence closed his eyes, awestruck by Geoffrey's heroic gesture. In giving his light he had ceased to exist directly—his life force was with Lawrence. 'Thank you, my dear, dear friend,' he muttered. He stood in silence for a reverent moment before bounding up the remaining steps.

He entered Luna's control room that occupied the head of the cat.

'Ah, Lord Boreas, you've arrived,' said Luna.

She stood with her back to him, looking out over the square through one of the cat's giant eyes. It was early afternoon.

'My lady,' said Lawrence and glanced about the room. It was like a celestial planisphere. He felt as though he were standing in space, able to see every star and planet. Floating in the centre was an ethereal sphere of Earth about which swirled a series of cyclones.

'Property,' she said calmly while gazing out at London. 'That's what upsets me most—that they think they actually own anything here… the water, the land, stripping it of its beauty to build these lifeless monstrosities they call cities, grey like their shadows.'

Lawrence said nothing.

'I'm going to make them suffer, Lord Boreas,' she continued in the same chilling calm. 'Not just the fat ones hiding within their mansions, but all of them. All are to blame. All must suffer for their cowardice, their failure to take responsibility.'

She turned to face him, her green eyes shining powerfully.

'I've been experimenting,' she said as she walked about the sphere of Earth, a subtle smile playing upon her lips. 'Through this sphere I can summon whatever weather I wish.'

Still Lawrence said nothing, disturbed by her mood.

'Given how passionately they cut down trees, humans obviously love deserts. So I'm going to cover some cities in sand. Others shall be swallowed by the earth. Just like that!' she said as she tapped the sphere with a finger—a city in China.

It flickered for a few moments then disappeared.

'The actual city?' asked Lawrence.

'Gone, my dear Lord Boreas—in a single glorious gulp.'

A chill ran through Lawrence.

Luna appeared to shine brighter as though the souls of the swallowed city had already arrived into the vault on her ark.

'And when these pitiful humans are gasping for thirst,' she continued, 'having themselves robbed all the water from beneath the ground, I shall rise from the sea and rain down from the mountains with such force that they shall be washed away, the soil and crops included. And then I shall freeze the world, eclipsing the sun for an aeon. Maybe that will encourage them to turn inwards. What do you think, Lord Boreas?'

A silence fell between them as Luna waited for a response.

'Who are you really angry with?' Lawrence dared to ask.

Luna studied him, a quizzical light in her eyes. 'Are you going to tell me, Lord Boreas, that we are where we place ourselves, including myself? That everything is just how it needs to be in order to evolve?'

'Is it not true?'

Luna smiled her enigmatic smile. She twirled a finger over the United States and created a hurricane that manifested immediately.

'How does it feel to create that?' ventured Lawrence, treading the finest of lines.

'Satisfying.'

'Is that enough? Is it not ecstasy we need? Without fear that it will come to an end.'

The amused light in Luna's eyes grew brighter as she beheld Lawrence.

'You think me a psychopath, Lord Boreas—a tragic tale of one who was once so open, so sensitive and trusting that the pain of the world was too much for me. And so I closed up and built a fortress around myself to stop further pain from getting in. Is that it?'

Within the lights of her eyes was not only amusement, but great danger. Lawrence drew a deep inward breath before boldly continuing.

'Do you not think, my lady, that behind reckless acts of destruction is a yearning to once again feel... to feel something... above all, to feel genuine love of which pain is part and parcel?'

'Do *you* love me, Lord Boreas?' countered Luna.

Her tone was playful. But there was something else: the subtlest tremor, the slightest crack, no more than a hair's breadth through her defences, but deep enough to reach the Core—the heart of the cosmos, the heart of the matter, the heart of Luna's plan and the fear behind it.

The opening was fleeting, yet timeless if the love was pure. But any love Lawrence might feel for Luna wasn't pure and he knew it. To claim otherwise would be fatal.

'If I could know you more deeply...' started Lawrence, but the moment had passed. The opening had closed once more. He could see it in her eyes. The shields were up again.

Luna smiled wryly.

'It is they, Lord Boreas, who are psychopaths,' she said referring to humans. 'Everyone of them, scrambling to be in control, scrambling to reach the top. And of what? A pile of excrement of their own making.'

She and they have become one and the same, thought Lawrence, supposing it had been her own fear of pain and fear of being alone at the Core that had originally contaminated humans. He thought of the sylph. If it was the symbol of humankind's deeply buried consciousness and potential, along with its fatal indifference, perhaps Luna had become the symbol of their ignorance. Perhaps the sylph truly was Luna's shadow, an expression of the depth of her pain.

'I have a job for you, Lord Boreas,' said Luna, concluding Lawrence's attempt to take her within herself.

'As you wish, my lady.'

'You're to relieve the sylph of its duty.'

Though Lawrence's expression remained impassive, his heart leapt for it would make his mission infinitely easier.

'You mean for me to enter the holygate, my lady?' he asked calmly.

'I'm sure it'll present no problem to a god of your power, Lord Boreas.'

'But the sylph, my lady—what makes you think it will listen to me?'

'Words will not be necessary, Lord Boreas. All you need do is slay Nestor Tusk.'

Any optimism Lawrence felt evaporated instantly. The colour drained from his face.

How am I to impress the sylph with a symbolic sacrifice of myself to my son if, before I even get the chance, I'm to slay my own dad right under its very nose? The hypocrisy will infuriate it! he panicked in thought. *As if the task isn't difficult enough!*

'Are you alright, Lord Boreas?'

'Yes, my lady,' said Lawrence, regathering his wits. 'I just wonder if it'll be that straightforward.'

'The sylph will return to where it came from,' said Luna. 'What else has such bitterness to do but destroy energy it has no faith in? And you're to carry out these instructions this evening.'

This evening! he thought as the image of the treacherous ridge up the icy mountain loomed in his mind's eye. Before he could be sacrificed at the hands of Jake, he had to reach its summit. The timing had to be perfect.

'Enter the gate when it's dusk on the Surface,' continued Luna, 'when Nashoba will be most vulnerable.'

'Nashoba? The oldest of the shepherds?'

'The departure of the sylph will create momentary chaos throughout the cosmos. I intend to use it to take Nashoba's light. Now go, Lord Boreas and do as I say.'

'My lady,' said Lord Boreas.

Following a bow of his head, he departed.

Once he was gone, the Guardian Commander stepped from the shadows.

'I sense rebellion in Lord Boreas,' she said. 'Follow him into the holygate. Make sure he carries out my instructions and slays Nestor Tusk. And once he has done it, you're to slay him.'

The Commander nodded and without a word disappeared.

As Lawrence descended the stairs, he reappraised his instructions.

I shall simply disobey them, he decided. *I must focus on my mission with Jake and impressing the sylph, hoping that it releases Dad. Two shall be saved. Yes, it makes the act even more powerful. Dad saved and my son released from the bonds of his ancestors and their unconscious destruction. And all done in defiance of Luna.*

Lawrence dwelt on the father-son myth and the distant summit he had yet to reach. He realised his greatest threat was not Luna's instructions, but his own unconscious and what he might do to Jake if overcome by one of his own demons.

Get out of my fort! echoed through his mind from the time he had spied Jake on the cliff from the beach. He still struggled to believe that such hatred and anger could well up from inside him, aimed at his very own son.

Lawrence's attention was suddenly hauled to another dimension. The part of him resting with the yeti cubs had been on the verge of dozing off when he heard movement in the part of the cave which led to the entrance higher up the ridge. The cubs also sensed it and cried out. Their mother was returning.

Lawrence on the stairwell grew suddenly faint.

Geoffrey's light—it's almost gone! he panicked and realised just how much had been used to deflect Luna's power.

In the cave he hauled himself up. He searched desperately for the exit through which he had arrived. It was no longer there.

A barrel-chested growl reverberated through the darkness as the mother yeti sensed an intruder. There was no escape. He summoned his fading strength and wits.

His gain, paltry though it was, came at the expense of Lawrence on the stairwell of the cat temple. His head spun. His legs buckled. He collapsed towards the temple wall—except there was no wall. As chance would have it, he lost his balance adjacent to a window halfway up the stairwell. Glassless, it stood fifty metres above the ground and as Lawrence passed out, he fell clean through it.

CHAPTER 69
ACCEPTANCE AND DECEIT

JAKE AWOKE TO THE SOUND OF TORRENTIAL RAIN. IT WAS DAWN at the fort and the first thing he saw was the sword on the bed beside him.

It wasn't just a dream! he realised excitedly and sat up.

He gently stroked the misted stone crafted into its hilt.

The excitement of the night before came flooding back, above all that his dad was alive. He cast aside the grim images of suffering and the appalling odds of survival. If his dad was alive then Jake would help him, just as he would save his granddad. It would all happen in the holygate.

Rain beat down onto the patio beyond his room. Pure and cleansing, it beckoned him. Leaving the sword on the bed, he put on his kilt and walked bare chested into the rain.

Within moments Jake was soaked. It felt wonderful. He walked up to the top of the ramparts and gazed out over the savannah. It had become a wetland. Small mammals had fled for the cover of the trees while elephants and buffalo waded about, egrets and herons fishing from their backs as the spoils of the lake spilt forth.

There was something fitting about the scene. As Jake dwelt on the revelations of the night before, it was as though nature were reflecting his emotions—the grey sky and the rain giving voice to the ocean of tears he had bottled up in his heart. And yet the rain drops were so large and drove down with such force that when they struck the surface they seemed to leap up in celebration.

If it was an expression of death and what it meant then it was a more complete one than Jake had previously understood. He glanced back into his room at the sword on his bed. Yet again one of the lines of the riddle came back to him, though it took on a deeper meaning.

In words (sword) pain for some, for others perhaps bliss.

The sword of the anagram had not referred to Caladcholg which had been thrust by Lord Boreas through Lawrence's heart. It referred to the one he was currently looking at and to what he would have to do with it.

Accepting in action is both the cruel and the kind.

The pain would be Jake's. The bliss, the release, would be his dad's.

But how can I do it? he agonised once more.

The image of bats flew through his mind and reminded him of his first meeting with Frost.

Initiation was how Frost had described the symbolism of bats. *The start of a hero's journey*, the meaning of which Jake was only just starting to understand: a heroic acceptance of what must be done in order for the journey to deepen.

'But why?' he asked again—not why his dad must die, for he understood that only death could heal a fractured soul, but why things had to be the way they were.

'Because you are part of the whole,' came the voice of the sword inside his head, its voice so pure that it resonated as though spoken. 'Because the sylph is ancient and its language is mythic. Because one's family is a powerful portal for changing the world.'

What do you mean? asked Jake in thought, awed and reassured to hear her voice.

'The act of sacrifice holds great symbolic power. On one level, the father is the symbol of custom—the unconscious inheritance of selfishness and destruction, of corrupted male power.'

But Dad doesn't represent that, refuted Jake.

'Not to you. But to the sylph he does, as do all fathers in modern times, just as mothers are symbols of corrupted female energy—for their failure to take responsibility for their part in their own disempowerment. For their failure to recognise that male and female energy exists in all humans. For manipulating through submission and blame, playing the part of the victim, or becoming just as aggressive as men. The sylph is sick of families. It's sick of the walls humans build around themselves, fighting and competing with the world, instead of using the family as a portal to unite with it. The sylph has had enough of modern ways and all their distortions.'

A family is a portal?

'A portal to reach through and embrace the world as one's complete family, one's complete Self. Assuming one can break from custom and do so with love and forgiveness.'

How do you mean?

'As I said last night, Jake, when you slay your father you must do so with mercy, with complete awareness of what it represents, with total love and not a trace of anger. If you can do this the sylph will take note. Because your father plans to offer himself with the same awareness it will increase the power of an already powerful act. But if either of you show the slightest anger then much will be lost.'

But how on earth does Dad plan on getting me to do this? asked Jake.

'You have been made aware of what to do, have you not?'

Yes, but...

'The cosmos works in mysterious ways.'

Jake released a heavy sigh.

And it's with you that I must slay him? he asked.

'You may use any weapon,' she replied, 'but your chances of success will be highest if you use me.'

Jake hesitated. *If I may ask, why is that?*

'Because I understand,' was her sparing reply.

Jake wanted to ask why that was, but had the sense that the powerful soul inside the sword had said all it would on the matter.

Instead he raised his face to the sky and rain. He thought of Brock and the grace of his fall—a being who had assumed the great responsibility of becoming Overlord despite the suffering it brought him.

I don't know how I'll do it, said Jake, *but if I am Dad's best chance of an end to suffering, if it impresses the sylph enough to help end the world's suffering...*

The weight of the task was immense. He couldn't say for sure if he could do it or not. An end to his dad's suffering would mean an unbearable-seeming burden on Jake's conscience.

I can only say that I'll do my best.

Just saying that brought relief. He felt a lightness, as if a door had been opened and the stifling air had cleared a little.

Following a final look at the peaceful scene of the wetland, Jake returned to his room, dried off, got dressed, ceremoniously took up the powerful sword and worked out a way to strap it across his back. Having tied his turban, he was about to leave when his gaze fell on the book of totems on his desk. Out of curiosity, and with Asclepius in mind, he quickly looked up the vulture.

The vulture is probably the most misunderstood of birds, he read. 'Misunderstood! Like the wolf!' he exclaimed.

A bird of dignity, despite its appearance, it soars with grace. As a totem it symbolises purification, death, rebirth and new vision… To the Egyptians it is a symbol of the Great Mother… By consuming what would otherwise be harmful it restores harmony and allows other life to sustain itself.

Jake skimmed the rest until his attention fell on the last paragraph.

In alchemy, the vulture held out the promise that all current suffering was temporary and necessary while a higher purpose was at work, even if not understood at the time.

His thoughts returned to the task ahead of him, comforted by the words in the book.

He recalled his and Frost's secret visit to Asclepius's laboratory.

Despite knowing so much of symbols and never ashamed of showing off, Frost had made no comment about what a vulture meant. Why? wondered Jake.

It had also been about that time that Jake had started to wonder about Frost, horrified that he might have invited a trixy into the fort. But Frost had later laughed at such a thought and confessed that he was in fact a pixy.

With an uneasy feeling in the pit of his stomach, Jake headed for the kitchens. He needed to talk with Merrywisp, the pixy chief cook.

As usual, Merrywisp was standing amid steaming pots and her company of sprite helpers.

'Hello, Jake love!' she cried cheerily on seeing him. 'Fancy some breakfast? Take a seat at the table. You can have it here if you like.'

'That would be grand,' said Jake, taking a seat.

'I expect you'd like big bowl of porridge on a day like this,' said Merrywisp.

'Perfect,' said Jake.

A whoosh of sprites later, a bowl of porridge and steaming coffee appeared in front of him.

'Merrywisp?' he asked.

'Yes, love?'

'How can one tell a pixy from a trixy?'

Merrywisp gave Jake a curious glance.

'To humans we would appear the same unless one knew what to look for. Of course, I can spot a trixy a mile off—the way they move and that tricky glint in their eyes.'

The ominous feeling in Jake's stomach grew worse. The description fitted Frost perfectly.

'But what's a trixy's function?' he asked. Though he had heard it described twice before he wanted to hear Merrywisp's version.

'It's usually to do what humans call *lead one astray*. Between them and us pixies you find your way. All roads lead to Rome, a trixy will say and they're right. It's just that some are more winding and far more eventful.'

'Would a trixy lie?' asked Jake.

'They wouldn't think twice about it!' exclaimed Merrywisp and barked with laughter. 'Except, of course, they would never call it a lie. They would say something clever about half-truths being far more useful than complete truths, which can't be grasped by anything less than a wise person. That's true, but it's how they say it that counts.'

Jake could imagine Frost saying just such a thing.

'A trixy would say they're tricky-true,' went on Merrywisp, 'and that humans are tricky-ignorant or pretend ignorant, preferring to turn a blind eye and thus humans are the trickiest species of all. Again, this is true, during these times at least.'

'My God,' muttered Jake, no longer able to ignore the facts. 'He *is* a trixy.'

'He's not just a trixy,' said a voice that caused Jake's heart to leap.

Both Jake's and everyone else's head in the kitchen turned to the doorway.

Standing within its frame, bow across her back, the rain beading off her bark coloured skin, was Rani.

'He's a prince,' she continued, 'and heir to the Kingdom of Earth. The corrupted kingdom of the corrupted tribe that secretly rules all that takes place on the Surface and has done so for thousands of years.'

A deathly silence followed. Jake looked at her aghast. He couldn't believe his ears or rather didn't want to because following an instant's reflection it made perfect sense.

Jake cursed in thought. *He knows everything!* he panicked as the ominous feeling in his stomach exploded throughout his entire being. *About Dad, Boreas... everything!*

'I'm sorry, dear,' said Merrywisp, looking bewildered. 'but who may I ask are you? I wasn't aware of any guests today.'

'You may call me Rani,' she said, standing proud. 'And I *am* a guest,' she continued, 'just not a very well-known one.'

Rani, gasped Jake in thought. Just the sound of her name brought him back to the present. Finally he knew her name. It was only then that he wondered at her walking about so openly.

'Well, come in, Rani dear, and have something to eat,' said Merrywisp.

'I'd rather stand,' she said.

'Suit yourself, dear, but what's all this talk of a trixy prince?'

Jake drew a deep breath and summoned his courage.

'I invited him into the fort,' he said plainly.

'You did *what*?' exclaimed Merrywisp, looking thunderstruck.

Jake came clean and gave a quick summary of how it had happened, though steered clear of his dad's secret.

'Well,' said Merrywisp, once he had finished, 'that certainly explains all the pilfering of food!' She also glanced in Rani's direction, who chose at that moment to study an owl perched in the rafters.

'If it is the son of Count Frost, whose name is Byzin, then Rani is right. The title Count is a vast understatement and a cover. Effectively he's a king and a very dangerous one.'

Feeling terrible, Jake thought back to Frost's claim that his dad was the richest man in the world. Incredibly, he had been telling the truth. That Frost had said so gave Jake hope.

'He helped free me from Renlock,' he said, reasoning out loud, realising as he said so that only a trixy or a guardian could have untied the cords of inner-force that had bound him. He cursed himself for not realising before.

'In order to win a greater prize,' said Rani.

'Like what?' asked Jake.

'I don't know, but there's something about him, something that seems different from the rest of his kind, something super-tricky, which makes him less predictable and even more dangerous.'

'I know what you mean, but I'm not so sure,' said Jake, remembering that while inside Deuteronomy's stomach, Frost had caused the blackthorn to flower, something a trixy wasn't supposed to be able to do. 'I understand the tricky-truth stuff, but he really has helped me work out where Granddad is hidden along with many other mysteries.'

Both Rani, Merrywisp and the sprites were looking at him doubtfully.

Jake was almost swept up in doubt himself when he remembered a comment from Frost just the night before.

Remember what I am. Remember I have my nature, he had said with that strange intensity as though he were trying to say something, though not outright. *And I must answer it!* he had continued. *I've been extremely negligent since meeting you.*

'He has helped me,' said Jake resolutely, 'in as much as his nature and his tribal loyalty would permit him. I really feel he wants to be friends. I don't think he has any.'

Rani snorted in contempt at Jake's naivety, but Jake ignored it. Instead he thought of the vulture. He then realised that Frost hadn't said anything about it in the laboratory in order to nurture the deception of Asclepius's betrayal. Had he not, then too much would have been known too soon, perhaps resulting in a premature interference in the subtlety of Jake's dad's plan. That Frost had been so aware was something admirable.

And yet Jake couldn't be sure of Frost's motives. Perhaps Rani was right. Frost was leagues ahead of all of them and perhaps sought something, some secret power or object Jake wasn't aware of. Or maybe he was leading them into some terrible trap.

His thoughts turned to Braysheath and how each time Jake had tried to tell him about Frost he had been interrupted. At that time Jake had thought Frost a pixy. That Frost was heir to the corrupt tribe of trixies, and that Braysheath probably knew he was in the fort, was another truth almost too large to swallow.

'Are you sure you won't sit down for breakfast, Rani love?' said Merrywisp, stirring Jake from his reverie.

'No thank you,' said Rani. 'I have to go. And so do you,' she said, casting Jake a stern look.

'Go where?'

'On a mission.'

CHAPTER 70

THE SECOND EAGLE

IN THE SPLIT SECOND BEFORE LAWRENCE STRUCK THE LONDON pavement, having passed out through the temple window, something swept through the falling snow and saved him. It was his winged horse.

While it carried his body back to Renlock, the part of him in the yeti cave was cornered. The light leaking from his navel was weaker than ever. But it was enough to light him up along with the furious yellow eyes of the mother yeti as she entered the cave.

They fixed on Lawrence and hardened to certain death. She released a roar that shook the cave, reared up and roared again. Taller and leaner than a bear, she looked like a giant human covered in dark hair.

Terrified, Lawrence's mind raced.

There's no way out! It must be a test, but of what?

He hadn't the energy for anything elaborate like shifting shape. He barely had enough to think.

The towering yeti approached him still roaring, the lethal claws of her forepaws extended and ready to swipe.

Lawrence's hand reached for one of the two swords he still carried, though he refrained from drawing it. To attack the yeti not only seemed futile, but wrong.

He didn't know the symbolism of the yeti. He deferred to the bear.

The bear, he stammered in thought. *Something to do with the unconscious... awakening... awakening its power, yes! Perhaps even more so for the yeti—it's rarer, more mythical. The bear is also a symbol of alchemy! Transformation. But of what?*

She was almost upon him. Only seconds remained before she ripped off his face or tore open his chest with a single swipe.

'Fear, of course!' he exclaimed. 'What else is there to transform except fear?'

Lawrence closed his eyes in surrender and stood his ground.

The yeti roared louder than ever, announcing her attack. The heat of her breath and spittle blasted Lawrence's face. His eyes were closed. But in his mind's eye he saw it all. She was about to lash out.

Lawrence then did something incredible. He leapt forward to embrace her.

There was a terrific jolt, a blinding flash of light, a gruesome tearing, followed by a terrible numbness.

Silence filled the cave as the echo of her fury subsided. Not even the cubs could be heard.

Lawrence opened his eyes, expecting to find himself bleeding to death on the floor. And yet, despite all he had just felt, he was still standing.

Spent though he was, he released a joyous gasp. The yeti, along with her cubs, was gone. He was embracing an apple tree, so lush that it glowed.

Lawrence stepped back and marvelled at it.

Though only two apples hung from its branches, they were so golden that they shone like miniature suns. Just the sight of them brought a weak smile to his face.

'At last!' he cried.

Without a moment's hesitation he picked one and took a bite. The energy immediately flowed from the magical apple. He devoured the rest of it and felt his strength return—perhaps not enough to take him all the way to the top of the mountain, but hopefully enough to carry him to the next testing ground and stash of energy. He was sorely tempted to eat the second apple. Instead, he prudently stowed it in one of his coat pockets.

'Thank you, my friend,' he said and patted the tree.

Thinking of bears, he thought of salmon making impossible-seeming leaps up through rapids as they journeyed upstream to return to birthing places. It felt similar to Lawrence's own journey back to his true origin—back to innocence. Unlike the salmon, however, he was less prepared for the cold.

Two more rapids, he thought. Now that he had resisted the temptations of the chair, fire and food, and passed the test of the yeti, two of the four eagles remained unaccounted for.

He looked down at his navel. With the boost of energy gifted by the apple, the light was leaking strongly again. He had to get moving.

'I won't be needing these,' he said, drawing his two swords.

Lawrence closed his eyes and visualised two ice-axes in his hands. It worked. With just the knife through his belt as the last of the weapons gifted by the woman, he passed through what remained of the cave and out onto the narrow ledge.

It continued a short distance around a large crag in the centre of the ridge. The drop was so precipitous that he couldn't see where it ended.

Lawrence rounded the crag. The weather cleared for a moment, enough to glimpse the ridge ahead. Except that it wasn't a ridge. The ridge was a hundred or so metres higher. In between was a sheer face of ice.

CHAPTER 71
BRAYSHEATH'S REQUEST

Jake followed Rani across the waterlogged lawn. The rain drove down. They were heading in the direction of the spinney, which appeared to have expanded, for other trees had gathered around. Their presence was heavy, adding weight to the burdensome thoughts racing through Jake's mind. Chief among them were those relating to Frost. Jake couldn't work out how he really felt about the trixy. Had Frost been loyal or had he betrayed their budding friendship? Like the sky, everything seemed grey and unclear. Only time would tell, he decided and tried to focus on the upcoming challenge.

'What mission are we going on?' he asked as they passed through the first of the trees, but Rani only glanced back without a word.

They entered the inner-circle of the spinney where no rain penetrated the dense canopy of trees.

Odin's Council, thought Jake, noting the same shadowy gathering as before. Though this time he could see some of their faces, they were no less mysterious while the atmosphere inside the spinney was even more oppressive than outside

'Lord Tusk!' bellowed Odin in a hearty greeting, the only one who smiled. On noting the hilt over Jake's left shoulder, his right eye grew distant and his left one brightened.

His right eye sees into the future, thought Jake, recalling what Frost had said.

Jake bowed his head before catching sight of a collection of menhirs arranged in the manner of a clock between the trees. Embedded in each was what appeared to be a gate. No one was the same, their form delineated by many stars. Three immediately stood out—the mouth of a roaring lion, a hollow tree and an arch made up of two hands touching at the fingertips.

'Replicas of the stolen Tusk gates to the Outer-Peregrinus,' explained Odin. 'Braysheath created them. They work just as well as the originals.'

It was then Jake noted another gate, by far the most chilling. It was the head of a man, palms pressed to his temples. The gate was his mouth mid-scream.

Before Odin had a chance to explain, Braysheath strode into the spinney with a sense of great purpose, accompanied by Asclepius.

'Right, my friends, everyone knows what they have to do. Do your best to stay in your assigned pairs and for those of you going through gates, you'll be under the charge of Ti. Try not to return until you've built up a sufficient resistance from amongst the inhabitants of each world. Dryads will be there to help you,' said Braysheath.

Jake was shocked at the pace of proceedings. Only then did he realise that he had missed the second part of the Council's first meeting and wondered why no one had filled him in on the details.

'Braysheath, I must talk to you,' he said, daring to interrupt, adding in thought, *I must tell you about Dad.*

Braysheath's attention fixed on Jake with the intensity of a hawk. For a dizzying moment his gaze bore into Jake, but was cut short when the spinney suddenly darkened.

'An eclipse,' remarked Asclepius and the lanterns in the trees lit up. 'On the Surface and throughout the cosmos. Luna's making her move.'

'There's little time,' muttered Braysheath in an ominous tone, maintaining his distant gaze on Jake a moment longer.

He doesn't want me to say it, realised Jake. *Like the times I wanted to tell him about Frost. He knows, but doesn't want to interfere.*

It wasn't a comforting realisation, for though Jake had the sword, he desperately wanted Braysheath's opinion.

'Asclepius will come with me and keep watch,' continued Braysheath, returning his attention to the rest of the gathering, 'while I enter the conductor—'

'Conductor?' broke in Jake yet again. 'What conductor?'

'Thanks to Rufus we know how Luna is capturing the lost souls,' said Braysheath.

'The war room in Renlock,' explained Rufus who suddenly appeared beside Jake. 'She's modified a unicorn horn to act as a transmitter. What we don't know is where it leads to.'

'And so I'm going to hop into it and have a look,' said Braysheath.

'But Braysheath,' came a female voice from the shadows, 'I'm still not convinced. The risks are too high. What if you become trapped? The effects on the cosmos would be catastrophic.'

'I'd be delighted if someone else would do it,' said Braysheath cheerily. 'Alas, I fear I'm the only one here vain enough to cling on to his identity once slain. And slain I must be in order to pass through the transmitter.'

'But who could slay you and with what weapon?' asked the same voice. 'You can't do it yourself.'

'This is true,' said Braysheath. 'There is, however, one sword I have found that is powerful enough to do the job.'

Jakes innards somersaulted as Braysheath's gaze once again fell upon him and the hilt of the sword across his back.

'Jake, would you mind drawing that splendid-looking sword of yours?' asked Braysheath.

'Hang on a second,' said Jake. 'While you lot are leaping through gates what am I supposed to be doing?'

'You have a very important job,' said Braysheath. 'Asclepius has suggested, and I quite agree, that you're to hold the fort.'

'What?' exclaimed Jake feeling humiliated. He glanced about the menhirs and caught sight of Asclepius. The god was looking at him, his expression blank.

While Braysheath leaps through the conductor, doesn't he realise that I must enter the holygate? Doesn't he realise what I must do there? Jake wondered.

'Glabrous and Rufus will remain here to help you,' said Braysheath before glancing at Rani, his eyes twinkling. 'Along with our most recent guest.'

Jake looked at Rani whose osprey had appeared on her left shoulder.

'Your first job, however,' continued Braysheath, 'is to draw that sword.'

Jake looked at him questioningly, though obeyed. As he drew the sword it released a ringing so perfect and so powerful that everything about him tensed, the trees included. All except Braysheath, whose eyes shone with fascination.

'Excellent,' he said. 'Now be a good fellow and strike me with it, will you? As hard as you can.'

'I'm sorry?' said Jake, thinking he must have misheard the request.

'How about a good hearty thrust to the stomach. I can't say I'm too keen on losing my head—tricky things to put back on.'

'You're joking, right?' he said and glanced about the rest of the gathering for help, but none of them shared his astonishment except Rani.

'I assure you, Jake m'boy, I'm quite serious,' said Braysheath. 'And we're rather pressed for time, so come on, chop-chop.'

At the reference to time, Jake thought of his granddad. He looked into the darkness of the eclipse beyond the spinney. *Luna's making a move*, he thought and recalled what he had heard in Renlock—how she planned to get rid of Nestor. Jake, however, had never stabbed someone before. It was bad enough that he would have to stab his dad, but he certainly wasn't going to start with impaling one of the most powerful beings in the cosmos.

'It's the sword that's powerful not me. Someone else should do it,' he said and held out the sword to the gathering.

Without exception, the gathering shrank back from him.

'You're the bearer of the sword,' said Ti. 'It must be you, Jake.'

'Couldn't someone have warned me about this?' said Jake curtly.

'You would only have worried,' said Braysheath. 'The element of surprise—that's the ticket!'

Struggling to comprehend what was being asked of him, Jake looked between the blade and Braysheath, who simply nodded.

Sword, he thought. *What must I do?*

'You must do as Braysheath says,' she replied telepathically. 'His soul must be freed from his body so that he can enter the conductor.'

Jake closed his eyes for a moment and took a deep inward breath. Trusting the sword, he stepped towards Braysheath and placed its tip against his stomach.

'You'll be alright?' he asked.

'I'll be more than alright,' said Braysheath. 'I'll be immensely grateful.'

Braysheath, Jake said in sombre thought, remembering the importance of intent. *I do this for the sake of my granddad, for the sake of my dad... for all our sakes... for the sake of the cosmos. Good luck and please come back to us.*

Braysheath's eyes were shining.

Before Jake lost his nerve he closed his eyes and thrust the sword forward with such strength that it passed clean through Braysheath's stomach and out through his back.

The shock was immense. Light blazed out from the spinney and countered the eclipse. Suns flickered. Stars fell. Galaxies shifted as the shockwave rippled throughout the cosmos.

To Jake it felt like he was the one who had been stabbed. For a fateful moment everything seemed to come apart. He wanted to yell though couldn't. He desperately wished to release the sword but was submitted to a force far greater than himself. All he could do was hold on, watch on, note how the stone in its hilt had become an eye—a furious orange like that of an owl while the blade blazed the same green as Braysheath's eyes.

With the explosion of light, Braysheath had become like a phantom as the surge of power grew more intense. It felt as though all creation were charging out from the shepherd, through the blade and through Jake in a cacophony of trumpeting, barks, roars and screeches.

He was on the point of passing out when it suddenly stopped.

As the eclipse returned, finally Braysheath wrenched himself free of the blade. Though Jake saw no wound or blood, Braysheath's eyes were wide with shock. He staggered backwards towards the gate with the image of the screaming man.

As Jake came back to his senses, he stared on mortified. He dropped the sword which had suddenly become incredibly heavy.

'Go,' gasped Braysheath. 'Everyone... go!'

He then fell backwards through the gate and was gone, promptly followed by Asclepius.

The others followed suit, leaping through the other gates in pairs until all that remained was Jake and his company of four.

CHAPTER 72
BEST SEAT IN THE HOUSE

EVEN THOUGH IT WAS LATE-AFTERNOON AND MIDWEEK ON THE Surface, otherwise known as rush hour, London was oddly still. The eclipse continued. Snow fell. A sombre crowd was gathered in Trafalgar Square. Prostrated in prayer or staring into the half-lit distance, they appeared like refugees.

Walking through them with the detached air of a doctor striding through hospital wards was Frost. Excitement shone in his eyes as he made his way to the oasis about the fountain. Still it defied the snow and was so lush that it seemed to glow—a place of promise amid the bitter cold.

As Frost approached, one of the four giant statues of lions sprang to life, jumped down from its plinth and blocked the way.

'No one passes inside the oasis,' it said gruffly.

'My father is Count Frost and this is his city,' said Frost with an air of authority. 'Step aside.'

The lion studied Frost for a moment longer then dipped its head in a reverent bow and let him through.

Passing under the ancient trees, Frost arrived at the fountain. His face lit up at the sight of it. A raven landed beside him and released a caw.

'I know, Silver. I've sensed it too!' he enthused.

He kneeled beside the fountain and placed the palms of his hands upon the surface of the crystalline water. He closed his eyes, breathed slowly and deeply then began to mutter a chant in a strange tongue.

The air vibrated. Trees creaked and rustled as a wind blew up. The tropical birds of the oasis sang vibrantly. With an ominous quake, the pool underwent a miraculous transformation.

No longer was it merely a pool, but as deep as a lake. Beneath its surface was a city. Lit by lanterns, it appeared Dickensian. A vast yew tree stood at its centre, lending it the air of a graveyard. In its crown was a strange light, shadowy as though obscured by something.

'I knew it!' cried Frost on opening his eyes. 'Down there is the holygate to Hunter! This pool is a secret portal. It's how Luna releases souls to the Surface.'

Silver released another caw.

'If my instincts serve me, which they always do, our dear friends Jake and Rani will shortly enter the gate. And not only them.'

Frost leapt up on the edge of the pool. 'Ah, how exciting! The twisted myth, Silver! Whatever happens, this is a great day!'

CHAPTER 73
THE MISSION

For several moments Jake stood stunned. Without a word, he walked from the spinney into the rain, the cool of its touch once more restoring some calm. He looked up at the dark sky and wondered at Braysheath's instructions.

The others joined him.

Rani studied Jake then also looked up at the sky.

'Well,' said Rufus, 'I suppose we'd best put the fort on alert just in case something comes through one of those gates.'

'No—wait,' said Jake calmly, struck by an idea. 'Glabrous, what are the boundaries of the fort? The *real* boundaries, I mean.'

Glabrous studied Jake a moment before answering.

'The true boundaries are without limit for the fort is a microcosm of the cosmos,' he answered, confirming Jake's intuition.

'And what would you say it means to *hold* the fort?' added Jake.

'Oh aye? And what are you gettin' at?' chimed in Rufus.

But Jake didn't answer. His attention remained on the thorsror.

'To hold,' said Glabrous, 'is to take care of something.'

Jake drew a deep breath of the cool air. He felt a surprising degree of stillness, along with an unshakeable certainty about what had to be done.

'The greatest risk to the fort is Dad,' he said plainly.

'What?' exclaimed Rufus.

'There isn't time to explain all the details, but Dad passed through the god gate just after Boreas. He was mortally wounded. His body didn't survive, but his soul did. It's been battling Boreas's for possession of Boreas's body—a battle which, against all odds, Dad has been winning. His soul is fractured, however. And as he grows weaker, the greater risk is not Boreas, but a demon even darker. A demon of Dad's. If possessed by it, he'll invade the fort. And that's just the start of it.'

'Glabrous?' said Rufus, seeking the thorsror's opinion.

Glabrous raised his nose and licked the air with his forked tongue while his eyes took on a distant light.

'It's true,' he said at last.

'Bloody hell,' cursed Rufus.

'Our mission is not here,' continued Jake, 'but in the holygate to Hunter where the sylph is using granddad to block it..'

'Now calm down, laddie,' said Rufus. 'I'm impressed at your deductions, not to mention yer courage, but what yer suggestin' is madness.'

'Perhaps, but I'm going. First to save Granddad and then to… to *save* Dad,' said Jake, without elaborating on what that meant. 'He plans to enter the gate on business of his own.'

'You'll never get in alive,' said Rufus.

'If my gut feeling is right, Luna wants me there. She'll ensure that I do survive, at least initially. And I have the sword.'

Rani was watching Jake. She couldn't help but be impressed by his calm authority. It was as though he had suddenly aged ten years and become a man.

'We should wait until Braysheath returns,' counselled Rufus.

'Luna will not wait. She intends to slay Granddad in order to release the sylph. And Braysheath might not return,' said Jake. 'Besides, this is Braysheath's true intention. I feel it. Asclepius's too. It's a test of bravery. I must make the decision myself in order for it to have enough power that it might work. And so I've made it.'

'Ach, Jake lad, these are noble words, but all the same—'

'Rufus,' broke in Jake. 'Regardless of Braysheath's intentions, I would go anyway. It's not about being a hero. It's about doing what I *must* do. And I *must* try. If I don't then what sort of life will I have, knowing that I turned a blind eye? That I left Granddad to the merciless whims of Luna. That I left Dad in his hour of need. I'd rather die trying to help than live the life of a coward.'

Glabrous was regarding Jake. He had in his eyes something akin to a glimmer of pride.

It was reflected in Rani's too, along with something deeper. The image of the warrior bathing in the lake flashed through her mind and for the first time she could actually believe that the warrior had been Jake in a past life.

'I also think it was Braysheath's intention that we go together,' said Jake, realising as he said so what a unique company they made. 'Together with the sword we are six. Whether you decide to join me, however, is up to each of you. I'll respect your decisions. But I intend to go. And now.'

Complete silence followed. There was only the sound of rain beating down on the trees and buildings.

Rani was the first to break it. Her mind had been in torment as to what to do until she touched the glove tucked through her belt. It tingled. She knew then that Jake had spoken the truth, that it was indeed Braysheath's intention that they should go together.

'Bin and I will join,' she said.

A rush of warmth swelled through Jake's heart. He smiled at Rani.

'As will I,' said Glabrous.

'Ach balls,' cursed Rufus, his version of *Count me in*.

Jake studied them in turn, knowing each of them to be utterly dependable. Again his heart swelled with pride then contracted with a grave sense of responsibility for their lives.

'So be it,' he said and went to collect the sword from the spinney.

Though not as heavy as before, it was still far weightier than it should be. *Stabbing Braysheath must've used up a lot of her energy*, he thought, hoping it would recover in time for their task.

When he returned to the others, Tancred the butler had appeared.

'Tancred, in our absence I place you in charge of the fort,' said Jake. 'Along with all the grizzlies and other creatures, I'm sure you'll be fine.'

'My lord!' beamed Tancred and bowed deeply.

Jake led the company to the gate of the screaming man.

'The quickest way to Renlock is through here.'

'Straight into the war room? Are yer nuts?' said Rufus.

'You know the way from there to where the holygate is kept, right?' asked Jake.

'Aye, but—'

'Good,' said Jake. 'Once we arrive we must move as quickly as possible before too many guardians are alerted.'

'You're assumin' that the arrival of Braysheath and Asclepius went unnoticed,' remarked Rufus.

'I'm hoping it did,' said Jake. 'If not, we must still go and do our best.'

Sword in hand, Jake prepared himself to leap.

'With respect, my lord,' said Glabrous, 'permit me to go first in order to clear the way for the rest of you.'

'I'm the one who's nuts,' said Jake, glancing at Rufus. 'And it's my crazy idea. I shall go first and clear the way for you.'

A crow landed on Glabrous shoulder and spoke. 'You needn't worry about all the pigeons, Lord Tusk,' it said in a strong male voice. 'We'll create a distraction for you.'

An entire flock of crows appeared as though from thin air, cawing wildly, smothering the branches of the trees.

'A murder of crows is without match,' said the same crow once the din had died down. 'I am Nook, son of Orad and Chief of Gladsheim's Crows. Odin has put me at your service.'

Jake bowed his head in thanks. He opened his amulet and plucked out three stones, one from each of the planets of the Outer-Peregrinus and popped them in the pocket at the front. A powerfully positive energy swept through him and added to his courage.

'Here, take this,' he said and held out the amulet to Rani. 'It'll protect you from the imbalance of inner-force on Renlock.'

Jake's gesture completely threw Rani. It came at a point where she was already confused, for the more Jake spoke, the more radiant he became.

'No,' she said softly, having recovered herself.

She took Jake's hand in her own and closed his fingers about the amulet in gentle refusal.

'I have lived my whole life with trees, with outer-force. I'll be fine.'

Revelling in her touch, Jake smiled then took the amulet back and hung it about his neck.

'I have no rousing speech for you,' he said to all of them steadily. 'No huff and puff... no battle cry about one side's freedom being more valid than the freedom of the other while ignoring the cost to all... while ignoring the grander scheme where nothing changes, one war following yet another. I don't even want to fight. But let us do what is necessary to save those dear to us and help restore balance for everyone else... Luna and the sylph included.'

There followed another silence. The sword tingled in his left hand.

'Ready?' he said.

'Aye, lad,' said Rufus, unable to disguise the emotion in his voice.

'Then let's go,' said Jake.

Following a deep breath, he turned to the gate of the screaming head and leapt through it.

CHAPTER 74
DEADLY PATIENCE

LUNA WAS BACK ON THE MAIN DECK OF HER ARK. LOST SOULS continued to flow in through its unicorn horn mast. The ark was so full of light that it glowed, illuminating the ice sheet and the arctic night.

There was little to do but wait. The Commander had been dispatched to the holygate while Count Frost had been given orders to ramp up the flow of inner-force to the Surface, increasing imbalance yet further. He did this by bringing shipments of highly-charged precious stones from the Inner-Peregrinus to the central banks of the Surface. The stones were so powerful that their essence contaminated the air. Humans would become even less able to sense the subtle song of the dryads through the trees. In other words, authentic hope, calm and intelligent action would become even rarer than it already was.

'The moment draws near,' she said to herself, with a satisfied glint in her eyes.

She was gazing up at the stars, reading them like the map they were. Raising her left hand, she was about to shift the makeup of a certain constellation when she hesitated.

'I wonder. It's tempting to open the way a little,' she said, referring to Jake's entrance into the gate. 'Yet the value of his light will be far greater if I don't interfere. And this female presence I've felt within the fort—it's getting stronger. I sense the hand of Braysheath in her destiny just as I sense the hand of Nemesis in the young Lord Tusk's.'

Instead of shifting the stars, she clutched at the air in the direction of the unicorn horn mast. An orb of light, a lost soul, veered from the mast and shot into her hand. She marvelled at it for a moment then inhaled it, as though it were nothing more than air. Her eyes shone with the stolen energy. A snack.

'Perhaps the heroics in the gate will unlock the secrets hidden in Lord Tusk, for tough times bring out the best as well as the worst in humans. Just a little more patience. And then, finally, I shall set sail from this failed place.'

The flow of souls into the mast suddenly faltered then reconnected with the violence of thunder and lightning.

'Ah, Braysheath!' said Luna with another smile. 'I've been expecting you!'

An instant later she transformed to light and flew up through the stream of souls.

CHAPTER 75
OLD HAG

Lawrence gazed up at the sheer face of ice. If he had more energy he could create crampons, without which the climb looked impossible. His fingertips were numb, but to grip the ice axes he couldn't risk wearing gloves.

Numbness, he thought and remembered something the pirate had said—that emotional numbness, and the fear behind it, was the true cause of evil. Whether the ice was symbolic of frozen emotions or something else, the obstacle was real and there was no way around it.

The hairs on the back of his neck suddenly shot up.

Lawrence glanced back. He sensed a presence, though nothing emerged—not from the sky nor from along the ledge.

'Boreas,' he muttered, for he instinctively knew that the weaker he himself became, the nearer the tiger drew, patiently waiting for the auspicious moment to strike.

Lawrence returned his attention to the rock face. To make matters worse, the light was fading as dusk approached. Unable to find a route up the ice that was easier than the rest, he simply summoned his strength and, with both axes in hand, began to pick his way up the face.

The going was painfully slow. Without crampons he had to make an extra effort to cut foot holds into the ice. Neither could Lawrence risk placing too much weight on his feet and his arms quickly grew tired.

Through pure determination he made it halfway. He stopped for a moment to catch his breath in the thin air. He dared not relax his grip. His burning muscles cried out for relief yet there was not even the slightest ledge on the smooth ice face for a decent rest.

Without warning, Lawrence almost blacked out. He lost his grip on one of the axes. He lost his footing and dangled by a single grip.

Back in Renlock, the winged horse had landed on the cliff, below which was Lawrence's office. As it did so, the Lawrence which had fallen from the cat temple slowly came to. It was the strain of being conscious in two dimensions at once that had caused him to almost fall from the ice.

For a dreadful moment it seemed that both parts of him would slip to their ruin, one from the ice, one from the saddle and off the cliff.

'Jake,' both muttered, as the strongest reason to recover awareness.

'Jake,' they repeated.

As the image of Jake filled Lawrence's delirious mind, little by little, breath by frail breath, both came back from the brink.

As Lawrence on the tower sat up in the saddle and looked out through tired eyes at the stormy sea, so Lawrence on the ice face drew on hidden reserves of strength and swung up his free arm to grab the other axe.

'I must not fail!' he said as he clung to the ice. Through gritted teeth he resumed his climb.

The other carefully dismounted and headed for a secret entrance and stairwell down to his office in order to prepare for his entering the gate.

Two-thirds of the way up the ice face, Lawrence was beset by yet another great challenge. Dusk had become night. The only source of light was from a waxing moon when, out of nowhere, ice nymphs appeared.

Like the sirens on the pinnacle, they flew about him in a seductive whirl, singing their enchanted song, willing him to rest and whispering lovingly in his ears. Their sweet perfume was intoxicating. He almost believed he was in a spring meadow and that if he let go he would simply fall back into lush grass. Unlike the wood nymphs, however, they didn't grab at him. Had they, he would have fallen.

Keep climbing, Lawrence! encouraged the part of his awareness in the office as he warmed his hands about the fire. *Soon you will be able to rest but not now. Keep climbing! These nymphs are not real. Listen only to your heart!*

'Rowena,' gasped Lawrence on the ice, though it was the image of his helper in the island palace which filled his mind and he realised that, on some level, they were the same—symbols of purity that would help him become whole.

Digging ever deeper to find more strength, ignoring the nymphs, on he climbed. With grim determination he swung his axe. When it struck the ice something strange happened. It shattered.

Lawrence gasped as he beheld an ice cave.

At last! he cried in thought. *A place to rest!*

The nymphs gave up and flew away.

Hardly able to believe his eyes, Lawrence dragged himself inside.

At long last he rolled onto his back and gasped in relief and pain. He lay there recovering as long as he dared.

When he finally sat up, it wasn't only from fear of hypothermia and frostbite. It was something else. He was suddenly aware of a pungent smell—one of human decay.

Instinctively he leapt up and reached for his knife.

He stopped short of drawing it. An old woman hobbled from the shadows. When she passed into the light of the moon, Lawrence started back in shock. She was so ugly that at first glance he wasn't even sure she was human. In fact, she looked more like an old witch, from her stubbly warts and hooked nose to the matted grey hair which framed her face like rotting reeds round a swamp.

Lawrence took a closer look, noticing her eyes. There was something unusual about them. Though dark, they shone with the brightness of a child, fixing on Lawrence with a curious light. The more she gazed at him the brighter they grew until a toothy smile broke across her face.

'Got any food for a poor old dear?' she croaked and stepped closer.

Lawrence hesitated, suspecting that there was more to the old hag than met the eye. He thought of the old hag in the desert cave who Rowena had become and wondered if there was a connection. He couldn't find one. This hag was too different.

'I have but an apple, old woman,' he replied honestly, 'but as you can see I am almost done for and have far to journey.'

Her smile broadened, though it wasn't a comforting sight. 'And I have almost arrived at my journey's end and yet I have nothing,' she replied and reached out an empty hand. 'Without a little something to help me on my way, I might as well have never left.'

'Who are you?' asked Lawrence.

'Just a simple old woman,' she replied. 'Think of me like yer mother, for all us mothers are the same. Would you not help her out if she were on her last legs?'

Lawrence sighed, not believing she was simple at all.

'Ordinarily you'd be welcome to whatever I have, but my journey is very important. I cannot afford—'

'More important than mine?' broke in the old hag. Her smile grew menacing.

Lawrence closed his eyes for a moment and tried to gain perspective. The cold was clouding his clarity.

The third eagle. Surely this is a test. But whether it's a trick, whether I stand to lose all or gain something greater in return, I cannot tell.

'I'll tell you what,' he said. 'Let's share the apple.'

As he took out the golden apple her eyes lit up, reflecting the same golden light.

'It's wholeness I'm interested in,' she said greedily. 'Half an apple is not enough.'

'You ask too much, old woman,' replied Lawrence.

The old hag simply stepped closer and continued to hold out her cupped hands.

As Lawrence battled with what to do, the part of him in Renlock was carefully descending the staircase on his way to the holygate. To pass inside it without being destroyed he would need as much energy as possible. Both parts of Lawrence needed the magic apple.

Lawrence in the cave looked out at the moon.

Faith, he thought, recalling Geoffrey's advice. *It's more important than anything else, even the apple. Whatever it is the old hag represents, who am I to judge the importance of her journey? Perhaps her need is greater. And did Geoffrey not also say that everything I see is ultimately myself?*

He looked back at the old hag and smiled weakly.

'Here, take it,' he said gently and placed it in her hands.

The old hag released such a delighted cry that Lawrence thought it was a trick after all.

'The proof is in the tasting!' she cried.

'What proof?' asked Lawrence.

'Whether you gave from your heart or from guilt. For if I taste the slightest hint of guilt, both of us will be destroyed. The same will happen if you gave expecting something in return.'

Lawrence watched on in anxious silence as she sank her teeth into the golden apple, unsure whether guilt and expectation had played parts in his decision.

Suddenly her eyes widened in horror and terrible gargling came from her throat. Lawrence prepared for the worst when she suddenly cackled with laughter.

'Only joking!' she wheezed before wolfing down the rest of the apple. 'It's pure! You passed the test!'

Lawrence breathed a sigh of relief.

'And though you didn't ask for anything in return, of course I must give you something.'

Lawrence waited patiently. *Thank God!* he thought.

'Let's see,' pondered the old hag. 'Yes! Of course! I shall give you a kiss!'

'A kiss?' said Lawrence uncertainly, eyeing her rotten teeth.

'Yes, a big juicy kiss! Come 'ere!'

Good God! thought Lawrence, once more recalling Geoffrey's advice never to judge by appearances and to kiss all crones.

'Come on!' encouraged the old hag. 'It's been an age since I had a good kiss! Especially from a handsome one like you! It'll do you good, I promise.'

Realising he had to go through with it, Lawrence leaned forward. Her eyes lit up in anticipation. She stuck out her hairy lips to greet his. Lawrence closed his eyes to make the job a little easier, bracing himself for a blast of rotten breath.

Yet, as their lips touched, far from being prickled by hairy warts, it felt as though he were kissing an angel. Her lips were soft and full of love, her breath as sweet as honey. Before he knew it, he surrendered fully to the kiss.

Half-way through he opened his eyes expecting to find her transformed. He pulled away in shock. She was the same old hag, her eyes crossed in ecstasy.

'Wonderful,' crooned the old hag. 'How about another?'

'I think that'll do,' said Lawrence.

'Are you sure?' she asked with a wise light in her eyes. 'They're powerful.'

'In what way?' asked Lawrence, for he felt no different than before the kiss and once more wondered whether he had been tricked.

'You'll see. When the time is right, you'll see,' she said and with a wink she transformed into a goose and flew out into the night.

Lawrence watched her fly away, mystified as to what it was he had gained from her.

His awareness returned to the part of him in Renlock who stood alone before the holygate. Lawrence in the cave knelt down and readied himself for the shock.

'Faith,' he muttered and focused on the things he held dear—his family, his friends in the House of Tusk, the beauty of nature and the great potential of humanity.

As the silhouette of the goose passed across the face of the moon so the Lawrence in Renlock placed his right hand over his heart and bravely stepped into the void of the gate.

Lawrence's faith was strong, but the shock was too great. The gate hauled him inside, crushed him to pieces, or so it felt, then spat him out unconscious.

Lawrence in the ice cave collapsed completely. He released a deathly groan. If his life flashed before his eyes, he hadn't the energy to see it. He had only enough to open them one last time, in the same moment something large and lethal leapt into the cave.

The Siberian tiger.

Lord Boreas had finally arrived, bristling with power.

A weak sigh of resignation escaped Lawrence. There was nothing he could do—no energy for fight nor flights of the imagination. Only the energy to witness and barely that.

Lord Boreas tittered.

'An admirable effort, dear Lawrence, *ex*-Lord Tusk, *ex*-human being, *ex*-imposter. Really quite admirable. I've enjoyed your vain attempt to take control and I thank you for stealing the gates. I doubt I could've managed it. Things have really turned out rather well. I couldn't have asked for more.'

The tiger stepped forward and sniffed around Lawrence's head, whose body shivered with the chill of dark intent. As the fight left him, his aura became visible and created a portal above him, allowing Lord Boreas access to his body in the reality of Renlock.

'Yes,' purred the tiger, 'the time is ripe.'

He took a step back. His body tensed, ready to leap.

'I would say farewell,' he said, glancing about the icy hell of the cave, 'but I doubt you will. Alas, Lawrence Burton, your time is up. And mine is just beginning.'

Lord Boreas released a victorious roar and leapt into Lawrence's aura. With a flash of light he was gone.

Lawrence's vision turned bleary with exhaustion. His eyelids grew heavy.

'Jake,' he mumbled with a final breath.

He had scarcely finished the word when his eyes closed and body went limp.

The collapsed body before the gate calmly stood up. Its ice-cold eyes shone with the same lights as the tiger's. Lord Boreas had repossessed his body.

'That's better!' he beamed and took a deep inhale.

'So, Luna wishes Nestor to be slain,' he said, having accessed Lawrence's memories. 'That I most certainly can do. And with pleasure!'

With a resolute stride and a pulse of energy, he disappeared through the gate.

CHAPTER 76
MORRIGAN AND THE STAFF

JAKE'S COMPANY ARRIVED INTO A SCENE OF TOTAL CHAOS. THE maelstrom of war had long since burst beyond the confines of the menhirs, as trees, creatures and hunters tore through one another. The wind howled. Leaves battered. The air cracked with the explosions of freshly severed souls. Light forked upwards as they were sucked in through the unicorn horn.

It seemed to Jake like the whole world had been turned on its head, as though the chaos of a whirlwind had been squeezed into the thunder cell of its creation—inner and outer, upper and under clashing together before their time.

Nook and his regiment of crows battled to fly as they streamed through the gate. They were so many that for a moment they were all Jake could see when something large burst through them.

A lion.

Claws extended it leapt for Jake. It was too close, happened too fast for Jake to do anything, but freeze. With a flash of a paw from Glabrous it was sliced clean in two. The explosion of light was blinding. Jake just managed to stay on his feet. He had scarcely recovered when a sword hurtled through the air towards his head, but an arrow from Rani deflected it just in time.

'We gotta get out of here!' cried Rufus and swept up Jake. 'This isn't our battle!'

An instant later Rani was atop Glabrous, Bin on her shoulder, horrified to see trees fighting.

All of them fled for the wall which led to a corridor, deflecting missiles as they went.

Jake searched for Asclepius, but found no sign of him. Glancing up he noticed a gallery overlooking the hall. His gaze locked with a guardian, whose bright eyes flashed with alarm.

With a powerful growl from Glabrous a portal appeared in the wall and they leapt into a stone corridor.

The crows went through with great speed and burst along the corridor like a flash flood of black rain.

With a growl from Glabrous the portal was resealed.

'Follow me!' cried Rufus and they sped after the crows towards the great wall in the vast cavern of Renlock.

They had only made it halfway when a company of guardians appeared at the far end and blocked their way. Jake and his friends maintained their pace. The guardians were mounted on winged lions and in a whir of silver they raced to meet their foe.

As the tail end of the crows mocked the guardians, Bin took flight and expanded before their eyes, plucking two from their saddles and casting them into the cavern at the corridor's end.

A guardian cast a pulse of inner-force in the direction of Jake's company. A roar from Glabrous cast it back and the attacker erupted in a flash of blue light.

Rani was too busy firing arrow after lethal arrow to revel in the sensation of riding a thorsror to battle, though not too busy to realise that her quiver of arrows wasn't depleting.

Braysheath! she thought. *He's done something magical to it!*

'Focus yer minds on the dryads of the outer-force!' cried Rufus just moments before the two companies clashed. 'Your attack will have higher impact. Think balance!'

Jake not only thought of dryads and trees, but of Brock spiralling down into the crater over Africa. The sword tingled as he clasped it in both hands. In that fateful moment he knew her name, but it wasn't the name Rowena.

'Morrigan,' he said and she suddenly grew lighter. *It must be the name of the silhouetted woman on the mountain.*

A moment remained to appreciate the scale of what swept towards them. It was no longer a single company of guardians. It had been joined by a stream of reinforcements—a glittering force just as lethal once slain.

With Jake's next breath came the clash.

Glabrous leapt forward. His giant paws and claws destroyed two riders, mounts included. Rani's knives were equally effective.

Two guardians sped for Jake at the same time.

The moment had arrived when Jake would have to slay something. He gripped the sword tighter and gritted his teeth.

But his heart wasn't in it.
Resolution wavered.
Time warped.

Images from his nightmare in the woods flashed through his mind in a blaze of murder. Revulsion and torment poisoned his every atom as his body recalled what his mind could not.

But he had to fight. What else was there to do?

Included in the blaze of images was everything Ti had taught him—that the opponent was simply a reflection, like a fortress hiding his true Self. The walls needed to be smashed down, sliced open in order to free it.

To his mind it made sense. The expressions of the guardians were cold and remorseless and Jake was keen to be rid of them. But in his heart there was something in Ti's words that jarred. To cut, to stab—even if the intent was wholesome, the action was violent.

Torn between extremes, resisting the fight in the face of death, something strange happened to his vision—a quake, a momentary splintering as though the integrity of what he saw was under question. As though another world were bursting through.

The guardians swords were arced back ready to sever. The claws of their lion mounts were outstretched ready to slash. There was no time and yet there was—time at least to recall one more thing Ti had said.

A true warrior doesn't kill… There will come a time when you see everything as part of yourself, even your opponent. Everything becomes a projection of your inner-landscape… all change takes place within… there is nothing to fear. Without fear there is no anger, only compassion for all you see… Surrendered to the divine, you let nature decide the outcome of all encounters.

As the blades swung towards him, Jake not only understood what Ti had described, he felt it. Morrigan was no longer just an object, a separate soul within a blade: he and she were one, the divine feminine now part of his left hand—receptive, trusting, compassionate.

She was helping Jake. Just as Ti had said, if a weapon recognised the great potential of its wielder they could lead the way.

With a powerful vibration, she amplified Jake's feeling to the point of revolution. Lines blurred. The guardians dissolved into bodies of light moving through darkness though were also part of it.

Jake stood tall as blades, claws and everything else washed through him as glittering particles of light—more a greeting than an onslaught.

He was reminded of the web of light he had witnessed during the theft of the gates except this was deeper, more fluid, more harmonious than then. And it had come from the present, not the druid. The distinction, however, was blurred by something else. Clasped in Jake's upheld hand was no longer a sword but an ancient-looking staff of dark wood, the special stone forged from the six worlds of death reverently held within its tangled top.

A staff! Like a wand, but more powerful! thought Jake, recalling what Ti had said—that such things were an evolution from weapons like swords until one could duel empty-handed.

Light beamed out from the stone, lit up the corridor and most of Renlock. It shone through and became part of everything, like a sun whose energy was in all things—the guardians, the granite, the air, the crows, Rufus and Glabrous. Jake felt them as separate but also as part of himself. And Rani—her presence felt like a wind, unable to be grasped and yet with the power to cause great destruction, but also great beauty. She had the power to change everything.

THE GUARDIANS WERE THICKENING WITH CONTINUOUS REINforcements. Rani had never fought so hard. Despite being mounted on Glabrous, she wondered how they would ever make it through the corridor when everything suddenly disappeared from sight as glorious light shone about her. For a moment she thought she had been hit, that her time had come. The guardians lost form. They glowed, not blue with inner-force, but pure like stars. She gasped in bliss as one of them shot into her and filled her with its energy.

Is this death? she wondered and glanced about her comrades but the same thing was happening to them. Starlight was shooting in all directions—into the crows and Bin, into Glabrous, into Rufus. Everything shone. All except...

Again she gasped. The stars didn't touch Jake. He didn't need their light for he shone brighter than all the rest like a beacon of peace, transforming the guardians into balanced energy for those who sought balance. She tingled in awe at what she saw—the sword had become a staff, held out with gentle authority.

SUDDENLY JAKE WAS STANDING IN FRONT OF HER ON RUFUS. Their company was at the end of the corridor, the great cavern of Renlock yawning wide before them. Crows wheeled in the air mocking the pigeons.

'Are you okay?' he asked.

Though his staff was no longer beaming, Jake was radiant, as was she.

Not knowing what to say, she simply nodded.

Jake was short on words himself. He was unable to make sense of what had just taken place—his opening up, his intention and what had flowed through, outer-force combining with inner-force in a subtle shift of time and space. He modestly credited Morrigan with what had happened.

Glabrous was looking at Jake. For the first time, Jake saw a smile in his eyes.

'I'm not sure what just happened, but I like it!' gasped Rufus. 'Still, we'd best get moving.'

Jake looked down into the cavern where once the image of Brock had been. In its place was a magnificent oak tree along with the symbol of Luna—a giant green cat just like her jade temple in London except this one was alive. Before they had arrived, it had been curled up in front of a sumptuous fire of light. Now it was staring at Jake with intense fascination, licking its lips.

Jake glanced upwards. Standing outside his office was Wilderspin, studying Jake and his company with a similar expression.

'Where's the holygate hidden?' asked Jake.

Before Rufus could answer, a dreadful din of warbling broke out. Pigeons streamed in through every landing in such number and so tightly packed that they appeared like a wall.

Glabrous sprang forward and released a roar so powerful that the wall of pigeons disintegrated before their very eyes. All that remained were the crows along with freshly arrived guardians who, after a momentary cowering, continued their rush towards them from all directions.

Bin swept down from above, knocking several of them from the stairwell. As she swooped past Jake's company, Rani jumped down from Glabrous and deftly leapt into the cavern and onto the osprey's back. An instant later she was skilfully felling guardians with her arrows.

'Follow me!' barked Rufus and shot off with Jake.

As they rocketed down and around the swiping cat, guardians on the great wall cast out pulses of energy. Others took to the air on their winged lions. Some hurled their swords and knives which Jake deflected aided by Morrigan who had transformed back into a sword. Those he didn't, Rani did, as Bin flew with the agility of a swallow through the protective murder of ravens. Glabrous, meanwhile, bounded down the stairs, slashing, biting and roaring his way through the rest.

Jake wished he could repeat what had happened in the corridor, but that had been born of spontaneity which couldn't be engineered. The best he could do was improvise.

He and Rufus had almost reached the corridor where the holygate was hidden when the giant cat pounced.

'Is that real?' cried Jake.

'I don't plan to find out!' shouted Rufus and shot forward.

At the same time the cat pounced, Glabrous made an awesome leap from the great wall across the cavern. As the cat closed in on Jake and Rufus, he sprang off its head, the distraction buying them the critical instant to sweep into the corridor, swiftly followed by Rani on Bin, along with some of the crows.

While the cat whined in fury, probing the corridor with a great paw and Glabrous dealt with the handful of guardians, Rani used the glove to open the way into the secret room.

'Fare thee well!' cried Nook the crow as Jake's company passed through it.

'Thank you, Nook!' said Jake and bowed his head.

Jake was last to pass into the room. Before he did, he glanced back down the corridor to find a giant eye of the cat, glowing green, staring right at him. A chill ran through him. The light in its eye was Luna's. He felt her joy. He was heading exactly where she wanted him. Refusing to be intimidated, Jake bowed his head and leapt from the corridor.

CHAPTER 77
RUFUS'S SECRET

FOR THE BRIEFEST INSTANT THE COSMOS DIDN'T EXIST. SOMEWHERE between the war room and Luna's ark, two beings of immense power had collided.

The cosmos was restored, though with one key difference—a new world had appeared. Consisting of no more than a clearing in woodland, it was a small world, but what took place within it would decide the fates of all.

It was dusk. At the clearing's centre stood a tree. Next to it, several paces between them, were Luna and Braysheath. His expression was grave. Hers was jubilant.

'I've been waiting for you,' she said playfully. 'Your timing is perfect.'

'Perfection is a process,' replied Braysheath calmly. 'Something you've yet to understand.'

'And you would wait until all energy is destroyed?'

'Were you not so attached to your image then all would be in balance.'

'This is my universe and these are my laws,' said Luna with authority.

A breeze blew through the woods and rustled the leaves.

'The only law is change,' said Braysheath.

'And so I have changed my laws, changed my *plan*.'

Braysheath closed his eyes for a moment and inhaled deeply.

'Patience,' he counselled. 'Go back to the Core and have faith.'

Luna snorted in contempt.

'I've been patient enough! Today I leave and I shall be taking your and Nashoba's light with me whether you surrender it or not.'

Braysheath smiled warmly.

'And where will you go?'

'We're about to find out,' said Luna and with a wave of her hand the wood transformed to light.

HAVING STOLEN INTO THE HALL WHERE THE HOLYGATE WAS hidden, resealed and re-encrypted the rock of the wall they had arrived through, finally Jake's company could catch their breaths. Within moments the guardians could be heard trying to get in.

'It won't fool them for long,' said Glabrous, turning his attention to the only object in the room—the holygate. He strode up to it, sniffed and licked the air.

'Only a force or high wisdom can pass inside. Rufus will survive but you won't,' said Glabrous looking at Bin. 'You must stay and guard the gate.'

'But she won't stand a chance against so many!' protested Rani.

'The odds for all of us are slim,' remarked Rufus.

'What about Rani and me?' asked Jake, keen to get moving.

'Nothing is certain,' said Glabrous. 'But with that sword you have a chance. As for Rani...'

'I have the glove,' she said.

'Its power comes from Braysheath,' said Glabrous. 'For what he now faces, he'll have little energy to spare. The glove cannot be relied upon.'

'Then... ?' said Rani.

There was a moment's silence, save the quaking wall as the guardians got closer to breaking through with their mysterious chants.

'I shall lend you my light,' said Glabrous plainly.

'No!' shot back Rani, both awed and horrified by the idea of such a responsibility. 'I couldn't possibly take it!'

'I said *lend*, not take,' corrected Glabrous. 'It's more important that you enter the gate than me, for all your sakes, especially Jake's. The alchemy of man and woman is high wisdom. For this reason it's important that you stay close to each other.'

'Aye,' said Rufus dryly. 'But I'd hardly say their alchemy was balanced.'

'It's evolving,' said Glabrous, 'and in the gate it will evolve yet further. Whether it's enough will depend on the mood of the sylph.'

'Thank you, Glabrous,' said Jake with deep gratitude.

'But…' began Rani, though was cut short by Glabrous leaping towards her and releasing the most fearsome roar she had ever heard. The whole tower appeared to shake.

Jake watched on astounded as the thorsror's light erupted from his mouth into Rani's gasp.

Glabrous's body slumped to the ground.

Jake was dumbstruck not only at the sight of the thorsror, who looked dead, but at Rani. She shone like a goddess.

Rani quivered with rapture as the thorsror's sensual power flowed through her. Her perceptions burst to life in a way she hadn't thought possible. She saw Jake as she had seen him through the net of light—one with the potential to be a true king and a strange and novel yearning rose up from deep within her.

'We must go,' said Jake, tearing his gaze away from Rani. The wall was starting to vibrate as the guardians got closer to entering the hall.

'Are yer ready for another shock?' said Rufus.

'What?' said Jake.

'Though my knowledge of the forces will protect me, I won'ay have the power to sustain flight.'

'So what are you going to do?' asked Jake, wondering how he was going to carry Rufus as well as do everything else that was expected of him.

'This,' said Rufus and transformed into a human.

Jake's jaw dropped. It wasn't just any human. It was Bill.

'Ach, that's better,' he said. 'And no more need for that bloody English accent.'

'Bill! Rufus!' exclaimed Jake. 'Why didn't you tell me before?'

'Time and a place, laddie. On which note, let's get crackin'.'

Jake couldn't believe it and yet it made perfect sense—Bill hugging trees and other strange habits not to mention how a carpet could catch fish, drink Vicar's Tea and butter toast, all the while keeping watch over Jake. His spirits soared just when he needed it.

'Right, I'll go first, you two follow,' said Rufus. 'Stay close and stay present.'

Rani glanced back at Bin and realised that Glabrous had also imparted a little of his light to her.

'Farewell, Bin,' she said, her eyes welling.

'You too, Rani dear. Fight well!'

'Okay, let's go!' said Rufus, just as the concealed entrance to the hall became almost transparent and revealed the busy guardians.

Side by side, Jake and Rani watched Rufus pass through the star-encrusted gate. Before he disappeared from sight, his legs buckled from the shock.

'Ready?' said Jake and held out his hand.

Rani nodded. She looked at his hand then gently took it.

A complex tingling swept through both of them and summoned nervous smiles.

Following deep breaths, they stepped into the gate.

LAWRENCE HAD LOST HIS BATTLE TO SUSTAIN PRESENCE IN TWO dimensions. There was a positive however—he was able to recover in one. But only just.

When he finally stirred in the ice cave, he was shivering violently from the extreme cold. He was trapped there. His connection with any reality outside of his unconscious was broken. It was like being stuck in a nightmare unable to wake up from it.

Pale and matted in ice, he looked deathly. It was night time. A full moon shone into the cave. The first things he saw on opening his eyes were his fingertips. They were black with frostbite. To move meant hypothermia, but he had to make it to the top of the great mountain. But when he tried to get up, his body refused.

Lawrence lay back and groaned. His toes were numb, just as frostbitten as his fingertips. He felt his body willing him back to sleep. He desperately wanted to close his eyes and drift off once and for all.

'M-must g-get up,' he stuttered defiantly.

He had come so far and suffered so much, he had to finish what he had started. Yet try as he might to battle his fatigue, Lawrence's eyelids grew so heavy that they finally closed.

His body relaxed. Despite the cold he drifted off.

Before fully passing into sleep, a voice came into his head.

'Get up, my love,' it said sweetly.

'R-Rowena...' mumbled Lawrence through his drowsiness.

'Get up. You can do it. Just a little further to go and then, my love, you'll finally have peace. But first you must get up. Jake needs you.'

'Y-yes... J-Jake...' muttered Lawrence and managed to open his eyes, realising that the voice had come from the real Rowena.

With a great effort he hauled himself up to a seated position and, following several deep breaths, finally dragged himself to his feet. He blew into his hands and walked some life back into his frozen body. A little less cold than he was before, he mustered whatever strength he could, picked up the two ice axes and walked to the cave mouth.

The moon lit up the sheer face of ice. Having glanced down into the gloom, he leaned out and looked up. Though it was little more than twenty or thirty metres to where the ridge continued, it looked like miles.

Gritting his teeth, Lawrence bravely set out for the summit.

The effort was Herculean as he picked his way up the final part of the face, twice losing his foothold and almost falling.

At long last he made it to the top of the ice face. He hauled himself onto the relative safety of the ridge and collapsed, panting for air, his hands frozen around the ice axe handles.

C-can't hang around, he reminded himself. 'M-must k-keep going.'

Lawrence stood up and gazed at the moonlit, snow-covered knife-edge ride. Though it posed a great challenge, he couldn't help but marvel at its beauty.

'J-just a l-little f-further,' he mumbled, the recollection of Rowena's voice gifting some strength.

Taking great care not to slip, Lawrence set off steadily up the ridge.

Oh, for that second apple!

The moment he completed the thought, an almighty crack shook the air. The ridge shifted. Lawrence lost his footing. Swinging both axes into the ice he just caught himself.

He stared ahead in disbelief. Yet another challenge separated him from the summit.

A crevasse had appeared.

THE SHOCK OF ENTERING THE HOLYGATE WAS SO VIOLENT THAT Jake felt as if he were being dashed against the cliffs by a ferocious sea. Rani felt it too. Though Glabrous's light was holding her intact, it was draining fast.

'Are you two alright?' shouted Rufus through the tumult, placing a reassuring hand on each of their shoulders.

Eyes wide with shock, Jake and Rani nodded their heads uncertainly, doing their best to adjust to the constant way the gate wrenched them in all directions.

It was dim. They were in a burrow-like tunnel, roots poking through the earth. Unlike the inkwell, the holygate felt more physical, though it was a reality their human bodies weren't designed for.

Slowly but surely Rufus led them along the tunnel. A twist and a turn later it was shot through by a blaze of light coming from a shaft ahead.

'It's the blockage caused by the sylph!' explained Rufus. 'The light is from all the souls waiting to return to the Surface!'

Before reaching the shaft, they came upon a staircase of tangled roots.

'Up here!' said Rufus and led the way.

A short while later they arrived through the surface of a misted lawn. Beside them was the largest tree Jake had ever seen—a yew tree. Its girth looked as wide as the ramparts about the House of Tusk. It stood within a pristine private garden, surrounded by a square of elegant townhouses. It was twilight and candle light issued from the windows.

Though the atmosphere above was less violent than below, it still weighed heavily upon them. They took deep breaths to help adjust to it, which helped slow Rani's loss of Glabrous's light.

'Come,' said Rufus. 'We must keep movin'. To linger in such a place is to become part of it.'

As Rufus made for the trunk of the yew, Jake suffered a terrible chill. Standing on the other side of the square was a shadowy figure—the only one around. He was holding a lantern, looking directly at Jake. It was the phantom form of the red-bearded druid.

Rani also saw him. There was no time for doubt. She wrenched him by the hand and dragged him away.

As they made their way to the yew, a pulse of energy erupted from the crown of the tree. A heron flew out with a ball of light in its beak.

A soul, deduced Jake. *One released to a new worshipper of Luna on the Surface.*

He watched it spiral upwards over the houses, realising that each house symbolised a family on the Surface.

They caught up with Rufus at a well-disguised stairwell that wound up and around the yew within its giant bark. As they ascended the great tree, they noticed how quickly the smart houses about the square deteriorated into a ramshackle sprawl of squalid quarters. It was a different expression of the vast cemetery Luna had witnessed through Pandora's Box. The sprawl stretched to the horizon and towered so high that it seemed like that the slightest breeze would bring it all crashing down.

'The sacrificed shepherds,' said Rani, referring to the slums.

Jake struggled to imagine how the sight before him was what had become of Braysheath's brothers and sisters. Despite the atrocity, there was something perversely marvellous in the ocean of lantern light amid the squalor, as though the stars had fallen from the sky.

Will the shepherds ever become whole again? he wondered, imagining, wishing, that one day the billions of souls might somehow regather themselves through the worlds of death.

A few steps later, his ponderings evaporated into the rapidly thinning air. Climbing the tree became increasingly difficult. Every step felt like a hundred metres of high altitude ascent. The others felt it too. Their pace slowed along with Jake's as they trudged up and around the mighty tree.

Just short of reaching the crown, Rufus stopped.

'Boreas is here, I can sense him,' he whispered, his breath ragged. 'Along with a powerful guardian. They've probably sensed us. Prepare yourselves.'

Weapons ready, Jake and Rani looked at each other. Though they made no sound, the wild lights in their eyes said it all. They spoke of fear, of hope, of racing hearts and other feelings more complicated—too new and too old-feeling to make sense of.

They nodded their good luck to each other.

Braced for battle, with a final nod to Rufus the three of them bound up the remaining steps and leapt onto the large flat area of the yew's crown.

Then halted, spellbound by the astonishing scene before them. Sitting upon a shaft of light at the centre of the crown was the sylph—a vast dragon of shadow.

Through shadowy eyes it studied the new arrivals and released to the sky an ear-piercing shriek of excitement.

Jake noticed an altar stone between themselves and the sylph. A dread chill gripped him. Lying upon it in the manner of a sacrifice, unconscious, emaciated, deathly pale and encased in a strange blue flame was his granddad.

Jake took a step towards him, but Rufus held him back.

'He's not dead,' he said.

'He's alive?' muttered Jake, scarcely able to believe it.

His hand grasped the amulet about his neck. A wave of hope rushed through him—authentic hope, for Jake had every intention of acting upon it.

Starved of such a rare thing, the sylph's awareness bore down upon him with the weight of thunder, demanding attention.

Tearing his gaze from his granddad, Jake bravely beheld the sylph's gaze. Its intensity was immense, even greater than Braysheath's. It shot through Jake like lightning. He felt its anger, its bitterness and wondered how five beings who had been so wise could become so lost. He also wondered at Luna's power in creating such pain.

The sylph reared up and stretched its wings. It glanced excitedly at the lantern-bearer standing down in the square then at Morrigan in Jake's hand and released another ear-piercing shriek.

Rufus tightened his grip on Jake.

'You cannae touch him,' he said, referring to Nestor, 'not before the sylph releases him. They're connected.'

'Or until he's slain,' came a menacing voice.

Sword drawn, the guardian Commander, Luna's other henchman, stepped into view. He stood as though waiting for something.

It was then Jake realised who was missing.

'Boreas,' he said to the Commander. 'Where is he?'

The guardian smiled.

Morrigan vibrated with alarm.

Jake glanced up, but too late.

Something powerful swept down, grabbed him fiercely and flew off with him.

'Jake!' cried out Rufus, unable to transform and fly after him.

'Slay them!' barked Jake's assailant to the Commander as a company of guardians leapt upon to the crown from the stairwell. 'But Nestor's mine!'

'Bin!' cried Rani.

Reinforcements meant the osprey had been overwhelmed. Swallowing her torment she fired an arrow at Jake's kidnapper but the shock of their separation suddenly hit her and the arrow missed.

They had lost the protection of their alchemy.

Jake's strength failed him. Slung across the withers of the winged horse, he peered back through bleary vision as guardians encircled Rufus and Rani.

'Lord Tusk!' came a powerful and harsh-sounding voice. 'Finally we meet!'

Jake looked up at his captor. Confusion gripped him. It was Lord Boreas, yet there was something different about his eyes. Like his voice, Jake didn't recognise them. Their lights were fierce, bright and as cold as ice. His skin was so pale that it was almost blue.

'Dad?' said Jake.

'Dad?' barked Lord Boreas and roared with laughter. 'Dad! Your dad is gone! Gone for good!'

Jake tightened his grip about Morrigan.

Regardless, Lord Boreas kicked her from Jake's clasp.

No! cried Jake in thought as he watched her fall towards the slums.

Separated from her as well as Rani, he passed out.

CHAPTER 78
MOTHER OF SHOCKS

As dusk thickened to night about wintry Trafalgar Square, Frost was beside himself with excitement.

'What fine lines, Silver!' he cried and leapt upon the wall of the fountain. 'The Great Father Myth is in the balance! Whatever happens will affect the entire cosmos! The sylph will make sure of it!'

He cartwheeled about the wall.

'Oh to be able to see what's become of Jake's dad!'

Just then a loud creak issued from a nearby oak tree and an ominous rustle escaped its leaves. Flocks of birds took to the skies, not only in London, but across the entire surface of Earth.

Frost spun around and studied the oak. His eyes widened. The trees roots had altered. Now entwined, they looked like a woman and a man embracing, she reaching up from beneath the ground, he reaching down from above.

'Their embrace, Silver!' gasped Frost as it shifted a little. 'It's weakened! It symbolises the Tree of Life—the two trees of Eden united. Eve's roots mirrored in Adam's branches. If they separate completely then the human experiment is over! Humankind's spirit, its potential, will finally separate from body and mind.'

Silver released a loud caw.

'Yes, Silver, that's exactly what it means! Not only is it tied to the gate and whatever's happened to Jake's dad, but Braysheath and Luna have at last come head to head!'

What Frost had seen in the oasis was indeed a reflection of the tree standing between Braysheath and Luna. The wood had not only turned to light, but its every leaf, its every insect, its every detail, the sky included, had become the most intricate geometrical design, all life force connected.

Braysheath shone like the sun.

Luna glowed like a blood moon.

It was she who made the first move. She struck a hand out as though casting a spell. Not at Braysheath. Her intention struck the fabric of the woodland which suddenly shifted. It became the image of Jake's face then shifted again through many other faces as she plumbed the mysteries of his lightline.

Eyes closed, Braysheath calmly reached out in the same direction. With a twist of a hand he shifted the image to that of her ark. As he reached towards it, the image changed at lightning speed, revealing the way to find it.

Before her secret was revealed, Luna re-exerted her power. She brushed aside the image of the ark and replaced it with that of a man on an arctic mountain—a Native American with long, steel-grey hair and a strong, strikingly peaceful face. It was Nashoba, the oldest of the shepherds, doing his duties at the North Pole. She cast up her other hand in the direction of the sky. The clouds transformed into a twilit ocean storm. A tsunami towered up and rushed for one the Surface's coastal cities, striking a blow at Braysheath's weak point—his love of humans.

The wood became like a giant and magical canvas where the only limit was the power of visualisation. What took place on the canvas took place in reality.

Luna sprouted two additional arms. A wave of their hands later, volcanos erupted across the Surface. Floods burst forth from shattered dams and tore through valleys towards the settlements below.

Lord Boreas landed on a hilltop commanding a view of the sprawling gate and the yew tree in the distance. He plucked Jake from the horse and threw him to the ground. There Jake remained, too weak to get up.

Lord Boreas stood tall, surveying the gate.

'There are some who believe that everything, absolutely everything, belongs in this cosmos—every new godforsaken child despite it adding to the imbalance, every pitiful concrete dwelling to house its witless parents and ever-multiplying siblings, spreading across the Surface like vermin, wasting all the water, consuming all its beauty. *It all belongs. It's perfect!* they cry,' mocked Lord Boreas and barked with ironic laughter. 'What do you think of that, Lord Tusk? What do you believe?'

What Jake couldn't believe was that his dad was dead, destroyed. But he had to be, otherwise how could it be that Lord Boreas had re-inhabited his own body? If not destroyed then he was lost in one of an infinite number of hells.

'Well, Tusk?' pressed Lord Boreas, peering down at him.

'I believe in balance,' said Jake. 'It evolves.'

Again Lord Boreas barked with laughter.

'Said like a true shepherd's apprentice! Oh yes, of course, on one level it all works out... *eventually*. All is energy, yes, yes, I've heard it all before. But in the meantime, what sort of life is this?' he said, gesturing to the slums. 'Do you see anything of quality?'

'Is it quality to surrender to your weaknesses and pass through the god gate, to take what you think is a short cut?' countered Jake.

Lord Boreas snorted.

'Everything has its time and this age of humans has gone on too long. It's time to start afresh.'

'Through stealing light?'

'Cleansing light,' clarified Lord Boreas.

'How can it be clean if someone unclean controls it?' asked Jake referring to Luna.

'You dare to judge Luna?' spat Lord Boreas.

'Yes,' said Jake plainly. 'And aren't you forgetting that you too are human?'

'I'm a god, Tusk, as you will shortly find out.'

'You are a *false* god,' said Jake bravely, 'and so you will fall. That's the destiny of all humans who pass through the god gate. It's a trap. Don't you realise?'

Grinning menacingly, Lord Boreas drew his curved blade and approached Jake who managed to sit up.

'I admire your courage,' said Lord Boreas. 'Unlike your father, who was cowardly and weak.'

'My dad was brave and strong,' said Jake who, making a great effort, dragged himself to his feet. 'Strong enough to defeat a god within the god gate and take possession of his body. Smart enough a human to fool a supposedly powerful goddess.'

'But not strong enough to accept death,' said Lord Boreas.

'What are you talking about? Of course he was,' retorted Jake. 'He would've fought to the bitter end but ultimately, when death came, he would've accepted it. I know.'

'His own, perhaps,' said Lord Boreas in a smug tone. 'But what about his wife's—your mother's?'

At the reference to the mother he had never known, Jake's head spun with confusion.

'My mother died. What else could Dad do but accept it?'

'What else indeed?' said Lord Boreas in a knowing tone.

Jake looked at him searchingly.

'You know,' said Lord Boreas, presenting the tip of his blade to Jake's stomach, 'in the gate we saw something of each other's truths—of each other's secrets. Or at least I saw one of his. A rather fascinating one. One I'm very much looking forward to telling Luna. It'll be the perfect accompaniment to the gift of this sword containing not just your soul and shortly your grandfather's, but your father's too. His soul is already inside it,' lied Lord Boreas and pressed the blade so that it pierced Jake's shirt.

Jake stepped back from the sword, scouring the god's eyes for hints of deceit, though was unable to read their smug fierceness.

'I can see you're dying to know your father's secret, but are too proud to ask,' snorted Lord Boreas. 'So I'll ask you a question. What do you think your father did when he found your mother lying dead on a mountain top above that quaint little farmhouse of yours?'

'Exactly what you normally do when someone's slipped to their death—'

'Slipped to her death?' barked Lord Boreas. 'Is that what your father told you? How dull that would be! No, my dear Lord Tusk, she was torn to shreds by wolves.'

'There are no wolves in England,' countered Jake.

Lord Boreas tittered. 'Have you learnt nothing?'

Everything is possible. Braysheath's words once again echoed through Jake's tormented mind, while talk of mountain tops reminded him of the peaceful-looking woman in the mad mansion.

'So, I ask you again. If you had been your father, *Lord* of the House of Tusk, a lord of gates and all the knowledge that comes with it, what would you have done? Imagine the scene—your ravaged mother, you within her protective clasp only moments after she had given birth to you—'

'You're making this up!' protested Jake. 'A woman about to give birth wouldn't, couldn't climb a mountain!'

'Your mother was no ordinary woman,' said Lord Boreas. 'She worshipped the mountains as resting gods and dragons. She was a woman of great beauty, especially inside. It's why your father couldn't accept the loss of her. Imagine his torment, his resentiment. His hatred! His hatred for you! That you survived, but his beloved died.'

'Hatred?' muttered Jake, not wanting to believe it until he recalled the rage of his dad on the beach deep within his unconscious, ordering Jake to leave the fort.

'Oh yes,' said Lord Boreas inspecting the exquisite blade of his sword. 'Ashamed of such hatred, naturally he repressed it, but the hatred is there. Believe me, I've seen it. Enough hatred to fuel an army! But enough about you. What of your poor mother? What was Lawrence to do? Oh, how he adored her! Oh, how unfair the cosmos was! Oh, how cruel this God Almighty!' said Lord Boreas with great drama. 'But wait! God! That's it! Suddenly your father was feverish with excitement, feverish with hope. *The god gate!* he dared to imagine, for naturally all Lords Tusk have known of it. Could he? Should he? What would happen to her, to him? What did it matter? To hell with everyone else!'

'He wouldn't be able summon it,' countered Jake.

'Oh, please! The gate has intelligence. It's designed by trixies. At the prospect of such mischief, it would have gladly revealed itself.'

Jake's mind reeled. If it were true...

'Oh, how love can blind,' continued Lord Boreas. 'And so your wretched father secretly tossed the remains of your mother into the god gate. And what do you think became of her, young Lord Tusk?'

Suddenly it all made sense—horrible sense. The woman on the mountain. Her appearance had changed, her name, Gwendolyn, had changed, but not her soul. If there was any doubt, what Rufus had said echoed through his mind—of something Lawrence had done sixteen years ago that had upset Braysheath. It was what Frost, unbeknown to Jake, had also discovered in the now-destroyed god gate records.

'Rowena,' he gasped, looking out over the holygate.

'Yes,' delighted Lord Boreas. 'The Goddess of Pride no less. One wonders at the genius of the gate.'

'Then what happened to the existing goddess?' challenged Jake.

'A wonderful synchronicity, naturally. She was called to the Core the very instant your father threw your mother into the gate. The cosmos works in mysterious ways, Lord Tusk.'

'Luna,' said Jake as the full implications sank in.

'Oh yes, how wonderfully ironic that she should choose to possess the soul of your mother, the wife of Lawrence Tusk. It'll be a joy to inform her. Not that there'll be much left of your mother's soul. The longer Luna inhabits it, so its light becomes her own.'

With an almighty click, the outstanding mysteries slotted into place.

The sword! thought Jake. *The swords in the mad mansion—the one in the corridor relating to Dad, the sword in the corridor relating to me... and Morrigan... Rowena's secret object of power where the greater part of her soul was hidden... They're one and the same! Gwendolyn, Rowena, Morrigan! It's all the same! They all sound Celtic. Mum was Welsh!*

A rush of warmth flowed through Jake and forced aside his fatigue. He thought of the peaceful woman on the mountain. Jake had seen the soul of his mother and had felt her energy tingle through the hilt of the sword. She had helped him resolve the riddles.

And the white dove in the chamber and again in the white tree of my dream—peaceful like the woman on the mountain. That too must have been her! Guiding me!

It suddenly struck Jake that the soul in the sword was much more than his mother. His mother was simply the soul's last incarnation. He thought of what Ti had said of the fort's dwarf-smiths—that the soul inside was so powerful that they dared not touch the sword.

But where is she now? he sighed in thought. Lord Boreas had booted her into the slums. *How can I get her back?*

Instinctively he turned his head in the direction of the square about the yew. There among the many lights he picked out the druid patiently waiting for something. For a moment his lantern brightened as though acknowledging Jake's attention.

Stay present, he warned himself, wishing he could do what he had done in Renlock and draw on the power of nature, but he was in a holygate, desperately weak and without Morrigan.

Lord Boreas was regarding Jake with a curious glint in his eye.

'The truth hurts, does it not?' he said and once again pressed the tip of his blade to Jake's stomach, this time piercing the skin.

As Rufus and Rani battled the guardians to protect Nestor while the Commander watched on grinning from the side, Asclepius was back in his lab desperately searching for a way to reach Lawrence. Though Lawrence's journey was one he had to make on his own, Asclepius had a horrible feeling that, at the critical moment, Luna would interfere. If she could, so could he. Yet try as he might, Lawrence was so deep within the Inner-Peregrinus that Asclepius couldn't reach him, not through scouring the galaxies, not through the turtle, nor through the white wolf, which lay comatose in the oak.

THE CREVASSE SLICED THE RIDGE COMPLETELY IN TWO. WITH NO ropes or any other special equipment the only thing to do was leap, but it was at least ten metres wide. Even if Lawrence hadn't been exhausted and half-frozen to death he couldn't have made it. He peered over the edge. It was so deep that it far outreached the moonlight.

Lawrence cursed. It was his wishing that he still had the second golden apple that had caused the crevasse.

I gave it to the hag because, in my heart, I wanted to, needed to and without any sense of duty or guilt. But, fool that I am, I then wished I had it back.

He wondered at the old hag's kiss. What power was it supposed to have gifted? '*You'll see,*' she had said. '*When the time is right, you'll see.*'

And why, he wondered, *did her kiss feel so incredible? Like the mythical crone, her ugliness was a disguise or a symbol, perhaps both, but of what? Beauty hidden behind something ugly, such as jealousy or hatred, but of who? Not Jake,* he reasoned, recalling the painful revelation on the beach, *otherwise surely she would've been male.*

After his recent exertion, again the cold was becoming unbearable. The colder he got, the harder it became to think. He was keen to get moving.

Whatever the crevasse represents, I have to cross it.

He reminded himself that he was deep in the unconscious where on one level everything was very real. Yet on another level, everything was an illusion. Lawrence thought of trying to close the crevasse through will power or sprouting some wings and flying over it, but his instinct told him not to try. Not only would the effort be a waste of valuable energy, but it wouldn't work.

It's a leap of faith, he realised.

Once more he looked down into the abyss of the crevasse.

Think positive, he thought.

Too cold to waste another moment, Lawrence took a few steps backwards, gripping the ice axes in his hands.

'And so I m-must have f-faith,' he stammered through chattering teeth, though he felt the weight of his doubts as he said so.

As Lawrence took a final deep breath, the image of Rowena filled his mind.

'F-for you, my love,' he said, rushed forward as fast as his aching body would carry him—and leapt.

CHAPTER 79
LAWRENCE'S DEMON

As Luna attempted to shake apart the Surface, so an eight-armed Braysheath sought to hold it together—parting the seas to contain tsunamis, creating lakes from flash floods, directing lava into mines, doing his best to preserve life, all the while shielding Nashoba at the North Pole, an image Luna refused to release.

The oldest shepherd was on his knees. His hands were held out to the sky as the world's darkness streamed through them and was recycled into hope. Luna, however, was massively increasing the burden. Pure inner-force erupted from volcanoes. Human fear rocketed and vicious circles spiralled out of control. Nashoba was buckling under the pressure.

With one of his hands, Braysheath drew off the excess shadow and so shielded Nashoba from Luna's attack, though not without consequence. His radiance dimmed.

With another hand he summoned about Luna a flock of hummingbirds. Flowers sprouted up about her feet, showing her the beauty she was bent on destroying. In contrast to the wood of light they shimmered with colour. She hurled them back at Braysheath in the form of poison ivy.

As it ensnared his body, he simply became the ivy, maintaining his focus through its tendrils before transforming back to his usual form.

Once more he tried to locate the ark, but she distracted him with another attack on the Surface. With a wave of a new hand, images of Surface temples filled the woodland. With a second wave, they exploded.

Gripping the fountain wall with rapture, Frost's head was virtually in the pool. Tearing his focus away from Jake for a moment, he focused on Rani.

'What a woman!' he exclaimed, for though she and Rufus were losing the initiative to ongoing reinforcements, she fought magnificently.

'She has the glove,' said Frost to Silver, 'but it's not working! And the flow of reinforcements is too strong. She and Rufus are tiring!'

He looked up and about the oasis.

'It's even lusher than before,' he noted. In fact it was glowing, as was the cat temple. 'All except that oak. It's shedding its leaves and look, Silver! The embrace of the roots has come apart some more!'

Frost gazed up at the stars. Some flickered. Some dimmed. Then everything flickered, including London. For a moment the entire scene disappeared—buildings, streets, all except the oasis. Surface reality was under threat.

Frost jumped to his feet, his eyes sparkling with life.

'It's Braysheath! He too is losing the initiative! It's why Rani's glove isn't helping. He can't spare the energy. He's too stretched!'

In contrast to the chaos, a brace of swans flew across the London sky.

'But what's this, Silver? Two beautiful swans! Two symbols of divinity. It comes not from the gate. Could it be Lawrence? He and Rowena? Yes, surely! But does he live? That's the question! Or has he passed on?'

Before Frost could work it out, an almighty explosion shook London. The upper half of a church steeple plummeted towards the fountain. Frost was directly in line. Nimble though he was, he wasn't nimble enough.

Having tasted Jake's blood, Lord Boreas's blade vibrated as it prepared to swallow his soul. Again Jake stepped away. His heels met the cliff edge and the great drop to the slums.

Lord Boreas tittered. 'Nowhere to go, Lord Tusk.'

Jake struggled to apply what Ti had taught him—to draw on the power of nature and to respect his opponent—but in a holy-gate amid the symbolism of the slums and tormented by his dad's destroyer, he found it impossible.

Again the lantern about the square billowed brighter. The red-bearded druid was holding it up in the manner of a lighthouse warden looking out to sea and Jake found himself wondering what it meant.

No! he repeated, *I must stay present* and clasped hold of his amulet for encouragement.

'What's this?' sneered Lord Boreas and ripped the amulet from Jake's neck.

'Give it back!' barked Jake and tried to grab it.

'An amulet! Ha! Another toy from the House of Tusk!' laughed Lord Boreas and slung it over the precipice.

'No!' cried Jake and anger flashed through him.

He was saved from venting it by a mysterious male voice in his head.

One can only be present if one's at peace with one's roots, it said.

The voice was authoritative, almost harsh. It sounded wise in a similar way to Braysheath's. It also sounded familiar.

Jake looked back at the druid and remembered where he had heard the voice before—during his interrogation by the oracle, the druid had floated before Jake and the mysterious door, offering his power.

'Time grinds on, Lord Tusk,' said Lord Boreas. 'If you have any last wishes then make them now.'

THE INSTANT HIS FEET LEFT THE SNOW, LAWRENCE KNEW HE hadn't a hope of getting anywhere near the other side of the crevasse. He was so tired that his momentum carried him only a metre or two before he plunged into the icy darkness.

The odds of landing without fatal injury or death were slim. So too were the odds of clawing his way out again. Regardless, Lawrence braced himself, axes at the ready to gain purchase on the ice wall.

The crevasse appeared without end. Yet as he plummeted, his mind was still. Lawrence had faced death too many times to panic. He simply waited.

As he fell he was beset by a vision. It was of the old hag. She was smiling mischievously as she held out something in her hand.

The apple! cried out Lawrence in thought and almost willed it into his hand. But he caught himself just in time. *It's a trap! I mustn't take it back!*

As Lawrence continued to plunge ever deeper into the crevasse, he closed his eyes. 'No,' he said to the old hag grinning in his mind's eye. 'I gave the apple to you. It's yours. With all my heart it's yours. Forgive me.'

No sooner had the words parted his lips than the old hag transformed. Lawrence's spirits soared. The glorious sensation of the kiss suddenly made sense.

'Rowena!' he gasped.

The next instant he was on his hands and knees on the other side of the crevasse as though the plunge had never taken place.

He stood up and felt new strength.

'The old hag had represented Rowena after all!' he cried out.

She looked different from the hag in the desert cave because I'm deeper in my unconscious.

'Rowena,' he muttered as he slowly absorbed the full implications of what the symbol meant. That he was harbouring an unconscious hatred of Jake was shocking enough, but of Rowena, the woman he loved? It was too much.

Lawrence shook his head in dismay.

How could I have unconsciously hated her? Perhaps blaming her for my hatred of Jake? For leaving me so suddenly...

It was possible, but still Lawrence struggled to believe it.

As the cold bit deeper, he was keen to get moving.

Whatever the reason, the foundations were false, he decided, realising that the hatred went back thousands of years, that Rowena and Jake were simply symbolic of a long line of male and female ancestral fear, rage, control and conditioning that was projected through all families.

And now it's been atoned for, surely? The gift of the apple was a gift of forgiveness in both directions. It's why it couldn't be given out of guilt, but only out of compassion—given from the soul and not from the conditioned mind.

Lawrence looked back at the crevasse.

Only one not weighed down by guilt or pride could have made the leap, he realised.

Feeling lighter, he set off up the knife-edge ridge. He dared to imagine he would make the summit when a portentous boom echoed from behind him. Lawrence spun around. It had sounded like thunder but the night sky was free of cloud.

The crevasse, he thought. Yet it hadn't shifted. On reflection, the boom had sounded like a great door being barged open.

A door up here? he thought until he remembered where he was.

Lawrence waited as still as stone for any movement.

A blizzard blew up without warning. In a matter of seconds the crevasse was lost to sight. He was about to continue his journey when something caught his eye. Lawrence thought he saw a man though couldn't be sure. It was too shadowy to make out.

A terror beyond measure suddenly seized him. Though he couldn't see what moved through the blizzard, he felt it.

The fourth eagle! The demon! The steel door in the mad mansion—it's been opened!

He recalled Geoffrey's warning along with the pirate's that if he so much as gazed upon the demon, he would be dragged off to the deepest hell for eternity.

It must have come from the crevasse, but why? The crevasse represents Rowena and forgiveness.

Lawrence edged backwards up the ridge. A great battle raged inside of him. One part of him was horrified. The other demanded to see the demon's face. He had to know what it looked like, regardless of the consequences.

Paralysed by indecision, Lawrence halted. The demon drew closer. Its presence shifted to a woman's form, though at the point of becoming completely visible through the blizzard, she stopped.

Lawrence stared on, spellbound. He caught glimpses through the snow. Within the darkness was a cloaked figure. Snow-matted dark hair obscured her face while clasped in her right hand was a long sacrificial-looking knife dripping with blood. There was a powerful whiff of magic about her, like a dark priestess. She was more unnerving, more haunting than even Luna.

For a fateful moment the blizzard cleared. A moonbeam penetrated the shadow and shone upon the demon. Again the image changed. The moonbeam revealed not a woman, but a man, suggesting the demon represented both energies. The hair about its rough-hewn face was grey, dreadlocked and wild like his beard, wild like the furs that covered his body. Barefoot, he stood like a savage from the woods.

But it was his eyes that struck into Lawrence the fear of God. Broad set and narrow, they glinted with a light as piercing as the tip of the knife in his right hand—the same knife held by the woman and still dripping blood.

He held Lawrence in his stony gaze, impassive and unhurried. Lawrence's curious part dared him to approach the wild man. But it was his cautious part that won out, the part that understood his terror. It knew that for Lawrence there was no greater threat. Because it was *his* demon. His darkest. It couldn't be escaped. Neither in that moment could it be approached, at least not with an ordinary weapon. Lawrence had to get to the summit. It was his only chance.

When the blizzard returned, he spun around and rushed up the ridge as fast as he could. The blizzard blasted him head-on. Lawrence battled to make way, glancing back every few steps. The demon had no reason to hurry and Lawrence knew it. The summit could be reached only by the ridge while on its other side would be another sheer face. It had to be that way—the mountain, like the journey, was mythical.

While the wild man pursued Lawrence from behind, his aspect as the dark priestess haunted Lawrence's vision from the front as he pressed on through the storm. Fierce and furious, her dreadful eyes promised vengeance. His frozen body aching with fatigue, Lawrence wrestled with who she might be. Perhaps she was gatekeeper to the demon, perhaps the part of his soul he had in some way betrayed. Perhaps the blood on the knife was hers or a premonition of his own doom. Whatever she was, she fuelled his dread. On he sped.

Finally, on his last legs, Lawrence reached the summit. The blizzard howled, though fortunately the pinnacle had a flattened top. Lawrence caught his breath, barely able to believe he had made it and yet now that he had, despite the approaching demon, it felt like an anti-climax.

He noticed something through the snow—an open tomb. At its head was the statue of a man. Lawrence started back in shock when he realised it was himself except for one detail. The posture of the image was one of arrogance, like that of a conqueror. He read the inscription on the tomb. His brow furrowed in confusion.

Here lies Lawrence Burton who hated his son and all humanity, who demanded exclusive love even though it could never be given.

After a moment's thought, he understood.

'This part of me must die. Today, this moment, it must die,' he decided.

'That's right,' came a voice through the wind that made Lawrence jump.

A bishop arrived from behind the statue. Dressed in a red cassock with a mitre atop his head, he appeared unaffected by the extreme weather. In his right hand was a staff. Mounted on its top was a gold disk which glowed like a miniature sun.

'Who are you?' stammered Lawrence, gripping the ice axes, alert to any deception.

'Just as this tomb represents the womb of the Holy Mother, so I symbolise the Holy Father.'

Lawrence looked in the direction of the ridge, wondering where the demon was.

'It's taking its time because it knows what awaits it,' explained the bishop. He held out his staff to Lawrence. 'Take this. With this symbol of divinity it can be slain. There is no other way.'

Lawrence studied the bishop. His face was stern, though not unkind. His voice was one of authority.

Following a moment's hesitation, Lawrence tossed down one of the ice axes and took hold of the staff. Immediately it transformed into a golden spear. It felt light and powerful. It felt right that he was holding it.

'Gold is a symbol of purity,' explained the priest.

Just then the demon appeared. He stopped short of passing onto the summit. Its stony expression and the intensity in its heartless eyes remained unchanged.

'Now's your chance,' urged the bishop, unable to contain his tension. 'Slay it before it's too late!'

GIVEN WHERE THEY WERE, GIVEN WHO THEY WERE—SYMBOLS OF the distorted male in all humans—and given the sylph was watching, the fates of Lawrence and Jake would determine the fate of the entire cosmos including the shepherds.

Braysheath was under immense pressure. As Lawrence prepared to use the spear and as Jake's soul was on the verge of being swallowed into Lord Boreas's sword, the darkness of the Surface took a quantum leap and continued to intensify at an exponential rate.

Braysheath siphoned off as much as he could, but it wasn't enough. Nashoba was close to collapse. His body, which had shone like a beacon of light, was darkening.

Luna continued to attack the Surface. Apart from the symbolic tree of creation, little could be seen of the original woodland. It had become a theatre of mass destruction. Every temple of every faith on the Surface other than her own was shattered to smithereens. Tsunamis rose up in the centre of every sea and raced for the coastlines. Volcanoes continued to erupt. Mountains shook and cities swayed. The air was thick with ash and fire. Flash floods tore through the valleys as Luna melted what remained of glaciers.

While she sought to reduce the Surface to rubble, Braysheath continued to remake it. Landscapes were reformed to something even more wondrous than before. The air was purified. Rivers sparkled. They ran deep and wide in the absence of dams. Temples were restored to stone circles before their shattered pieces reached the ground. When the gravestones cracked in the sprawling cemetery of Pandora's Box in a damning statement of failing hope, Braysheath transformed them into a lush meadow of trees, flowers and singing birds. For a glorious moment it shimmered with life. The next, it was shot through with a scorching desert storm incinerating all life save the charred angel who watched on with rapturous laughter from the top of his pyramid.

Braysheath and Luna stood like many-armed conductors vying for the upper hand in the symphony of destruction and preservation. Luna searched for the decisive blow. Braysheath sought to maintain the flow. He was learning more about Luna with each attack, though he was too burdened to utilise the knowledge.

If there was any doubt as to who had the upper hand, the appearance of a python dispelled it. The remaining leaves of the central tree suddenly fell and there it was. It wound down about the trunk. As it passed over the roots their symbolic embrace loosened further. The python then slithered off, shedding its skin as it went.

Emboldened, Luna cast out a new arm and, with a burst of great power, opened a new image in the chaotic canvas. Braysheath faltered and a great rift tore through Delhi. Tsunamis raced towards New York and Beijing.

Luna had reopened Jake's lightline—the ancient part that she had seen in Wilderspin's mad mansion. At the end of a path lit by lanterns was the same ancient-looking wooden door festooned in blackthorn. It was the door she desperately sought—a door to a strange temple beyond. The move, however, was merely a feint. Braysheath was so stretched that in order to deal with it he had to reduce his focus elsewhere. Again, it was only a moment. But a moment was all she required. As Nashoba continued to buckle under the sudden increase in darkness, Luna lunged for his light.

CHAPTER 80
OBLIVION

Frost was dazzled, horrified and utterly awed when, in the split-second before the church steeple flattened him, it transformed into a cawing flock of ravens.

Frost howled with delight.

'Braysheath!' he cried and marvelled at the containment of Luna's destruction about the London skyline.

A meteor tore through the atmosphere. The fiery rock raced towards the capital. It struck the city as a shower of autumn leaves which fell poetically upon the snow.

'How long can he keep it up?' pondered Frost as he noted a further unfolding in the embrace of the oak's roots. 'Much depends on our dear friend Jake!'

Lord Boreas looked out into the distance. Quakes rippled through the gate as ramshackle tower blocks collapsed.

'Well, Lord Tusk,' he said, 'if you lack the imagination for a last request then prepare yourself. It's time to leave this place and I've still your grandfather to deal with.'

'No, wait!' said Jake. 'I do have a last request—a question, in fact.'

'A question?' snarled Lord Boreas impatiently. 'Just one. Get on with it.'

Jake had had a brilliant idea. He finally accepted that his only chance of escape was the druid—but at what cost? He needed a little more time to make a decision along with some help in making it.

Why not ask Boreas? he had thought, turning a danger into an asset.

Regardless of the fact that Lord Boreas had been corrupted by Luna, as God of Greed he had a profound understanding of the cosmos. Just like Frost's tricky truths, one simply needed to be aware of the god's perspective. Depending how he answered, Jake could decide to go along with the advice or do the opposite.

'If you had a choice to access ancient power, but couldn't be sure of the consequences, what would you do?' he asked plainly.

'What are you talking about?' said Lord Boreas, a glimmer of greed in his eyes.

'You see that lantern light about that square in the distance?' said Jake.

The lantern glowed brighter.

'Yes, I see it. What of it?'

'Do you sense anything unusual about it?' asked Jake.

Lord Boreas studied Jake with a sceptical expression before focusing on the lantern light.

Lord Boreas's eyes widened.

'A ghost!' he gasped. 'And a druid!'

The god looked back at Jake with a mixture of suspicion and confusion. 'How did you know?'

'Because it's part of my lightline,' said Jake matter-of-factly, feeling a little stronger for having the initiative.

Lord Boreas looked ready to dispute the point. Instead, his fierce gaze plumbed Jake for deception.

'So what would you do if you were me?' pressed Jake.

Lord Boreas grinned.

'Your question is not clear. If you mean were it me, with my soul, in your shoes, why naturally I would accept such powerful light. But had I your soul, weak vessel that it is, I wouldn't dream of it. The druid's light would destroy you.'

'Why would you accept the light? Because it's dark?'

The god scoffed at Jake's ignorance.

'It's not a question of darkness, not in the way you and other fools mean it. Druids have knowledge of dark-seeming things because they're not afraid of darkness. They explore the abyss, using their light to show the way. The deeper they explore, the wiser they become.'

Weak though he was, Jake smiled inwardly. He felt the truth in Lord Boreas's words. He recalled his nightmare at Nemesis's tree when he had approached the ghosts in the fog.

Now is not the time to take that path, Nemesis had warned him. *One day, yes. One day soon perhaps. But not now.*

Jake drew a deep breath.

That day had come. It was time to confront the druid, just as Frost had said he should.

Once decided, it was as though a great weight had been lifted from Jake's shoulders—the irrational fear of the druid he had felt as a child, which had returned to haunt him on the death of his dad.

He focused all his attention on the light in the lantern.

Who are you? he asked.

The lantern billowed.

My name is Oblivion, came the far from encouraging answer.

But who are you?

Part of your past. Part of who you really are, answered Oblivion.

What do I get if I accept you?

Freedom.

At what cost? asked Jake.

Everything.

Oblivion's profound answers surprised Jake. With an anguished click, another mystery slotted into place—the critical link that had alluded him in the vault just the night before. During the break-in, it had been Oblivion's power that had disintegrated the arrow Rani had fired at Lord Boreas, except that it hadn't been the god, but Jake's dad. Oblivion must have known all along.

'Questions over, Lord Tusk,' said Lord Boreas. 'Time's up.'

What do you mean by everything? Jake asked Oblivion.

Jake waited for an answer but none came.

DARKNESS POURING IN THROUGH HIS CROWN, HIS BODY TURNING to shadow, Nashoba, the oldest and most powerful of all shepherds, finally collapsed on all fours.

So too did the human race. Luna's merciless attack on the Surface multiplied by the moment. Fear shot even higher. For the first time in history, no longer aided by Nashoba, they felt its true weight.

Sensing a presence before him, he raised his weary head. A unicorn had appeared, sent by Luna. With great ceremony it lowered its head, not only in reverence, for the mystical creature knew who Nashoba was, but in order to collect something.

Battling to contain himself, Nashoba closed his eyes. The pressure, however, was too great. A wisp of light seeped from his forehead and spiralled towards the horn.

The demon took a single step forward onto the flat-topped summit. The night grew darker. Thunder rumbled overhead. The blizzard thickened and the wind howled.

'Now!' commanded the bishop. 'Throw the spear! Slay this abomination of nature before it's too late!'

Lawrence gripped the golden spear as fear gripped him, reached back and was about to hurl it, but hesitated.

'Throw it, you fool!' boomed the bishop. 'Throw it!'

The demon took another step closer. Another crack of thunder summoned in Lawrence yet greater terror. Again he almost hurled the spear. Again he hesitated. The same old great battle raged within him. He held the demon's harrowing gaze. Within the steely lights of its eyes was something else, something that mirrored the very part of Lawrence which resisted throwing the spear. Something searching.

'You coward! You're not ready for this!' spat the bishop and lightning forked through the blizzard. 'Everything's at stake! *Everything*! But you're not ready for this great step! You're too weak!'

'Ready for what?' barked Lawrence, maintaining his gaze on the demon.

'To become a true king! A true master! The ruler of your destiny!'

The gate, the sylph, Jake! thought Lawrence as the urgency of his mission gripped him.

'Leave this mountain!' ordered the bishop in disgust. 'You're not worthy! You're nothing!'

The demon took a third step forward. Only a few paces remained between them. It raised the bloody knife and pointed it at Lawrence.

Lawrence's fear threatened to consume him. He changed his grip on the spear, ready to thrust it. He took a step forward and was about to do so when a voice echoed through his mind.

It was Rowena's.

Let it go, love, she said. *For all our sakes.*

Let what go?

What's behind all your projections of hatred—of me, of Jake, of Nestor, of your departed mother, of everyone.

Lawrence glanced between the bishop and the demon, wondering what she meant. With the brightest flash of lightning yet, finally he understood.

Hatred of myself! he cried. *A confused child's hate of itself, believing that it's not worthy of love—of exclusive love that could never be given by parents who had their own shadow, though who gave as much as they could.*

And? Urged Rowena.

The child grows into an adult, unconsciously hating itself for what it's become—for all the self-images it creates as it strives for a false idea of perfection, for approval and recognition, all the while betraying its true nature, its true magnificence, fearing scarcity, fearing abundance, no longer trusting in life.

Everything suddenly made perfect sense. Just like humans who felt inferior and so hid behind masks of superiority, so his daring role as Lord Tusk had provided the perfect mask, covering an unconscious cowardice to face a truth—a wounded child's fear of loss, of its mother's love and any love that followed, clinging on to it to the point of suffocation. But Lawrence also saw the beauty. All masks were flawed attempts to protect a divine child from further pain. The masks, however, were no longer needed.

'Slay the demon or leave!' cried the bishop. The tension in his voice had become crazed.

To slay is this manner is denial, said Rowena. *Instead, sever the cord and set us free.*

The cord? questioned Lawrence. *Cords which bind... karma... the bonds of karma!*

For the first time Lawrence dared to look away from the demon. He gazed out into the storm. Immediately the blizzard cleared along his line of sight. In the far distance, lit up by the moon, he saw a coastline and a ship anchored in a harbour—not Luna's ark, but the pirate's vessel Lawrence had sailed on to reach the island.

The ship laden with guilt, shame and pride.

'What are you doing?' barked the bishop.

Lawrence looked at the bishop. 'Why are you so angry?' he asked.

'Are you mad? Were you not listening? Everything's at stake!'

Lawrence looked at the demon. The searching light in its eyes grew brighter. There was something about their brightness and the demon's greying hair which reminded Lawrence of wolves— an impression reinforced by the howling wind. He thought of his totem the white wolf and his long and arduous journey to reach the summit. He thought of the pirate and one thing in particular flashed through his mind. It was what the pirate had said on finding Lawrence as an adder under the log. *Lift a rock and you will find me. Split a log and I am there.*

'Everything...' he said to the bishop.

'Yes, everything!' bawled the bishop once more. 'Everything will be lost!'

Everything is one, thought Lawrence and truly felt it.

Immediately the blizzard relented.

'What's happening?' panicked the bishop.

Lawrence said nothing. He studied the demon. The old grinning hag once again loomed in his mind. How harshly he had judged her appearance when all along she was part of his soul. Suddenly the depth of his fear made perfect sense.

What's more terrifying than shadow? he asked himself. *Light! Love! One's true nature! Infinite potential. What's more terrifying than death? Life! To truly live! To truly love and be open to its pain. To understand this divine play of life, to see through the illusion of separation, to stop projecting our shallow dreams and weaknesses onto others and to wake up to who we truly are.*

He looked back at the bishop. For the first time in his life he understood what it meant to feel compassion.

To someone caught up in a distorted world, who seeks to control life rather than trust in and surrender to its glorious flow, someone who unconsciously derives pleasure from controlling others—to such a person, what could be more terrifying than life?

Lawrence saw the bishop for what he was. He saw through his rage to the fear of pain behind it and the fear of being alone. He felt the pain and understood it at the same time—that it was simply a confused child's cry for love. And though he couldn't clearly see the bishop's potential amid so much anger, he understood with perfect clarity what he had to do in order to release it.

Following a steadying breath he looked back in the direction of the distant ship.

'What are you doing?' cried the bishop.

Lawrence looked him hard in the eye.

'It takes courage to love,' he said simply.

He fixed his gaze on the rope of the ship's anchor. It glowed like a thread of silver beneath the moon. Then, casting aside all boundaries of what was possible, he leapt forward and hurled the spear.

'No!' cried the bishop, as though Lawrence had hurled it at him instead.

He leapt forward to stop Lawrence, but it was too late. The spear flew from Lawrence's hand and arced over the great distance as though thrown by a god.

The bishop and the demon watched on as it descended towards the ship. Lawrence focused not on the spear, but on the rope. His entire will was bent towards it.

The spear obeyed and the rope was sliced clean in two. As the anchor sank to the bottom of the harbour, the ship shone with the same gold as the spear. Freed from the island, it drifted to where the harbour met the sea. There it waited as a rising sun cast back a portion of the night.

Just the sight warmed Lawrence's heart. For the first time in what seemed an age, he felt peace.

Before the light of truth, all disguises fell away. When Lawrence returned his attention to the mountain top, he found not a bishop, but the Emperor of the distorted Paradise island. His haughty façade had fallen away, revealing the fear behind it.

The demon meanwhile hadn't moved. His knife still pointed at Lawrence.

'Thank you,' said Lawrence to the Emperor and meant it sincerely.

The Emperor said nothing.

'Don't be afraid,' said Lawrence. 'We're just the surface.'

He turned back to the demon, held out his arms in surrender and closed his eyes.

'This is who we really are.'

LAWRENCE'S HEROICS, THOUGH GREAT, HADN'T THE FORCE TO break through Luna's chaos to the Surface. Nashoba continued to lose light to the unicorn. His loss was Luna's gain. With the burst of power, her perceptions grew even sharper. She sensed a great threat from somewhere deep within the cosmos, from a world she hadn't felt before—the hidden world of Lawrence where he surrendered to fate.

There wasn't a moment to lose. Casting out another arm she opened a portal and released a deadly arrow.

ASCLEPIUS HAD TRIED EVERYTHING TO FIND A WAY THROUGH TO Lawrence. At the end of his wits, he slumped forward onto a workbench and released a despairing sigh.

'Forgive me, old friend,' he lamented. 'But what more can I do? What more? What use is it being a god if I can't even help a good man? A man who's truly suffered. For is it not a god's duty to answer the prayers of those who suffer?'

Asclepius lay there, his forehead resting against his grand experiement, breathing deeply when he suddenly leapt up and thumped the bench.

'Of course!' he cried out. 'Of course!'

Gathering himself, he knelt down facing the oak at the centre of his experiment and drew a deep breath.

'Sacred Mother,' he said with great homage. 'Forgive my arrogance, my impatience, my weakness. Forgive me, I beg of you! Strip me of this godly status, this pretence! Damn me, destroy me, send me back to the Surface in whatever form you see fit, but before you do, Great Mother who gives so much, I ask of you just one thing. Send me first to Lawrence. He needs me. In the name of balance, in the name of harmony, in the name of love and truth, I beg of you! Send me now.'

Stillness followed. Even the fizzing flasks of the elaborate apparatus fell silent.

A soft wind blew through the laboratory and ruffled Asclepius's robes. Still he remained bowed.

Suddenly he looked up. The constellations above the experiment had shifted. A black hole appeared. An instant later he was sucked from the fort.

STILL NO ANSWER CAME FROM OBLIVION.

Lord Boreas readied to thrust his soul-absorbing sword into Jake's stomach. Yet again he was halted by another question.

'If I told you that in receiving a gift of power you would lose everything, what would you say?' asked Jake coolly, continuing with his plan to both stall for time and seek advice.

Lord Boreas cursed.

'Won't you shut up and die quietly?'

But Jake's question, like the first, was too tantalising for the vain god to ignore. Once again he glanced between the distant lantern and Jake, wondering what was going on.

'I don't seek everything,' replied Lord Boreas. 'If I did then I wouldn't have become a god. Everything includes the riffraff, the irretrievably ignorant human scum. I seek pure light which, thanks to Luna's cleansing, is on the rise. Light which you'll shortly be joining, my inquisitive Lord Tusk.'

Just then, as Lawrence's spear severed the ship from its anchor in another world, a cache of long lost energy was set free, coursing through the karmic veins of the cosmos to those whom it was due. To Jake, suddenly relieved of a great burden he hadn't realised existed, it came as a burst of clarity.

Every-thing, he repeated. *It makes the world sound like every-thing is separate. But the word 'nothing', that makes much more sense. No-one-thing separate but all connected. To give up every-thing gains you nothing. Or rather, to give up an illusion is to see reality as it truly is. All is one.*

'Goodbye, Lord Tusk,' said Lord Boreas, tired of waiting.

He glanced a final time at the lantern, a glint of uncertainty in his eyes.

Jake imagined himself riding atop Braysheath in the form of the eagle, soaring over the crater during Brock's fall. It would serve as a place of power. He then focused his mind on the lantern.

Oblivion, he said in thought. *I accept you. For the sake of my family, for the sake of my friends, for the sake of all creation—help me.*

IN SURRENDERING TO THE DEMON, LAWRENCE HAD GIVEN IT permission to do whatever it wished. As it took a step closer its eyes lit up. The subtlest of smiles broke across its otherwise stony face. The razor-sharp edges of its knife glinted in the light of the rising sun. He prepared to thrust it into Lawrence's heart when the Emperor leapt forward.

'No!' he screamed. 'No!'

As though in answer to the Emperor's scream an arrow tore through the air. It was no ordinary arrow. The tip was cursed, charged with the power to damn for eternity and aimed at the demon's back in the precise area of its heart.

Ignoring the Emperor, unaware of the arrow, the demon's eyes fixed on Lawrence's heart. Its grip tightened about the knife. Muscles tensed. Its right foot lifted for the final step and thrust.

Luna's arrow, however, had the lead. Nothing in that world could stop it.

In the instant before it struck, the air flexed. A portal opened from another dimension. Something large and dark swept through it. It was a vulture—Asclepius.

The arrow flew with such power that it passed clean through the great bird's body. The force of his interception, however, had altered the arrow's course—instead of hitting the demon it struck the rocks below the summit. No one noticed except a furious Luna.

As the vulture's limp body plunged towards the crags, the demon thrust the knife clean through Lawrence's heart.

CHAPTER 81
SINFUL EYRIE

Rani and Rufus fought valiantly to protect Nestor as he lay unconscious on the altar. Blue light exploded about the crown of the yew tree as guardian after guardian was slain. Yet there seemed no end to the reinforcements. The air was thick with inner-force, taking its toll on both Rani and Rufus.

The Commander and the sylph gazed out across the gate to a distant hill, fascination glinting in their eyes. They were watching Jake and Lord Boreas.

Rani glanced in the same direction. The loss of focus cost her dearly. A guardian gashed her arm.

It took light to unlock light. And it took great force to break open a heart. For Lawrence it took the demon's knife.

The instant its tip pierced his heart an exquisite light shone out from the summit, brilliant yet gentle as though the sun and moon had merged. Before its radiance, the demon transformed. He closed his eyes. A blissful smile spread across his face. Freed from the Emperor's control, his entire appearance softened. When he re-opened his eyes they were so full of rapture that he glowed like a saint—not a tainted saint, but a true one. Following a warm nod to the Emperor, the demon disintegrated into pure light. It flowed through the knife and into Lawrence, followed by the knife itself which also became light.

His arms outstretched in surrender, Lawrence shone even brighter.

The Emperor watched on astonished as the blizzard calmed to softly falling snow until that too finally stopped.

At last Lawrence lowered his arms. A halo shimmered about him and when he opened his eyes they radiated compassion.

The Emperor beheld him with a look of great expectation as though his very life depended on what Lawrence would say.

WITH A DEEP EXHALE, JAKE SURRENDERED EVERYTHING. HE FOCUSED on the lantern, visualised its candle and the eye within its flame and inhaled it as though it were right in front of him.

The effect was immediate. It flowed through Jake like an icy stream of fire. Everything seemed in reach, as if all opposites understood one another, though for some mysterious reason maintained a subtle distance, a subtle tautness. Two stood out—anger and peace. Though fear and love were at their roots, these were the words that stuck in Jake's mind.

A-n-g-e-r-p-e-a-c-e, came the voice of Oblivion, whispering the sound as though the two words were one and so softly it was like wind through trees.

Jake felt himself swept up by it, but was hauled back by a terrible jolt.

Lord Boreas had finally thrust his sword through Jake's stomach so violently that it came out through his back.

Jake's mind reeled in confusion.

A-n-g-e-r-p-e-a-c-e, continued Oblivion as Jake gazed up at the sadistic relish on Lord Boreas's face, dreading the onset of pain.

Each time Oblivion spoke, the tone was subtly different, spiralling up and down through different scales as though to suggest that peace evolved from anger and anger from peace. Each time their characteristics were slightly different, always changing, always exchanging, always heading somewhere.

A-n-g-e-r... where does it come from... where does it go? said Oblivion, confirming Jake's intuition.

Lord Boreas tittered at Jake's confusion.

You're connected to power, added Oblivion, *but the choice is yours. What will you do with it?*

'Now, Lord Tusk,' sneered Lord Boreas as he waited for the sword to absorb Jake's soul, 'join your cursed father. Be gone!'

In something of a daze, Jake looked down at the sword hilt then back at the god, his expression free of pain.

Lord Boreas looked unnerved.

'What is this? Swallow his soul!' he commanded the sword and shook it within Jake.

When still nothing happened, he wrenched the blade out. To his amazement the wound healed. There wasn't even a scar.

Suddenly Jake felt the power. Just as it had in his duelling lesson with Ti, it burst up from deep within him like an erupting volcano. An image filled his mind. It was the silhouetted man in the fog, along with the sleeping bear the oracle had tried to wake. By accepting Oblivion, Jake had accepted a whole lot more as though the druid were merely a gatekeeper.

This time there was no denying it—distant and ancient, the fury belonged to Jake's lightline. Its proportions were global and the God of Greed was the perfect target.

In an attempt to control it, again Jake visualised himself riding on Braysheath the eagle over the crater of Brock's fall, imagining Lord Boreas as part of the whole, even part of Jake himself, but it was useless. The idea of union, he realised, was just that—an idea. It was something he had heard from Braysheath, Ti and others. It was something he accepted in his mind, but didn't feel. He couldn't—not then, not there.

The anger flashing in Lord Boreas's eyes was nothing to Jake's fury. Out of desperation, the god was readying to strike Jake a second time.

Connected to his lightline and the great depth of its experience, Jake made a second momentous decision. The god was a menace and would remain so unless something was done. He was better sent off to the next life or to Luna's vault or some distant hell than left to run free in the Peregrinus. If that meant Jake's soul was in some way damned then so be it. He would bear the responsibility.

The decision appeased the anger, held its power in check a moment longer—in his wrists, in his neck, in his every fibre, ready to explode at the first signal.

'You killed my dad,' he said plainly.

'Your father was a *fool*! A meddling idiot!' spat Lord Boreas and swung his blade at Jake's neck.

Despite the threat, Jake felt a remarkable calm. He felt the druid. The bear was awake. All doors to power were open.

As Lord Boreas's blade arced for his neck, Jake gave the signal. He opened his left hand and exerted his will.

A pure sound rang through the air. An instant later, Morrigan was in his clasp, as light as a feather. Holding her in a single hand, Jake effortlessly blocked Lord Boreas's blade.

The blades whined as the powerful swords came into contact. The light in Lord Boreas's eyes grew wilder—with confusion, with fear as he glanced between Jake and his sword.

He came at Jake with all he had—hard, fast and ruthless with kicks, knees, elbows and knuckles.

None of his blows made their mark. Utterly composed, Jake stood his ground and parried every attack as though he were fighting a child despite Lord Boreas's physical prowess.

Without a break in his fierce attack, as God of the North Wind he summoned a storm. A tornado swept across the gate directly for Jake. Before it tightened about him he simply held out his right hand. The tornado shrank in size and passed onto his palm. Jake held it within his fist as though it were nothing more than a ball.

Next came an icy blast of snow.

It was absorbed into the same hand.

Lightning forked down for Jake's head, but was absorbed by Morrigan instead, who glowed with power.

Sensing it was time to finish the duel, Jake upped the ante, forcing Lord Boreas towards the edge of the precipice. Sweat broke out on the god's brow. He struggled to gain the initiative, but the harder he tried, the clumsier his strokes became.

His heels at the cliff's edge, he attempted a feint. He swung his blade for Jake's head while drawing a dagger and thrusting it at his ribs.

Neither worked. Morrigan severed his sword clean in half. The dagger disintegrated.

The souls set free from the broken blade howled with joy and torment. Lord Boreas ignored them. Empty handed, chest heaving, he stared at Jake in disbelief.

'Who are you?' he said in barely a whisper.

Jake's mind re-engaged. He heard an answer echo through him from the distance, though gave it no voice. He sensed its desire for destruction, sensed the common ground with his own anger and a demand for revenge on the very being who put his dad through hell.

Jake struggled to centre himself. This time it was the image of Rani that came to his aid. She was struggling in the battle on the yew tree. Jake sensed it. But the Rani deep inside of him was something yet more mysterious. Her presence made sense of the great distance along his fractured lightline, softened the blow of its dark message into something shadowy, though not quite clarity. It was grey like the elephant she rode through time.

Jake drew a deep inward breath and once again managed to control the fury.

'Any last wish?' he asked Lord Boreas in an ironic tone. 'A request for forgiveness perhaps.'

Not to be defeated in words as well as duelling, Lord Boreas snorted in contempt.

'Forgiveness? Who are you to judge? I played your father like a witless trout,' he said, going directly for Jake's sore point. 'I allowed him to possess my body while it suited me, let him do my dirty work, for who better to steal from the House of Tusk than the Lord himself?'

'You're weak,' observed Jake.

As he saw through the lie, the fury deepened and became harder to control.

'I simply waited patiently and once he'd served his pitiful purpose,' boasted Lord Boreas, 'I slayed him like the dog he was—loyal and stupid.'

Jake was silent. He battled to stay centred while half of his awareness remained in shadow.

'My dad had the courage to face his demons,' he said looking straight into the god's spiteful eyes.

He glanced at the storm in his right hand. Lord Boreas followed Jake's line of sight and his fear returned.

'And now,' continued Jake, 'it's time for you to face yours.'

With a flick of the wrist he cast the tempest at the god's chest.

THE EMPEROR WAITED FOR A WORD FROM LAWRENCE, BUT Lawrence said nothing. Eyes shining, he simply held out his arms in embrace.

Through that simple gesture something shifted—something momentous. It was felt throughout the entire cosmos. Trees rustled. Rocks sighed. Frost leapt for joy while Luna released an anguished scream.

As Lawrence's arms opened to the Emperor, a sacred geometry spread from his hands out across the mountains, the sky and all they encompassed, linking them in a way that could not be ignored. So too it embraced the Emperor.

His appearance changed a second time. Once a bishop, no longer an emperor, he returned to his original form—that of the pirate, except the lights in his eyes, far from mischievous, shone with peace.

In a mark of reverence, he prostrated himself before Lawrence. As his forehead touched the rock, he, like the demon before him, transformed into light that flowed back to whom it belonged.

Lawrence shone so brightly that the snow melted and spring swept forth across the wintry landscape. Flowers sprang up. Birds sang. Sparrows flitted about him. One landed on his upturned hand.

With a look of completeness, Lawrence turned to the precipice.

Following a blissful inhale of the fresh air, he stepped into the abyss.

Lawrence's surrender was felt by all. Luna wavered. Braysheath forced back the tsunamis and held off the other catastrophes for critical moments. Though Luna was quick to recover, the battle was now more equal.

Rani and Rufus received a vital burst of energy to their flagging defence. With fearsome battle cries they tore into the guardians.

The exception was Jake. Contained by the cool fury of his distant past, he watched Lord Boreas turn to ice.

Leaving no space for hesitation, Jake thrust Morrigan at his heart.

Then, in the split-second before impact, something strange happened. Jake suffered the full force of his inner conflict—between a coldness which felt no humanity in Lord Boreas and so no remorse in slaying him, and the part which felt the god's potential to be something great.

The split-second splintered. Through that infinitesimally small fraction of time burst a brilliant light. It shone out through the ice of Lord Boreas's body and dazzled Jake.

Whatever it meant, Jake's momentum was too great, his anger too strong. Morrigan vibrated with flawless power, carrying the stroke forward with yet greater force.

The sword drove home.

Ice shattered.

Light shone out across the gate.

A shrill cry rang out as the sylph reared up and took note.

Frost barked with delight in Trafalgar Square.

The battle that raged about the yew's crown halted for a critical moment.

Morrigan's eye flashed open and blazed.

So did Jake's eyes except, where Morrigan's was fierce and focused, his were full of horror. Standing before him was no longer Lord Boreas. It was Lawrence, his dad, a blade through his heart.

Despite it, he stood radiant.

Any hope that it was a trick was shattered by the anguished roar of a tiger. Close, yet somehow distant, it reverberated through Jake's entire being. He instinctively knew that it came from another dimension, that Lord Boreas and his dad had once again exchanged places.

The sword was driven through Lawrence to the hilt. Jake tried to withdraw it, but couldn't. He tried to release it, but Morrigan, eye still blazing, blade glowing, wouldn't allow it. His horror, revulsion, love, regret and confusion escalated beyond his worst nightmare.

Lawrence shone brighter as he beheld his son.

'You... you weren't destroyed?' stammered Jake. 'I thought... Boreas said... my God! What have I done? Dad!'

Something Jake had dismissed as nonsense suddenly besieged his mind—the prophecy of the Norns. *On sinful eyrie your power buoyed, mind your intent and what's destroyed.*

The sense of tragedy tore Jake apart. How could he have dismissed the prophecy? How could he have allowed his anger to get the better of him after all Ti had tried to teach him? And what of his dad's great plan to untwist the father-son myth and win over the sylph for the sake of all? It was ruined. Lord Boreas had tricked Jake into believing his dad was done for when he had only lost the initiative for a while.

Despite Jake's torment, still Lawrence shone. He reached out and gently held Jake's hands. It was a touch that wrenched at Jake's heart, a touch that said all that needed to be said and made amends for all of Lawrence's absences.

With a serene smile, he slipped free of the sword and tilted over the precipice. Morrigan had released him.

'No!' cried Jake and dived forward to grasp his hands, but he was too late.

Lawrence plunged towards the distant slums.

Jake watched on in disbelief. Time seemed to slow, lengthening the horror. Two tears formed in his eyes. They were his reply to his dad's touch—an embrace, a declaration of love and a plea for forgiveness sealed in a suffering so pure that when they struck the earth, rain would fall throughout every world.

'Forgive me,' he whispered as his tears fell. *Take my light, please! This is all my fault. Let us trade places!*

Eyes shining, body glowing as it fell, Lawrence brought his hands together in prayer, as though to say there was nothing to forgive.

Geometrically patterned light which had flowed from him on the mountain now flowed from him in the gate. Beneath him blossomed a giant lotus flower. Smaller ones appeared throughout the gate as though the ramshackle city were suddenly floating upon a lake.

Real time snapped back. Lawrence disappeared into the light of the lotus. Thunder rumbled through the gate. A cloud of smoke rose up in the distant sprawl. The gate was collapsing.

Jake paid little attention. Emotionally exhausted, he got to his knees.

I'm in a place of death, he thought as a calm detachment washed through him. *Perhaps I should embrace it.*

He looked back at the yew tree, too distant to see how his friends were faring.

'Death, destruction' he muttered. 'I'm not afraid of it. But life and its losses and its cruel twists...'

He thought of all he had seen since passing through the inkwell, above all what he had seen of himself, including his past. He then understood Oblivion's words: that the only way to truly live was to be at peace with the past. Jake realised that to find peace, to become peace, involved a journey which took great courage and great patience.

To be destroyed was easy. For a moment, Jake envied his dad. He watched the geometry of light spread through the gate and light up an intricate web of life.

'Life,' he muttered and thought of his granddad who had always been so full of it. He thought of Braysheath, Rufus, Rani and of Frost. He thought of spring mornings at the farmhouse and chirping birds, of Brock, of flowers springing up and celebrating the sun. The great challenge, he realised, was to surrender to life's flow, to dance with the great mystery and to trust those you shared it with.

Despite his love for these things, a great weight took hold of him.

'Let them go,' came a deep and dispassionate voice.

Jake looked up. A vast but pale sun was rising. Silhouetted before it, standing like a giant amid the mounting chaos of the collapsing gate, was the terrifying man from the fog—the one whose power Jake had just used to unwittingly slay his own dad. Now he felt its full force. He was becoming part of it, just like in his nightmare in the woods. Raw infinite-feeling power.

'No!' commanded Jake, battling to stay conscious. 'I'll have nothing to do with you. Leave!'

The man tittered. 'How can I leave what is part of me? How can I leave you to this Luna, this poisonous spirit who sent Boreas to slay your father?'

'Your power slayed him!'

'Power you chose,' said the man and glanced down at Oblivion in the square. 'What you did with it was also your choice.'

'I chose Oblivion, not you,' said Jake, tormented by an inner-conflict. Had the druid tricked him, or did he see so deeply that what was happening was somehow necessary?

'The power wasn't pure. I felt your will,' continued Jake. 'You wanted Boreas destroyed.'

He tried to stand up in defiance but collapsed on all fours. The power was slithering through his body and mind, reaching out for his soul. Regardless of what Lord Boreas had said about dark wisdom, Jake felt only the darkness.

'You want to destroy Luna, don't you?' said the man.

'Yes! No! Not destroy, but...'

Jake's mind was becoming cloudy. He struggled to think straight. A growing part of him demanded revenge. The fading part knew it to be pointless.

'Join with me,' said the man and reached out a giant dark hand. The closer it got, the more seductive the power became. 'Whatever you wish, together we have the power to achieve anything. The collapsing of this gate—you could stop it right now if you wanted. Just take my hand.'

Jake didn't doubt his words. But in the slither of consciousness left to him he doubted everything else about the man, knowing that he would possess Jake and reek ruin.

'And what is it that you want?' he asked.

The man took a slow and giant breath. For a moment the destruction in the gate disappeared. Though the man remained silhouetted, the hand reaching out for Jake became human.

'Silence,' said the man. 'Peace. These are what I seek.'

With the sincerity in his voice the seduction was all but complete.

Oblivion? appealed Jake, the only one he could turn to.

Oblivion's only answer was a brightening of his lantern. The decision had to come from Jake.

The sight of the flame reminded him of another link—Rani. Jake knew nothing of alchemy. He knew nothing of the man's power that he inhaled with each fatal breath. What he did know was that Rani, the Rani of the present, was in his heart. Whatever poison he inhaled, her light transformed it into something pure.

The man's hand seemed to soften. In that subtle gesture was a silent appeal—for connection, for warmth. Within the immense weight of the man's power was a flicker of pain, just a flicker, but enough to almost destroy Jake. Jake's eyes streamed with tears. He was so deeply connected with the man that the held out hand was actually his own. His heart contracted. His heart swelled. He yearned to take hold of the hand. He almost did, but knew in his heart that it couldn't be done, not there, not then, not like that. The pain would overwhelm him and ruin would follow all the same.

Or perhaps the pain was just an act, a powerful trick.

As the world closed in about him, as the gate collapsed, Jake pressed his right hand to the cool earth. His left hand tightened about the hilt of Morrigan. The love of the mother flowed through both.

The man's hand moved closer. Its appeal grew louder.

Jake's mind cried out for reason, flailed blindly for all that Ti had taught him. Instead he stayed with the wisdom of what his hands already held, stayed with the wisdom in his tears, stayed with the wisdom of his heart. With a giant breath from its light, he leapt up, roared with wildness and hurled Morrigan at the giant man's heart.

CHAPTER 82
SYLPHILANTHROPY

As London flickered in and out of existence, Frost who understood the symbolism of all he saw, was completely still, awed by the sight of Morrigan spinning through the air. His eyes welled with the power of Jake's roar—a roar of the purest frustration, of wanting to accept life's challenges, to accept his past, to feel compassion, but not knowing how to. The honesty was pure. It was a thing of great beauty.

'Well done, Jake,' he said softly. 'By casting away the sword, you've passed the test of power. And it's not gone unnoticed.'

The sylph was watching Jake with great interest.

'And look, Silver!'

Frost could barely believe it. Morrigan had carried the great distance to the silhouetted man. At the point of contact, two things happened: the image of the man faded back into the past, and Morrigan sliced a hole in the geometry of the gate and disappeared clean through it. She was shortly followed by two swans.

'Could it be Lawrence's soul, guided by Rowena?'

Braysheath's duel with Luna had reached the critical point. Tsunamis that towered over Beijing, New York and other coastal cities finally broke and bore down upon their targets. Delhi surrendered to the rift. The unicorn's horn had absorbed the greater part of Nashoba's light while Braysheath's body, like London, flickered on the verge of extinction as he battled to maintain presence on too many fronts.

The Tree of Life told the same story. Adam's embrace of Eve had almost ended. Just one of their many-rooted arms remained in contact though only by the hands—hands which slipped through one another, fingers across palms, fingers through fingers until only their tips touched.

A dreadful moment of stillness remained. Next, the collective spirit of all humans would snap free of their collective mind and into the hands of Luna.

Yet fine threads and milliseconds meant little when love was pure—as pure as the light of the brace of swans that suddenly appeared and flew through the chaotic woodland.

They released a cry, melancholy and mythical. The geometry of the woodland brightened to the frequency of divine light. It was the frequency of hope—true hope born of action. Something momentous had happened in the holygate.

The effect on Braysheath was immediate. He shone like a beacon. Light pulsed out through his many arms. Waves were cast back from the point of mass destruction. Delhi was restored. The lantern-lit path of Jake's lightline was waved away. Nashoba was relieved of Surface shadow.

Luna summoned the unicorn with its hornful of light, but the hope was so potent that Nashoba immediately recovered it. He blew a kiss at the unicorn which disintegrated before his eyes only to reappear before Luna, shining brighter than even Braysheath.

It was the purest light in the cosmos—too pure for Luna to touch. Just the sight of it subdued her. Braysheath, meanwhile, had absorbed enough of her blows to align with her frequency. A deathblow against him would be a deathblow against herself.

An ironic smile spread across her face as she watched the rooted arms of Adam and Eve re-embrace. With a click of her fingers, she was gone.

WHILE THE TSUNAMIS ON THE SURFACE HAD BEEN CAST BACK, THE tsunami in the collapsing gate was mounting by the moment. A monstrous amphitheatre of rubble was closing in about the yew. Entire sections of buildings appeared like pebbles surging up through the deathly wave.

With gashes to their bodies, dodging the debris of the collapsing gate as it was sucked into the yew through the ghostly form of the sylph, Rani and Rufus were on their last legs.

Throughout the battle, Rani had kept an eye on the Commander. He had been watching the summit of the distant mountain where Lord Boreas had carried Jake, apparently waiting for something.

Suddenly he drew his sword. He glanced up at the sylph. The mysterious creature was thoroughly captivated by all that was happening. Seizing the moment, the Commander marched for Nestor.

Lord Boreas must've been slain! Jake lives! deduced Rani.

'Rufus!' she cried, alerting his attention to the Commander, slaying another guardian in order to reach him.

It took their combined effort to hold the Commander back, but it wasn't enough. They were exhausted, he was fresh, having absorbed the inner-force of the slain guardians. Following a flash of blade strokes, he dismissed them both with powerful kicks.

A leap later he was at the altar. His blade raised over Nestor's neck, he gave a final glance up at the sylph. It was gazing directly at him, then glanced out at the gate and back again, its eyes ablaze with intrigue. It made no attempt to intervene.

Rani and Rufus tried to get up, but the gale of wreckage was too dense.

The Commander drew back his blade and, following a contemptuous sneer in the direction of Rani, swung it towards Nestor.

Rani's heart sank. She had never met Nestor, yet his life was somehow vital—a link between all that had been and all that could be. He was a true elder, for only a true elder with a light heart could have borne the darkness of the sylph for so long.

And now his time had come.

Rani's eyes closed as the blade descended.

Then flicked wide open with the resounding ring of steel.

It was Jake. He had swept in on a winged white horse. Not only had he blocked the Commander's deathblow, but struck his sword clean from his hands. As he sprang to recover it, Jake flew over Rani, knocking down guardians.

He leapt down from the horse and stood in front of his granddad. Rani marvelled at how the lethal storm of shattered concrete, which prevented herself and Rufus from intervening, avoided Jake completely.

It must be the sylph! she thought. *It's holding space. It's collapsing the gate, though keeping the players in place. It's still deciding whether to take sides.*

Neither did the concrete bother the Commander. Having recovered his sword, he studied Jake. With a wave of his hand, the sword Jake had found in the saddle of the horse vaporised into thin air.

Again Rani tried to get up to fight, but the storm of debris wouldn't allow it. Rufus transformed into a carpet to try to get through, but was swept off the crown by a boulder. The wave of the imploding gate towered higher and higher, just moments away from collapsing on top of them.

'Goodbye, Lord Tusk,' said the Commander, his icy voice cutting through the tumult.

As the Commander approached his prey, savouring the moment, Jake simply closed his eyes. His face was a picture of peace. Ignoring Rufus's earlier warning not to touch the lethal blue flame, he reached through it and held his granddad's hand.

A shiver ran through Rani as she watched on, awed by his courage, awed by his vulnerability, awed that he appeared unharmed. She tried to crawl towards him to help defend him, but a great lump of concrete almost severed her arms.

'Jake!' she cried out in frustration.

A step away from Jake, the Commander drew back his sword.

Jake didn't move, making no attempt to defend himself.

Tears welled in Rani's eyes.

This is it, she thought then caught herself.

No! Live, Jake! she willed with all her heart, daring to imagine a future different from all the destruction that tightened about them like a noose.

'Live!' she cried out through the storm as the Commander's blade reached full stroke.

Live, she heard from another place within her, except that it wasn't her voice. It was Frost's, calm and powerful.

Instinctively she looked up and saw the strangest thing. It was Frost's face filling the sky, distorted as though he were gazing at her through a pool. His palms were placed reverently on the water. Eyes closed, his lips moved. He was praying.

Rani was so aghast that for a moment she quite forgot where she was. She wondered at the great risk he was taking—a trixy prince, whose father was aligned with Luna, directly intervening in a place where great power saw everything.

A blissful warmth burst through her as Frost's prayer took effect. It was swiftly followed by a shudder of power. She understood what it meant. He was amplifying her will-force.

The Commander's body tensed to strike, eyes bright with relish.

'LIVE!' she cried again and felt its force boom from her belly and reverberate through the depths of her soul.

A fierce trumpeting rent the air and merged with a shriek from the sylph. The image of the bull elephant Rani had seen in the woods filled her mind's eye. Its dark eyes blazed with power. They became her own. She inhaled a vast breath which filled her heart with light and connected her to Jake.

Sensing intervention, the Commander rushed at Jake and swung his blade.

With Rani's exhale, the powerful light in her heart shone from Jake's, so bright that it was like a star.

The Commander's blade stopped short of Jake's neck, held up by a superior force. Rani felt it—the force she knew better than any other. It was the force of trees.

Outer-force! she cried.

It was more than that. It was the five forces united. It was love. Real love—the very force that held the cosmos in perfect tautness for life to exist.

Jake hadn't moved. Still and serene, he shone like Lawrence had only moments before. The image of the golden key filled Rani's mind and she finally accepted its meaning. As Luna suspected, as Frost had said—he, Rani and Jake were like a key, one which held great power when their wills were united through the heart. Combined, they became true warriors. And a true warrior, just as Ti had told Jake in his duelling lesson over the ravine, required no weapon.

Unperturbed, the Commander took another stroke, but still his blade couldn't touch Jake. He swung his blade at Nestor's body instead, but the light which flowed through Jake also flowed through Nestor. Again the Commander was foiled.

The remaining guardians closed in about Jake and Nestor to unite their force when something even more extraordinary took place.

Rani gasped.

From Jake's aura stepped dryads of light. Male and female they shone with such brilliance that the guardians backed off.

The tsunami of rubble, however, was seconds from collapsing on top of them. Rani shuddered as the giant branches of the yew coiled upwards, grew to yet greater size and held it back for a critical instant: the instant it took for two of the giant twiggy hands to reach out through the maelstrom and guide back something flying towards them.

At the sight of it, the Commander sneered. Following his lead, the guardians dived through the gate in retreat.

Rani's eyes were wide with wonder. Flying through a beam of light projected by Jake was a creature of myth, not one of shadow, but one of flesh and blood.

It was a dragon, black-skinned with blazing green eyes.

As it drew closer, the glove tingled back to life.

'Braysheath!' cried Rani.

She jumped to her feet. Any debris which slipped through the protection of the creaking branches dissolved before her as the glove worked its magic.

The dragon released a sombre cry which echoed through the gate. The sylph replied. In a blaze of light released from the world of Hunter, it flew up from its roost towards the dragon.

Braysheath roared out a jet of green flame. Before reaching the sylph it transformed into hummingbirds. As they flew through the sylph its shadow dissolved. Nothing remained of it save a fresh wind which washed over Braysheath.

Under the weight of the tsunami, the branches were at snapping point. With a single flap of his wings, Braysheath was at the crown. So too was Rufus. As Braysheath swooped down and swept up Rani and Nestor in his great talons, Rufus swept up Jake. In the split second before the gate imploded, they shot through the crown into the blaze of light.

For the first time in his life, Frost was dumbstruck. His perspective of the collapsing gate had been that of a god. From above, he had seen it all.

As a mushroom cloud of dust rose up from the collapsed gate, his attention shifted. Ever-intuitive, he had been watching the passage of the sylph, especially at the point where it seemed to have vanished. Instead of peering directly into the fountain, he studied the reflection in its surface. There, just as he suspected, he caught an image—a glowing ship setting sail on a great voyage from a lotus-strewn harbour towards a setting sun. At the helm, looking serene, was Lawrence.

Frost wondered at the breeze which had washed over Braysheath as the sylph had dissolved. Was it the same wind that now billowed in the ship's sails?

'What could it mean, Silver?' he whispered as the image faded. 'For where does Lawrence sail? Has his sun finally set or will it rise once more? Or does he sail with the sun? And what about the sylph? Will it return to its other half, the charred angel confined to Pandora's Box? How boring if it did!'

A dry playful laugh reverberated about the oasis.

'It's him!' cheered Frost. 'The charred angel!'

Silver released a sharp caw.

Frost turned to find a parrot in the branch of the oak.

'The parrot, the pirate,' he said with a smile. 'A creature of imitation, though ultimately a bird of the sun—a teacher of hard truth. A healer.'

Frost leapt up on the fountain wall, his eyes shining.

'Ah, Silver, it's truly wonderful! This radiant parrot is a symbol of Lawrence's fine work. The pirate was his severest teacher, his strongest demon, but through courage, wit and determination, he won back its energy. Perhaps more! It's the same journey that Jake must one day make, though on a far deeper, far greater scale.'

A breeze blew through the oasis and ruffled Frost's hair.

His eyes brightened as he glanced about the oasis. He was bursting with so many secrets and so much excitement that he looked as though he might explode.

To expel some energy, he sprang up into the reformed tree of Adam and Eve, right to its upper branches and gazed through the falling snow, revelling in the stillness of London. Silver joined him.

'Luna still reigns up here,' he said. 'And she's pleased! Dear Jake has revealed his fitness for power. And it's power he needs if he's to find and unlock the gate she seeks. And what of that gate, dear Silver? Who knows what it really is or where it leads?'

CHAPTER 83
FEAST AND REBIRTH

ONCE IN THE SHAFT OF THE HOLYGATE, BRAYSHEATH HAD USED his power to transport everyone back to the House of Tusk, collecting Bin from Renlock. The osprey was alive. Other than a broken wing and a concussion from being knocked out, she was fine. Neither were any of Rani's wounds fatal. All the same, she and Bin were taken back to Wrathlabad to be treated by their own healers.

Nestor, Rufus and Jake had all been taken straight to the healing hall in the House of Tusk, tended by sprites. Asclepius hadn't returned, something which caused Jake great sadness, not to mention guilt for having unfairly accused him of treachery when he had been so loyal and brave. No one knew exactly what had happened to him, not even Braysheath.

Jake and Rufus had been discharged after just two days while it was several more before Nestor finally came round and was fit to receive visitors.

The rest of Odin's Council had more or less returned in one piece. Companies of resistance had been successfully installed on Roar, Leaf and Hunter, though it would take considerable time before the tide was turned, such was the scale of the battle.

As for the Surface, though Luna had retreated to her ark, she remained Overlord. Humans, humbled though ignorant of what had really taken place, flocked to her cat temples in ever-increasing numbers. While the natural disasters had stabilised, it was only a temporary reprieve. As Braysheath had explained to Jake, such things as tsunamis and earthquakes were nothing more than manifestations of a collective inner-turmoil—surges of emotion, quakes and fiery explosions of rage, droughts of feelings and so on.

Despite the precise location of Luna's ark remaining a mystery, the operation was deemed a success. Odin had insisted on a feast and so it was agreed that one week following the fateful events, a small celebration would be held in the woods of the House of Tusk.

THE GREAT DAY ARRIVED. TO JAKE'S DELIGHT, NESTOR WAS DUE TO be discharged that same afternoon. Taking some freshly picked fruit, Jake paid him a visit.

As he descended to the healing hall, Jake reflected on how the fort felt as much like home as the farmhouse. The difference was in how he was greeted. Regardless of what Jake felt of his performance in the holygate, the staff, the sprites and the many other creatures about the oasis thought it worthy of respect. In their own way even the trees paid their dues. As Jake passed by, the air grew light as though they had rustled up a breeze just for him.

Having Nestor in the fort made a world of difference. Just knowing he was there, even while convalescing, filled the place with a cheerful light that shone through one and all.

Jake passed into the healing hall, passed the jungle of patients until he found his granddad in the far corner. His bed was beneath a beech tree in autumn colours, next to a window that commanded a view of the great lake.

After a week of Merrywisp's cooking, Nestor was almost back to normal. His eyes were bright again. He even had his deerstalker hat back on.

'Jake!' he cried on spotting his grandson. 'How are you, fella?'

'You look great!' laughed Jake and gave him a hearty hug.

'You know me—never one to miss a party! Take a pew. How are you doing?'

Jake sat on the side of the bed, immensely happy and relieved.

'I feel older,' he said finally and smiled.

'Nothing wrong with that. What've you been up to?'

'Just relaxing. Making the most of this brief spell of peace and trying to get my head around everything that happened in the holygate.'

'Everything? Sounds ambitious. How have you got on?'

'Well, not quite everything,' admitted Jake.

With a shiver, he thought back to the terrible anger that had welled up from the distant past along with what he had done with it.

'Oh, Granddad…' he sighed, gripped by the same guilt which had tortured him all week. 'How will you ever forgive me for what I did to Dad?'

'Forgive? There's nothing to forgive, Jake fella!' exclaimed Nestor without a moment's hesitation and gave Jake's hand a gentle squeeze. 'Lawrence lived a full and remarkable life. He was extremely proud of you and ultimately extremely grateful. Whether you see it or not, you set him free.'

Jake looked out of the window at the beautiful tree-fringed lake. The rains had stopped and the savannah was back to normal. 'I wonder what happened to him,' he said at last, wiping back a tear.

'Who knows, Jake? But I'll tell you what. Let's imagine that Lawrence was sent back to the Surface, perhaps as a new born child, perhaps as a tree, perhaps in all the elements—the wind, the rain, in the very rock beneath our feet, with us every step of the way. That's much more fun and a far more useful thought because it doesn't really matter what you believe as long as it works. Not just for you, but for everyone.'

'Works?'

'In other words, as long as what you believe keeps you open to life in all its forms.'

'What about the truth?' asked Jake, who already knew that Nemesis hadn't had contact with his dad's soul since the fateful day in the gate.

'Ultimately, that is the truth. We're in all things, in all the elements and all the elements are in us.'

Jake beheld his granddad's twinkling eyes, when something clicked.

'I've just realised!' he said with a rush of joy. 'In your riddles the reference to *untied or titan'd*—untied is an anagram of united! So maybe he has been united with nature!'

'My God, you're right! That's the good old subconscious for you.'

'Really? You didn't realise?'

'No. Funny things words. There's great mystery behind them. Like *a part* and *apart*. What a difference a single movement can make! Or the word *scared* —if you can *c* forward just one momentous step then scared become *sacred*, while a *life* without f's become a lie.'

'F's?' questioned Jake.

'Fun, frivolity, fire!'

'Fighting, fear, frozen emotions,' countered Jake.

'Them too,' agreed Nestor. 'But as you've no doubt learnt by now, the focus must be on the fight within yourself in order to find the real life.'

Jake nodded in agreement.

'Humph! United! Well done, Jake fella.'

'I still can't believe how you could have guessed at so much,' said Jake, referring to the riddles.

'The middle way is the one I find most useful, between probability and possibility, your wingtips in both extremes... along with great faith in the cosmos, that when one follows their heart, it conspires to help in a very conspicuous way.'

Jake studied Nestor. 'You knew about Frost, didn't you?'

'Of course,' said Nestor matter-of-factly. 'Count Frost lives in Harkenmere.'

'And you didn't tell me because it would have interfered with the flow of things?'

'Precisely.'

'And what of corrupted trixies? Are they also part of the natural flow?'

'The way of things today, yes, though like all things they're constantly evolving. Never be too quick to judge, Jake. Help can sometimes come from the most unexpected places. Sometimes it has to. After all, did he not help?'

Jake nodded. 'In as much as his nature allowed him.'

'And unless I'm much mistaken,' continued Nestor, 'your friend Byzin Frost is a little different from the rest of his tribe. Perhaps a lot different.'

'You mean because of who his dad is?'

'That might have something to do with it, but I think it's mainly to do with who he is. And you, of course.'

Jake tilted his head questioningly, for Nestor had touched on something he felt himself.

'We all have our gifts,' explained Nestor. 'And given your respective positions in the cosmos, you and he have wisdom to share with each other that may prove critical in how you both develop. In how we *all* develop. Remember, there are no coincidences, only synchronicity. But you must both take great care. Your destinies are in the balance. You may become each other's greatest ally, or just as equally, each other's greatest foe. Perhaps both, one before the other.'

Jake tried to imagine what might cause such a rift when the image of Rani popped into his head. Since his journey with Rani into the gate, something had changed. Something deep inside of him had been stirred to life. The idea of fighting over a woman, however, struck Jake as absurd.

'Do you remember anything from your time in that strange blue flame?' he asked, shifting themes.

It was Nestor's turn to draw a deep breath and sigh.

'It was like the strangest of dreams—one I can't remember, the symbols too deep to apprehend. It was as though they came from another cosmos altogether, another time, another type of existence.'

Jake's skin prickled as he recalled the sylph dragon and its ghostly eyes.

'But let's not worry about all that now,' said Nestor, lightening up. 'It's time for a party! Give me a hand, Jake fella. I've been cooped up in here too long!'

Come dusk, Jake was standing in front of the mirror in his room. In stark contrast to the last time he had gazed into it, his reflection was a picture of spring, a pair of thrushes making a nest in his hair, which had become even shaggier since his entrance into the fort.

He was in excellent spirits, excited not only about the feast, but mostly about seeing Rani. As soon as he thought of her, horns sprouted through his reflected hair and sent the thrushes flying.

'Strange mirror,' he said and studied a snake which had appeared about his reflected neck. He touched his chest where his dad's amulet had once hung. Jake was sorry to have lost it. Yet it had served its purpose in helping him to pass through Renlock and enter the gate.

He picked up Morrigan who had mysteriously appeared in his room just the day before. The mission to save Nestor had left its mark on everyone and she was no exception. She felt even more powerful than before. It wasn't just her—the connection between them had deepened. With Morrigan in his hand, Jake felt as though there was nothing beyond him. Almost nothing. The images and feelings of that ancient darkness was never far from his thoughts. Like all shadows, it was destined to follow him until he mastered it. Even then it would follow him, though would no longer dominate him and that would make all the difference.

What happened in Renlock when Morrigan had become a staff, and what had saved Jake in the holygate, had been gifts of power. The first gift was from nature, the second from the druid, brought about as much by circumstance as by Jake himself. The challenge ahead was to be able to summon, control and sustain such power in places even deeper and darker than a holygate.

'Morrigan?' he said, wondering if she would answer.

She hadn't said a thing since their episode in the gate and Jake had many questions. He especially wished to talk with her about herself, how she had been his mother, though sensed it wasn't the time. Her only reply was a gentle vibration of acknowledgment.

Jake gently kissed the misted gemstone in her hilt and sheathed her across his back.

He had just finished tying his turban and slung his cloak about him when Rufus appeared in the doorway. He was in the form of Bill and dressed in a kilt.

'Ahoy there, fancy-pants!' he cried. 'Ready for a party?'

'I certainly am!' said Jake. 'You?'

'Aye! Ach aye I am! Hop aboard!' replied Rufus and transformed into a carpet.

Jake hopped up and they shot out over the ramparts and into earthy aromas summoned by the silvery night, over the howdah-mounted elephants and the camels of arriving guests.

A SHORT WHILE LATER JAKE SPOTTED THE LIGHT OF A FIRE IN THE clearing of the woods. They flew down.

The feast was a sight to behold. Jake was immediately swept up in its festive rhythm. Trees danced through their shadows cast by the light of a great fire. Creatures of the wood were as much guests as anyone else. There were owls in the boughs of trees, boar and deer grazing amongst the dancing sprites to name but a few. Delicious aromas wafted through the air while the faces of Odin's Council, no longer concealed in the shadows of the spinney, were full of tales of brave deeds.

Braysheath noticed Jake and beckoned him over.

'Jake Tusk!' bellowed Odin. 'Come, sit with me!'

Jake walked over and sat down between Odin and Braysheath.

'Odin, son of—'

'Never mind all of that. Have some food!' bawled Odin and thrust a plate into Jake's hand. 'And something to wash it down with, of course.'

Odin was about to hand Jake a flagon of mead when, noting his own was empty, he suddenly stopped.

'Hold on a second, Jake—this one looks off. I'll just have a quick taster. Could be poisoned!'

Odin drained half the flagon in a single swig, came up for air looking uncertain, then finished the remainder and belched heartily.

'My mistake. It was fine! One can never be too sure. Mead!' he bellowed to the sprites.

'But you're a god,' remarked Jake. 'If it was poisoned, surely you wouldn't notice.'

Odin studied Jake for a moment.

'That's a good point,' he said at last. 'You'd better hurry up and become one!'

'Or a carpet!' added Rufus in human form, tucking into some food.

No sooner had Jake a flagon of mead in his hand than he almost dropped it. Another guest had arrived. He had only seen her dressed as a warrior. Now she was elegantly wrapped in black and turquoise silks, her dark hair flowing freely about her shoulders. She was riding queen-like atop one of three powerful-looking black panthers, Bin perched on her shoulder. It was Rani. The sight of her left Jake breathless.

She cast him a haughty glance then looked away, though failed to conceal a smiling light in her eyes.

'Welcome Ezram and Rani! Welcome friends!' hailed Braysheath.

The largest panther, the one walking beside Rani, transformed into human form—that of an elder, powerful and peaceful with a face that reminded Jake of the Himalayas.

He and Braysheath exchanged salutations.

The feast was soon in full swing and Jake, when not having a laugh with Rufus and Odin, did his best to catch Rani's eyes or move closer for a chat. She, however, was one step ahead and seemed to do her best to avoid him.

Another time he caught her glancing into the shadows of the trees as though searching for something, a wistful look in her eyes until they met with Jake's and she suddenly looked down embarrassed.

Is she looking for Frost?

Jake wondered whether his invite to Frost still had the power of concealment and whether Frost had the audacity to return. He also wondered at his own emotions. While part of his mind demanded a sense of betrayal towards Frost for his deception of who he really was, Jake's heart understood his fascinating friend and willed their reunion. As for jealousy, there were no grounds for it. All the same, Nestor's warning echoed through his thoughts.

Rani, he sighed.

She looked up as though she had heard him. This time she smiled shyly before turning away.

Jake's heart soared. It was the first time she had smiled at him in that way. The effect was magic. Any darkness between them was cast aside. All he saw was a goddess.

EVER SINCE SHE HAD ARRIVED IN THE FORT, RANI HAD BATTLED with a sense of imbalance. Now she not only accepted it, but surrendered to it. The music played its part. Wild, raw and sensual, as the drum picked up pace and the dancing grew more frenzied, so too did her heartbeat, her temperature and she craved to leap up and join the others. It seemed to bridge a gap within her and restore a balance of a different kind, one more human—a novel feeling for Rani who had grown up with the creatures of the jungle.

She glanced at Jake when he wasn't looking. He also had a wildness about him that had the same effect, both enflaming and grounding at the same time. Since escaping the gate, his wildness had become tempered—more present, fuller, inclusive and more useful for those around him. It was the wildness of nature, the type Rani loved. No longer did he seem like a lost cub. Jake had become a man with a lion's heart. The darkness of their pasts was still there, but rather than waste energy in resistance, it had become a mystery to explore.

HIDING IN A TREE A SAFE DISTANCE FROM THE FIRE WERE FROST and Silver. He knew better than dare to join the feast. Few of Odin's Council would understand the part he had so far played. Frost's power lay in the shadows, in the secret passages of the fort and other such places, operating behind the scenes, but on the ground, well-informed and deadly.

His bright eyes fixed on Rani's.

'She loves Jake,' he said to Silver, 'It's plain to see. But she fancies me. And I wouldn't have it any other way.'

Silver was busy cleaning his beak on the tree, apparently disinterested in Frost's thought.

'It's been a fine start, Silver. I'm overjoyed! But much work lies in store. The rubber band must be pulled taut before being released if it's to make the distance. And the distance is great. Everything must be taut, the heartstrings included—taut to the point of snapping if doors are to be found and burst open. Everything must be razor sharp if attachments are to be cut loose. And cut loose they must be in order to venture where Jake and Rani must go.'

Silver gurgled an ominous-sounding response.

'Indeed, Silver, us too! And as we all delve into the murkiest depths of the cosmos, towards that mysterious door, so the depths will rise up to the Surface and kick those sleepy humans heartily in the arse.'

Frost watched excitedly as Jake and Rani stole glances at each other when the other wasn't looking.

'Yes, my iridescent friend,' continued Frost to Silver. 'It's time to fan the flames of love, to fan the flames of war and unleash the most brutal, the most blinding truth the world ever saw.'

FINALLY BRAYSHEATH GOT TO HIS FEET AND CALLED THE FEAST TO silence.

'Dear friends! If you'll permit me, I'd like to say a few words,' he beamed and all the guests cheered.

His gaze swept across the gathering before he continued.

'Friends indeed, for at times like these we truly realise what friendship is and the true value of life.'

'Hear! Hear!' bellowed Odin and was joined by the others.

'So let us celebrate!' continued Braysheath. 'No matter how dark the days become, remember that in every breath you inhale light, life, love... togetherness.'

Everyone cheered.

'For that is reality,' said Braysheath. 'When you take responsibility for your breath, when you breathe life into all that surrounds you then, my most cherished friends, you become a true creator.'

There was a moment's silence as the gathering nodded in agreement.

'And now!' cheered Braysheath. 'Let us raise our flagons to one who truly took responsibility. A true man! To one whose sacrifices we shall never fully know, the burdens he bore, as ever without complaint. Let us make sure they were not in vain. We owe him much. To Lawrence!'

'Lawrence! God speed! Strong may he journey!' cheered the gathering with the exception of Jake who closed his eyes a moment and wished him peace in silence.

'And let us raise our flagons to a living testament to the power of blood, to its marvellous potential, a testament to nobility and how it can warm the bitterest of hearts. To a dear fellow we have toasted many times before. To Nestor!'

'Nestor!' cheered the gathering. 'God speed! Strong may he live!'

As Jake roared the toast, he finally spotted his granddad. He was cosied up with Merrywisp, a huge grin across his face.

'Let us raise our flagons a third time!' cried Braysheath. 'To one of the finest warriors I've ever seen—a tribute to her tribe already famed for its skills and courage. A true daughter of the earth and Protector of the House of Tusk and someone who, I dare say, will play a yet greater role in the portentous days ahead. To Rani!'

'To Rani!' cheered the feast. 'God speed! Strong may she live!'

Though Rani maintained a graceful humility, her eyes shone— and with it Jake's soul.

'And last, but by no means least...' started Braysheath when he suddenly stopped.

He looked out into the darkness of the wood as though he had sensed something.

A suspenseful silence hung in the air as the gathering followed his gaze.

Before whoever it was drew into sight, a joyous smile spread across Braysheath's face.

'May I have the honour of making this toast?' came a gravelly voice which caused Jake's heart to leap. It came from a peculiar radiance of soft light which emerged between the trees and cast back the shadows.

The light came not from a god. It came from someone else, one who had passed through the dark night of his soul, confronted his shadow and embraced it in light. It came from a man. As he passed into the clearing, the gathering sighed with delight. It was Asclepius.

'Where have you been?' gasped Jake as he jumped to his feet.

Asclepius walked up to Jake and held his hands in both of his. The warmth of friendship flowed between them and a great burden lifted from Jake's shoulders.

'It's a long story, dear Jake, but I can say this—I'm no longer a god. Neither is there a god gate. And I can't tell you how good that feels.'

'But... ?' started Jake, realising he had too many questions and the feast wasn't the time to ask them.

'Jake,' said Asclepius warmly for all to hear, 'your dad was one of the greatest men I have ever known. Honest, patient, attentive, understanding... strong... and immensely brave.'

Asclepius's words struck Jake straight through the heart and he closed his eyes for a moment to control his emotions. Asclepius gave his hands a gentle squeeze.

'And you, Jake,' he continued, 'you are so much more than a worthy heir. Never be ashamed to call yourself Lord of the House of Tusk. You've truly earned it.'

'To Lord Tusk!' roared Odin.

'To Lord Tusk!' roared the rest. 'God speed! Strong may he live!'

After an embrace from Asclepius and as the festivities erupted back to life, Jake slipped away into the shadows. He needed to be alone. He walked until the music blended with the sounds of night, found a giant oak and sat between its roots. Suddenly tired, he closed his eyes, drew a deep breath and rested.

He hadn't been there long when something touched his shoulder and frightened the life out of him. It was Rani, crouching in front of him and smiling—not a shy smile, but one which shone and lit up the woods. It sharpened and sweetened every sound and smell, creating a moment of union which rippled throughout the cosmos in subtle and beautiful ways.

'Hi!' said Jake, too enchanted by her beauty to say anything else.

Rani said nothing. Her expression grew suddenly serious. She took hold of Jake's right hand. With great ceremony, she placed one of her kukri knives in his palm and gently closed his fingers about it. While still holding his hands, she closed her eyes and whispered something like a prayer in her native tongue.

Before she released his hand, Jake put his other hand on top of hers. A blissful electricity flowed through him. He longed to embrace her.

'It's a gift of friendship,' she said, her mood still grave.

'Thank you,' said Jake, deeply touched, realising that for a warrior to give away a weapon was something momentous. He wished that he had something fitting to give in return.

'Friendship,' said Jake in almost a question, not sure what it meant exactly.

'Yes,' said Rani smiling once more.

Jake searched for hints of a suggestion, though found only mystery.

Before she withdrew her hand, Jake gently kissed it and caused her to blush.

With a shy smile she got up and rounded the great tree.

His body abuzz, his heart aflutter, Jake leapt up to follow, but having rounded the tree, once, twice then running back in the opposite direction thinking she was playing, there was no sign of her.

'Rani?' he called out.

Sensing a presence, he spun around.

It was her. With a playful smile, she reached a hand to his cheek and placed a soft kiss on his lips.

The electricity was overwhelming. Chaos, calm, thunder and lightning, the most beautiful aspect of every season, the most joyous cries of every creature, they swept through Jake like an ancient and immortal tide.

Lips parted. Breaths were short. Their eyes reflected the same serene confusion, the same feverish questions tearing through a world of bewildered knowing, thirsting for answers bursting with play, never more than a step away, though always out of reach— capering, laughing, revelling in joyous mystery.

His heart racing, Jake cupped her face in his hands and kissed her with such tender depth that all questions evaporated in a rush of heat. It welled up from volcanic depths where passion and compassion were never apart.

After a tight embrace, Rani stepped back from Jake, her eyes shining. Their hands ran through one another's like the sea through the shore, an ebb that promised to flow yet stronger on its return as she withdrew into the shadows of the trees.

His arms longing to hold her tighter, Jake stepped forward, but with a glow of light, with a glow of love, she was gone.

WHILE JAKE WANDERED OFF INTO THE WOODS IN A HEAVENLY DAZE, Rani reappeared in a part of the oasis yet further away from the festivities where the trees were the most ancient she had ever seen. Their presence was so brooding that Rani could almost hear their thoughts. She shivered with awe. Only the hoot of an owl broke the stillness.

Braysheath, she sighed in delight, her heartbeat still racing from her encounter with Jake.

She had been embracing him when the glove had tingled. The timing had been perfect. They had parted in exquisite torment. It felt so alive and magical that it seemed as though she were floating.

With a great effort, Rani tore her thoughts away from Jake and glanced excitedly about the moonlit trees for Braysheath. He had never spoken with her directly. Their only communication had been through the glove. There was no sign of him, however.

Just as she sighed in disappointment, a familiar voice from right beside here made her jump.

'I do like trees, don't you?'

Rani leapt round to find Braysheath, not realising that another part of him was also sitting about the fire, regaling Odin and the others with wonderful tales.

She hugged him tightly.

'I love them,' she said. 'Just as I love you.'

'Dear child,' he said returning the embrace. 'Dear woman. And we all love you.'

Rani tingled with the sincerity of his words and felt his love flow through her.

'Come,' said Braysheath, 'Let us walk a little. It's a beautiful night.'

Rani was in bliss as they wandered through the stillness of the night. If Ezram was her dad then Braysheath felt like her wise old uncle, someone she had known forever.

She had so many questions she was bursting to ask him, but was loathe to disrupt the silence. One, however, forced its way through and demanded attention.

'When I was a baby in that place on the Surface called Kashmir, why did you take me from there and entrust me to Ezram?'

Braysheath put an arm about her shoulders.

'These are deep mysteries,' he replied. 'I could say that the wind blew me there, but what is wind but a phenomena for restoring balance, escaping high pressure and seeking the low.'

'Do you mean that I am part of the restoration of balance—that you gave me to Ezram to protect me until this time?' asked Rani, hungry for a constructive perspective on all that had happened.

'Precisely.'

'What else?'

'What do you mean, what else?'

'There must be more to it than that,' she said, frustrated by his vague answer.

'I'm sure there's a lot more to it,' said Braysheath with a smile.

'But you know so much. You must know everything, surely. I mean *everything*,' she said, looking at him intently, with Frost and Jake in her forethoughts.

'My dear, the longer I live, the less I know.'

'But you act, Braysheath—on knowledge,' pressed Rani.

'Do I? When called to action I try not to think at all. It causes terrible confusion! I try and be empty so that nature can act through me. Don't you do the same?'

'Well, yes, I suppose so, but not like you,' she said.

What she really wanted to ask more directly was whether Braysheath was orchestrating events between Jake, Frost and herself. She could no longer deny that something was happening between Frost and herself. If it was chemistry then it felt like a dangerous experiment. And there was Jake. He felt sweeter and stronger in a more dependable way. But then there was Jake's past making its way into the present—potentially something far more explosive than even Frost.

Both Jake and Frost coursed through the ocean of her being like two currents, competing and yet not, one cold, one hot, then both warm and getting warmer, deepening, stirring her up, dancing through one another, mixing her emotions, creating a frenzy like the intoxicating rhythms of the feast. The only way to release the tension was to dance to the rhythm of this new life, but she didn't know the steps.

A reassuring squeeze to her shoulder from Braysheath brought her back and said all that needed to be said. *Patience*.

Rani looked up and apologised with her eyes for doubting him.

'Seen any big elephants recently?' he asked.

Rani's eyes shot open. The image of the powerful bull elephant filled her mind—the one she had first seen that mysterious night in the woods, along with the bat and the fox when Braysheath had passed into a boulder.

'You know who it is?' she asked excitedly.

'I must confess, sometimes I do know things,' said Braysheath.

'Who is he?'

'A force.'

'Not inner-force?' cried Rani.

Braysheath released a knowing rumble of laughter.

'No. An even deeper force, the counterbalance to the pull of gravity. The force of time.'

'Time, a force?'

'Of course. That tick-tocking infernal bleeping that humans call time is just another one of their inventions that drive them mad. What I call time is the force that creates the challenges that allow us to grow so that gravity has something to take hold of and pull us towards the Core.'

'Then it *is* inner-force,' sighed Rani.

'Similar. But while inner-force works on us within a lifetime, time works through all lifetimes. It's longer-wave and more subtle.'

'Why an elephant and why is it showing itself to me?' asked Rani.

'He, for time is a masculine force, is very fond of elephants. If he decides to manifest as a creature they're his first choice. I suppose it's because elephants look a bit like boulders when viewed from a distance and rocks are very patient and wise. As for why he has revealed himself to you, I imagine it's because he has an interest.'

'Why?' asked Rani, warming to the idea of having a relationship with such a great thing.

'That's for him to answer. But for quite some time he has shown a close interest in both you and Jake.'

A shiver ran through Rani. She thought of the visions Frost had revealed of some of the past lives that she and Jake had shared. The word *challenging* certainly seemed to fit them. In some lives they seemed at war with one another. In others they had felt like lovers.

'But I don't understand, Braysheath. Why Jake and me?'

'Don't be in such a rush, dear Rani. Just follow your heart.'

'Please, Braysheath, tell me *something*,' she implored. 'So much is happening, I need something to hold me steady. Of course there is beautiful nature, but please give me some words.'

Braysheath stopped and looked gently into her eyes. 'You're forcing me to make assumptions.'

'Yes,' said Rani, not believing Braysheath needed to assume anything. He simply didn't like to be too specific, preferring to keep the present open. 'Please assume.'

'Alright, I'll have a go,' he conceded with a smile. 'You and Jake have great potential. You as a woman. Jake as a man. Ultimately you are symbols of the masculine and feminine energy in all humans, but you two especially have the courage to live your message.'

'Why?'

'Because of who you are, who you've been and the long journey you've shared together—wisdom you must now share with all humans, leading by example. When you and he finally unite—'

'Unite? How?' asked Rani, blushing.

'However you see fit. But when you do, so long as your message is freedom, great magic will be unleashed.'

'Magic?'

'The magic of togetherness. What some call love, though most confuse with entrapment. When the rest of the cosmos follows your example, everything will be possible—not through time, but in the moment. An Age of Truth will have returned. The Great Dance! And with a bit of luck, it'll happen in this lifetime. Because it needs to.'

'The Great Dance,' muttered Rani, thinking of the confusion and fusion of energy that Jake and Frost caused within her.

Her other burning question was about Frost. She was dying to know how much Braysheath knew of him when a loud shriek and flapping made her jump. An owl had taken flight from a nearby tree.

He doesn't want me to ask, deduced Rani, disappointed.

'Isn't nature marvellous,' remarked Braysheath.

He knows, at least, she thought, which was some comfort.

'And so in this Age of Truth,' she continued, 'everything will make sense?'

'Everything,' agreed Braysheath. 'It always does.'

Rani took a deep inhale of the crisp air. As Braysheath gave her shoulder another gentle squeeze, all her worries seemed to dissolve.

'Thank you, Braysheath,' said Rani and gave him another hug.

'Shall we get back to that feast before Odin scoffs all the goodies?'

'Do you mind if I join you in a moment. I just want to be on my own for a while.'

'Of course, my dear. Come when you wish. I dare say that nifty glove of yours will help you find the way,' he said with a wink.

He then bent down and kissed her forehead.

Rani closed her eyes, so full of joy that again she felt as though she were floating. When she re-opened them, he was gone.

Once alone, she remembered something else she wished she had asked. It was about Glabrous. She was especially fond of him despite their short time together. He had lent her his light, but his body hadn't been found on their return through Renlock.

She crouched down beside a yew tree and stroked one of its roots. Tears welled in her eyes.

'I wish I could bring you back, noble and beautiful creature,' she said softly, her heart full of sadness.

She took out her remaining knife and held the blade to her left palm.

'Your light flows in my blood,' she said and pressed the blade until it drew blood.

She let two drops fall onto the yew root followed by two tears which fell from her cheeks and mixed with the blood.

'Salty tears from the magical sea that flows through all of us.' Rani leaned forward and kissed the yew. 'I love you, Glabrous. Thank you for your great gift.'

As she repeated her wish that she could bring him back, a gentle breeze rustled the trees about her.

Suddenly sleepy, Rani lay down on her back beside the tree and closed her eyes. Her thoughts turned to Jake. She revisited the lake of her vision except this time the man was Jake in his current life, the woman herself as she was now. She silently slipped from her robes, joined him in the water and wrapped her arms about his back. Jake turned. He gazed intensely into her eyes. As he took hold of Rani, electricity coursed through her like a wild storm. In a moment that seemed to take forever, he leant forward and kissed her.

Blissfully lost in a watery dream where lines blurred between light and dark, hot and cold, between all things, finally Rani awoke. She had been floating weightless on the lake, looking up at an evening sky when a beautiful sweet smell called to her.

On opening her eyes, she was back in the woodland. It was still night time. There was a difference, however. Surrounding her and the yew tree were the most perfect red roses.

With a gasp she sat up and marvelled at them.

'How is this possible?' she muttered. 'Could it be a symbol of my dream with Jake?'

Rani was enchanted with the idea when a chill gripped her.

'Roses!' she hissed.

The image of the rose that Frost had left her in her secret hideout blazed in her mind—a decapitated rose that had infuriated Rani at the time.

She jumped up, scoured the branches above her and the surrounding shadows, but found no trace of him.

Relaxing a little, Rani studied the roses. Unlike the one Frost had beheaded, these were so vibrantly alive that they seemed to glow despite the night. She touched one, inhaled its delicate fragrance to make sure they weren't a trick.

'They're perfect,' she sighed. *Trixies can't create such beauty.*

She wondered if there might be some other explanation, but knew in her heart that Frost had something to do with it. He had been there and seen her sleeping. Rather than disturb her, he had somehow created the roses.

Though perhaps not alone, she thought.

Rani recalled what Frost had said of the alchemy between the three of them and their joint destiny. Perhaps the three of them had created the roses—while Rani had dreamt intimately of Jake, Frost had been nearby or beside her. Perhaps their connection was so strong that it had been enough.

However the roses had come about, Mother Nature had been part of it, which made her feel better. Studying them she wondered at their symbolism—their deep red, their sweet fragrance, the immaculate way the petals unfolded like many layers concealing an inner-secret. It was such a sensual flower. And it had thorns. Nothing of value was gained without pain—a loss, a shedding, like a drop of blood.

Whatever it meant, the word that danced through Rani's mind was *love*.

Kneeling down, Rani cupped a rose in each of her hands. Both buds were on the verge of opening up their first layer of petals.

Two unlikely heroes, she thought.

It suddenly occurred to her that both were mirrors to parts of herself. The revelation came as a shock. In fact, she saw that they were all mirrors to each other—revealing the shadowy aspects one would rather ignore, along with great gifts to be drawn out.

She inhaled the scent of one.

'May I embrace my past as you have begun to embrace yours,' she said softly thinking of Jake. With a leap of her heart she kissed the rose.

As she inhaled the fragrance of the other rose, Rani closed her eyes. She thought of Frost and felt her own trickiness, how she had denied her feelings, hiding behind fight. But then, how did she really feel about him? What was Frost to Rani? What gift was he drawing out of her?

An image filled her mind—his face in prayer, peering into the holygate through a pool.

He understands the Surface so well. He's so bold and rebellious. And yet he's wise in so many other ways, she reflected, realising that Frost had revealed only a fraction of what he was capable of. *Sometimes he seems so old, yet he looks so young and strong.*

Rani released a sigh.

He's a mystery, she concluded and as long as he remained one, so also would her feelings towards him remain equally mysterious.

Following a final inhale of its delicate scent, she touched her forehead to the rose and released a gentle sigh.

EPILOGUE
TOO BIG TO BELIEVE

Dressed in his kilt and a woolly jumper, Rani's knife tucked through the back of his belt, Jake climbed one of the steep-sided mountains above the farmhouse. He and Bill had decided to take a few days well-earned break on the Surface.

As the rising sun crested the adjacent ridge, Jake rested up on some crags near the summit. Thanks to Luna's interference in the weather, snow still blanketed much of the world, and northern England was no exception. Ill-omened or not, it was a glorious sight. As Jake poured himself a coffee from a flask, he took a deep satisfying inhale of the crisp mountain air.

He shook his head in wonder at all that had taken place since the last time he had climbed the mountain. In many ways it still felt like a dream. And yet, as his breathing calmed from the climb and the stillness embraced him, he had a different impression: far from a dream, the world about him appeared more real—intensely so. It felt larger, brighter and vastly more alive.

He stroked the boulder he was sitting on.

'Hello, my friend,' he said.

A chough swooped past him, releasing a sweet-sounding cry, lending its voice to the mountain.

It felt like an age had passed since he had disembarked the train in Harkenmere just a few weeks before. During that time, Jake had learned a lot about the symbolic way in which the cosmos spoke—symbols that we many layered, ever-evolving and alive. As he beheld the snaking river in the valley below and the dragon-like spine of the mountain ridge before him, he understood the purpose of symbols more deeply. The ancient people had imbued the landscape with meaning so that they would never forget that it was sacred. They were always alert to the many ways in which it spoke and guided them through the journey of life. He thought of the wind as one of its tongues and a breeze stirred from the stillness and embraced him in confirmation.

We don't own anything here, he thought to himself as he gazed down at the farmhouse in the valley. *We're here as caretakers of this magical land. Our responsibility is to know it as deeply as we can and so know ourselves—to listen to the land and our bodies which never forget.*

He thought of the collapsed holygate, relieved that it would take some time to rebuild it. The drop in population would give Mother Earth a chance to breathe and encourage humans to focus inwards in order to find deeper meaning to their lives.

Jake remembered the bats he had seen on the bridge following his first meeting with Frost. His friend had been right about their significance. If there was one word which summed up all that had taken place since Jake passed through the inkwell it was *initiation*. He had left the farmhouse, his place of birth, in search of his family. What he had found was himself, or at least part of it, and what it belonged to—a family yet greater. Jake had returned from a voyage to discover that all humans were part of his family.

The sun grew suddenly warmer. His body tingled and eyes welled.

He gazed about the summits in awe and understood why it was that so many humans in the past had believed that the mountains were the homes of the gods. Seated where he was, Jake felt godly. From there he could look over the valleys, their settlements and see that all were connected—by the wind, the collective breath of all worlds, by the flight of the birds and their sweet song, by the grass and rock, by the streams and rivers, he at their source. It was all one vast community. Seeing it that way, feeling it, brought Jake great peace.

Perhaps the broken holygate will give humans a chance to feel this too, thought Jake. *To broaden their idea of family and to find the security and peace we all yearn for. Peace that comes from trust.*

He reached into his knapsack and took out his breakfast—two pieces of toast and marmalade sandwiched together. He was about to take a bite when a voice from behind made him jump.

'Hello there! The last time I was in this spot there were lions,' said the familiar voice. 'I was almost eaten!'

Jake swung round to find the welcoming sight of Braysheath.

'That wouldn't be marmalade, would it?' he enquired.

'Don't tell me you smelt it all the way from the fort?' exclaimed Jake.

'I do have a rather good nose, I must admit. But heavens no, I would never prey on unsuspecting marmalade eaters! No, I simply popped out here. Must have been your gravity. But since you do have two slices, which does seem a trifle excessive for one person, we may as well share.'

Jake prized the sandwich apart and, shaking his head with a laugh, passed one to Braysheath.

'Thank you!' said Braysheath and took a hearty bite. The cobra about his neck writhed with pleasure and an eagle cry rang out in the sky.

They sat in contented silence, sharing the cup of coffee. Jake hadn't had much of a chance to catch up with Braysheath at the feast. Now that they were together, something which had continued to trouble him reared its ugly head again.

'Braysheath?'

'Humph?'

'You remember the prophecy of the Norns that I told you about?'

'Indeed I do.'

'Well, there were three parts. The first came true.'

'Yes, I suppose it did.'

'Then so might the second part. You remember it? *In ark in ice best think twice, if madness for a maiden is too dear a price.* Well, the only ark I've heard of is Luna's, but what do you think *madness for a maiden* means?' asked Jake as the image of Rani filled his mind.

Having polished off his toast and thoroughly licked his fingers, Braysheath turned to Jake and held him in his gaze. Stony faced, his eyes widened slightly and his pupils dilated. He gazed at Jake for an uncomfortably long time, the pools of his eyes growing deeper and deeper. Jake was at the point of becoming dizzy when Braysheath finally relented.

'Madness isn't quite what you think it is,' was his cryptic response.

'What do you mean?'

Braysheath studied Jake a moment longer before answering. 'Madness is not a condition. It's a place.'

'A place?' queried Jake. 'So, according to the prophecy, I might have to make a choice between a place and a woman?'

'Possibly, though it's far too soon to get lost in such ideas. Besides, prophecies and riddles, as you've discovered for yourself, tend to have more than one meaning.

'*At fiery gate when hope seems spent, love thine enemy and they'll repent,*' said Jake, repeating the final part of the prophecy.

Another image filled his mind. This time it was the strange gate he had seen on escaping the chamber—a gate of black fire along with the white wolf of his dad and his mum the dove.

'That makes me think of the door Luna's seeking, which has something to do with me.'

Braysheath had taken out his pipe and was packing it with tobacco as was his custom during heavy matters.

'You know, Jake m'boy, every human in each life, without exception, fulfils some great task to help the cosmos evolve. First, however, we must take responsibility for all that happens to us.'

A chill ran through Jake.

'Are you saying that I must open that door and pass through the gate?' he asked.

'Doorways and gates are made to be passed through,' said Braysheath. 'Though who passes through and in what state and with what intention will prove critical for all.'

In what state, repeated Jake in thought. With another shiver he recalled the anger that had coursed through him in the holygate.

'In the holygate I accepted the help of one of my past lives, a druid ghost by the name of Oblivion.'

Braysheath said nothing. He lit his pipe and took a long draw.

'But I'm not sure he did help. If anything, he opened the way to... I can only call it an ancient anger, a terrible fury which I knew was mine and yet...'

'The fury that took hold of you is what allowed your dad to truly shine,' said Braysheath, his tone distant. 'It amplified his forgiveness to a brilliance the sylph couldn't ignore. It was vital.'

'Do you think Oblivion understood that?'

'A lantern bearer sees far.'

'But the source of the anger—what about that?' pressed Jake and remembered the lethal flicker of pain his past life had revealed, along with the thought that perhaps it had been a trick.

Braysheath took another puff on his pipe.

'Patience, Jake m'boy,' he said at last. 'In time these ancient wounds will come to the surface. Until then you must have faith. Accept that you are human and being a human means far more than you realise. Humans contain infinite power when united through the heart.'

Jake looked back out at the glorious view. His thoughts turned to Morrigan whom he had left at the fort. Now that Lord Boreas was effectively gone, Braysheath was the only one other than Jake himself who knew the truth about the soul inside of the sword. Jake was sorely tempted to raise the subject. But he held back. Rocks, plants, birds—all could hear and especially pigeons.

Luna must never find out, he thought. Perhaps a time would come when he and Braysheath could talk about Morrigan, but there on the crag was not it.

'Humans are far more than I realise?' he said instead.

'Of course! Having the courage to change is what makes humans so noble—to not be crushed by life's challenges, but to see them as wonderful opportunities for grace. And at the end of what seems such a perilous journey, one realises that the need for courage was just as illusory as the fearsome perils one thought one faced. There is no fight. The journey is ultimately a safe one. You're never alone. You're always held, always guided, for absolutely everything is nature speaking to you. And you're always loved, deeply, purely, even if at times you can't feel it.'

Jake took a deep breath and felt light again.

'So stay present, Jake m'boy, in this great dream we call life. Relaxed and alert! And dream a beautiful dream, for if you can't imagine wonderful things then they'll never happen.'

'You make it sound so easy,' remarked Jake.

'Because it is, dear fellow! Just don't let others tarnish your dream with fear. Remember—beliefs create reality. Your duty, your joy, is to shine. To simply shine! A light unto yourself and unto others.'

'You said before that now was an exciting time to be alive,' remembered Jake out loud.

'And I was right! It's a terrifically exciting time! A time for all of us to wake up and pass through the final part of shadow, to grow through our relationships with all things and leap into a new dawn—one of balance and truth!'

'But what about Luna?' said Jake. 'Who is she? You said before that good and evil are from the same source, but if all she seeks is destruction, is she not evil?'

Braysheath took another draw on his pipe.

'Evil is a cry for help, dear Jake, never forget that. The greater the evil seems, the greater the despair behind it. And when someone we call evil is unaware of their hidden despair or indifferent to it, then that person becomes very dangerous indeed, to both themselves and others. But remember—the anger they project onto others is always anger at the parts they hate within themselves, the parts they don't yet wish to see, not realising there is something beyond those parts—something immense and truly wonderful. And when people talk of evil as a force, blaming something outside of them, it's simply the collective despair inside all humans.'

'We must shift the fight to below the Surface,' said Jake, reminding himself of his conversation with Nestor, 'taking responsibility rather than blaming others.'

'Exactly, dear fellow. Some call it a battle between good and evil but I prefer to call it a struggle between awareness and ignorance, between an elder and a confused child.'

'A child?'

'In many ways, yes. Luna has become her belief. All she sees in humans are spoilt children beyond hope. She can no longer see the beauty. She's forgotten where she's from. Her impatience, her doubts that she has passed on to humans have spiralled out of control. She is the embodiment of all human weakness disguised as strength, though as long as she fails to see this she's extremely dangerous.'

'And the sylph, what does that represent?'

'It's a deeper expression of the same thing. Yet, given its origin, the shepherds, it's also the link to what she has forgotten, if only the sylph could emerge from its bitterness.'

Jake took a deep breath of the pure air.

'But this,' said Braysheath, indicating the valley and beyond, 'this is just the reflection. Never lose sight of that.'

'So where is Luna reflected in this landscape?' asked Jake.

'She's reflected in almost every human thought and word, be it an expression of false hatred or false love. She's the blockage in all throats, the tension in all muscles that prevent the heart from being expressed through touch. She's the confusion in every mind. She's the fear behind all futile human attempts to control and the failure to trust in love.'

'Then,' said Jake after a moment's thought, 'if all humans can wake up to who we really are, drop all ideas of separation, then we can defeat her?'

'Transform her, Jake m'boy. Thoughts of defeating *evil* are just as absurd as the idea that we are separate from it. The energy Luna represents must be transformed into something beautiful through something beautiful—the reality of togetherness that you so perfectly described.'

Jake looked at Braysheath and realised just how amazing it was to be sitting with such a being, to be having such a conversation, to be living such a life. *If everything is a reflection,* he pondered, *then is Braysheath a mirror to the wiser part of myself?* He recalled Ti saying something similar. Such a thought was like a ray of sun. Though it sharpened the shadow he sought relief from, it also connected it to something wholesome.

'But don't you worry, Jake m'boy,' said Braysheath, giving Jake a reassuring pat on the shoulder. 'Everything will work out. It always does, one way or the other. And that's a promise.'

Braysheath stood up and took a deep breath of air.

'Well, time to crack on,' he said and made to leave. 'Thanks for the marmalade!'

'Wait a second. Luna, where did she originally come from?' said Jake, but just as he turned Braysheath disappeared in a gust of snow.

Returning his attention to the valley, Jake caught sight of the moon. There was something marvellous about seeing it in the sky at the same time as the sun, reflecting its light.

Luna, he thought and ran through all he could remember about her.

Frost had said she was from the sun. Wilderspin had said she had lost her faith. Geoffrey had said that her weakness was her pride. It made her sound so human and yet how could she be? Neither was she an ordinary goddess.

So if not human, if not a goddess or a soul that's passed to the Core yet she can visit the Core at will, powerful enough to almost overpower the combined strength of the last two shepherds, then what and who is she?

Jake gazed out over the sun-dappled lake at the same moment a V-formation of geese landed upon its surface. His mind went blank.

Weaving its way into that blankness was the outer-tendril of terrible revelation. A chill ran through Jake as he waited for the rest of it to emerge.

Humans sustain Luna through ignorant beliefs and actions, but who created her? he wondered.

His conversation with Braysheath in the farmhouse kitchen came back to him, how the Creator was like Humpty-Dumpty who threw himself off the wall, perhaps to create company, perhaps to see if he could pull himself back together again through the co-operation and co-creation of his separate parts.

But where did the Creator come from? battled Jake.

The best he could come up with was that perhaps the Creator had emerged from a flow of no-thingness, where nothing was known to be singular, and that he had willed himself into existence as part of a long term cycle or spiral of evolution—an act of singularity, of separation. It struck Jake as an imperfect start for a Creator—an original sin maybe, from a being most assumed to be perfect.

Yet what followed—the act of creation, in other words the cosmos, was perfect, at least initially when things were in balance. So too the process of evolution as humans journeyed towards union.

The Creator, however, hadn't been able to surrender himself. Not fully. He kept part of himself back to keep watch, unable to fully let go of his image, unable to fully relinquish control, creating shepherds as an insurance.

Ancient humans worshipped the land, realised Jake. *It was paradise, heaven on Earth. There was no need to journey to the Core, not how the Creator had imagined it. The shepherds, meanwhile, honoured the process of evolution. And so the Creator got bored waiting at the Core where it thought heaven should be. He grew lonely, bored, bitter, angry, lost his faith in an experiment which was all about faith—became a shadow of himself, forgot his true Self and origin and became a destroyer, though one without compassion.*

Like a thunderbolt from the sky, it struck Jake.

A flock of crows flew up raucously from trees about the lake. A sharp gust knocked over his flask of coffee as a cloud hid the sun.

Jake knew.

Without a shadow of doubt he knew who Luna was. It was suddenly so obvious, so terrifyingly, so earth-shatteringly clear that the only reason he hadn't realised it before was because it was simply too big, too shocking to believe.

'My God,' he muttered. 'She's the Creator.'

GLOSSARY OF TERMS

See start of book for illustrations of the Lantern universe. This glossary of terms is non-alphabetical. It starts with the big picture.

Atom Universe —the structure of Lantern's universe is like an atom. The macrocosm and microcosm reflect one another. The neutron is the Core, in other words the residing place of the Creator and those souls that have joined Him. The Inner Peregrinus equates to a cluster of positively-charged protons which, along with the Core, account for the majority of the atom's mass, or rather its meaning. The Outer Peregrinus equates to negatively-charged electrons, orbiting at great speed. Through time, evolution and presence, the opposites unite—electrons and protons collapse into the neutrality of the Core. Such a phenomenon cannot be measured or weighed, which is perhaps why science still struggles with finding a Unified Field Theory, uniting Einstein's Theory of Relativity with Quantum Theory, uniting the macro world with the sub-atomic world.

Peregrinus—derived from the verb to peregrinate, the Peregrinus is the spiralling spine of the universe through which the soul journeys, from the surface of Earth to the Core, from unconsciousness to consciousness. The planets in outer space are a reflection, a secondary reality, of the primary planets which make up the Peregrinus. Everything is within, the only place where true change can happen. This is the key metaphor of the trilogy. Thus, planet Earth is symbolic of oneself. Each planet of the Peregrinus can be likened to a chakra or archetypal energy system within a human body. The Surface equates to the primal energy of the root chakra. The Core equates to transcendence, existence beyond the crown chakra. But nothing is hard and fast. Everything ebbs and flows, twists, turns and evolves.

Outer-Peregrinus—in the secondary reality we take as fact, this relates to the outer-mantle of Earth. It represents the cycle of rebirth that may go on for millions of years before a soul is ready to pass to the Inner-Peregrinus. Here there are four worlds or dimensions. The surface of Earth is the great laboratory where the soul is put to the test. Between each life on the Surface there are three death worlds where the soul recuperates. In the world of Roar, souls incarnate as a creature and remember honesty. Which creature depends on their soul's specific requirements at a given point in time. In the world of Leaf, the soul is born as a tree or plant and remembers compassion. In the final death world of Hunter, the soul incarnates in human form and remembers how to live in mature community in harmony with nature.

Inner-Peregrinus—in the respective worlds of Fear, Greed and Pride, the soul is put to yet hasher tests than those on the Surface. The fire and lava science have detected within Earth are a secondary reality, symbolic of fire's power to transform. Once the soul has passed to this inner realm it doesn't return to the outer worlds of rebirth unless it fails the inner tests, in which case it starts all over again. Though in theory the inner part of the Peregrinus follows on from the outer part, in practice it can seem as though the leap to the Core happens from the Surface. This is because the nearer one gets to the boundlessness of the Core the more time and space warps. Thus, a million years in the Inner-Peregrinus can appear like a blink of an eye in the outer worlds, or a single night's dream.

Core—otherwise known as heaven, nirvana and similar names, this is the home of the Creator, the residual portion left of Himself after He created the rest of the universe. This is the origin of truth, symbolised by the sun above the Surface and the boundlessness of outer space. Truth, or gravity, is what draws us from the Surface to journey deeper within ourselves. Through time, gravity should grow stronger as more souls arrive there. However, due to a mysterious series of events this has not been the case and the exponential expansion of outer space is a symbol of a collective loss of centre and how human potential is moving beyond reach. Other galaxies, planets, asteroids, dark energy and so on are also symbolic of changes within our collective inner-universe (e.g. new places to become lost in as our true Earthly reality fractures and splinters due a loss of presence).

He and She—masculine and feminine are of equal value. Both energies are contained in equal measure in each human, regardless of the physical body's sex. The energies are symbolic. Feminine energy symbolises, amongst other things, the gift of intuition, feeling and compassion. It's a nurturing energy. The male gift is focus, action and accomplishment. When things work in balance, first a human feels (through the heart, not the conditioned mind), then acts compassionately. The idea of the Creator being masculine derives from an Eastern idea that consciousness is masculine, while all forms of energy are female in essence. First the Creator becomes conscious of itself. The action of creation is masculine, though what it creates is ultimately feminine, a nurturing energy, regardless of outer appearance.

The Five Forces—science currently maintains that there are four forces—gravity, the electro-magnetic force, strong and weak nuclear forces. In The Book of Lanterns there are five. All are different aspects of the master force which holds all levels of reality together—what some call authentic love, or the authentic togetherness of mature community. When just one human awakens to authentic love, it has an immeasurable binding effect on the universe.

1. **Outer-force**—the force of the Outer-Peregrinus, made up of the combined song of the dryads, the tree people who exist on each of the three death planets of Roar, Leaf and Hunter. Most humans on the Surface will not hear this force as a song but as a feeling, a yearning to slow down, rest under a tree and be present.

2. **Inner-force**—the force of the Inner-Peregrinus whose constituent parts are the precious stones and metals from the three planets Fear, Greed and Pride. They are carried to the Surface by the Zarzanzamin, special creatures resembling dragons. Sometimes they are carried to mid-oceanic ridges, the force released gently. At other times they are released directly into the air through volcanic eruptions. More recently, a corrupted tribe of trixies have been accumulating precious metals and stones in the vaults of central banks across the Surface. This has disrupted the natural balance of destruction and creation.

3. **Time**—in the Books of Lanterns, time is a force not a dimension. Some might liken it to a rolling stone through a Creator's dream, or a certain elephant's patience for humans to enter the present. (Time sometimes manifests as a bull elephant.) Time plays and dances with Gravity, creating the tautness we call life in a longer wave and subtler equivalent of the inner and outer forces. Effectively time and gravity hold space for the shorter wave forces to play.

4. **Gravity**—the subtle force which coaxes human souls to journey from the Surface towards the Core. See explanation for *The Core*.

5. **Spark force**—the essence of what is known as water, all of which flows from the Orijinn Sea, the mother ocean. Though the ocean is created by the clash of inner and outer forces at the mid-point between worlds, it's a force in its own right and reaches the Surface through the dreams of whales. Crystalline water mesmerizes and reminds us of our potential—to be pure, clear, indiscriminate like the river, nourishing all and holding on to nothing. Its sparkle sparks something to life within us as we journey as droplets towards union with the ocean. When the rivers and seas are polluted it reflects our collective inner-pollution, our emotional turmoil.

Guardians—manifestations of inner-force, appearing as either winged silver-coloured lions or in humanoid form, dark robed with silver-coloured skin and lion-like facial features. Their function is to ensure inner-force is distributed throughout the universe in the correct amounts. Some of them, however, have become corrupted by a powerful being disguising itself as a fertility goddess by the name of Luna.

Dryads—tree beings who inhabit the Outer-Peregrinus and whose combined song creates the outer-force. Though dryads oppose Guardians, the two ultimately work together.

Trixies—while Guardians are confined to the Inner-Peregrinus, trixies act as their hands on the Surface. Half-force, half human, they create obstacles to test humans in order to ensure all souls learn the lessons of life thoroughly. Though their influence is menacing, they are a vital part of the whole.

Pixies—in modern times most humans are not subtle enough to sense the outer-force, hence the existence of pixies. To an ignorant human they appear like any other human but are actually half human, half force, similar to trixies. However, while trixies create obstacles for humans, pixies work in subtle ways to guide humans through them. When a human encounters what they call a coincidence, there are usually pixies behind it.

Druid—the philosophers, teachers, medicine men and magicians of the ancient Celtic world. The word druid is said to derive from *they who know the oak*, the words for tree and truth being interchangeable. Mistletoe, which inhabits oaks, is said to have been their most sacred plant.

Menhir—a large upright standing stone, often tapering towards the top, either found on their own or in a group (e.g. forming a circle). They are widely distributed across Europe, Africa and Asia and are thought to have religious significance.

Nemesis and the Scribes—Nemesis is the modern name for the ancient Goddess of Justice. She manifests as the Tree of Life, connected to every one of the original human souls created by the Creator. Since the sacrifice of the shepherds, five more trees have appeared—Nemesis's Scribes. Their function is to weigh the goodness of each soul at death and determine the starting point in the next life which will best serve the soul's needs as it evolves towards wholeness.

Shepherds—the seven original beings the Creator created before humans. Together they contain half the universe's total energy. Their purpose is to gently shepherd evolution back to wholeness, never interfering in the Creator's experiment too directly. However, around ten thousand years ago, during the retreat of the last Ice Age, something mysterious and abominable took place—the youngest of the shepherds was sacrificed and split up into hundreds of millions of souls. Since then, four more have been sacrificed, accounting for the explosion in human souls on the Surface. Only the two oldest remain—Braysheath and Nashoba.

Sylph—a unique being, modern in the making, ancient in essence and with the power to destroy energy.

Zarzanzamin—ancient dragon-like creatures able to withstand the great burden of pure inner-force that they carry from the Inner-Peregrinus to the Surface, whether releasing it through the mid-oceanic ridges or directly into the atmosphere through what are known as volcanic eruptions.

Printed in Great Britain
by Amazon